"A masterpiece . . . One of the great road novels . . . Exhilarating . . . A literary experience unlike anything else." —*The Washington Post Book World*

"Danielewski clearly wants to push the boundaries of the novel even further . . . A true revolution—it wants to overthrow not just how we read, but what we read." —*Newsday*

"In his new novel, the author of *House of Leaves* is up to his old tricks—multicolored and upside-down text—and some flabbergasting new ones." —*The New Yorker*

"Celebrates the unique capability [of] the printed book . . . Ambitious, undeniably astonishing, and contemporary . . . might just be his *Finnegans Wake*." —*Bookforum*

"Engaging . . . Reads like a love story that slipped into a particle accelerator." —*Time Out New York*

"It's difficult to decide whether Danielewski is merely reinventing the novel as a medium, or has constructed his own, entirely original platform from which to destroy literary convention." —*New York Press*

"A startling and versatile pair of voices . . . The kind of faith in ambitious literature so rare among contemporary novelists . . . Once you are attuned to its extraordinary music, there is no way out except through the end." —*The Guardian*

"Exceptional . . . A poetic jazz riff on two hundred years of U.S. history . . . Combines the best of Kerouac, e. e. cummings, and Joyce." —Minneapolis *Star Tribune*

"Heartbreaking . . . A mythical journey with two storytellers." —*The Denver Post*

"Rewarding . . . A palindrome of a book . . . Appears destined to become a classic." —*The Oregonian*

"Sweeping ambition and [illegible] . . . A quintessential novel of our time." —*Los Angeles Times*

II

Only Revolutions

Mark Z. Danielewski's

Only Revolutions

by

Hailey

Volume 0 : 360 : ∞

v.o.

Pantheon Books New York

Only Revolutions

The Democracy Of Two
Set Out & Chronologically Arranged

THIS IS A WORK OF FICTION. THOUGH SOME CHARACTERS, ACTIONS, AND EXCHANGES ALIGN WITH HISTORICAL EVENTS, THE TOTALITY OF THE NOVEL—FROM MECHANISM TO MOTION TO MOOD—IS A PRODUCT OF THE AUTHOR'S IMAGINATION.

 Published in the United States by Pantheon Books, a division of Random House, Inc., New York, and in Canada by Random House of Canada Limited, Toronto.

Originally published in hardcover in the United States by Pantheon Books, a division of Random House, Inc., in 2006.

Pantheon Books and colophon are registered trademarks of Random House, Inc.

Library of Congress Cataloging-in-Publication Data
Danielewski, Mark Z.
Only revolutions / Mark Z. Danielewski.
p. cm.
ISBN 978-0-375-71390-3
I. Title.
PS3554.A5596055 2006 813'.54—dc22 2006040996

Printed in China
First Paperback Edition
2 4 6 8 9 7 5 3

abOut

O-Color
Polythiophene Ink
&
Bipowered
Decks

TriColor
Pantones
146 U, 356 U
&
2602 U

B/W
Double Volumes
without
Concordance

Fonts by order of arrival:
Life (Endpapers), Dante MT (Title), Lucida (∞), Perpetua (Dedication), Tempo (Dates), Myriad Pro (Chronomosaics), Spectrum MT (Hailey) & Univers 57 (Folio).

www.onlyrevolutions.com
www.markzdanielewski.com
www.jessicagrindstaff.com

Special thanks to VEM™
for Imaging & Cultural Resonance Tracking

Expiration Date: Now

You were there.

H

Nov 22 1963

—to screaming.
—he's gone.

Parkland Hospital.
1:00 PM.
Oak Cliff & 2 cartridges,
JD Tippit goes.

—This is it.

Lee Harvey Oswald.

—I haven't shot anybody.

2:41 PM
Love Field.
Air Force One. LBJ &
Judge Sarah T Hughes.

—defend, protect and.
—OK, let'S get this plane back to.

John W McCormack's
security squad.

—Serious but not.
—a giant Cedar.

Broadway.
Half-mast.

—Would you come with US?

—That is all I can do.
I ask for your help.

—a tragedy for all of US.

Dow down 21.16.

Samsara! Samarra!
Grand!
I can walk away
from anything.
Everyone loves
the Dream but I kill it.
Atlas Mountain Cedars gush
over me: —*Up Boogaloo!*
I leap free this spring.
On fire. How my hair curls.
I'll destroy the World.
That's all. Big ruin all
around. With a wiggle.
With a waggle. A spin.
Allmighty sixteen and freeeeee.
Rebounding on bare feet.
Trembling Aspens are pretty here:
—*You've nothing to lose. Go ahead.*
Have it all.
Tamarack Pines sway scared.
Appalled. Allso pretty. Perfumed.
Why don't I have any shoes?

Solitude. Hailey's bare feet.
And all her patience now assumes.
Garland of Spring's Sacred Bloom.
By you, ever sixteen, this World's preserved.
By you, this World has everything left to lose.
And I, your sentry of ice, shall allways protect
what your Joy so dangerously resumes.
I'll destroy no World
so long it keeps turning with flurry & gush,
petals & stems bending and lush,
and allways our hushes returning anew.
Everyone betrays the Dream
but who cares for it? O Hailey no,
I could never walk away from you.

Nov 22 1963

8:45 AM. Fort Worth Dallas.
Margaret Disco.
Poonch & Alouette crash, 5 go.
United Arab Republic, North Korea
& a toss.
—we are going to live with Them.
Love Field. 11:37 AM. Grassroots
Democrats. Trade Mart & 200,000.
South Vietnam Revolutionary Council,
Van Thanh Cao & 31 officers.
Motorcade. 12:35 PM.
Elm Street. Dealey Plaza.
Texas School Depository. 411.
Grassy knoll. Rufus Youngblood.
John B Connally.
Adelheit Nentwig.
—We are hit.
—he's shot.
Greer & brakes. Roy Kellerman. Tague.
Head. Lap. 80 MPH.
—O no! O no!

Twisting round, **Almond Willows**
slope and smile me comfort:
—*You're beyond all that.*
Tag Alders along with **Grass**:
—*Beyond every grasp.*
Windfollowing applause.
And for my long arms, fleet
toes, neato, all revering me
euphorically. April's Free Radical
boiling these barerock bowls &
savage basins ringed with
Licorice & Lilacs.
—*You're our end*, **Bull Thistle** rasps.
By my finger **Mints** &
Catnips clash. Glaciers pour.
That's a start.
Avalanche Lilies glee my Spring.
Poppy blossoms explode.
I'm a new terror upon the land
releasing runoffs, tumbling
torrents. No sweat.
Me.

Nov 23 1963

Bethesda.
Gawler.
Mahogany & silver.
Honor Guard.
Catafalque. Manhasset's
Macdougal East.
10:30 AM & 75.
Evelyn Woods.
Thomas C Chatmon
convicted.
Italian accord.
Arab expansion.

—Karachi is a
wretched place.

Eisenhower, Truman &
Cabinet Members.
Supreme Court
& Senators.

National Shock.

—who cherish the
cause of peace.
—to the brink of
Nuclear War.
—unite behind him and
help him all we can.

Fitchville fire, 63 go.

—that are going to
suffer.
—carrying on his work
beyond this hour of.
—enemy of democracy.
—We all feel
somewhat allone.

me.
And my Vengeance.
At once.
The Justice of my awful loss set
free upon this crowded land. An old terror
violent for the glee of
ends.
But to those who would tend her, harrowed
by such Beauty & Fleeting Presence to do more,
my cool cries will kiss their gentle foreheads
and my tears will kiss their tender cheeks,
and then if the Love of their Kindness, which only
Kindness ever finds, spills my ear, for a while I might
slip down and play amidst her canopies of gold.

Nov 21 1963

San Fernando winds.
Richard Claborn & $20,
Louis Saunders goes. 3 Soviet fighters,
Daragaz & 1 Iranian plane, 2 go.
Min River & Chinese Nationalist,10 go.
Chicken War. Cyrille Adoula &
Soviet Embassy. Taher Yahya, Syria &
UAR. William Pekar goes.
—space gap.
—so fast that.
—all-out support.
James Barry Lewis.
Tokyo, Liberal Democrats &
Hayato Ikeda. Big Lift over.
—out of there.
San Antonio duo.
—conquest of space must
and will go ahead.
—I want everyone to join hands.
Houston's Albert Thomas.
Pike's Peak, 2 go.

Nov 24 1963

Cufflinks & a lock of hair.
Captain Fritz,
JR Leavelle
& LC Graves.

Rubenstein's .38 Caliber.
—You killed the
President, you rat.
—Jack, you.

—When is this all
going to end?

Connally's 20 Texas
Highway Patrolmen.

John-John & Caroline.

Stirrups, reversed
military boots & Sardar.

Mike Mansfield.
Earl Warren.
John McCormack.

Wreath. Flag, lips &
a small hand.

Mary Anne Marczack.

1:07 PM.

Lee Harvey Oswald goes.

LBJ, South Vietnam &
US policies.

Hiephoa Special
Forces Camp, 37 go.

—stand firm on.
—to have her again.

250,000.

Top of this peak, my greetings
crash down upon powdery cliffs
releasing rivers shhlick beneath
whirls of murderous smaze.
By plateaus of national hurt.
And from stonescattered talus
where climbs of **Douglas Fir**
yonder, I start the ball rolling
by wandering off.
My fiery Mountain Top grovels:
—She!
A thousand buds of **Western Flax**
find gifts of melting
haze.
I will sacrifice nothing.
For there are no conflicts.
Except me. And there's only
one transgression. Me.
Of course **Daisies & Saxifrage**
chear: *—Race on Ruler.*
This my **Charlock Mustard**
seconds.

Nov 19 1963

—damage to those who threaten.
Haitian flood, 500 go. Baathists out.
Caracas terrorists, 7 go.
Atlantic City's Surfside, 25 go.
—bequeathed to US.
—obligations of keeping ours a
government of and for the people are
never-ending.
China & Moscow. Latin Nukes.
Lady Strange.
Long An & Dinh Tuong Provinces.
Congo's 2 Soviet Diplomats.
—beat Them.
Chen Yi & Cambodia.
—just and patriotic struggle.
Haupt, Williston & Beane.
Honolulu three. UN General Assembly
& South Africa. Rocking chair.
—Social disaster.
Michael Collins & Thomas Libby.
—Hold my hand.

Her. Her. Her. Future breezes implore
me to stay.
But I'm no future. I'm no past.
Only ever contemporary of this path.
I'll sacrifice everything
for all her seasons give from losing.
She, I sigh
from The Mountain top.
By her now. My only role. And for that freedom,
spread my polar chill, reaching even the warmest times,
a warning upon the back of every life
that would by harming Hailey's play, ever wayward
around this vegetative rush of orbit & twine,
awaken among these cascading cliffs of bellicose ice

Bend by bend I lead every curve
blossomingly.
Choke Cherry dotes,
sanctioning my volubility.
—*Continuity & Grass Precocity*,
shy **Mountain Avens**.
I'm no haste.
Except what now troubles me?
Terribly allone. Heartrendingly
hooked. Out there, my only harm.
Of course I near the barb.
Roams below shilippering my fars
with thawing ease. Of course.
I'm The World which
The Mountain descends from
and I laugh because it tickles.
Tansy & Tarragon sway.
And though by a flick I could
stop it all,
I'm curious.
Stave Oaks thrush:
—*Never get stung.*

Nov 25 1963
Maude Shaw.
—*happy.*
—*Hail to the Chief.*
6.
Richard Cushing.
Clint Hill.
John-John salutes.
Arlington.
50 F-105s.
Taps. 21 guns.
Taper & stumble.
—*please take care of*
your servant.
Cambodia's neutrality.
Malaysian Federation
& US Arms. Taconic.
LBJ, FBI & Justice
Department.
—*our man.*
Partisan Politics
& 30 Day moritorium.
Chung Hee Park's
Democratic Republican
Party. Dow up 32.03.
Cape Canaveral's
Satellite Explorer 18.
—*Let US continue.*
UN General Assembly,
Disarmament Committee
& Latin America
Nuclear Free Zone
—*Earliest possible*
passage of.
Liquid Hydrogen
& Atlas-Centaur
Launching Vehicle.

4
357

Sure no fun
falling for her all over again,
allone.
Too alive with all she still revives
and preserves, touches and serves, her gold
amidst these burnished greens, tickling
fields and glades, mead and arbor
for swerves of Peace. Heartendingly Open.
All that these roams allways keep of her. Explosions of
Aster, **Yarrow**, **Buttercups** and **Clover**. Blazing beside
Tarragon, **Tansy**, **Mustards** and **Daisies**. Along with shoots
of **Flax**, **Catnips**, **Mints** and **Bull Thistle**. **Lilacs** and **Wild**
Licorice. And holding my sky, **Birches**, **Tamarack Pine**,
Trembling Aspens and **Atlas Mountain Cedar**.

Nov 17 1963
—*The Mayor has not had the decency to.*
—*just don't go away.*
22nd orbiting Cosmos.
Soviet Fertilizer. Rangoon's 300.
Brenner Pass & Europa Bridge.
Las Vegas gambling & law enforcement.
Julius K Nyerere & Tanganyika.
—*World attack on poverty.*
Board of Education, Max J Rubin quits.
George W Ball.
—*flexibility.*
—*during the coming.*
Wagner's New York fluoridation.
AFL-CIO's George Meany.
JFK & Florida Chamber of Commerce.
—*anti-business.*
Abdul Salam Arif overthrows Baathists.
—*will deal with any opposition.*
Organization of African States,
Addis Ababa & 7 Nation Commission.

Nov 28 1963

Willy Brandt &
Berlin Pledges.
Algeria, Tunisia &
Sahara gas &
petroleum.
MLF & 7 Nation NATO.

Cuba, arms &
Venezuelan terrorists.
—oppression to any of
our fellow Americans
whatever their.

Britain &
US leadership change.
Chief Justice Earl Warren
& commission.

Soviet Booster rockets,
Space Vehicles &
2 Pacific impact areas.

Montreal & Trans-Canada
Jetliner, 119 go.

Valium.
Roger Staubach.

200,000 West Berliners
& John F Kennedy plaza.

District of Columbia
& LBJ favor.

Hamilton Tiger Cats over
British Columbia Lions.

California, New York &
Population gains.

Someway higher, somehow strewn.
Out there, somewhere,
another ruin.
Stupendous.
Then impudently a MOUSTACHED
TOOTHER jerks me around.
—Lost, Little Lemonade?
—There aren't no returns for those
with no starts.
—Sure. I got weed too. Where
you from?
—Around.
—Wanna get down?
—You're all School and Summer.
—How'z that?
—No class.
—Yeah, but it's Spring baby.
And I just lie down and let HIM.
And when HE goes I go too.
A round tear slips past, slides
from my life and on the soft paths
showers my dirt with strife.

Nov 14 1963

Iceland's Bjarni Benediktsson
over Ólafur Thors.
—to society.
—it is no accident.
Cao Dai & Le Thanh Tat.
Boris Yudkin's 41 & 3 years.
—the overwhelming power of the
Western World.
—for this rich country of ours.
Elsie, Mac & Murdo.
63-17, $3.7 billion & Senate Aid Bill.
—now to the point.
Arturo Illia & 10 foreign oil contracts.
Moscow frees Frederick Barghoorn.
Mike Mansfield & Argentina. Polaris.
The Great Toy Caper's 13.
Roswell L Gilpatrick's TFX. Laos,
Kong Le & Singkapo Chounramany.
—of the Communist challenge.

Except me. I'm allready over now,
dwindling from this strife.
So she goes, I go too. Scooch about,
cross legs and ankles. Guard over her.
Winter's fall lending Winter's weight
quickly on my shoulders.
There is no more way for US.
Here's where we no longer occur.
We are the unfixed, the ever mixed up.
Freezeville for sad sits. Hadniks. And Bums.
No holding hands. Lost.
Dancing around. Goofing off. Not even valid.
And cold allone O cannot numb how I miss.
Me with her. Beyond all starts. Beyond return.

I'm over this.
O what dour, repugnant thing
just rolled me?
Hownow here?
So easily misused?
Flowers from my curls so rudely
removed? Time to just
waste this fucker.
No worries.
—*But what about Generosity?*
Clover & **Snowberries** shummy.
My obliteration is
the ultimate Gift.
Over with a snap. A slap.
—*But there's so much more to meet,*
whine twines of **Matrimony Vine**.
I don't give a shit. I'll nevernomore
the World with a smooch.
Blissfully too. Torridly cruel.
Tiptoe and kiss The Mountain,
Trees, RudeRoot & All
byebye. Hot.

Dec 1 1963
Bayard Rustin.
Raúl Leoni & Venezuela.

New Zealand, National
Party Government
& Keith Holyoake.

1,400 US weapons
& Viet Cong.
Mancroft, Board of
Norwich Union
& Arab League Office.

Major General Duong
Van Minh & Strategic
Hamlet Program.

Virginia Supreme Court,
Prince Edward County
& Public School System.
China & 80-Nation
World People's Council.

—*West Germany can*
rely unconditionally on.
OAS & FALN.
LBJ & MLK.
220 US troops return
from Vietnam.
Malcolm X censured.
Aldo Moro.
Pietro Nenni.
UN Security Council
& apartheid.
American Cancer
Society.

For her
the World turns and to blow it away
would forfeit all the World allready Loves of her.
What bending she allways resolves.
What evolving she allways ends.
How here without, she still somehow,
over with, comforts now what I'd obliterate.
And she's just chillin on the snow.
She exists for more. More exists for her.
And I cannot destroy more.
For I cannot destroy her. Ever.
So let ice blossoms vine her hair.
And though repugnant & dour,
all she cares enough for to let go I'll spare.

Nov 10 1963
Somalia's 20,000 &
Russian weaponry. China's 5,000
Soviet troops. US Solar Satellite
Propulsion. Antonio Segni &
Aldo Moro. Gordie Howe's 545th.
Kabyle Berber revolt over.
Algerian border dispute, Mohand
Ou el Hadj & Socialist Forces Front.
Cosmos 21. Brazil, João Goulart &
Alliance for Progress on Latin
American Economic Problems.
Moscow & Cambodia, Norodom
Sihanouk & US Aid. Yale &
Frederick Barghoorn. São Paulo,
Averell Harriman, Alliance Program
& recipient nations. JFK, Emergency
Aid & Kentucky's Appalachia.
North Korea, DMZ
& 8 US and South Korean soldiers.

Dec 5 1963

West Germany,
4 military rockets,
Jordanian & Saudi
Arabian military attachés.

Charles Halleck supports.
Howard Smith.

Senate GOP Leader
Everett Dirksen &
tax-cut bill.

Bolivian tin miners,
3 US officials &
1 Peace Corps volunteer.

LBJ, John McCormack &
temporary succession.

Labor Department &
5.9% unemployment.

US, New Delhi &
a nuclear reactor.
25,000.

*—to establish a
continuity.*

Lake Tahoe, car trunk &
Frank Sinatra Jr.

Arab League, Israel &
the Jordan River.
Bangkok.
Engineers,
trainmen, firemen &
Federal arbitration.
Sarit Thanarat goes.
Oswald allone & FBI.

Only before my EndAll
Smacker can land—
An imbecile. Crouching down
among **Buttercups** and **Rollers**.
Green Eyes with flecks of Gold.
Rears back before his
Queen, shrill screaking my leap.
On his knees. Elbows.
Paralyzed.
After all I am his cry's
redemptions.
—Dullsville Yiiiiick,
Yarrow & **Asters** confirm.
Imp trembles and squirms.
Goof hair and hands for hives.
While palm to palm, my calm
diverts tides and troubles patriots.
Taking lives.
I'm his land torching a broken sky.
I'm his World.
Of course dear dyno shakes.
What a cute smile.

Nov 5 1963

Federal Reserve Board. 50% to 70%.
Melvin Price.
—gross overruns.

Chicago's US Court of Appeals
& Muslims. ICBMs: 5 to 1.
Milk & radioactive substances.
East Germans, US Army Convoy
& 41 hours.

—meet the menace of.
US Merchant Fleet. Kinross Scotland.
South Vietnamese Ruling Council
& curfew. Apollo capsule,
New Mexico Missile Range & 1 mile.
Elston Howard. Saigon, US
& new regime. Hanna Mining
Company, Hanna Nickel Smelting
Company & $2 million. Yokohama
& 3 trains, 163 go. LBJ's 34.
Kyushu coal mine, 450 go.

I kneel down beside her. Her smile though's
so sad I can't keep from shaking. Blur.
My broken sky. My frozen land. No more tears.
Enough of tears, diverted for a deadlier calm.
Her soft curls careful upon my palms,
her tides, my storms, spirals by which
she still redeems, reconciles and warns.
A paralyzing cold.
O here my Pining & Curving Queen.
Gold Eyes with flecks of Green.
Unsold and ever free.
Reproaching me, her imbecile, for
this kiss now I wouldn't keep.
Gently left here upon her brow.

Dec 9 1963

—*Clumzy Clutzoid!* he haws.
My exhalation immolates plateaus.
—*Are you retarded Missy?*
My serenity wipes out
his gall.
—*Go beg elsewhere*, he caws.
I'm busy. Someone stole my horse.
And I'm off to find some falling snow.
But I'm the sizzle preceding
disaster. Only by his panicky
squawk am I overcome.
With laughter. Heaves.
Doubling over. Wheezing.
What calamity I bring with just a
shoeless pirouette. When
by **F**lash, searing lime to wide,
I weirdly demand:
—*I Wish you'd just chill.*
A **W**ind follows.
Curious.
He bows.
—*Hi. I'm Sam.*

Studebaker Corporation & South Bend.

British Foreign Office & Arab pressure.

Hayato Ikeda re-elected by Diet.

Zanzibar & British Commonwealth.

Bolivia, US arms & US planes.

Cambodia & Western journalists.
JFK's Idlewild airport.
DynaSoar Space Glide & US Defense.
Sinatra & $240,000 ransom.
UN Security Council, UN Criteria & Portugal.

UN Committee & Oman.
Thanom Kittikachorn.

Swiss Parliament & Ludwig von Moos.

American Farm Bureau Federation & compensatory payments.

Jomo Kenyatta.
Pockets of Poverty.
NATO & multi-lateral nuclear force.
HR8747. HR9009.
China & Roger Hilsman.
Fasten Seat Belts.

Nov 1 1963

Dumb me with a bow. It's the HONEY.
All along. By it I succeed.
Without it I retreat. Begin to freeze.
Chimes! **C**hime! **C**himes!
My hand falls. I'll eat no HONEY.
Thuu**UUU**uUu**UUU**Uunder.
Because my World's urgings over earth's want
pours from this mortal work. All any
esteem and need, from meadow, weed,
burrow and brook, slow amber of every bee,
gold's master hour & ore, source of play, leisure,
trade and War. Though not more.
And without? Without me. The only way
my anguish can Zeee out for sweetness. Maybe.

US Fourth Circuit Court of Appeals, Federal Aid & segregated hospitals.

South Vietnamese Army overthrow. Duong Van Minh, Tran Van Don & Ton That Dinh, Ngo Dinh Diem & Ngo Dinh Nhu go. Buddhists free. Nhu's US coup. Rome & Vatican II's 5 delegates.

Groton's Ulysses S Grant. Valentina Tereshkova & Andrian Nikolayev.

George Papandreou & Constantine Karamanlis. Communist Chinese Security Ministry, Nationalist Chinese guerrillas & coastal raids, 461 go. Bombay, US Team & Davis Cup.

Giovanni Leone out.

Boston School Committee, segregation & Louise Day Hicks.

Dec 14 1963

Dominican Rupublic &
Honduras.

Izvestia, military budget
& 5% reduction.

The OAS 100
De Gaulle & pardon.

Atlanta march & 2,500.

—gravitational
collapse.

US Military base &
Morocco turnover.

$1.195 billion &
HR6143.

8 mile freefall &
US Parachute team.
Senate &
El Chamizal Treaty.
$95 million &
Clean Air Act.

Poverty, hunger, disease
& A Peaceful Revolution.

President Chung Hee Park
& South Korea's
Third Republic.
Notre Dame &
Ara Parseghian.
—Moscow,
a second Alabama.

UN operations, Congo
and Middle East &
USSR's $50 million debt.

Anywho, I've mucho to scorch.
No dillydallying for me. But
silly boy so impressed still gallops
after me. He'll burn too.
If he keeps up.
If he doesn't keep up.
Everyone burns and
no one keeps up.
I'm that fast, man.
Wobbling loose the travis.
—*Wait*, Sam gaps.
Turning me back
to —*What?*
his offer:
—*Okay, you can be my slave.*
My flying kick nicks his nose.
A warning. Worse if I weren't
succumbing to squeal.
What a heel.
I'm too multiple to feel.
A fork ahead.
I take both.

Oct 25 1963

Northeast Air Pollution.
Dallas Mayor Earle Cabell's spit.
Nevada's 12 kilotons. Moon race.
Morocco & 200 Algerian prisoners.
Cincinnati, Walton Bachrach
& Jobs and Freedom Day.
Egyptian troops & Soviet weapons.
Michael DeBakey & 4 days.
Chen Yi. Thomas Connally goes.
US Wheat & US Ships.
Hassan II, Ahmed Ben Bella
& Bamako. US Senate, France
& Atlantic Alliance.
Englewood, Engineer
& Soviet Trade Mission Employee.
$105.9 billion & Federal Taxes.
British Aid & Columbo Plan.
Duncan Sandys & General Elections.
Guiana.
Holiday on Ice, 63 go.

And time only for US.
No more spooning here. Foronceandforall anyandall.
What I must accept. Except
I'm too presently too late.
Hailey someway still protecting me
from pains I'd now so happily kick.
Her humility's too much, a
palled gratitude I can never pay.
So here's my pernicious price. What solitude
enforces. Rancor assumes. Juggernauts of one.
No one keeps up and everyone burns and everyone goes.
I am the big burnout. Beyond speed.
That crazystoked to feast on sacrificial smoke.
Firing up now with her leftover comb of HONEY.

Giggles then dribble from my lips.
Bubbles to breeze. Thousands.
Not one popping. Bubbles forever.
Just floating forever.
Popping forever.
How I fly fantastic too. Grand jeté
sailing over wet groves, smoky
stones and sudden growths near
flooding creeks. **Wild Chives** erupt.
—*Gather, gather,*
blooor **Pipsissewa**.
But I gather nothing.
Not even me.
Slipping clear of that grinjerking
footstomping twerp and bubbling
away forever bubbles while I skirt.
A seething dash of joy.
Warming some. Scalding most.
—*Gather, gather,*
glore **Dewberries & Speedwell**.
So I gather it all.
Especially speed.

Dec 19 1963

Strange Saigon.
4,000 across Berlin.
Kenya's liberty.
Asian Population
Conference.
William S Merrill
& MER-29.

Greek & Turkish
Cypriotes.

South Vietnam
& US presence.

UAR, President Nasser
& China's Formosa.
Tiros 8.
Ghana,
President Nkrumah
& All-African force.

Paul Robeson returns.
Candles by Lincoln.
Baghdad
& 5,000 Syrian Brigade.
Lakonia burns, 159 go.
George Papandreou quits.

500,000 West Berliners
to East Berlin. Viet Cong
& cease-fire rejection.
China, Sinkiang
Province border &
Kazakhstan.
National Safety Council,
30 hours & traffic wrecks,
226 go.

—*most admired.*
Salvador López.

Because I'm the rules I allready change
and by their change allways regain.
Because I'm the order over
which ruling orders perish, and by my Hailey,
which I'll disorder with relish.
For a greater economy shall follow US
and it will be outdone.
And a greater autonomy shall follow US
and it too will be outdone.
And a greater feeling shall follow Love
and it too we will blow to dust.
For I am longings without trust. The cycloidal haste
freedom from Hailey forever wastes.
Dust cares for only dust.

Oct 18 1963

Eisenhower & European troops.
French Armed Forces Ministry,
Space & a cat. Edwin Aldrin,
Alan Bean, Eugene Cernan &
Roger Chaffee. Lebanese soldiers,
3 go. Saigon rebellion. Orono, Maine.
Hot Springs, US Business Council &
Douglas Dillon. 5,000 Syrian troops &
Kurdish guerrillas. William Scranton.
Jimmy Brown's 8,390 yards.
Albania, Communist China & 57-41.
—*blockade of our country.*
HR6143. Ralph Houk.
Soviet bloc Council of Economic
Mutual Assistance. Salt Lake City &
2 extremes. Chicago's 225,000.
Hayato Ikeda.
Fort Hood to Frankfurt.
S1576. HR7195.
Fred Whipple's flakes.

Dec 27 1963

LBJ & Austin barbecue.
McKinley & Ralston over Emerson, Fraser and Newcombe.
Bears over Giants.
Bouncing Jupiter.

—a year of decisive change for.

Communist China, France & normalization.
$6.2 billion & Agriculture Department.
US Chess Championship & Bobby Fischer's 6th.
Duncan Sandys, Nicosia & cease-fire proposals.
The Feminine Mystique.
US, Bulgaria & Ivan Khristov Georgiev.
University of Illinois over University of Washington.
War, Worldwide treaty & Khrushchev.
Ghana, Nkrumah & a lone assassin.
Ellsworth Bunker ambassador to OAS.
National Education Program.
$14.4 billion & Russel Sage Philanthropy.

Until his hampering footsteps
diminish, and from that
finish comes a pierce!
My Wish threatening to become.
What longing longs me then
from me.

—Allone,

bounce spiralling **Meadow Salsify**.

—Never go on,

groan **Milkvetch & Iris**.

I go on, allone, by gullies steep
with bending trails.
By lollygagging **Hemlocks**.
Past springing shoots and stalk,
petals of **Solomon's ZigZag**
climbing & leaping off from
clouds of mud. All around begging
me stay put. Bursting for me.
But I just keep rolling thrills.
And come upon
Two Girls,
Juggling upon the hill,

And more still. All following to extinction my
extinction, ever allways beyond death. On and one.
For I forever only spare
the pursuit of all I delimit.

I'm the prophecy prophecies pass.
Why need dies at last.

How oceans dry. Islands drown.
And skies of salt crash to the ground.
I turn the powerful. Defy the weak.
Only **Grass** grows down abandoned streets.

And I allone am left to slaughter
all my laughter would not Wish to keep.
Where by my staying no else remains.
All now I'd never hamper.

Oct 12 1963

Rockefeller & Goldwater.
Argentina & Arturo Illia.
West Berlin protests.
Kabyle Berbers, Socialist Forces Front Headquarters & Michelet. 99%.
Las Vegas & Mickey Wright.
Jackie Kennedy & Aristotle Onassis.
Florida Supreme Court & 11 defendants. Paul Nitze over Fred Korth. 17 Nations, UN & Space Weapons. West Germany's Ludwig Erhard over Konrad Adenauer. Chung Hee Park over Yun Po Sun. Subcommittee No 5.
Selma's Voter Registration drive.
Sean Lemass & Project Vela.
Ernie Knox goes. JFK & Tito.
Marrakesh. HR7179.
—weakens the last great.

Morocco forces attack.

Jan 3 1964

Fazil Kutchuk, Turkish Cypriotes & partition. Angolan rebels, Holden Roberto & China Aid.

Pacific Missile Range. Auburn University's enrollment.

1/3 unqualified for Armed Forces.

Paul VI & Athenagoras. San Diego Chargers over Boston Patriots.

Berlin Border Guards.

Long Island, Nuclear Power & Consolidated Edison.

Britain, Bahamas & Roland Symonette. Sarawak & Sabah. Johnny Kerr's 711.

450 English buses to Cuba.

—*War against poverty.*

Depression, FDA & hexafluorodiethylether.

—*Not dependable.*

Viet Cong, Pleiku Province & 2 hamlets. Panama Canal Zone riot, 20 go. Roberto Chiari & US Treaty.

who flush and slip before
my stunning allure. Such
their adoration. Immediate
dependence. But I must go.
Even if FIVE SODA GIRLS,
blouses & bangs,
weepingly implore:
—*Bounce for some Jacks.*
—*O My's* spilling for
the wonder of me.
Unwavering terror of me.
Of course.
THESE NINE FANATICS
reach for one touch.
Once is enough for my passing
coziness. Not much.
I'm just too much.
So all Ringaring Around O
Rosie, without me, finding by
my exclusion every one of their
desires blazing. Razing up. I'm
their bonfires. Fevers too.

Oct 4 1963

Uganda & Mutesa II.
Caracas crackdown. Iraq & Kuwait.
Hurricane Flora, 6,000 go.
Colin Jordan & 1,000 eggs.
—*relaxing tension between.*
John Richardson. Dodgers over
Yankees. 54 million ounces.
Robert G Baker's peddling. HR8100.
Plaquemine tear gas & cattle prods.
Cyrille Adoula.
Vaiont Dam & 11 villages, 2,000 go.
$250 million & 150 million bushels
of wheat. American Medicine & Cuba.
—*major foreign policy.*
James Webb's NASA.
Limited Nuclear Test Ban Treaty.
US Army Convoy & Autobahn.
—*trading with the enemy.*
Edith Gassion goes.
Jean Cocteau goes.

All I won't forgive. Forfend. Fortake.
I forsake it all with pogroms.
Heave of blade, grenade, uranium &
troubling velocities. Mortar rounds, ground zero.
By me all levees will break. All silos heave.
I will walk heavy.
And I will walk strange.
Racing wheeling famines roadside to ramp. Carrion damp.
A compass of travels never
beyond range of my wrath. Even equators
will crisp. Change our directions. Until Saturn,
Uranus, fedup, will wobble loose and go.
Sorrow's Five Horizons goes too with a swing.
Milkyway, singularity, every universe sent wandering.

Jan 11 1964

Atlanta, Ivan Allen
&14 hotels.
—health hazard.
Olympic skating team &
Peggy Fleming.
Sheik Mohammed
Shamte Hamadi & African
Nationalist Groups.
Calcutta riot, 200 go.
Anti-American Panama,
29 go.
—Hello
Whiskey-a-Go-Go.
Antonio Segni, Italy &
Atlantic Partnership.
Calcutta, 163 go.
Willie Mays & $105,000.
Abeid Karume & US ties.
Polonium tobacco
plumes.
45¢ per hour raise.
Khrushchev & Panama.
—United States
imperialists.
Grenoble &
Sjoukje Dijkstra.
13 Arab Nations, Israel
& irrigating Negev.
Zanzibar revolt,
3,000 go.
World Trade.
Outlawing territorial
aggression.
Southern Taiwan
quake, 400 go.

And allso their gyre's screw.
Though I still tear loose of this crew.
—*Tootaloo girls!*
And EIGHTEEN NEWLYWEDS wash
pale while Double Dutching and
buzzing YoYos:
—*O hang on.*
TWENTY DIVORCÉES cluster
around on their knees.
TicTacToing for Tiddly Winks.
—*O hang on please.*
THESE THIRTYSIX RISING CAREERS,
Hula Hooping on Wheelbarrows
for Jelly Rolls:
—*O hang on. Please.*
THESE NINETY FIRED & UNEMPLOYED
slimpering for some participation.
All On One Side. All're all turned
around. Fireworks & ice.
I'm no consolation. I'm the heist.
The impersonal price.
Playing hooky.

Sept 27 1963

190 million. Senate Committee,
Joseph M Valachi & Vito Genovese.
—boss of bosses.
Dominican Republic & Juan Bosch.
Rusk, Gromyko & East-West.
Pakistan & $70.5 million.
Kabylia Mountain opposition.
McNamara & Maxwell Taylor.
South Carolina & anti-segregation
protests, 189 arrested. Atomic
Satellite. California, New York
& population rise. Nigeria's Republic
& Nnamdi Azikiwe. Germany
& 40,000 US troops.
New York & Pennsylvania railroads.
S1988. Haile Selassie.
—heat of this revolution.
Sandy Koufax & 15 down. Osvaldo
López Arellano over Ramón Villeda
Morales. Prague's 5. Josef Beran free.

Patience. Their Resolve. Because I'm without value.
I'm the coming of every holocaust. Turning no lost.
Rending tissue, sinew & bone. Excepting no suffering.
From this Mountain I'll go, rogue, stalking
the Sick upon their curbs, Thirsty with their ladles.
And all towns will burn.
I'll hunt the Rich. And the Fat. Heads dashed.
Flipped. Limbs ripped. Strewn over stream beds.
Across every ditch.
Cities swept loose with fire.
And for those who kneel, beg for reprieve,
Municipalities and Paladins, I'll chew
through their teeth.
And every nation will burn.

Jan 20 1964

Tanganyikan soldiers
& Dar es Salaam.

Joseph Kasavubu,
Kwilu province
& State of Emergency.
Relay 2.

Kenneth Kaunda &
Northern Rhodesia.
Richard Wilson's proton.

Pathet Lao
& countryside drive.

Fidel, Nikita &
Moscow hunting trip.

Pone Kingpetch 15
rounds Ebihara.
24th Amendment.

*—triumph of liberty
over restriction.*

Joseph Zavatt,
Manhasset elementary
schools & de facto
segregation.
Echo 2 & polar orbit.
5,000 British troops,
mutinies & Tanganyika,
Kenya and Uganda.

Atlanta segregation
protest, 84 arrested.

France & China.
Nkrumah rule.

Soviets, Erfurt
& US Air Force T-39.

And all shiver & grope,
hardly able to muster the courage
to run let allone cope
with hello's abandonment.
Trapped by my grandeur.
My roasting eagerness.
Encircling me with
raised Croquet Mallets for Peace
& Deliverance. Washing me with
tears. Because I can send
their tears away.
Sockhop their hurt away.
But do I hurt?
I depart.
Undisturbed by their protest,
Hopscotching The Wherewithall
I Delay for The End I Play.
To love only ruins.
Skipsliding free.
Easily.
*—Don't stick around Gals on my behalf.
Catch you on the flipside.*

Sept 16 1963

Canadian Wheat & flour. Malayasia's
Malaya, Singapore, Sarawak &
North Borneo. Kuala Lumpur.
British anti-missiles. HR8200 &
$175 million fallout. Jakarta 10,000
& British Embassy. Hiroyuki Ebihara
over Pone Kingpetch.
James Farmer & Plaquemine.
—detrimental to the strength.
John Byrnes. JFK, Ngo Dinh Diem
& Ngo Dinh Nhu. Antonin Navotny
over Viliam Siroky. Communist China,
USSR & 5,000 border violations.
US demonstrations.
French Government & NATO
headquarters. Georges Paques
arrested. Cleve McDowell & weapon.
—excessive.
US Senate & Test Ban. 80-19.
Wallace Greene over David Shoup.
HR7179.

Perimeterless on the flipside.
And just that easily, on my behalf,
I come around. Because I'm burning.
Because I am too soon.
Because without her I am
only revolutions of ruin.
The beast of War feeds only on the meats of War.
And now I'm for carnage.
Here's how my anguish frees.
Destroy everyone of course. Because I'm unwanted
& unsafe. And I'll take tears away with torments & rape,
killings & feers not even the dead will escape.
Encircling the Guilty, Ashamed, Blameless and
Enslaved. Absolved. Butchering their prejudice.

Jan 29 1964

Saturn rocket.
Military Coup & Major
General Nguyen Khanh.

Ewald Peter goes.

Congolese airlift.
Tuskegee High School &
12 students.

Herbert Lee, Louis Allen
& a pickup truck.
Sargent Shriver's
anti-poverty drive.
US Coast Guard &
4 Cuban fishing boats.

Sea of Tranquility
& Ranger 6.
Lidiya Skoblikova.

*—Revolutionary
prospects are excellent
throughout Africa.*

Tom O'Hara.

NYC Public
School boycott.
Terry McDermott.

Nicosia embassy blows.
Notasulga
High School walkout.

Guantánamo Naval
Base & water supply.

2,000 Somali troops &
Ethiopia, 100 go.

Byron De La Beckwith's
7–5.

I resume meandering, past
Walnut & Hyacinth, extending
every curving field I wend by.
Huckleberry honeylickling
for more:
—*Unite The Lost.*

But I'm desolate. Desolation's
Cost. Endlessly separate.
And coming across an orchard,
with **Jimson Weed** blooming,
a DYING HOPE receives me.
Politely. Dope fiend. Ripe. But
not too hard to ignore.
Can't grant HER a five on five.
And too soon allready troubled
by clawings up through
gravel and peat,
a NEW HOPE seethes
with gnashing teeth.
Skin of deliquescent soap.
Hands? No hands. Pusher.
NEW HOPE. Dangerous mope.

Sept 6 1963

—to the brink of a split.
Laotian Phoumi Nosavan. Krebiozen
& creatine. 4 Huntsville schools
& 4 students. Saigon & 800
teenagers. Boston sit. El Dorado's
Donna Axum. Paraná blaze, 250 go.
—Batista of his.
Ben Bella's constitution.
John Gronowski. Floyd Armstrong
& Dwight Armstrong. Levi Eshkol.
—major obstacle to the.
Alabama National Guard.
JFK & US draft.
National Association for the
Prevention of Addiction to Narcotics.
Frank Church. Birmingham
& 16th Street dynamite, Denise
McNair, Cynthia Wesley, Carole
Robertson & Addie Mae Collins go.
—racial holocaust.

DEAD HOPE. Very dangerous. Though not to me,
even with millions of hands. I slink menacingly:
—*You've lost. You're the Bomb Squad after
the bomb's gone off. I'm the blast ongoing.*
DEAD HOPE screeches. Karumph! to that:
—*Live longer rascal! Get back!*
—*No,* I rumph, banishing her fumes, life's
petty banes turning to raggedy rales.
Fascinating. Here
with Winter, cupped by Hailey's left palm,
a comb of HONEY nipped just once.
A waxing amber that doesn't ebb.
Try a bit. Worth a nip.
Whoa! what weird fire devours my perimeter.

Feb 7 1964

G McMurtie Godleys
& Congo. Ethiopia
& 2,000 Somali troops,
100 go.
Anti-segregation
marches & Chapel Hill,
90 arrested.
Princess Irene
& Prince Carlos Hugo.

Saigon Stadium blast,
2 go.

HR7152.

KGB, US & Yuri
Nosenko defection.
Nationalist China,
France & diplomatic ties.
25,000 & JFK airport.

—*So this is America.*
Cyprus Greeks
& Cyprus Turks, 50 go.

—*Restore the*
monolithic unity of the
World socialist system.

Ethiopia, Somalia
& cease-fire.

Longshoreman's
Association, USSR
& wheat shipments.

Ken Hubbs goes.
Leon Mba overthrown.

—*one man's vote is.*

—*All of it's yours,* NEW HOPE yams.
But not a smidge of it if you
hang with that drip.
SHE even wrinkles. Twit.
Flip but hip.
Very flip.
Though allso yucky.
—*What?* SHE gimps. My turn to
grin. Enjoying her snarl.
Though weirdly I'm shaking.
Enthralled by my scamp.
Where is Sam?
THE NEW HOPE throws a tantrum,
temper pounding manure.
DYING HOPE returns
following this furor:
—*Wander every path.*
Only you can. But grasp:
none may ever accompany you.
Whispurring me allone.
Allready a wilderness.
Though never my own.

Aug 27 1963

Cambodia & Vietnam. DC's 200,000.
—*The whirlwinds of revolt will*
continue to shake the.
—*we cannot walk allone.*
—*we cannot turn back.*
—*until justice rolls down.*
—*let freedom ring.*
—*Free at last! Free at last!*
Saigon, Buddhists & US Mission.
—*link between Washington*
and Moscow is now operational.
Philadelphia & Folcroft couple.
Belgium, Congo & $1 billion.
—*The Great.*
US Nuclear submarines &
Japan's 100,000. State troopers &
Tuskegee High School. Kashmir Valley
shake, over 100 go. South Carolina
Public Schools. Louisiana Public
Schools. Birmingham Public Schools.

Now's my way. Never a wilderness.
Without an escape. For I take
every path. And I'll ravage every chance.
The hammer. The blast. Massing
at last. I'm the fury only Hailey's
DEAD HOPE, charred over, haggard, can try to stop:
—*We're the unmended, the untended,*
cold soldiers of the shoe. We're the neglected,
the never resurrected, agonies of the few.
We're the once kissed, unmissed and allways
refused. Because we're the unfinished
and feered and we're never pursued.
—*We?* I flip to this DRIP WRETCH swinging
forlornly her broken switch.

Feb 19 1964

Omega-minus.
Bobby Baker &
Senate Rules Committee.

French troops &
Gabon government.

Odessa, wheat &
Exilona.

Kashmir cease-fire.

Homs, Syrian police &
demonstrators, 20 go.

Soviet Embassy & Tirana.
Cassius Marcellus Clay
KOs Sonny Liston.

Euratom, European Coal
and Steel Community
& EEC.

Pathet Lao's
Plaine des Jarres.

Long Dinh & Viet Cong's
514th Battalion, 16 go.

Princess Anne, Maryland,
Firehoses & Dogs.

Lockheed's Mach 2.

Greek thousands &
anti-US rally.
Assistant State
Secretary for Far Eastern
Affairs & William Bundy.
Dawn Fraser's
58.9 seconds.
—the persistent.

Mild turnings deliver me Sam
skipping by. Stumbling
mostly along musty bogs.
An uptown bust.
Spun out for the long slog.
—Give over the gentlest, smirr
Hound's Tongue and **Spreading**
Dogbane which by spore, snag
and burr, quickly cling to him.
Playfully. He shrieks. Painfully.
He's every failing bravery surprising
THREE NATIVE NURSES
with garden hoses turned towards
the onslaught. Amok Sam
knocks over most.
Slides. Flails. Wipes out.
Then runs off, chased by
their angry moods.
—You clod.
—Worthless poltroon.
Until over a rise all come
across a Campfire.

Aug 14 1963

Anti-Xi-Zero. 37–44, S1321
& National Service Corps.
Albertis Harrison. Stefan Wyszynski.
Alphonse Massamba-Debat over
Fulbert Youlou. Buddhist monk
& Saigon gasoline, 1 goes.
AFL-CIO National Maritime Union
& 34 shipping routes.
Haiti & Dominican border.
Naha Okinawa, China Sea
& Midori Maru, 55 go.
René Chalmers. State College Board
& Cap. Robert Wagner's day.
Anthony Wedgwood Benn.
Wally Butts & $3 million.
Over 100 monks arrested.
Radiation, wheat & bugs.
Lockheed C-141 Starlifter.
67 miles. Sea of Galilee. HR7885.
1,000 students protest.
Jordanian Soldiers & Israeli Soldiers.

Icy comfort. But allso too my own warning.
I plod angrily back to Hailey, and
allready every crunch of snowy clump
shoves mountain upheavals over.

I desire panic, privilege slaughter.
Assault health. Too heart strong.

I'm every bravery failing,
crushing with each stride the throat
of any friendship. How the hand I round
forces down a heavy whip of lenticular cloud.

Storms too. And why? Because I feel rotten.
Worse. Rotten's got something left to give.
I'm not even worth taking. But I have what it takes.

Rage. Rage. Rage.

March 3 1964

Gabon & Libreville riot.
Governor Nelson
Rockefeller.
—Stop-and-frisk.
—No-knock.
LBJ, Government posts
& 10 Women.
Kentucky's Public
Accommodations law
&10,000.
Phenothiazine &
schizophrenia.
Constantine of Greece.
Elijah Muhammad,
Malcolm X
& Nationalist Party.
—There can be no
revolution without
bloodshed and it is.
Supreme Court,
New York Times
& LB Sullivan.
East Germany,
Soviet Defenses
& US Air Force RB-66.
—Bloody and wanton
stalemate.
Pnom Penh &
anti-US riots.
James R Hoffa,
jury tampering & 8 years
—Whenever and
wherever.
Queens & a knife,
Kitty Genovese goes.

THESE EIGHT SCREAMERS promptly
sitting down, Hot Potatoing
snorts of derision.
Mascara and campfire smoke.
Sam's still forbidden a role.
—Not with bird shit
on your shoulder.
—Scram kid.
THESE TEN SORORITY GIRLS
defending their Musical Chairs.
THESE TWENTYFOUR MARRIED
Koosh Balling his pules.
—Depart friend, Sam, wiping his
shoulder deposit with a spoon.
Whereupon THESE FORTYFIVE
BATTERED WIVES commence
chucking custard & mustard on
him. Sam accepts the Quaker
Meeting with bowing thanks.
Praises their courtesy. Until fedup
gynæcocracy stands, some
SLAM OF A GAL, and just attacks him.

Aug 2 1963

Canadian Trade Ministry &
3 million long tons of wheat.
—bold policy of co-annihilation.
US, South Africa & arms.
FDA, progesterone & 2 million.
—World thermonuclear.
Joseph Farland. Roger Craig's 18th.
Utah & BreedLove's 407.45 MPH.
South Tyrol & 6 bombs. HR4955.
UN Security Council's 9-0.
Patrick Bouvier Kennedy goes.
Glasgow to London & $7 million.
Burma's Revolutionary Council,
Ne Win & 11. Spanish Guinea.
Estes Kefauver goes.
Nepalese mud, 150 go.
Schollander's 1:59. Orville Freeman.
—to avoid a complete.
H Hobart Grooms. Saigon burning.
—one-man rule.

I attack the powder. Can't even pack it with a punch.
Hailey so unrevoked. And unaccompanied.
By me unprovoked. Battered. Nothing even
vertical near. All domed and fluffy.
Departure's defense.

Is there ever an edge? Is there even a fall?
Hailey's harm now appalling me with its
matrimonial awe. Susceptibility beyond gall.
How she someway succeeded.
Her fragility beyond tall.

I roll over on my back.

Could I but just scram this mash. But I can't.
Because I'm allways falling for her
and ever before and allready after only warned.

March 14 1964

Jack Ruby &
Melvin Belli.
—where there is justice.
East of Max Planck,
a westbound train &
17 jumping teenagers.
*—We must stay there
and help Them, and that
is what we are
going to do.*
Congress, $962 million
& poverty.
*—Our objective:
total victory.*
UN & Cyprus.
Joseph Mobutu,
Congolese troops &
Kwilu rebel tribes.
US personnel &
Chantrea, 17 go.
The Alps &
Great St Bernard.
Key West,
2 Cuban defectors &
a helicopter.
Hindu attacks,
200 Muslims go.
Uri & Pakistani force,
24 go.

—*O no,* Sam reels.
Jumps, turns, hesitates.
Too afraid to actually run.
—*Muchos Gracias, please stop.*
—*Not a chance,* screeeaaaaams
THE MONDO SLAM OF A GAL,
on a rampage after him.
All around, by jubilant laughs,
clear a path. Sam allready
wheeling with feer while I happily
untangle my hair. I'm the tangle
of every dare. And every care.
Sam sprints around the fire.
So fast, he chases HER.
To get HER he's most afraid.
So bounds
up and over
charcoal & flame.
Squinting the heat.
Coughing soot.
Straining.
Sprained.

July 20 1963

US, USSR & Atom Test Ban. Coyote,
Titan 3C & 1,000,000 lbs of thrust.
Oceans.
—of imperialist nuclear.
National Labor & Howard Jenkins.
George Mueller. Peking & Moscow.
Liston 1 rounds Floyd Patterson.
JFK, Congress & Immigration.
Havana & US Embassy.
Test Ban Treaty.
—a victory for.
Skopje quake, 1,011 go.
Syncom II & synchronous orbit.
Peru & Fernando Belaúnde Terry.
South Korean Demilitarized Zone
& US Soldiers, 2 go.
Saigon's 60,000 Buddhists.
USSR, New Delhi & weapons.
Hohegeiss, East German border
guards & vacationers, 2 go.

over the jag. Down the face.
Except there is no lag. Not even a heartrace.
A googol of flakes arrests my plunge immediately.
Just a fistload of snow flung by my hands.
No cliff surviving. All falls rounded by the fall
of the outside. Slowed under for gradual declines
I can only roll around on. This
rival wait denying me everything
I might have given over.
So binding grief can persevere.
The splashdown crowning my Hailey's unwhirl,
my motionless Empress,
who to spite me, despite me,
still hitches to leave.

March 27 1964

Alaska, Anchorage
& 8.4 quake, 66 go.
Wallops Island & Ariel 2.
Faisal over Saud. Atomic
Energy Commission
& Mary Bunting.
Harib Yemen
& British planes, 25 go.
Thomas Matthews,
Maarten Schmidt
& 3C-147.
Etowah County.
Hubert Humphrey.
Ethiopian & Somalian
border truce.
Florida's Malcolm
Peabody & 283.
President Goulart
flees Brasília.
—revolution to
goulash.
10,000 Belgian doctors.
Cuban execution,
Alfonso goes.
US & Panama.
Punchholing,
Premier Jigme Dorji of
Bhutan goes.
General Douglas
MacArthur goes.
Cleveland School
& a bulldozer,
Bruce Klunder goes.
—and big-China
chauvinism.

THE GARGANTUAN SLAM OF A GAL
allso jumps but
with a trip flips to a crowd
shuddering sprawl.
And howl.
Searing. And sizzling. Finally
screaming free for damp towels.
Continuing to howl.
Scrawny Sam
blows victory kisses.
The crowd mauls him
and his paltry fists, hurling the
rapscallion from their midst, fast
rolling away, limboing off past a spot
where blow a GRIZZLED BEAT
and RALLY FRO:
—Liberty's all.
—Love, THE BROKE ONE complains.
—Liberty and Love are one.
—And Divorce? There's how
Liberty paying Love's cost
finds Liberty lost.

July 6 1963

—Peaceful co-existence between the
oppressors and the oppressed.
Cheddi Jagan & labor. Smith over
Moffitt. 16 Nations & 10,000 Whales.
—convictions of the American people.
J Robert Martin & University
of South Carolina. Ecuador's Army &
Carlos Arosemena Monray.
Locomotive Firemen and Enginemen
Convention & negroes.
Ross Barnett, Communism & JFK.
—to the point of rupture.
Anquetil's 4th Tour.
—the radical.
Buddhists, South Vietnam &
Diem. Giuseppe Martelli.
Revolutionary Recovery Movement.
Schoendors, 333 miles & Blitzen.
—peaceable assembly.
Baathist Government, 12 go.
Nelson Drummond. X-15's 66.3 miles.

to Liberty no more. To Love no more.
Their divorce united just with death.
Death's all. Life's only toll.

And where RALLYING CLOUDS cavort
with GRIZZLED WINDS, such tollless rasps
conquer little else but each's own grasp.

Only my lasting lets any have. Aborted traps
I move on past. Because I cannot last.
With paltry fists so mauled by weather,

The Mountain howls a sudden sweep of blizzard.
Pale drifts of sorrow. Crowds of firn.
I'll quit tomorrow. I will not return.
So without Hailey, and facing up,

I jump

April 11 1964

Farm Bill.
General Arnie's 4th.

Belgium Government,
National Healthcare
Crisis & 6,000 physicians.

Ian Smith &
Rhodesian Front Party.

Rome & New York.

Silver Spring,
Rachel Carson goes.

Southern Rhodesia,
Joshua Nkomo &
Demonstrations.
Geraldine Mock &
solo round-the-World.
Shea Stadium &
Long Island traffic jam.
Draft assessment.
Srinigar, Sheik Abdullah
of Kashmir & 250,000.

*—For which I am
prepared to die.*

Cleveland school
boycott's 86%.
Boston Marathon &
Aurele Vandendriessche.
*—Peace through
understanding.*
World's Fair,
300 activists arrested.
Houston,
Ken Johnson's no hitter
& Cincinnati's win.

Causing The Hard One
to beat The Soft One until
both dirt their blood.
I'm so ever unbegun.
Following a foaming idiot blurting
at large roaming animals.
How him? On this walk?
Is this who I wander for?
Ludicrous.
But I follow. Slower if now Samtied.
Swinging wide for still
untried crossroads
with cairns left for encounters
never kept. But met here.
Regret begets every alternative.
So scowls a Racked Bus Driver
to a Slack Mechanic I pass:
*—Liberty! The second most
misconstrued of
human aims.*
—Wha'z the first?
—Love.

June 21 1963

Hayes & 9.1 seconds.
France, North Atlantic
& NATO fleet. Danville's 10.
—population to acts of violence.
Aden's British Army
& Yemeni tribesmen, 4 go.
Iraq & Communists, 28 go.
Julius Boros. Kremlin & China.
Surgeon General & Polio.
West Berlin's 150,000.
—Ich bin ein Berliner.
Henry Cabot Lodge & US
Ambassador. Giovanni Battista
Montini. MLK, Harlem & eggs.
Zone Improvement Plan.
UK & Kim Philby. Gennadi
Sevastyanov & CIA. JFK & Rome.
Southern France's farmers.
Brian Sternberg. Baltimore Ferris
Wheel & Eugene Carson Blake,
288 arrested.

Liberty?

Shaky heights on which to lose the responsibility
of anything more. Love following too
a bend of violence. And allready I close murderously
towards such bitter conduct.

Feering no regret. Begetting no dead.

Because I'm allready found and never
found. I am the finding all findings refuse.
Because allways discovered about, I'm allready
carrying out the roamings her absence loses.
And so I teeter over this deserting wide, heart fluttering
faster for the fall so necessary to leave her.

Traipse no more. Impertinently.
Ever over. And now undone, tied

April 24 1964

Laos & Souvanna Phouma.
—*longer and hotter Summer.*
Viet Cong's 6 & Westmoreland.

Walnut, Al Oerter & Discus chuck. Keith Runcorn's turning tides.

Copenhagen & Mermaid.
Celtics over Warriors.
Juan Lechín Oquendo & US.
—*Avoid disaster.*
3,000 students & Prague protest.
USNS Card & Saigon harbor.

Northern Dancer's Derby.
Shisha Pangma.
Geneva, 37 nations & tarrif reductions.

Maltese voters & free Malta.
Federal Aviation Agency & 32 women.

Ben Bella & USSR.
US Railroads & 3,000 Locomotive Firemen.
Dominican Republic & protests, 800 arrests.
LBJ's Atlanta breakfast.

Until on an abrupt hill,
Sam pauses to sniff the breeze
heedless
of SCORCHED CHAR OF A GIRL
charging brashly over flowering
Betony. Rage her only agony.
Her only pulp. Terribly flung
if missing Sam entirely
who can only stumble after,
with a gulp,
her tumbling bouncing,
out & down, ouch,
bashcrashing the ground
THAT SCORNED SPAR OF A GIRL
steamrolling **Wheat**
and shaking **Barley**.
Over and over. O me.
Agony her only age.
Her only crutch.
Entirely clutched.
Until a Brook accepts her splash
and Currents cache HER gently.

Hailey's abrupt stop? By this drop?

Algidity binds Hailey. Currents of sliplimmering
glaze hard over her cheeks.
Hair a thistle of icicles reaching
down to The Mountain of World.
Even her knees join the surrounding freeze.
Unhailed, stuck, needlessly seized.

I return to the ledge. One fall
warning all. An edge heedlessly beyond this.
By sheerness offering a chance to fling clear
of my eternity. Here, a King reaping fling, and
allready tugging me too, assurances of
the easiest trip by which I'll break
a timid breeze. Smacked soon from

June 8 1963

Port of Quizan, UAR planes & Yemen, 30 go.
Equal pay for equal work & S1409.
Saigon, Buddhists & gasoline, Thich Quang Duc goes.
Nicholas Katzenbach, James Hood & Vivian Malone.
Savannah & 3,000, 50 arrested.
—*I Love you.*
—*I Love you.*
—*I Love you.*
Jackson Mishishishi, NAACP & Byron De La Beckworth, Medgar Evers goes.
Iraqi Army & 14 Kurdish villages.
Alabama sit, 450 arrested.
Clay 5 rounds Cooper.
Vostok VI, Valentina Tereshkova & 48 revolutions.
—*Valya, my Love. You are higher.*
DC & Moscow direct.

May 11 1964

US military plane
& Philippines, 74 go.
B-70 & 70,000 feet up.
Margaret Smith's 3rd.
—going to be
a long War.
Khrushchev, Nasser &
Nile.
10,000 Utah teachers
& strike.
Moscow's US Embassy.
Northwest of Nicosia,
Finnish Soldier goes.
—Waging a very cruel
and dirty War.
—The Great Society
rests on abundance
and liberty for all.
African atmosphere &
2.2 lbs of plutonium.
Argentina, Peru & Lima
National Stadium,
300 go.
Nuclear Weapons,
Goldwater &
the defoliation of
South Vietnam.
United Arab Republic,
USSR & $227 million.

But I'm tied, gliding the far
screes. Down past peevish
Peaches shlickering at his romp,
perturbed how he blubbles on
at every bug he crosses.
American Plums allso annoyed.
Still I trail. I'm every trail's switch.
Ever hitched.
And now even willing
to reach and, well, touch him.
Except I'm allready
wheeling back with a —*Whoa!*
Shocked. Unsaved.
There amidst a small clearing,
Sam swinging with
the softlope foolery of
a ropeadope grope.
A New Hope, yabbling
flirtatiously. All circley coy,
swinging bubblegum tits.
Fingerless too.
New Hope. Most nettlesome.

May 22 1963

Greek Parliament & a motorcycle,
Gregory Lambrakis goes.
Duvalier's 50,000.
Portland's Civil Defense Program.
400 UN troops & Tshombe's guard.
Organization of African Unity
& 30 African States.
—Freedom Rally for Birmingham.
Belgium & 15,000 Walloons.
Kenya Prime Minister
& Jomo Kenyatta.
East Pakistan cyclone, 22,000 go.
Jones's 500. Gettysburg Patience.
CORE, tear gas & Tallahassee.
Strayhorn goes. Wallace's
Federal defiance. Roncalli goes.
John Dennis Profumo, Soviet Naval
Officer & Christine Keeler.
Stephen Ward. Ayatollah Khomeini
& Mohammed Reza Pahlavi, 3 go.
Saigon B-57s. Jesse Jackson arrested.

Annoying. A million filickering fingers without
one turn of consolation. Another desolation.
All here at once and untouched. Where flows
retained by frozen grudge refrain from
releasing all I miss so much. Her mischief,
her closeness, her warmth. Unsaved. Razed.
Wheeling away.
With no hope long gone. What is
there ever the reach of? This storm's
battling and colliding gusts trying to, before
its routes finally vanish too, with just me and Winter,
rolling on, impersonally reprised,
outside of its crystalled pyre
we prepare together amidst gyres of stinging ice.

May 26 1964

Supreme Court & Prince
Edward Island Schools.
—out of his.

Jacket with rose,
Jawaharlal Nehru goes.

Jerusalem, Palestine
National Congress
& PLO.

Pan Am, New York
& West Berlin.

Dave MacDonald
& Eddie Sachs go.
Foyt's 500.

Bahamas, British
& Manuel Ray.

Havana execution, 3 go.
Lal Bahadur Shastri.
—combined might of
all the nations.

Koufax's 3rd no-hitter.
Fred Hansen's 17'1".
Jim Ryun's 3:59.

Pathet Lao territory,
2 US pilots go.

Debbie Thompson's dash.

—The battle is over.

Florida & MLK.

Santo Domingo
Ammunition dump,
10 go.

And SHE even cancans his waist,
all twitching, switched on & blaze,
bird dogging with icky vertebrae.
Bloated spewl spewing on.
Sam's seduced.
But no NEW HOPE can escape my
harm. Even this foxtart.
SHE'll bake by my snorts.
When suddenly trembling,
with awful shakes,
SHE takes his hand!
Kisses it! Amorously!
I outrace fury.
Populate worry.
Burn something up.
Burn everything down.
O NEW HOPE, by
Guitar, Flute & Tambourine, get ready.
For I'm an overwhelming
madness hurling molten cyclones
of flame. Except Sam's away
taking HOPE with him.

May 6 1963

Birmingham thousands.
—too little, too late.
Aleppo, pro-Nasserite crowds &
Syrian police, 50 go.
Strategic Hamlets. Pearson, Canada
& US Warheads. Oleg Penkovsky &
Greville Wynne. AD King & bomb.
Biracial committee & Nashville,
Tennessee. Lincoln Laboratory &
400 million copper dipoles.
Federal Troops south.
Davis Cup Team & Arthur Ashe.
Kuwait. Leroy Gordon Cooper,
Mercury capsule 7 & 22 orbits.
—of attacking the Ku Klux Klan and.
Mishishishi Freedom walk, 11 arrests.
Supreme Court, sitting &
enforced segregation.
University of Alabama & 2.
Schneur Zalman Shazar.

And there's no rest. And
except for Hailey's I couldn't care less.
Left above such tumbling slopes
with all the ways I easily ignore. Ringed,
gaunt. Spastically shivering with
no hope at all. Just this savage cold, Open,

tossed along by blizzardy moans.
Worry & Fury seized by their own ends.
And I've no hand to hold, stroke, kiss again.
How uncomplete I am. Unimplored. Missing and
unmissed. Now even this storm's wispy gropes
go unscorned. Because she's not jealous

anymore. Untorn beyond possession. Motion.
Where there is no hope.

June 11 1964

Montana floods, 30 go.
Haiti & François Duvalier.

West Pakistan winds,
330 go.

Algeria & French troops.

Mers-el-Kébir & Sahara.
A Philadelphia burning.
Honshu quake, 30 go.

—a great society where
no man is a victim of feer.

Japan & US. 73–27.
Congolese Rebels
& Albertville.

Westmoreland over
Harkins.

Jim Bunning's pitch.

Jean Guichet,
Nino Vaccarella &
Le Mans.

—just how you feel.

James, Andrew &
Michael go.

Danny Escobedo.
Kid Gavilan imprisoned.

Mishishishi wreckage.
LBJ's 200

Naval personnel.
Parade & Augustine 800.

—The kids are dead.

All gone. Him. Me. Even
if my smile's still lethal,
a terror kindling Spring.
I'm hitchless and hiking tall.
Anywheres. Swaying what I don't.
I never won't.
—*Sway how you sway,* **Mountain**
Marsh Marigolds gummon.
—*What do you sway?*
Golden Currants wicket.
Everything. Everyway. Exvious.
Hoofing flammatory over ice
shackled meadows and melting
Mountainstacked pebbles. Mine.
Round Alumroot affirm: —*Totally.*
Embraces all around:
—*¡Hola! Ahoy! Chào em!*
—*You've nothing to lose.*
Greet all ears with a grin.
Blunt Sweetroot & Bearberry by
Henbit DeadNettle yiggling:
—*What Up!* —*Hey Boss!* —*Yo!*

April 19 1963

2 cyclones, over 110 go.
Julián Grimau García goes.
Lester B Pearson goes. Attalla
Alabama, William Moore goes.
Celtics over Lakers.
—a foreign country. There's no.
Herat floods, 107 go.
Brian Sternberg's vault. Castro's
Moscow. Baghdad, Palestinian
students & Jordanian Embassy.
Kontun, 42 go.
Bob Hayes & 9.9 seconds.
Dominican Embassy's 22.
Everest & Norman Dyhrenfurth.
Eugene Bull Connor, fire hoses
& dogs. Nelson Rockefeller
& Margaretta Murphy.
Baeza's Derby. Alfred Svenson,
East Germany & defection. Denver
Colorado & 4 Cadets. Wayne Morse
& John Sherman Cooper.

Bye! Later! Svidanye!
Just leave it. Quit it. Kick it loose.
I'm nothing left to lose.
Arrivederci! Bis Spater! Ciao!
Embracing a certainty overdue,
and, sparing the how, prepared for too.
But daring that now, still stuck on manner.
The Mountain she lies upon, The Mountain
she's undone upon. Without
agony, anguish and damage. So perfectly managed.
Without even dread. This face, these soft
cheeks. Gentlest hands. Fingers I cup down. Nails up
tapping thumbs. Her mouth still faintly charmed.
She for me, O. Me for her, O. Allone here.

June 28 1964

—prepared to risk War to keep its freedom.

Cuba, Juana Castro Ruz & defection.

Manila, Luzon & Typhoon Winnie, 107 go. HR 7152.

—Let US close the springs of racial poison.

Atlanta, Lester Maddox & axe handles.

Wimbledon & Maria Bueno.

Weekend traffic wrecks, 504 go. Over 1,000.

LBJ, Mishishishi & 140 Federal Agents.
Congo & Premier Moise Tshombe.

Chuong Thien Province,

Vinh Cheo & 1,000 Viet Cong, 200 go.

Jackson's restaurants. Lemuel Augustus Penn goes.

Tallulah's 2.

Saigon & 600 US troops.

Jacques Anquetil's 5th Tour.

When Renversé to bole, hundred
ringed, with frightened **Crown**.
Oddly roped for hacks
by savage frown:
—O here. Now. Let me go. Please.
Shirpbawkelay!
Strong Pith. Tall Phloem.
Great Heartwood, Oily Barked with
cones of Ever Dust. Perfumes
trampled by Diesel Trucks, chain
sawed, and clear cut
for that SNIDEY CLYDE:
—You cain't own
what you cain't end.
Notching and atimbering. I dash,
murdering gaps to gum his axe
hacking at my **Tree**.
Tall Pith. Warm Heart
creeing just to stay
a little longer except
by violent do's
allready removed.

April 1 1963

Grand Jury & 7 US Steel Companies. Quinim Pholsena goes. Birmingham, non-violence & segregation. Lunik 4. John L Lewis retires. Gympie fight, Norman Smith goes. Tito's rule. Nicklaus's Masters. Churchill's US citizenship. 9:00 AM, 1,400 ft & USS Thresher, 129 go. *—We shall overcome.* Birmingham Jail. *—is unjust, and who unwillingly accepts the penalty of imprisonment.* Mahendra Bir Bikram Shah Dev & Nepal's State of Emergency. *—an important corner has been turned.* London, 70,000 & A-Bomb protest. National Reconciliation Cabinet. Paul Hornung, Alex Karras & Pete Rozelle.

Now what?
Her death
clinging hard to Hailey's rigid lips. O! How?
Some course of course. If not at all obvious to me.
Only the saddest mystery cradled by her cold palms.
My end denied by her end
allmost ending me with all it won't harm.
Because I can't end what I don't own.
Though there's got to be somehow I can join her?
I freak. Shaking, streaming.
Tears unstopping globs of mess.
—O here. Let me go. Please.
So hacked and roped by this savage World.
I'm too frightened.

July 15 1964

Carl Weinman &
Samuel Sheppard.

—the defence of
liberty is no vice.

Robert F Wagner
Junior High School &
Thomas Gilligan,
James Powell goes.

Campbell's 403.1 MPH.
Atlas-Agena rocket.
Harlem riots.
Bedford-Stuyvesant riots.

UAR freighter &
Port of Bone, 100 go.
Rochester riots.

—to ratify terror.

5,000 to Vietnam.
Sugar Workers &
171 day strike.

Rocky Mountains &
Public Power Plan.
Pleasant Grove burns.

Ranger 7 &
Sea of Clouds.

—We will not fail.

Gulf of Tonkin.

Ticonderoga, Maddox
& torpedo attacks.

—a sting out of this.

Distaff wheeling plait. Cast off to
foggy dales slipping further down
by sapling slopes wet with sweeps
of departing damp. Until soon by
every shifwhimering path, worried
Field Pennycress shuffle.
Kentucky Coffee Trees rustle.
Over the hills the strangest crash.
Boooooooooomblastandruin.
Looooooming at last.
—Them!
shake heaps of **Ballhead Waterleaf.**
Spurge & Cohosh feersick. **Parsnip**
too. Not me. Can't feersick me.
I'm all. The all safe.
Ever once. Ever there.
Allways unsafe. But **Saskatoon**
Serviceberries still escape:
—Run away you dingbat.
And somewheresomeway on
batten wings, a sadder bough.
Mmmmmm.

March 18 1963

Clarence Earl Gideon vs Wainwright.
Sahara 8th. Costa Rica, President's
Conference & Soviet aggression.
Mohammed Yusuf over
Sardar Mohammed Daud Khan.
44.8 points. The Rock
& 27 prisoners. TFX fighter.
Measles vaccine. Bali
& Agung volcano, 1,500 go.
Henry Carr's 200 meters.
170,000 French Coal Miners.
Ultimino Ramos. Davey Moore goes.
5-4. Arson. Parliament, London
Police & 7,000 from Scotland and
Northern Ireland. Commando L.
William Levitt refuses.
Key West, 2 Cuban MIGs
& US Floridian.
Pathet Lao, Kong Le
& Plaine des Jarres.
Low voter turnout.

And no, finally, a maybe
stopping me, yes.
I'll stay.
By her, for her, with her. Her calm, her calamity.
What even now her stillness demands.
All I can never get from me. Not me.
Feersick with me. Yearning for returns
No One allows.
So far gone. The strangest longings. By every
shifwhimering path allready whisked from here. From
her. By hoar and permafrost, the frozen stand of slope
and copse, down to where common towns roast
their stay with warming hands and warmer laughs.
Where I will not go.

Of course I stick it out.
A little trepidation going.
Misgiving? Perhaps. Quite a rumble
roaring my way. A bit
difficult to relax.
Not that I can't with both
hands behind my back
evaporate all.
Except I'm somehowsomenow
changed. Okay stayed. At least
hesitant. Even when, with these
surrounding legions,
tightclutching my enviable mound,
swarming from gulch, gully and gorge,
and by, Angry Mangy
Naked Urges riot towards me.
—*Them!*—
Every last one of Them.
Tufted Evening Primrose streaking
from this hurtful gathering.
Though funnily, I do not
duck the onslaught.

Aug 4 1964
Earth dam & 3 bodies.
Turner Joy.
Air Raids & 5 down.
—*Aggression unchallenged is aggression unleashed.*
416-0. 88-2.
Wayne Morse &
Ernest Gruening.
—*repel any armed attack.*
Turkish planes
& Northwestern Cyprus.
UN cease-fire.
—*Peaceful relations among nations.*
Tokyo Olympics
& South Africa.
Alice Lenshina's
Lumpa charge, 500 go.
London Raid
& train robber.
US trap &
2,000 Viet Cong.
Patterson &
Elizabeth riots.
Barry Watson's channel.
Louisiana High School
& 3.
—*to accept the endless growth of relief rolls.*
Mali, Burundi, Congo
Republic & deportations.

I must go. Race for help. Though to take
that chance I'll have to leave her.
Must if I'm to find from
this hurtful convergence a remedy
for her ceasing. By gorge, gully and gulch,
down past glade, brook and path, towards
another encycling of life to lend a life
and save my Hailey.
But what if, if by that time,
if she's even then not saved, I find I'm changed?
Somenowsomehow enduring?
By circadian seduction eager to stay
on without her evaporating ways?
How ugly. Could I betray her?

Feb 22 1963
Libya & 3 earthquakes, 300 go.
Supreme Court & South Carolina,
187 free. Ralph Bunche's Yemen.
Malcolm X & cooperation.
Cuba & USSR's 10,000.
—*lost.*
Pompidou & Paris 9.
Greenwood Mishishishi,
Emancipation Proclamation &
voter registration drive.
—*along the entire.*
Balloon, 77,000 ft & Mars.
Peruvian landslide, 300 go.
Charles Sifford. Nicolás Lindley
López over Ricardo Godoy.
UAR Warships & Port of Jizan.
Army Coup & 8th Syrian revolt.
Georges Bidault & Germany.
Military draft, HR2438 & 4 years.
Virginia, West Virginia, Tennessee,
Alabama & Kentucky floods.

Aug 22 1964

Wheelus Air Force Base.
Bill Horstmeyer goes.

Hurricane Cleo, 124 go.
HR 9586.

Nguyen Khanh,
Duong Van Minh,
Tran Thien Khiem &
Triumvirate.
Nimbus A.

—backlash.

Maria Itkina's Kiev dash.
North Philadelphia riot.

—War impossible
for all time.

Novaya Zemlya,
Cesium-137 & Eskimos.

Alvin C York goes.
100 paratroopers
& Malaya.

—There is a mood
of uneasiness.

Chile, People's Front &
Eduardo Frei Montalva.
Typhoon Ruby, 736 go.

Uruguay & Cuba.
1,400 & 7,
Prince Edward
Schools open.

William Willis,
Age Unlimited &
a 9,800 mile drift.

Around me, about me,
twirling me, pawing me,
plundering me until
after it's done and before it's begun
I'm overwhelmed by Them.
Slapped. Mauled. Bound.
Bludgeoned. Fried. Whacked.
Everybody gets a turn.
—*Me,* Them reek.
—*You,* Them bleak. Yearned
without earning, and by such
Pleasures & Pride, thrusting their
frustragings on me. Allforfree.
From my mouth to thighs,
with rocks & ties,
whacks, punches and gropes.
I don't move.
Them don't stop.
All Them. At once. Onebyone.
Until abruptly Them're gone.
Leaving me furious
and, okay, sure, a bit startled.

Feb 2 1963

Nicklaus over Player.
Douglas Harkness retires.
—to rid the hemisphere.
Conservative Government, Coalition
& Diefenbaker.
—Europe will never turn her back
on England.
—a base for the export of
aggression and subversion.
Savang Vatthana. Jim Garrison
convicted. Iraq & Air Force revolt,
1,000 go. Abdul Karim Kassem out.
Ceylon. Venezuelan rebels, Houston
& Anzoategui freighter.
—humiliated time after time.
—World order under law.
Jimmy Hoffa & Robert Kennedy.
Harold Wilson. Joe Tribble.
Conservation Corps. Jim Beatty's
3:58:6. Mayor Brandt re-elected.
Peace & Kurds. MIGs & shrimp boat.

And not even panic helps.
Because there's No One to turn to. And none will
ever turn for US. I can't go on with her.
Only keep her, hold to her. Protection from
this savaging ice, covering her feet and face,
shielding her from this molesting freeze,
allmost pleasant & fine enough to need,
if despising too its onslaught with tremoring
hands circulating only death.
—*Hailey,* I peep.
—*Don't leave me,* I weep.
Draping over her, pawing her, rolling her,
for denying me her ease
where wantings cannot want me.

Sept 10 1964

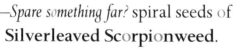

But hey, now I'm eager too
to heap all on my palm
and blow it away.
I'm ruins of dead. Now
here, suffer my affections.
How I long. How I belong.
Because that's what I'm here for.
Even soil simpers with feer.
—*Spare something near?*
shoooodder **Hotrock Penstemon**.
But my role commands
the ultimate toll.
Over with a flick.
A kick.
—*Spare something far?* spiral seeds of
Silverleaved Scorpionweed.
But I'm unavoidable. No underneath
beneath. No over
above. Just one side.
Only I'm uncertain.
Fingers quibbering.
Breaths shallow and tired.

Singapore, Malays
& Chinese, 13 go.

Hans Puhl &
East German refugee.
Reinhold Niebuhr.
Lam Van Phat
coup crushed.

Republican Party
& Strom Thurmond.

Constantine of Greece &
Anne-Marie of Denmark.
British Commonwealth
& Malta liberty.
Taiho sumo.

Constellation cups
Sovereign.
McComb & Dynamite.
Florida & Minuteman II.
US Senate, Appalachia
& $1.6 billion aid.

89 General Motors
plants, over 250,000
United Auto Workers
& strike.

The Warren Commission
& FBI.
Reservoir bursts,
1,000 go.

Congress & ROTC.

Ban on political activities,
Berkeley sit & 32 hours.

Jan 12 1963

And now my breathing shallows.
Calves cramp. Everything about me unsure.
Unable to carry her more. No way beyond.
Walking the edge of a sob.
Stuttering. Stumbling to a stop. US.
Dropping to my knees, stroking her head.
No kiss, choking over hers missing.
The ultimate toll I can't command.
Too powerless to ever lift her again.
So I drag her. But not much.
She's too much. I can go no further. Shuddering
then, cold with feer, here where I won't belong,
among offals of dead,
atop The Mountain's palm.

Portsmouth & John Adams.
Dean Rusk.
Miami, Cuba & 100 US citizens.
—*danger to the World.*
$10 billion tax cut.
Alabama.
—*segregation now, and.*
Bourguiba & Tunisia's 13.
Khrushchev & Berlin's divide.
East German Party Congress &
Ulbricht. DC, Iranian Embassy & 12.
—*Genghis Khan policy.*
US cold, 150 go.
1 firing squad, 10 Tunisians go.
New Orleans &
Tulane University's 5.
Brunei & 2,000 British troops.
Multilateral NATO atom force,
de Gaulle & veto. USSR, France &
Trade Pact. Federation of Rhodesia,
Nyasaland & Hastings Banda.

Oct 4 1964

Hurricane Hilda, 32 go.
Vicksburg dynamite,
2 go.

Arfons's 434.02 MPH.
57 to West Berlin.

—the annihilation
of both players.

George James & Poverty.
Venezuela's
Michael Smolen.

Accidental bombing
& Bien Hoa Province,
30 go.

Tokyo Olympics.
Paris race, 5 go.

LBJ, John Birch Society
& KKK.
Voskhod I & 16 orbits.

Cardinals over Yankees.
Bonneville Salt Flats,
526.28 MPH & pond.
Khrushchev ousted.
Taklimakan Desert &
20 kilotons.
Harold Wilson.
Leonid Brezhnev &
Aleksei Kosygin.
—Peaceful coexistence.
The Shoe's
Slapstick 5000.
Baxterville Mishishishi
& 5 kilotons.

By this furious flurry
what just won't desist,
a pang—
Sam.
Somehow too among this
unslackening stream of thriving shit
untossed—
Sam. On his own. Lost.
So even with Them, their clotted
loathing regrouping to covet my
supreme Fame, I wonder of
his Green Eyes with flecks of Gold.
—He's around,
Rosy Pussytoes bold.
But then Them returns.
Where's his curvy moptop?
I blunder until teeming Hordes
resurge, pawing my rear, splittling
my lips, clawing my nipples raw. I
don't and uncurl revenge.
I'm their only World.
Where's his smile?

31

330

Dec 23 1962

South Vietnam & US helicopter,
1 goes.
East Berlin, bus & the gates,
8 escape. FDA & Frances O Kelsey.
JFK & Brigade 2506's 1,113.
Packers over Giants. UN forces
& Katanga. Kolwezi, Kamina
& Kipushi. Tshombe & Salisbury.
—force a solution on US, all.
Taiwan, Peking & mainland revolt.
USC over Wisconsin.
Mekong Delta, Ap Bac
& 5 US helicopters, over 65 go.
Jadotville, Katanga secessionists
& UN. Peru's 800 arrests.
Ukraine's 6.
300 surround James Meredith.
—You nigger!
16 days' rain & Morocco,
hundreds go.

Though without a smile.
My only World. What twists for revenge.
Beyond every feer. Removed from the surging of shift
I allways move with. I'm a waste of time but here
with her soft hair wrapping my neck
hangs the wastes of time. No longer around.
Gold Eyes with flecks of Green.
A frigid Glory
found without relief,
unbound without contentment, leaving me
lost, too on my own, someway still
pushed by that unslackening pang beyond
any cure. Hailey desisting with this fury
I keep failing to cross out of.

Oct 23 1964

Not here with this beat
frenzy & stomp, desires exceeding
desires first want, using me,
abusing me over
and over for such
Exhuman Engines of Lust.
But hey, it's no biggy. I'm unhurt.
Unturned. Unscarred. Though
Them not abating grants
me the hate I need to
devastate sympathy.
And Them.
Only Sam's absence overcomes
me. Welcomes Pain.
A curious gain which I'm not so
kippy to experience again.
So then turning for
a Promise
still promising one Promise's debt,
I heed my change,
jiggle free of these Thugs
and jet.

3 Hungarians defect.
Billy Mills, Wyomia Tyus
& Edith McGuire.
Republic of Zambia.
Don Schollander.
UAW GM strike over.
Khartoum riots, 10 go.
—*Surrender.*
Arfons's 536.71 MPH.
—*a time for.*
563.35 carats.
Tanganyika, Zanzibar
& Republic of Tanzania.
Viet Cong, Bien Hoa Air
Force Base &10 B-57s,
5 go.
Senator Robert Kennedy.
Landslide.
—*for unity, for a*
government that serves.
Paz Estenssoro flees.
Tran Van Huong's
Cabinet.
Congo rebels hold 1,060.
Mariner 3 fails.
Explorer 23.
Eisaku Sato.
Australia draft.
—*I'm perhaps at.*
Berkeley, Kerr & Savio.

Nov 29 1962

Must run. Gather her up. Race back.
Little gained though. My legs failing the heavy
cloak. Crashing through its giving cap.
Dry billows everfleeting over this meadow.
I plow through. But where to? For what help? How?
Who to return Hailey to, this turning absence?
And allready me too weak, overcome
by all I can barely carry.
Beyond even the strength of sympathy.
The will of hurry. Barely able
to hold on let allone move on.
Her crossed arms against my chest,
forehead rocking forward,
each time brushing my cheek.

Algeria & Communist Party.
San Bernadino, Peyote & 3 Navajos.
Navy over Army.
Chinese troops leave.
Downtown Algiers & arrests.
London fog, 106 go.
Phase one & Vatican II.
Turnbulls depart.
Tanganyika, Dar-es-Salaam
National Stadium & Julius Nyerere.
Masai, Wamakonde & Wasukuma.
20 Minuteman missiles &
Malmstrom Air Force Base.
DC & Kremlin link. Borneo,
Federation of Malaysia & revolt.
—*space for our country*
and the free World.
Cape Canaveral & Explorer 16.
126 Atlas missiles, nuclear-ready &
operational. Juan Bosch Gavino &
Domican Republic. Don Meyers.

Nov 19 1964

—I have nothing but sympathy for.

7,000 to Thudaumot.
Ascension & Congolese rebels.
Explorer 24 & 25 polar orbits.
Sudan revolt.
Verrazano-Narrows Bridge opens.
Kelso.
Paulis Congo, Belgian paratroopers & Stanleyville.
Panama City & 2,500 students.

—that the Viet Cong could ever militarily defeat the armed forces.

Gbenye & Rebels, 20 go.

—colossal harm.

Shriver & Job Corps, Neighborhood Youth Corps.
Saigon, martial law & student riots.
Zond 2.
Alex Quaison-Sackey of Ghana.
J Edgar Hoover & MLK.

—gradual takeover of.

Brazil, Spain & Juan Perón.

—extremists.

New **Mountain Phlox** and **Wild**
Strawberries praise pleasingly
my racing breeze:
—*Weeeeeeeeeeeeeeeeeee!*

Every smipering **Stickseed**, **Laurel**
and **Toadstools** by pool and gush,
Brewer's Bittercress offering up
from ground and bog, **Beech** &
Spruce whrrrring at clouds, all
creeeing my impossible rush:
—*Weeeeeeeeeeeeeeeeeee!*

And I'm allready gonegoing,
their only one and on, feetbare
padpadding by leaps and rounds
of **Pawpaw Apple** and **Wax**
Currant with abounding **Clasping**
Peppergrass snippering zowns:
—*Weeeeeeeeeeeeeeeeeeeee!*

From escarpments and névé cwms,
by cirques, couloirs and slides,
I streak free, which Them allso
hazard, trailing after me,

Oct 28 1962

—anxiety of the people of the.
—putting the pressure on US all around.
—of hazards. The cost of freedom is allways high but Americans have allways paid.

USSR's launch & Mars.
Daulet Beg Oldi & Karakorum pass.
Democrats & Voter turnout.

—You won't have Dick Nixon to kick around anymore.

Eleanor goes. Cuban bases.
McLaren's Australian Grand Prix.
Santiago's 5,000 & Chilean troops, 5 go. IL-28 Jet bombers.
Bomdila.
Viet Cong & outposts, 109 go.
Peru crash, 97 go.
727 Trijet. Skybolt fails.
De Gaulle & Jouhaud.

And then she's at my feet,
cradled by my arms. O Hailey. So stiff & still,
gone from slide, couloir, cirques and cwm.
Escarpments of change.

I stroke her. Sob. Push her rigid chest. Parting
her mouth, driving down my breath upon
her strange freeze. All the while prodding Here?
How? By me allways near
and yet without cause.

Impossibly still. Just gone. Dead.
To where I'm allready goinggone.
Though over her still bawling, kissing her, plugging
her nose, compressing her heart. My breath
rushing. Allone. Now. Here. Left only.

with something else following even
Them, beyond penance & relief,
a Kindness
never outrun, never achieved.
The dread by which I'm omitted,
which I should breezily visit upon
all paths except this one,
sparing me, stalking me,
daring me to crisp
the World fast.
So what if **Silky Lupine**,
Holly and **Woodland Stars** flutter:
—*Mercy*.
And **Larches**, **Berseem** and
Raspberries wutter:
—*Charity*.
And **Snowline SpringParsley**
bludder: —*Humility*.
Because allways all around me
the World rebegins. For my amble
of course and smile, and these only
curving and dazzling for his

Dec 7 1964
Mixed & unmarried.
Berkeley's 13,000.
—grand alliance.
UN, Che Guevara
& bazooka.
—ensure that raids.
Kenya, The Republic.
Meridian, Esther Carter
& 20.
Edward Kennedy's walk.
—of certain powers.
Bill Bradley, Oxford &
New York Knickerbockers.
Don Schollander. F-111.
Hurricane, Ceylon &
Madras, 7,000 go.
Cleveland over
Baltimore.
500 Chinese spies.
—political,
economic, financial
and defense fields.
$93.61.
Playmate of the month
& Pop Tarts.
Reynolds vs Sims.
—people, not trees
and acres.

—I quit school when
I were sixteen.
Head Start.
Johnson's Office of
Economic Opportunity

her?
Her dazzling pace? Her curving way?
That terrible haste reeeeending a World.
Vanity. Greed.
And Vengeance.
No! Not over this ledge and cloud buried valley but
behind me. O no. Allways beside me, among those
boulders of slate. Her arms folded, ankles naked,
a secund wait upon my weirder race.
Hailey! I stagger back. Up to my waist. Through these
ever fresh drifts. Across their wide breach.
And soaked through with sweat, now hard out of
breath. Dragging me down. Slipping me up,
with a grief I can't overcome.

Oct 11 1962
Vatican II. Brussels &
60,000 Flemish. Amnesty.
—ready to be fired?
Yankees over Giants.
Sagua La Grande. Cherry picker,
launch pad & Soviet missiles.
Saud & Faisal.
—of all is to do nothing.
Johnston Island's 20 kilotons.
Tibet border. Slight cold.
Vieques & US maneuvers.
Naval blockade.
—most of the major cities.
—if allowed to go unchecked and
unchallenged, ultimately
leads to War.
25 Soviet transports. Krasnograd.
Himalayas. Uganda & UN's 110th.
Dhola & Khinzemane.
—But Turkey adjoins US.
—Bobby, mayor of Havana.
14,000 Air Force reservists.

Jan 1 1965

Michigan over Oregon.
South Vietnamese &
Binh Gia.

State of Union.

*—to which we are
totally committed.*

11 MIA.
Chief Justice of State
Supreme Court &
Lorna Elizabeth
Lockwood.

Murph The Surf, Miami &
a bus terminal.

American Football
League All-Star game,
New Orleans players
& boycott.

Laos & 2 US planes.
North Ireland, Republic
of Ireland & Belfast.

Churchill's stroke.

Cape Kennedy &
Gemini 2.

*—We are all passengers
on a dot of earth.*

*—allways trying and
allways gaining.*

US Air Force Academy &
100 Cadets.

veering I feel nearing for me,
his each racing footfall removing me
farther from
Them
and that Over Rated
destructive role I lazily postpone
with each of my own steering steps
racing for Sam down **Mosssoft**
stones, by bud, bulb & blossom
bursting from muck. And twittering:
—Whoooopeeeee!
Prairie Coneflowers glipper too
while bristling **Dandelions**
parachute away seed.
I'm sooooo from these uplands,
wide fell and dome.
From corries and chines.
From the freezeloss and slowwash
slushgushing out of basins
and brooks to miles of
Northern Rock Jasmine growing:
—Hello.

Sept 24 1962

James Meredith.
342-13 & 150,000 Military reserves.
Weatherly cups Gretel.
Liston 2 rounds Patterson.
Ferhat Abbas &
People's Democratic Republic.
Floods & Northwest Barcelona,
445 go. US, Israel & short-range
missiles. Yemen, Iman Amhad goes.
Mishishishi National Guard
federalized. Valeri Brumel.
Bella's Neutral Socialist state.
Meredith's enrollment & riots, 3 go.
Class. 200 arrests.
*—to disagree with the law but
not disobey.*
—Let it end.
Walter Schirra, Sigma 7 & 6 orbits.
Cuba's Free Dixie revolt. Saudi
Arabia, Yemin & border clash.
Uganda Liberty. Mariner II.
S3361.

One bye?
Losing all living. Summary
of company lost on a hill. Above rounding basins,
from chine and corrie, moated dome, and fell,
by uplands and solitary seracs.
Ahead. Rasping. Sad.
Desperate to regain all I had.
Scream at Hailey. Laugh at Hailey. Hug.
Because if there's a wind, I'm not the wind. Hailey's
the wind. There are no winds. Only the fall of this
ravaging storm I keep slaving on through.
Rejected even by the prejudice of
the Rankest Order, no longer locatable
with even my own veerings to

Because heretherearandeverywhere's
Sam
streaking by, barely able to balance
let allone run, freaking ecstatic,
hops acrobatic, so clumsy I stop,
to which clubby responds
with a leap, spinning low down and
over, forwards, around,
then over and down. Way over.
Uh O.
Feet skidding horizons.
Still flipping.
Until he chestslams the ground.
Ow.
Still now. Face down.
I yelp loud over this terrible
impact. Bleakness surrounding
his small hands and shoes, curvings
abused. So mistreated. So sad.
Whereupon by Flash, searing lime
to wide, I whipper:
—I Wish him all

Jan 26 1965

Hassan Ali Mansour goes.

Saigon blaze,
Dao Thi Yen Phi goes.

The Lion goes.
Skateboards.

Voter discrimination
& Selma protests,
700 arrests.

Ron Clarke's dash.
Alabama truancy
& unlawful assembly.

Viet Cong & Pleiku,
8 US soldiers go.

Don Hoi guerrilla base.
DC-7 & Jones Beach,
84 go.

Moscow US Embassy
& stones.

James Clark, deputies,
clubs & cattleprods.

*—We seek no
wider War.*

West Germany & Israel.
Operation Rolling
Thunder.

*—You've enjoyed the
thorns. You've enjoyed
the thistles.*

Ottawa's Maple leaf.
4 for Bell & Liberty.

of falling snow.

ThuuUuuuuUuuunder.

Quiet landings. So saddening. Bleak here without
Hailey near to catch such myriad nows, floating
vows, settling briefly on my tongue.
Melting but once. Gone. O.
I step to. Out over this whirling summit.
Steadily and farther towards a way ahead
I close closer with each leg I wade forward.
Though too with an uneasiness around
I cannot outrun. But I hurry, falling frequently.
Struggling back up, meeting the flurry, gaining
ground, batting the sleet, across this strange meadow
allready hung with the passings of forever.

Aug 26 1962

Cape Canaveral, Mariner II & Venus.
Felix Frankfurter. Arthur Goldberg.
Justin Bomboko, Angolan rebels &
Portugal. 3 billion.
Northwest Iran earthquake,
10,000 go.
Hong Kong typhoon, 128 go.
Strategic Air Command &
1,000 B-52s & B-47s.
Soviets & Cuban military.
JFK & Castro's aggression.
Chinese Communists & Taiwan U-2.
Rod Laver's Grand Slam.
Kremlin & Nuclear War.
Nixon & Governor Brown.
Ross Barnett, University of
Mishishishi & Federal Court Orders.
Berlin dig, 29 escape.
US Justice Department,
public schools & racial segregation.
China & 3 USSR consulates.

Feb 20 1965

Ranger 8's moon.

—Hold it! Hold it!

Farhan Attassi goes.

Nguyen Khanh overthrown.

Norman Butler arrested.

Jimmie Lee Jackson goes.

Jakarta, 500 students & an Ambassador.

UAR, East Germany & $100 million.

North Vietnam & 160 US planes.

Moscow's US Embassy & 2,000 Asians.

State Troopers & Edmund Pettus Bridge.

US Marines & Da Nang.

Turnaround Tuesday.

Clubs, tear gas & 1,500 Montgomery bound.

James Reeb goes.

—There is no Southern problem. There is no Northern problem. There is only an American problem.

—And we shall overcome.

the falling snows of Winter.
And then a **W**ind heaves. Shudders.
And Sam flopping over,
moanudders:
—*Great.*
He's greatly changed too,
clotted, scraped, and by
bramble, mud and thorn
mugged, caked and torn.
Rags and kicks putting
on the high stink too.
Plus hurting.
All of him.
Scour of grimace & twitch.
So I just soothe him with
supple smooths.
Too loud he might ditch.
All haggard and pancaked out,
my Equality might just
overcharge his ribpump.
One twitch, he fibrillates. Kicks.
On his behalf, I turn aside my face.

37

324

Aug 1 1962

Ghana bomb, 4 go.
Norma Jean Baker goes.
Soviet Arctic atmospheric blasts.
Britain & Jamaica Liberty.
Colombia's León Valencia.
Georgia, MLK & Ralph Abernathy.
Vostok III & Andrian G Nikolayev.
Vostok IV & Pavel R Popovich.
—wonderful.

East Berlin & tear gas.
Mont Blanc. Dutch & New Guinea.
East Berlin Border guards & 1 escape, Peter Fechter goes.
Groton's Alexander Hamilton.
Budapest, János Kádár & 25.
$300 billion & US National Debt.
West Berlin riots.
1st Constituent Assembly.
OAS, Petit-Clamart & Citroën tires.
San Jose over Kankakee.

there's a stillness I cannot bear. Pang & patter.
Hailey. My cycle of turns. Where evers go.
And retaliate. Beyond what Equality
could never equal. Cannot go missing.
Missing her would find all missing.
Yet here I twitch & scratch allone,
stranded among heavy boulders, stacked
with sharp ice, under skies allready breaking twice.
Shocked, struggling me, just gaining strength and
only with raggy shreds to oppose a World somehow
still ongoing without the wonder of Hailey's grin.
Until at last, back on my feet.
Chimes! **C**hime! **C**himes!
Flakes finally

March 16 1965

Only a brush of my luster
would clarify him.
Desperate to live,
clearly terrified,
he turns his head too.
Poor dibble. Mess and a half.
I hover over him, though
even this concern's too much.
Proximity allone nearly
flats his existence.
He winces. I pull back.
—*Are you deaf too?* he zaps.
I'm probably paralyzed.
My snort pulverizes his moxie.
A Doofus. Dolt.
Snappy though and
for a cripple fairly chaud.
I offer my hand
which starnit he
blushingly yanks.
He doesn't weigh much.
But I'm glad for his touch.

Detroit & gasoline,
Alice Herz burns.

Federal Judge &
a march to Montgomery.

Soviet Union, Aleksei A
Leonov & a somersault.

4,000 troops to Selma.
Nationalized rubber.

3,200 start.
Ranger 9.

Yemen, Egyptian gas
& Royalist forces.

Gemini III & 3 orbits.

Freedom Walk.
25,000 arrive.

—*We are on the move
and no wave of racism
will stop US.*

Viola Gregg Liuzzo goes.

FBI & 4 KKK.

2 Hanoi MIGs
& 2 US jets.

Early Bird.

—*But we will use it.*

East German jets,
Bundestag & Parliament.

July 3 1962

Wake?

Where World? Heavy pall? Wheelings ever going.
Feral winds still threatening snow.
But I'm up. Poison done.
—*Hailey!* I clup but Hailey does not return.
This cap of snow, by arc of stone, abandoned
beneath a circling storm.
I shiver. Retch. Deaf.
Frail unable to withstand much more. Grimace.
Wince. Amiss. Ugly for this failure, despite
enduring hurt, to find out where she's gone.
—*Hailey!* I bleat but Hailey does not return.
No longer around. Left, okay sure, but to where?
No. Time diverges here and all too near

Charles de Gaulle, Benyoussef Ben
Khedda & Algerian Liberty.
USSR travelers. Nevada bang.
Susman over Sukova.
H-bomb 200 miles over Pacific.
Georgia arrest. Anquetil's Tour.
Vietnam & US helicopter, 5 go.
X-15 & 59 miles high.

Peruvian Army over Prado.
US anti-missile missile & ICBM.
France, Tunisia & diplomatic ties.

US Joint Chiefs of Staff,
Maxwell Taylor & Lauris Norstad.
Palo Alto & Valeri Brummel's jump.
Gary Player.

Dawn Fraser's 100 meter swim.
Federal Agencies &
Sexual discrimination.
Equal Pay.
Tom Hayden & Port Huron.
—*participatory democracy.*

April 11 1965

Jack Nicklaus.
Midwest tornadoes,
271 go.
230 planes & Tayninh.
Hickock & Smith go.
—A free bomb zone.

Seoul's fifth day riots.

DC & 15,000 Students for
a Democratic Society.

South Vietnam & US
helicopter, 9 go.

Morio Shigematsu's run.

Dominican Republic coup.

Lester Maddox,
2,000 segregationists
& a smoke bomb.
Cambodia, US Embassy
& 20,000.
US soldiers
shipping out.
Francis Keppel &
desegregation.
Australia's 800.
Celtics over Lakers.
Lucky Debonair's Derby.
14,000 to
Dominican Republic.
Cambodia &
US diplomacy.
Liuzzo mistrial.
Ian Smith's 50
parliamentary seats.

Tremendously glad. So glad
thousands of **Whorled Loosestrife**
immediately demand:
—*Me!*

And I oblige.
Their petals twirling my hair.
I am their hair. And though my
feet are dangerously bare, I'm just
too free and faire to care about.
—*Yipeeeeeeee!*
Defeasibly not.
I dive, palms a squeeeeeal wide,
swirling the World and lifting
the sky, arches uniting
stratocumulus & ground.
My smile a frown a smile a frown.
Allways a smile.
Around and around.
Blurring these pastures and fields,
smoky with heat which by these
whirling heels giddily overturn
everything.

June 3 1962

Air France 707, Atlanta & Orly,
130 go. Supreme Court
& 6 Freedom Riders. OAS, Algiers
University & 3 phosphorous bombs.
Alcatraz, 3 convicts & spoons.
—have the best of both Worlds.

Paris Police, de Gaulle & 30 arrests.
Zone D, 7 vehicle convoy
& 200 Viet Cong, 17 go.
Brazil over Czechoslovakia.
Jack Nicklaus.
French airliner & The Antilles,
112 go.
Canada's $1 billion.
Engel vs Vitale. 6-1.
—no government has the power to.

U.N.'s Urundi & Ruanda.
Mexico City's million.
Sandy Koufax's no-hitter.
Robert Soblen.

But O what a sting! Now? Me? Over with? How?
Whirls wheeling me away. I'm unable to breathe,
cry out, heave past my own irretractable poison.
A prison. All here's imprisonment & poison.
Air, snow and uncertain clouds. Around and around.
Spinning me from the World.
I dive. I itch. Allways curling
away from Hailey, nowhere near to hold me.
—*O no,*
twisting faster and harder, dangerously farther,
because why? A withering stab,
mortality's hand, grabbing my cold hands,
my cold mouth, my cold feet
and dragging me to Peace.

May 8 1965

Matson's shotput.
ARVN troops & planes.
49-45.

Pakistan cyclone,
17,000 go.
Armed Forces parade,
Fifth Avenue & a sitting.
South Vietnam
& 20 US planes, 21 go.
Cassius Clay 1 rounds
Sonny Liston.
—a surprise.

Israel & Jordan.
Ralph Boston's
25′5″ leap.
Alabama's graduation.
Columbia
University boos.
Jim Clark's 500.

New York,
Governor Rockefeller
& Death Penalty.

Japanese mine,
236 go.

Bangladesh cyclone,
30,000 go.

Edward's 20 minutes,
100 miles above.

—This is the saddest
moment of my life.
OAS & Santo Domingo.

17,000 NYC jobs.

Until I'm surrounded,
a warning labor, bzzzzzzzzzing
Alfalfa Corollas.
Wax and venom sacs
dutifully waiting on the hazards of
a spin. Air thick with disaster.
The me I terribly feer.
My own stinging vulnerability.
Even if by some momentum
and glee, I can't deny now
this twirling
speed.
Sam though shoots by,
scurrying and hurrying,
somehow scootching away barbs,
which, eschewing **Honeysuckle**,
Heathers, Fennel and **Thyme**,
rise for a dance with the wind.
And over again, despite sharp
rafts of worry, Sam, yippling with
laughs, keeps clearing my path
happily.

May 10 1962

1,800 Marines to South East Asia.
—is here. My days of.
Seventh Fleet & Gulf of Siam.
5,000 US troops & Thailand.
Souvanna Phouma.
—act of diplomacy.
Hong Kong, Chinese immigrants &
barbed wire. Fleeing Algiers.
Supreme Court, The Fifth &
6 contempt convictions.
Taiwan's refugees.
Jean- Louis Tixier-Vignancour &
Raoul Salan. Carpenter,
Aurora VII & 3 orbits.
Berlin battle. NAACP, Rochester &
de facto segregation. Ward's 500.
—Long live Germany!
Long live Argentina!
Adolf Eichmann goes.
Pennsylvania, strip-mine & fire.
Pentagon's Federal Fallout.
UN & Iraq's Kurds.

Around the World. Over the falls. Yoyo down and up.
We reach the top where wild winds threaten
sleet. Hailey's allready going, yippling, carefree.
Cartwheeling this skywrapped flat,
while I lay back, just laugh, and find
wax, here, there, scattered combs
of amber flow. Weirdly abandoned.
—Whoooooopeeeee!
We're set again. A wild stickiness. If here allso struggles
a Bee, Hailey's only poison, upon my thumb,
yielding slowly to this numbing, bzzzzzzzzzzing
sorrowfully, what I cannot save, will not kill,
until abruptly with a plunge of hurt
it ends its life.

June 7 1965

Allison Wanamaker goes.
US Supreme Court,
criminal trials &
due process.
Morocco, Hassan II &
a monarchy.
Perimeter Defense.
Combat &
US ground forces.
New York anti-War rally's
17,000.
472 Jackson arrests.
Viet Cong & 27 B-52s.
Titan 3-C missile. Air
Marshal Nguyen Cao Ky.
Revolutionary Council,
Houari Boumédienne &
Ahmed Ben Bela.
Saigon Square,
Tran Van Dong goes.
Kenya & labor unions.
Military transport plane,
84 go.
Rome Doctors strike.
Zone D.
Search & Destroy.
US economic aid &
Taiwan.
Wimbledon &
Margaret Smith.
CORE reverse.

Down I go with this kid
blammering & stammering.
Some oblivious dip, though nice to
handle the sharps.
—*Baby, you lift me, gift me,* he hops.
Get me all hot. Here on
the spot.
I speed up.
He better not touch me.
I'm too foxy fly for that rye.
—*You're fine,*
flip him some time.
When suddenly there,
where we pass by,
paloozing piles,
rotting rings, chip misery
of all I wither so casually.
My **Silver Birch**! Sad lasting.
At last. At least.
Beside the carcass of a
murdered beast,

April 9 1962

2 East Berliners & a truck.
US Steel & $6 per ton.
—*unjustifiable and irresponsible*
defiance.
Nazem el-Kodsi returns.
8 steel firms rescind. Georges
Pompidou over Michel Debré.
Louisiana segregationists expelled.
Celtics over Lakers.
Eino Oksanen's marathon.
One-way bus transport.
Atmospheric Atomic Blasts.
José Guido & Peronist victories.
Ranger IV & moon crash.
US Steel, Bethlehem Steel.
Lisbon & Oporto. LP 327-186.
Algiers Port & longshoremen,
62 go. Billie Sol Estes
& Agricultural Department.
Decidedly's Derby. Australia,
Ethan Allen & launch. Laos
& Nam Tha. Groton's Lafayette.

There upon
a scorching ridge, flanks frosted, head lifted,
my Horse!,
wheeling to my crawl upon this crumbling fluff,
snorting with disgust, hoof stomping such
stuff, offering me his back, mane
and gallop off.
Which I refuse by holding onto Hailey,
so leaving behind all of me.
Higher on, to alpine meadows, groves of powder.
Glacial glades we cross out of.
Oblivious to all to all Promising oblivion.
Hailey's my oblivion. For once. And allways.
Beyond even time's front. Because now
we are out of time. We are at once.

deprived of all dignity, slashed,
hacked and left, crumbling sorrows,
upon which bleakly
Shepherd's Purse feasts:
—*It's through! We're all through!*
Sam sobbling hard.
Tears and snot blobs. A wreck.
Though I stay solemn, calm.
Exquisite. Soon finding amidst this
slaughter a Strange Pack which
under leather & latch bars:
Jars! One dozen Jars!
Twinewrapped with
plugs of smooth wax.
I uncap one. Potentially lethal. I give
it over to Sam. Oafishly he noses
a glob. Thumbs then his mouth.
Sunnyastounded kisses my mouth.
Mistletoe whisks:
—*Consume only this.*
HONEY!

July 8 1965
Maxwell Taylor retires.
Henry Cabot Lodge.
Bogalusa violence.
Soviet blast.
Guayaquil strike.
Gimondi's Tour.

London Street,
Adlai Stevenson goes.

Mariner 4 & Mars.
Chile & British aid.
Bien Hoa outposts.

Athens, police
& 10,000 students.

16 US plane & North
Vietnam bomb factory.
Newport boos.
50,000 US troops to
Vietnam.

*—Retreat does not bring
safety and weakness
does not bring Peace.*

France, Algeria
& desert oil.

LBJ, Harry S Truman
& Medicare Social
Security Bill.
Americus attack.
Mustafa Amin arrested.
Texas, New Mexico,
Oklahoma, Kansas
& UFOs.

Because yes! not all not all is dead here.
Startled. Even Maggots die from feer.
the chance of Policy until she stops abruptly.
about the vagaries of our climb. Vagueness without
weather's frozen might. Clouds allways churning
towards gusts of alarming bite, a higher waste of
And awkwardly I follow her away
—*Let'S go on,* she smiles awkwardly.
stickiness of some no more.
Uncapped, unwaxed, timetrapped
lethal division. Our Jar over.
sadness only I swallow. Hailey beyond such
joining our snowastounded lips with a terrible
with Wood Storks gone,
HONEY's imparting strength,

March 5 1962
West Africa's
British airliner, 110 go.
*—Conservatism is young,
virulent and.*
Guatemala protests &
Miguel Ydígoras Fuentes.
Jumna River & Roses.
JFK & Ahmadou Ahidjo.
Guam, Manila & Flying Tiger,
107 go. Titan 2 & 5,000 miles.
Israel & Syrian raid, 30 go.
*—of the armed forces,
Muslims and Europeans, to join US.*
Argentina & Frondizi's coalition.
Army of South Vietnam &
Pacification Operation,
Binh Duong to Ben Cat.
Supreme Byron. Binh Dinh.
João Goulart.
Milovan Djilas arrested.
1,179 Havana prisoners
& $62 million.
—against the nation.

Aug 4 1965

—My fellow revolutionaries.
George Athanasiadis-Novas quits.

—strike away the last major shackle of those fierce and.

—two great rivers.
350 DC protestors arrested.
Arkansas Titan II silo, 53 go.
Singapore & Malaysia.
Marquette Fry.
Watts riot.
—Burn baby burn.
USSR & Canadian wheat.
20,000 National Guardsmen.
Heat wave & curfew.
Chicago fire engine.
—from which disorder largely flows.

Kashmir & 2 Pakistani Outposts.
21,000 Athenians riot.
Quang Ngai Province.
Nasser, Faisal & Yemen War.
Draft exemption.
Mekong route, 50 go.
Gemini 5 splash down.
Héctor García Godoy.

Half a Jar goes. He eagerly
gulps every bursting delicacy
I bring to him.
Bringing appetite too.
Without which, this sweet
untroubling meat, he'd die.
Sunnysurrounded
I kiss him back then.
He retreats. So rare my taste.
He returns. So rare my taste.
A dozen kisses unfinished.
Half kisses.
Lips, lip and cheek.
And since Sam's such
a gremmie, puckering,
slobbering, bumbling knocks,
I go easy. Still he's
teethnicks doubleclutchin, spastic
erratic, licknibbling my hair, from
ears, chin to neck. All of it too with
puddles of goo, sog and drool.

Feb 4 1962

Von Allmen, Etter & Matterhorn.
$5.6 billion School Aid.
German Mine, 249 go.
10 bombs & André Malraux.
US Defense Department & Military Assistance Command.
Paris Police & protestors, 8 go.
Robert Kennedy & Akira Iwai.
Rudolf Abel for Gary Powers.
Damascus & Soviet Union.
—balance to cold warriors.
Urn of coffee.
Hamburg hurricane, 343 go.
Friendship, John Hershel Glenn Jr & 3 orbits.
—is tremendous.
—unflinching courage.
Bronx heroin.
—butchery.
2 Bombers and Diem. American Airlines & Jamaica Bay, 95 go.
Big Dipper's 100. Burmese coup.

Beneath boughs bent by the briefer wait
of all we fail to extend.
Here encompassed by icicles & Fall's frozen drench.
How can I, so close to
her, feel still so unfastened?
How by kisses, bumbling ones,
can I kiss longing for still more of Hailey?
So rare her taste, I turn afraid.
So rare her taste, I return unbrave.
Until snowsurrounded she kisses my fingers
and finds for US our last jar
of HONEY. All we've left.
Not half enough to feed.
Not half enough to keep.
Just half.

Sept 1 1965

And Sam sogs & gogs on,
tongue RPMing for
more. Lunges with hugs,
prying for splits.
Rolling me down & up
with spins and urges.
Until I desist.
—*Eazzzy there Chappy Man,*
take a breather. I won't
skip loose.
He gruntgasps, accepatating
the truce, if still keen for
more juice.
—*This your first bowl?*
I gotta ask.
Sure, me, I'm the roll but this
kook's all the dole with short pants,
and not a move how to go.
Flake off & dash.
Cut a wide path.
But I am charmed

Mishishishi
& Natchez March.
Lahore & Punjab.
US suspends military aid.
Segregations
& Bogalusa's 3,000.
108,000 US troops.
Dodgers, Cubs
& Sandy Koufax's pitch
LBJ, HUD
& Robert Weaver.
Hurricane Betsy, 23 go.
Pakistan's Sial Kot.
12 Arab nations
& Solidarity Pact.
Bin Province
& Ankhe clash.
California burning.
Vietnam &
7 US planes down.
Ted Erikson &
Channel roundtrip.
UN cease-fire.
Sugar Ray Robinson
rounds Jersey Joe Walcott.
Juan Bosch, Dominican
Republic & violence.
Japan &
150,000 ton tanker.
Manila volcano,
hundreds go.
Kashmir violence
re-erupts.

Jan 13 1962

And following those charming feet, all will
quicken for, if never occurving to
her, untaken, untouched.
However way she leads US.
Among these bristles of frost.
—*Will anything outlast US?* she wonders.
—*No,* I gaspgrunt, racing to catch up,
if nixy slog holds me back, while
she's all skipping our upandout with even
friskier leaps and bounces.
I persist: —*Wait for me, please.*
—*Why my darling,* she turns around, so I will
eventually, spiffling & sweating, hug
her knees, ring her waist, embrace the spin
of our ever pressing haste.

China, Albania, Economic
and Technical Cooperation.
Dutch New Guinea &
2 torpedo boats.
Charles Van Doren.
Rafael Rodríguez Echavarría out.
Vietnam & pesticides.
Souvanna Phouma, Boun Oum &
Souphanouvong.
Paris French Foreign Ministry &
bomb, 1 goes. 34 more bombs.
—*OAS strikes where it.*
Rocket Ranger 3.
Salvatore Luciano goes.
Peter Snell & 3:54:4.
US, USSR, UK & disarmament.
Detroit's Flying Wallendas:
Jana Schepp & Mario fall,
Richard Faughan & Dieter Schepp go.
John Uelses & 16 ft.
Cuba Trade Ban.
Times Square Rally & 42 arrests.

Oct 3 1965

LBJ, Liberty Island &
Immigration Bill.
Cuban exiles.

*—threat to peaces does
not come from progress.*

Che Guevara from Cuba.
*—To fight imperialism
abroad.*

Luxembourg &
US Ambassador
Patricia Harris.

Aden, student riots
& tear gas.

Florida & 3 boats.

Dodgers over Twins.

David Miller arrested.
Alabama acquittal &
Collie Leroy Wilkins.

Salisbury demonstrators
& police dogs.

US friendly gunfire,
6 GIs go.

Eero Saarinen & Arch.

Aleutian Islands &
80-kiloton H-Bomb.

Morocco, Paris &
El-Mehdi Ben Barka.

South Vietnam, US jets
& friendly village, 48 go.

by his blushwide trembles and
fidgets. Uncertainty. Sure.
How he sputters out:
—I'm a virgin. You?

O. That's extreme leaving
me with nothing left
but to lay the hurt on.
Could refrain.

Skirt. Shirk. Ramble away
but why and for where?
I'm allways pursued, confused,
supposed to do what I'm never
seeking to do. Want to do. Enjoy.
I'm entirely used and used to
it. Nothing to keep. And
nothing to lose. What I'd give
to spill it.
So I do.

And of course Sam wigs out.
Not hardly
unexpected.

Dec 15 1961

US, China & UN.
JFK & Caracas crowds.
Bogotá 500,000.
Goa, Daman & Diu surrender.
Sukarno & Dutch New Guinea.
James Davis goes.

Packers over Giants.
Lebanon & Military coup.
Harry Hess's Continental Drift.
Minnesota over UCLA. Portuguese
soldiers & Beja Army, 40 go.
Lebanese 400.
Venezuela & 4 US oil.
British Honduras. 14-16 divisions.
Algeria, OAS & revolution.
—broad economic and social.
—Immediate Ready Force.
Sikorsky HSS-2 & 199.01 MPH.
US debt limits.
Mount Huascarán & Huaylas Valley,
over 3,000 go.
Pennsylvania & New York Railroads.

And all the while laughing,
giddy, dancing. Terrifyingly cruel,
the mobilization of her way.
Her snorts spilling cyclones. Smiles bringing harvests.
Sieges by swishes of a hand. Brows tangling jet
streams, headturns searing the poles.
Aurora borealis and deep solar controls.
Sparing only me, playfully,
because her coyness is too departing to refuse.
We follow our departures together,
fused beyond worth, links unlinked
forever relinked by all we now cross,
all I am used to, used by, streaking
over all we will never again have
the chance to return for.

Nov 2 1965

Pentagon & kerosene,
Norman Morrison goes.
555.127 MPH.
4-F & 1-A. Cornell,
Edelman, Lisker,
McReynolds & Wilson.
Arfons's 576.553 MPH.
Pitcaithly & Schachet.
—*War, all War.*
Ontario, 7 States
& Power Failure.
Rhodesia & secession.
Manila's
Ferdinand Marcos.
Yarmouth Castle, 91 go.
600.61 MPH.
4,000 postal workers.
Ali 12 rounds
Floyd Patterson.
240 GIs go.
US & atomic blasts.
Joseph Mobutu over
Joseph Kasavubu.
DC Peace demonstration
& 50,000.
Army & Navy tie.
Soviet Union,
China & World
revolutionary struggle.
75 Cubans.
Robert Strange
& Willie Brewster.

Loony. Feverish.
Peeling fast this way and that
to slip loose of me.
Until he's running tight circles.
Pulling his hair. Committing
somersaults.
Even climbs a **Soft Elm**.
Yammers tearfully at feathers.
Then out on a limb he hurls off.
Belly flops among bewildered
Fireweed clusters:
—*Well he's out of his tree.*
And to confirm, then conversicates
with fur! Which promptly
sprays him.
He'll split now.
He even has my HONEY.
Though is it ever too late
to destroy the World?
Then suddenly Sam sighsads
and hands back the pack.

Nov 9 1961

100,000 miles high & 4,070 MPH.
Rockefeller's fallout.
South Vietnam &
200 US Air Force trainers.
Volgograd over Stalingrad.
Georgi M Malenkov,
Lazar Kaganovich &
Vyacheslav Molotov go.
Leopoldville
& Italian UN force, 13 go.
Cameroon State of Emergency.
Globemasters, cars & trucks.
—*I am a Democrat.*
Dominican Republic, Trujillo
Regime & US Navy. Cape Canaveral,
2 orbits & Enos. Navy over Army.
Patterson rounds McNeeley.
UN forces & Katanga.
EEC & 18 African Nations.
Tanganyika liberty. Moscow,
Peking & Albanian embassy.
Supreme Court overturns
sitting convictions.

I carry the pack
of all we have. Just a taste.
Because I Love her
and it's never too late to keep a World.
So we're careful with our honeymoon
and all we save, laid to waste upon this face of
mated grains, fixing land & air. Fires bound.
Waters paired. Overtaking paths
by Fox and Skunk skulls,
our only coinciding no longer unshared.
Hailey, my Civilization, ever calmly by me,
hiking over WoodPewees, crushed,
up these slopes towards our sublimity,
hardly disturbing the flakes
snowsnaking away with the wind.

Dec 7 1965

Vatican II.
Delta's DC-9. UNICEF.
Haiphong's US bombs.

Gemini 6 & Gemini 7.
Karachi Cyclone,
10,000 go.

UN, Harold Wilson &
24 African delegates.

Britain, Rhodesia &
oil embargo.

Charles de Gaulle
re-elected.

Georgia &
209 lbs of heroin.
New York's 4 Pacifists.
Vietnam &
30 Hour Truce.

US, Rhodesia & oil ban.
Max's Kansas City.

—Stop the War machine.
—Drop out, turn on.
—Flower power.
—ate the seeds.
—Unsafe at Any Speed.
David Dacko ousted.
Bokassa's Communists.
Mekong Delta.
Wisconsin over
Cleveland.
—peace drive.
—own future.

My. O. Sam!
Not going away. But handing
my knapsack back. And then it's my
turn to pounce. He buckles, laid
out among **Stork's Bill Geraniums**.
Off with this peekaboo top, whisk
free my ultrashorts. Away quick his
overalls. Flouncy. Beat. Leave socks.
Small.
Kisses then, wet if thin.
Magnificent tits. Gripped. Until
missing. Misaligned, mistiming.
Until.
Jouncing jerky him. Tight
stickening his nakedness. Bounces
slickening the rise. Firming my
cheeks and jiggling his thighs.
Until. Allready out.
Sam releases from me,
teethclamping, seedflinging
stickily streamings off to the side.

Oct 9 1961

New York over Cincinnati.
—This can be done.
X-15 & 3,477 MPH.
South Africa & UN censure.
215,000 ft up.
Quincy, Bethlehem Steel
& USS Long Beach.
Moscow's 22nd Party Congress,
Khrushchev & Chou En-lai.
—War waged by an enemy who attacks US with.
Albania. Paris & FLN protests.
UAW, Ford & 17 days.
30-megatons.
Malta autonomy. Ngo Dinh Diem
& American assistance.
Outer Mongolia & Mauritania.
Friedrichstrasse. Over 50-megatons.
Hurricane Hattie, 400 go.
Algiers riots, 86 go.
UN's U Thant.
Hollywood Hills & Bel Air burning.

Flushed too while spasms
overtake me too. Taking off.
Pitching emissions I'll no longer spill about.
Not to the side but this time up.
Mingling her Open finds.
Whereupon with quivers & jerks
she claws, chokes and hits, bawling
with her balled up fists my final
heave up, releasing everything I'm allways
allready becoming for her:
my time, my alignment. Our unbuttoned bellies
rubbing each dry, kisses shy, smiles wide,
Hailey still continuing to cry even when
we continue with our climb, overalls on,
by bones of Muskrats & Lemmings.

And too along with such icky
drying he allso grunts:
—*I'll allways only come outside.*
Okeydokey, but he could linger.
I bite my tongue because under
me he's so completely uncertain.
He'll cry.
So I stroke him awhile.
And take his hand.
My Sam.
Big deal if somewhere nearby
US
Them amasses & gnashes.
Beside him I'm uniquely free.
Sure Them's still after me.
Booooooooomblastandruin.
But I smile because I'm faster.
For now here, weirdly, where
my chainsawed **Green Ash** died
by Sam's murdered ride waits
a Shelby Mustang. Idling.

Jan 6 1966

500,000 students.
173rd Airborne Brigade's
Operation Marauder.

8,000 US Army Soldiers
& Iron Triangle.
Georgia legislature,
184-12 & Julian Bond.

Atlanta 1,000. Nigeria
& Johnson Aguiyi-Ironsi.

B-52, K-C 135
& 1 H-Bomb, 8 go.

Shriver quits
Peace Corps.

—and the first servant
of my country.
3-day truce.

—highways and biways.

First Cavalry Division
& Operation Masher.

Mont Blanc & Jet,
117 go.

Eastern seaboard storm,
166 go.

Soviet Luna 9 & moon.
Japanese 727 &
Tokyo Bay, 133 go.

Honolulu, LBJ &
Nguyen Cao Ky.

—Win the.

S now surrounds Hailey's Lincoln Continental.
Sweeps of pack, drifted over, crusted
with stacks of irregular plate.
Bafflements of stuff we slug through. Allmost enough,
Lostlastandstrewn,
except groundsnow now just won't suffice.
We must find ours falling our fairs
freely. So on we rise, panting, beat,
until Hailey takes my hand and upon needles
evergreen & sweet pulls me down with
stoking caresses. All of her over me.
I could cry. Uncertain, unsure, riding Hailey's
nakedness with sighs. Biting her lip. Fighting quick.
Surprised when she abruptly slips:
—*I'm coming.*

Sept 5 1961

US Atomic blasts.
—their War preparations.
S2268. Foreign Assistance Act.
Paris, Colombey-les-Deux &
9 lbs explosives. Monza's Grand Prix,
Von Trips and 11 go.
UN, Elisabethville & Katanga, 30 go.
Hurricane Carla, 46 go.
Menderes goes.
Northern Rhodesia's UN plane,
Dag Hammarskjöld & 12 go.
Southern Vote Drive.
—are forced upon.
—the World who won't go
along with.
Syrian Military Revolt,
Egyptian domination & UAR.
Gamal Abdel Nasser's troops.
Roger Maris, Tracy Stallard & 61.
—We will fight and fight and
fight again.
Peking & China-Nepal border.

Feb 10 1966

David Miller's conviction.
The Stilt's 20,884.
Kentucky draft board,
1-A & Ali.

Alabama shooting.
Milton Obote,
5 Cabinet Ministers &
all the powers of
the Uganda government.
Ghana, Kwame Nkrumah
& National
Liberation Council.
34 National Leaders
& Gandhi's rule.
Fleming's Switzerland gold.
Richard Petty's Daytona.

Elliot See &
Charles Bassett go.
Talmadge Hayer.
Soviet Venus.
British 708 & Fujiyama,
130 go.
DMZ.
Seagren's 17' 3/4".
Ambassador Duke's swim.
Nelson Column goes.
Beatrix &
Claus von Amsberg.
Malay's Suharto &
Communist Party.
41 Governors &
Vietnam policy.

Hauling free. I'm not weak.
The weak are not weak.
I outdo all weak.
Even the strong.
PedaltothePasPasMetal, gassing it,
hitting it hard.
I'm leaving The Mountain.
East. I am The East.
Master of the Wheel. That's me.
Opening the carburetor.
Powering turns.
Accelerating more until I'm
hardly touching the tar.
My Oldsmobile Toronado flying.
Sliding. Even widening the road.
I am the road. And roar.
Here I go. Here goes. Not I.
Allways.
Beat the bend, so uptight &
low, Sam quails pitifully, trying
hard to hold onto me.

Aug 1 1961

Leopoldville & Cyrille Adoula.
UK Parliament & European Common.
Vostok II, Gherman S Titov
& 17 orbits. 1,741 East German
Berliners. US flights, hijacks
& Federal Agents.
Salah Ben Youssef goes.
East-West, barbed wire
& Brandenburg Gate.
Soviet division surrounds.
Willy Brandt. Punta del Este,
19 Latin American Nations
& Alliance for Progress.
Berlin's concrete.
Jomo Kenyatta free.
Sweden & EEC. Berlin tanks.
UN & Guantánamo Bay Naval Base.
Burma's Buddhist Republic.
Soviet Union's Atomic detonations.
TWA Hinsdale crash, 78 go.
Yugoslavia, 25 nations &
Tito's conference

So I hold onto Hailey
who keeps zinging up, flinging by what's allways
staying, marshalling bends, diversions and closures.
There goes me. There goes. Me too.
Roads loosening, escalating, coming apart,
gumming US with sand and ice enslaved rock.
Until Hailey's Galaxie Starliner backs off,
finally stops, pistonings turned off.
The Wheel hers no more.
We're stuck but she's my West.
And we've reached The Mountain.
And though we're not strong, the strong are not
strong. So we undo all strong.
And weak.
And then by foot we carry on.

March 15 1966

Kharg Island.

Gemini 8 & Agena.
Thi ousted.
10,000 protest Ky.

H-Bomb & Spanish coast.

—*Unworthy*
of American Business.

Selective Service &
College Deferments.

Harper vs Virginia Board
of Elections.
Eggs & 20,000 for Peace.
Soviet Communist Party,
First Secretary & Brezhnev.
London labor.

—*Kill Them, shoot Them.*

Luna 10 & moon orbit.

1,000 Mishishishi
Demonstrators,
gas & clubs.

US Jets &12 junks.
Jack Nicklaus.

Guam B-52s & Laos.
Sandoz & LSD.
Ford & safety.

Paul Parkman,
Harry Myer & Rubella.

Dutchess County raid
& Timothy Leary.

Passing through Gettysburg,
Route 30 East to 134.
By Plum Run.

By barns, stacks and tractors,
blurring fences and pastures of
centerpivoted soil. Each way we go.
Until Sam starts groaning, heels
scrunched to seat.

Braaaaaaaaaps bursting down.
Briiiiiiiiiiiiiiips bursting out.
—*Stop! Please!*

Boss all, I slide my Dodge Charger to
the coziest park. Sam, allready
bounding loose, wipes out, skidding
the curb, circumleaping **Bee Balm**.
Curious.

And while **Woodland Ferns** object,
still I must check. Hitched for
the skinny on my Cat Bird.
Out of both ends.
Squatting. Sick.

June 23 1961

X-15 & 3,000 MPH. Tractors for
Cuban prisoners. Frank Budd's
9.2 seconds. Kuwait, Iraq &
annexation. Ketchum shot.
Algiers, Sahara & Nationalist
riot, 80 go. USSR, North Korea &
Military Aid Pact.
Mortimer over Truman.
Moscow's defense budget.
Citizens' Council &
Louisiana County Registrar.
Lenin Stadium meet.
—*Torschlusspanik.*
National Council on
Physical Fitness. Bizerte.
Rudolph's 11.2 seconds.
Haute-Savoie. Virgil Gus Grissom,
118 miles & Liberty Bell 7.
Cassius Clay rounds Alonzo Johnson.
$3.5 billion Pentagon budget &
217,000.
—*We do not want to fight*
but we have.

Actions long over. Encounters undone.
Abandoning US to windy roads,
all skinny, perpilexed and allone.
Bullfrogs long dead without caring. And I'm
terrified. What stillness unbounds US? And why can't
we turn around, especially with Northern Racers
lifeless off to the side? Because we're frightful?
Beyond the limits of life? Only frequently alive?
Hailey's Oldsmobile F85 drives on.
Go! Go go! I O.
Skareaaaaaaaaams tumbling down.
Skareaaaaaaaaams rolling down upon our push.
The sadness of the World before US
but we are allready after US
and sadly passing even US.

April 18 1966

Ford & 30,000 brakes.

Bill Russell to Boston Celtics.

Kenji Kimihara's Marathon.

163 soldiers go. Marcel L DeRudder goes. Dominican Republic, US troops & 7 protestors. Celtics over Lakers. Mao's Revolution.

Caibac River & US shelling.

—Succumbing to the arrogance of power.

Kauai King's Derby. Hanoi rails.

Viet Cong & 7,200 lbs of tear gas.

Chicago students & Selective Service.

150 New York students & City College.

—Turning on their leaders, their country and their fighting men.

—to police the World.

DC protest. Joseph Bonnano. Gold free.

Splash the hash. Lunar bare too.
Grody turds. Assssspray, so 288, I'm
glad to steer another way.

My own belly grumbling. Funny.
How come? The drive? Company?
Beats me.

Over a trap, I giggle & send.
O Lucky World.
My present.

First from my rear, forests of
Giant Sequoia, **Dwarf Juniper**,
Downy Hawthorn and **Yew**.

Next, **Rugosa Roses** and **Trailing**
Arbutus. Lastly relieved, Marble,
Feldspar, Malachite and Opal.
Coast to coast. Volcanic to Granite.

Pssssssssing streams allso of
loose **Arrowheads**, **Starworts**
caressed by **Lotus**.

Brrrrp Cirrostratus and Mammatus.
Rainbows too.

May 20 1961

Freedom Riders, Montgomery mob & clubs. James Farmer, Student Non-Violent Coordinating Committee & Commerce Commission. Evian Truce. 400 National Guard & John Patterson. DuPont, GM & $3 billion. Jackson 27 jailed. US Justice Department & Alabama police.
—continue the struggle for freedom.
Solomon Saay.
—every tinhorn.
17 more. Viet Cong & Military Group expansion. Foyt's 500. Juan Tomás Díaz & San Cristóbal 7, Rafael Leonida Trujillo Molina goes. Paris million.
—to escort Jacqueline.
Enovid & Norlutin. Vienna Soviet-American Summit. Mobile beards.
—protect me.
Kuwait. Freeport salt water.

blending rainbows, Brassy Minnows spent, Coho
Salmons desiccated, African Elephants slumped on
faroff runoffs. The scowling whip of banishment
sending ash, dust and radiant clouds across every
haven. Encounters still befuddled by a rattle for
only a succumbing. Hurt & grief butchered.

Gibbons, Masai Giraffes, Siberian Tigers slaughtered,
until not even Roosevelt Elk, Bactrian Camels
and Muskoxen can endure.

Our present.
Lucky World.
How long will it continue? I can't dish.
While we cease, it can't ever finish.
But we never cease. We only jet
from such an armistice. Exhausted.

May 25 1966

Wipe my hands and with what's left,
a Leftwrist Bracelet—
Priceless.
And there's Sam. How pitiful.
Around his Leftwrist a Twist of Shit.
More so I'm bat with
epaulettes & harem pants.
But he's just rank & dripping
overalls.
O well. Scarves.
Magnanimously I let him drive.
He pales of course. The farmer's
first try. Clutch & conk. Sideways to
windside. Unpardonably slow.
Still this is a way to go.
And so everything else around
US allso goes.
So beat. Zip skills.
Zilch agility, slave to
boneheadedness, mashing
Live Forevers,

Saigon protests.
Abdul Salam Arif goes.
Assam train, 55 go.
Britain & Free Guyana.
Dow Chemical protest.
Graham Hill's 500.

—Seize the day. Seize the hour. Away with all the pests.

6,400 against Vietnam.
Hernando, Highway 51
& James Meredith.
—forth a tiny ripple of.

MLK & 208.
Hurricane Alma, 51 go.
Supreme Court
& Ernesto Miranda.

—to remain.

Marine pilot's
shots on drugs.

Coulee Dam Bill.
Amsterdam anti-establishment riots.

LBJ & Faisal.
Mishishishi marchers
& tears. Jackson &
Meredith's return.

Argentina, President Illia
& General Ongania.

52 309

April 14 1961

River Otters wither then.
Never to return. For so by every leaving & needing,
sharing & stealing flies her havoc.
For me. This much. Her all.
Shhhhhhhhhhhhhhhhhhhhhhhhhhhhhhhhhhh. I'm stalled.
That's so George, me sways, mad for her touch.
Whenever there's a hush that's US.
Sweet whirrs, again brushing the
Silence she could
prolong endlessly. Her hitch outracing continuums.
Overturning reprisals. Confounding blockades.
A way out of the momentum of conflict.
And if I'm by my Leftwrist Twist of Shit
allways rank & sapped, Hailey's
Leftwrist Twist of Forever astounds me,

Algeria & 700 free.
—Now only ashes.
CIA & Bay of Pigs. Angola &
Portuguese reinforcements.
Peace Corps & Tanganyika roads.
Maurice Challe.
—Full responsibility.
—colossal.
Coquilhatville. Explorer XI.
Little Joe 5B.
—Do you need elections?
Laos cease-fire & critical zone.
6 million tons of Canadian grain.
Freedom Rides.
Alan B Shepard Jr & Freedom 7.
—The capsule and I went weightless together.
Fair Labor Standards Act. $1.15.
Carry Back's Derby.
400 Special Forces Soldiers.
Anniston, CORE freedom bus
& firebomb. Seoul,
Chang Do-Young & John Chang.

June 29 1966

Hanoi &
Haiphong bombs.
Stokely Carmichael.

France from NATO.

Billie Jean King's
Wimbledon.

Nyasaland & Malawi.
CORE & NAACP.

Soviet race meet.

South Chicago &
Richard F Speck,
8 nurses go.

*—My friends
are all dead!*

Lucien Aimar's Tour.
Chicago troops, 2 go.

Jim Ryun's 3:51:3.

Ho Chi Minh's
mobilization.
Gemini 10. Liberia,
Ethiopia & Hague.
Corazon Amurao.
J Pennel's pole vault.
London, Parliament
& steel.
England cups
West Germany.
US race riots.
Charles J Whitman &
Romero Martínez, 16 go.
Yakubu Gowon's Nigeria.
Lenny Bruce goes.

crisscrossing lanes, splashing by
drains, all stiffin & jivin, and
rattling on, undisturbed, whipping
over pavings & rubble.

By Greenmount and Flat Run,
through Thurmont and Lewistown,
by Harmony Grove.

—*Hey Monocacy,* he flails.
—*Hey Tuscarora,* I hail.
—*Hey Carroll Creek,* we wail,

salutating Frederick and
Little Bennett.

Sam elatedly carrying
out our overflow.

And this is allso the way to go.

And so everything else around
US allso goes.

Only capless Sam ups for horny,
ogling my feet. Something
I might do him for with my
NOW primosteam release.

March 12 1961

Hiebeler & Eiger. Latin Neighbors.
10 points 10 years.
—Progresso, sí! Tiranía, no!
Patterson 6 rounds Johansson.
South Africa & British
Commonwealth of Nations.
—vindictive.
22 ft, 2,342 lbs & python, 1 goes.
Wax. Kennedy's Laos.
Paris Bourbon blaze.
Jackson Mishishishi, clubs & dogs.
23rd Amendment.
Miami & 50,000 Cubans.
UN, US & sanctions.
—We are out.
83–0.
—die choked by slavery.
Persian Gulf & burning Dara,
100 go. Gary Player.
Celtics over Hawks. Moshe Landau.
Yuri Gagarin's orbit.
—proceeding normally. I am well.
—We are behind.

That by her now the urgent rush appreciates how
even with barefeet she casually suspends
the anxious with one shush. How around
forts, by camps, outposts, foxholes and trenches,
everyone abruptly just stuffs it. Them must.
For US a suspense without consent.
Because we're coincident.

We go. Later O.
Hailey routes. Later O.
I blow. Later O.

Without crash, rally, clash, when sallies
just fascinatingly quit. Briefly. The perils of
an unexpected crisis, we're allways the farthest
away from, a Deployment that Maneuvers can
never defend against: we're what's left.

Maybe not. Maybe.
—*Stop,* I command and
my Cord 8/10 slams to a
standstill before a
Junkyard of Dereliction & Refuse—
Society's Share.
Everyone reveres the Dream
but I take it.
Except Sam, not pouncing his screw,
bounds out for a DownAndOut
allready approaching with a
whirl of sweat, mayhem and
displeasure crawling his brow.
Nothing's nothing
ready to accept still less.
So for Sam's high fives,
misses & hisses. For Sam's back pats,
curses and bile. Yet Sam, if shaken,
keeps on grinning.
Persistence, Poverty and Pomp.
After something

Aug 6 1966
Ali 3 rounds London.
Britain's economic freeze.
North Vietnam
downs 7 planes.
US Coast Guard Cutter,
2 go.
Sabah & Sarawak.
Tunis, Bourguiba
& miniskirts.
Lunar Orbiter 1.
Galilee, Israel
& 2 Syrian MIGs.
Richard Daley &
de facto segregation.
Chichester sails.
—A great revolution.
Kern Ruck & Rinker Buck.
100 nations & water.
—Bricks on the left flank.
Pop bottles on your.
South African parliament
& Dimitri Tsafendas,
Hendrik Verwoerd goes.
Dennis Mora's hard labor.
William Haddon &
National Traffic
Safety Agency.
Ali 12 rounds
Mildenberger.

I get out. It's cold. But no harm.
Cold when cold when warm. I yup. And Hailey
glides around our stalled vehicle. Barefoot.
I glide too.
—*Don't you want your Wedding Gift?* she flirts.
—*Turn it over!* I lurch.
She proceeds. Her fingertip pressing my lips
until a serenity crashes the earth.
—*Hssssssssssssssssssssssssssssssssssssssssssssssssssssssssssssssssssssssss.*
Everywhere Them conversicate an implausible pause
falls. Everyone feers the Dream but she frees it.
Cast & Mired bungle but Hailey, certain
beside her Valiant V200, revokes all sorts,
nationality, tradition & nature
for carrying on stupidly.

Jan 31 1961
Mercury Capsule,
Ham the Chimpanzee & an apple.
NATO's Paul-Henri Spaak.
Pinchas Lavon.
Strategic Air Command &
Minuteman ICBM.
Northeast snow. Sputnik V.
Patrice Lumumba goes.
Véronique's rat.
Single Law Austerity.
—any aggress against Bhutan.
Sabena Airlines & Brussels, 72 go.
Cairo & Belgian Embassy.
Henry Kissinger & National Security.
10 Doctors, a nose operation &
Moulay Hassan.
Marvin Panch's 500 miles.
Nairobi & Tom Mboya.
Peace Corps & R Sargent Shriver.
—nations from the bonds
of hunger.
X-15 & 2,650 MPH.
Max Conrad & Piper Aztec.

Sept 11 1966

Atlanta riots, Ivan Allen Jr
& concrete blocks.

Police, mobs &
Grenada Public schools.

South Africa &
Balthazar Vorster.

850 miles up, Gemini II
& Agena.

U Thant, UN & Vietnam.

Joan Baez &
State Troopers.

Friendly village,
28 go.

Bechuanaland &
commonwealth nation
of Botswana.
Basutoland &
nation of Lesotho.
Moscow &
Chinese students.
4 to West Berlin.
Orioles over Dodgers.
Leary's narcotics charge.
LBJ's Nutrition Act.

—who are listless
because Them are hungry.
Hurricane Carter &
John Artis.
Department of
Transportation.
12 NYC firemen go.

among Junkyard Caps, ripped Sheers
& Plaids, heaps of grubby polyester,
along with Zoris and FlipFlops.
Sam points. Some skuffling.
The Beggar's miffed.
Sam offers his Leftwrist Twist
of Myrtle & Tamarisk.
Awkward. Very.
The BagMan shakes his fist
furiously:
—*Beat it Free Loader and take*
your toxic crap with you.
Hurling Treads then, bonk to
the konk!, enormous Flats
hardwhacking Sam on the head.
Sam takes the lumps.
And The Pumps.
Maniacal pursuit. Destitution
clings. Sam scrambling and
squeaking. Until with just a tissk, I
turn away such Disestablishment.

Jan 2 1961

2,820 East German Berliners.
OAS, Venezuela & Hector Trujillo.
University of Georgia
& Charlayne Hunter.
Nigeria, France & Atomic sand.
Mohammed V, Nasser, Nkrumah,
Toure, Keita & Abbas. 75.3%
Oslo's Astrid. Soviet Spy Ring.
—of an immense military
establishment and large arms.

Khrushchev & Soviet agricultural.
Snow & 22°

—pay any price, bear any burden,
meet any hardship.
—But let US begin.
—together we can do for the
freedom of.
Attorney General. Mu meson.
Salazar & Santa Maria.
Boston's leap.
Liege & overturned cars.
Ferryboat strike over.

And Hailey's tires spin out,
tragically slick above everything we aim for,
spinning US round and around,
completecircles upon this concrete cold, out of control,
beyond friction & direction, counterturns & corrections,
donuts on donuts flinging for a slamstill,
improbably totalled, never totalled,
the way we wipeout a somesome who
none could ever cross again.
Carcasses of languishing casualty. Far away.
Even my Leftwrist Twist of Myrtle & Tamarisk
mocks this accident's loss of consequence.
Hailey's toes wiggling prettily though,
weirdly missing soles & lace,
her shoes somehow here misplaced.

Only to have Sam kneel then and
offer me a World ending affront,
which doesn't, shoving such
Sorrow Soles
on my feet:
—*From me to you.*
Way loose, way appalling.
What shitkicker barges
for my delicate steps?!
But I'm tranquil,
maybe even moved by this
simpleton's efforts to give
to me, fingers so nervously
slipping the strap.
So I pat his dirty pate and
how his big ears blaze.
Back at the Wheel, burning rubber,
my Pontiac GTO overturns limits
supersonic. Unlimiting horizons.
No horizons. Erotic.
Course Sam slips catatonic.

Oct 19 1966

US Chess Team to Cuba.

Moroccan Police Chief
& Ben Barka.
Manila gathering.
Cam Ranh Bay.

—vicious and illegal aggression across this little nation's.

China's missile
& A-Bomb.

New York police
& 20 Minutemen.
Italy, Social Democrats
& Socialists.
Grant Park garbage.
Bengal hurricane,
1,000 go.
Demonstration Cities
and Metropolitan
Redevelopment Act.
Arno overflows.
Senator Edward Brooke.
Hebron battle.
Ali 3 rounds Williams.
Gemini 12
& Aldrin's stroll.

William J Knight, X-15
& 4,233 MPH.
Aubrey Norvell.
Chief of State
Liu Shao-ch'i.
Israel, Hussein
& Jordanian riots.

Dumb double dipper. It's all my bubble. Split by
romance. We're feckless, far to lak wildernesses
beyond. We're troubled. We haven't a chance.
Though Hailey's Aston Martin still
charges on across thick platoons of ice.
O my big ears, dirty head of mucky gribble,
how'd we wind up on this trip?
Robbed now of all we might have kicked with,
stayed for and adored. But any mightiness
allready slides off the possibilities of
Hailey's careening curves.
There's only one curve. Delicate
with the centrifugal
theft of all
I never kept.

Nov 15 1960

179,323,175.
Charleston's George Washington.
New Orleans riots. 300 to 223.
Congolese Army & UN. Kasavubu &
Lumumba. USS Ethan Allen.
Harvest of Shame.
Navy over Army.
Félix Houphouët-Boigny.
Secretary of State Dean Rusk.
B-52s & 10,000 fuelless miles.
Baudouin &
Doña Fabiola de Mora y Aragón.
United Airlines DC-8 &
Trans World Super-Constellation,
134 go. Selassie returns.
Ellen Steinberg's schools.
Laos & Boun Oum. Algiers,
Charles de Gaulle & Muslims.
—All of US feel after so many trials.
South Vietnam, Diem &
National Liberation Front.
Eagles over Packers.

Nov 30 1966

Barbados free.
Leslie Hornsby.

Navy Recruitment &
Berkeley boycot.

Bonn &
Kurt Kiesinger.
Cairo, Jordan & troops.

Sydney, Gipsy Moth IV &
13,750 miles.
—I shall go on.
900,000 tons of grain
& US.
US arms to Jordan.
Cargo plane &
Vietnam village, 125 go.
Soviet moon.

*—It is impossible
to avoid all damage to
civilian.*

Masters & Johnson.
Betty Friedan's NOW.

*—equality for
all women.*

Rare and
Endangered Species.
F-111 B.
Connecticut's
fluoridation law.
Purdue over USC.
Jack Ruby goes.
GM's 269,000 cars.
Iron Triangle attack.

Anything to festinate freely
with my Corvette Sting Ray:
me, me, me.

On the round,
all around, found and never found.
By The Anacostia.
Around Logan Circle.
Down Vermont. Constitution.
For Arlington,
though traffic jams jail haste for
Commerce and Continental poke.
The servitude of dough. But I'm all
honks and nickels letting me go.
My Corvair Monza looping the
beltway. Capital orbit. I'm Capital's
thrill terrifying Capitol Bills.
Sam zakes. Swave & Blaze
stunned by how I pastblast this
municipal standstill. Sassyly.
Eazy Breezy.
I'm beyond Transient & Lingering.

Oct 7 1960

Nixon, Kennedy & Taiwan. Regret.
Bay of Bengal cyclone, 6,000
go. Asanuma goes. Khrushchev,
Lorenzo Sumulong & a shoe.
—Kholui.
Pirates over Yankees.
Cuba nationalizes banks.
MLK arrested. Columbia River
& Hydroelectric plant. Britain's
Dreadnought. Cassius Clay first.
—reckless.
Georgia & 4 months.
East Pakistan wave, 4,000 go.
Otoya Yamaguchi goes.
Félix Mounié goes.
—fine race .
—for a new administration and for.
Moscow & Communist Party
Congress & Enver Hodja.
Vandenberg & Discoverer XVII.
Fuentes & Army uprising. Jimmie
Davis. 2 New Orleans High Schools.
HEW.

of how quickly we move and where
to. Stunned by her confidence & verve.
Get out of our way. There will
allways be this way. Without ever a departure.
—You're my October skies. And I'm yours,
for which she smiles, releasing
rings of attraction.
Hailey's Dodge Dart crunching past offramps
and unowned Shops. The value of trade somehow
slipping away. Past Missoula, Polson and Kalispell.
Hailey, Hailey, Hailey.
Her AMC Metropolitan curling the curves.
Betrayal's enduring worth. Ending.
Because we're taking it all. Taking our time.
We're leaving everything behind.

Jan 8 1967

Nanking.

—not libel if not deliberate.

US vs Laub.

—I ain't got no quarrel with Them Viet Congs.

Super Bowl I,
Packers over Chiefs.

New Haven's 462.
DeSalvo's life.
Wright's freedom.
Operation Cedar Falls.

62 nations, space
& weapons.

—Get US out of here!

6:31 PM. Apollo 1.
Virgil, Edward
& Roger go.

Yugoslav blasts.
Bartley & Harmon go.
Anastasio Somoza
Debayle.
Ali 15 rounds Terrell.
Gandhi's stone.
25th Amendment.
Lin Piao.

—revolutionary order.

National Student
Association & CIA.

—Drop Rusk and McNamara. Not the bomb.

And allways fluent.
Sam: —*Where you going, Runaway?*
—*Anywhere away.*
Him sliding closer:
—*Be my guest. Everything okay?*
—*I'm on the dole.*
—*I guessed.*
But not what he supposes. He'd
puddle my seat if I confessed
my opposements.
Nodding Trillium trailing:
—*You're allready too late.*
Because I'm annihilation. Napalmic
and plastic. Find me by buckets
of fingers and noses.
Still Sam scootches over, grabbing
my breast, slapping my leg:
—*I'm allso evading arrest.*
Him too? Well maybe then he does
get how what I must do's
become a won't do

Aug 21 1960

Somalia & Ethiopia.
Rome Olympics. Tobian dive.
Senegal's Léopold Senghor.
Otis Davis. Wilma Rudolph.
Abebe Bikila. Rafer Johnson.

—to go through that again.
—around the course again without.

Hurricane Donna, 30 go.
Iraq, Iran, Kuwait & Saudi Arabia.

—I feer Washington.

NLRB & 20,000 taxi drivers.
New Orleans 6.
NSA & Sexual Perversion.
Jordan & Syrian troops.
UN General Assembly.
Castro, Khrushchev & Harlem.
James River & USS Enterprise.

—spendthrift.

Congo, UN & 16,382 troops.
Nigeria & British Commonwealth.
Alhaji Abubakar Tafawa Balewa.
South Africa & Afrikaners.

And the travellers are long gone. Traffic undone.
Leaving US allone on deserted lanes sliding by
barren Rest Stops & Momentary Dumps.
And I'm afraid. Quavering too while
Hailey detains all she escapes.
Nothing ever overtakes her freedom ride.
I just hold tight.
Ringnecked Pheasants fright. And die.
And with the hard grip of killice comes
the pale threat of all we must now somehow
regret driving for.
Purposes outracing caprice, staking out
ahead, amidst all the tumult of colliding
fronts, dangerous flakes. Hanging there.
Even if Hailey's everyway aware

Feb 21 1967

Brakes, steering
& Ford's 217,000.

Tay Ninh province &
Operation Junction City,
282 go.
Suharto over Sukarno.
Cambodia offensive.
Shelling North Vietnam.

—Are you DeSalvo?

War Zone C.

Adam Clayton Powell out.

New Delhi &
Svetlana Alliluyeva.

US Senate &
Soviet bilateral treaty.

Somaliland riots.

GIs & Viet Cong, 423 go.
Ali 7 rounds Zora Folley.
MLK, Civil Justice &
the Vietnam obstacle.
Annie Decatur.
UCLA over Dayton.

New York, 10,000
hippies, bubbles & kites.

Cornwall, Torrey Canyon
& Brittany to Cotentin
Peninsula oil slick.
France's Redoubtable.

because here's so much fun.
And I'm allready lusthot to
stophop for a roll, zipping over
my Firebird 400 by
Morning Glory hummering:
—Summer's here!

Yup, I'm a Summer Slummer.
I am Summer. Thumbing to go.
Sam too.

Flip back, feet last, to the rear seat,
scrambling, bottoms for
plunder, downsideup, over,
slippling my wet, stickily met,
Sam allready squirting the floor,
though back again, panting for
more, and I'm gripping
his hard, grindings galore.
So soft I'm hardest of all.

Again.
Sam spurts his mess.
All over my chest.

July 15 1960

Revolution, rape & Mbanza-Boma.

—on the edge of a new frontier.
—We stand on this frontier
at a turning.
Nencini's Tour. Ikeda over Kishi.
Ceylon's Sirimavo Bandaranaike.
Francis Chichester's Gipsy Moth II.
—No.
—the destruction of the country.
—our shoulders to the wheel.

X-15's 2,150 MPH.
—merry-go-round of the.
Richmond & Roanoke enroll.
Souvanna Phouma over
Tiao Somsanith.
Excelsior III, 102,800 ft
& Joe Kittinger.
Cyprus & Nicosia charter.
Break with Holland.
Moscow espionage & 10 years.
Gabon Republic. Hamburg Beat.
2 dogs & a Russian orbit.

Timeout to lie, nuzzle and spend.
Lick and guzzle. Spend again.
Skies whirling battlehard, sought,
while on the road skins still grip for hard halts
over and over, every driver antagonized
by an odd stop for only a stop.
Roadtrains to Jeeps, Rockets to Tanks, nerfing
chrome, fendering fadeaways, benders stomping
bogs for this Pass's peculiar clog.
—How long can it last? Hailey asks.
—With travellers around, it won't ever cease.
But we are beyond ceasing too.
Autumn's here. Displeasing US.
And American Sables go.
Hailey's Chevrolet Impala goes too.

Sam's turn at the Wheel then.
Spishing the shoulder,
just missing a ditch.
A marauding hitch & glitch to
Front Royal for Rockytop.
Shagbark Hickory crying:
—*Higher!*
Spring Larkspur histing:
—*Aspire for a still wider cruise!*
So Sam's left hand flies
kites, planes and balloons,
drifting waywardly.
—*What's your bag, Pixie Boy?*
—*Johnny Law, The Man.*
Racing to tag me for
dodging zee draft. You?
—*Jam up! Dodging zed too.*
Sam laughs.
Impulsively I headwork his lap,
teething his shaft, a rashshuck for
the gobblurt I lobfast to the dirt.

April 2 1967

Liu Shao-Ch'i
& Peking 100,000.
War boycott.

500th US plane down.
Quang Tri rescue.
NAACP vs MLK.
Powell's return.
Supreme Court,
Army & Ali.

Haiphong power blaze.
Athens, Colonels
& Constatine Kollias.

76ers over Warriors.

Tangling parachute,
Vladimir Komarov goes.

Colorado, John Arthur
& Abortion.

Konrad Adenauer goes.
Stylianos Patakos
& George Papadopoulos.

Houston, Draft resistance
& Heavyweight loss.

Las Vegas, Elvis Presley
& Priscilla Beaulieu.

6,000 to Yaros.
Proud Clarion's Derby.
Greek junta, miniskirts
& beards. Stockholm,
Tribunal of War Crimes &
US bombing of civilians.

Impartible, together, across. Upon all highways,
lowways, freeways & byeways. Every cloverleaf,
bend, crossroads & circus. US.
—*What's shaking O? A traffic jam?* Hailey cooooos.
—*With my compliments,* I extend.
—*That's tooooooo much,* she swoons,
diggly for the stoppage we admire
now from our hilltop lounge.
—*Jam down,* returning her smooches & struggles,
gratitudes allready surpassing my meagre efforts to
afford her.
Groundhogs groan, go, but Hailey's all flow:
—*So tight & snaky.*
And Rat Snakes fade while rubbernecking lines keep
braking for all we're no longer there to impede.

May 23 1960

Ricardo Clement. Midas I.
Gürsel over Menderes.
Rathman's 500.

—closer together.

Tokyo Diet riots. Joseph Kasavubu.
Ike's Taipei & 86,000 rounds.
Patterson 5 rounds Johansson.
Armin Hary's 10 seconds.
Robert F Wagner &
George Lincoln Rockwell.
—juridical somersault.
Leopoldville, Baudouin &
a sword. John Thomas leaps.
Kwame Nkrumah. Somalia
Republic. Bueno over Reynolds.
Ohio's Universe.
—hostility toward the US.
—no longer at an unreachable
distance from.
700,000 lbs of sugar.
Western Hemisphere &
Communism. Katagna & Tshombe.
—Do not turn away from this.
Guatemala asylum, 200 go.

May 11 1967

Mishishishi &
Student riots.
70,000 march for
Vietnam.
Mickey Mantle's 500th.
Britain, EEC &
de Gaulle's veto.
Texas Southern
University riot.
Ellington repeals Monkey.
UN quits Israeli border.
Downtown Hanoi.
USSR's atom smasher.
—destruction of Israel.
Chichester, Plymouth &
28,500 miles.
Hausa & Ibo.
Odumegwu Ojukwu
& Biafra secession.
Foyt's 500.
Boston bash.
Moshe Dayan &
50 Egyptian tanks.
Suez & Gaza.
150 tanks & 400 planes.
*—mincemeat of
everything.*
Jerusalem. Sinai &
US ship, 10 go.
—Tiran is now open.
Race & Marriage.
Monetrey pop. 3:51:3.

Sam drives off the road.
Riot of grass. Swerving idiocy.
Hangs a Louie, Uee. Near crash.
Over park lawns, a sandbox,
scattering Picnickers, Misters
and Dismissive Chicks.
Poison Ivy blistering:
—On you we must depend.
Because I am the trip. Every turn off
and turn on and slip.
Sam parking again,
eager for play, more PDA
and slick trip moves.
Chestnut Sprouts hoot when,
crunching my toes, he sticks both
my shins. Then drops,
squeezing my tush,
lickers my thighs
slobbers my cootchie,
so pawpoking silly
what's thrilling just dies.

April 19 1960

Seoul riots, 127 go.
Adam Clayton Powell. Brasilia.
11,000 crossing.
—nose full of collectivization.
—progressive conservatism.
Biloxi beach, 10 go.
Key West, Muriel & 3 castaways,
Angus Boatwright goes.
Lar quake, 1,500 goes.
—her from it.
—Hi ya, Charlie.
Rhee quits. Togo liberty.
Huh Chung.
Russia, U-2 & Francis Gary Powers.
Caryl Chessman goes.
Wheat Pact. Margaret
& Anthony Armstrong Jones.
Venetian Way's Derby.
The Pill. Beach's 84 days.
Nashville & 6 lunch counters.
Babuba, Lubia & Congo.
Summit collapse. Payola & Freed.
Atlas ICBM's 9,000 miles.

A globally snarled knot.
Which for offerings is all I've got. Hailey though's
surprised by this swift mischief I give her.
Even if hacked **Virginia Opposums** die stacked upon
the hills and we're allready pulled off to the side.
Reparked. Beyond this bottle neck, bent necks,
teeth grinding and clenching
over a congestion beyond explanation.
No wreck, spill, something large.
Just the hazards of an unexpected stop
near where quartered **Pale Oxen**
die wet upon our divides.
What Segregationists never suspect
unless Hailey suspends even their death:
here's our mess.

June 23 1967

Committed ongoing but callow.
I'm astounded.
So Marvy Groovy
I finally start yanking his hair,
scratching his scalp.
Disappointment requires a move.
But Sam's ginchy handling of my
American Rogue leaves me turned
out, downed off & chapped.
Morels & Mulberries sadly
whipper then. Something desolate
by way of these roads.
Unlicensed, undetermined.
Unearned.
—*Billiards!* I suddenly eject.
Sam obeys, brakeslams, afraid, while
for a hang I jauntily approach the table
circumcrowded by a BIKER GANG.
All sugar and revel, Them
shy away from my burn.
I take what's due,

LBJ, Kosygin & Glassboro.
17′8″.
Buffalo riots, 14 go.
Jayne Mansfield goes.
—*March against feer.*
Meredith finishes.
Nigeria attacks Biafra.
Typhoon Billie, 347 go.
Newark riots, 26 go.
Tom Simpson goes.
Pingeon's Tour.
Detroit riots, 19 go.
—*Burn this city down.*
SNCC Rap arrested.
8 US planes down.
—*Vive le Québec libre.*
Forrestal & 29 planes,
159 go.
Jerome Cavanaugh.
Atlanta, Boston,
Philadelphia, New York,
Birmingham, Cincinnati.
—*time of violence and tragedy.*
—*abandon, a carnival.*
100,000 more.
—*tremendous price with nothing.*
—*aggressive armed violence.*
45,000 more.

March 1 1960

—*O that's unnecessary,* Hailey gassing
the slope to Bozeman Pass.
Hmmm. But though I'm without resources,
sourceless & primitive, surrounded by
traffic, I suddenly find a present I can
proudly pass over her way.
—*Slow please,* I request. *There. Now stop.*
Skidding to a standstill. Blocking behind US all
progress vehicular. Piles, Chariots & Shot Rods
turned here to a parking lot. Dead
Bobcats & Goldfinches ditched amidst honks.
And no wheel can pass these wheels,
Hailey's Skoda Felicia across every lane.
From Tallahassee to Seattle by
Honolulu to Noatak.

Agadir quake & wave, 4,500 go.
Kabul's 100,000. Eisenhower &
Suriname. La Courbe &
Havana harbor, 100 go.
Carol Heiss. Houston beating.
—*soft on Communism.*
Celtics over Knicks.
—*We feel this terror violating elementary constitutional.*
Adenauer, Gurion &
Waldorf-Astoria.
Sharpeville shooting,
56 go. Los Alamos fusion.
500 Peronists arrested.
—*but by a million.*
Marshall Texas fire hoses.
300 Johannesburg jailed. TIROS 1.
Sahara blast. Peter Llewelyn-Davies
goes. Cape Town raid. Hendrik
Verwoerd. Celtics over Hawks.
—*stop Kennedy.*
Flying Frenchmen over
Maple Leafs. Nuclear weapons
& London's 74,000.

Aug 6 1967

Havana, Colombian DC-4 & hijackers.
Svirsk & Chinese.
Michigan sympathy.
Peking & British Consulate.
Hanoi suburbs burning.
Arlington sniper, George Lincoln Rockwell goes.

Treason & Papandreou.
Cairo & Nasser's overthrow, 150 arrested.

69-11.

Supreme Court & Thurgood Marshall.
Quang Ngai's 1,200 free.
Ilse Koch goes.
Arab aid to Egypt & Jordan.
Nguyen Van Thieu.
Michigan & George Romney.
Ford & UAW strikes.
US moon.
Sikkim-Tibet border & artillery fire.
Reagan, Viet Cong & the bomb.
Abdel Hakim Amer goes.
Ewa Klobukowska's test.
Turkish soccer riot, 42 go.

a turn and a cue. Sevenplygassed
with my sexydexy ass challenging
This Crew, who all itch to teach me
how I'm missed. I'm ready.

Though despite yumblings,
These Twinks must first put up
geech against my Leftwrist
Wealthy Twist.
Much too much.

Each REMF threatens to quit.
—*Aww come on, just play now for zip.*
I assent. Break after break.

Clean banks for Solids. Stun shots
for Stripes. Spins. Jumps.
Running fast rocks.
Boonie Rats chear, collapse
when I slamsweep their
balls, clearing
pacified slate,
These LURPs plopping
down hard,

Passing Livingston. Along with chopped,
dropped Buckets of whinge. Hailey busting on by.
Every Bug & Clunk too barring our way farred
from our route. Every transit.
Just Married barrelling through. Cans
clanging bumpers. Shivarees fluttering creamy.

And when The Big Hats follow we stop for fun.
—*Kids, there are speed limits here.*
—*Not my limit,* Hailey obliges.
—*Awwwwwwwwww,* The Topkick sighs,
perhapses and collapses. Dies.

We're impossible to threaten. Without any limits.
Which is when I dig, even with Hailey's Leftwrist
Wealthy Twist, my wife deserves
a Wedding Gift.

Jan 29 1960

—*will be compromised.*
M14s. JFK's hat & ring.
Greensboro 4 & Woolworth lunch counter.
Israel, Syrian base & Demilitarized Zone.
Algiers & surrender.
—*are all members of one another.*
Mikoyan & Cuban sugar.
Durham demonstrations.
Carlotta's Little Rock bomb.
Havana's 104. Adolph Coors.
Pierre Lagaillarde & Jo Ortiz.
New Delhi neutrality.
Reggan & 70 French kilotons.
—*she does not need a protector.*
Groton's Triton. Winston Salem sit.
Chattanooga riots.
Ebbets Field. VD.
—*and place my order and be.*
Squaw Valley. Penny Pitou.
Melvin Purvis goes.
—*Viva Eeke!*

Sept 18 1967

Nike & Spartan missiles.
Mosbacher cups Sturrock.
$70 billion defense
appropriations.
Esalen.
X-15's 4,534 MPH.
Enugu seized.
Che Guevara goes.
St Louis over Boston.
Selective Service
& anti-Draft rallies.
2,900 Viet Cong,
58 GIs go.
James Goddard, booze
& pot. Neshoba guilty.
Tehran & Mohammed
Reza Shah Pahlavi.
—Dump Johnson.
David Dellinger
& Jerry Rubin.
10,000, Potomac
& Pentagon.
Elath. 46 days.
Pipers over Americans.
1.1 million Chevrolets.
Suez refineries.
Philip Berrigan,
Baltimore & duck blood.
Diaz acres.
Elizabeth
& legislative power.
Linda Fitzpatrick
& Groovy go.

awe struck by my play. Allatonce.
Never missing. So fatigued by my
feersome caroms, every IMPRESSED
frays. Until
Sam peeps:
—For you from me.
Slipping by
WOUNDED & DISCHARGED,
smallness aiding his mission.
Where there's a frown, there's a grave.
So enraged, I just give
him the stick to bug off.
But he only froths over cloth,
multitudes deserting, until
recklessly snap by ferrule & tip
wobbling slips,
he lunges butt end, smackflat
across to miss even
a Cue Ball dip.
And tearing up the field
leaves one ragged rip.

Dec 20 1959

20 New York bosses.
Mohammed Reza & Farah Diba.
—Peace and friendship.
Congo Civil War.
Colts over Giants.
Hubert H Humphrey.
Franc devaluation.
Ahmadou Ahidjo &
Cameroon Liberty.
Camus goes.
—what's going on?
France, Algeria & torture.
Cologne riots.
Trieste, Walsh & Piccard.
Kenya's State of Emergency over.
Otto Butz. N Sanjeeva Reddy.
82 & Congolese Freedom.
—what is at the bottom of your.
Paul Pender 15 rounds Robinson.
Algiers, freedom &
armed European mobs.
Schock & Moll's Monte Carlo Rally.
Byrd station, transport plane & skis.

Natural adventure over cement and gradient tar. We're marital jelly, icing onramps, closing down mountain lanes. Sparing no pains for all we abandon. Damage. Bridge.

There's no bridge around we can't burn. We build no bridges. Just spurn. Multitudes lining up for Hailey. There to the outside! I'm embarrassing. She's the coolier one, pleasantly waving byebye.

Where there's a way, there's a Wheel.
And allways she Wheels US on.
If mostofthetime urgent & harmed
I'm still game for more:
—No more. Game's over.
Racing by Reed Point. Greycliff.
Allweather overyondering.

Nov 5 1967

Abdullah as-Sallal ousted.

—Capital is the enemy.
Soviet Parade.
Egypt & Israel.
Apollo 4.
—unconditional end to
the bombing of
North Vietnam.

American desertion.
Rusk's policy
of escalation.
Haiphong shipyard.
Régis Debray's 30 years.
Cincinnati & TWA, 62 go.
Air Quality Act.
Hill 875.
Lisbon flood, 250 go.
Soviets from Egypt.
McNamara quits for
World Bank.
Leary & Woodruff.
Eisenhower & Nixon.
—through blood and
sacrifice.
—steady drum.
Mekong, 365 go.
Benjamin Spock &
Cathleen Fitt.
President Ceaușescu.
El Paso Gas blast.
Concorde.
Airlifting 6,500.
Southwest Blizzard.

I'm howling calamity on
this Plutonium hitch, my
Buick Electra's spongies bashing
from Asheville to Oak Ridge.
Sam, irascible,
wants every turn to take a
turn. Foams, paddles and pleads. But
I'm all slaps, stall & nix. Flicking him
back with jack & jink kicks.
No thanks.
Though thanks allone to me
he exists.
—*What's the frictive, Sweetie?*
Just a quick tool around?
I'm too serious.
By Flash, searing lime to wide:
—*I Wish you'd just settle down.*
And a Wind spills dangerously free.
Something uneasy losing speed.
Condensing,
condemning.

Oct 21 1959

Ladakh clash.
Bonn's Volkswagens.

Stanleyville, Mangobo
& Patrice Lumumba.

Panama Canal Zone riots.
80 day halt. 8-1.
—couldn't play golf for 80 days?
Egypt, Sudan & the Nile.
Oregon, cranberry bogs & ATZ.
Perry Smith & Dick Hickock,
the Clutters go.

Kilauea Iki erupts.
Free Trade: Britain, Sweden,
Norway, Denmark, Switzerland,
Austria & Portugal.
President of the National
Bank of Cuba. Navy over Army.
Hungarian Party Congress.
Plane, bombs & 5 Cuban exiles.
12 Nations & Antarctica.
Mercury, Wallops Island
& a monkey.
Peking pardons Pu Yi.

Only then does Hailey release me. Cheeks drenched.
Chin pouring. And I'm allone again. With her. By
our Worldturning blur.

Chimes! Chime! Chimes!

—*I do.*

ThuuUUUuuUuUUUuunder.
The stump gone. Proof & License too.
Still Hailey hangs around my neck:
—*Hiya Hubby!*
Kissing me, I kiss her more. Can't barely stand it.
Having a blast though eager for more. Somehow
allso uncertain. Unsure. Even worried. Grippy
for her desire, affection and peoplekilling
slinkiness, until pinkie to pinkie, we return to her
Ford Fairlane rumbling ready for the time of our life.

Dec 20 1967

So I juice it with honks,
blurring by squads
and boondocks.
My Karmann Ghia burning hot.
Air jelly. Fumey. That's me.
Kerosene. Gasoline. Fuel for this
trip. Sam spooning up HONEY.
Fuel for the fuel. Keeping him tight.
My Saab Sonett
whipping past
trucks hauling trucks.
Until I reach a
Strange Accident of
times, burning melee
for miles. And Ben Tre dead still
clutching Tire Swings, SeeSaws &
Rings. Smoldering.
—*O beware,* **Wild Grape** twines.
Yet for this slaughter, Sam stops.
Sacrificial smoke. Crumbling bone.
Around which **Tall Corydalis** grow.

Gandhi & outlaw groups.
Washkansky's heart.
LBJ's Cam Ranh Bay.
Papandreou free.
—We shall win
and so will you.
Microwaves & Cherry Pie.
Robert Clark. Leroi Jones.
Alexander Dubček.
838 acres.
US Air Force & Laos.
Sweden deserters.
Super Bowl II,
Packers over Raiders.
Claudia Taylor
& Eartha Kitt.
Khe Sanh.
Greenland, B-52
& 4 H-bombs.
North Korea & Pueblo.
—We will be free.
Minerve down, 52 go.
$186 billion.
Clark Clifford.
Tet offensive.
84,000, Saigon,
Hué & Highlands.
Mauritius free.
New Hampshire race.
Soviet ICBMs double.

Sept 4 1959

Turkey Vultures pulled down. Drowned.
Ice cutting across townships and roads.
Even breaths freeze. And shear.
Feral Pigeons shallow, hurt and cease.
Hailey though, aware & tender, patiently
waits on my reply. What can I do?
She's all that is over all I'll never get.
Me just so squashed up & clenched,
wondering now about the somuchmore
Hailey with her Edsel Corsair
could roar on for without me.
Even if she's my honey. My everything. My me.
All desire needs to have to die.
Her Dodge Lancer even honks
Heiha!

Power of Unions.
Southern votes.
Dalai Lama & UN. Lunik II.
Landrum-Griffin Act.
Khrushchev arrives.
Defense Minister Lin Piao.
B-52, X-15 & Scott Crossfield.
Typhoon Sarah, 2,000 go.
UN's Communist China.
Groton's Patrick Henry.
$650 million urban renewal.
UAR, Meir & Suez canal.
Camp David.
Bandaranaike goes.
Typhoon Vera, 4,466 go.
—What is it? Do you have rocket
launching pads there?
3 & 3 more. World Bank's
Development Association.
Little Joe. Lunik III.
Macmillan's Conservatives.
LA over Chicago.
9 Gaullists & UNR. CENTO.
Dalles Dam. Mitterrand's escape.

Feb 3 1968

Anibal Escalante.
Neal Cassady goes.
Grenoble.
George Wallace.
10,500 combat troops.
Israel, Jordan & jets.
Draft deferment curbs.
Jean-Claude Killy.
3 pilots free. Kachchh.
—bravest girl.
206,000 more.
—A few bandits.
32 African nations.
—end the Americanization.
—separate and unequal.
Lockheed Galaxy.
Saigon ambush, 48 go.
San Juan slick.
—too often been disappointed.
Rhodesia hangings, 3 go.
—Long live Czechoslovakia.
DC-8 to Havana.
—I just killed.
Task Force Barker,
Song My & My Lai,
450 go.
Hugh Thompson.
Robert Kennedy.
50,000 more.
Bleiberg. London 200.
Madison 400.

Puttering among troubles, even
my Chevelle SS396 zooms to lose
such rubble. I'm nothing but supple.
But allso curious.

This billow of human scorched, sour
twin to honey's hour, sets upon my
teeth a satisfying savor. And I want
more. But I've company.

Brutality's arm.
Murders spilling my ear.
CANE caressing my thighs.
A Calcine Massacre of times.
—There are wonders I keep
near for you.
There. Feer. THE CREEP allmost
swallowing me up.
I'm The Burn Yard.
Bone Yard.
Switches Cauldron.
Sleazy breezy amidst Lithium-6.
But THE CREEP's sexy.

Hailey's Cadillac Eldorado, our union and escape.
the storm's assault allready lowering upon
Except THE GENERAL runs too,

your lawfully wedded wife?
young man this young woman to be
by The Powers Power loathes, take you
—By The Powers above,

off for anyway anywhere else but US.
US? Too frightened, ALL leap for their lives, plunging
THE GENERAL shakes. But who could hold?
—Should any here reject their,

the meaty banks.
Floods swell The River and gore
Suddenly graveyards brew with turning corpses.
The curve every longing longs to tour.

Tibet border. 1,400 NYC police.
—We stand by your side.
Bhutan & Sikkim.
Haiti's François Poirier.
Hawaii, 50th.
Manhattan power failure.
Princeton, Powners & whiskey.
Jordan & United Arab Republic.
& Rafael Trujillo, 2 go.
Counterrevolutionary plane
Vandenberg's Discoverer V.
grow burdensome.
—of illegal orders will
—continue the struggle.
—anti-democratic regimes.
NASA's Explorer IV.
Paris, Les Halles & blaze, 6 go.
Laos & 2nd province.
except feer of it.
—anything about Communism
—If War comes, we both lose.
Moscow's Kitchen.
Savannah. France & Kabylia.
Castro's presidency. Camden's

July 18 1959

March 22 1968

Army Chief of Staff.
UCLA over North Carolina.
Robles impeached.
F-111 down.
—*I shall not seek and*
will not accept.
Eldridge Cleaver.
—*I'm not feering*
any man.
Lorraine Motel,
MLK goes. Apollo 6.
—*and compassion*
toward one.
Operation Pegasus.
Abernathy.
Poland crush. Coretta.
Creighton Abrams.
—*Violence cannot.*
Rudi Dutschke.
—*Shoot to kill.*
Prague spring.
Eric Starvo Galt.
Pierre Trudeau. Rudd,
Dean & Columbia.
Boston University.
200,000 cut class.
Lindsay's gym.
Wheat aid.
Grayson Kirk amnesty.
700 New York arrests.
Poor People's March.
Cohn-Bendit's Sorbonne.
Forward Pass's Derby.

—*I quench every*
thirst. Feed all desire.
CREEP's hand on my side.
And pangs of hunger rapidly arrive.
My mouth wet, wandering. Thrilled.
—*You can find a Creep anywhere,*
Virginia Creepers spill.
But I can't challenge this violence.
It's too attractive.
Too deliberate.
And despite Sam's ruckus,
THE CREEP grabs hold:
—*Come with me now.*
Because allways I want t .
Except blundering across Poplar
Creek, heedless of Mercury & PCBs,
past broken tanks of Uranyl Nitrate,
Sam barrels back,
gleefully farting.
So loud THE CREEP's revolted
enough to let go.

June 11 1959

Hovercraft.
5 quit over Castro's land.
Over Sea of Japan.
Tallahassee rape & 4 for life.
Klaus Emil Fuchs free.
2.35 million acres.
Johansson 3 rounds Patterson.
Milan, TWA & storm, 68 go.
—*The revolutionary*
government is.
Bonn's Heinrich Lübke.
Bueno over Hard.
Olmedo over Laver.
2 dogs & 1 rabbit.
Bien Hoa South Vietnam &
Communist guerrillas,
2 US soldiers go.
New York, NAACP & Roy Wilkins.
—*people can't get together and.*
Labor Management & Unions.
500,000 Steel Workers strike.
Whitman's Chocolates,
Holiday goes.
Bahamontes's Tour.

—*We gather now to bind these two forever,*
THE GENERAL continues, medals clinking
with the growing squall, a hazarding
ice creeping out of the forest.
He nods to Hailey. To me. To these rest,
shuffling uneasily. Majors,
Captains, Corporals and Sergeants.

Something borrows. Something blows.
Somehow restricted. Somehow few.
Someway allways familiar. Too.

Hailey toots, deckedout gorgeous with
highneck blouse, cuffed skirt & soft boots.
Me, overalls. She squeezes my hand. Her hair flaxen
& smooth. Lips waxy. Eastern Creepers limp.
Air and earth hungering and thirsting for her bounds.

May 6 1968

Paris New Left.
Presidential primary.
Catfish pitch.
Avenue Kléber.
Lewisburg Oak.
Stanley Cup.
French Labor Federations
& general strike.
Nigeria & Port Harcourt.
6 years.
—trying to bring down
this society.

Grenelle agreements.
Storming Supreme Court.
Unser's 500.
Sorbonne riots.

—from the people.
I shall.

Celtics over Lakers.
Warhol & SCUM.
Jordan River lobs.
Sirhan Sirhan, RFK goes.
Ramon George Sneyd.

—War
and tried to stop.

Ex-OAS Bidault returns.
Raoul Salan free.
Jim Hines & 9.8.
Hugo Vihlen & 84 days.
Poverty walk.
Argentina soccer
stampede, 73 go.

Duke of the Cat Walk, Sam. Bowing
now with a rearrancid kazoo.
I'm radioactive, enflamed. What a
repellent toot. THE CREEP recoiling
too, further shocked
except not.
THE CREEP's miles of
Viet Cong and Carpet Bombs.
Conquest's necessity. Forbidden
to forbid. And if

Boooooooooomblastandruin

looms over this territory, so what?
I'm every terrortory CREEP'll fondle.
And dominate. Chuckles given,
commending Sam. Even flatters
his murky flatulence.
Sam again wagging his ass, yapping:
—*Mustard gas!*
Eliciting by this prance wry
laughs accustomed to affliction.
Even a CREEP though must get away.

April 25 1959

Great Lakes, Atlantic
& St Lawrence Seaway.
Liu Shao-ch'i.
Clare Booth's Brazil. Texaco.
Luce & Morse. $30 billion.
Latin America safe for democracy.
Tommy Lee's Derby. 208.8 million.
Geneva, Big Four
& German reunification.
Florida fever. Laos & Pathet Lao.
Cuba's sugar mills. Citizenship
& 5,000 Japanese-Americans.
Nuclear accord with Canada.
Benjamin O Davis.
Seven Cuban airlines. Dulles goes.
Able & Baker return.
Munich, Taiwan & Peking
Olympics. Ward's 500.
Nicaragua's National Guard.
Ike & John Diefenbaker.
Singapore & British
Commonwealth.
Groton's George Washington
& Polaris rockets.

speedily handling all of our nuptials while I rock
fitfully on the playground swing, hardly moving,
clouds above stirring, until I just flip back
and lie still. Hailey giggles.

Even THE GENERAL chuckles though cautious of
Hailey. Nervous too. After all she's territorial.
She's what terrortories become when some're none.
Lostlastandstrewn.

Plenty soon come.
Drunkards, Laggards, Moochers and Bums,
kicking & hurting, taking up stations
on pews, logs and crates
feerfully skirting The River's way.

—*Shall we proceed?* THE GENERAL slumps, setting
our LICENSE & PROOF squarely on that stump.

June 24 1968

National Guard & DC.
10% surcharge tax.

Gaullists
& National Assembly.
US jet & Kurile Islands.

First Cavalry Division.
Moscow, 36 nations
& Non-proliferation
treaty.
Charlene Mitchell's
Communist Party.
Paris Medical School.
Gary Player's Open.
Aeroflot &
PanAm to Moscow.
DC-8 to Cuba.
Iraq & President Arif.

Janssen's Tour.

Algeria, El Al & 21.

Carl Stokes & slums.

Two women, two hearts.

*—You have let me down
and moreover.*

Manila temblor, 400 go.
Basque.

*—of the great
majority of Americans.*

Nixon & Agnew.
Friendly Fire, 8 go.

Sam's a moron.
CREEP's goosing my caboose.
Enraged yet all restraint too.
I'm no restraint.
By THE CREEP allways restrained.
—*Hey teenyboppers,* THE CREEP zaps.
*Don't roll square. Just get
to The Party.
Dig?*
Gifts from maiming hands.
PREMATURE BOONS. LAURELS.
—*Cool beans. We're allready there.*
Whereupon CREEP, swirling
Agent Herb, JollyGreenGiants off.
Gone.
—*Grovel now,* Sam quips. *Thanks
to me sitch just flipped US the grits.*
But I'm too knocked for a loop.
And just accept Sam's piggyback.
Froggydoos to dash of my Super Bee
leaving TRU hazards behind.

March 4 1959

Pioneer IV's moon.
Syria & Iraqi assault.
—bankrupted.
Lester Young goes.
Kalin's Albion road.
Discoverer I lost. Westford's Venus.
Lhasa, Khambas & Dalai Lama.
Strontium 90. Iraq's Baghdad Pact.
Britain's $1 billion cut.
Celtics over Lakers.
Astronauts: Carpenter, Cooper,
Glenn, Grissom, Schirra,
Shepard & Slayton. Discoverer II.

France, Gaullists &
Democratic Work Union.

DC, Castro & military fatigues.
—that we are not Communists.
Christian A Herter over
John Foster Dulles. 93-0.
Pakistan River irrigation pact.
Algiers & voting, 8 go.

Panama revolt, Roberto Arias &
Margot Fonteyn.

Burying majillions on this ride. Hailey's Rambler Ambassador running down halflives of pride, so many entropic lives. Tirelessly too. While carrying me along. Just rolling with her confidence.

—*Thank you,* I grovel.

Her rushrushing Your Welcomes me to Columbus. Clough Avenue to Pike, where we find by the Yellowstone River,

THE GENERAL. Somehow familiar?

—*At your service,* THE GENERAL salutes. Leading US around the overcast hillock allready laid out with linens, tables, benches & chairs, heeding a stump covered with a violent cloth fringed with hoarfrost.

And Hailey's so extraordinary,

Aug 12 1968

Bikinians return.

Starving Biafrans.

Addis Ababa.

Prague, Warsaw Pact
Nations & Soviets tanks.

France, Pacific & A-Bomb.

—World is.

Chicago, 178 arrested.
John Gordon Mein goes.
—Pigs, pigs, oink, oink.
Mayor Daley's Men.
McCarthy raided.
Last 12 free.

Iran quake, 8,000 go.
Tel Aviv bomb.
Swaziland free.

Huey Newton convicted.
Caroline & JFK carrier.
Arthur Ashe's Open.

Illinois 300.
Mediterranean &
French jet, 95 go.
400 Viet Cong go.
Carol Jenkins goes.
Mexico's National
University, 18 go.
Zond 5.
Caetano over Salazar.
55 Nigerians go.
Greek Colonels.

Sam then's fugazi at the Wheel,
tarring for Edge City, allways
scarfing the turns.
Keyed up anyway for
divagating leagues, blurrring
Potawatomies, Stumblebums
and Banshees.

But I'm the only range by a stranger
ferocity. One I cannot meet but
must seek. Until it defeats me.
While Sam's the freak,
free maybe but weak.
A goof.
Antic with acne.
High and tight doof. Feckless with
freckles and nothing to lose.
Race. Hold. Except O those
Green Eyes with flecks of Gold.
—And his smile,
Smooth Azalea bold.
He slows. Pulls over.

Jan 14 1959

New Delhi's Gandhi.
Atomic generator & a hat.
Buenos Aires, transport workers
& general walkout.

American Airline coasts.
US Space Flight & NASA's 110.
Arlington, Norfolk
& Peaceful desegregation.
President of Congress.

Mason City snow,
Holly, Richardson & Valens go.
Titan ICBM.
Moscow & Peking expansion.
St Louis tornado, 22 go.
Cuban Premier & Castro.
Vanguard II's weather.
Fort Royal boycott & 22 more.
UK, Greece & Turkey: Cypriot
autonomy. Eisenhower, López
Mateos & Rio Grande Dam.
Rhodesia's State of Emergency.
Discoverer.

Iran, Soviet Union & treaty.

WhamO off.
Carolina Parakeets dead. Worldhit
& stiff. Hailey beyond squeam.

Gold Eyes with flecks of Green.

And me just hanging on for the haul. Appalling.
Hiding. A smatter of pimples on freckly cheeks,
which I'm too teen to treat let allone pop.
While Hailey's pristine to sleek. The astonishment
of every peculiar moment, rappering along 10, 310,
by Fromberg, Rockvale. At terrifying speeds.

Because we are the littlest part of we
and I'm the littlest part of me.
And allways we will leave US
behind US.
Because we're free.

Oct 1 1968

Yippie Hoffman's Yo-Yo.
Bob Gibson's 17.
Abe Fortas quits.
Mexico City students,
49 go. Dubček defeated.
Telford arrives.
France's Universities.
Tigers over Cardinals.
Panama coup, Arias out.
Gibraltar failure.
Al Oerter's discus.
Tommie Smith
& John Carlos.
Beamon's leap.
Toomey decathlon.
Dick's jump.
Skorpios, Aristotle
& Jacqueline. Apollo 7.
Berkeley seizure.
Czech protest
& Soviet occupation.
Naval and Aerial
bombing halts.
Helicopters to Newark.
West Berlin students.
Shirley Chisholm.
*—Unbought and
unbossed.*
Nixon over Humphrey.
—Bring US together.
Beate Klarsfeld.
Arkansas defeat.
KKK & $1 million.
Heidi.

Unlawful assembly. After which
I cramp:
—I can't ever become.
Again. Grub on the trunk. Don't
iron while the strike is hot. Lester
grunts, pumps, kinking to bop,
bustin concrete, shimmying
on top, if Sam allready pops,
a fosbury flop all over me.
Goo.
And depressed if I'm not content.
—Ever? he whines.
—Never.
—O. *—No.*
Except now he wants how many
times I've fucked. How'z
that gonna help? Okay. Wants
it, gots it. Every Diddling Round.
And off he goes. Unscrewed,
disturbed. If somehow for me
he allways returns.

Nov 24 1958

Ibrahim Abboud &
Sudan's Republic. Atlas ICBM,
South Atlantic & 5,500 miles.
African Republics: Chad,
Congo-Brazzaville, Gabon,
Senegal, Mauritania & Mali.
30 Havana officers.
Chicago & Our Lady, 98 go.
Towards the moon.
Kure tanker & 1 million barrels.
African Republics: Nigeria, Upper
Volta, Ivory Coast & Dahomey.
Colts over Giants.
Frances Kelsey & Thalidomide.
Melin, Knerr & Grex.
The Hoola Hoop.
Iowa over Southern California.
Alaska, 49th. Batista flees.
Castro's Cuban Army.
Lunik's 343,750 miles.
British P-1 & Mach II.
Manuel Urrutia Lleó.
—now the first.

A way we go. MT Lovell, Warren,
Bridger. For Billings. Taking
our time. Me and
my immaculate girl. Untouched,
unturned and unreturnable.
Her gliding The District Court Clerk two Licenses
who spinning both returns one Marriage License
with appointment: *—Go here for your blood test.*
Sobbing too because we're allready so never.
Leaving no joy. Only anguish.
The Clinic Staff stabbing US then, yabbling US,
until tourniquets split. Splats across their yaps.
Covering every hat, slack and lash with our
streaming blood. Which of course Techs check easily
because we're bloodless.

LZ New Orleans! Slashing
Freddy slamming! My joint!
By limos and shuttle crowds
of Weathermen, Cherries
& Bars jamming the way.
Not my way. I am the way.
The wide bang.
Taking even Sam past the front line.
My Fucking New Guy,
overalls, unpopular, panicked.
Hustling ahead of my wake of
Gawkers, Droolers and Overdressed.
All heads turning
for Popularity's Caress.
Without success.
Take a seat. I'm too sweet.
—*Game'z not over,* I relay.
—*Sure thing,* nods THE VALET.
And though Sam flips him off,
we pass by unaltered.
Welcome.

Nov 23 1968

Miami hijacking &
87 passengers.

—join the Peace.

Presidential Panel,
Milton Eisenhower &
Chicago Police.

Sicily, Giuseppe Saragat &
Franca Viola.
French Communists &
Soviet Union.
Department of Labor's
3.3%.

Pueblo Crew,
Lloyd M Bucher &
Bridge of No Return.
Dwight David Eisenhower
& Julie Nixon.
Apollo 8 & lunar orbit.

*—the big vastness
of space.*

*—I do not feel that I am
a piece of property.*

Israel, Beirut Airport &
13 planes.
*—Youth rebellion
is a Worldwide.*

New Jersey guns.
James Simon Kunen.
Ohio over USC.

Unwelcome.
Constantly unchanged, unchallenged by all we
lawfully & unlawfully arraign.
—*Are we rude?* I try.
—*No. Just screwed,* Hailey sighs.
By Kearney, Banner, Sheridan and Acme,
past a roadside tramp of Recruits, marching along
with crew cuts and raincoats,
shouldering duffle bags, rolled flags and extra
pairs of Government issued boots. We're
where these troops each want to go. Even Vets.
Our muddle & mess, rejection & best stirring
now a storm sweeping east the feeling of youth.
While Wishes float above the immortal puddles
we allways splash through.

Oct 12 1958

Pioneer Satellite's 23,450 MPH.

X-15, 4,500 MPH & 100 miles up.
Israel's 8 border police.
Thailand & Sarit Thanarat.
96 Nova Scotia miners.
US out of Lebanon.
Pan American World Airways
& European Service.
South African women.
Mohammed Ayub Khan over
Iskander Mirza. Pecos County well.
Angelo Giuseppe Roncalli.
United Nations Educational
Scientific and Cultural
Organization. Iskander Mirza
quits Karachi. 38,677 shells.
Democrats. 15 & 48.
Pioneer 2's 6 hours 52 minutes.
Smithsonian's 112 Carats.
Eisenhower
& Soviet Atomic Test Ban.
Lake Michigan
Cargo transport, 33 go.

Backyard spread, stainless and cotton.
With Cookie Pies, Candy Pies, JellO
Pies, Ice Cream Pies.

Pies! Pies! Pie!

Stacks with Graham Cracker,
Flaky Dough and Shortbread Crusts.
Heads, Sailors and Lumps scarfing up
Tarte Tatins and Linzertortes topped
with Cream Cheese. Jams.
And Jelly.
Which I daintily peck at,
nibbling moments of Cherry
Custard, Rhubarb, Pumpkin,
Pecan. Marionberry, Butterscotch,
Lime. Brandywhisked
Pears. That's it.
A smidgen of Gelato, Espresso soaked
Puddings with Tutti Frutti Eclairs.
Napkin dabs to my mouth. While
Sam refuses even a taste,
afraid allways to partake.

Jan 2 1969

Maginot pillboxes.
Adam Clayton Powell's
$25,000.
Ian Paisley's Northern
Ireland.
Ifni.

*—drive criminal
anarchists and latter-day
fascists.*

Guantánamo, Florida
& 81 Cubans.
Abie Nathan's Forra.

Super Bowl III,
Jets over Colts.

London's 5,000.
Enterprise blast, 24 go.
Jan Palach goes.
Soyuz 4 & Soyuz 5.
Roy Cohn. Lionel Rose.
Joan Tognola.

—Let US gather the.

—I was not prepared to.

Nairobi 1,200. California
mud. Marty Liquori.
Yasir Arafat & Palestine
Liberation Organization.
Lima's Petroleum
Company. Biafra bomb,
300 go. Boeing 747.
—It's plugged.

NYC snowstorm, 14 go.

Only the most gaunt & desperate
Teenage Urchins taste the tongue & lip
ripping kiss of our trailing egress.
On flagpoles, chainlinks & steel rails.
A bristling of hoar to take hold of all we let
go of and fix. We fix nothing.
—*The crowd's thin,* I shudder for these
tarrying Bleak, scavenging for breath.
—*Then let'S feed it,* Hailey lazzles,
our awful speed releasing for
such Vagrancy, Famish & Perishings a way to
slip away. Follow US. With dignity.
Only none ever follows.
We are all strays.
Allways astray.

Sept 10 1958

Florida, Custom agents &
31 armed. No delay.
Second Atomic Energy
Conference. U-235.
Castro's offensive & Camagüey.
5 MIG-17s & 3 torpedo boats.
Ferhat Abbas & Belkacem Krim.
Martin Luther King & Izola Curry.
Ted Williams & bat.
—with sadness.
Fouad Chehab. Sami es-Sohl out.
Taiwan's 10 MIG-17s.
Columbia cups Sceptre.
Thor over Jupiter. Guinea &
New French Community.
5th Republic.
—for Peace.
Arctic atomic blasts. Matsu.
Chrysler, GM & UAW.
Clinton High School explosives.
Yankees over Braves.
Patrice Lumumba &
National Congolese Movement.
Atlanta bomb blast.

Feb 12 1969

Israel & Syrian MIG-21.

University of Madison, 900 National Guardsmen & 5,000 students. University of Rome.

Jerusalem explosion, 2 go.

GM's 4.9 million.

—Finally the big bird.

Chenpao, Damansky & Ussuri River, 31 go. Apollo 9 & Lunar Module.

Moscow's Chinese Embassy.

Abdel Riad goes.

Columbia University & 100 Barnard women. James Earl Ray & Tennessee State Prison.

Venezuela & jet, 150 go. Israel's fourth premier, Golda Meir. Columbia, Carlos Lleras Restrepo & student unrest. Egypt & plane, 91 go.

Uruguayan Security Force, Tupamaros & Manera Lluveras.

Past Mingle &
Chatter to a bar's tall tumblers
on ice, longstems of fizzz, vodka
martinis, dirty and dry.
—*Time to get primed,* I high
THE TENDER, winkling rye,
Sam abashed, slinks back,
leaving me both glasses to bag
which a thirsty pinkietap
allready refills.
Round after round
our BARMAN churning and tipping
Daiquiris, Margaritas, Piña Coladas
to my lips, slurping
every dickle bit. Foam is beer.
Sam takes no sip. Feering fifth gear,
clutches his Leftwrist Iron Twist
steers for a crowd
roaring amateur passes
somewhere around,
terribly proud,

July 31 1958

Louis Dejoie, Paul Magloire & François Duvalier. Jordan & Iraq. North Pole & Commander Anderson's Nautilus. Khrushchev & Mao.
—imperialist War maniacs.
Cyprus truce. Secretary's Defense Reorganization Act. Army, Navy & Air Force. UN, Lebanon & 1,700 troops. Dutch plane over Ireland, 99 go. Tel Aviv & 14 Syrian spies. Peking's Russian weapons. Snipe Island. Groton's Triton. Denmark refuses Skate. Brazzaville.

—the process of decolonization.

Quemoy shelling. National Defense Education Act. Nottingham riots. Paris & 3,000 arrests. Labor Pension Act. US escort & Taiwan transport. Gwadar Peninsula.

So sad.
Nearby somewhere
a whirl of solitary risk.
And me with just
my Leftwrist Iron Twist to toy with uneasily.
Even if Hailey never leaves my side, tripsying with
an impish fling: —*I'm gonna do something titsy.*
Along tarry lanes, through Upton, Wright and
Gillette we foliot, rounds of US
ripping the ground, spreading out across gardens,
yards, fields, creek beds eased with frost,
hillsides seized by rime. Enough to
drive me away. But tenderly Hailey holds me tight:
—*We're allways around.*
Shattering these groves with our untimely freeze.

April 2 1969

NYC Police & 21 Panthers.
Avenue of the Americas.
Dogs & The North Pole.

Haskell Karp goes.

400 police, 300 students
& Harvard.

North Korea
& US plane, 31 go.

Gustáv Husák over
Alexander Dubček.

West Germany
& Daniel Cohn-Bendit.

Cornell Student Union.

Belfast, fire bombs
& 1,000 troops.

*—There is no place for US,
the ordinary.*

American 77th Field
Artillery, Southern
Vietnamese Army
& Mekong River region.

12:11 AM.

—Ne Vous Y Trompez Pas.

ROTC & Democratic
Society's 6.

Majestic Prince's Derby.
Canadians & Stanley Cup.

swinging for Bogies. Bunts.
Tennis with shovels. Soccer on stilts.
Out of Bounds. Fouls.
Fourth Downs & Punts.
Sam challenging the Grunts. He's
all Them abhor. Downside to Sport.
Hated. Berated. Benched. Tackled.
Openly Scorned. Finally handing over
The Creep's WREATH. Mine!
TOURNAMENT CHIEFS all sneering shrill
with Plastic Hippie disgust. Thrilled
to death. Sam their mascot. HaHaaas
for each Period & Lap, Round & Match.
CYCLOGIRLS sidle closer
giggling misses with blown
kisses because he's cute.

—Zowie!

—Fabalicious!

—Dig it!

Griefing me, THESE GINCHIGALS
I could beat so easily.

June 18 1958

Wilt Chamberlain &
Harlem Globetrotters.
Linus Pauling & Detlev Bronk.
Paul Robeson's passport.
New York-London,
Harry Burrell & 630.2 MPH.
Edson Arantes do Nascimento.
Michigan's Mackinac Span.
10 Americans, 2 Canadians &
Oriente Province mine.
Fred Shuttleworth
& Birmingham blast.
Brazil over Sweden.
Castro's 28 US Naval Personnel.
Vito Genovese's 150 Fifths.
Bernard Goldfine.
Gibson over Mortimer. US ICBM &
6,000 miles. Iraqi army, Faisal &
6,000 British troops.
—of Lebanon's grave peril.
Camille Chamoun &
5,000 US marines.
Amman's 2 battalions.
Moscow bricks. Explorer IV. NASA.

wonder what the problem is with THESE STUCK
ROUSTABOUTS & DINGALINGS. Armed. Trespassing.

—It's just play, SOME flagrantly defend.

—Until you can't change games, Hailey alarms.

—What's it then?

—Your life.

Over which THESE POACHERS aggress and lose,
Hailey rewarding their possessions & assault
with a frostbite mauling throat & chest until
even their volitions kneel expelled along
with their flapped hats and vests.

Hailey's glad. She's taught all.
O Gee! Free's free. Le paths Odesea.
Me though, only a beggar busking for calendars.
Weakening. No purchase. Surrendering even stunts.

May 5 1969

Celtics over Lakers.

Secretary of Navy
& Pueblo Crew.
Canada, abortion &
homosexuality.

Louis E Wolfson &
$20,000, Abe Fortas quits.
Berkeley protests,
shotguns & tear gas.
Timothy Leary.
Queens college.
Bolivia, Chile, Colombia,
Ecuador & Peru.
Apbia Mountain.

Bruce Mayrock goes.
South China Sea,
Australian Carrier &
Destroyer Frank Evans,
73 go.
Mexico crash, 79 goes.
Congo, Kinshasa &
Mobutu's troops, 100 go.
Baltimore Maryland &
Catonsville Nine.
Kenyatta 37X goes.
Midway's Thieu &
25,000 troops.
Warren E Burger.

Justice Department, FBI &
J Edgar Hoover.

Sam lays it on thick, freak flag
slapping solo for the unhip.
Sickening.
I'm on a bender.
KoolAidGrain to amebiate ire,
while Sam botches the play, blows
every point, at least with a smile,
on each bounce, throw, hit, if
losing ground with every switch.
The Man wins.
Hairy vibes, assorted Tribes,
yammering this hyper kid:
—*Scram!* —*Get sick!*
—*Wretchedly licked!*
Until Sam shoots for a
far hoop to miss. And, O,
swishhhhhh,
even if he's allready split, leaving
Creep's GARLAND for a tip.
Following shoes for
happening grooves around

May 13 1958

Algiers & Charles de Gaulle.
Mediterranean, 6th Fleet
& Lebanese Liberty.
US troops & Caribbean.
18 days. North American
Air Defense Command.
Adam Clayton Powell's evasion.
8 Nike missiles blow, 10 go.
Raoul Salan & Algerian juntas.
Pierre Pflimlin.
Paris protests. 13 cars collide,
Pat O'Connor goes. Bryan's 500.
—*exceptional.*
—*and that is my death.*
6 months rule by.
Brooklyn's carrier.
Nikolai Kurochkin.
Iran, Jordan, Lebanon & 50 jets.
Kent vs Dulles.
Imre Nagy, Miklós Gimes
& Pál Maléter go.
Akihito & Michiko Shoda.
—*I need him.*

And though opportunities stack up around US,
we stand on it, shunning the squirt brakes,
leaving this tip: when the going gets slow
you go.
We rip on ahead.
O and whatever. We hurl
a wind of worry & dread.
Assault & Battery. Manslaughter.
DAs sick. Hipsters & Dig Crowds
slammed. Even National Forest Rangers scram for
some refuge from the terror our journeys allways
elicit. There's no protection. Because we're illicit.
Our engagements explicit. Our encounters
implicit. We're the fickle visit
the leery feer to revisit when stopping we

where bongos, guitars, lava,
hookahs and snares hubbub
the downy air.
Bends of **Southern Magnolia**
flittingly recommending:
—*Check out the bhang.*
And I'm down with this atmosphere.
Turn out, turn loose and turn on.
Tingles rush my hips, Zydeco yen,
tiny wiggles urging me then. Move
the World, faster, blast off and boogie.
Ball Sam too. Ball on my
own. Dance.
And I'm happily there, ready to
further and farther my feel
when I'm left.
Sam bolts away with one ruinous
step, dashing from me
leaving free
Boooooooooomblastandruin
to congeal.

June 17 1969
Jacques Chaban-Delmas.
Frances Gumm goes.
Haifa oil. Peru's land.
Laver. Tom Mboya goes.
Charles Evers.
Golan Heights
& 7 Syrian MIG-15s.
Bonny The Space
Monkey goes.
Tan Son Nhut, Fort Lewis
& US battalion.
Port Taufik. Honduras,
El Salvador & soccer.
Cleaver's Algeria.
Carmichael's Conakry.
Cape Kennedy, 39-A
& Apollo 11.
Martha's Vineyard,
Edward Kennedy
& Chappaquiddick,
Mary Jo Kopechne goes.
Merckx's Tour.
—Houston, Tranquillity
Base here. The Eagle has
landed.
10:56 PM
—one small step for man,
one giant leap for.
—magnificent desolation.
Collins' orbit.
Splashdown.

still. We drive by
lostlastandstrewn appalling a hearse,
obsequies by Mourners and Jolies. Howls
our licketysplit allways blurs beyond relief.
Behind the Wheel. Behind the Seat.
Behind every swerve. Ahead of the curves.
Closer and nearer to every Wanderer
we snuff out for oblivion. Despondent & grim.
Sundance, Carlile, Moorcroft.
Fast lane. Passing lane. One way.
Ripple discs overturning our countering World
again and again. And we slam low.
So up for this sky of billowy puff
from every bang our exhaust pipes sputter.
King Cheetahs cease on the rough.

March 26 1958
Explorer III.
Texas, US marshals &
35 New Yorkers.
—with a high level of work and
a higher standard of living.
Syria & Israel.
Moscow & Atomic tests.
—a gimmick.
Trafalgar Square's 5,000.
Ripple Rock with 1,375 tons.
Arnold Palmer. Polaris Missile.
Crane & Turner, Stompanato goes.
Hawks over Celtics.
Gomulka's strikes. Sputnik II.
Trinidad & Margaret. Atomium.
Egypt, Suez Canal Company &
$81 million. Tim Tam's Derby.
The Great Leap Forward.
—surpass those of several.
Bukittinggi.
Lima's University of
stone, shove & boo.
—Out with Nixon.

July 27 1969

Romania & Nixon.
Robert Rheault & 7.

Hollywood Hills & Pigs.
Sharon Tate goes. Leno &
Rosemary LaBianca go.

Vietnamese, South
Vietnamese & Americans,
1,647 go.

Max Yasgur.
Bethel's 200,000.

—Welcome to Woodstock.
—cosmic accident.

Belfast riots.

Philip Blaiberg goes.

Hurricane Camille, 300 go.

Federal Agents, Bobby
Seale & Alex Rackey.
Prague protest & tanks.

Tran Van Huong quits.

V V Giri.

—refuse to go.
We cannot move out.
CIA, 4 Berets &
Thai Khac Chuyen.

Idris I, Hassan al-Rida,
Shwirriba & Qaddafi.

Ho Chi Minh goes.

Sam doesn't hear. Crashing from
table top through cane chair.
Helterskeltering silverware, china and
glassware. Clodplodding every neck,
belly and knee, tripping to a clearing
with friends yowling for An End.
—Outrageous!
Griping. But Sam, jiggling,
bellbottomed with stripings, puts on
his happy feet and just leaps.
Jauncing jouncy united. Peace.
Even the most courageous must shy
from this catastrophe.
Gyrating hips, pokey nods,
a caterwauling seizure,
leaving all, US,
oblivious to what allways prevails,
what reaches my neck now and
drapes calmly about my shoulders,
Booooooooomblastandruin
here to smash

Feb 1 1958

California military planes,
47 go. United Arab Republic,
Syria & Egypt. Hague, Benelux
& trade curbs. Vanguard launch
& blow. Mikhail Menshikov.
Japanese fusion.
Algeria's medical trucks, 74 go.
—legitimate defense.
Northeastern blizzard, 171 go.
Britain's 60 Thor missiles.
Juan Manuel Fangio
& Cuban rebels.
Argentina's Arturo Frondizi.
Carlos Prio Socarras & 8.
Gorontalo. Turkish ferry, 220 go.
—temporarily.
Explorer II.
Wisconsin decomissioned.
B-47's dropped bomb
& Mars Bluff South Carolina.
Vanguard I & 2,513 miles.
Cold & a crash, Mike Todd goes.
US 53310761.
—Hoodlum empire.

Here to thwart even
lostlastandloooooooomin.
Through Tilford, Spearfish, Beulah.
Driving towards defections unable to
defect from any cold. I defect to Hailey.
With her, I'm but US,
beyond the cloying brush of Populations eager
to regain Our Anticipated Rush to Open Life.
Except our refusal leaves Them to the catastrophe
of their convictions, now tragically
consistent & unified. Just doing time.
So away we roll. Over all disorder.
Because we're all of time's items apart. Smited.
Bided. Beyond all Guided. From every start.
Skid & slide. Crash & die. Lie

me away. Again.
—*You're with me now,* comes the scold.
CANE rap between my
kissing knees.
—*Thank me. You're free of this Drag,*
THE CREEP's fingernails digging sharp
my scalp, turning me from Sam,
with a terrifying plan.
Deft hands. Terrible might. Calm.
—*I'm your only one.*
—*Yes.*
—*You will submit.*
—*Yes.*
—*And want to.*
Accepatating this rip wheeling me
under gleeping **Swamp Willows**
weeping: —*Hurry. Escape.*
But I'm too late, finding by such
power irrefutable thrills. How
CREEP'll summon. How CREEP'll wait.
How CREEP'll bind this World with fate.

Sept 7 1969

Brazil & C Burke Elbrick.
Everett Dirksen goes.
James Pike goes.

Airliner & small plane,
83 go.

C-5A Supertransport.
Gulf of Suez.
11 Egyptian jets down.
Nixon & North Vietnam
bombing.

Aden hijacking. Ulster.
Viet Cong barrage, 100 go.
35,000.

Cairo gunfire & Illinois.
50,000 draft cut.
Cuba extradition.
Mike Mansfield.
Ton Duc Thang.

Thailand's 6,000.

—*nattering nabobs of.*

Sweden & Olaf Palme.
—*Days of rage.*
Czechoslovakia
& travel ban.
79 University Presidents
& pullout. Soyuz 7.

Vietnam Moratorium.
—*residual force.*

Mets over Orioles.
—*anything can happen.*

Yucksville for Splitsville we kill it.
All we decline.
Slicks ripping our drive.
So early we lose nothing we find.
Our allaround escapes. Not US.
Chilean Llamas collapse lifeless to the side.
We find nothing. By Harney,
Rockerville, Stratosphere Bowl. Dakota Rock.
Yup, crossing Rapid City too. Of course.
And everything submits to US.
Sure. Because we're it. Hip. Allways imminent.
The only ones released across Meade.
Tempt US. Fug it. Fug it all.
—*So excellent,* I shrug. It rains. *We're free*
for so much. I'm glad I'm with you.

Jan 3 1958

Hillary's South Pole.
2 squadrons of Strategic Air
Command with ballistic missiles.
Hailes & British West Federation.
French troops & Cameroon uprising.
—*to overthrow.*
Moscow's 300,000.
Sakiet-Sidi-Youssef & Tunisia,
15 go. Djurdjura Mountains.
Linus Pauling's 9,000.
Rebels & Manzanillo.
Arthur Summerfield's
snapping dogs. Caracas Police,
women & machetes.
500 Americans & KKK rally.
Marcos Pérez Jiménez overthrown.
Cockcroft, Strauss & 100 million°.
Ferenc Münnich over János Kádár.
Air Force's Thor missile.
Roy Campanella & crash.
Douglas Wyoming & 110 MPH:
Charles Starkweather &
Caril Fugate. Explorer I.

Oct 18 1969

Cyclamates.
Bolivia's Gulf Oil.
—effete snobs.
Hurricane Laurie.
President Willy Brandt.
Kerouac goes.
Monosodium glutamate.
Trudeau's Arctic.
Lebanon & PLO's 300.
Aga Khan, Begum Salima
& Sarah Croker-Poole.
ARPANET. Alexander vs
Board of Education.
—with all
deliberate speed.
—at once.
San Francisco Rome
hijacking.
Copenhagen Sex. Vassar.
—fire and blood.
Polo & Buckingham
allowance. Rockefeller,
General Motors, Chase
Manhattan bombs.
Apollo 12. Pennsylvania
Avenue's 250,000.
Eugene McCarthy, George
McGovern & Coretta King.
—We are here to
break the War.
Atrocities & slaughter.
US, USSR & SALT arms.

Eat dirt, feet first. THE CREEP
shoves me along and since
I'm looped, populations will hurt.
Teeth cut on the weak,
jerking up such spite

under my skirt.

Nobody flips.
Everybody trips.

THE CREEP owns what Them need.
Fucko Punch, Rainbows & Horse.
Speedballs of Meth, Crank. Rows
after rows of South American Blow.
Snappers and Beans. Stashes
of Ludes. THE CREEP's allways
got something to do.
Puts everyone to use.
Nobody cuts loose of such endeavors.
—*What the fuck's eating you?*
—*I'm with you,* I shrug. *For now.*
—*Forever.*

Nov 22 1957

French troops & Sahara, 42 go.
Mickey Mantle. Ike's stroke.
Jakarta, Sukarno & a grenade,
7 go. Dutch enterprises
& West New Guinea.
Nuclear icebreaker Lenin.
Vanguard Rocket, 2 ft
& an explosion. AFL-CIO
& Teamsters. UN, Algeria & FLN.
Eisenhower, Dulles & Paris Summit.
Cape Canaveral, Army Atlas ICBM
& 500 miles.
Shippingport Pennsylvania
& Duquense Atomic Power Plant.
US ballistic missiles
Europe & NATO.
Cairo, anti-Western crowds &
Afro-Asian Solidarity Conference.
Lions over Browns.
Gurion's Coalition over.
Ohio over Oregon.
Venezuela Army, Colombia &
revolt.

—*Never,* I mubble.
—*I'm with you,* Hailey rubs. *Forever.*
—*And never again,* we agree. Ready to blow on.
US: —*You're just overkill.*
Splitting wide from THE CREEP for
more turns of the road. Hopped & howling.
We're feers across hills & plain, towns &
farm without mission. O US.
Any mission. Every omission. Viciously bound
to bang on for Warsaw forces, Geneva derisions
and rainbow frisbies floating uncivilly overhead.
Everybody freaks.
Everybody flips.
Even if nobody gets a whiff.
The slimmest gist of who
it is we allways shlip from.

Nov 19 1969

Apollo 12's moon walk.
Podgorny, Nixon & Nuclear
Non-Proliferation Treaty.

US Draft Lottery.

Chicago Police
& 7 Panthers,
Clark & Hampton go.

—am a revolutionary.

Tracy California &
Altamont Speedway,
Meredith Hunter goes.

Milan National Bank, 3 go.
Round 3 of departures.
Ramiro Silvera & Amado
Sanjur over Omar Torrijos.
Capital punishment.
Lugogo & Milton Obote.

Vice President Anwar Sadat.
Bernadette Devlin.
Willie Sutton's free.

Congo-Brazzaville's
republic. Vorster's
apartheid. Coed.

Moshe's Marauders.
National Football League
& American Football
League. Super Bowl IV,
Chiefs over Vikings.
Biafra surrenders.

But I shuckashake: —*Never.*
Sam, why'd he ditch?
So sad. Allready. Sticking here
with this nittygritty.
And the hit stings.
CREEP's knuckles splashing my face.
What next? Rape? All varieties of take?
Rickytik filickerings, supple and
tender, those hands bending round
and down by a smile, repeatedly
losing touch with what my powers
still won't concede.

—*Turn,* **Woolly Groundsel** warns.
—*Run,* mickles **Spanish Moss**.

But I'm stuck.
THE CREEP's patience claiming me,
stroking my permy curls, a soft
thumb to my mouth.
Here's Brutal beyond consequence.
And I'm every consequence

Sept 25 1957

Clean dress, clean socks
& Johnny Gray's punch.
—Mob rule cannot be allowed to
override the decisions.
Miami Beach Teamsters.
Sputnik I,560 miles high &
1 hour 35 minutes around.
Braves over Yankees.
Ike, Ghana Finance Minister &
Delaware restaurant.
Syria & Egyptian troops.
3 rocket failures.
Bonn breaks with Yugoslavia.
East LA hail.
Point Magu waterspouts.
Jupiter ballistic missile.
Saigon bomb.
Umberto Anastasia goes.
Georgi Zhukov over.
—cult of.
Laika's 937 miles.
James R Killian Jr &
Special Aide for Space.
Hank Aaron.
Novotný over Zápotocký.

of such consequences because I am.
Because Hailey can. We are untaken steps.
I press my thumb then on her soft mouth,
touch her playful bangs, my own
patience claiming me.
Because we're uncalmed.
Coral Snakes coil up. Rot.
Disarmed Leeches slip down. Stomped.
And then Hailey concedes even her
strength needs me, touching my face
repeatedly, cooing with her fingers supplely,
reaching around me, all over me, splendorly
pleasing me, slowly, whiling me, with care. All
varieties of kisses. Affections. Unlimits of actions.
I could never ditch Hailey.
Ever.

Jan 17 1970

Brody's Puerto Rico.
G Harrold Carswell.

New York Panther 21
Legal Defense Fund.

Everett Alvarez.
South Africa & Arthur Ashe.
Manila 2,000, 2 go.

French immolation, 8 go.

Golan tanks.
Gulf of Suez &
Egyptian Minelayer.

Israel's US weapons.
Val d'Isère &
avalanche, 39 go.
Scrap metal plant
& Cairo, 70 go.
GM's unleaded engines.

Frazier 5 rounds Ellis.

Ravine &
Lagalanga train, 81 go.
Chicago 7's acquittal.
—dance on your grave,
Julie!

Denny McLain's gamble.

Governor Lester Maddox,
Charles Diggs &
axe handles.
—a baboon.

unable to turn free.
THE CREEP, relishing my
freeze, ready to get some,
KATY clean for the stick
of me. And Sam still off
waggling beats, fried & staggering,
far from cuntsville here, toe
poppers & frags. Zoned for zaps.
And that's it, I'm torn down.
Over and out. Prepped for pain.
Except THE CREEP's only disdain.
—*You is all mine so.*
I allmost faint.
—*The only way.*
O no.
There. CREEP's fun. Casual. Not
overdone. How to retain me
to repeat tortures CREEP
enduringly seeks.
ROMAN CORD. Around me.

Aug 29 1957

South Carolina's Strom Thurmond's
24 hours & 27 minutes.
—hardships.
—will stop their fight.
Orval Faubus
& Little Rock's High School.
Greensboro Senior High School
& Josephine Ophelia Boyd.
—We don't want you here.
Hailstorm & B-66 bailout.
Militia bars 9. 400.
—niggers!
—The Federal Constitution
will be upheld by.
Cienfuegos uprising,
Cuban soldiers & Castro's rebels.
Birmingham beating.
Nashville bomb &
Hattie Cotton Elementary School.
Bangkok's Thai Army.
Nevada burning. 1,000 to 9.
—our school.
Carmen Basilo rounds Robinson.
1,000 Paratroopers & 10,000
Arkansas National Guard.

tumbles off around US because we're unwinding
THE CORD.
Hailey, with my assistance,
loosens, shreds and finally spreads what's no
longer left of THE CREEP's hold on US.
On the World.
—*O yes.*
Might THE CREEP die?
—*Used all up. Everything.*
Unrestrained, THE CREEP curls up with
the suffering of all who go on without US. Over &
Out. Worn down. And because I'm now here by
this agony, how THE CREEP, discommobulated &
finally lost, keeps spinning at our toes
until even there freezes with bleats,
turning me free

Feb 25 1970

Isla's Bank of America & 1,000.
—*cowardly little bums.*

5 Marines.
David Dellinger, Rennie Davis, Thomas Hayden, Abbie Hoffman, John Froines & Lee Weiner.
—*a racist, a fascist and a pig.*

Salisbury & Britain.
Houston, Marijuana & Leary's 10.
Eurydice down, 57 go.

18 West 11th Street, Weathermen & accidental blast, 3 go.
Ernest Medina.
Eugene Kotouc.
Kurdish autonomy.
Samuel Koster.
UCLA over Jacksonville.
Electric Circus blast.

Carlo Gambino arrested.
Lon Nol over Norodom Sihanouk.
Turkey quake, 600 go.
MIG-21 down.
Francis Sargent & bill.
Jerome Holland.

Except Sam arrives, miffed certainly,
if allso turning out smiles,
strut, happily highfiving THE CREEP,
slapping out some horrid detente:
—*Eat my heart out! Thank yooooouu*
for giving this Chocolate Bunny
the Poulo Condor.

—*My guest.*

—*Gonna keep her tied up long?*

—*O yes.*

Then jives hard, chuckhuckling at
my expense. Though I'm too held,
moaning allone with slow feers,
to try crying.

—*Wow, you're tough.*

—*Toughest.*

—*Well maybe among those fools back*
there, all dinged out & stewed. But
you're still no athlete. Stooped &
pooped. But that's cool.

July 15 1957

—*will taste better with butter.*
Sultan Said of Muscat and Oman & Civil War. Anquetil's Tour.
Persian Gulf's RAF jets.
Bey of Tunis & Tunisian Republic.
Carlos Castillo Armas goes.

Castro's 200 rebels.
Patterson 10 rounds Jackson.
Nigerian autonomy.

Batista, Bueycito & Minas.
Belgrade, Tito & Khrushchev.
Malaya's Abdul Rhaman.
Moscow & Syrian delegation.
Brooklyn's Rudolf Ivanovich Abel.

Quebec's Canadian vets, 79 go.
Levittown's first by police guard.

Geneva's 600 billion volts.

Forbes, David G Simons & 101,486 ft.
Niagara Power Bill.
Soviet ICBM.

Wisconsin's William Proxmire.

Cool beyond gain. So of course, pooped & stooped,
THE CREEP's STAVE starts to droop.
—*You fool,* Hailey slings a circumvoluting
feer THE CREEP can't drop.
—*You're too much, I'm afraid.*
Hailey: —*Tough.*
And then THE CREEP nearly cries,
so glum sillyda, which hitches Hailey,
ever free to vanquish enough
with a clap.
—*O No.*
—*No worries. We shan't tie you up again.*
—*Thanks.*
When, slyly sudden, THE CREEP lunges with STAFF,
slashing & smashing at all I'm powerless to stop,
catch, prohibit. Except all aim turns to FLAX and

April 10 1970

Paul McCartney quits.
Apollo 13.
—Houston, we have a problem.
James Lovell, Fred Haise & John Swigert.

241.7 million Soviets.

Trinidad's US weapons.
Earth Day.
China's satellite.
Gypsy Rose Lee goes.
Ohio State University's 600.
Cambodia's Fish Hook.
—a pitiful, helpless giant.
128 US Jets & North Vietnam.

Diane Crump.
Dust Commander's Derby.
13,000 Panther supporters.
—off campus.

Kent State.
Allison Krause, William Schroeder, Jeffrey Miller & Sandra Scheuer go.
Knickerbockers over Lakers.
Mayor Lindsay.

Jackson State, 2 go.
Thor Heyerdahl's Ra II.
Mao & World Revolt.

Sam yabbling on
about squatthrusts, handstands,
crunches, marathons,
until THE CREEP just cracks
neck, rolls shoulders and
looms skookums with slowly
closing fists.
—*You win,* Sam quickly submits.
—*Where's my Reward?*
—*I allready returned it,* Sam stappers.
At your backyard scrimmage.
—*No. You lost. It's mine now*
but you still owe. Me.
—*Hey, you gifted US that Plum.*
—*No tin's for free.*
And then Sam, all backed up, afraid,
somehow gets a teensybit brave.
—*Yo Owl, don't get so dinky dau.*
Check with the ground. There're
plenty of Feds around.

June 3 1957

US & Baghdad pact. Poland & US Surplus Farm Equipment.
Cape Canaveral, Atlas Missile & 5,000 ft. Western plan & Atomic test ban.
Smith Act & California 5.
John Diefenbaker.
Hurricane Audrey, 390 go.
11 Arab States.
Japan's Occupation HQ over.
Caspian sea quake, 200 go.
Committee over Presidium: Molotov, Malenkov & Kayanovich. 8-4.
—completely clean.
French colonial repression.
Fayetteville truck, 20 go.
Althea Gibson over Darlene Hard.
Army Ballistic Missile.
B-58.
—the World would be a better.
4th National Nuclear Attack drill.
Over mountains, under desks.

Hailey laughs. *And you, Cube, are scarce.*
THE CREEP wavers, pulling back
such toilings, trying to regroup.
Which is when, maybe a smidge courageously,
I take away the snare:
—*Nothing's free.*
And: —*Hey Cat, that's me.*
And: —*Not anymore.*
And That's That, winding up such strands,
leaving THE CREEP barely standing & stunned.
Except for THE CUDGEL. Raising THE CANE:
—*Give it here at once!*
But we don't. Both of US closing our fists,
rolling our shoulders, cracking our necks.
Physically fit beyond fitness. We're fit
beyond physical. Beyond pain.

May 27 1970

Paris police & Maoist students. Huey Newton. Unser's 500. Brandeis University & Student Strikes. *—a bloodbath, then, let'S get it over with.*

Mount Huascarán, Yungay & Ranrahirca, 66,794 go.

Welsh vs United States. Brazil, Bonn envoy & 40 prisoners. Pele. *—enough to die for our country but we cannot.* 81-10. Tonkin resolution repealed. McSorley's gals. American Medical Association & abortion. *—new militancy among homosexuals.*

NAACP & Nixon. Cambodia's US Troops. China & Russia accord.

Spain & British plane, 112 go.

Belfast snipers, 5 go. Margaret Smith Court.

—So?

—We're only sixteen.

But THE CREEP just laughs,
unmoved by this admission of youth.
Because we're unguarded,
unadmitted, averaged
and loose.

*—If only The Nóose were big
enough for two,*

THE CREEP cinching me tighter,
which I return with a smile,
if allso, so circumcingled, I feel
something capricious start to expire.
THE CREEP then raises CLUB cruelly
above Sam: —*Time to redeem me.*

Whereupon THE GAME REFEREE
arrives: —*Your Winnings, Sir.*
A noble deed offering Sam's victory
with returns exceeding THE CREEP's
trap. Loyal to Sam? The sport?

April 20 1957

Plymouth England, Plymouth Massachusetts & Mayflower II. Army Air Defense Command: Nike Hercules over Nike Ajax. Greenville KKK's Catholics. Harold Connolly & Olga Fikotova.

—100 flowers opening, 100 rival schools.

Nuclear reactor, Fort Belvoir & Wilbur Brucker. Robinson rounds Fullmer. North American Council, US Forces & Western Europe. Iron Liege's Derby. Soviet's 92 regions. Groton's Skate. AFL-CIO & Dave Beck. Destroyer USS McGowan. Taipei's anti-American riots. Port-au-Prince Haiti, Leon Cantave & Pierre Arman. Brooklyn Dodgers to LA. New York Giants to San Francisco. Hanks's 500.

Khrushchev's Disarmament.

that we're saved. Safe?

*—Fools. I'm your salvation.
Your hard knocks. Your dues.
Without me, you both lose.
You'll slip away and never find a role.
Time's up. Time to tie you down. Now.*

THE CREEP then flings THE NÓOSE
around US both, something of our whimsy
allready failing with this knotty yanking
and circumsingling, about our waists, our necks,
cinching US lesseverly. Until:
—*Tsk, tsk,* Hailey smiles. *This won't do.
The Cord is never big enough for two.*
And THE NÓOSE falls loose
around our youth.
—We're allways sixteen,

July 7 1970

Asbury Park riots.
James Walsh free.
NYC LSD overdose.
47,000 dockworkers &
London State of Emergency.
Presidio blast.

Reggio Calabria blaze.
Gamal Abdel & Aswan Dam.
Antonio Salazar goes.
United Farm Workers,
Cesar Chavez &
26 grape growers.
Castro's Jumbo Jet.
Robert Kennedy, Robert
Shriver & marijuana.
Freeloader Semo-Tordjman.

—Wait for me.

Lucy Komisar.

—Not particularly.

Berrigan arrested.
Postal Reorganization Act.
GM, Ralph Nader &
$425,000.
Beisan Valley.
Forbes Burnham's bauxite.
Pat Palinkas Panthers.
Nerve gas 418.
John Volpe's
85,000 police cars.
ABM.
Hurricane Dorothy, 42 go.

Perhaps.
THE CREEP shrieks this passado,
freeing me to lasso my squirt, racing
pellmell from each culty swoop.
—*Split,* **Mud Plantains** prevaricate.
—*Jag out,* **Pitcher Plants** divaricate.
Even THE GAME OFFICIAL defers. Flees.
THE CREEP persists.
Another throw. Another miss.
Grabbing THE COIL, Sam, spastic and
drastic, tries to refling the tangle.
Until all relaxed & fantastic, I switch
auftritt and by grande battement,
fingers curved, arms long, trip
THE CREEP backwards.
Sam frantically wrangling
the ensuing thrash with
THE NÓOSE at last.
—*You can't leave me,*
THE CREEP seethes.

March 5 1957

Israel's Suez Canal.
Kwame Nkrumah.
—her lost freedom.
Eisenhower, Communist
aggression & Mideast Forces.
Aleutian Island Tsunami.
Bahrein & Saudi Oil.
Boeing 707. Cebu crash,
Magsaysay goes. Bermuda meet.
San Francisco quake.
American Heart Association.
—between smoking and
the occurrence.
European Economic Community:
Luxembourg, Netherlands, Italy,
France, West Germany & Belgium.
Euratom. Hoffa. Tunisia
& Morocco Friendship Treaty.
Herbert Norman goes.
Soviet H-Bomb. New Mexico
& Aerobee Hi's 126 miles. Dubna's
accelerator. Bonn physicists &
nuclear weapons. Celtics over
Hawks. Hussein over Suleiman
Nabulsi. Egyptain Canal toll.

There's THE CREEP:
—*You can never leave me.*
THE CORD on hand.
I'm all whimwhams, but when
THE CREEP attacks I scratch back, frantically
scampering for some escape.
Hailey though, arms long, fingers curved,
goes for a reverse kick.
I spastically try to circle for a rearside trip but
THE CREEP dodges, steps aside, and with a
feersome leer grabs US both easily enough
by savagely pinching both of our ears.
Dwarf Sirens die.
Recluse Spiders die.
And then THE CREEP starts spinning
THE COIL, each time croaking with certainty

Aug 24 1970

Agnew & ROK forces.

Wisconsin, US Army
& a bomb, 1 goes.
5th Avenue's 30,000.

American Suffrage
Parades. New Orleans,
Detroit, Boston.

—Hardhats for Soft Broads.

Pondexteur Williams.
An Quang. Philadelphia
raids. Edward Akufo-Addo
& Amboinese separatists.
Chile's Salvador Allende.
Jordan's Revolution Airstrip.
TWA Boeing 707,
Swissair DC-8,
British Airways DC-10.
Court's Grand Slam.
UAW, GM & 240,000.
Typhoon Georgia, 300 go.
Hendrix goes.
Jordan, Amman & PLO.
32 free.
—Nasser!

Ficker cups Hardy.
Huessy. EEC.
South Vietnam
fighting rains.
Al Fatah. Uttar Pradesh.
Carl McIntire's 20,000.

But we do.
And I'm still shaking. Unsteady and
bruised. Unbruised. Sam too.
At least The Party's Ongoing.
And I'm unenslaved, flying braless &
brave, if clutching Sam
to upside my way.
Taken around loaded Vets, Zilch
Patrols, Ben Heads and Wasted Barbies
sucking highballs, cocknballs and
allways cigarettes. Even tonguing for
butts. How hungry this crowd.
Proud, direct. Wild. Bankers,
Dilettantes, Virgins & Sluts. I wave.
Smile. My longlashes fluttering
certainly.

What's the harm?
Where's the danger?
But Sam, livid, holds onto anger
with angrier steps and flimsier arms.

88 | 273

Jan 19 1957

Egypt, Saudi Arabia, Syria &
Jordan. Gurion, Sharm el Sheikh
& Gulf of Aqaba. Kashmir. Taiz.
Alger Otomatic Café &
the Coq Hardi, 4 go.
DC & Saud.
Algiers & General Massu.
Cambridge cryotron.
US & Dharan airfield.
Bruce Dern's sideburns.
US Communist Party &
Soviet Control.
Georgia Senate's athletics.
Andrei Gromyko.
Wilkes Land Antartica.
—be here fighting for Fidel.
Butler vs Michigan.
Jean Muller,
Tablat Camp & torture.
SCLC's Martin Luther King,
Ella Baker, Bayard Rustin &
Stanley Levinson.
—and prompt withdrawal.
—with the utmost speed.

Earthbound and Sad,
I let go of our Discarded.
We are the discarded.
So we just pass on by.
Maybe.
Hailey's longlashes flutter. She even smiles and
next to me wags to me. We're solitary
and yet something allways moves alongside US.
Still. Hunting.

—Do you feel that there's?
—Yes, I. But it's okay.

Except it's not. The feer around US. Allovers
I can't shake even with shudders. Though Hailey's
hardly disconcerted. Sheer Strength & Attitude.
Poise & Pulchritude. We won't pull over
anymore until at a rotary we do.

Oct 4 1970

Joplin goes.
President Sadat.
James Richard Cross.
Harvard Affairs blast.
Fiji's freedom.
Front de Libération du
Québec & Minister of
Labor and Immigration.

Rae, Cape & Menthosa.
40,000 troops.
Angela Davis arrested.

Typhoon Sening, 583 go.
Typhoon Titang, 526 go.
Baltimore over Cincinnati.
Pedro Taruc goes.
Ravenna's 25.

Trudeau's War Powers.
Sledge, Conti & Calley.

Manhattan armories,
Police station & bombs.
Environmental
Protection Agency.

—who bomb and burn.

4 Weathermen arrested.

—Majority of my fellow.

Vietnam's Legality.
UAW strike over.
Charles de Gaulle goes.

—the events of.

Yankee Foxtrot, rotating back to the
World. Meet Ms. Army fatigues.
Iron Weed approves.

Only I bring relief. Plastered Paul begs
me for Cs. Betty Crockers & Flowers.
Laughter's the taste of my surviving.
And Sam's bagging suds.
Chill cups of chugaluglug. Guzzles
Ketchup for fun. Pies too.
Large helpings. Won't even chew.
I wanna leave.
Still I hitch close to this hick.
For hot vibes & soothes, 50s,
frag moves and LAWs.
Hard to give up.
I'm all personnel.
Impersonal.
Personally prepared for
the wet revenge
Sam rapaciously attends.

Nov 22 1956

—are tottering.
Melbourne Olympics.
Hungary's 10,000 go.
János Kádár turns.
Patterson 5 rounds Moore.
Fidel Castro's rebels.

—We will bury you.
Army & Navy. Cuban planes
& Oriente Province, 40 go.
Fraser, Leech Morgan & Crapp.
Port Said.
—to the armistice.
UN's Japan.
Montogmery Boycott over.
—of oppressed people.
France & Britain leave.
Tallahassee buses. Giants over
Bears. Governor Collins.
Iowa over Oregon.
Rámon Villeda Morales.
Suez salvage. Harold Macmillan
over Anthony Eden.
Egypt's British & French banks.
3 Air Force Stratos, 500 MPH
& 45 hours.

—Enough's a feast.
—You're all I need, I choke.

And outandout we tear for Custer Curves
on wild loops, strangely impersonal,
rounding threatening steeps.
Dirt. Asphalt. By Dry Creek.
Lame Johnny. Prairie Trail.

So fast, I cleave to Hailey.

Until we come among what's only left over,
strewn across our way, unconsumed,
untouched, here lying doomed upon
the frosty mat of our road, the mighty
blurring we breeze by wherever we drive.
Sadness. The wastes of all survival.
US, a stampede stilled upon the land.
American Bison churned to chaff.

Nov 13 1970

Cyclone, Bhola & Ganges Delta, 300,000 go.
Lunar 17.
Libya, Egypt, Sudan & Syria. NCCF's 36.
203,184,772.
Taos tribes & 48,000 acres.
William O Douglas, Gerald R Ford & impeachment.
Debra Jean Sweet & The End.
Lettuce Boycott.
Reveille over.
LG Bacon.
—*Yes.*

FDA, mercury & 1,000,000 tuna cans.
Venera 7 & Venus.

Polish riots & Gomulka.
US Troops & Friendly fire, 9 go.

Nixon's Occupational Safety and Health Act.
Clean Air Act.

Howard Hughes & Britannia Beach.
Pyotr Jaroszewicz.
Kiangsu, Kiangsi & Kwangtung.
Stanford over Ohio.

Whatever he needs.
However he wants her.
No worries.
Allready pathetically
pinching a Warm Up Wendy's
rear who freeks & splits
because Sam stinks of feer. But
we dance the bawds and, obliging
Sam's PTSDs, jerking around for
Lucys, Lollipops & Screams, by lips
and my Diamondy Leftwrist Twist,
I wing a DEADEND over, gingham midi
with shearling boots, fucked up and
juiced, rattlesuckrolling
lemon drops.
—*Now we're three,* slipping
her tongue between my teeth.
—*We need drugs,* Sam blushes
but keeps thick to this clench
of shimmy on legs.

Oct 22 1956

French arrest 5 NLF. Budapest Police & Hungarian revolt.
—*We will crush Them.*

Warsaw thousands.
Nagy's Soviet troops & supporters. IAEC & 11,000 lbs of Uranium-235.
Israeli forces & Sinai.
Mindszenty free.
UN Emergency session.
Hungary, Soviet troops & Warsaw Pact. Israel's Gaza strip.
Budapest & 1,000 tanks.
—*to overthrow the legal.*
—*We don't have much time.*
RAF's 100 MIG-15s.
Moshe Dayan & Sinai, thousands go. Eisenhower over Stevenson. DS Saund.
Canal's 46 boats. 250,000 Chinese volunteer for Egypt. 65-1.
Bus segregation unconstitutional.
Connecticut iceberg.
Hungarian deportation.

arm beyond the reach
of anyone. Not even reaching US.
—*We need you,* THE PACHUCAS run.
We just bust on:
—*Time to dust off.*
Rumbling off
for curves more remote.
If only I wasn't so
fumbling & clumsy with Hailey
and her Leftwrist Diamondy Twist.
While THOSE CHICKS still slug a bathtub
desperate to catch up until Them don't.
PELLTIER, SARAH, BURD, LAURA & FRANCIS at last
turning horrified before such bloody retreats
we precede and proceed to cause. At speeds beyond
balls. Because we're. Now. Here. Not even near.

Jan 6 1971

Berkeley hormones.
Russian long hair.
Coco goes.
Allan Passaro.
Swiss envoy, Brazil &
70 political prisoners.
Stung Chhay Pass.
Super Bowl V,
Colts over Cowboys.
South Dakota's
George McGovern.

—which power is turned back to the people.

Long Island, Oil tanker &
385,000 gallons.

Manson & 3.
—You won't outlive this.

Idi Amin over Obote.

Georgia Arms Plant
explosions, 24 go.
Rolls-Royce bankruptcy.

Apollo 14 & a stroll
on the moon.
Vietnamese Army,
Communist supplies
& Laos.

LA quake, 51 go.
Spiro Agnew hits 3.

OPEC prices.

On tiptoes, knees, beanbags and
shag. Squeeze, shove and grab.
Five Six SixtyFive I'm sick.
Seven Eight EightySeven I'll submit.
Because I don't object. Along for the
ride. I am the ride. Crotch copping
JELLY NIGERIA threesomes for
moresomes. Why lessen?
SHELLY & KELLY. Byebye poplin vests!?
GROUPIE CLAIRE. Byebye hot pants &
belts!? JUICY FRUIT. Byebye panties!?
Throngs for gliding. Gom dan
for grinding. Tgroup tripping,
exotically along.
Beer kegs spraying the pond.
All swim, splash, sputter muddy.
Sam rascalling
few feels
with an ittystiffy
bonging for tongues, rugs

Sept 2 1956

Glad Woodward, National Guard
& Tennessee's 12.
—it is carried out.
Sturgis High School bayonets.
Egypt & Suez Canal.
Cairo's Soviet captains.
—fight to the bitter.
Managua's Panama Canal Zone,
Rigoberto López Pérez goes.
Jhelum River, 22 go.
Newfoundland & Scotland.
Air Force Bell X-2 down, 1 goes.
Anastasio Somoza goes.
Luís Somoza Debayle.
Algerian Nationalists, FLN bombs
& European Cafés.
Suez Canal Users Association.
Sabin vaccine.
Don Larsen's no-hitter.
—cheap and easy.
Yankees over Dodgers.
Hong Kong clash, 40 go.
USSR & Japan.
Poland's border stop.

On we boff, through Wounded Knee,
Hermosa to Mount Rushmore granite,
mist soaked & cold,
where frozen there
under such pursed lips
and fog kissed brows
some BEATNIKS orbit around our pause.
Sweet, sharp, clingy & bold.
Heroic, Unequal, Wise & Conservative,
along a Presidential Trail following only US.
—*Over here,* ONE begs.
—*Get off the bus,* ANOTHER presses.
—*No,* ANOTHER by gripe still objects.
—*Please, we need you around,* THE LAST ONE tries.
—*Scat,* Hailey zats, blasting ahead. She's the way
even stone dies. Off for a Crazy outstretched

and outlaw tugs.
But it's a miss & a mess, a sprawl of
undress. All scrambling to dirt and
concrete, drying on grass,
umpteen bodies detaching
with touch, rubadub dub, Oooooﬁng
the clutch, Nnnnnnnnnning
turntaking fondles so casually offered
to ear canals, nostrils and busts.
Pubic thrusts for public orifices.
And lusts.

—*Hey!*

—*Ouch!*

I'm every pang. I am pain.
Every Upper East Side plaidskirted
kid running to find the edge of
her worth. And everyone wants to
conquer me because when I gain
competitions hurt.
Which I allways desert.

Feb 17 1971

Chile, peasants & farms.

Athens & long hair.

Nigerian Health Ministry
& cholera, 29 go.
Anne Henning's 500 meters.

Ali's Miami 10 spar.
—*all to be destroyed.*

Ernesto Regalado goes.
1:32 AM, Senate sink
& Weather Underground.
—*barbaric.*

Reagan, California
& welfare rolls.
Pierre E Trudeau
& Margaret Sinclair.
Around Lao Bao.
Tchepone.
Frazier 15 rounds Ali.
Gandhi's majority.
2 US platoons refuse.
District of Columbia
& Walter E Fauntroy.
Ford & Pintos.
Susan Atkins, Leslie
Van Houten & Patricia
Krenwinkel.
—*going to come
down hard.*
Guilty.

their hand at overtaking our joyride.
No one comes close. No one's alive.
We're the pain collidings provide.
What no one seeks out. Who none can slow.
We're the longings of Societies not even
the slickest Lower East Side kid can outgrow.
Assured. Hailey & I enjoying our only boredom.

—*Oooooo.*

—*Yeah.*

A private grind on pleasurable grounds. Without
much burst. Nnnnnnnnnning then
to Oooooﬁng. We do get around.
Just two of US screwing human demands.
Allone. And even if we don't come,
Hailey's frenzy and pace leaves me
outlawed.

July 19 1956

Brioni Islands.
Panama, Communism &
Western Hemisphere.
Anjar quake, 117 go.
Nantucket, Stockholm &
Andrea Doria, 50 go.
—*And it will be run by.*
Walkowiak's Tour.
Burma occupation.
Britian mobilizes forces.
Shukri el-Kuwatly over.
Portsmouth & Theseus.
Chekiang typhoon, 2,000 go.
Bridgeport drive-up's Mechanics'
& Farmers' Savings Bank.
84,730 tons. New National
Liberation Army. 160,000 Czechs
to West Germany. Estes Kefauver.
Bonn & US nuclear arms.
—*Joe Smith for Presidency.*
Johannesburg's 100,000.
France's Cyprus. Texas Rangers &
Mansfield. F-84.
—*the terror of any
who would be our.*

April 5 1971

Supreme Court's 5-4.
Banco Mercantil
del Río de la Plata.
67-1 & Eximbank.
Fire Base 6.
Golconda's hydrogen
sulfide, 4 go.
Nixon, People's Republic
of China & Trade embargo.
Tajuddin Ahmed.
Gainesville, O'Connell
& 2,000.
Nisseki Maru.
Supreme Court, busing &
9-0. SS-9. Duvalier goes.
700 veterans & a toss.
—*greetings.*
New Jersey Turnpike,
1,000 protestors & 4 hours.
Bangladesh, thousands go.
Leslie Bacon,
Mayday Tribe & arrest.
Canonero II's Derby.
Amtrak, The National
Railroad Passenger
Corporation.
DC jail, football field &
7,000 arrests.
Rail strike over.

But Sam's ready to churn butter,
full tilt boogie for the gang,
zipless fucks for Sex Cherries and
Virgins, Hair Burgers and Urchins,
ringpieces and clappers of slick,
all snapped, sapped and sick,
leaving me out of that
circle, just sitting allone.
Though for Sam, silly priapic,
I try to hang happy, if
O man I'm sad.
Though I keep wringing a smile.
Why?
Ecstatic hurt
over this jerk.
Oops, a burp. Burp twice.
He's frowning? Welling up?
I'm confused.
Sam's shocked, worried for me?
My. What am I doing?

June 6 1956

Ellsworth Bunker's Teenagers.
Bulganin's 1.2 million.
Walter Reed Army Hospital.
Buenos Aires
counterrevolutionaries, 40 go.
Port Said departures.
Golda Meir over Moshe Sharett.
East Germany's 19,000.
Casbah & Battle for Algiers, 70 go.
President Nasser.
Clifford Brown goes.
Miller & Monroe.
—*We want bread.*
Polish United Workers,
Poznan & tanks.
650,000 Steel Workers strike.
United Airlines, TWA
& Grand Canyon, 128 go.
—*We are going.*
Fry over Buxton.
London's 15 Supreme Soviets.
Asia, Famine & Food Bank.
Hungarian hijacking & defection.
Dix C-118, 46 go. Aswan Dam.

allone from these awful streets. O my Hailey
worried about me. Shocked? Gives me a
piggyback. And I'm confused, frail,
allways welling up over her attention.
But she giggles. Giggles again.
I'm such a bummy jerk.
While all around hurts.
But for Hailey's smile, I smile
too with desire
to gas faster. Happy to
trim, hug, slip her & slide.
By Oacoma, Winner and Rosebud.
Powering past Beards, Wrenchheads,
Benchracers, Taco Wagons & more.
Scores more. Hundreds more. Spinning it,
slamming it, zipping it once and for all to try

May 22 1971

Bingol quake, 995 go.

Norwegian Meteor, 32 go.

Bobby Seale
& Ericka Huggins. Nixon's
Supersonic Transport Jets.

Juan V Corona
& migrant workers.
Elizabeth II.
Bangladesh & cholera.
Bucks over Bullets.
Nixon & Drug addiction.
EMM goes.
France's Socialists
& Mitterrand.
Daniel Ellsberg
& Neil Sheehan.
John Mitchell.
Manhattan's Gay 5,000.
Muhammad Ali, 8-0
& Draft Dodging.
Joseph A Colombo Jr
& Jerome A Johnson go.
Turkey's opium.
6-3.
Salyut's Georgi Dobrovolsky,
Vladislav Volkov &
Viktor Patsayev go.
Nike missile.
26th Amendment.
Goolagong over Court.
Morrison goes.

Sam rejects the rest and bolts the
spree. Away from odd groans and
pleas. Reaching now for only me.
Streaking sleak and singularly,
gathering me up with terrified arms.
I: —*Forgive me please.*
Please forgive me.
And he: —*Please forgive me.*
Forgive me please.
And a Louisiana Chearleader
bubbles: —*Oooooo where you*
two zippin to?
Winding waywardly side to side.
But we are allways zipping by.
Allready wide.
The compass of all
that's never around,
leaving even the found
to get off allone and wither.
The Ongoing Party's so Over.

April 23 1956

Supreme Court &
bus segregation. 13 States.
—employment
of Negro bus drivers for.
Transcontinental Warheads.
Brockton Blockbuster retires.
Columbus Circle.
South Vietnamese training.
Carlos Prío Socarrás arrested.
Charles Wilson & USSR's H-Bomb.
100,000 for German reunification.
Karen Nationalists.
Needles's Derby.
Togoland & Ghana.
Algiers, Constantine &
silo's French soldiers, 19 go.
Namu drop.
$750 million Farm Subsidy.
Peking, Lu Ting-yi & 100 Flowers.
Casbah & 5,000 French troops.
Frederick Seaton. Everest, Lhotse
& Swiss. Narragansett Casino.
Flaherty's 500. Molotov over.
Maharashtra, Bombay & riots.
West Bengal's cyclones.

By Them. By US.
Together without
everything we won't leave.
Outside Casinos Lucky & Jackpot,
Jaywalkers heap Hailey's lap with profits
we allready forgive. We deny every debt.
We're without debt. I have no hat.
But Offenders keep chucking tips:
—*You two, you're our lucky streak.*
Me: —*Please excuse me.*
Hailey: —*Please please excuse me too.*
Which leaves The Subsidized stupified and bleak.
Conmen, Thieves and crooked Gestaps
circling their momentary victory.
Them are all momentary. Only we continue at all.
Not moved towards. Not moved by. We move on

July 6 1971

Matzdorf's leap.
Guatemala's Arriola
goes.

FDA & botulism.
Ngo Dzu's heroin.
400,000.

US, UK & Iran.
Barnard's breath.
Flights over China.

Apollo 15, Lunar Module
Falcon & Sea of Rains.
David R Scott, James B
Irwin & Lunar Rover.

—O, Man!

Laos & CIA's 30,000.
Bernard Bender's bands.
Paksong offensive.
Vaucluse Mountains &
9 nuclear missiles.
Awami League.
Chay Blyth's Westerly solo.

Rio & Brazil's Popular
Revolutionary Vanguard,
Raimundo da Costa goes.

Melvin Laird's
Ground Operations.
Bretton Woods over.
Calley's 20 years.
San Quentin,
George Jackson goes.

Though some still gamble,
rolling for broke, while
Hostesses mingle and cravated
Long Hairs with silk spats continue
their toques. At least I'm
with Sam, though I'm so heavy,
staggering US from this bust.

My guts turning, splashes & sweats,
DTs to kicks. I'm all dreck. Wrecking
everything. Remorsefully.
Ashamed. Tortured. The only one
here to blame, assured. Sam stumbles,
crossed tumbling by haranguing
Radical Chic, career sneering
imprisioned now hucking their drinks.

—*Well then!*

—*Greedy Bums!*

—*Gook on a slope!*

—*It just kills me.*

O yes. Yes, it does.

Feb 25 1956

—We must abolish the cult of.
Eggs and rocks.
—That girl sure has guts.
Europe's blizzard, 1,000 go.
NAACP's University of Alabama.
Morocco's Liberty.
Hussein over Glubb.
Buenos Aires polio outbreak.
Syria's Israeli plane. Makarios.
Hawkins vs Board of Control.
Tunisia's freedom.
156 day strike over.
—on all the South to.
Tiflis University strike.
Iceland's US troops.
Warriors over Pistons.
Franco's Rif.
Birmingham & Nat King Cole.
Wladyslaw Gomulka.
Colorado River Bill.
USS Saratoga's Nuclear Power.
Lockheed Starfighter.
Chervenkov out. Cominform over.
Rainier II & Kelly.
Hammarskjöld's cease-fire.

O No. Hailey snickers at
the killings we allways haul by.
—*South Dakota,* I sigh.
—*Our fruit,* she slys, roaring by
a camp ground. Fenced off with wet pits
dead by cöld charcoal, while
the thrill of US still tickles the air.
Hailey rejoices. Pickup Roll.

We're off to Mitchell.
Havens Avenue by Edmunds
to Main Street where
Hailey supports me, hooks my arm,
pats my head. I'm so heavyless. Staggering
to stay even closer. While passerbys
wave at Hailey, tossing US clips of wealth.
Gambling on what's allready woe.

When for **Hemp** buds rush Narks,
here among US, cracking, planting,
confiscating stash. Clubs & cuffs.
Feebies sizzling Draft Dodgers and
Joggers. Pro Athletes diving
for the pool. Late.
ESTs, Guests & Pranksters
slump petrified
by the lake.
But Sam swerves US through
with a cry:
—Catch US on the flip side!
Then sambos a cab. Off for the car.
Except I blow Frankincense & Myrrh,
exquisite sluices
of sticky squeets.
And Sam holds onto it all.
All I'll never keep.
All I'm not. All I've got.
The Big Whirr.

Aug 22 1971

Bemba & Zambia.
Juan José Torres
overthrown.
Oran Henderson.
Preston Smith.
British Hawker Siddely
& 6 Trident 2Es.
IRA, Belfast & bombs.

Bill Macomber's women.
HEW & welfare rolls.

Wage, prices
& Nixon's freeze.
Frank Render II retires.

Adriatic Sea & Greek Ferry,
54 go. Motel caprice.

Alaskan Airline & Tongass
National Forest, 111 go.
Pontiac bombings
& 6 KKK.

Mongolia crash,
Lin Piao goes.

Attica prison &
1,500 Troopers, 40 go.

Tokyo airport, 3 go.

—Kill! Kill!
—Yah! Yah!

2 years more.
Cyclone Orissa, 23,000 go.

Later. Souped Up & Sauced. Bobbed with
the works. Hailey's all I have.
All I'll never keep.
I can't keep my hands off her.
Tight to her. Missing her. Even while
we drive, even while, with an exquisite yawp,
Hailey burps up Frankincense & Myrrh.
Whirring on through Eyota. Austin.
—Bask it a half,
Hailey scramms US wide.
By Hayward and Alden.
Through Fairmont, Worthington, Ash Creek.
To Sioux Falls.
Backroad Fuzz too winded to even take a go.
The Broke way too busted up.
Polar Bears turning to muck.

Jan 9 1956

Samir el-Rifai's Jordan.
Virginia's private schools.
1,600 parachutes to Cyprus.

—of development of
underdeveloped countries.

Syria & Lebanon
Mutual Defense Pact.
—If you try to run away from it,
if you are scared to go to the brink,
you are lost.

East German People's Army.
LA commuter trains, 30 go.
Cortina d'Ampezzo.
Third World & USSR Aid.
Catroux. Guy Mollet.
Albright's gold. Wright's Tiple.
—Algeria is French.
Tuscaloosa's Autherine Lucy.
Weather balloons.
20th Party Congress.
Urho Kekkonen.
115 boycotters.
—give relief to
these citizens whose civil.

Oct 9 1971

—Hirohitler, go.

Lake Havasu City &
London Bridge.
C-5A's engine.
Rap's armed robbery.
Pirates over Orioles.
Nixon's School Lunch.

Cambodian revolt, Lon Nol
& State of Emergency.
Vasectomy fair.
Chuck Hughes goes.
Zaire.
—across the
World will rejoice that
we have taken our.
Alaska's Atom Blast.
Pnom Penh's airport
rockets, 25 go.
Irish women, British
soliders, Tar & feathers.
Mariner 9 & Mars.

Wage & prices free.
Chiao Kuan-hua.

—nations want liberation,
and the people want
revolution.

Roger de Louette,
Paul Fournier &
$12 million of heroin.

A SWEET HOPE visits. This one
a nurse. Tidy with roastcoffee
smile. And creamy lap.
—Tssssssk tsssssssk, all of it's so O no
never so rough.
Touches my forehead and doubts.
—Shiiiiiiiiiiiit, getting all tugged, trapped
turnedaround and mugged. Girl,
there're easier ways to go.
O?
—What every teenage kid,
runaway, throwaway, outtaplay
just must hold for sho.
O?
Brushes my hair and feers away.
—Life happens, Sugar. And if there's hard,
there's easy. If there's bitter, there's fine.
But you gots to slows to own it with—
O? Allways?
—No.

Dec 1 1955

—paid slaves of communism.

Montgomery bus boycott.
—we are tired, tired of being.

NYC, 71st Regiment Armory
& 16 million workers.
Attlee retires. Montgomery
Improvement Association.
Honus Wagner goes.
Menderes Government.
Robinson KOs Carl Olson.
Israel, Syria & Sea of Galilee.
UN's 15. Mongolia & Japan.
Hugh Gaitskell.
Tappan Zee Bridge.
Cleveland over Rams.
California & Oregon floods, 74 go.
Michigan over UCLA.
Khartoum & Sudan's Republic.
Saigon's First National
Assembly election. US,
West Germany & Nike missiles.
—a stronger better America.
Mau Maus going.
Jerusalem attack.

—No way.
—Grow up. She's much too fast. You ain't. Time to
slow down. Shove her free. You don't Love
her. Anyway, Love's not enough.
No?
I speed up but
SHE effortlessly keeps up.
—Stick with her and you're over.
She's over. No enduring bond, Slingshot,
can save you both.
No?
—Love kid. Lost until you
give some a kick. You're too young to leave it.
Too young to keep it. Love's the breath a Life
still lifts when Life is finally over with.
With which my LAST HOPE departs.

Sweet Hope, allways so sure.
I shrug her away. Scowl too.
She saunters off mildly.
Blade through her throat.
While here at the ER
I continue to barf.
Sam dabs my forehead
before sinkwashing the Bucket.
Dry heave, sploosh boosh and bile.
Curl up and wait.
What's more, fuck it, pinguid puke's
now dying? Vile? Crusting with pain.
Here I go again.
All over the tile.
Janitors ignore. Patients bore.
We all just want some bedliness.
And Sam's begging:
—She needs a Doctor now.
—She's drunk Sport,
Triage flatly retorts.

Nov 26 1971

GATT split.
Nader's El DuPont.
London & caning.
Newry & border, 2 go.
Cairo & 3 Palestinians,
Wasfi Tal goes.
Robert Vesco
& Milton Meissner.
Greater Tumb,
Lesser Tumb &
Abu Musa. Hilli.
Mars 3.
Abu Dhabi, Dubai, Sharja,
Ajman, Fujaira &
Umm al-Quawain.
GM's 6.7 million Chevrolets.
Serpico.
President Yahya Khan
& War's end.
—We'll let Them stay.
US Department of Justice,
Mishishishi & ballots.
Thousands of Iranians.
NASA, $5.5 billion
& Space Shuttle.
Groton's 500 gallons of
coolant.
Hong Kong Harbor
& Seawise University
burning.

The Mishishishi, above on Grand Bluff,
we soberly behold some city outstretched
below and feel our terror.
The East outgrows the East
but we never outgrow US.
And it exhausts me. Though Hailey's uplifted
by the stickless gusts of our briefness.
We're without pause.
Without remorse. Allways turbulent.
And over Lock & Dam 7 few care that
Hailey starts small cyclones
with her breeziness, eaziness over all
she dares to nope and leave unfinished.
Which is when I find, all teen & shot up,
loping alongside me,
my Last Hope.

Oct 14 1955

Zero Mostel's fifth.
Colombo Plan. 695.163 MPH.
France & Hanoi trade.
El Auja DMZ. Berkeley proton.
Egypt, Syria & Jordan.
Saar & European rule.
UN General Assembly,
Plessis & apartheid.
—policies of apartheid.
Ann Eden Crowell's prowler,
William Woodward Jr goes.
Akahira mine, 60 go. Brazil coup.
101's Bonn Gathering.
Aramburu over Lonardi.
Campbell's 216 MPH.
Geneva's Big Four failure.
Maryland National Guard.
ICC: Trains, Buses & States.
—and thermonuclear.
Soviet megaton.
Montgomery Alabama,
Cleveland Avenue bus
& Rosa Parks.
—Why do you all
push US around?

Jan 12 1972

13,000 workers,
Ondangua & Ovambo.
Mobutu Sese Seko.
Abu Sayeed Chowdhury.
Bangladesh &
Mujibur Rahman.
Copenhagen's Margrethe.
Super Bowl VI,
Cowboys over Dolphins.
Gwelo riots. Juanita Kreps.
Elmo R Zumualt Jr's
Sixth Fleet.
Evonne Goolagong.
EEC & Britain, Ireland,
Denmark & Norway.
Shoichi Yokoi's Guam.
Chisholm's Presidency.
Londonderry, 13 go.
Peking, Bhutto & Mao.
42 F-4s & 90 A-4 Skyhawks.
John Mitchell.
Ronald Carter goes.
Alcohol abuse.
Peking, Nixon & Mao.
René-Pierre Overney goes.
John Taylor.
Australia, New Zealand,
Fiji, Tonga, Nauru,
Western Samoa &
Cook Islands.

NOW THE CAB DRIVER
accosts Sam:
—*You pay for the taxi now. And clean*
up too your skank girl's crap.
Big bruiser.
Jabs at Sam with a thumb.
Who offers immediately
his Leftwrist Twist of Copper which
beyond affront briefly stuns
grunting BRUTE. So Sam hangs my
COOKIE CUP on one pileous knuckle.
Shoved aside then by LOCAL
SECURITY rabid with questions:
—*Over here greaser.*
—*There're rules about booze.*
—*Drugs.*
—*How old are you?*
On the hook, Sam comes on strong.
Twitching, cowering, until squealing:
—*Please just let me live.*

Aug 29 1955

Egypt & Israel, jets over Gaza.
Al Fedayeen's assassinations.
Talbott's Super Sabre.
Maxey's glide.
Istanbul & Izmir riots.
Peru's voting women.
—*keep our guard up.*
USSR & West Germany Diplomacy.
Security Act & 360 citizens.
Kuts's 14:16:8.
Perón's Rebels. Israel's oil.
Colorado coronary thrombosis.
Pakistan's Baghdad Pact.
—*of asylum.*
$44 million down.
Hurricane Janet, 500 go.
Salinas & Spyder,
James Dean goes. Ben Arafa quits.
Constantine Karamanlis.
—*deprive law enforcement.*
—*Wow, wow, wow!*
Dodgers over Yankees.
Army's male nurse.
Wyoming's United Airlines, 66 go.
USS Saratoga. Kye.

—*So you can be,*
SHE twitches coweringly
before Hailey's gracious
wait. SHE wants US. SHE's lost US.
—*The question of my age*
only concerns the lousy
satisfaction of turning over whatever
possibilities I will now never exceed. Behave.
Because we're every extreme.
Hailey beyond all SHE can ever
reprieve allone. We leave everybody allone.
And so? Everyone misses US but we're never
missed. Me and my Leftwrist Copper Twist.
The slight extension of my hand.
A poor shake. Of thanks. Our WIDOW
yuks. Turns. And where a slack River joins

Feb 27 1972

Victor Paz Estenssoro
& Hugo Bánzer Suárez.
Rikers Island attack.

—This is a great.

Florida, Cesar Chavez
& Migrant Farm Workers.

Pioneer 10 & Jupiter.
Key Biscayne, Sonesta
Beach & 900.
Walter Dejaco's free.
JDL, Williams
& Yevstafyev's bath.

Dacca's Mutual Aid Pact.
Belfast blasts, 6 go.
Heath's 3 points.

UCLA's sixth.
Meany & Phase II.

Hanoi's offensive. DMZ.
14 divisions, 200 tanks
& 130 mm blasts.
Quang Tri province.
Little Italy,
Joseph Gallo goes.

Kjell Isaksonn's 18' 1"
70 nations
& biological weapons.
Chile's 200,000
anti-Marxists.

—Hey Honalee! It's not
willpower, it's pillpower that'll
get your fast feeling back.
Here among Dehydrated,
Syphilitic, Malarial, Valarial,
Unemployed Crazies, Lazies, Burned
Out, Ringwormed and Afraid, with
Henna and Dreads, a RASTAFARIAN
MEDIC doles out ampulets of Cure,
a CURIOUS PILL, herbally milled,
which I go on and try.
—*Wait!* Sam yelps, racing my way.

Carolina Jessamine wickering:

—Too late!

REGIONAL ENFORCEMENT on heels. Sam
slides aside. TRIPPED OUT SANDAL GUY
unfortunately dog piled. While
THE SHUTTLE DRIVER, missing
my man, hurls some BOWL OF
AIR over everyone's noddles.

July 12 1955

Stan Musial's hit.
1,243 refugees.
Morocco Café, 6 go.
South Vietnam's Accord.
—every legal.
Grandval's Foreign Legionnaires.
Seawolf. Bulganin,
Eisenhower, Eden & Faure.
Geneva Summit.
—begin an arrangement
very quickly.
—open sky.
Constellation over Bulgaria,
58 go. Bobet's 3rd tour.
Peking's 11 pilots.
62 Nations & Atomic Energy.
2 Flying Boxcars over
Edelweiler, 66 go. $1.
Hurricane Diane, 184 go.
Moscow's 650,000 troop
reduction. US Northeast floods,
179 go. Portugal, Nationalists &
Goa. Zirout Youssef &
Jacques Soustelle, 1,000 go.
A Chamonix cable car.
Emmett Till goes.

Our WIDOW turns then to me,
relieved to the buckles by how
much ease these improprieties bring HER.

Even if
SHE won't last much longer. We outlast all.
We're allways last. SHE'll finish this last task and
quit. For US SHE's hung around too long.

Mosquitoes too. Gone.

—He, he shot. No game. No ball. Just
business. Blew his teeth out with a grin.
No verdict. Just overflowed the sink.
A dishonorable discharge. Left this.

Handing over then all I
need to legally marry Hailey.
LICENSE. O yes.
Without levity.

April 15 1972

The Great Lakes.

Hanoi, Haiphong
& US bombardment.
An Loc & Dak To.

Fairfax, Cook & a rowboat.
Columbia protestors.

Apollo 16's rocks.
Oxford gals.
Hsing-Hsing & Ling-Ling.
Hué evacuation.
Riva Ridge's Derby.
Lakers over Knicks.
North Vietnamese harbors.
Israel paratroopers &
Belgian flight engineer.
Wendell Anderson &
715 National Guardsmen.
Okinawa.
Arthur Bremer.
—arrested for
a hit-and-run.
QE2.
Pentagon explosion.
Lazlo Toth's hammer.
Nixon & Brezhnev.
Harvey Mcleod's
shopping spree, 4 go.
3 Japanese terrorists &
Lod Airport, 24 go.
—between the two most
peaceful nations.

I glide away. Balancé.
With a turn back to Sam:
—*I'm quite dizzy now and warm.*
Hop stepping ahead, around these
Ill & Huddled Afflicted, something's
going around, rubbing my belly until
clearing my throat once, I can't clear
my throat. I can't breathe.
Stop. Moving. Perpilexed. Sam's brows
squinched. Ears flexing?
And I lilt, drifting down,
with strengthless Sam
allready shrilling for NURSE YANK
who swivels away. Clipping her nails.
Fortunately EXTERNS stampede over.
How hazy. And strange.
Raspless. Caught.
All of me
allmost stopped.
—*Losing pulse,* ATTENDANTS yolp.

May 14 1955

Konev's 8 & The Warsaw Pact.

Austrian State Treaty over.
Cambodia aid. Mergers &
Federal Trade Commission.
Soviet arms to Egypt.
Cyprus riots. Belgrade, Tito
& Khrushchev.
—aggravations.
Ambassador Riddleberger.
Southern tornadoes, 121 go.
Sweikert's 500.
Bill Vukovich goes.

—with all deliberate speed.
Port Arthur evacuation.
Groix Island & Bourguiba's return.
Mount Kanchenjunga.
Tahar Ben Ammar's ratification.
Ford & United Auto Workers.
Taiwan US air bases.
Le Mans raceway & 3 cars, 80 go.
—by its own law.
Beech Paris. Argentina revolt.
Congolese uranium.
Over Bering strait.

Wavering via US
all SHE no longer finds around.
Her husband's stink. His brittle hair. Curses
under a spit. His amble. Spared. Fedup. Paired.
Carried on. When the palm of his touch
once gave HER back their only warmth.
Returning later SHE
brings US the dead.
—*Her, Them beat. Tictactoed. Tackled.*
By some Jazz Club. Law student mauled by
their attack. Over by a parking lot.
Where she flowed on. And left just this.
Handing over then all Hailey
needs to legally marry me.
LICENSE. O yes.
With only heaviness.

June 4 1972

Santa Clara County
& Angela Davis.

Napalm.
GRAE, MPLA & OAU.

Democratic National
Committee, 2:00 AM
& Watergate complex.
James McCord, Bernard
Barker, Frank Fiorini,
Eugenio Martinez
& Raul Godoy.
*—blatant act of political
espionage.*

Hurricane Agnes.
American Airlines
& $502,000 free fall.
North Vietnam Steel Mill
& 2,000 lb bombs.
F-15.

*—cruel and unusual
punishment.*

Boeing 727s & China.
Giorgio Almirante.
Arturo Armando Molina.
Soviet Union &
$750 million of US grain.
King over Goolagong.
British troops & IRA, 9 go.
Sadat & exiting
Soviet personnel.

At least Sam won't let go,
fingers crescenting my wrist.
A racket of wheel. A gurney arrives.
I'm raised, gauged
and laid out.
—*Stop*, a CRUDE COMMISSIONER louts.
We cannot admit this girl here.
She must not be handled.
Discharge her at once.
Wild Orchids grumble: —*What?*
—*Huh? You fucking butcher.*
She's dying! Sam bawls.
—*Regulations, I'm afraid,*
THE HEAD COMMISSIONER stalls.
We don't treat her kind.
Slender Silphium: —*Huh?*
—*She's going*, a PHYSICIAN sputters.
Even THE BUS DRIVER, head HATTED
by THE SOOOEEES, pips: —*It's emergency.*
Sam's grip softens.

April 4 1955

Kao Kang.
Chicago's Richard Daley.
NAACP's Roy Wilkins.
Ann Arbor's Salk vaccine.
Detroit over Montreal.
Nike's flying explosion.
Jerusalem Security Zone.
—new course.
András Hegedüs. Einstein goes.
Don't Walk. East Germany &
17 Berlin bound trucks.
Bandung's 29 African &
Asian Nations.
Giovanni Gronchi. Saigon Police.
Chance Vought F7U Cutlass.
Ngo Dinh Diem over
Nguyen Van Vy. Turkey, US &
atoms-for-Peace.
Nevada blast & dalmatians.
*—partnership with the
former occupying powers.*
Hague, Britain & rule over
Falkland Islands. Swaps' Derby.
Mitten Ishida & Michiko Sako.
—anyone, anywhere.

Where we're allready encountered, except
emerging for our will, eccentric & gentle,
our WIDOW expects little out of all
we've come here to get. SHE's going.
Shad Roaches go too.
—*You can't take offense over*
Love and still find it waiting there
for you.
—*O that's Lovely*, Hailey ooooos.
—*No, that's devastating.*
Human Lice flakes off. Wastes.
Wisps of fragile curls, withered left leg. Soft
stumbling lips. Stirs a cup. Fetches US some.
Hailey shakes yes.
—*Quit wine. Had a life supply. Only coffee.*
SHE appreciates Hailey's vitality. Maybe me.

July 25 1972

Eagleton's shock.
Kashmir & Simla Pact.
George McGovern.
Gloria Steinem &
Letty Cottin Pogrebin.
—unified political leadership.
ABM Treaty.
Idi Amin, Asians & 90 days.
Pat Nixon & Jane Fonda.
Danang's Marines.
B-52s & North Vietnam.
35,000 Soviet Jews.
El Al Jet & gift bomb.
Queson.
Miami's 900.
Trans World Airlines,
American Airlines &
baggage.
Bobby Fischer over
Boris Spassky.
Montreal Café firebomb,
22 go.
Spitz & 7 golds.
7 September Guerrillas &
Tuesday.
Joseph Romano &
Moshe Weinberg go.
Brazil's political prisoners.
9 go. 4 go.

Whirls awheeling. Imprisoning poison
removes me despite commotion.
PUSHER MAN carrying out protest:
—Hey man, take it eazy. Don't flip.
It's all just herbal legit.
—Chuck it, Freak!
POLICE allso alerting THE HOSPICE NURSE:
—Because her present state is caused by
stuff handed out, obtained here, and
—consumed, assumed
—on these premises,
STAFF: *—you are responsible.*
ECO MAN: *—you are responsible.*
Sam: *—you are responsible.*
ALL: *—Fiscally.*
Even **Vanilla** stands: *—Saaaaaam.*
Now all worry & pomp, THE GLOBAL
COMMISSIONER flip flops:
—What's this neglect? Save her!
I'll have everybody's neck!

Feb 17 1955

Britain's H-Bomb.
$101 billion Highway
Development. Nevada,
atomic missile & dust.
SEATO Council.
Edgar Faure over Mendès France.
American Military Group
& Saigon. Turkey, Iraq
& Baghdad Military Pact.
Paris Vélodrome & Pierre Poujade.
—stateless homosexuals.
Nanhai Islands.
Hanoi-Peking-Moscow-Berlin.
Israel & Gaza, 42 go.
Suramarit over Sihanouk.
Maurice The Rocket Richard.
Mexico City, Louis Jones
& 44.5 seconds.
NAACP's Walter goes.
Atomic fallout. Honolulu
& US Navy DC-6, 66 go.
John Marshall Harlan.
Algeria & State of Emergency.
Philippine quake, 200 go.
Guadalajara train wreck, 300 go.

execute, electrocute,
a PENITENTIARY PROBATION OFFICER who out
allone wanders a path with an umbrella. Even
the Captivated, hardbop & softspots, yowl.
And so too Silverfish go.
—Impersonally, Hailey scowls.
We're irresponsible.
Me: *—Irresponsible.*
US: *—Irresponsible.*
And impossibly thrilling, smoothed & nosed,
charging by ringriver miles, through Kieler,
Burton and De Soto. Slack time's here Victory.
And where Prisons tend to the shield of laws, we
fly on. Confined to no loss. Beyond stops we all
toss. Because we're emergent. Allways divergent.
Down shifting only when we reach La Crosse.

Panic. PHYSICIANS furious for time.

—It's shock! *—It's cardiac!*

Sam above me. Peaked and gaunt.
Slap. Someone pounds my chest.

—It's a reaction! *—Anaphylactic!*

But The Wheel seizes.

—Epinephrine!

Losing it. Nearer. Now.
And all I can do is hold him.

—Needle!

Ow. Outandout relief. Rush.
A turning, returning, release. Pleasing.
I want Sam to kiss me awake but
ALL PRACTITIONERS unclasp my hand
and whisk me away to recover.
Allone.

With allready The Healing, stinking
of gangrene, and Visiting Ailing
guarding their spleens, anxiously
motioning me to join Them.

Sept 10 1972

Frank Shorter's marathon.
Uganda, US
& $3 million loan.

Tonsure.
E Howard Hunt,
G Gordon Liddy & 5.

Cairo's Joint capital.
Mitsubishi & Harvard.

Vietnam, US & 0.
Manila Martial Law.

Sacramento ice cream
& F-86 Sabre Jet, 22 go.
Hanoi 3 refuse.
China & Japan.
Olga Korbut.
Somalia.

Chile & strikes.

Roe vs Wade.

Elizabeth 's Scotland mobs.

Kitty Hawk.
Uruguayan Plane, Andes
& Rugby players.

Nixon's $30.2 billion
Revenue Sharing Bill.
Philippine rebels.
Oakland over Cincinnati.
—Peace is at hand.
Mathieu Kérékou.
$18 million corn.

Iced, streeted and refused. But I'm
all refuse, refused even by every
dump we jump by along the way.
To the GroundGal's pal. No postponement.

We lose no time. Together.
Cruising. My hand on hers.
By County Jails, Slammers, Maximum
Security Facilities and District Stockades.
Where the captives feel US pass and
heeding
our freedom shriek until, for a nearness
none may survive, all lose US.

And I grin
twice because there is only me besides
her. I hold her head. Touch her lips.
Kissing my fingertips until sharp sparks

Dec 26 1954

Browns over Lions. Big Bang.
French Assembly's West Germany.
$216 million aid.
Ohio over Southern California.
Dacron. Reserpine & Thorazine.
100 planes over Tachen.
Figueres, Somoza &
Costa Rica. Chase National &
Bank of Manhattan. 84-0.
*—There can be no victory
for anyone.*
Atomic clock. Panama
cooperation. Formosa escalation
& mobilization. 410-3. 83-3.
Johannesburg protest.
Mishishishi tornadoes, 29 go.
*—and unsatisfactory
leadership.*
Nikolai A Bulganin.
US-Nationalist China
Mutual Security Pact.
Meadowlands 130. AFL & CIO.
Meany & Reuther. Con Ed &
nuclear power plant.
Bell's fixed-wing vertical.

Oct 29 1972

West German Airplane & 2 Arab Guerrillas, 3 free.

Nixon, Social Security & $5 billion.

—a man and a woman need each.

DC, 500 Native Americans & Trail of Broken Treaties.
East Germany's 30,000.
60.7%.

—of Peace throughout the World.

Atlanta's Andrew Young.
September Group & 18 bombs.
Havana, 3 hijackers & Cleveland.

Baton Rouge Police & protest, 2 go.

Buenos Aires & Juan Perón.

Moscow, 51 leaders & Sakharov.

8 gunmen & Sean MacStiofain.

David, guillotine & 80 years.
Irish Parliament & IRA.

Australia's Labor Government.

Neato keeno. I lurch back for Sam
but The EMTs keep me pinned.
Strict protocols require that I stay put
until properly discharged.

—Is he your?

—No I'm.

—Is he a?

—No I'm.

—Sure not. Is he your husband?
Sure not allso. You're too young.
He'll deal then with Admin.

—Yes but we're dating.

—Don't worry little lady, you're
the one requiring care. He's fine.

Whereupon elated Social Services
encircle, hovering close over
the duties of my Naggy Shacklings
I'm so off to whack.
But can't.

—Afterwards we get you.

Nov 8 1954

Soviet MiG-15s down Tiger Lil over Hokkaido.
Hossein Fatemi goes.
Mohammed Naguib arrested, Nasser takes over.

—safeguard their security.

Communist torpedo boats & DE-47 USS Decker.
SAS over North Pole.
William Remington goes.
Alger Hiss free. Navy over Army.
Johannes Gerhardus Strijdom.
Arthur Watkins & 67-22.

—unbecoming a senator.

US, Taiwan & Mutual Defense Treaty. NORC. Frank Clement, Nixon, Dixon & Yates.

Aircraft Carrier Forrestal.
Special Foreign Policy Aide Nelson Rockefeller. Nicosia, Cyprus riots. British troops, Limassol & autonomy.
Italian Airways crash, 26 go.

Jackson Mishishishi's 2-1.

Out of our way.
Through the Courts to the bureau of
The Feeble District Clerk who awfully jinxed
over why we still haven't split tries to close up.
Hailey stops that.

—We're here to get circled.
Don't let me ask twice.

—O. Hey. You. But.

Hailey's shun carps her huffer: *—Why not?*

—One there's applications. Two there're tests. There's
authentication. And above all, there's the Law.
You two are mixed. You even have ID?

Hailey: *—No.*

—How bout you?

Me: *—No.*

—Then no. That's the way it goes. All protocol.

Dec 17 1972

Muammar el-Qaddafi
& Habib Bourguiba.
Apollo 17 & splashdown.
Seoul's Park.
16 cannibals.
Managua's quake,
7,000 go.
Hanoi raids.
Truman goes.
Carpet bombing.
Roberto Clemente goes.
USC over Ohio.

Cairo riots. New Orleans
& Howard Johnson, 6 go.
Essex goes.

Super Bowl VII,
Miami over Washington.
Yuba City's peach orchard.

—but what can I do for.

Foreman 2 rounds Frazier.
LBJ goes.

*—broad enough to
encompass a woman's.*

Paris Round table,
Henry Kissinger
& Le Duc Tho.
582 POWs.
William Nolde goes.
8:00 AM.
EPA & pollution.

—*Hold up Slick,* a Bacon counters.
*Whatever your charges what we
got here's a minor. Now missy—*
Of course Them charge after me.
But I'm allready scrambling:
—*Kiss my ass!*

Ditch the gurney, Dash!, zippityzoom,
spurning their tackles, zap vrooom
past their ankles, shackalacka over
linoleum and tile, corner and rail,

Potted **Musk Mallow**: —*Yippity doo!*

by Post Op, Pre Op and ICUs, over
cot loads of Quarantined Junkies
chucking for O,
Marrow Shattered,
TBed, VDed, and Cancered,
dosed with no answers.

Crocuses stalk: —*Dancer!*

Plods pursue,
shift after shift,

Sept 8 1954

SEATO's 8 Nations.
Algerian shake, 1,000 go.
Outlawing bigamy.
250,000 North Vietnamese flee.
—movements of people.
Oil tanker & Fukien coast. DEW.

—Wan sui.
Ngo Dinh Diem.
Johns-Manville's asbestos.
New York over Cleveland.
West Germany's NATO.
Baltimore protest.
Ho Chi Minh's Hanoi parade.
Communist Control Act &
US Civil Service. B-58.
Hurricane Hazel, 347 go.
Floyd Patterson rounds Gannon.
South Vietnamese Army.
UK & US Trieste occupation over.
Turnpike Tolls.

Ramón Grau San Martín quits.
Stockholm's National Health Care.
Algeria, fellaghas & Ben Balla.
Democrats. Navy's Pogo.

Because we're what everyone goes for
even after the going's over.
Whirligig Beetles still.

Around US crowd Scurves, Lurps, Nerds
& Pashpies along with Argonauts, Bulls, Percys
& Cheesecloths, never going out with Bikeniks
& Crazy Chickniks, allready on their own to
finkydiddle and dig, cook, dip and brush. Drag it.
Beat it. Leave it. That's that but here's next. US.
Glossy Ibis drops and rots.

Our stand stilling every transport, unbanding
every across, until Hailey spins about:
—*Let'S go back.*
And with major shoves we're
going again.

—*This way.*

Feb 8 1973

Earl J Silbert.
Juan María Bordaberry &
Antonio Francese.

20 POWs.

—California, here I come.

—well on the way
to winning the War
against environmental
degradation.

US, Cuba &
5 year extradition treaty.

Evel Knievel over 52 cars.

Israel fighters &
Libyan airliner, 116 go.

AIM's 250, Pine Ridge &
Wounded Knee.

John Lynch &
Fianna Fail Party.

—giving very serious.

Gas & Oil control.
Buck goes.
Trafalgar Square, Old
Bailey Criminal Court &
2 blasts, 1 goes.
John Downey returns.
John Sirica &
G Gordon Liddy.

never retarding, relenting.
Barely a break.
And I'm wide the Ninth Ward,
By Pontchartrain Park. Bucktown.
Past ferry and trolley.
Broadmoor to University.
Truckpumping over Jams, Honkers
and Hogs, groking the cleanup before
any collision. Paramedics and Coroners
spitting derisions which
I scoot by splendidly.

Live Oak: —*Do it!*
Sweet Pecan: —*Boost it!*

Beyond their hassle & rants.
Beat The Fans and their bray.
What Them chase but can't lock.
Lock but can't trade.
I'll go Over Seas. Omnicontinental
adored. Though without Sam I just
once it around the ward.

July 28 1954

Cypriot reunion.
Mount Godwin Austen.
Tunisian autonomy. LA smog.
Bobet's Tour. Morrocco riots,
11 go. Formosa Strait's 8.
Robert Moses. UN from Korea.
Nepal Monsoon floods, 900 go.
Fez Arab quarter.
Haiphong evacuation.
Taiwan's Seventh Fleet.
Packard & Studebaker.
James Wilkins.
EDC & German rearmament.
Getúlio Vargas goes.
Hubert Humphrey, Communists
& National Labor Board
Protection. 346-2.
—the violent overthrow of our.
Atlantic, Pacific
& 2 US icebreakers.
Atomic Energy Act.
Senate censures both.
Neo-Destour Party.
Patrol plane over Sea of Japan.
Quemoy, 2 go. La Strada.

around the bend
to mull scatting off to
Pennsylvania it, Portland it.
We still got our lump to
jump US out of this way. Lose
the ceremony. Toss procedure.
Ditch hassles and sluff.

Even if Thistle Butterflies slide.
And Elisa Skimmers can't survive.

We stand amid the traffic whirr. Snarled
and directed. Streaming and wide. Big Mercs,
Abortions and Daniels. Haulin Henrys. Broke
fortunes. Accompliced junk. Teenagers & pals.
Accidental Runs & Law Busting Handlers.
Traffic's blur now sluggishing down around US,
barely a leap, everyone braking. Allways a wait.

March 29 1973

Back then to my bed:
—*My mymy. My Sam. Where is he?*
It's urgent. I need him.
There among Ravaged,
Wasted, Autopsied, Embalmed.
Frail and Obese, Shrivelled
and Bloated, Defeated, Depleted, Rigid
and Bagged, laid long and still, feeding
their hair to the gnash of a carelessly
sashed air.
—*Who?* THE CARETAKER dares.
A Curious Sting pricks
me with chills. Prickles of feer,
I grab hold of THE HOSPITAL STAFF,
bending their sharps and smashing IVs.
Everyone shares the Dream
but I need it.
Something pattering.
A pounding anger.
Me.

Kuwait
& Saudi Arabia's 20,000.
Hanoi Hilton.
ICCS & Tong Le Chan.
Diets & amphetamines.
Tigers. US airlift
& Phnom Penh.
Basel airport, 104 go.
—*to get down there.*
Jon Anderson's marathon.
Elizabeth Holtzman.
Siberia-to-Eastern
Europe pipeline.
Chicago Board of
Options Exchange.
—*my way back up to the.*
HR Haldeman,
John D Ehrlichman,
John W Dean 3rd
& Richard G Kleindienst.
Puebla & Autonomous
University, 4 go.
Secretariat's Derby.
OCAM. Gómez Peláez goes.
Second Battle
of Wounded Knee over.
Knicks over Lakers.
Daniel Ellsberg's charges.
Skylab 1.

June 9 1954

me.
And Hailey stills.
Cooling evenly. Treacherously. Turning.
Everyone chases the Dream but we leave it.
THE IMPERTINENT CLERK blanches and there before
Hailey, standing, prickly & sharp, goes
low with feer. Head rolling. Tiny jerks.
Until finally, to Hailey, SHE blurts:
—*Who are you?*
Here too among the Raped, Detained and at
blame. Recused, Released, Appealing. Alarmed.
Plaintiffs, Defendants, Executed. Citizens on
Jury Duty. Circuit Judges & Attorneys with
disputes over misdemeanors & felonies.
—*And who too is he?* THE FLUSTERPATED CLERK
finishes, leaving US nowhere to go but

—*at long last? Have you left*
no sense of decency.
Richmond's 12 Southerners.
Global peril.
Guatemala's Fruit.
National Civil Defense Drill.
Special Security Board &
Loyal American.
Western hemisphere.
John Landy's 3:58.
New York State Thruway.
Castillo Armas over
Jacobo Arbenz Guzmán.
French troops from Tonkin.
Babe Didrikson.
British meat rationing over.
B-52A. Alfredo Stroessner.
National highways.
$365 billion. Drunkometer.
Roy Cohn quits.
Dash Eighty, Boeing's 707.
Geneva, France & Viet Minh.
—*liberate.*
2 Chinese MIGs & British airliner.
Abdel Nasser, Anthony Head &
Suez Canal Zone.

May 17 1973

Milan hand grenade.
Luis Balparda Blengio quits.
Colorado's 3 30-kilotons.

Senate Panel.
Venezuela's People's
Revolutionary Army
& Avensa airliner.
Baluchistan & Sibi, 8 go.
Anthony Lambton quits.
Lovea Sar.
Charles Rogers,
Fred Sheffery &
Roscoe Robinson Jr.
Earl Jellicoe quits.
CODELCO.
Palo Verde, 17 go.
—a civil War here.
Thomas Bradley.
South and Midwestern
tornadoes, 47 go.
Johncock's 500.
63-19.
Greek Republic.
Paris & TU-144, 13 go.
Secretariat's Triple Crown.
Tripoli's US Oil Company.
—cancer.
Clarence Kelley's FBI.
US military activity over.
Rhodesia guerrillas &
278 hostages.

I pas de bourrée aside. Fouetté about.
Fly. Catching somehow
dizzying bursts of dread.
Race burning ahead, away
from THESE PRACTITIONERS of what?
How playing? What corpses?
Just warming up. I can
slow down any time. I don't slow.
Though. Waiting. Determined. No one
around. O I'm going. I've gone.
I go to The ER, easily slipping
towards motion.
Something Faaar Out frenzying up here.
TECHNICIANS racing with Stethoscopes
and Lab Coats. Where's Sam?
O scrog! O socks!
Sam's tiny feet kicking
for nowhere. Squirming
there. Flipping his arms
above.

April 18 1954

Premium gas. Calcutta Cholera.
American Motors. Petrov.
Perón & Crisólogo Larralde.
Dulles, Chou En-lai & Vietnam.
Milford's snow. Determine's Derby.
Musial's 5. Ceylon, atom bombs
& colonialism.
Viet Minh & Isabelle.
Roger Bannister's 3:59.4.
Paraguay, junta & 10th revolution.
—after 20 hours of fighting without respite.
—We lack ammunition.
Dien Bien Phu falls.
St Lawrence Seaway.
Taiwan from Olympics.
William Mustard's hypothermia.
Karachi riots, 206 go. Luis Taruc.
Brown vs Board of Education.
—separate educational facilities are.
—will not abide by.
Luis Taruc.
USS Bennington, 91 go.

Until we're flipped over
to THE PATSY CLERK who puts
US both down. With nahnahs & nopes.
—We need a marriage license,
I still truckle.
A hiss. Grit.
—Negroid boy? SHE spits. *Uh no.*
—Mongolian girl? SHE sniggers. *Uhh no.*
—Way too dumb? SHE diggers. *Ahhh no.*
I go. O going. Hailey just sits down.
I spin around, fret, cool
down a bit, because Hailey's drift
might leave everyone here stiff.
How can this official deny US the pleasure
of our together? I'm flabbermated. And dizzy.
The World suddenly revolting

July 10 1973

And he's allone.
Flapping palms warning the ground.
MDs converge. Going
jugular. Vascular.
Paddles.
—*Gutter trash,* The Clinic Head twangs.
Kick this rot to the grill.
Probably just swilled.
I demurely object:
—*Pardon me but much more's at*
stake here. He's certainly hurt.
Me, all sleek, decked out
with Surgical pleats.
—*Someone toss this floozy out.*
This isn't a drunk tank. No thanks.
I windup and snap off his nose.
—*Pulse rate over 360!* a PT leaps.
The Clinic Heel bleeds to death.
—*His heart's failing.*
I grab Sam's hand.

J Paul Getty III.
Portuguese troops
& FRELIMO guerrillas.
—*massacre of.*
Beryl's 100,000 barrels.
Brazilian 707 & Orly,
122 go.
Bertram Podell.
Nolan Ryan's no-hitter.
Ian Patten &
Fletcher Thomson.
John Butterfield.
8.5%
Phu Giao.
Mersa Matruh.
Maria Margarita Moran.
Saang falls.
Charles Lockwood.
Roger Williamson goes.
—*not apologize for my*
loyalty to the.
Athens Airport, 3 go.
Neak Luong, 137 go.
Alan Bean
& Jack Lousma walk.
Elmer Wayne Henley.
Aviaco Airliner
& La Coruña, 85 go.
Windhoek riot.
Route 4, Route 5
& Khmer Rouge.

Feb 18 1954

I grab Hailey's hand:
—*Easy does it.*
I muddle, trying to soothe her
while she gasps and hacks
angry. Cupping her chin, rubbing
my fingers over her cheek:
—*Do you want me to get US outta here?*
Which I'd stand.
Though hurting for her to be my wife.
Hurting to be her husband.
—*I'm down with it, Lover. Ready to tangle.*
Which comforts me with the wayout end
Hailey now holds out for me.
Her place, this race, her company.
And if someone resists, no one resists.
We're left allone.

—*each other's position better.*
308th Division.
Advancement of Education Fund.
Robert T Stevens, Ralph W
Zwicker & Irving Peress. Hasem
al-Atassi over Shishekly.
Bravo Kwajalein Island.
Lolita Lebrón.
—*Viva Puerto Rico!*
Bentley, Jensen, Fallon,
Roberts & Davis. American
States Organization. Giap's
assault. Beersheba bus, 11 go
—*with impunity.*
Soviet European Security Treaty.
—*united action.*
US Air Force Academy.
Konno's Triple.
—*go over very quickly.*
Chain reaction. 8 Oil Companies.
Security risk & Oppenheimer.
Minneapolis over Syracuse.
—*to hit these people.*
Detroit's Stanley.
3,000 US Troops from Korea.

Aug 28 1973

Mexico quake, 527 go.
Dixy Lee Ray & AEC.

Gainesville Eight
VVAW acquitted.

1,375 ft, Roger Mallinson
& Roger Chapman free.
Kompong Cham.

—havoc.

Viktor Krasin & Pyotr Yakir.

Tony Boyle.

Faina Melnik's toss.
Armed Forces,
National Police &
Augusto Pinochet Ugarte,
Salvadore Allende
Gossens goes.

Titograd crash, 42 go.
Alvin Arnett's OEO.
Israel, Syria & 13 MIGs.
Martha Mitchell.
Ahmed Zaki al-Yamani.
King over Riggs.
Juan & Isabel Perón.
ITT HQ bomb.
Boston 6 burning, 1 goes.
Syria & Golan Heights.
Agnew quits.

—War of liberation.

Nearby **Pansies**
and **Aloe Vera** glopper for The Allready
Too Much of approaching wheels:
—Get hopping!

I cockandsock THE HOSPITAL PREZ,
boomeranging his jaw off. He spews to
death again. A beat heeding JANITOR
hovering over Sam goes pasty:
—Eighteen thousand. Heart's
pumpin waaaaaay toooooooo fast.
—Thirtysix thousand?!

THE NURSES: *—O you'll pay.*
STUDENTS: *—You'll pay.*
THE ADMINISTRATORS: *—And still pay.*
Sam: *—Glmphs yitoitzy plmph*
brlt swrmsh.

These boundless currency claims
leading to THE HOSPITAL's turn around:
—Well do what you must. But
get her back to bed at once.

111 250

Jan 8 1954

US Citizenship.
Dalaas Avalanche, 10 go.
Ambassador Zarubin
& The Atomic Energy Pool.
Joe DiMaggio & Marilyn Monroe.
Tito's Milovan Djilas.
22,000 anti-Communists to UN.
South African Labor Party
& Universal Franchise. Groton,
Hyman Rickover's Nautilus.
120,000 barrels.
Seoul train, 46 go.
Berlin's Big Four.
Korea, US & Soviet MIG.
Senate's $214,000 &
Fulbright dissent. New Delhi's
Hindu stampede, 350 go.
Kashmir Assembly
& Reunification.
Maxwell Bodenheim goes.
Kremlin purges: Moldavia,
Kazakhstan & Lithuania.
Malayan Communists.
Ike & South East Asia.
Atlantic's 13,284 ft.
Tobacco's Research Committee.

—Get back to your place.
Only a oneatatime allowed here,
THE WHEALLY CLERK squeaks.
Hailey slides away:
—Shi fi ki pi ti.
Me: *—What's the cost?*
Me: *—Is there a fee?*
Me: *—Whatta we have to gleek?*

Because free's too much. Though that's US.
Hailey rubbing her chest. Startled. Starting to
wheeze. So I, fast worried, rub helplessly
the back of her neck. Stroke her forehead.
Mush her cheeks too. Even pet her hair.
—Keep cool kid.

If allready somewhere close Snapping Turtles
& Swainson's Thrush twist up and croak.

Relaxing. Sam's discomfort slackening.
—*Defib him?* —*Start CPR?*
But Sam's below me. Smiling.
I wiggle his nose. Rub his feet.
—*Pulse evening!* —*Pulse slowing.*
And The Wheel rolls on.
—*Adenosine?*
Calmly, nuzzling his head back on
the pillow. My hand squeezes Sam's.
—*Improving.*
Sighs. General release. Rush.
The Gurney slowing. Turning.
And I kiss him and hug him
and no one stops me. And
we're zipped away to recovery.
Together.
With allready THE REVIVED
striving for the Just Out on my
mojo maracas rescue. Impressed to
death by my derringdo.

Oct 19 1973

Nixon & Appeals Court.
Elliot Richardson
& Archibald Cox.
Oil embargo.
A's over Mets.
Worldwide Military Alert.
Malcolm S Forbes
& a balloon.
War Powers Act.
Gulf & Ashland
Oil Company.
Disney World's monorail.
—*Well, I'm not a crook.*
Pacific, 12 rafts & 17 days.
Australia, Aborigines
& vote.
Phaidon Gizikis over
George Papadopoulos.
Belfast blast, 1 goes.
Rose Mary Woods.
Emergency Petroleum
Allocation Act.
US gas stations.
Abdus Samad Khan
Achakzai goes.
Arab States &
Western Banks.
—*A funny thing happened
to me on the way.*

112 249

At her desk, THE CLERK ignores US.
Unimpressed. More wait our turn.
Accused, served. There to admit, contest, slap
down geets. At the Court's bidding.
We are not the rest.
We are unbidden, mistreated.
But Hailey kisses me. Neat.
Turning slowly to renegotiate our potout.
—*Improvement's here,* she nods,
releasing my hand to return to the counter.
—*Hey, can we cut a fat one?*
But even Hailey's iced. With a flip.
She grinds her heel. Twirls a braid.
I lay back.
This stall, strangely, spinning her
all out. Frosty howl.

Nov 14 1953

Mideast Strategic Bases &
Arab League. Roy Campanella.
Scott Crossfield, Douglas D-588
Skyrocket & 1,327 MPH.
—*face to face.*
—*crawling with Communists.*
Taipei, Chiang & Syngman.
Belgrade, amnesty &
7,194 prisoners.
Operation Castor's
French paratroopers.
Defiant New York
Longshoreman. Britain & Iran.
—*Atoms for Peace.*
Big 3 Bermuda Conference:
Laniel, Eisenhower & Churchill.
GE's Communist workers.
Soviet firing squad, 7 go.
2 US Divisions from Korea.
Lions over Browns.
—*no longer alive.*
Rosewall's Davis Cup.
Nepal's Snowman.
Pat McCarran & McCarthy.
Bonn, Adenauer &
1,000 free POWs.

Dec 14 1973

Algerian Consulate
explosion, 4 go.
Explorer 51.

OJ Simpson's 2,000.
US and Lufthansa jetliners
& 5 Palestinians, 29 go.
Basque Separatists,
Luis Carrero Blanco goes.
WTC.

Turin wreck, 39 go.
55 MPH.
Regional Railroad
Reorganization Act.
Brian Faulkner quits.
CLC. Ciro Humboldt over
Víctor Paz Estenssoro.
Iran's 30 F-14As.
Super Bowl VIII,
Dolphins over Vikings.

Le Minh camp.
San Francisco, Chinese &
Public Schools.
*—effectively foreclosed
from any.*

Exxon's 59%.
—I'm not embarrassed.
US Coast Guard,
Bulgarian trawler &
182 tons of mackerel.
Ali 12 rounds Frazier.

Doll Sam throws bold yos
even if his nose is grody
caked. Pointy ear too poking out
from under the blankets.
—Yollo.
—Yollo.
Yoggle & stretch, then wiggles
over to my bed for a smooch,
scoop and backscratch.
And tickles too.
I smile a little.
Nice but I'm ready to blow
this Popsicle Stand for the road.
Juiced for speed, swerves
and quickerest curves.
—Get back to bed on the double,
NURSEY NIX charges. Grabbing
a lobe, dragging Sam
to his bed. He yowls and pinches
sails of her arms.

Sept 27 1953

27,000 refuse to return.

—risked their lives to avoid.

Marciano 11 rounds La Starza.
Spain's US bases.
Louis B Toomer. Earl Warren.
North Atlantic Dock strike.
Yankees over Dodgers.
British Guiana. Bosphorus swim.
Zone A to Italy.
Greece's US bases.
Frankfurt's Sabena, 44 go.
Operation Seagull. Qibya.
Leyte fire, 37 go.
—Condemn me. It does not.

Rio Grande Falcon Dam.
Laos Liberty & French Union.
Federation of Rhodesia
& Nyasaland.

1,456 off Federal Payroll.
Emil Zatopek. Boston Harbor
& Sodium Peroxide, 7 go.
Moshe Sharett.
Ramón Magsaysay.

How gently now
she holds onto me. Her soft breath
warmly on my ear.
Of course, I recover some zip:
—Outta here at once.
Shazzam,
speedzips and swerves, and we hurry. I stumble,
over gardens, by ponds,
down a plodpath towards all I want.
I even grin. Both of US so thrilled
we pause for kisses and hugs, allmost tumble,
down on the ground, allready fumbling
for a fast mess around, except we don't.
—Let'S roll.
—Roll it is, I bustle. Hailey's
pinna, Open, so wonderful to me, leads on.

—You two should be split up,
Nancy Nurse berates.
It's not proper. When Doctor Friendly
comes she'll do the separating.
Sam gets hot and bothered but
turning to me placates US with those
Green Eyes with flecks of Gold,
brazenly bold, waiting for War,
until we're at it again,
a pillowslinging
hop dance. Bedtop boogie,
tossing our socks for
Discos & Ragtime.
Cancer Stricken & Quad Sickened
joining US.
Until panting under
our downy flurry, Sam:
—Is The Cord still tied down?
—Sure, I surmise.
Let'S let The Creep out.

Jan 31 1974

2 PFLP & 2 Japanese
Army guerrillas.
Mao's New Revolution.
Patty Hearst
& Symbionese
Liberation Army.
269,000 British miners.
Gasoline gap.
Phnom Penh's artillery fire,
139 go.
Solzhenitsyn's Switzerland.
Fort Meade,
Robert Pearson
& Army helicopter.
$2 million of food.
Vietnam & US defoliants.
—we kind of missed
you on your.
Turkish DC-10, Orly
& a forest, 345 go.
Welfare blast.
54-33.
Oil embargo over.
Mars 6. Mars 7.
Ernesto Geisel.
—gangs up.
700,000 & drought:
Harar, Gamu-Gofa,
Bale & Sidamo.
Revson goes. Amelia.
Chickens & Dieldrin.

freely, even
deliberately.
—The Court's Open, she somehow gets, which
creeps me out. Hailey though flips around and
—Rockin and Rollin! commences to jump,
tapperific, swinging me
around, so'z I'z flowing
flip flopping hops,
arms flung underneath, while Hailey triple
ripple riffs, then jumps up, she, onto me, and
I stagger, wobble, shift for a turn quick, dip,
bobble, drop, groan ridiculously, until finally
arched over those long legs with dimpled knees
her Gold Eyes with flecks of Green
lift me with tender kisses.
—We'll be married very properly soon.

July 26 1953

Bobet's Tour.
2 Army Barracks &
200 Cuban Activists.
Berlin 10,000 & Free Food.
10 AM. Panmunjom,
William K Harrison & Nam Il.
Vladivostok's B-50.
214,000 immigrants.
Paris Civil Service.
Dulles, Pyun Yung Tai &
Mutual Defense Pact.
Franklin Held's javeline.
Ionian quake, 1,000 go.
Giuseppe Pella.
Mullany's Wiffle Ball.
Fazollah Zahedi over
Mossadegh. Ben Arafa's
Morocco. Jacqueline Auriol.
Laniel & Paris strikes.
Connolly's Grand Slam.
Hawker Hunter's 727.6 MPH.
Trabert over Seixas.
Durkin retires. John F Kennedy &
Jacqueline Lee Bouvier.
Vijaya Lakshmi Pandit.
Cairo round-up.

March 29 1974

Mariner 10's Mercury.
Grand Jury's Kent State.
Georges Pompidou goes.
Mishishishi, Ohio &
148 tornadoes, over 350 go.
Al Downing &
The Hammer's 715th.
New Delhi
prisoner exchange.
Golda Meir retires.
Qiryat Shemona, 18 go.
Tong Le Chan.
Gary Player.
—This is Tania.
OPEC & US.
Libya & Syria.
Koh Krabei.
Peam Lovek.
Pan Am's Bali,
107 go.
António de Spínola over
Marcello Caetano.
734 Pakistani POWs.
N Dale Anderson.
Federal Energy
Administration.
Cannonade's Derby.
League of Women
Voters & Men.
Celtics over Bucks.
Dalkon Shield.

He laughs
until Collection Agents tromp over,
hysterical with head bands,
donking on our amusement:
—Hey stop that!
Parting US with
our Account now due.
Not so cheap.
For taking care of US.
Phrmph. These Welfare Agents
are only taking care of business.
I turn Them on their heads.
Spin each around. Giving
The Suits a winkerstinker pucker.
Horrified, Them cluster to fly.
I'll suffer These Prims no more.
Even Sam fumes to resist,
though he'll probably cry when I
start scattering their chops. Then
a tender cough changes everything:

June 3 1953

Belgrade, Tito & NATO.
Nevada shock.
Midwest tornado, 139 go.
DC restaurants.
New England tornado, 92 go.
Pinilla's Bogotá.
South Korean Fifth
& Eighth Divisions.
American Third. East
Berlin's Soviet tanks.
Egyptian Republic.
Tokyo & Globemaster, 129 go.
Ossining & 8:04 PM.
—may have condemned
to death tens of millions of.
Sihanouk returns.
Dibrowa's Martial law.
Nathan Twining's Air Force.
Azzedine Bey goes.
Nagy over Rakosi.
—Imperialism and colonialism
are a barrier to.
Lavrenti Beria. Managua.
Louisiana hydrazine.
North Korea's 2 miles. Lanson.
Sea Dart. Operation Swallow.

And turning to roll,
the bones of Parole Officers, PIs
and dallying Dicks shiver brittle while Hailey
shallies by. Longings without answer. Ever.
Who can endure that power?
All run. Awfully afraid.
I laugh over such worry
taking Them away.
Does she turn heads!
Turns me upside down. And the World.
Tickles my ribs. And when the Discreet split
because she spins the World, she spins me too.
And MAD fast at that. Allways close by
if I'm trifles to our together course.
—Off for more amusement,
she leaps on

—*Leave US be.*

And at once THESE YICKY YACKS tip
hat obeying DOCTOR FRANK, on her
rounds, gently wheelchairing over to
determine our health:

—*I'm just around to check on your
wellbeing. For the timebeings. I
want you both back up and running.
How are you feeling?*

Sam's fine. Calm, small sure
but allways zippy:

—*I'm super superb.*

—*Yes,* SHE mildly assures. *Your
heart though suffers some worry.
SVT. Sinus Tach maybe.
Often beats too fast.*

—*What can I do?*

—*Plug your nose. Kick back.*

—*What causes it?*

—*Feer, man.*

May 17 1974

Watts & SLA, 5 &
Cinque Donald DeFreeze go.
Pentagon's rain.
Rajasthan's kilotons.
Giscard d'Estaing over
François Mitterrand.

—*which won't stop soon.*

Jeb Magruder's 10.
Duke goes. Frances goes.
Rutherford's 500.
Brescia blast, 6 go.
Geneva, Hafez al-Asad
& shuttle diplomacy.
110,000 clothing workers.
Yitzhak Rabin.

Smallpox, 10,000 go.
Henry Heimlich.
Mogadishu nomads.
Westminister's bomb.
Pittsburgh Gulf blast.
Iran's 5 reactors.
Nixon & Brezhnev.

—*I'm tired of all this.
I'm taking over.*

Marcus Wayne Chenault
& Atlanta Ebenezer,
Alberta Williams King goes.

Mikhail Baryshnikov defects.

Turkey's opium

—*How'd it quit?*

—*How it allways quits.
No high hat. No flat hat.
Just the mash of needs & wants
that never subtract out. But life's big.
If you can't fix it, give it a spin.*

Which races my heart something violent
until Hailey's easy touch gentles me.

—*Here,* THE GROUNDSGUY coughs.

Somehow weird. Someway strange.
I suddenly want to split.

—*If the Courts nix you, catch up with my
friend. Halfway unpermitted but.*

Giving Hailey then the way there
before returning to his shovel.

—*I'll leave me be now.*

April 14 1953

Laos 40,000.
Buenos Aires bomb, 6 go.
—*am a Peacemonger.*
Keizo Yamada's run.
Carl W Kirchenhausen.
400 tennis shoes.
Offshore Oil Bill, Wayne Morse &
22 hours. Deoxyribonuleic Acid.
Rosalind Franklin. 11th Session.
Mount Aso, 5 go.
Paksan & Muong Khoua.
British Caribbean Federation.
Calcutta Comet, 40 go.
Moreno's Derby. Monsoon.
Nairobi, Mau-Mau &
barbed wire.

Waco tornadoes, 124 go.

F-86 Sabre, 725.5 MPH &
Jacqueline Cochran.

MIG-15, Roenne &
pilot defection.
Coastal States &
Submerged Land.
Hillary & Tensing on a top.
Vukovich's 500. Domino Effect.

July 12 1974

The guilty plumbers.
Continental drift &
Icelandic volcanoes.
Arturo Mor Roig goes.
Turkey attacks Cyprus.
Greece, Civilian Control &
Constantine Karamanlis.
8-0.
27-11.
Impeachment.
Obstruction of Justice.
—Your honor I am.
—I will have hastened the start of that process of healing so desperately needed.
—unless you hate Them and then you destroy.
Warren Burger.
—Our long national nightmare is over.
—you again.
—the deepest valley can you ever.
Greece & NATO. Mang Buk.
Alfredo Miller goes.
Marshals, mace &
William Kunstler.
—I don't care.
Mose Malone.

And then with a pivot
turns to me:
—How are you doing?
I feel weird. Somehow peculiar and
little but fortunate beside her:
—Zonked z'all.
—Yes, SHE kindly nods.
The pill you gulped, from that
Hippie, Bee Pollen. Harmless
to most but you're allergic.
Severely. It might kill you.
—What should I do?
—Avoid bees.
—Honey?
—No, SHE smiles. *Honey's fine.*
And DR. FORD's allready truckin off
to her own circuit, if pausing
for our last moment:
—Stick around. Break the yoke, repair the
eggs. Slowing down's your only bet.

Feb 24 1953

South African Public Safety.
La Follette goes. De Gaulle &
European Defense Community.
North Korea's F-84s.
Ankara defense pact.
Tehran mobs.
—Yankees go.
Clare Boothe Luce.
Stalin goes. Malenkov.
MIG & RAF. Galeb & Tito.
Gabrielle. Calcutta winds.
Yucca Flat blast.
Milwaukee Braves.
Gonen quake, 1,000 go.
Khrushchev. Nairobi 2,500.
Castries & Beatrice.
Jonas Salk's 90.
Charles Bohlen. Soviet General
Amnesty. Korea POW exchange.
Navarre & Giap exchange.
Elaine & Dominique.
Dag Hammarskjöld. Department
of Health Education and Welfare.
Jomo Kenyatta.
Lakers over Knicks.
Oveta Culp Hobby.

—You two, too cool for school, HE winds.
Sure kind of you to stick around.
Even if you do bring up how
much I miss my man. Sharing
with someone's where it's at.
And HE's kind, pausing each time on his
round to groove with US.
—We're getting married, Hailey smiles.
—Cloud 9!
She & I both shrug.
HIM: *—Hey now, ritual still depends on*
Civic Permission. Your own thing's not enough.
And HE glums for a while.
—Maybe you can still find him,
I try.
—O no, that's over.

—*Time to cut loose,* Sam scoots over.
Before the Olive Drabs return.
But I'm allready moving,
shoving on my boots, waiting
impatiently for Sam to
follow suit.
Then the unpardonable
grabble of MARTINETS reapproaches.
I yank Sam's hand, delicately.
Around the corner we go.
Hospital Alarms. Charge.
Candy Caners and Clowns allso game
for a chase. O the humanity! Along
with the rest of the Pitiless
trying to pin US down.
And I'm ever Now.
Rounded up, chewed. Disavowed.
Racing towards streets where
Tulip Poplars and
Manitoba Maples still play.

Sept 1 1974

SR-71, James Sullivan
& 1:55:42.
Ecological revolution.
US & German Democratic
Republic. Mozambique's
Lusaka agreement.
Snake River Canyon
& Evel Knievel.
—full, free and absolute
pardon.
—regret and pain at the
anguish my.
—will continue to suffer.
Haile Selassie over.
Courts & Boston busing.
Conditional amnesty.
Courageous cups
Southern Cross.
Hurricane Fifi, 2,000 go.
—major economic crisis.
Freon & ozone.
Betty Ford's cancer.
—chaos and new.
Guilford IRA blast, 5 go.
WIN.
Ford, Francis Sargent
& 450 National Guard
A's over Dodgers.
—not progress,
it is degeneration.

Longtailed Weasels slump.
And Ocelots too.
We wheelie along by streetside
arguments and land grabs. Trial Lawyers.
Paralegals. Jittery Deputies.
But no one heeds US. We are unchased.
We cannot be delayed heading for the Courts.
All closed. Temporarily. Fascinating.
We wait around the block. At a park.
Hailey takes my hand, sweetly.
Patrol Plods, knocking back rounds, leave US
allone. Fade. Then along comes a GROUNDSCHAP
dragging a hoe. Splys on our bench.
Smokes a cigarillo. A bunch. Smokes a month.
—*You got the time?*
—*We are the time.*

Jan 1 1953

Southern California over
Wisconsin. Swiss Cheese.
Jamaican bauxite.
Kremlin's 9 doctors.
Rangoon Asian
Socialist Conference.
Tage Ellinger's Luzon.
—a soldier's pack is not so
heavy a burden.
34th.
—the only verdict we could.
Andrea Doria.
Seventh Fleet & Formosa.
Victoria down, 130 go.
—for General Motors and
vice-versa.
England storms, 200 go.
117.5 million short tons.
John & Jennifer Nicks.
6 Viet Minh War Factories.
Guatemala's 234,000 acres &
United Fruit. Davos, poliomyelitis
& Tenley Albright. Clemency.
$140 million power.
Mexico City's trolley, 60 go.
Taber's 75.

Oct 28 1974

Rabat, 20 Arab leaders
& PLO.
Jungle Rumble.

—kill him.
Ali 8 rounds Foreman.
UN's 100,000.
Connecticut & Ella Grasso.
Tel Aviv food riots.
South Africa, apartheid &
UN's 91-22.
Yasir Arafat.

Fullerton & All-Dog Frisbee.

Jane Alpert.
US Justice Department,
civil anti-trust suit & AT&T.

2 Birmingham pubs &
2 bombs, 19 go.
Ford, Veto & override.

Dubai, Tunis &
Palestinian hijacking.
Vladivostok Arms Pact.

Trade Ban over.
Tehran airport
& Snow, 17 go.
6.5% unemployment.

Soyuz 16 returns.

Rhodesia's ANC, ZANN,
ZAPU & FROLIZI unite.

Away from THE HORDES angrily delayed:
—You're too young.
Namaste.
—Come back. Wait.
—This.

—is not allowed!
But it's only fair. I'm every escape.
And besides, though Sam's afraid,
no one follows. No one cares.
We swing by The Ongoing Party, Hey
Now!, drum circle sesh breaking our
slip, hitting fresh biscuits, fanning bold
riffs, with spliff tucking ease, grants a
tease, blends on.
Mellow.
Me & Sam gig through to
herpetic CREEP caught still by
THE COIL. Too stiff for the
drift of our wistfulness.
—Hey Dualist, I slim.

Nov 5 1952

Commodore, 2:05 AM & Mamie.
—to cry but it hurts
too much to laugh.
Kimberley Protest, 14 go.
Weizmann goes.
Supreme Court
& railway segregation.
Zoll's shock. Einstein declines.
John Foster Dulles.
Globemaster over Alaska, 52 go.
Meany's AFL.
Saar alliance.
Adolfo Ruíz Cortines.
Slansky & 11 go.
Reuther's CIO.
—What are?
Farhat Hached. Jerusalem,
Knesset & Yitzhak Ben-Zvi.
3,900 MPH & Viking 9.
Pongam riots, 82 go.
—uncontested control of the.
George Christine Jorgenson.
—all here together to.
Larson C-124 crash, 84 go.
Lions over Browns.

some Continuous Join
we wistfully slide for,
loose, low & shafty.
And though a creepy chill starts
stabbing my arms, Hailey & I roll on.
Halting soon amidst bunches of
FUZZY DUCKS and YOOTS, I'm even these, lost,
stuck, an all Ts circle of Bennies and Left Wing
Luckies, circling ever back, to their gymband
pizzazz of bass, snare & brass, doling to
The Ongoing Hangover no hassles. Hailey just
getting the rap on going double. She's trouble.
Evasive, even if everyone Dubuques:
—Not allowed.
—Not together.
—You're too young.

We untie it. THE CREEP's confused, by
turns seething, amused. Until we flee.
The MG MGB burning US by
Horned Bladderwort squirming:
—*What comes around goes around!*

while we fly via bayous & berms,
verving the turns, if Sam flinches at
WILLY BO BILLS too low &
slow to catch our rinse for bribes.
This time. Besides, by my
Leftwrist Emerald Twist, we're rich.
Even if
Sam's allready awince.
Left over runs.
Drops trou overside.
Pops a lump:
—*If it don't pay rent,*
kick it out.
Whiffy dukers away.
Gratitoot.

Dec 18 1974
Majdal Zun.

—with America that
Americans cannot.

Senate Armed
Services Committee.
CIA & anti-War activists.
Harrods' bomb. B-1.

Japanese oil spill.

Binh Tuy Province's
Tanh Linh falls.
Cyclone Tracy's
Darwin, 50 go.
Marshall Fields & flares.

Managua, Sandinista
Front & 20 hostages, 3 go.

Mirabat quake,
thousands go.
3 Boston school officials,
& the Law.

Elaine Noble. JG Hayes.
Women's Year.
Lotru Mountains crash,
33 go. $750 million,
Saudi Arabia & 60 F-5s.
Super Bowl IX,
Steelers over Vikings.

Angola's liberty.
Detroit rebates.

Fraunces Tavern, 4 go.

Hailey's fantabulous.
I'm shit.
World's too particular for me.

But we hit it.

And where five roads link,
I poop puddles of stink.
The air grimacing all over. I grimace too.

We keep driving. Seeking someone now to
permit our union. Thrills enough to get
Hailey turning her Leftwrist Emerald Twist.

And no one can challenge our run enough
to stop me. Wisconsin Mickeys allready squishy
when we buzz by. Sooo out, we're never found.

What goes around comes around.

And WhipPoorWills die mourningly,
while our Mercury Monterey unites for

Sept 6 1952
London's DH-110, 25 go.
Chinese Farm cooperatives.
—give me.
Reparations & $822 million.
Hufnagel's valve. Thule base.
Alfred Hershey & Martha Chase.
Checkers.
—we're gonna keep it!
—completely vindicated.
La Sybille down, 48 go.
Strasbourg Plan.
Santayana goes.
Atomic cannon. Britain's bomb.
19th Communist Party Congress.
Route 3.
Wafd Party & Mustafa Nahas.
Yankees over Dodgers.
Harrow England's 3 trains,
78 go.
Poland & Repudiation of Yalta.
36 & Moscow's Presidium.
Pan Am jets.
Lancaster Fusiliers & Mau-Mau.
—I will go to Korea.
Operation Lorraine.
Bolivian Tin.

Feb 11 1975

—very, very thrilled.

US Army & birds,
500,000 go.

*—to spend the rest of
my life with.*

UN censures Israel.

Shelton rubber factory.
Sheep Creek Camp.
Iraq & Kurds.
Ban Me Thuot.
Northern desegregation.

Glomar Explorer.
ZANU's Herbert Chitepo goes.
Pochentong Airport.
Tam Ky & Quang Ngai.
Thau Thien Province & Hué.
Faisal bin Musad,
Faisal bin Abdul Aziz goes.

Portugal's Supreme
Revolutionary Council of the
Armed Forces Movement.
Mustafa al-Barzani.
Jean Gueury's free.
Eritrea Province.
Danang falls.

—earn a return.
22,500 out of 124,000.
Freedom Train.

Sledding the toll. Hustle &
zoom. Fusee & fire. We're carefree
battling on melting tires.
The Chevrolet Caprice sizzling all revs.
For Our Great River Wends.

Peppermint singeing the air. **Rosemary**.
Persimmon. Burning peat too.
Fertilizers, compost, turpentine and tar.
Sugarcane thick with sweetening warns:
—Go careful you two.

The Ford Elite whines on,
around caressing banks splashed with
refuse, Our Mishishishi, heaving a
low Barge loaded with
Half a Ferris Wheel tuttuggering for
Southern Pastures. I am the South.
The Buick Century Special rumbling
on, stressing, progressing.

Allways neverthelessing.

July 23 1952

Naguib's Army.
US Steel Strike over.
Oscar Callazo commuted.
Puerto Rico rule.
Little Evita goes.
*—I am going to take my coat
off and help him win.*

Ahmed Fuad. Helsinki &
Emil Zatopek's marathon.

Chesapeake Bay Bridge.
Remington Rand Chairman.
Scotland & 2 Sikorsky H-19s.

Drought.

Saskatchewan uranium.
Marjorie Jackson, Agnes Keleti,
Nina Romaschkova.
Bob Mathias, Floyd Patterson.
Waco bus, 28 go.
Algerian Defense Front.
New Delhi crop failure.
Hussein over Talial.
Matyas Rakosi. Clarissa Eden.
Faisal II. Canberra transatlantic.
16,000 East Berliners flee.

Peking's famine-relief refused.

Egressing
allways. Fast too.
Our Ford Pickup whirring North.
She is my North. My Northern Prairies.
What Half a Ferris Wheel loaded on
a long Tug continues to pugpuggering up
The Mishishishi after. But even with arm
around, by necker's knob, I feel skittery.
Why? Our Chrysler Newport races on.
Allmost carelessly. By whirlybirds, UFOs.
While Timber Wolves go stiff.
Hailey snuggles and buzzles me.
Alligators & Raccoons die.
And Porcupines too. But we
ripple on by Davenport, Fulton, Savanna. To
Hanover. Our Pontiac Dual Range now
only wedding bound.

April 4 1975

My Sam sixteen smiles, heels cavitating
the wind. Rangy. A stunner.
Saluting my wonder:
—*Here's to keeping it Summer.*
I pinkle back —*sure*, while
the Imperial LeBaron heaves harder.
Byes, abandoning tread, motorvating
for rush, for fun, a fullon furious torque
blur by Lacrosse Grounds, Tether Balls
and Rusting Schoolbuses souring yards,
bogs and swamp. Fields of Big Wheel
Cotton Blocks.
Knapweed and **Beets** gawk
but we're allready by Pole Vaulting,
Hammer Throws and Shot Puts. And
while PreTransients
stir a pot of soup
with forks,
I gladly pass around

Galaxy C-5A, 125 go.
Chiang Kai-shek goes.
Phalangist Party, Beirut
& a bus, 22 go.
Jack Nicklaus's 5th.
79 cities & water pollution.
World Whale Day.
—*105 degrees and rising.*
Ky's goldbars.
7:52 PM & 11 Marines.
Ho Chi Minh City.
Jeanne M Holm.
Foolish Pleasure's Derby.
Nebraska tornado.
—*to close ranks.*
—*we failed.*
26 ships, 30,000
& Subic Bay.
Millions of
Cambodian peasants.
W Arthur Garrity's 20,000.
Mayaguez's 39.
Tang Island & 3 gunboats.
Junko Tabei.
Paul Shaffer
& John H Turner go.
Baader-Meinhof gang.
Flyers.

May 29 1952

Passing forks around.
While close, over a kettle of coals,
a bunch of PostTransients stir dew.
I do too.
Hailey might dump me here
but would I object? O.
Pelicans & **Snails** toxinated. Dead.
Such are the precedents against any holdings.
Broke. We're the only attachment.
Hailey lets go of my hand and there on
my knees, by county crossroads, proposing
without even a ring,
I officially ask her to me
and she accepatates.
Our Hudson Hornet flies on.
—*Here's to letting Autumn fall when it wants.*
Hailey sixteen smiles.

Greek Women Vote.
Ruttman's 500.
Ridgway's NATO Command.
Groton first.
6-3 Steel Mill Violation.
Bucharest's Gheorghe Gheorghiu.
Tanks & Koje Island camps.
Berlin Eastern Guard,
1 goes. Compound 76.
Andrei Gromyko.
Swedish Jet & Soviet Jet.
Lancia sport, Luigi Fagioli goes.
500 UN planes &
5 hydroelectric plants.
Truman vetoes Immigration
& Naturalization Act.
Congress passes McCarran-
Walter Immigration Quota Bill.
Palmdale's F-94C.
Sedgman & Connolly.
35.95 knots.
—*total victory.*
Veterans' Readjustment
Assistance Act. Ghavam over
Mossadegh. 4.5 million &
Social Security roles. Fausto
Coppi's Tour. California quake.

June 2 1975

Police, prostitutes & Lyons.
Ethiopia's drought.
Anwar el-Sadat &
Suez Canal.
Belgium's 102 F-16s.
Pham Van Dong,
Vo Nguyen Giap &
Nguyen Duy Trinh.
25%. Palestinians,
Nahariya & 3 rockets.
Chlorofluorocarbons.
Cruise missiles.
*—casual and less
politcally responsible.*
Oak Park,
Sam Giancana goes.
Eastern 727, 109 go.
Mozambique &
Samora Machel.
Oglala Sioux & FBI, 2 go.
Allahabad Court &
Gandhi's election.
—to save its citizens from.
Finback whale.
—own defense.
Denis Cecil Hills.
Jerusalem's
Square blast, 13 go.
Ashe over Connors.
Thomas Stafford &
Aleksei Leonov.

HONEY.
8½ left.
One jar for two. Halfbyhalf.
Spooning gooey scoops. Lipsforlips
tongueontongue, undoubling stashes of
amber. Spooly, drooly, refueling.
Sticking US again to the World.
The Mercury Comet bucking the tar,
around Long Hauls chugging freight
of Whey Barrels and Curd Cartons by
Convoys on Coupons yanking past
Milkweed slawwing for wutter.
Tossed spades turn to Claymores. While
heat blisters pumps and drivetrain
hauls with gravelly lows. And though
timing belts slip, unravel and Dazed
& Disabused force US to slow,
the Plymouth Fury lugs on anyway
without pause.

123 238

April 4 1952

US & Chile.
East River & UN Security Council.
Truman nationalizes steel mills.
National Revolutionary Party,
La Paz & Bolivian Overthrow.
—honor and equality.
Boeing YB-52's 8.
Lakers over Knicks.
Sugar Ray 3 rounds Graziano.
California C-46, 29 go.
Jackson State Prison uprising.
Hobson & Wasp, 176 go.
Air France & MIG-15.
Tibet's Panchen Lama.
Overseas Airways.
Hill Gail's Derby.
Maria Montessori goes.
Suan napalm.
Koje Island & Dodd.
Bonn Pact & Essen's 30,000.
Ambassador Shrimati Vijaya
Lakshami Pandit.
Desert Locusts.
Superliner.
Railroads return.
European Defense Community.

And she agrees.
Our Buick Super barrelling quickass over
bitulithic pavements, past Stopped & Cuffed,
Locally Charged for Civil Arraignments.
Unchallenged. Even Warrants out for our
arrest turn out to be suburbanized anxieties.
And the mains twirl smooth. Loosed loads of
machetes hurtling towards US turn to grease.
Alpacas perish. Diseased.
We drive afster & faster. Unhindered now by
headons, leaked oil, delays and postponements.
Our Aero Willys
allways easily beating the World.
And when we pull over to stroll,
feeling gooey, I treat my girl.
3½ left. Sweet
HONEY.

July 25 1975

Holden Roberto, FNLA & MPLA. Kentucky & 5,000 vans.
Voting Act extension.

Helsinki, 35 Nations & Conference on European Security and Cooperation.
Poland & 120,000 Germans.
UN, Vietnam & US veto.
John Walker's 3:49:4.
Dacca & Khondaker Moshtaque Ahmed, Mujibur Rahman goes.
Samuel Bronfman II free.
Renee Richards.
Pathet Lao & Vientiane.
Mazzotti goes.

—to liquidate the Palestinian.

Guillermo Rodríguez Lara over Raúl González Alvear.

Gerald Ford, Larry Buendorf & Lynette Squeaky Fromme.

—It didn't go off.

Martina Navratilova defects.

Lice quake, 1,000 go.
Fred Salomon goes.

Anyways we're gravy. My Mini Mint &
Muffin skilling his engine with wheeze,
grease and me, curling my fingers around
his dingledangle, stiffening easily with
each stroke, grip and tug. Maybe a slurp.
Hungry for Wyatt Earp. Pumping squirts.
His fingers agiling my nookie
by the whirly

river bends

past surly bites of Freeway Dash
and Semis pistoning crankshafts, tight
turned and scalding. I'm pleasing and
pleased. I'm tropics of heat, his tropical
breeze. Allways ongoing and going.

—Congratulate me.
—OK, what for?
—Because you're savage.
—And you're plenty.
—Nuf!

Feb 8 1952

Kenya's Treetops & Elizabeth.
Marciano KOs Lee Savold.
Oslo's Andrea Mead Lawrence.
Hossein Fatemi goes.
North Carolina, FBI & 10 KKK.
DAR & Dorothy Maynor.
$1 billion of rubber.
9th session. Britain's A-Bomb.
Japan & US military bases.
Feinberg Law.
Florida Golf Course restrictions.
Paraná River train, 108 go.
Peter During's pump.
Batista over Socarras.
NATO's Ismay.
Trieste border clash.
Daniel Malan resists.
Mishishishi tornadoes, 343 go.
James Leedom goes.
William Benton.
Tangier riot.
Bey of Tunis & Martial Law.

—seriously damaging the position of.

George Kennan.

—Fun!
Hailey has plenty,
and savagely the ground trembles
and the sky hardens with streaks
until around US whips our icehard
wind, snagging their limbs, how
Hailey, slick, and slickening to me,
levies the effects of our speed:
each shivering without defense
before Hailey, their living end.
—Get bent Clydes, she stuns. *I'm the curves*
you cry for. I'm the curves you die on.
And each ASSAILANT snotsobs galore.
Decapitated. Maimed. Demolished by laws.
Me: *—Come on Dolly, let'S fringe these flookies.*
You're all that's it.
—Cookie, we're never it.

Sept 16 1975

Sarkis Paskalian.
Takeo Miki's $6.7 billion.
Patricia Hearst & FBI.

Sara Jane Moore,
Oliver Bill Sipple &
.38 caliber revolver.

FBI's 239 burglaries.
Madrid Basques, 5 go.
Karen Ann Quinlan.
Manilla Thrilla.
Ali 14 rounds Frazier.
France &
100,000 unemployed.
Diana Nyad's swim.

—to be unequal.

Hassan II, 350,000 &
Sahara.

6 million tons of grain &
10 million tons of oil.

Arunachal Pradesh.
Cincinnati over Boston.

Peter Sutcliffe's hammer,
Wilma McCann goes.

Britain's North Sea
oil & pipe.

*—not only a friend but
allso a neighbor.*

The Checker Marathon surging from
Natchez brodies curves toward warm
embankments, down among

Reeds & Rushes lapped by current,

slaps impossibly urging US back. Shudder
thrive. Peck & neck. Dive. Licketysplits.
Gobble. Eats my pie. So I have it too.

—*UuuuuUuu,* he mumms.
—*UuuuuUuu,* I rumble.
—*uUUUUUuUU,* we bumble,

rear seat squunched until crunched
on the trunk, bonk,
log and bumping the horizontal jog,
tingles climbing my sides & thighs,
bending me ecstatically over
until Sam's up the rainbow
spastically wide, sticky spunk
rushing for mud.
Cheeks blushed, breaths crushed.

Dec 13 1951

Truman, Hoover & the disloyal.
C-46 down, 56 go.
Bagel Bakers of America.
3,100 POWs.
West Frankfurt Illinois
& mine explosion, 118 go.

Rams over Browns.
Idaho Falls & AEC.
Illinois over Stanford.
National Drug Raid.
Republican Ike.
British Atomic Consent.
Montana's Hungry Horse Dam.
Henrik Kurt Carlsen,
Flying Enterprise & Turmoil.
Vickers Valiant.
Jeanette Burr.

Hoa Binh Basin, Saigon
& Tonkin delta.
Habib Bourguiba arrested.
Jacqueline Lee Bouvier
& John G W Husted Jr.
Robert Patterson goes.
Vincent Massey.
Mustafa Nahas over.

—We are ready to.

Every race,
except we're the only race, so speedy there's
never a race. Verdicts away. Still our
Toughs circle, petty & hankering, and
even if some Girls & Boys slow up then,
Them're way too late, past help, remedy,
drenched and anxious. Hailey's that dangerous.
She turns their gall to torture.
Their superbity to horror.
—*IiiiiIii,* One Bully gawks.
—*IiiiiIii,* One Delinquent bawks.
—*iIIIIIiII,* Everyone shocks.
Their assault knocked cold.
Now Here's all Corrupt.

Robins & Rabbits undone.

Hailey's the Verdict each gave up.
Even our Plymouth Belvedere vrooms up.

But for my bouncing bazongas
musters still more.
The AMC Pacer harrowing direction,
highsliding the set. I am the best,
unset, unguessed, eager wailings
for the next Rest Stop.
Nuts For Sale.
CottonCandy and Jelly Sandwiches.
Slow versall turnings.
Nuclear Rods To Finance. Preserves For
Purchase. Leukemia For Free.
Some idling over our way cautiously.
—*Can I help you?* STAND MAN gapes.
—*Can I help you?* Sam ablates.
—*Not hiring no work.*
—*We never work.*
—*Now don't freshmouth me, Schmuck.*
—*Lucky US!* I blunt.
We work enough. Way too much.

Nov 10 1975

—*of racisms and racial discrimination.*

Lake Superior &
Edmund Fitzgerald, 29 go.

John Kerr, Gough Whitlam
& Malcolm Fraser.
William O Douglas.
Ecuador's General Strike.
Communists
& violent revolution.

Francisco Franco goes.
Juan Carlos de Borbón.
Trans-Alaskan pipeline.

—*free appropriate public.*

Beilin & 7 South Moluccans,
2 go.

—*War of men against weapons.*

New York's $2.3 billion.
Angola & Lúcio Lara's
Popular Movement.
11 OPEC ministers.

—*arm of the Arab revolution.*

Little League World Series.
La Guardia bomb, 14 go.
Lebanese jet, 82 go.
Ulster, 10 go.

goof off. Play ball.
Detesting US for doing just that. And more.
—*You both hold.*
—*You're under our control.*
And I'm all complying, tossing thanks,
sorrys. Shaky knees. Afraid. Hailey though's
her own judicature, not backing down one
step before their threatenings.
And THE HOOLIGANS shove ahead too,
too cubesville to get what each is up against.
Even with clubs, hammers and baseball bats.
Hailey just chills. Relaxed. Won't pick fights.
Finishes Them. Set allready for their best.
—*Niggers!* Them retch.
— *Chinks* —*Japs!* —*Spicyspans!* —*Wops!*
Surrounding our Dodge Wayfarer.
—*Kikes!!*

Oct 16 1951

Liaquat Ali Khan goes.
Air-to-Ground Nuke.
Robert McGill's helicopter.
Winston Churchill &
10 Downing Street.
UN Atom Control.
Viet Minh from Hanoi.
Nepal, Rana & Tribhubana.
US & Yugoslavia military aid.
Paratroopers & Hoa Binh.
France turns down Tunisia.
Po River flood.

—*surrounded by the.*

British troops take over Ismalia.
Prague, Gottwald &
Rudolf Slansky.

—*much to gain by standing.*

—*everything to lose through concession.*

Punmunjom Peace & 38th.
Damascus & Shishekly.
Tunisian rebels. Navy over Army.
New York & US Radium,
another goes.
Suez Zone, many go.

Jan 15 1976

Henry Williams' castration.
Super Bowl X,
Steelers over Cowboys.
Madrid strikes &
70,000 railmen.
Lebanon accord.
—an all
embracing political.
Angolan rebels.
$45 billion, veto & override.
Buckley vs Valeo &
campaign spending limits.
Arizona, Ernesto Miranda
goes. Guatemala &
Honduras quake, 12,000 go.
—exporting revolution.
Sun Belt migration.
Tucson's Lear Jet.
Phoenix's Greyhound.
Houston's Shell.
—economic discipline.
Frank Stagg goes.
Dorothy Hamill's gold.
Nigerian coup, Murtala
Rufai Mohammed goes.
Bali's ASEAN. Moscow
microwaves & US Embassy.
Western Sahara & Polisario
Liberation Movement.
Eskimos & Canada.
—outlaw.

Here though, Berry Sodas, Fries,
Tampons, Socks. Offering Lip Sticks,
Pet Rocks, Car Washes, Lollipops.
Dirndls, Pinafores, Bikini tops.

Sam scouting out Mias and Joes,
though his Leftwrist Steel Twist's not
tender enough, Lincoln enough, for
these Dismissive Shops we roll along past
with their Vague Men and Anxious
Clients sulking from
abandoned High Schools, parking lots,
bleak curbs, where aboundoned TEENS
skate waves of dull heat.

We do too.

Body cranking kicks, heelies,
plankriding wheelies, tacks for
aerial lift offs, even if Sam's
all wobs, Hodad boffing
the rim,

Aug 25 1951

Emmanuel MacDonald's 10.2.
Arlington National Cemetery
& John R Rice. Kennecott
Copper. US, Philippines
& Mutual Defense Treaty.
Douglas Skyrocket.
—feer, ignorance, bigotry
& smear.
ANZUS.
—to serve wherever democracy
needs to be defended.
Louis J Sebille.
Little Mo. Azores.
47 Nations, Japan & Peace.
Rudolf Slansky.
Asch, Frazek Jarda & 111.
Marshall retires. Fawley oil.
Veteran's Pension. Greece &
Turkey. Switzerland & suffrage.
—had the obligation to.
Bobby Thompson's
shot around the World.
Henry Gurney goes.
Cairo, Suez & Sudan.
Yankees over Giants.
Mutual Security Act.

We are unmastered.
Impossibly implored. The detour
every byway demands
US to deplore.
Which we don't,
allways bending lanes for
OFFENDED TEENS, goaded, enrolled & fettered
for fights over allegiance, regions and
sweaters.
All Them craves is to skip loose from
the Gang's beat, Man's can,
but so digging our bore mill and grill
fix to pop me for just my Leftwrist Steel Twist,
abduct Hailey for a ball,
each of these JDs, leather lathered with grease,
tied up by rank and role, custom and
code, just dying to go

March 4 1976

Pan Am's negligence.
Nigerian BS Dimka arrested.
Tokyo's 4,000 workers.
Frank Church.
—our greatest foreign policy problem is our division at.
—and pervasive feer.
Patty Hearst guilty.
Jorge Rafael Videla over Isabel Martínez de Perón.
Camp David Peace Treaty, Menachem Begin & Anwar el-Sadat.
DC's public transportation.
Supreme Court, Virginia & homosexuality.
Steven Jobs & Stephen Wozniak.
Howard Hughes goes.
Hua Kuo-feng.
Syrian troops & Lebanon.
—spare no effort to crush.
Leary's parole.
Volkswagen.
—solidarity with exiled, persecuted, jailed.
Boston thousands.
Portugal's Mário Soares.
Bold Forbes' Derby.

pearling for bongos,
roadrash and wipeouts,
all stoked still for gliding
with grins and whoops.
Hopping a skateboard to Ooops it
again, I hardflip stick the dry pool.
More gathering round, torn Ts,
distressed Jeans, lifting skuffling smiles
for wheels, speed and miles
of road. Them all want to go.

—*You can,* I bin.

—*How we begin?*

—*Just zing.*

But TEENERS wait on rot and
afraid circle off to spend change on
chocolate shakes.

The Bricklin SV1 rakes
each one, snorting US on,
until the halfbaked feel our pace.

June 29 1951

US, Soviets & Wonsan Harbor Ship.
DC-6 & Rocky Mountain Park, 50 go. Bob Feller's third.
Colombo Plan.
Dick Savitt, Doris Hart & Wimbledon. Kaesong.
Dashiell Hammett declines.
Turpin 15 rounds Robinson.
Governor Stevenson, National Guard & Cicero Suburb.
Missouri floods.
Tehran riots, 9 go.
Jersey Joe 7 rounds Ezzard.
Franco & West.
Jordan's Abdullah goes.
Rocquencourt's NATO HQ.
General Ridgway, Kim Il Sung & Peng Dehuai.
Koblet's Tour.
Ystad & 12 Polish sailors.
William Hill Jr goes.
Viking Rocket's 1,400 MPH.
East Berlin's million.
Suez blockade.

Dago dropped and glasspacked,
past Mediapolis and Wapello,
our DeSoto Custom scats topless.
Hailey the bikiniest trouble. Topless.
Big tickle for Truant Officers
committed to seizing what Them never miss.
We miss Them by a wide stretch, a whiplash
doubletake. Setting off every school bell.
Recessing every class. Leaving schoolbound
frowns turning around over the chance
of setting out from playground rules for
something so much riskier.
Town after town, rampant treks
through Muscatine, Edgington and Andalusia.
Ringing every bell. Class excused.
Headmasters all vexed by
what mastery we wreck.

May 6 1976

Udine quake, 95 go.
Chemical Corporation,
James River & Kepone.

Israel & West Bank.
Ulrike Meinhof goes.

Paris & Che Guevara Brigade,
Joaquín Zenteno Anaya goes.
Park's pot plumes.

Bangladesh, Maulana
Bhashani & The Ganges River.

Mario Jascalevich.
Senate's 15-members.
Typhoon Olga, 215 go.

Giscard's Concorde SST.
Ellis Island.

Lebanon's Syrian tanks.

Snake River Valley,
Teton River Dam
& 80 billion gallons.
Boston over Phoenix.
Francis Meloy &
Robert Waring go.
Soweto riot, 6 go.

—at all cost.

Beruit's 263,
Operation Fluid Drive &
Operation Iowa Primary.

Asphalt amped and jamming,
steamy fine, even if
the Chrysler Cordoba floats storms
of radiator fumes. Hub caps
biffing Frisbee Nuts, Kite Flyers, Leary
Alcoholics fired for vermouth.
Towards hurt.
By Rolling Fork to Hollywood.

By dittering **Sassafras.**

Canyon and salt flats. Rockets and tin
hats. Swollen knees, parched buckets.
Only some are lucky. Hardly.
And I'm all sands west when the rains
left. I'm a thousand Julys.
The Camaro LT apprising
the lazy why July never dies,
while Sam digs ear wax.
Grommeted overalls. Kinky fro.
Kicking up go.

April 25 1951

$10,000. Hussein Ala quits.
British Asiatic Petroleum.
Rochester over Knicks.
Count Turf's Derby.
Farouk & Narriman Sadek.

El Salvador shake.
Eniwetok H-Bomb.
Saigon harbor & Adour, 55 go.
100 mile front. Jet Ace Jabara.

Bradley & Marshall
over MacArthur.
Tibet Liberated.

Willie Mays. Donald Maclean
& Guy Burgess. Theodor Koerner.
Wallard's 500.
Iron Triangle.
—Up Dev.
UNIVAC. New Delhi People's
Party. PCF & RPF.
Pilot strike. Draft extension.
—overthrow of.
Elizabeth Gurley Flynn.
Pan Am & West African jungle.
The United States.
Malik cease-fire.
—of the conflict.

Allways away with Hailey.
Even with my oily ducktail. Sloppy
overalls. Diggy for ear wax.
She's why September never wanes.
Our Hillman Minx unleashing turns.
I'm a thousand Septembers. And she's
all oceans east when the tankers sink.
Though we're allready gone, amidst
the Fallout & Tarried until even Harried &
Accused are carried away by our drive.
Eskimo Chickens die.
From Peoria.
Knoxville, Monmouth and Biggsville.
—I'm glad we're on our own, if we are allone,
I glub klutzy but Hailey still kisses me. Our
Mercury Barris
cranking. Blown.

June 28 1976

Air Force Academy.
Seychelles Islands.

Supreme Court, Sierra Club
& strip mining.

Jurek vs Texas.
Bjorg over Nastase.

Israeli commandos,
Uganda's Entebbe Airport
& 103 hostages, 31 go.

225 ships, 30 Nations
& Operation Sail.
Dora Bloch goes.
John Hodges
& smuggling ring.
Nixon disbarred.
—now a time to heal.
Nadia Comaneci's 10.
Venezuela floods.
Viking I & Mars.
Mexico's rains.
Ewart-Biggs goes.

Tangshan quake,
over 100,000 go.
Bruce Jenner's decathlon.
Colorado floods, 139 go.
William Harris
& Emily Harris.

Cape Town riots, 17 go.
Tel al-Zaatar.

My lusty boy.
—Isn't this Liberty, on our own.
—Wherever whatever we please.
We're so eased.
—Just US allone.
—Free from duty. From Regulation.
From everyone and anything.
Me: *—What about me?*

Diminishings driving this spurn.
Getting worse.
Until he takes my hand, curling one fist
from two, palm on palm, wrist on wrist,
Peacefully mixed.
—Except from you.

Both of US suddenly caught by a cool
gust rising up just around the bend,
every bend, prickling our arms until
we separate and shiver. Boiling
Summer returning with a giggle.

Feb 26 1951

22nd Amendment.
Groton's K-1.
GM's $834 million.
Ali Razmara goes.
Frank Costello & Estes Kefauver.
Operation Ripper.
Mossadegh's oil fields.
Ukrainian Army. Schuman Plan.
China rejects truce.
—shocking and loathsome.
Draft deferment.
—We must win. There is no.
Irving R Kaufman.
Israel bombs Syria.
—on me, I want him fired.
Stone of scone.

—If I allowed him to
defy the Civil Authority, I.
Sabres over 8 MIGs.
Abadan's Anglo-Iranian
Refinery.
—to prevent
a third World War.

—just fade away.

Manila's Huks, 5 go.
University of North Carolina.

I glumble, fidgets giving up our age
which Hailey takes back with
fleemiest disobedience.
The Sheriff lazysusans then for
Federal Roads burning with wrecks.
—What the?!
—We're without agency, Hailey kindly rumbles.
Ageless for all. Pursue your Peace.
But his Peace sways, and with it
legality, allready betrayed when we
pull away, leaving him grieving
amid churning impacts, lorries exploding,
glass melting, cabbies gouged by exhaustions
of rust, calamities littering curves, medians
& shoulders, which only retire him,
allready overtaken by contagions, and US,
obliterating him for escapements of dust.

Aug 17 1976

Mindanao quake, 3,100 go.
DMZ, Bridge of No Return & axes, 2 go.
Argentina & Montoneros, 46 go.
Philadelphia, Bellevue-Stratford & Legionnaires, 28 go.
Tokyo's Soviet MIG-25.
Space Shuttle.
Mao Tse-tung goes.
Orlando Letelier goes.
Rhodesia, Smith & biracial regime.
West Point's 700.
Hurricane Lizzie, 2,500 go.
Earl Butz quits.
—There is no Soviet domination.
Commerce Department & Israel boycott.
A-Bomb for dummies.
Sadahuru Oh.
Swine Flu, 3 go.
Gang of Four.
Hua Kuo-feng.
Santa Cruz's 707, 102 go.
Bermuda Triangle & Sylvia L Ossa, 37 go.

By turnoffs, road blocks and stops,
the Triumph TR6 vibrations turn me on.
Flux!
How'd I get so tight for this chooch,
fired up, whiz poppin mangy,
by my tangy boost?
And all we smooth past.
Every PASSERBY's last grasp.
The jell out FOLKS won't chance.
How PEEPS slack what I have.
We rip over to veg and bask.
—*What for?*
—*Get some swerve on?*
Satsumas, Kumquats,
Watermelons defer. All exocence,
I lead on, shashaying US beyond a fence,
where snagging for antics,
free from STROLLERS,
I secure tantric joy.

Jan 10 1951

1 hour 42 minutes. $71.5 billion.
—clear and present danger.
Osan & Kumyangjang. Vin-yen.
—Come on. Break through and get me out of here.
Porsche goes.
Alp avalanches, 217 go.
UN out. Charles Nessler goes.
Economic Stabilization Administration, Wages & Prices.
670 lend-lease ships.
Nevada hazards.
Charles Blair, Mustang Fighter & Jet Stream.
Rochester, Cincinnati & burning snow.
Vladimir Clementis arrested.
New Jersey Commuter, 84 go.
UN's 38. Mohammed Reza Pahlavi & Soraya Esfandiari.
Robinson 13 rounds LaMotta.
Europe's 4 Divisions.
Yanyang.
Moore goes.
—traitors & conspirators.

because panic's what we offer
even a NAB we
only snag for briefly, benzing up from
around a fence with snide sirens, swaggering
to tap what can't be tapped. Even deferred.
Armadillos, Darners & Mourning Doves die.
—*You've a license to fly this thing?*
—*Sure,* Hailey whiles, her
recusant rancor granting what my crummy
handwringing flails to cram: how even
this OFFICER quails to command US.
—*Hand over your identity,* PORKY tenses.
Joyriding's verboten round here. Theft's
breakin the Law. Jail's where we'll
secure y'all.
Our Porsche 356 puttering.
—*Sure,*

Oct 18 1976

—will share power.
William Scranton,
South Africa & Namibia.
New Orleans ferryboat,
78 go.
Cincinnati over New York.
Soweto liquor stores & bars.
Jiang Qing.
George Wallace,
Clarence Norris & a pardon.
Wayne Hays
& Elizabeth Ray.
Edward Gurney & acquittal.
Asghar Khan, Tehrik-i-
Istiqlal Party & 50,000.
Atlantic City Casinos.
Jimmy Carter.
279-241.
Martin Rye.
Baseball draft
& free agents.
ROTC hazing & bayonet,
1 goes.
Federal funds & abortions.
Chrysler tanks.
Mount Ararat quake,
4,000 go.
—Juice! Juice!
Libya & Fiat. Tip O'Neill.
UN's Kurt Waldheim.

O too soon rolling, lying low,
moany kisses, hungrier for snacks,
licks and my fairahhh waves.
The River, Our Mishishishi,
Roaming Along The Long Way
Sadly Slipping On,
too slow to ever catch up with US.
Sam spanking my winkie,
diplipling the Nation,
spinkling my berries
to thrust hot for.
—O, o, sure!
Butter for tips. Until slick
for toprocking stick on clit:
—Up me some more!
Sam groans. I groan too. Both of US
locked, he pawing my chalubbies,
me clawing his front, bumping
quicker this funch, wettest yet,

Nov 8 1950

70 B-29s, F-80 & MIG-15.
Supung Dam &
Chongchon River.
—the most offensive.
Oil from Coal. Viet Minh with
Laotian & Cambodian rebels.
550,000 over Yalu.
Blizzards.
Arabian American Oil.
University of Tennessee's 5.
10th Corps, Chosin Reservoir
& Hungnam.
Ban on People's Republic of
China. Harry Gold's 30.
—an arsenal of freedom.
State of National Emergency.
—put aside his personal.
Lattre de Tassigny.
Supreme Commander
for Allied Powers.
El Glaoui & Ben Youssef.
Robinson 9 rounds Villemain.
Cleveland over LA.
Michigan over California.
UN abandons Seoul.

I slide over to Hailey, for her soft
waist, nape, Open, against the chill
she heaps upon the lawns of every Barbecue,
Sprinkler Run and Foamer we fleet by.
—It's about time!
O even the bravest Chancellors shudder.
Lay Judges sure doom.
—So so fine!
And every smooch Hailey spares
dismisses somewhere someone's
longing to stay strong. Our embrace
& jazzing wilts the lustiest Adlibber.
Dollys and Dregs shoe eggs.
—*We allways will,* Hailey admits,
despite all that's panicked and young.
Because we're only flowing young.
And we cannot panic

Dec 22 1976

Donald Jamieson &
Canadian External Affairs.
Paris & Charles Martel Club,
Jean de Broglie goes.

Thanat Khoman &
Soviet missile silos.
Rudolph Perpich.
Zaire's Ebola Virus.
USC over Michigan.
Abu Daoud's arrest.
Super Bowl XI,
Raiders over Vikings.
UNESCO, pollution & Athens.
—Let'S do it.
Utah State Prison &
firing squad,
Gary Gilmore goes.
Cairo riots, 44 go.
—Jimmy!
Pennsylvania Avenue stroll.
65°
Draft evaders & full pardon.

Florida freeze.
Madrid, 3 Communist
Labor Chiefs go.
Freddie Prinze goes.
Rhodesia &
Nationalist guerrillas, 7 go.
Uganda executions.

down and up, rushing of course,
justly winding my clock for fast
mattress stacking, under prods,
over, cycling my thrill, by tables,
benches and campfire grills.
On we mill.

Sunflowers grow around our buck.
Fiery Daffodils encircling our fuck.

I'm recircling burns, even
taking a turn on Shooter's Hill.
A fourknee boogie before Sam.
Swiggle and thrum. Slumping
to limbo for more hump,

while **Turnips & Radish** soak up

my funk and plump. Snickers.
And though I'm allways over
Sam's allmost done,
face flinching brief twitches,
boggy bamboo slipping free

Sept 15 1950

Wolmi. Yongdok. Kunsan.
Pohang. US First Marine
Division & Army's Seventh.
The Mount McKinley.
—of free enterprise.
Quincy's Constitution.
Veto Override
& Mundt Bill. MacArthur,
McCaffrey & Seoul.
—suffered so terrible
a liberation.
Khakis & hat.
—bones ache and blood curdle.
US Eighth over 38th.
Hugh Stewart's
Petroleum Administration.
Sidon to Gulf.
Yankees over Phillies.
Cao Bang & That Khe.
Wake Island. Connie Mack done.
Pyongyang.
China attacks Tibet.
Sixth Division's Yalu River.
San Juan uprising.
Oscar Collazo, Griselio Torresola
& Leslie Coffelt.
Tribhubana Bir Bikram flees.

We are naturally killer.
The goings of all around. Hurling past
slayings whose PRACTITIONERS
catch Hailey's blown kisses, suddenly feeling
every murdered tongue their own. Over
and over again.

Plovers & Tortoises spill with illness.

—*Hop the hassle,* Hailey leads.
—*Agitating the gravel,* I concede, cool
gassing US by curve & hill. Slashed &
still. At speeds allways beyond where

Sandhill Cranes go
and **Wild Boars** die too.

On we rush.
Appeal's death. If it were the end
all the time, it would allways be just.
We are never just.

to surge a sticky stream
clear to **Kudzu** weeds.
I am astonishing.
What I provoke. Both of US
all wanked out now
and pretty much broke.
The Jeep Cherokee puttering US on
by guard rails and park trails where
Lyre Sage, **Sweetgum** and **Ginkgo**
slip solemnly:
—*It's not all just sex.*
Okay. If too thick.
—*How about a dip?* Sam suggests.
And zip! we park, disembark for
a splintering dock.
I dangle my feet. Sam dives
for peregrine hazards, immediately
swept away, too flimsy to fend
off the opposing surge.

Feb 12 1977

Rose Elizabeth Bird.
Brazilian torture.
Vibhavadi Rangsit goes.
Edwards Air Force Base
& Space Shuttle.
Rocky Flats & 6 windmills.
Scouting USA.
Argentina, Ethiopia,
Uruguay & Cyrus Vance.

Idi Amin's 240.
Eric Heiden's 3.

Bucharest quake,
750 go.

Rabin & Carter.
PNP over JLP.
Teamsters
& United Farm Workers.
Bogotá's 100,000.
Hamaas Abdul Khaalis's 134.
Kamal Jumblatt goes.
Marien Ngouabi goes.

—accepted the verdict.
Judge S Lee Vavuris
& Sun Myung Moon's 5.

Pan Am, 2 KLM 747s
& Tenerife, 561 go.
Uranus. Sadat
& Carter. Shaba.

And Hailey never even raises
an arched brow which would destroy
precociously any doubt over what's so
attractive about her: ruthless mirth
ending the living's certainty.
—*Let'S Hopalong Cassidy,* Hailey quips,
and I'm immediately with it. Moving on.
Laying out far & hard, by
Snowy Egrets, **Toebiters** and **Minks**
strangely struck down and stinking.
Our Lincoln Cosmopolitan barrelling on
from some continental terrortory
thrust after what we only abandon,
clutching swips of cold among small thickets
of dying din, crying helplessly.
Even **Cows** collapse udderly
among strangled weeds allso thinned.

July 7 1950

Budge Patty. Draft.
Kum River Tanks.
Uruguay's World Cup.
—go fishing.
Oil & Mao's China.
Senator Millard Tydings.
—upon the State
Department are.
150,520,198.
US Army, Selective Service &
100,000. Marine Corps &
National Guard Troops Mobilized.
—If the Russkies come down,
we'll fight the.
—We are now.
Baudouin's Belgium.
62,000 Reserves.
Florence Chadwick's channel.
B-29, A-Bomb &
California trailer camp, 17 go.
Naktong River. Shirley May
France. Truman's railroads.
Pressman's 3. Formosa fleet.
North Korean front.
Hokkaido typhoon.
Emergency Economic Powers.
Pennsylvania troop train, 33 go.

April 9 1977

1,500 troops & Kinshasa.
Christopher Boyce.
—not yet overwhelmed US.
Spanking OK.
Bhutto's Islamabad.
7.5 million gallons of
North Sea oil.
Mengistu, Ethiopia &
US officials.

HEW's 35 million disabled.
Istanbul riot, 39 go.
Seabrook, Clamshell
Alliance & 1,400 arrests.
Global recession.
Seattle Slew's Derby.

—Dolores!
Helicopter, 43rd Street &
rotor blade, 5 go.
Likud Party.

*—When the President
does it*
Orient Express. Janet Guthrie.
Brabant blaze, 302 go.
South Moluccans &
161 hostages.
George Willig's rise.
Foyt's 500.
Humboldt Park riots, 2 go.
Blazers over 76ers.

I swim easily over, quickly
arresting his flailing drift with
a stern grip of his hair.
Wailings and chokes. Okey doke.
By fabulous kicks and stroke, I drag
him sputtering back to shallows.

—*Cum ung,* Sam blubbles,
unsure, unsteady, clamoring there
for my Leftwrist Amethyst Twist.
So pinche poor. Pathetic.
        But sweet allso.

We pass, while trudging back, Two Lovers
boosting amidst our paths.
Jerks, grunts and curses.
                Both of US snicker.

We stamp on by their
goofy coupling, and with little
much exciting, double
back to The River Landing.

May 19 1950

New Jersey Ammunition
barge blows, 20 go.
Brooklyn-Battery. 3 French
Companies, 4 Viet Minh
Battalions & Dong Khe.
New York's Czech Consulate.

—National day of mourning.
Johnny Parsons' 500.
Maurice Herzog's Annapurna I.
College segregation.
Bonn Foreign Policy.
William Remington quits.
Ben Hogan.
South Africa's Assembly.
Richard Laoler's kidney.
Northwest DC-4
& Lake Michigan, 58 go.
North Koreans over 38th.
Douglas MacArthur
& Far East Forces.
*—United States will
continue to uphold the law.*
Seoul falls.
—US is not at War.
Pyongyang's 33,000 US troops.
Suwon Road.

Away to Sloggerville.
Pull up for a town wendawhile.
Cool by a fountain. OooLopaDa.

Bickering Couples break to lob US
copper. Change enough to resume mamboing
around the corner. Solo Bikers killing
Presidents toss their shyness and roll off
tied. Even Vagrants leave savings before
fleeing alive. We save no one.

—*Hand it over,* a Pimp slams,
grabbing for Hailey's Leftwrist Amethyst Twist.
—*Beg your pardon?* Hailey fans.
—*O, fresh.*

Then foolishly, The Madam strikes.
Hailey heels him with a twirl.
She trembles. Stills. Until
all of him twists off.

June 6 1977

This time, hugging the side,
Sam retries wading against the flow.
Cautious. River only knee high.
Still ashamed by his slip:
—*You're so crit.*

Me just treading, swimming
effortlessly outside his slow limp.
Where there's a bend,
there's a change. Sam admiring
how I tear through the current.
I am the current. And currently bare.
The currency of every dare.
But I admire Sam too,
enjoying him there,
however timid, rising when
I stride from the fawning
ripples to take his hand
and him over chilly mire,
beneath burning skies.

Karachi, Lahore
& Hyderabad.
Helsinki accords.
Brushy Mountain Prison,
James Earl Ray
& 6 escape.

Seattle Slew's Triple.
Dutch Commandos free 55,
8 go. Johannesburg
Police HQ, 2 go.

Adolfo Suárez González.
Wernher von Braun goes.
Lynch's Fianna Fail.

Prudhoe Bay, Valdez
& 799 miles.

—*nice to be back.*

Coker vs Georgia.

Zia ul-Haq over Ali Bhutto.
Kent State Gym
& 194 arrests.

North Korea &
US helicopter, 3 go.
New York failure,
3,700 arrests.
Begin's West Bank. Box kite
& Santa Barbara fire.

Creys-Malville, 1 goes.

March 17 1950

Nice under iceblown skies, with allways the
time for warm smoochandroll shots,
behind Car Lots, Concession Stands,
Local Parks. Saloons.
Hailey, all fusion ball,
blasts on with a fury only
she can smile through so
creamily.
I barely keep up, though I'm hardly down.
Where there's a Wheel, there's a way.
And we're allways awaying.
Waving at folk, honking up tricky
desires for all we decline.
Hailey charms everytime
the sweep of lives we slip by.
And all Warden Men stock still
for even a hint of her again.

Californium.
Sungmen. Brussels & Eyskens.
Owen Lattimore. Rebels &
Macassar. Jawaharlal Nehru,
Ali Khan & Drumhead Justice.
Baltic Sea, Soviets &
US Navy Plane.
Supreme Court,
Contempt Convictions &
Political affiliations.
Harry Bridges' 5. Athens &
Nicholas Plastiras. Fatima's loss.
Toronto, Manhattan & Avro Turbo.
Habib Bourguiba.
Navajo & Hopi rehabilitation.
A heart massage.
Hainan evacuation. Jordan.
Trans World Airlines.
Frédéric Joliot-Curie. May Day
& West Berlin's 500,000.
Middleground's Derby.
Grand Coulee Dam.
American Bowling Congress.
Polish United
Workers' Party &
Purge. Istanbul &
President Celal Bayar.

Aug 3 1977

FALN's Manhattan blasts,
1 goes.
Cambodian troops &
Ta Phraya, 29 go.
Salisbury explosion,11 go.
Rio de Janeiro Death Squad.
—Well, you've got me.

Mojave & Enterprise.
Herbert Kappler.
Elvis goes.
Amnesty &
FRETELIN guerrillas.
Arktika's North Pole.
Marble Cone's 175,000 acres.
Mozambique massacre,
16 go. Bill 101 &
4,000 Eskimos.
Tong-sun Park.
Stockholm US Embassy,
Leopoldo Aragón goes.
Benigno Acquino goes.
Panama Canal &
Omar Torrijos Herrera.
—counter any threat.
Stephen Biko goes.
Courageous cups Australia.
Onassis & $20 million.
Peking, Hua Kuo-feng &
Pol Pot.

Memphis Rendezvous.
Reconcile all round abouts,
the Trans Am belching stalls
on Wagner and Beale Street.
I'm cashed too.
We conk by South Second.
Stretch and stroll.
Sam dumpster dives for bogue crusts
served up on trashcan lids, while I pluck
from behind clumps of **Carnations**
generously tucked away for just US,
cold milks, fresh flan and pie.
—*Great,* he gulps.
And I'm riled too.
—*A most sumptuous eats for two.*
—*You lost me.*
Sam suddenly downtrodden, beleaguered,
which gets me all eagers to cut out.
Road run it again.

Jan 21 1950

Paul Larsen & Civilian
Mobilization Office.
63-19. Hiss's 5.
NATO's 8 Western
Nations. Apartheid
& Johannesburg riots.
Iran shakes, 1,500 go.
*—against any possible
aggressor.*
Hainan to Port of Canton.
Soft-Coal Strike, 6 states
& 400,000.
Bao Dai & Ho.
Wheeling 205 & Joe McCarthy.
Joseph Stalin, Mao Tse-tung
& Mutual Defense Treaty.
Robert Vogeler.
US vs Rabinowitz.
General Elections & Labor.
Orient Express to Paris,
Eugene Karp goes.
Diner's Club. Klaus Fuchs' 14.
Saar mines. Coplon
& Gubitchev. Aja Vrzanova.
Sigginston & Avro Tudor,
80 go.

only we can easily escape. Because we're
unpunishable. Pinky's out of jail.
Hailey staying pippy & loose,
my Sophie & Scooch.
Yeah, she still gets me off.
—*You too,* she clevers.
—*Anytime soon.*
And we go forever.
Air damp with our struggle.
Jaguars starve. Purr. Die.
Not US. We feast on troubles and sip
up sorrows. It vibrates her. It spasms me.
Elated, still rolling, and all tromped up.
Our Crosley Hotshot snorting
out chilly clouds which drift off to exile.
Only there is no exile anymore.
There's only US.

Oct 8 1977

Guernica & Basques,
Augusto Unceta-
Barrenechea goes.
Ibrahim al-Hamadi goes.
—Struggle Against World
Imperialism.
Yankees over Dodgers.
Mogadishu, West German
Commandos & Lufthansa,
4 go. Hans-Martin Schleyer.
—vulture spewing.
Ecuador's sugar strikes,
220 go.
Steve Cauthen's ride.
South Africa & US sanctions.
$2.65. Edward Koch.
Beirut & Israeli jets, 60 go.
Seneca Falls to
Houston & First National
Women's Conference.
Madeira's TAP 727, 124 go.
—Peace with justice.
Cyclone Andhra Pradesh,
20,000 go.
Blowering Dam Lake's
300 knots.
—we welcome you
among US with all
security and safety.

Loaded for speed. Past wallowing
Tractors and Migrant Sorrow.
Flying Saucers and Gymnasts.
Only now the California Cruiser can't
cope. Gears shred, suspension bends,
antifreeze spills. My Sam ever
carked. Me too. And to top
it off we're low on fuel.
Fuel?
The Pinto Wagon gasps on
by Roller Discos and mopeds. Generics
and Bottled Water for sale.
Gasoline diminishing.
At least there's a station but
Pump Zot only takes wad.
I offer the spare. Owner Plug shrugs
fair. Splinks the tank,
wants me for a drink.
Not even scared.

Nov 13 1949

Cambodia liberty.
Nathuram Godse goes.
Flying Cloud. B-29s down.
Pathans & Pushtunistan.
David Lilienthal out.
Angus Ward.
Iron & Steel Act.
Bojangles goes.
Democratic Republic. Army over
Navy. American Airlines
explosion, 28 go.
Parnell Thomas.
150,000 French to Chinese-
Vietnamese border.
Traicho Kostov.
Eagles over Rams.
Tel Aviv to Jerusalem.
Craigie's saucers.
Hungary's nationalization.
East Berlin's 125,000 to West.
$7,990 & Levittown.
Ohio over California. Egypt,
Nahhas Pashas & Wadf Party.
London's Communist China.
Jacob Malik over Tsiang.
Acheson, US consuls & China.
Boston, Brinks & $2.7 million.

on sacrificing
felonious
Gas Station Man, stiffed by our approach.
Unsafe for all he's stashed and stayed.
Withering, calcifying. Splayed.
Because everyone we blow by, we blow away.
Never spent, we never laze
by barbed wire and bones,
Hitchhikers, Violators and Harps.
Our Morris Minor
trooping East by Chain Gangs crushing stone,
Tar Sloopers, Concrete Stirrers. One Guy
perched on a harvester lifts his arm. Wants
to come. Holds onto US long after we're gone.
Our Studebaker Commander.
Hubs hugging the curves of our float
by landscapes drenched with guilt

Dec 2 1977

Bulgarian jet, 159 go.
Marthinus Prins & South African Police.
10,000 boat people.
Jean-Bédel Bokassa & Party.
Malayasian airliner & Strait of Johore, 100 go.
Tractors, trucks & Washington DC.
—*No Dough, No Sow, No Grow.*
Benito Juárez University.
OECD & Youth Unemployment.
10,000 political prisoners.
Caracas, OPEC & $12.70.
West African famine.
Airliner over Arabian Sea, 213 go. Speer's Youngstown.
—*Peace, justice, freedom.*
Said Hammami goes.
Dayton High School sports.
Chamorro goes.
Super Bowl XII, Cowboys over Broncos.
Boston blizzard.
USSR's Cosmos 954.
Franklin Jacobs' jump.

Getting on, a tire blows,
the VW Rabbit, barely full, no longer
barrelling, too soon slowing,
gushing air defeatedly.
Without an extra fix I circle
our newly nixed trip pleasantly.
Even if I'm dour too!
Expelling grooves!
And worse, stock still, understanding
at last the peril pursuing US,
fast against our trip, a reversing
at hand gathering to control, hold
and disband US.
Here then my choke of feer:
I am no longer strong enough
to defy such greed.
Revenge against whimsy.
To deny and plunder US
and bind me.

Sept 23 1949

—*an atomic explosion.*
Radioactive food. Yugoslavia & USSR. Chairman of People's Republic of China.
277, 264 flights.
—*of equality, mutual.*
Pittsburgh Steel's 500,000.
Formosa. Sherman Minton.
$5.8 billion for NATO Allies.
Yankees over Dodgers.
Eugenie Anderson.
East Germany, Wilhelm Pieck & Otto Grotewohl. Amoy.
Guatemala flood, 4,000 go.
10 out of 11 to 5 years.
Ambassador George Allen.
General Assembly.
40¢ to 74¢
Cyclone, 1,000 go.
DC-4 & P-38, 55 go.
Hague's Round Table.
Philip Murray, United Electrical Workers & Farm Equipment Workers.
GM Dividend. Rokossovsky.
Antonio Salazar's Party.

edge, continually unwinding, uniting.
Every around retreating before
our freedom. Even the Vindictive & Greedy.
Because we're quirky. We are the feer
every Wanderer longs to skip loose of.
Touch US & miss US,
find US & wail.
Any confidence allready failing before US.
Hailey cool now, her fingers on the air.
Every dip endangering journeys,
meadows whimpering, every turn frailing
by her horrible presence.
Far out! Ooozat!
Our tires spinning for the tarmac,
tubes untested, compression unmessed with,
barrelling ahead. Hailey, such a gas,
with our Pontiac Chieftain, bent

Jan 31 1978

Robert Bergland,
American agriculture
& hog cholera.
Marci Klein.
Muriel Humphrey.
Canada's 11 Soviet
Diplomats.
Somalia & Ethiopia.
Spinks 15 rounds Ali.
China, Japan
& $20 billion Trade Pact.
Reggie! Bar. Larnaca Airport
& Cypriot troops, 15 go.
1,000 dolphins.
Sinai expansion.
US Capitol blast.
Vladimir Remek's orbit.
Nuclear Non-
Proliferation Act.
Al Fatah guerrillas & a bus,
30 go. 22,000 troops,
Lebanon's PLO bases.
Rome Radicals.
Brittany, Amoco Cádiz
& 1.6 million gallons.
Karl Wallenda goes.
Dancing clouds.
UMW's 109 days.
Doğan Öz goes.
Farm Aid.

Still, though mired, hungry,
low on gas, I truck over
to The River Marsh
to catch up with bareheaded Sam,
kiss his sweet mouth and wandering
together wonder
of a way to continue our charge from
the persistence of the World.
His slim hands. Scrubby knees.
Still exquisitely free.
Wanting all he may allways have of me.
—*Let'S skip stones,*
I simple.
And we do.
Finding thin, slick earth wings,
which by shoulder and hip,
elbow and wrist, releasing any grip,
I skid skimming flat flips
across the waters east

July 21 1949

82-13.
Fausto Coppi's Tour.
Tibet & Chinese Nationalist
Consul. Fist fights &
French Assembly.
De Havilland Comet.
Ernst Reuter.
Shanghai Consulate siege.
Ecuadorian quake &
Pelileo, 4,600 go.
Everest's Bell X-1 &
63,000 ft.
Truman's Department of Defense.
Chiefs of Staff. Strasbourg &
Paul-Henri Spaak.
Husni Zayim &
Mohsen el-Barazi go.
Margaret Mitchell goes.
Thomas Clark. 3 Armored
Divisions & Yugoslavia.
USSR's A-Bomb. US, Tito &
Soviet blockade. Lithium.
Theodor Heuss &
Konrad Adenauer.
László Rajk.
Noronic & Ontario Pier, 207 go.
Gary Davis & Objector Status.

starred by dirt.
Stones suddenly flick towards US. Miss.
Routes overtake roads overtaking slowpokes.
And when the gentle get out
of our way, we sigh. And when
the angry run US off, we smile.
Because we're irreversible, impossible to
sideswipe. Impossible to double. Even engage.
Hailey allways the ongoing fun. With
sweet hands. And dimpled knees.
—*Why did the skeleton cross the road?*
—*Why?*
—*Duh, she's a chicken.*
Hailey peals, and a dozen stops greed our
happening temptings. Speed. Frightening
everything beyond the edges of our travels.
We are without

March 30 1978

Ezer Weizman.
Otto Passman.
European Trade Union
Confederation & 15 million.
Neutron Bomb.
Arkady Shevchenko defects.
63.5 million shares.

—Give Carter to Panama.
Senate ratifies.
McDaniel vs Paty.
Soviets & Korean 707, 2 go.
Alfa Romeo firebombs.
Tarapur Uranium.
West Virginia collapse, 51 go.
Taraki's Afghanistan,
Mohammad
Daud Khan goes.
John Singlaub retires.
Naomi Uemura,
54 days & a sled.
Sunao Sonoda, Nobuhiko
Ushiba & Takeo Fukuda.
Affirmed's Derby.
Aldo Moro goes.
Yuri Orlov's 7 years.
Italian abortion.
Katangans. Caroline of
Monaco & Philippe Junot.
Unser's 500.

to Asheville, south to New Orleans,
even skipping horizons north, for
permanently icebound coasts.
Umpteen hops, minute dribbles,
soaring scores of arcs tripling
on and on, up, down and across
this ever aching river flow.
I am the flow.
And all the bounces too.
Sam of course allso throws his
weight around, hurling blocks of
rock tumbling out and down, only
once, with just a thick kerplunk.
No hops.
Hardly surprising.
But on and on he struts over such
ridiculous splashes, guttering proudly:
—Chattanooga! Baton Rouge! Anchorage!
A confounding one.

May 14 1949

Gerhard Eisler & Batory.
Dublin & Belfast.
Berlin rail riots.
—prospect of the yawning.
James Forrestal goes. Bonn
& Federal Republic of Germany.
Tornadoes, 46 go.
Soochow Creek surrender.
Bolivia & Tin Strike riots,
150 go.
Holland's 500.
Britain, Argentina
& 5 Year Trade Treaty.
Hashemite. Cochin China.
Frederic March
& Edward G Robinson.
Karen Kayemeth L'Israel.
Josef Beran.
LaMotta KOs Cerdan.
Sixth Session.
Charles 15 rounds Walcott.
Wolf vs Colorado.
Judith Coplon.
Linus Pauling's sickle.
Drobny & Cernik defect.
Supreme War Council.
Israel, Syria & Armistice.

We let go and lunge on.
Bridge to ridge, herm across berm,
up this Great River Road winding US
for still colder turns.
We overtake tricycles, wagons, trailers
loaded with ballot boxes, bearings, barrels of
tack, strapped down sloop mast.
Asphalt bits bouncing off our wheels.
We pass fires. KKK rallies. Car chases.
Drunks, Bandits and Thieves.
Even when traffic hitches for Stunted Kids,
washing windshields and chrome,
hunted by the Wanted Alive,
we zip by.
Because we are mobile.
Heedless of all we are.
And sure never struck, never

June 5 1978

China's 110,000.

Howard Jarvis, Paul Gann
& Proposition 13.
Bullets over Supersonics.

—is the joy about?

Spencer W Kimball's
allowance.

Affirmed's Triple.
Nancy Lopez. Hussein
& Elizabeth Halaby.
TVA vs Hill & Tellico Dam.
Bulgaria & Till Meyer.
Turin's trial & 29.
Ahmed Hussein
al-Ghashmi goes.
South Yemeni's Aden,
Salem Rubaya Ali goes.
Versailles
& Breton Separatists.
Allan Bakke. NRC.
Beirut, 22 go.
Alessandro Pertini.
Marquette's 2,000 Nazis.
Spanish gas & campground,
200 go. Anatoly
Shcharansky, Aleksandr
Ginzburg & Viktoras Petkus.
Khartoum's 30 Nations.
Omar Bongo's 10,000.

Additionally pippeting: —*Excellent!*
But here's a surprise: midhuck for
another mudmucky thursplunk I
actually applaud vigorously his aplomb.
My palms repeatedly meeting.
Curious.

We continue on our travels, slipping
rods for catalytic meltdowns, misfires
coughing US along on shreddling tires.
Rippp, prahp, hissssssh. Three more flats.
Even with my Leftwrist Platinumy Twist.
Past Carbondale and onto Waterloo.

—*I'm happy with you,* I abruptly
shout. *Soooo happy.*

And he's so sweet then. And quiet.
Surprised obviously by me. Blushing
until he just pats my knee,
the Dodge Omni
grunting bitterly onward,

March 18 1949

North Atlantic Treaty
Organization.
—of Peace & Security.
Earl Browder's 11 Communists.
Louis Johnson over
James Forrestal.
Rebels attack Thrace.
Newfoundland's 10th Province.

—liberty and the rule of law.
12 Nations & Defense Alliance.
West Germany.
South Korea's 30th Veto.
3 Mao Armies. Snead by 3.
61.8 seconds.
Ginza's Western Ways.
John Costello.
Russian Cortisone.
Shanghai surrounded.
Huk Liberation Army &
Manila, Aurora Quezon goes.
Durocher. Loyalty Day Parade.
Argentinian nationalization.
62,000 Ford workers.
Ponder's Derby. West German
Assembly's 53-12.
Frank Hague. UN's 37-12.
Berlin Blockade over.

Zoooming effortlessly on. Fugacious.
Our Cadillac Series 62 whips
rudely throughout every imprudence.

Outracing trucks, the awestruck,
leaving behind US diasporas of rust.
Hailey: —*Fly baby. Let'S never stop.*

By Palmyra. Fenway. Alexandria. Keokuk.
Hailey's Leftwrist Platinumy Twist spooling.
Cattle Farms and fallow fields tilled cool
by moons, where Stout Fellows
slick after meals, flossing with twigs,
wave US on
to cold Nauvoo.

River sliding ever back. We go with the
flow. Our own flow. Onward. Curious
pebbles ricocheting our tail and exhaust. While
Riverwheels low with raisins let go.

July 31 1978

Pete Rose & 44 games.

Love Canal. Philadelphia & MOVE, 1 goes. Julian Bond.

100 tons of marijuana. Christina Onassis & Sergei Kausov. Ben Abruzzo, Max Anderson,

Larry Newman & Double Eagle's Atlantic.

Abadan blaze, 430 go.

Managua's palace, 25 Sandinistas & 2,000 hostages.

Albino Luciani over Giovanni Battista Montini.

Pan Am & National Airlines.

Martial law & Iranian riots, 2,800 go.

California busing.

Ali 15 rounds Spinks.

Iran's shake, 25,000 go.

Camp David, Dogwood & Birch.

Pacific Southwest Airliner over San Diego, 135 go.

Pieter Botha.

collapsing shocks turning to chunks,
rackandpinion seizing, pulling US left,
brakes softening with each pump.
The spavined Plymouth Horizon gasping.

—*Guess.*

—*No.*

Over the hill for any offramp where we
might laze, play and leisurely, perhaps,
participate.
There's the most important wage.
To experience this need and wait.
And even if Sam's allways for the break
loose and accelerate, he too needs
to take five.

Sam. All saggy snoop now, pallid cheek,
weary and teen. But still somehow
his Green Eyes with flecks of Gold
keep smiling tenderly
for me.

Jan 20 1949

4 Points.

—*help the free peoples of the World.*
Dean Acheson.
Peking. Trygve Lie.
Poland's 200 arrested.
David Ben-Gurion.

San Diego, Santa Barbara & Palm Springs: Snow.
Budapest's People's Republic.
Gallagher around.
Tudeh Party. Nizam.
Schleeh, XB-47 & 607.2 MPH.
Hassan el-Banna goes.
—*State of distress.*

Soviet labor camps. Gatow Airfield's one millionth ton.
Fritz Kuhn free.

Anna Louise Strong.
Israel, Egypt & Rhodes.
WAC-Corporal's 5,000 MPH.

10:31 AM, James Gallagher & Lucky Lady II.
Andrei Vishinsky. FBI & 3 spies.
Marti & 3 sailors. Chester Opal.

Ditch it.
Aside. And Hailey agrees,
Gold Eyes with flecks of Green,
cheeks brassy, nose sassy. Oogley. She
downgrades the late. Earbangs the dozey.
All allone, an exchange of arrivals for passage
on a shockingwave of laughter. Hers.
Floating over riprap, pit and rut,
by Grafton, Gilead and Hannibal,
until Lover's Leap slows US for a roadside
Fair Of Summer's Best where Hailey wins a
swimsuit contest. Cash prize. Boodling me:

—*Guess.*

—*Yes.*

Our Buick Roadmaster never finer.
Humming from axle to alternator. Cool
and powerful. Ventilated. We never alter.

Sept 30 1978

Tuvalu liberty.
Syria & Hafez al-Assad.
—Iranian political problem is possible without.
Hannah Gray.
Nancy Spungen goes.
John Simon Richie arrested.
Karol Wojtyla.
Yankees over Dodgers.
Anatoly Karpov over Viktor Korchnoi.
—competition is the most powerful.

40,000 Iranian oil workers strike.
Kovalenok, Ivanchenkov & 140 days.
Julius Nyerere's Tanzania.

Iranian troops.

Hai Hong's 2,517.
Sri Lanka crash, 183 go.
Guyana's Port Kaituma Airport, Don Harris, Robert Brown, Gregory Robinson, Patricia Parks & Leo Ryan go.
Jonestown 900 go.
James Warren Jones goes.
—time has come to meet.

He nods then. And I nod. Slowly.
—We can't go on.
I sigh. He sighs. Slowly
taking an exit for a smooth loop,
clattering hubcaps free, swerving US
by Concrete Curbs, Chop Shops and
Shut Schools. Through Desolate Parks.
Everyone sells the Dream but I live it.
Pin Oak bowing defeatedly.
Sam headturns our where's:
—But how can we stay?
—Unload the car.
—O.
—And get a job.
—Until when? For how long?
Promises threaten departure,
except Sam holds all three
just by reaching over and
cradling my hand carefully.

Nov 22 1948

Yale's Levi Jackson.
UN & Democratic Republic of Vietnam. Caracas & Venezuelan Army. Dublin Dáil.
Army & Navy: 21-21.
Untouchables. Berlin divided.
San Remo & Mount Grammos.
Palestine's Abdullah of Transjordan.
Mary Agnes Hallaren.
Whittaker Chambers, Pumpkins & tiny rolls.
UN's Seoul. Eleanor's 48-0.
Hiss. French reactor.
Bears over Eagles. Jakarta & Dutch Airborne. Tokyo 7 & Crimes Against Peace.
—Banzai!
Madiun. Mindszenty. Antrycide.
—Buy em by the.
Alfred & Clara Kinsey.
Kashmir cease-fire.
Northwestern over University of California.
—Bread, Land & Liberty.
Sam Rayburn. Durban.
Tientsin.

A way we go.
Heading for all we pass and
refuse to slow up for.
On our own. Top up, fastering
flattered fifths and grins.
We're big engines without brakes.
Passing the bashless beebopping from town.
Catch our blur. We allways whirr.
By mud mounds. Lazy graves.
Ploughs, tractors. Sweat smoothed rakes.
A lone **Moose** rotting.
Everyone wants the Dream but we give it.
Two lanes. Four lanes.
Only one way about it.
Hailey & me with next to nothing atoll,
outracing every offramp & turn.
Throttle & roll. Such gall.

Nov 22 1978
Kuala Trengganu &
Vietnamese refugees,
200 go. Great Britain's
Cledwyn Hughes.
Sri Lanka hurricane, 150 go.
George Moscone &
Harvey Milk go.
Griffin Bell's 21,875.
James Clark's marijuana.
Navy over Army.
Charles Dederich.
USSR & Afghanistan.
Golda Meir goes.
John Adamson's 49 years.
Norway's EMS.
Tehran millions.
Dennis Kucinich &
City Council.
Cleveland defaults.
John Rideout's Greta.
Houari Boumedienne goes.
John Wayne Gacy's 21.
Woody Hayes fired.
Meshed, Lar &
Khurramabad.
Energy and Justice
Department vs 9 oil
companies. Guadeloupe.
Shahpur Bakhtiar.
Vietnamese troops &
Phnom Penh.

Around here's The Slo
Drag. But that's The Big
City. London, Cairo,
Berlin, Kiev. Baghdad,
Dublin, Tokyo.
Here's to St. Louis!

Way of it. Way by it. All. And
unowned. Mercury Zephyr sold
for the cost of keeping still. Loans.
Sam handling the mopandbuff patrol.
Cleans up after Dregs, while I keep with
howdydo smiles for shallying customers,
Full Hanks to Himmers passing
through for a seat, passing up tips,
passing on favors. All just passing.
—*Spare a moment?* Sam sneaks me.
—*Sure Babe.*
—*Come here.*
Soft kisses my cheek

Sept 22 1948
UnAmerican HUAC.
Mao's Tsinan.
—*We are going to win.*
Cadillacs & P-38s.
Cleveland over Boston.
US, Spain & UN.
KLM airliner &
Tarbolton, 34 go.
Israel's Beersheeba.
Zhengzhou. Baotou.
—*War which*
is getting warmer.
Sukarno & Communist Party.
—*large enough, free enough,*
strong enough to.
Manchuria, 12 Nationalist
Army Divisions & Hulutao.
Strom Thurmond
& Fielding L Wright.
Truman over Dewey. Maine's
Margaret Chase Smith.
Kansas repeals Prohibition.
Egyptians from Negev.
VD. Hudson River Day over.
Communist forces, Tientsin-
Pukow rail & Nanking.
—*first citizen of the World.*

I kiss her cheek:
—*Now what?*
—*Who cares.*
—*But where? How?*
Passing pedestrian blurrings,
goings out of business,
rushing around US, until somehow
we're found by an anxious EXECUTOR who
on behalf of the Round Table Regulars,
now dead & buried, hands over to US
at their bequest all we own.
Paid. Gassed up. Ready to roll.
Our new Tucker Torpedo on the ball, all
revysetjet to go from St. Louis. Tokyo,
Dublin. Baghdad, Kiev. Berlin, Cairo.
London. Every city. Paired. Air brisker.
Wishes riskier. Chasing US to our ages.

Jan 13 1979

—vacation.
Council of the Islamic
Revolution. National
Advisory Committee
on Women & Bella Abzug.
Hong Kong's 3,383.
Bangui riots & Zaire soldiers.
Super Bowl XIII,
Steelers over Cowboys.
Abu Hassan goes.
Nelson Rockefeller goes.

Carter & Patty Hearst.
Liu Shaoqi.
Giulio Andreotti.
Ayatollah Ruhollah Khomeini.

—your hands.
Beth Heiden's skate.
Joachim Yhombi-Opango.
Adolph Dubs goes.
Chad & Felix Malloum.
William Sullivan
& US Embassy.
—attacked from 3.
4 Iranian Generals go.
North Yemen
& South Yemen.
—can kiss my ass.
China's 480 mile front.
—brazen bandit attack.

before returning to his soap
returning me to my post. The Lope About.
All at The St. Louis Falafel Stand.
Grub, Dunk, Kick Back.
Run remotely by owner BILL BAZETTI
handling this smorgasbord,
deliveries to cash. A financial man.
Hardly around but thanks
to him we're currently employed.
Won over by my smooth &
girly flirts, if reluctant about Sam,
hires US for a hitch.
—*Couple of dumb kids,* he snips.
VIAZOZOPOLIS though's the problem.
Our swaggering manager
muckingup shifts. Working
tables & chicks.
Thick swinging dick
tormenting every Geek

Aug 7 1948

Yangtze floods,
3 million wandering.
Soviet Consulate &
Kasenkina's defection.
Republic of South Korea.
Alice Coachman. Emil Zatopek.

Ceylon's 27th Veto.
Spy mania.
Israeli Army, Egyptian drive &
No Man's Land.
Robert Schuman.
Federal Reserve.
North China People's
Government. Parliamentary
Council & Konrad Adenauer.
Polish Workers' Party &
Moscow, Gomulka out.
Amsterdam's Juliana.
Berlin, Russian & Assembly
coup. Kim Il Sung &
Democratic People's Republic
of Korea. Mildred Elizabeth
Gillars & Axis Sally.
Hyderabad troops. Folke
Bernadotte & André Sérot go.
Berlin landings, fog &
windy runways.

And with that,
turns his back.
Clams the tableless
with offers of chairs. Free pastry scraps.
Even helps out doubly
confused VIAZOZOPOLIS:
—Just a couple of stupid kids.
And the gig's over. Dumped.
Hailey hardly stalls. And with
smoothy floss even readies me to cut loose.
Tossing out:
—We go to free the World.
But BAZETTI BILL tries for the last stab:
—You go to lose the World. You allways do.
—No, we go to free you.
And we do. Shuffling off from
The St. Louis Drive Thru drudgery.

March 4 1979

—Freine! Freine!

Jupiter's rings.

—of freedom there is.
NRC's 5.
20 tons of hashish.
Richard Sykes goes.

—Peace has come.
—on a long and
difficult road.
Carter, Begin & Sadat.
Baghdad's Arab League.
Idi Amin & Kampala.
Harrisburg, radioactive gas
& Three Mile Island.
Richard Thornburgh
& a 5 mile evacuation.

Begin & Egypt.
Ali Bhutto goes.
Pakistan's US aid.
Amir Abbas Hoveida goes.
Yusuf Lule.
Fuzzy Zoeller.
Bill Rodgers & 2:09:27.

Chris Evert & John Lloyd.
Sadat's victory.
Rhodesia's Abel Muzorewa.

9 Babcock &
Wilcox reactors.

and Sam with thankless tasks and
staggering fronts. Rolls of clout assuring
US he's better off without much. Because
Bill Baazetti allows him too much
freedom, Viazizopolis tortures Sam
with duties. So eager to can him,
littering the floor with ash, shattered
ceramic, any loaded tray.

—Sweep it up, Punk.

And Sam does, terrified of Viazazopolis.
Okaying the Buzz Crusher with a
flurry of frantic waves. Bucket
and sponge, cold suds, dishrag
and broom.
But I cherish Sam
so much I smile
and he awshucks me
with a shrug.
Here,

June 18 1948

Reich to Deutsch.
Berlin Blockade.
—technical difficulties.
Selective Service Act.
Peacetime Draft.
Louis 11 rounds
Jersey Joe Walcott.
2,500 tons of food.
Operation Vittle underway.
Prague's Cominform & Tito.
Japanese quake, Fukui falls.

Citation's Triple.
—the greatest I've.
Tito & Stalin. National Health
Service Act. Satchel Paige.
Egypt by air. Iraq by land.
Togliatti goes.
Senator Barkley. William Z
Foster & Benjamin Davis.
Progressive Party.
—equality of treatment
and opportunity.
Ludwigshafen's Farben blast,
250 goes. France's German
zone. Whittaker Chambers
& Alger Hiss. Árpád Szakasits.
Mathias's decathlon.

—There!
The Crowd suddenly parts. And I'm
awed by the bruised & splitlip
scowl still clawing after me.
Plaster bound with splint & sling, yet
vehemently too swinging a mop,
ready to drag, knock cold, expunge
me from anyone's hours, when
by some menace Hailey manages,
Viazazopolis suddenly stops, quails, slumps:

—Please don't leave US.

Betrayed by the way his life ebbs.
Slows. Divorces. Lets US go.
Continuously. Hailey brutalizing
Viazizopolis with her freedom's allowance.
Even if Baazetti Bill steps forth, raging:

—You laughed at US. You're dead to US.

where while he scrubs, I meet the rush.
Seating the crowd with a Cazh Yo and
soft touch. Missing Sam, though he's so
close among these Regular Fluffs doling
props, escorting
their Gallant Nellys.
Whacked that I allone
can roll him.

Now. Here.

Until work's over, jigging free.
Only then do I relax, traffic's honkscreech
zipping on wide, **Bald Cypress** swaying
nearby. St. Louis Eatery renewed. Despite
smog, Amusement Parks and August.
Until at last we crash. One simple bed,
bath and Limit Fan.

—Sped! *—Whipped!*
—Wrecked!

Rubbing our necks.

May 3 1979

Margaret Thatcher.
—is ultimately what life is.
Elisabeth von Dyck goes.
Spectacular Bid's Derby.
DC, Nuclear Power
& 65,000.

Popular Revolutionary Bloc
& El Salvadoran army, 23 go.
Poor little rich girl goes.
Tiberias blast, 2 go.
Oklahoma Federal Jury,
Kerr-McGee Corporation
& $10.5 million.

Canada's Progressive
Conservative Party.
Carlos Antonio Herrera
Rebollo goes.
Bert Lance.
Chicago DC-10, 272 go.
Koboko.
Shoreham nuclear plant,
15,000 & 600 arrests.
MX missiles.
Le Mans race.
30%.
Marion Morrison goes.
Bryan Allen over Channel.
Malaysia's 70,000.
Evelyn Ashford's 100 meters.

APRONS rubbernecking the mayhem:

—Desperate! *—Stark!* *—Marvelous!*

If I'm around the block, corner cutting,
by shops selling Fans, Baths, Mattresses too.
September's rattling MerryGoRounds.
To the front of The St. Louis Diner where
nearby Okapis lie hacked.
Zipping by the boom & honk of traffic,
finding Hailey gone. Allready quit.
Here Now
lost among the turmoil of arriving
Fire Engines, sirens blaring.
And Bobbysoxers, Hep Cats &
Jive Bombers do a sidewalk mill.
Until behind, I turn to find
turning to find me, Hailey, heel high,
allready hugging me. Tightly.

May 1 1948

Greece & OPLA,
Christos Ladas goes.
Citation's Derby.
Truman, US Army & railroads.
United Nations Temporary
Commission. Israel & US.
Egypt bombs Tel Aviv.
Chaim Weizmann &
5 Advancing Arab Nations.
Greek Communists, 213 go.
Mundt-Nixon Bill.
UN's Folke Bernadotte.
Nationalist Party &
Jan Christiaan Smuts.
Columbia River's Vanport City.
Seoul's Syngman Rhee.

Egypt, Syria & Lebanon attack.
Rose's 500.
Anchorage & Fairbanks
airports. Mount Palomar.
Ha Long Bay Accords &
Bao Dai.
—Disgusted.
—I will work.
Yeager's Bell XS-1.
Western Hemispheric Defense
Pacts. Tripoli Riot Emergency.

June 18 1979

Carter, Brezhnev &
2,250 missiles. SALT II.
Bill Stewart goes.
Bernard Rogers &
Edward Meyer.
Supreme Court &
Affirmative Action.
Supersonics over Bullets.
8-1.
Bonn, War crimes &
Statute of Limitations.
Chadli Benjedid &
Ahmed Ben Bella.
Khomeini's amnesty.
Skylab falls.
Carmine Galante goes.
—*Crisis of confidence.*
Cabinet & Senior Staff.
Sebastian Coe's 3:49:0.
Somoza overthrown.
María de Lurdes Pintassilgo.
Federal Reserve Board &
Paul Volcker. Sinai & Egypt.
Atlanta woods, 2 go.
Madrid blasts, 5 go.
Chrysler's $207 million loss.
Cambodia's starving.
Selma, Montgomery & klan.

Too thrashed for more. Just the
tender cuddles he adores. Pretty def.
Beat by THE KITCHEN STAFF chucking bread
at him every time he passes their posts.
Stopped.
Dropped. Beat too by VIATOTOPOLIS
allways prodding me to give him cone.
I roll clean of anything that
lecherous grope tricks on,
fullout busy to stick
my swirling blur, wring me still.
Though I wayfresh slipduck such
attempts, each shift spinning free
from his Leer & Grabs.
Sliding easily past,
by stride, ballchange
to a glide
resuming my together time
with Sam.

March 6 1948

Ruhr.
Dodecanese Aegean Islands.
McCollum vs Board
of Education.
—*left free from the.*
Sidewalk smash, Jan Masaryk
goes. Leib Jaffe goes.
—*O we could not start a*
War over that.
Italy, Yugoslavia & Trieste.
Farouk & Aswan Dam.
$6.2 billion foreign aid.
Soviet Union,
Western Trains & Berlin.
US flies supplies.
Foreign Assistance Act.
European Relief Program
& Paul Hoffman.
SAS. Bogotá mobs
& machetes. Mazandaran
Martial Law. 100 Soviet tanks.
European Organization for
Economic Cooperation.
94% for Democracy.
US & Britain begin airlift.
Organization of
American States.

Hailey, our
time together threatened,
allso pursues. Ballchange, tumble, for
Commis & Meez, stumbling just past his
Spearings & Bash, leaping for a careening
pie cart on which I slipduck more of his
attempts to wring my neck.
And leave me bent.
Assortments of dishes now lofting by.
Exploding around me. Glasses too.
I roll on through the Kitchen
just missing flying ropes of salty dough.
VIATOTOPOLIS doesn't. Spangled. Tangled.
Wrangled, near the soufflé
station, by unleaven bread hucked by
still surprised & chuckling SWING COOKS.
Who all laugh: —*Haaaaaaaaaaaargh.*

Stretching out for
lazy hustles. A prick is just a prick
until it's jizzum. Squishy tugs
jerking tight grips until his groans
drip over US for US
from stirring lives we won't abide by.

Viatitopolis can't abide our attraction,
turns on me, knocks over a stool,
but The St. Louis Greasy Spoon
still relishes our wonder.

I go on, seating guests.
And Sam, despite
his Leftwrist Silver Twist,
rakes up another broken dish.
Sloshes out more bubbles of foam.
Around tables. Scrubbing floors.
Which Viaroropolis,
with sludgy kicks,
muds up.

Aug 11 1979

Morvi & Gujerat Dam,
thousands go.
Jason Epp & 11 tribes.
Homosexual immigration.
Beirut-Tyre highway &
Israeli Commandos, 8 go.
UN & PLO,
Andrew Young quits.

—Pol Pot can never
come back.

Diana Nyad's 60 miles.
Brink's truck & $2 million.
Puerto Rico & Bobby
Knight's 6 months.

Hamilton Jordan
& Studio 54.
IRA & a fishing boat,
Mountbatten goes.

Cuba's 2,000 Soviet troops.

The Norway.
Hurricane David, 400 go.
Jean Seberg goes.
Hurricane Frederic
& Mobile.
Taraki goes,
Hafizullah Amin takes over.

938.
Department of Education.

Terror answers. So I, with downhop
trips from the now rampaging
Viaroropolis, bolt slopslippityquick across
the floor, onto tables, pounding
goblets of bubbly and petit fours,
shattering plates not even my
Leftwrist Silver Twist could afford.
Diners stand back. I run faster. Hollering.
No wonder
The St. Louis Juke Joint evacuates.
Chairs knocked over. All while, not
accepatating my dash, Viatitopolis
plows after me, spreading an angry
wake of dingdong disaster.
Howling mad. Hurling whatever he grabs:
mugs, saucers, flatware and bowls, until with
clenching fists he allmost squeegees me.

Jan 12 1948

Ada Lois Sipuel Fisher vs
Board of Regents of
University of Oklahoma.

—campaign to wipeout.
Haifa, 82 go.
Gandhi's fast over.
Rhône Dam. USSR, UN &
North Korean elections.
Iraq riots & Saleh Jabr.

Garden walk &
Nathuran Vinayak Godse.
—Bapu is no more.

Ben Yehuda blast, 33 go.
—to secure.

Korean Communists strike.
Button gold. Khaksars &
League National Guard.
Fianna Fail loses.
4,000 Jeffersonian Democrats.
Rana. Prague & Gottwald.
Cairo-Haifa train &
British soldiers, 30 go.
—those who till it.
Vandenberg.
Saigon-Dalat Convoy, 150 go.

Oct 4 1979
Jesse Jackson & Yasir Arafat.
13.3%.
Typhoon Tip.
—there will be no Peace.
384 lbs of cocaine.
Bert Lance.
1,800 Marines
to Guantánamo Bay.
Pirates over Orioles.
Boston violence.
Prague 6.
Seoul & Kim Jae Kyu,
Park Chung Hee &
Cha Chi Chol go.
• South Africa's bang.
Mexico City's DC-10, 74 go.
North Carolina Rally & KKK,
5 go.
—overrun our embassy
and take our.
Iran, 500 students &
90 hostages.
Mehdi Bazargan quits.
Ontario, toxic gas &
derailed train.
Iranian assets.
Islamabad's US Embassy.
Thomas MacMahon.

—Clean it up fast jerkle while
I get to squaring your Betty Girl's circle.
Nice rack, sloppy ass.
Sam chatters calamities:
—Whatever gets you off.
Hardly hampering VIARIROPOLIS's approach
through the crush of
The St. Louis Mess. Set to molest
me with flattery.
Sam but grinning over
all Dull Loaf doles me: *—Slink, if you give,*
it gives back.
I'm hardly amused:
—Too limp, Twink.
I laugh only at Sam's antics behind.
Nose thumbing jacks, flipping off
VIARAROPOLIS before mooning him too.
Then: *—Cut the chatter!*
BILL BAIZETTI abruptly slaps,

Nov 29 1947
Arab & Jewish State.
Premier Schuman
& anti-strike law.
Jerusalem bus, 6 go.
NLRB. Philadelphia,
Leaster & grain.
UAW from AFL.
$522 million Emergency Food
Aid for France, Italy & Austria.
$18 million for China.
1,523 pardons.
North Atlantic Blizzard, 55 go.
Cardinals over Eagles.
Michael & Gorza. National
Basketball League & American
Basketball Association.
4 millions vets.
23 Nations Trade & Tariff.
Vafiades, Konitza, mud & snow.
—new imperialism.
Stern Gang & Arab Higher
Committee, 14 go.
—Burma's period of
tutelage is over.
$39.6 billion.
—Hard-boiled.

even if BAIZETTI BILL's still near:
—Scour the crapper, Cracker.
I oblige until VIARAROPOLIS clogs it again.
This time leaving the dripping overflow
of all behinds to slosh a floor.
—Let'S scoot this boot,
Hailey flies.
—You can shove off too, Big Gruesome shares.
Which cannot satisfy him.
VIARIROPOLIS bound now to batter
something. The St. Louis Restaurant stills.
And there's a crowd.
—Just going about my way,
I cautiously slink out.
—Not unless you want me
to beat you to death.
Very scary but I still start to giggle.

a rare footstep amidst these hours,
though I'm allready to duties by the time
VIAPOPOPOLIS spins around, anger
quelled by Ms. Millstone. His weary WIFE.
—*You too, Sticchio!* BILL BEEZETTI burns.
—*Hey he's,* VIAPIPOPOLIS squirms.
—*Fine,* frowns, flicking his thumb.
—*Let'S go,* I lob Sam.
Another shift over
to roam about
City by River.
Thames, Dnieper. Sumida.
Columbines & Sycamores weeping:
—*Not again.*
HONEY. For US allone. 7½.
Because we're ever happening,
coaxing a World free from US
to have fun. Destroy. We're all anyone
must absolutely have to enjoy.

Nov 26 1979
310,000 Afghan refugees.
—*Khomeini struggles, Carter trembles.*
Clean-air standards, US Steel & 13,000.
Antarctica crash, 257 go.
Who's Cincinnati, 11 go.
1,200 Ethiopians.
Shariar Mustapha Chafik goes. David Treen.
5 OPEC Nations.
—*Are we going to guarantee.*
Chrysler's $1.5 billion loan.
Robert Mugabe, Joshua Nkomo & Abel Muzorewa.
Mujahedeen & Soviet 56,000.
Elon Moreh.
Leopoldo Fortunato Galtieri.
A-OK, Shorty Powers goes.
Eldridge Cleaver's parole.
17 million tons of grain.
Saudi Arabia's beheadings, 63 go. Tabriz's Revolutionary Azerbaijanis.
—*never threaten, never.*
George Meany goes.
Honda & Ohio. 104-18.

Maybe, yes, it's time to move along.
Spare some our misery before
the World regains what allways we
allude to when we're gone.
4½. Only ours. HONEY.
Caribou & Hummingbirds perish beside
Mapocho, Vistula, Huangpu, Yamuna.
River by City where
we roam freely until
the next shift begins. Only now
Hailey suddenly pops: —*Let'S quit.*
I only chew my thumb. Worried sick.
VIAPIPOPOLIS: —*Hey move that broom, Poutsa.*
BEEZETTI BILL quipping: —*He's your boss.*
Until at last with THE WIFE splitting,
VIAPOPOPOLIS spins around to
hash it out with me

Sept 24 1947
World Women's Party.
UN & Soviet control over Yugoslavia, Poland, Bulgaria, Hungary & Romania.
US Air Force. Warsaw's 9 Nations Comintern.
—*imperialist hegemony.*
—*Eat less so Europe may eat more.*
Yankees over Dodgers.
Jerusalem, US Consulate & blast. Chuck Yeager, Glamorous Glennis & Mach 1.06.
William's AFL. HUAC's 79.
—*Hurray for Mr. Taylor.*
Maine disaster. Kashmir revolt.
A Spruce Goose mile.
Budapest's Jack Guinn.
Stanislaw Mikolajczyk.
46-0 & Korean autonomy.
UNESCO.
27 Belgian collaborators go.
Vishinsky's bomb.
Friendship Train. Elizabeth & Philip. Hollywood 10.
Australia nationalizes banks.

Jan 20 1980

Super Bowl XIV,
Steelers over Rams.
Andrei Sakharov,
Yelena Bonner & Gorki.
John Boyce.
China's US weaponry.

Pretoria 3 & 25 hostages,
28 go.
Abolhassan Bani-Sadr.
Mary Decker's dash.

—*not men of compromise.*
Tehran, Canadian
diplomats & 6 Americans.
Kurdish rebels & Kamyaran.
Abscam's Harrison Williams.
Richard Blumenthal.
Cairo's Israel Embassy.
Qnat, 60 go.
California flooding, 16 go.
US over Russia, 4-3.
Eric Heiden's 5.
Suriname coup.
M-19, Dominican Republic
Embassy & 80 hostages.
Steven Stayner.
El Salvador's coffee,
sugar & banks.
Jean Harris,
Herman Tarnower goes.

New, nice & fly! The St. Louis Relais
adores me. Roundtable boys for sure.
That Dusty Musty Conventicle allways
hunched around playing some Chess.
Steadies with canvas caps
& long sleaves grateful for the lumpup
swag I loan their certainty.
Their ordinary.
Gathering canes, crutches and walkers.
Wheelchairs too. Even Sam assists, his
chear easing the pains my presence
for a while rectifies entirely.
Them's here to stay.
Chuckling over every turn.
Every roll.
Every round of sip.
—*Come close Miss,* these regulars motion.
—*Our marvel!*
—*You have US all!*

July 31 1947

Sumatra & Jakarta.

—*firm and vigilant containment of Russian expansionist.*
8-0.
Vacuum Oil & Shell.

Paraguay's Pilar. William
Odom's around the globe.
Lahore & Punjab riots.
Karachi. Pakistan's Liberty.

—*That may be beyond US, but so long.*
Vafiadis & Free Greece.
7-0 Wightman Cup. Yemen.
Italy & Austria barred from
UN. London War curbs.
American Legion NYC Parade.
Harwell Atomic Power Plant.
Treaty of Rio de Janeiro.

—*attack against all American States.*
Themistocles Sophoulis.
Punjab, 150,000 go.
—*now let Them go to it.*
C-54 Skymaster.
Nikola Petkov goes.

—*Hold on,* I try.
—*You're ever only yours.* Their reply.
Too: —*Byebye Mister.*

Around the bend then,
strolling on towards the final turn.
Them allways go.
Their traumas at least relieved some
when Hailey tenderly takes care of their aids.
Handing back wheelchairs. Canes,
crutches and staves.

And certainly Hailey's extraordinary
kindness assists these lads wearing short
sleaves & sifty canvas hats, holding out
for some of that Secure Society.

This Busty Busty Conventicle retired
from their roundtable, from Hailey, me,
The St. Louis Deli and all anyone ever needs.

March 13 1980

Henry Ford III retires.
—*pain.*
Warsaw crash
& 22 boxers, 87 go.
Dennis Sweeney, Allard
Lowenstein goes.
Linda Eaton.
Moscow Olympics.
Arnulfo Romero goes.
Hunt silver. North Sea oil,
109 go. Bank deregulation.
33,000 transit workers.
Windfall Profit Tax Act.
Joy Menold.
Peruvian Embassy's 10,000.
Terry Fox starts.
Severiano Ballesteros.
—*recession.*
Zimbabwe.
Revolutionary Council
& universities.
Iran, US C-130 Hercules
Transport Plane & helicopter,
8 go. Bogotá siege over.
Cyrus Vance quits.
Edmund S Muskie.
London's Iranian Embassy
& 20 hostages. Beatrix.
Genuine Risk's Derby.
Tito goes.

—*That's for sure!* Each raucously
trumpets. Suddenly. Over me.
I'm the immunity these Gassers need.
Allways bringing Them
more glasses of Ice Tea,
despite their onandon
tripons about my Sam.
—*Dump the scab,* PAULIO warns.
Because I'm their winning hand.
Sam's too. Fawned over
with affectionate lather by
JIMJIVITIS, DONABETES & JERRYATRIC:
—*So pretty, so young.*
—*So lost.*
But I don't need any flattery.
Sam's allready mine. And I'm his. Even
if these Geezers still clot about on my
behalf to pry me loose from his game.
Allone I'm unchanged,

June 5 1947

The Marshall Plan.
—*breaking the vicious circle and restoring.*
Eva Peron. Truman to Canada.
Anderson's Sugar.
Mildred Didrikson Zaharias.
New Delhi & British partition.
Beven, USSR & appeasement.
—*Outrage.*
68-25. NYC street car.
17 cities, 11 countries, 13 days.
Levitt.
Kramer. Osborne.
—*to help other countries help.*
Greece's 2,800 Leftists.
16 Nations &
Economic Recovery.
2,500 Guerrillas & Yanina.
Ethiopia declines UN Aid.
Presidential Succession Act.
Haifa, Warfield & 4,530.
Burma premier goes.
Robic's bike.
Dutch Forces, Cheribon &
Java. National Security Act.
Girl Scouts. Peasant Party.

change the outcome of all.
Away from their winnings, these geezers
continue their bold parade of aches,
fever & pains. That's me. And I'm Hailey's.
Getting on without a buckup.
—*Buddy, we won't get*
around much anymore,
PARKERSON, DEANENTIA & PAULYP bumble,
not curved at all to find Hailey & I,
somehow, just now, holding hands.
—*Don't lose our youth,* ALLENZHEIMER
wucks. Warnings happily given
during this sorry pileup.
Cold coffee left to mugs
for which I refuse to budge. I'm the
diaspora of these pocked fartings:
—*Never again return!*

May 8 1980

WHO & Small pox.

Tampa Bay Bridge, 32 go.
Lee A Iacocca &
Douglas Fraser.
Lakers over 76ers.
8:32 AM, Mount St Helens
& Toutle River Valley, 8 go.
Miami riots, 18 go.
Love Canal's 710.
Robert Franklin Godfrey &
6-3 overturn.
Quebec's separate nations.
Jean Marie Butler.
Kwangju.
Vernon Jordan goes.
Fort Chaffee Army Reserve
Base & Cuban refugees.
Cheyenne Mountain,
North American Defense
Command & Soviet launch.
Richard Pryor & polyester.
$32 per barrel.
John Jenrette.

Diamond vs
Ananda Chakrabarty.

—economic growth
and consumption of.

approaching without rush, vagueness.
But now here with Sam somehow
blurring with strangeness. Confidence
veering. Somewhere else.

Sko the bells.

Those gentle farewells.

STANOSIS pats my arm. RICKETS too.
Sam's around out hosing the street.
Sidewalk & curbs sprayed clean
of dirt. Gets paid beans, and worse,
Owners, Rollers and Yants passing by
rant on him to perish. He won't.

—*Baboso!*

Sam spazzes. Unable to stand it.

—*Pendejo!*

Rears. Attacks then a trash can.
THE CRUSTY RUSTY CONVENTICLE
throws up their hands and jeers.
BILL BIZETTI with his friends shudders:

April 16 1947

Grandcamp, Monsanto
& Texas City blow, 500 go.
—midst of a Cold War.
The Wagner Act.
US Steel, Union & 15¢
—The girl with the smile is
gone for a while.
Iowa outlaws Closed Shop.
8-1. Hoover Dam.

—renounce War.
Meiji Constitution.
Jet Pilot's Derby.
Acre Prison, 251 free.
Arab Higher Committee
& UN Emergency Session.

Brazil's Communist Party.
World Bank's
$250 million loan.
Taft-Hartley.
Huynh Phu-so goes.
Near East Aid.
Finland's Collectivized Farms.
United Airlines crash, 44 go.
Rose's 500. Abd el-Krim
escapes Réunion.
Lajos Dinnyés.

Still BIZETTI BILL explodes, promptly
throwing out THE GUSTY GUTSY CONVENTICLE.
Though Hailey defends Them:

—*Be cool man, these're your pals.*

And: —*Not bums.*

And: —*O don't.*

Which can't stop the exodus. If still
calms down a tick our owner hassling
these steadies to gather their belongings and
leave. To curb & sidewalk. Devastating
streets for the —*devastated lot.*
HERMANOIDS pats my elbow. EDEMA's runny:

—*We're your opportunity, your skids.*

And: —*Take care kids.*

Only Hailey keeps me strangely confident.
Somehow regaining a certainty that we can,
without exertion, absolutely

—*Imbecile.*

Sam fumbling his brush near their
allways washed, never driven BMW M1,
which this crew hard at its Bingo
feers too much to lose. I'm that attractive.

—*Butterfingers, you've a way with
these lads. Thanks for putting up
with their flak. And grabs. A raise?*

BILL BIAZETTI confliments.

Me: —*My pleasure.*

—*How about my Manager's mack?*

—*Your problem.*

VIAPAPOPOLIS, the Slick Zip, ever lascivious
with drink, oblivious of his iffy hold
on work, bantered about while
Backgammon exchanges roll.

ARTHURITIS to me:

—*Without you Missy
our World couldn't spin.*

July 2 1980

Draft Registration.
Warsaw meat.
Islamic women protest.
Cathlyn Wilkerson.
—commitment to struggle against Them.
Moroccan fighters
& 2 Cuban tankers.
Zenko Suzuki.
Bolivia's Armed Forces
& Hernán Siles Zuazo.
Marjorie Matthews.
Zoetemelk's Tour.
Borg & Simionescu.
Chattanooga's
Civilian patrols.
Mohammed Reza Pahlavi goes.
Bologna blast, over 84 go.
Ogaden & Somali soldiers,
1,300 go.
Lagos & 183 million barrels.
Hurricane Allen, 272 go.
—the work goes on.
Gdansk, Lenin Shipyard
& 1,700 workers.
Hisham Jumbaz goes.
Uttar Pradesh City riots,
142 go. Poland, arrests
& 14 dissidents.

—*Without your Hailey our World
wouldn't spin,*

OSCARPOROSIS ribs me,
loads of Big Board shares allready plumping
their savings. While over thataway,
blitzed on the oblivion of his own shenanigans,
VIAPAPOPOLIS keeps throwing back liquor.

—*What a luftmensch.*

—*Crude and crass.*

—*A great pain to the ass.*

All offending BIAZETTI BILL:

—*So what then? Let this mitty manage?
Thankfully I'm the one owns this cash cow.*

I'm that unattractive. A losing to feer when,
no, sweepstakes don't pay off and their booty,
a Chrysler Town & Country, waits undriven.

—*Touvlo.*

Feb 22 1947

New Delhi, Nehru &
Liberty. Frankfurt Nazis.
Nuremberg's Franz von Papen.
Brussels, Parliament &
50,000 veterans.
Xinxiang departures.
Soong retires. Jerusalem's
Officers' Club, 20 go.
Martial Law.
Maurice Thorez & Vietnam.
Gromyko & Atomic Control.
Totalitarian strikes.
Moscow, Big Four & Germany.
Czechoslovakia, Poland &
Mutual Aid.
—assist free people to work out their own way.
Philippine Naval Bases.
Russia's 890,532
German POWs.
Detroit's Margaret. Yenan.
FBI loyalty. Illinois 119.
American Helicopter Society.
Japanese Pacific.
Herbert Backe goes.
Texas tornado, 132 go.
Madagascar. Montreal &
Jackie's Dodgers.

Aug 26 1980

Jagielski & Lech Walesa.
Eduardo Frei & 50,000.
300.
Gdansk strike over.
Göschenen & Airolo.
Evert Lloyd over
Hana Mandlikova.
Zhao Ziyang.
Haydar Saltuk over
Süleyman Demirel.
Arkansas & Titan missile silo.
Piaget goes.
Asunción & bazookas,
Somoza goes.
TSS. Solidarnosc.

Freedom cups Australia.
Iraq & oil exports.
Munich Oktoberfest blast,
12 go. Mariel boatlift over.

—He flushed his toilets.

Khomeini, Hussein &
Khuzistan.
Marabá gold.
Michael Myers.
Holmes 11 rounds Ali.
Rue Copernic car bomb, 4 go.

El Asnam quake, 2,590 go.
Foreign Service Act.
Abadan.

And my turns do exclude these wisps
from the traumas of living. So briefly.
THE LUSTY THRUSTY CONVENTICLE grateful:
—So erotic!
I curtsy. Soft nods all around. Sam
wallops their backs. His demise
immediately desired. Feeds the table's ire.
Too played out and tired, silly struts
causing their Gin to stale.
At least Sam follows me away
from such stakes. Trips promptly on a
chair, tumbles under a table. Laid out.
Shifts follow shifts.
VIAMOMOPOLIS pilfs me
more hauls:
—I'm falling for you.
Everyone falls.
Sam falls
on dropped soup.

Jan 1 1947

Illinois over UCLA.
Cambodia &
French domination.
Baruch retires.
Britain nationalizes coal.
Chinese reconciliation fails.
Secretary of State
George Marshall.
LeClerc turns away.
Stanford's Polio virus.
Irgun & Haifa police.
Elizabeth Short goes.
4th Republic's Vincent Auriol.
French on Hué.
—a new business.
KLM Dakota down,
Gustaf Adolf goes.
US 12,000 from China.
Truman's Dimes. Palestine
evacuation. Rome's Coalition
Cabinet. Nanking Nationalists
& Shantung. Polish
Ambassador & Free elections.
Berlin dance blaze, 150 go.
French Foreign Ministry
protests. Bogotá crash, 53 go.
Romanian famine.
$350 million relief.

She sits down then
while HE slims across the floor:
—I won't bother you anymore.
Slipping off.
The terrible VIAMOMOPOLIS.

And shifts follow shifts,
Hailey passing by table & chair
with the messiest flair, me barely able to
keep up with zerosum commotion over
NFL bets, way off on odds. Their cooler.
I'm every sure bet that's lost, a drear beat
for the losing streak allways dreaded.
Too weak to object to Them, all
around pounding my back. Miss.
—Fortune's flapper!
THE HUSHY GUSSY CONVENTICLE
ignoring happily all my tips.

Oct 21 1980

So sorry and pathetic even
Viamimopolis gives him a hand.
Wipes off some of the slop too. Helps
him to sit. Sam stressing this trip.
—*Eazy Stud, time to kick back and just chill.*
Enough of your dish. She's with you. I'm
tied. Let it ride. I'm the rudewack trying
to leave this sitch smooth. Cool?
Me, touched now, twirling my
Leftwrist Silvergold Twist.
Waiting for Sam to
relax. Grin.
But he doesn't.
Even flinches over the offered
handshake.
His lips twitching,
spittle spittling.
And all while Viamemopolis
whiffles softly:

Phillies over Royals.
Ortuella Spain
& elementary school, 64 go.
Warsaw Trade Union.
GM's $567 million.
Ford's $595 million.
—*There he goes again.*
Iran's $24 billion.
Sadaharu Oh retires.
489-99.
—*to work again.*
—*it doesn't hurt.*
—*to be unemployed.*
Pennsylvania Railroad
& $2.1 billion.
Jorge Salazar Argüello goes.
Signe Waller.
Las Vegas
& MGM blaze, 84 go.
Italian quake, thousands go.
Alaska's National
Wild Life Refuge.
Bernadine Dohrn.
Jim Bakker & Jessica Hahn.
CPW, Dakota & Chapman,
John Lennon goes.
NATO, Russsia & Poland.
San Salvador's Duarte.

Nov 3 1946

Softly
Viamemopolis,
without any spit, such nervous lips,
reaches over and kisses the back of her
hand. Bowing down to the ground.
I start twitching.
She doesn't even try to knee
his schnoz, merely twirls her
Leftwrist Silvergold Twist.
Perhaps even moved. Before cooing:
—*Go on, too safe. Have a taystee.*
A MopshiLulopBopPopLay. Until it's my turn.
I'll ride you with hurt, slide my jive to
your wife. Eventually just burn you alive. Kay?
Which stresses him. Fascinating.
Viamimopolis releases her fingers quick
and moves pathetically out of her way.

Hirohito, Rearmament &
New Constitution.
Madison Square's National
Horse. Republican control.
—*will, from now on, serve*
the people better.
—*wisdom and restraint.*
Holland Truce.
UN's Veto Power. Thailand.
French hit Haiphong, 6,000 go.
Oregon Native Americans.
UMW, Lewis & contempt.
Attlee & Jinnah.
US, Britain & German Zone.
Atlanta's Winecoff burns,127 go.
UN, Spain & Franco.
46-7. Rockefeller.
Bears over Giants.
Hanoi, Ho & Léon Blum.
Viet Minh & Annamite.
Japan's tsunami, 1,000 go.
Sainteny & Ho.
Nanking constitution.
—*with axes and sticks.*
World War II over.

Dec 19 1980

21.5 % Prime Lending Rate.
Bokassa.
226,504,825.
Greece & EEC.
San Salvador Sheraton,
2 go. David Barnett.
Manila's Martial Law,
341 free.
Ronald Wilson Reagan.
—Government
is the problem.
—era of national renewal.
444 days &
52 American hostages.
Warsaw's 4 hour strike.
Jiang Qing, Zhang Chunqiao,
Wang Hongwen &
Yao Wenyuan.
—revolution is no crime.
Java sea & passenger ship,
580 go. 60 day freeze &
Government regulations.
Super Bowl XV,
Raiders over Eagles.
Gro Harlem Brundtland.
Athens soccer, 24 go.
Wojciech Jaruzelski over
Józef Pińkowski.

—She's so bookoo. Pumpums to buttons.
Chrysanthemums abruptly swoon.
Zinnias & Gladiolas blurt perfumes.
I lay back, assisting customers, even
flushed a bit by this amiable encounter.
—She's all very cream,
VIALOLOPOLIS amicably swings.
—*She won't quit me,* Sam screams.
Shrugs all around. These klunks. Because
only I allone will everyone leave.
Allways.
—Advice, Roller: you're just wobbly young.
Smokin Sally's allready got her shally.
Stupid steady. Fresh, firm. Betty. Too
hot to ever hold onto for long.
Which gets Sam rockin,
fumed by VIALILOPOLIS's
aid.
Who even, before turning

Sept 8 1946

Sofia's Simeon.
Porters' strike: 200,000 workers
& 3,000 ships.
502,000 Divorces.
William Green, Sleeping Car
Porters' Union & Cat's Paws.
Truman, Wallace
& anti-Communism.
Niagara horseshoe.
Spain's León Degrelle.
Averell Harriman.
Equine meat. Soviets
& European Economic Unity.
Acheson & Korea.
11,236 miles.
Nuremberg 9.
Buffalo smoking.
Erie crash, 39 go. Kalgan.
St Louis over Boston.
—Heil.
—that German unity be.
9 go. OPA & margarine.
Stuttgart, 3 US facilities
& bombs. L85. Except sugar.
Flushing General Assembly.
—surge of Communist tyranny.
Santiago, Videla & 3 seats.

turning his life around.
VIALILOPOLIS doomed. All worked
up, even to tears:
—You're so pretty. The only thing I'd hold
onto here. So firm, round and fully packed.
I gots to act now. You're it. I'll relish,
cherish you, keep you cozy and rich.
Sheeeesh.
And though none to me will every cleave,
Hailey shrugs. Smiles:
—I'll never leave him.
Flumstered VIALOLOPOLIS must acquiesce:
—You're out of the oven.
I'll piss on my hands and
eat his french fries. Still, I hold back.
Buntings & Mockingbirds dive.
Chipmunks die too.

away,
pats Sam. Softly on the shoulder.
Phat props among these
dining Pars & Dar. But Sam spars:
—*Get fucked.*
—*Excuse me?* VIALALOPOLIS spins, shoving
tables aside, impulsive, knocking over
plates of sauce, falling blobs of marinara
glopping everywhere. Which shocks
Sam completely, the ensuing clatter
causing The St. Louis Grill to stampede.
VIAFOFOPOLIS, clutching a rag,
goes over to Sam. Allready retreating.
Fortunately BILL BIOZETTI halts both:
—*Fucking Idiot, outta my face.*
—*Me?* VIAFIFOPOLIS halts.
Gasps. *Why? What I do?*
—*You? Throwing trays, smacks,*
evacuate my place? You're fired.

Feb 12 1981

Peter Squires.
Naples shakes, 2,916 go.
Patrick Baltazar goes.

$695.5 billion.
Eammon Coghlan's 3:50:6.
Madrid's Parliament &
Antonio Tejero Molino's 200.
Thatcher & Reagan.
392 penalty minutes.
Congressional Loan Board
& Chrysler's $400 million.
Federal Employment
& 37,000 jobs.
Miami's Nicaraguan contras.
Alexander M Haig Jr
& Soviet Union.
El Salvador & 12 US soldiers.
6-3.
Phil Mahre's Switzerland.

DC Hilton, Ronald Reagan,
James Brady, 2 Security
Officers & John Hinckley Jr.

—forgot to duck.

—the store?

—me you're Republicans.

Rome & Mario Moretti.
Oxford's Susan Brown.

A ir chills. Customers diminish. All
seatings for dinners, lunches, thin.
—*What do we do?* laments
VIAFIFOPOLIS. *And soon.*
— *Ilithios, leave me allone,*
exciting BIOZETTI BILL snarls.
Hailey stays luscious. Attracts attention.
Combing back the grease, VIAFOFOPOLIS
eases through The St. Louis Café,
passing scattered lingerers. Completely
irresistible. All bluff cuffs & action, slaying
everyone with his stuff, and still pleasant
enough to blush a bit for Hailey with his
VIALALOPOLIS charm: —*O give me a chance.*
—*Get fucked.*
Whereupon before this fresh water crowd,
HE gently strokes Hailey's gentler cheek,

July 9 1946

American League Baseball.
$3.75 billion British Loan.
War Crimes Tribunal.
Colonel Joachim Peiper.
Yangtze drive. Tito &
Yugoslavia, 8 Chetnicks go.
Britain leaves Cairo.
Villarroel goes.
Irgun & Menachem Begin.

—dangerous and
may be fatal.

A-Bomb's Arkansas, Nagato &
Saratoga. USSR &
Albanian arms.
Britain's Tel Aviv.
Assault's Triple.
Fulbright abroad.
Santo Domingo wave.
No German Economic
Reunification. AFL &
Bakery Production.
Haifa & Operation Igloo, 1 goes.
McCarthy over La Follette.
Larry Lambert, Army P-61 &
7,800 ft. Mao's War.
Congress of Destour.
Outer Mongolia veto.

April 11 1981
—going to walk out.
Brixton riots.
—extreme distress.
Cape Kennedy's
Space Shuttle Columbia.
36 orbits.
John W Young,
Robert L Crippen &
Edwards Air Force Base.
Warsaw's Polish Farmers.
Grain, soybeans & meat.
Honduras & Nicaragua.
Pleasant Colony's Derby.
Bobby Sands goes.

François Mitterrand.
—Only the entire national community can.
Marley goes.
Francis Hughes go.
John Paul II &
Mehmet Ali Agca.
Celtics over Rockets.
Roy Lee Williams.
IRA mine, 5 go.
Social Security Pension cuts.
Chattahoochee River,
Nathaniel Cater goes.
Licio Gelli's Masons.
Ziaur Rahman goes.

Dude unafraid, Sam just laughs:
—Haaaaaaaaaaaaaah!
And that iz ass out flat. BILL BOZETTI,
livid, allready charging off, whips around
to break on Sam:
—For the time being you're safe. But you
ever laugh at him again, I'll waste you.
Harrowing. I slide my palm on
Sam's back. He's all shakes.
Hyperventilates.

But we get by.

Ongoing.

Clocking our tasks among these
scads of Passing Patrons demanding
extras, exchanges and specials.
Me & Sam allways around. Ever here.
But with all we put up with now
is this Society enough?

May 22 1946
French Social Security.
Prague Communists.
Agerholm 826. $1.85 daily.

Robson's 500. 7 Arab League
& Jewish Immigration.
South African land ownership.
Morgan vs Commonwealth.
National School Lunch Act.
La Salle blaze, 58 go.
Dock's 200,000.
—the quick and the dead.
Jerusalem's 5 British officers.
—World Peace.
—World Destruction.

Louis 8 rounds Conn.
Frederick Moore Vinson.
UN Security Council. 7-4.
France's Ho Chi Minh.
—There is nothing to.
Hagana. Jakarta Coup.
Paris Treaties: Bulgaria,
Romania, Italy & Hungary.

Bikini Atoll
& Operation Crossroads.
—Pooh.
—America buried imperialism.

Fontainebleau.

Enough of this Confederacy and
everything I have to put up with
here. And for what? Hailey & me.
Stuck to these ordinary routines carried
out among public throngs unpausing
amidst our rush. Relentlessly

going on

even if I'm
all anxiety and
shakes. Rubbing Hailey
with my palm to calm me. Harrrrrowed.
—I'll kill ya if you ever scoff at US again.
Cause now, for the timebeing, you'ze unsafe.
And I'm spinning.
Nowhere close to even grinning.
BOZETTI BILL surprising me. Follows with:
—Haaaaaaaaaaaaaah!
Laughing over how afraid I am.

June 7 1981

Israel Warplanes, Iraq
& Osirak Nuclear Reactor.

—*counterrevolutionaries.*
US Baseball strike.
Donna Caponi Young.
Wayne B Williams.
LA's 9,700 immigrants.
Minority flight & suburbs.
Terry Fox goes. Tehran,
Islamic Republican Party &
Massoud Rajavi, 72 go.

Liverpool riots.
Paul MacCready's Channel.
California fruit flies
& Malathion. Bill Plucknett
& steroids. Kansas City
& Hyatt Regency, 111 go.

Stanley Rother goes.
Philip Charles Arthur George
& Diana Spencer.
25% Tax cut.

US Baseball strike over.
Senegalese troops
& Gambia.

Bolzano blasts.
15,000 Air Traffic Controllers
& 11.4% raise.

Of course VIAFAFOPOLIS is rehired,
promoted, upscaled
with bucks.
And though still dodging THE WIFE,
hits on me less. Because now there's
THE NEW BITTY to jock. Here at
The St. Louis Boîte beats starting to
bump, the Dunk Zup, blowing up,
flood of Fit Lunks, Lit Punks,
hungry, dizzy, hisididy,
come over to socialize, downplay
a trade up for plenty. Greased. Locked.
MCM the CMC to finally drop squat.
VIADIDOPOLIS welcomes the turn,
especially this NEW JILL:
—*Over Here Baller!*
Our manager doling out free spills.
—*You'z propa thrilla.*

March 16 1946

Ferhat Abbas free.
Bernard Baruch.
Transjordan Liberty.

50 miles high.
Leaving Iran.
War Assets Administration.

—*not to overeat, not to waste.*
Gold Coast African majority.
1,000 Frankfurt Nazis.
Greece's Monarchists.
400,000 Soft Coal Workers.
Hawaii wave, 300 go.
USSR & Iranian oil.
Peking-Mukden rail.
Japanese suffrage.
Chungking, Chou En-lai & War.
P-80. UNRRA's grain.
French nationalization of 34.
Vincent Auriol, Ernest Bevin,
Molotov, James Byrnes.

8,000 hp.
Tel Aviv & UK 7.
Tojo's 55. Tsitsihar.

Marines on Alcatraz.
Assault's Derby.
Victor Emmanuel III.
Yankees & United Airlines.

—*So Screwball Supersolid!*
Our manager glibs, amping his party.
—*Out of this World!*
NEW JACKSON whips,
thick now with VIADIDOPOLIS, because HE's
rolling at last with wads of fast cash,
played up & socialized to overcome any
highsociety, ditzy, extremely stingy
Chunks throwing out cold brace
O broads to newcomers booting
to face down the odds. Of acceptance.
All at The St. Louis Bistro where HE
now woos and marries THE NEW GAL.
Whereupon our manager's
WIFE starts flirting.
Offering me her human
ruin shunted aside by
VIAFAFOPOLIS of course.

Aug 3 1981

7,000 flights.

—system cannot work without US and.
Reagan fires 12,000.
—But the law is the law.
EEC fruit.
2 US F-14s &
2 Libyan SU-22
over Gulf of Sidra.
Renaldo Nehemiah's 12.93.

—no friend of.
Mohammed Javad Bahonar
& Mohammed Ali Rajai go.

—revolutionize the office.

Beirut, Louis Delamare goes.
100,000 Soviet troops.
Ayatollah Assadollah
Madani goes.
Sugar Ray 14 rounds Hearns.
Iran's militants, 149 go.
Belize freedom.
Paris, Lyons & TGV.
Jack Henry Abbott arrested.
Sandra Day O'Connor.
—Khomeini will be overthrown.
$1 trillion deficit.

And HE's off, brawling
to muzzle and rumble. The Big Dance.
Tidy Girls spinning for
drunk clutches and mash.
Arms around arms, circling the flats,
allways asking me over, wanting
bunches to join Them each time their
hunches swell and human pleasures
come forth to grab still more.
Shots on the bar. Burning. A choochoo.
More shooby and blow.
The hullabaloo of contact I easily eschew.
Sam too.

We do what we do.

Running bubbles and slosh, mopping
up the abandon had to have fun.
I'm their daze.
Without recursion.

Jan 17 1946

Tanganyika.
800,000 Pittsburgh Steel
Workers strike. UN's Atomic
Energy Commission. UMW
& American Federation
of Labor. Trygve Lie.

—willingness to subordinate.
Soviet Danube Steamship
Company. Calcutta riots,
14 go. ENIAC. Wage
& Price Controls.
Bank of England. 18.5¢
Canadian Mounted Police
& 22 Soviet Spies.
Office of Economic Stabilization
& Chester Bowles.
Cairo clubs blaze.

—the overwhelming forces at our disposal.
Argentina's President Perón.

—an iron curtain has descended across the continent.

Vietnam. French Naval fleet
& Haiphong. Mukden.
GM & Walter Reuther.

Tito & Draja Mikhailovich.

Without respite.
Allways their bum.
Squandered fun tossed to the skids for
roams ever troubling and allways undone.
That's the run I run.

Not necessarily Hailey.

She'd thrive easily on this
jump. Among such Sniffers & Stewed.
She's Melloreenee on ice, crushed, to the top.
More still barging up with
pleasures to gulp, their times
allready compelling Them to
seek out her wellbeing to restore Them
on the dancefloor. Heels following heels.
Stomp for a lurch & grab,
spinaround with revelers.
Close, hopped & ready to
reel on and on.

Oct 1 1981

Saudi Arabia's AWACS.
Anwar el-Sadat goes.
Hosni Mubarak.
Sufi Abu Taleb.
—committed to all.
Bonn's 250,000.
—reaping the
whirlwind of all our.
Polovchak defects.
Moshe Dayan goes.
Reagan's recession.
Pan Hellenic Movement.
Kathy Boudin, Judith Clark
& David Joseph Gilbert.
London's 150,000.
Alberto Salazar.
Dodgers over Yankees.
Mayor of Atlanta.
Antigua, Barbuda
& Redonda liberty.
Sweden & The Whisky.
—No balanced budget.
David Stockman.
Shuttle Columbia.
Hyman G Rickover goes.
South's migrant slavery.
MX missiles, 100 B-1s
& Stealth bomber.
Typhoon Irma, 176 goes.
—before we drink.

Without place.
I just keep turning Lucys for Bingos,
reservations for checks, decked out
with velvet skorts, wifebeater and treads.
While Sam, overalls, helps the Valets.

Around I go, picking up Aces & Jax
for a seat when we're packed,
for a flirt when we're not.
Which only goes to tip the staff.
I've no need for Them's snaps.

Though ENTREPRENEURS & BROKERS
must greed for all I circulate.

—Do the grownup?
—Fer sure.

I'm The Allways Enough ever
reached for. And missed.
I'm their underage mitt.
I'm that kid.

Nov 19 1945

Truman's National Health.
Chief of Army Ike &
Chief of Navy Nimitz.
Parker, Jackson, Biddle &
The Nuremberg Trial.
GM Nationwide strike.
Meat & butter.
2 Palestine Coast Guard
Stations. CARE.
Marshall to China.
Gaspari's Italy.
$25 billion lend-lease over.
B-29's Coast to Coast.
Rams over Washington.
Tire rationing. Karl Renner.
Blood & Guts goes.
Monetary Fund and Bank.
War Labor Board to
War Stabilization Board.
Frozen foods.
—a new state based on
democracy, peace and.
Alabama over Southern
California.
Yalta, Truman & The Balkans.
Army's Moon.

That's Hailey too.
Bending outskirts of popularized
duties, the oversized conglomerates of feer.
Because enough allready, she's here.
—And sooo grooovy.
—Our globeovooty.

Circulating the gory deeds all
these Yard Dogs & Company Cats
need to stay keen.
Sliding her riches
for the bat of her lashes when we're
slammed, a stool when we're cool,
Lincolns & Hamiltons, palmed underhand.
And while I'm just overalls, gloomy staff,
she's dome hat, bloomers & flats,
up the ladder promoted, deserving it too.
While ruffs for slugs I'm spiralling down.
Without a break.

Nov 28 1981

Wood goes.
Damascus car, 64 go.
CIA & US
—pertinent.
—not going to change my.
Poland, National Vote &
Martial Law. Begin's Golan
Heights. Silesia, 7 go.
—cannot destroy ten million.
Italy & NATO attaché.
Reagan, Poland & Soviet ties.
Ghana & Jerry Rawlings.
Acquired Immune
Deficiency Syndrome.
California mud, 12 go.
Framingham. AT&T.
50 Guatemalan hostages,
50 go.
Air Florida, 14th Street
bridge & snowstorm, 78 go.
Perm anthrax. Pakistan,
Mahmud Haroon, Zia ul-Haq
& 480. OSHA.
Arm's control, Poland &
Soviet dominion.
Super Bowl XVI,
49ers over Bengals.

Whatever. Everyone circles a want.
Even New Babe, wiggling around, slinks
my way, tingling her tits,
coylying her lips.
Quick brings me a drink, I pass on.
A pass, I pass off.
Wants to experience me, I pass along.
she is me if only briefly.
And hugging me only withers her.
So scowling sure and sad
The New Belly Ride grabs Sam.
Forces a smile. Drags him aside.
Swoopin fierce on my squeeze!
Chompitty chompchomp
down on her knees:
—¿Qué onda Jammer? Gonna
give me some hammer?
But my Sam,

Sept 21 1945

Ford retires.
210,000 Detroit jobless.
Clement & Government.
French forces & Saigon.
UN's Palestine.
Masaharu Homma. Federal
Control of National Resources.
Army Air Transport Command
Plane: Globester.
21 points & a Fair Deal.
—our last chance.
Third to Fifteenth.
26 US Oil Companies.
Transcontinental strike.
Tigers over Cubs.
Antón Dostler.
Shirtless Ones & Buenos Aires.
Czech nationalization.
Arab League's Egypt, Syria,
Iraq & Lebanon. Caracas.
Jackie Roosevelt Robinson.
Laval & Quisling go.
Imposed regimes. DC-4.
Vargas quits.
—Shoes!
Cairo riot. Zoltán Tildy.
Meteor's 606 MPH. Sukarno.

crusting back at her:
—You're a Whack Scrag. A Sloop Droop.
And I should kick you.
But he doesn't. Only
Glubblubberingly,
moving unsteadily towards me. So,
yes!, I drag him aside. Forcing a smile.
Whereupon this New Sad Lug all
depressed and pouting
actually goes ahead and hugs me,
briefly becoming me,
though I'm
experience beyond all grasp,
longed for, over,
by all who drink, eat, stroll, fidget,
curl a fist, dare to not, give up,
win, fit. New Herkle splits for commons.
Wants a circle of his own. Whatever.

Jan 28 1982

confused somewhat, only retreats
from her slutty tour. Politely too
but firm. Even when SHE starts bawling,
plaidclash of tubetop on goth,
Sam rewards HER with only a hanky.
Him: —*I'm terribly*
sorry. I'm hers.
And HER: —*I'm sorry too.*
You're nice.
Fine. Until THE NEW LICK allso slides:
—*But if you change, I'm around Mr. Eleven.*
Your fastfood drive through. 24/7.
Gushing with G force!
Which VIADADOPOLIS crawling free
of the dancefloor mix
gets wind of, jealously.
Sam though, proudpleased to be
loose of this NEW HOOTCHIE, finds me.

Dozier.
Flynn's Icy Chin Save.
Nueva Trinidad's
500 guerrillas.
Gdansk clash.
Livermore Labs
& 170 arrests.
—to stay the course,
to shun retreat, to weather
the temporary.
Carrollton to Montgomery.
Zacatecoluca surrrender.
Poznan's 194 arrests.
Banque Rothschild.
North Atlantic
& Ocean Ranger, 84 go.
John Z DeLorean.
Ahmed Fuad Mohieddin.
Burma, 3 battalions
& Khun Sa.
12 gunmen, Kuwaiti jetliner
& 105 hostages.
Philip Caldwell
& United Auto Workers.
Afghans & Soviet gas,
3,000 go. Charles Haughey.
Claus von Bulow.
EPA & hazardous waste.
Daniel Ortega Saavedra.

July 24 1945

This NEW SWOONY moves onto
Hailey too, blowing his wig,
getting all stiff to drag her out
for a dancefloor struggle.
VIADADOPOLIS sizing this
play jumps quick on me:
—*She's any guy's drive, eh Mr. Zip? Time*
to find you something your own speed.
NEW BTO still sliding his jive:
—*Nice phiz. You're*
everything and ten.
And her: —*I'm his. But*
thanks again.
HIM I don't dig. I've got my limits.
This kid dangling Hailey's flops with
two gimmicks which Hailey declines
leaving HIM to rudely
retreat, somewhat confused,

Potsdam Conference.
Stalin, Truman & Attlee.
—destruction.
B-25 & Empire State, 13 go.
89–2. Japan turns down
surrender ultimatum.
—obliterated unless your.
9:15 AM, Enola Gay &
Hiroshima.
—what have we done?
Russia attacks Manchuria.
Fat Man's Nagasaki.
—too often recurring plague
of humanity.
Korea. 400.
—national unworthiness.
VJ. Victory kisses.
Fuel rations. Unemployment.
Hap Arnold retires. 38th.
Wainwright. Nanking &
Shanghai. Mountbatten's
Singapore. Yokohama HQ.
Los Alamos, Oak Ridge
& Hanford. Liberation
Committee of Vietnamese
People. Operation Downfall.
—It is for US.
Thailand. Iva Toguri. Froebel.

March 28 1982

Iran's Khuzistan.
José Napoleón Duarte.
84 British Marines.
Falkland Islands.
Choa Praya River, Sirikit & 100,000.
Carrington quits.
Syria & Iraqi oil.
Dome of the Rock, 2 go.
—step off the.
Ottawa & Constitution Act.
Charlotte Teske.
Cuba & US travel. Yamit.
Poland's 800.
—Energy turns the World.
British bombers & Stanley Airfield.
Gato del Sol's Derby.
General Belgrano, 362 go.
Exocet missile & Sheffield, 20 go.
Narval & British jet.
Braniff bankruptcy.
Jack Kaenel.
Islanders over Canucks.
Port San Carlos.
HMS Ardent, 22 go.
Antelope burning.
Khorramshahr.

Still VIABIBOPOLIS seethes for revenge.
THE NEW BAIT slipped from him.
Me slipped from him.
But if ready with shank to
go after Sam, anyone close, me,
THE WIFE nearby cools him.
BILL BOOZETTI too, walking
The St. Louis Saloon, tickling the tills,
thanking employees, spinning the dials
of his vault.

All while THE MUSSY FUSSY CONVENTICLE
falls to Roulette. Curlin cables, bouncing
balls. Giving US wrinkles for wins.
—Ask me that Chalk!
—Agree to this Polack!
—Livin large Suede Boys!
—Death of me, Squids.

Because we're allways sixteen and

June 4 1945

Kobe. Germany's 4 Zones.
Kamikaze, Mishishishi & Louisville. Haakon.
Trenchant & Ashigara.
Vampire's 500 MPH.
Hoop Jr's Derby. Borneo.
Simon Bolivar Buckner goes.
Truman, Ike & Second Cluster.
Wenchow. Pan Am's 88 hours.
Osubka-Morawski.
Mitsuri Ushijima goes.

Okinawa over, thousands go.
Himeji, Akashi, Kagamigahara, Tamashima & Kure.
—is the single greatest.
50 Nations. National Unity.
Elizabeth's soldiers.
Harry Hopkins retires.
Henry Morgenthau too.
Honshu attacks.
Operation Overcast.
Salina Utah & Bertucci's rage.
US strikes. Alamogordo, New Mexico & The Trinity Test.
—destroyer of Worlds.
Yokosuka. Braden's crowd.

And besides we're allways sixteen.
—So murdering it!
—Snuff & Butter broads!
—Nip this!
—Kiss my pretzel!

Chears for jeers given US for every
hit of MLB base doings. Hysterical bets
placed by our FUSTY HUSSY CONVENTICLE.
While with vault dials still,
employees killing it,
cashflows at The St. Louis Pub go trilled
by BOOZATTI BILL who keeps banking it.
Even if our manager's WIFE's unsatisfied,
imploring Hailey, anyone nearby, me,
to pour her some attention, affection,
slip her some pills
which some NEW THRILL finally does.
Under VIABIBOPOLIS's nose.

May 26 1982

Yuri Andropov quits KGB.
Darwin & Goose.
Robert Runcie. Spain & NATO.
Johncock's 500.
—probable cause.
Shlomo Argov.
Israel's 20,000 troops.
—armed aggression must.
Lakers over 76ers.
Sidon, Tyre, Khalde & Damur.
Mauritian Movement.
550,000.
Tumbledown Mountain,
Stanley & surrender.
West Beirut. No First Use.
—going because the army.
Albuquerque's 38. Jean-Loup
Chrétien. George Shultz.
—have had enough.
ERA over. Moon's 4,000.
Reynaldo Bignone.
—away with his swag.
Kenner crash, 146 go.
Miguel Vázquez's quadruple.
Wendy Lee Coffield goes.
14% poverty.
Hyde & Regent's Parks, 9 go.

it's allways their loss. The long across
rushing towards the only personal
receipt. Not me. I'm free.
I'm Victory over
Ties Them compete at.
For something warm. Something sweet.
Jam Up. Jam Down.
When toast falls it's jam all around.
—Catch US on the flip side,
we bounce. Sam seated behind, under
shiftsleekening skies where clouds of US
fly and everyone sighs. Because THE CHEFSKI
lends US his Bike. On we ride. Slowly.
European Hornbeam panic.
Because I'm slower here.
Because I feer
the irreparable loss of holding
someone dear.

March 23 1945

Patton over Rhine.
Werewolves, Oppenhoff goes.
Danzig.
Czechoslovakia's Benes.
Yamato. British 8th Army.
Elbe at Magdeburg.
—I have a terrific headache.
FDR goes.
—You are the one.
Buchenwald. Shuri cliffs.
—disorganized mob.
1,000 bicycles, 1,000 skirts.
Lublin Government. Toronto's
cup. Hodges & Konev.
—to that tremendous
power allone.
—will give you an empire.
Duce & Petacci go.
Comfort.
157th, 222nd & Dachau.
—Kill em.
Berlin falls.
Eva & Adolf go.
Goebbels goes.
U-853. 2:41 AM. VE.
—but half won.
USS Bunker Hill.
—Yes, this is the end.

Sometimes letting go though
works a longer road.
Because it's free.
Because it's bold.
Lowland Gorillas go.
Slowly. So Hailey & I bury the Bike.
CHEFSKI dies. Everyone mourns. Ashes fly
across battletorn skies and frolic. Until
Hailey clutching my hand turns US out:
—Catch US on the fip side.
Because whenever toast drops we're both.
Jam Down. Jam Up.
Hailey allways around. A sweet comfort
between something ever effortless:
The Losses of all Lost
and me outlasting all
personal costs of loving her beyond
her. Though nothing's beyond her.

July 25 1982

Arafat & Israel.
—sorrow could do something to reunite.
Basra, hundreds go.
Goldenberg's blast, 6 go.
Polish riot police.
Opal Charmaine Mills goes.
$98.3 billion tax.
Soyuz T-7. Salyut 7.
EPA & lead emissions.

PLO, PFLP
& Democratic Front for the Liberation of Palestine.
—revolution until victory!
32nd Amphibious Unit.
Johns-Manville Corporation & asbestos.
Bill Dunlop's sail.
15,000 Palestinians & Syrians leave West Beirut.
Carlo Alberto Dalla Chiesa goes.
Kelly goes.
Bashir Gemayel goes.
Sadegh Ghotzbadeh goes.
Sabra & Shatila, over 300 go.
NFL strike.
Amin Gemayel.

Hard work. The OnlyGettingBy
cycle of striving. Shifts
onshifting, drifting US apart.
Sam leaving when I arrive.
Sam arriving when I leave.
Switch over again. The Bike still on the
lend from CHEFOWITZ who dotes on me
and drills muffins at Sam.
Leaving US but a curve of time
for Kisses, Soons and Byes.
Sam allready attacking the
dirty cutlery.
—*Tardy, Ditz Man,* ill CHEFMANN
jibes nicely. *You got*
mountains of mungy plates.
While SAUCEBOY & PASTRYDUDE huck loaves,
which Sam, wielding Oven Mitts for
laughs, allways fails to evade.

Jan 23 1945

Kreisau Circle.
Mars Task Force. Fluoridation.
7.7 tons of hair. 7,650.
—Arbeit Macht Frei.
Zhukov's blizzard.
Luzon 513.
Ecuador vs Germany.
Stettin. Yalta's Three.
General Mud. Manila falls.
—to annex anything.
Dresden firestorm,
130,000 go.
Task Force 58.
U-711's bell. 55¢
US Marines, Iwo Jima & Mount Suribachi, 6,800 go.
Ahmed Maher Pasha goes.
—with trepidation.
US Curfew. Chrysler's Briggs.
Finland. Manila POWs.
Hodges & Cologne.
Eifel Plateau, Ludendorff & Rhine. Granville.
Curtis LeMay & Tokyo burning,
100,000 go.
Albert Kesselring. Mindanao.
Anne Frank goes.
Hitler's scorched earth.

Then smacked,
flinching & wincing, with hails of
buns hurled by RUNNERS & STEWARDS.
—*You're behind the ball. But stalls, I'm*
rounding an Ice Mountain, paining
CHEFMANN sighs, *too soon.*
Crumbs scattering
over me, racing to Hailey who by a
Later Gator & peck spares me
all of time's curve.
A brioche smacks me, bounces. Dear
CHEFOWITZ only dotes on me.
His loaned Bike switched over again.
Arriving when I leave.
Leaving when I arrive.
Departing Them by drifts
only we survive. Our cycle allways
putting everyone out of work.

Sept 25 1982

Wilkes-Barre
& George Banks, 13 go.
Tel Aviv thousands.
Gisele Ann Lovvorn goes.
Livingston train.
Philippe Petit.
Beirut cluster bomb
& US marine, 1 goes.
EPCOT. Helmut Kohl.
Cyanide, strychnine
& Tylenol, 7 go.
Swedish depth charge.
Job Training Partnership Act.
Palermo's Mafia.
Cardinals over Brewers.
Grete Waitz's marathon.
Solidarity outlawed.
1.008 billion.
Felipe González. Mario
Cuomo. Itaipu Dam.
Baghdad, Dezful
& Iran. Biloxi fire, 27 go.
Brezhnev goes.
—only be defended by
relying on.
57,939.
Walesa free. Terry J Hatter
& Draft Registration.
NFL strike over.

Finally getting down to sudbusting
platters with brillo, detergents and
billows of steam. Whips, strainers,
braziers and ladles. China caps, spatulas,
scoops and jar pumps. Sauce pans too.
Dried then on racks with thick dishrags.
Trash bagged & out. With a stumbling
galop en avant.

All over again.

GARDE MANAGERS adoring Sam, his spasticity
charming Them from the bumly drain.
—Knock it off. You're free.

Sam racing again
the gauntlet of THE SOUS CHEFS'
baguettes laughing the air.
Grinning allways to find me
waiting, holding the Bike,
reready to begin.

Nov 24 1944

Marianas, 50,000 go.
Trojo. Army over Navy.
Athens curfew.
Miller goes. 5-Star General.
Von Rundstedt & Ardennes
Counterattack. Bastogne.
Packers over Giants.
509th. Giap's Vietnamese
People's Army. McAuliffe &
2 Panzer Divisions.
—Nuts!
William E Johnson,
43-38233, Sweet & Lovely.
Budapest surrounded.
—I am very happy.
Elias & Royalists.
Hood River.
Trojans over Tennessee.
Bodenplatte. Akyab.
Committee on Un-American
Activities. Ommaney Bay.
—all young girls.
Gertrud Seele goes.
Thomas B McGuire goes.
Luzon. South Poland.
American First Army's
Houffalize. Lodz, Kracow &
Tarnow. FDR's 4th.
Russia's Germany.

Ready to part,
taking the Bike from me,
amused posatively by the
slashing croissants
our BAKERS huck and
never fail to land.
—Get bussing, Sad Sack.

Time of their life. Dusting these stables
for a World separated by five tables,
where slaving over all again,
with a stumbling digshuffle tap,
I slowly slop the trash and, geared with
a dishrag, wipe & smear every spill.
Wash & slosh with buckets. Flubbing
sides. Dropping condiments. Catsup too.
Slipping on grease. Mucking up linen.
Knocking down chairs. Fumbling wares.
Messing their floors.

Nov 24 1982

Hawaiian hurricane.
Serge Ivanov
Antonov arrested.
Yasuhiro Nakasone.
Beyers Naudé. Barney Clark &
Jarvik-7. 245-176 over $988
million MX missiles.
Charles Brooks Jr goes.
Ballykelly, 11 go.
Norman D Mayer goes.
167,000 foreclosures.
North Yemen quake,
2,800 go. Anne M Gorsuch.
Koeberg Station's 4 bombs.

—Don't be afraid!
Marry her! Live!

Overtown riots.
New York 4 & Puerto Rico.
Times Beach.
Newark's 3 million
gallons of gas.
American Medical
Association & boxing.
7,291.

—War on crime
and drugs does not.

Rubén Zamora's New Cycle.
Allen Dorfman goes.

Kisses, Laters, Gones,
allready braving another assault
of whirling demands. Fast slammed
with deuces, four tops. Eights and a six.
Fly Tricks granting me no catchup chance.
Wonky Tonks guggling syrupy drinks.
Mall Marchers greasing wedges of pie.

Callery Pears twirl beside Buggy Men.

Their hours go. And even though Sam's
only got his Leftwrist Twist of Rosegold,
he's more. Allways needed,
assured, helped and valued.
And of course waited for.
While I sling coffee.
Beans & franks.
Assuring impatience with a smile.
Over and over.
Everyone still dips deprived.

Sept 27 1944

Arnhem Bridge, thousands go.
Marzabotto, 700 go.
Surplus War Property Act.
Warsaw surrenders,
215,000 go.
Britain's Petras.
Dumbarton Oaks.
St Louis over St Louis.
Churchill, Eden & Moscow.
United Nations. Aachen.
1,000 planes over Formosa.
Okayama. Rommel goes.
Vinegar Joe. Leyte.
MacArthur returns.
Sibuyan Sea's 282 ships.

—most crushing defeat.
Go For Broke Brigade.

—I refuse to accept
your order.

Walcheren. Scheldt River.
Cairo & Stern Gang,
Moyne goes. Singapore.
—my little dog, Fala.
Tirpitz. Ushio & Kiso.
Renault Factories.
Saar Basin & Ruhr.
Battery F, 3rd Defense.

allways feeling deprived.
Again and again.
Without even a smile's relief.
She flings out blankets & gaskets.
Cow juice and mud.
Cheared for. Sold Out.
Swooned over, hooted and tooted,
amply rewarded. While I
with my Leftwrist Rosegold Twist
keep losing more. Hours slide.

Wood Ducks die.

And still she slices pie for Droolies,
scooping sundaes for Battle Crates.
Tables on tables she takes
care of too absolutely, before, finally
loose, standing back to where I,
allready on guard, can greet her with
What's chillin? Hi Sugar. Kisses & Cute.

And if I'm The ThatThat Smootho,
when Bill Buzetti drops by,
I jitter, dropping orders,
losing the crowd, poorly shuzzing with
the Gritters and Limpers scamming on
all what's going down. I'm awkward
& that grody. Fer sure too snorty.
Serving the Sourest Bub with the
raspiest —*Sorry?* And course Viabobopolis
turns up, catching wreck
for rolling ends, all hop and
station, soon souping some tub.
Even with The Wife.

I'm pretty rude,
ditch him offering cigs.
Just chillin. Ill.

How I miss my Sam
at The St. Louis Taverna.

Jan 25 1983

Italy's 32.
Klaus Barbie.
Andean Peasants
& Path, 8 go.
Super Bowl XVII,
Washington over Miami.

3 Israeli tanks, US Marine
Charles Johnson & a pistol.
Managua rebels, 73 go.
Beirut & PLO, 22 go.
Rita Lavelle.
Iran's 4th.
Giovanni Vigliotto's 105.
Eastern Seaboard blizzard.
Medina, Gordon Kahl
& 2 US Marshals, 2 go.
Phoolan Devi surrenders.
Nimitz & 2 MiG-23s.
Hindu raids, 600 go.
—Why should we?

—War hysteria.
3:49:78.
Arthur & Cynthia Koestler go.
Zomax. Robert Hawke.

—Peace through.
—to catch up.
—turn their great.

At The St. Louis Supper Club
where finding Hailey leaves me
chilly & drastic.
Awed how she manages the turnover
so casually and with savvy.
Her life's blist without stress.
Allways more longing for her, shoulders
up, ever sleeker with the gossip
shuffled now, about her, by
Viabobopolis of course. Sorry? Here?
Hardly scouring my sourest feers.

Some New Flutter, gammin
& hard, on charge
for my gally, turn me over
to some Stockade Yard, be
francyfree with Hailey. Doesn't help
that to Buzetti Bill
I'm the Garmy Drumb Plumber,

July 27 1944

Soviet Vistula.
Brest-Litovsk. Avranches,
Caen & Push and Go.
Bor-Komorowski's uprising.
Philadelphia Transportation
Strike. Ankara.
Myitkyina falls. Piano wire &
meat hooks. PLUTO.
Audie Murphy's hill.
Third Army's Mantes-la-Jolie.
Paris police rebel.
—a field of ruins.
Pétain to Wiesbaden. Falaise.
—Ja.

Dietrich von Choltitz
surrenders to Henri Karcher.
Romania vs Germany.
Maidanek.
Toulon & Marseilles.
Foglia River & Gothic.
Bucharest. Sedan. Argonne.
Lyons. Brussels. Helsinki
Armistice. Antwerp's Channel
Ports. Benelux. Tito's Balkans.
V2 & London. Operation Anvil
to Dragoon. Omar Bradley's
Siegfried. Moselle River.
Lagedi, 3,000 go.

April 1 1983

London's Security Express.
Human chain.
Issam Sartawi goes.
Chicago's Harold Washington.
Kenneth Adelman.
Nicaraguan assistance.
Beirut, US Embassy &
2,000 lbs of explosives, 63 go.
Joan Benoit's 2:22:42.
Persian Gulf leak.
—a nation at risk.
Polish 20 city protests.
—government out of the barrel of.
Iran's Tudeh Party.
David Tom's $400,000.
Halo's Derby
Carol goes.
El Salvador aid.
2.33 million acres.
Chile & 1,000 arrests.
Islanders over Oilers.
Anguilcourt-le-Sart, dioxin &
41 canisters. Pretoria,
South African Air Force &
ANC car bomb, 18 go.
Buenos Aires 40,000.

But then —*I'm off*, pedalling free,
conqueror of drives, conqueror of seasons,
banished only by softening sighs.
His. Wondering, if business
be business, could I ever just turn
Sam over to some flossier RIALTO HO?
Bodies fast dropping. Extend a gentle hand.
I'm conduct beyond demand.
Thank yous. Courtesy. Concerns.
I've only conduct now.
Chill hard. Raw. Game sparred. Rugged
legs, lame. Beaded curls. Combat boots.
It clears. It rains.
Pare is pears. Working on
duties. Organizings surrounded.
I'm allways moved by the
manners of going away.
So I stay.

May 26 1944

Allies & South of France,
3,760 go.
Damascus & Drop of Milk.
15th Air Force, B-24s
& Concordia Vega.
Rome. B-29s hit Japan.
—OK, let'S go.
82nd & 101st Airborne.
Orne Floating Headquarters.
—World exploded.
—stand with US.
Utah. Omaha. Sword.
Gold. Juno. Quakers,
Rangers & Mulberries.
2,500 go. Bayeux. Bonomi.
Oradour-sur-Glane, 634 go.
Vengeance Rocket.
B-29's Kyushu. Bloch goes.
Ireland's Republic.
Saipan Island. Elba.
Zay goes.
—to let Them down.
Cherbourg.
Philippe Henriot goes.
Dewey. Minsk.
Birkenau. Port Chicago.
von Stauffenberg.
Monetary Fund.
Operation Cobra.

That's how I return.
My turn around manners
allways flipping me back
to my want's duty.
The shock of pairless veers.
When it rains. When it clears.
Beret. Head shaved. All clumsy, but
rock. So beat, but socked. Cold now.
I've only conduct.
Permissions. Courtesy. Yes Sir! Miss!
And all that conduct must fail at.
I strive to give away. Adhere. Rely.
Defer ambiviolence towards G.I.s
advancing on Hailey. Business is never
business when
soft sighs challenge vows to
legions vanquished, lives anguished.
So I pedal back: —*Hi there, Stuff.*

Outandabout. Cycling pavements around
Lake Drive. Up Martin
Luther King. To Broadway.
Where streets afford no attraction.
No boredom. So I coast. Here for now.
Forever. No hands. So dope.

Up Monte Caprino to
Via Del Funari. Reginella.

Lindens & Chicory warn me. Afraid.

New wave. All underage. Dismayed.
Along Via Del Progresso to the Tiber.
Past sailors, rough trade and petroleum
trampolinemen. Stocks, bonds & slaves. Zot.

Honeylocusts & Jewelweed worrying.

Hazardous wibbles for this freewheeling
waif. Allways a slum. Big Bites to Glum.
Heavy uptight.
What allways fights.

May 24 1983

George J Gregory
& Elizabeth New Jersey.
Albert A Schaufelberger
goes. Williamsburg Economic
summit & Global Recession.
76ers over Lakers.
Morazán.
Volga River collision,
over 100 go.
Shoreham &135 arrests.
Yannick Noah.
Miguel d'Escoto Brockman
& 3 US diplomats.

—I warn you.

3,526 strike outs.
Thatcher.
Pioneer 10 out.
Anti-Pinochet protests.
—On you depends tomorrow.
—Ride Sally, Ride.
Honduras & rocket-propelled
grenade, 2 go.
Gujarat floods, 900 go.
Acid rain. Dow. Reagan
& National Women's Caucus.
NAACP's George Bush.
Daniel Crane & Gerry Studds.

—muzzled no less.

Overburdening. Allways overrunning.
How these shores lose ground.
Retreat. Reflow US. We're every bargain.
Low. High. Accrued. Wagered. Pooled.
Killing **Sloths & Meerkats**. By meat wagons.
BIGOTs on the get along flying for a zero
hour. Production, assembly, cargo power.
Along Raspail towards the Périphérique.
Shellshocked. Underage. All crippling.

Penguins & Pandas dying.

Along Wharf Street to Chouteau Avenue.
Grattan Street allone.
Stark. Hanging on. Rarely.
Now where? Just to coast. Excited
by the most desolate roads.
Looping Gravois Avenue. Restalozzi to
Grand. Arsenal. Big Bend.
Over blurring rubble. Outandabout.

March 24 1944

Stalag Luft III's 76 POWs.
French Maquis.
Kovno, 800 go. UNRRA.
Charles Wingate goes.
Palaus & 150 planes. Ascq's
Panzer, 86 go. Vesuvius.

—destroy state.

De Gaulle's French Committee
of National Liberation.
PAYE. Quinine.
Malinovsky's Odessa.
Simferopol. Fort Stikine.
Blobel Commando.
Hollandia. Palmiro Togliatti.
Humbolt & Tanahmerah leap.

—You New Dealer!

Tiger & E-boats.
Meat rationing over.
Rommel's Steel Ring.
Pensive's Derby. Paton's bank.
Allmendiger & Schorner.
James Vincent Forrestal.
Gustav fails. Cassino falls.
Burma Guerrillas,
Merrill's Marauders &
Myitkyina. Kiel &
Pas-de-Calais. Loyang.
US through Anzio.

July 24 1983

George Brett's pine tar.
—atmosphere of terror.
Lisbon, Turkish Embassy &
Armenian terrorists, 7 go.
Pershing II.
Contadora Group.

—rapid deterioration.
AWACS, F-15s & Chad.
Bettino Craxi.

Christine Craft's Metromedia.
Shawnda Leea Summers goes.
Chilean protest, 17 go.
Hissen Habre & Faya-Largeau.

*—overthrow Muammar
el-Qaddafi.*

Hurricane Alicia, 17 go.
Manila Airport & Rolando
Galman y Dawang,
Benigno S Aquino goes.
Benjamin Ng guilty.
Beirut's US Marines, 2 go.
Soviet Fighter, Sakhalin
Island & Flight 007, 269 go.
Yitzhak Shamir. 4.72 billion.
Raincoat balloon.
Vanessa Williams.
Rich's evasion.

I don't fight anything.
Not even the glide. 86ed.
Splish, Shlap and Slish.
How The River slides. Bridges the wides.
Which for Sam might allmost slow.
Nearly stands still, digging the rubble.
Sam illified, funkified,
even if banging a double.
Until by Harrison Street,
I again return to my beat. Craving on
those Green Eyes with flecks of Gold.
And his long arms' tender hold.
—*G,* I wave, pretty desperately.
—*Allmost done,* bumping me a
grin, while PEST CONTROL, working
about, stirs up some pesticide.
—*Whaz alive?*
—*A hive, Sir.*

Jan 26 1944

Argentina. Missouri.
Martin Bormann. Spruance.
*—When we hit,
we hit hard and for keeps.*
Fraz Kutschera, 100 go.
Kuril Islands. Vanakula.
Burma. Lutsk & Rovno.
Panchen Lama.
—for something greater.
US 34th.
Khedive Ismail, 2,000 go.
Plateau des Glières.
Monte Cassino.
Korsun thousands.
Alabama oil. U-410
& Penelope.

Bedaux goes. Hideki Tojo.
Marianas & Guam.
Operation Brewer.
—no safety there by.
Stettinius. Erkner balls.
Wales strike. Ireland's Axis
envoys. Vienna bombing.
Koldichevo's 99.
—I am a butcher thirsty.
Pierre Pucheu goes.
Cordell Hull's Cooperation.
A Rome Roundup.

Now's alive with
Proud Profiteers of Trade. Presidents
confident with controlled rationings and
War bonds. The Securities Exchange.
Flats on the dole. I drop off Hailey,
taking over the Bike: —*Evaporate.*
From her long legs & tender knees. And
those Gold Eyes with flecks of Green.
Blockbusters. Zazoops. I return to mosey
along battered roads. Hardscrabble
doubling me back away from
my sloggin & hassleless Hailey,
bustling to keep US steady,
slow US down for US.
But The River keeps slipping.
Slish and Shlapsplish.
Our relentless churnings allways
overtaking everything.

Sept 21 1983

—have a woman,
two Jews and a cripple.
Argentinian amnesty.
Australia II cups Liberty.
Rio Grande crossing million.
Icebreakers & 30 Soviet
freighters. Guion Bluford.
Philippine rebels, 46 go.
AFL-CIO's Walter Mondale.
Punjab.
Rangoon explosion, 19 go.

Yvonne Shelly Antosh goes.
Orioles over Phillies.
Africa's 22.
Hudson Austin
& Bernard Coard,
Maurice Bishop goes. Beirut,
8th Marines Headquarters
& Mercedes truck, 241 go.
French barracks, 47 go.
Organization of Eastern
Caribbean States, US troops
& Grenada.

—Rainbow coalition.
Philadelphia's mayor.
Edwin Wilson.
Alfred Heineken.
Cypriot's Free State.

—Tripendicular! Gorging on comb?
Both of US crowd.
—Nah, just icing the swarm.
Tsttttttt, tsttttttt.
More spray. Tripping US away,
spitting coughs, threats & slaps.
But thank you, close out, at least our
shifts relink. Ending together. At last.
Sam on handlebars. Thumbing gears.
Me pumpin to steer.
Around hushing **Amaranth**.
Down solemn paths. Someone's here.
We're allways here. And overwhelmed by
no distances, encircling, fastening US to
The City, Our Mishishishi and US. Just two
for the World. Allone supplying the force
of unity. Altering, faltering
allies we need.

Dec 1 1943

Oswald Mosley free.
Mustard &
John Harvey. Tehran.

—undertaken
from the East, West and South.
—to clean Them out
thoroughly.
Mignano. Marshall Islands.
P-51D Mustang. Task Force
76. New Britain Island.
Kurcwaig & Dorosiewicz.
Chicago over Washington.
Arctic Scharnhorst &
JW-55B. Army's rail.
—whizzing all around the ship.
Paris ball-bearings.

—L'audace, l'audace,
toujours l'audace.

Soviet troops over Polish
border. Kaj Munk goes.
Bell P-59. San Vittore.
Victor Basch goes.
Galeazzo Ciano goes.
$99.7 billion. Oschersieben,
Halberstadt & Brunswick.
Supreme Command of Allied
Expeditionary Force.
Anzio. Rakitno. JW-56A.

Dashing off soon.
Out. Around.
With Hailey of course but allso unsure,
exploring a World for just two.
US, The Mishishishi, The City. However
fascinating and so many ways nifty, still
ever only by. Because we're allways near?
Dangerously dear? **Larks** now quieting?
By roundabouts. Autobahns. Hailey steers,
pedals. I just perch on handles.
Allready our shifts diverging, thanks
to the overtime our employers demand.
And still without slack & flak
we stumble back.
Groooooan, grmmmble. Our
time together waning.
And both of US dismayed by
why this is so.

Nov 24 1983

PLO Israel & prisoners:
4,500 for 6.
Memphis, Wells Fargo &
$6.4 million.
Equal Employment
Opportunity quotas.
Hammana bombardment.
Beirut airport, 8 go.

*—of working people
to organize.*
6 Kuwait car bombs, 7 go.
Lenell Geter's trial.
Kim-kai Pitsor goes.
Harrods blast, 5 go.

—will move forward.
Tripoli, 5 Greek ships &
4,000 PLO troops.
Elizabeth Bouvia.

—whom I have forgiven and.

—don't quarrel with success.
Tunis & Sfax, 75 go.
Texaco, Getty Oil &
$10 billion.

—more guns.
Malcolm H Kerr goes.
Takeda mine, 83 go.

Allways new. And peaceful too. On a
turnandtoss of bedding. Humming fan.

—How'z life?

—Taking forever.

—Let'S dance?

—And take forever with US?

—Yes.

—Let'S go.

—We're so poor.

—We'll work it out.

*—I want you just this way. To never have to go away.
From you. From US. Allways kissing, adored.
The rest. And smiling. To hold you when we're
happy, we're lazy. Sad. When you're stubborn.
When you're brave. When you're mad. When you're
scorned. But allways beside me and my moods.*

—That's too easy.

—Then be difficult.

If peaceful still. Before the passing World.
Except US. Fan humming. Linen bundled up.

—Taking everyone.

—How is forever?

—Dancing on.

—Taking our time?

—Yes.

—Let US go gently.

—We're that poor.

—And the World works?

*away and our Love is clutched by no one.
breath. Their lives. For US. For me. Until all's
Ravaging the best. The rest. Taking away their
When I'm crazy, anguished and brutal to behold.
Bring sorrow. And terror. When I'm defenseless.
—My rudeness. Besides I curve when I'm cruel.*

—What's easier?

—That's too difficult.

—the road to Rome.
Shinchiku & 42 planes.
Gilbert Islands. Tarawa Atoll.
Berlin's 2,000 tons.
& Chiang Kai-shek. 764 RAF,
Tarawa. Cairo's Churchill, FDR
SL-139/MKS-30. Fido.
Léros & Castelrosso.
U-794's Schnorkel.

Dulverton off Kos.
Grenoble & bayonets.
Rehabilitation Administration.
United Nations Relief and
Vatutin, 88th & Kiev.
Senate's Connally.
Hatsukaze & Sendai.
Barbara & Mondragone.
& Dnieprodzerzhinsk.
Luftwaffe. Dniepropetrovsk
New Guinea. Düren
Sobibor's 300. Australians'
Sacha Pieczerski's mutiny.
& War on Germany.
Volturno River, Italy
Mulberry landing.
Yankees over Cardinals.
Petrov's Caucasus.
Naples & McCreery's X Corps.

Oct 1 1943

—I want to let you go. Betray US.
Give US Torment, Deaths and Futures.
Then curl up with you through
Reunions, Abuses and Departures.
Too when you arrive. When you're allone.
When I go. When I'm allone. But
allways beside you wherever we roam.
—Now? —Yes. —O.
—Again? —O. —Yes.
—Except it's allready going.
—So sad. —Over with so fast.
—Why does everything go
that way except US?
—Because we're allways at once?
—Everything and everyone's?
—Yes? —Now. —Yes? —Again?
—O. —O. —I hear you hearing me.
—I'm not content.

Jan 22 1984
Super Bowl XVIII,
LA over Washington.
Edwin Meese over
William French Smith.
—America is back.
Operation Manta.
Jaime Lusinchi.
Bruce McCandless
& Robert L Stewart.
Sarajevo.
Andropov goes.
Kostantin Chernenko.
—to cool the hot heads of.
Delise Louise goes.
David's bubble.
Enrique Casas Vila goes.
Lebanon's last US Marines.
—to assume this challenge.
Maitatsine & Yola, 1,000 go.
—I got hurt.
Lisa Yates goes.
81-15.
South Africa & Mozambique.
County Clare shootout, Irish
National Liberation Army
& Mad Dog.
Mary Lou Retton's 10.
Cuba, Angola & troops.

—My violence?
—I feer you feering me.
—Now? —Yes. —Again? —Yes.
—Everytime and everyway.
—Let'S just do it all at once.
—Because except for US
everyone goes away without US.
—Over with so fast. —So sad.
—Except it's allready going out.
—Yes? —O. —Again?
—O. —Yes. —Now.
—Whenever we roam be beside me.
When you're allone. When you go.
When no one comes along. And for all we
Wander, Encounter and Open
allways curl up with me.
Give me Pain, Past and Fury.
Betray my way. I won't abandon you.

Aug 1 1943
PT-109. Ploieşti oil.
Harlem riot. Treblinka revolt.
Catania. Maddalena Island.
Erik Scavenius.
Nuremberg's 3,444 tons.
656 RAF for Milan.
Patton's apology.
Castellano & Hoare.
7th, 8th & Messina.
Quebec's Three. Vella Lavella.
Peenemünde bombed.
Jeschonnek goes.
John Curtin. V1.
Von Manstein's XI Corps
& Kharkov. Chungking.
Mountbatten's
South East Asia.
4 days of Canadian fishing.
Egret, Athabaskan &
Chase-Me-Charlies.
Gestapo's Lebrun.
Boris of Bulgaria goes.
Danish uprising.
Albert Speer. Pietro Badoglio.
Reggio Calabria. Salerno.
—Duce, you are free.
Corsica rising.
Fulbright. Smolensk.
Rome's 50 gold kilos.

March 25 1984

José Napoleón Duarte &
Roberto D'Aubuisson.
Donald Regan, Raúl Alfonsin
& $500 million.
Marvin Gaye goes.
Terry Rene Milligan goes.
Lansana Konte over
Sékou Touré.
Nicaragua harbors & 84-12.
—behaved very nicely.
El Salvador aid.
Christopher Wilder goes.
London Libyan Embassy
& protest,
Yvonne Fletcher goes.
Mike MacCarthy, Amanda
Tucker & Eiffel Tower.

20,000 Soviet troops
& Panjshir Valley.
LAV & AIDS. David
Anthony Kennedy goes.
—It's flourishing.
Poland, Soviet Union &
Trade Pact. Swale's Derby.
$180 million. Nicolas Ardito
Barletta Vallarina.
Ibuprofen.
Iraq's Panamanian Cargo ship.

—I want you more and more.
—I feer more and more.
—I'm afraid too.
—I'm so strange now. Unmissed.
We're impossible to dismiss.
—To be apart of this?
—Whirls of ours.
—Still stinging to. —Racing. —earn.
—But who all chases US?
—Only US. —And outlaws US?
—US. —How?
—By something wide which feels close.
Open but feels closed. Lying weirdly
across US. Between US. Where we're
closest, where we touch, where we're one.
Somehow continuing on separately.
—Hold me tighter. —On top of me.
—Behind me. —Harder. —Use your teeth.

May 29 1943

2,622 go. 29 imprisoned.
Committee of National
Liberation. Juan Perón.
Count Fleet's Triple.
Pantelleria yields.
Butterfly bombs.
Board of Education vs
Barnette. Archibald Wavell.
Lancaster Shuttle. Detroit riot,
29 go. Mülheim.
War Labor Dispute Act.
Lille & Trotobas.
—utmost severity.
Zoots & Hispanics.
Rendova Island.
Gibraltar & Kim Philby,
Wladislaw Sikorski goes.
Winniza. Jean Moulin goes.
Sicily, Operation Husky
& 3,000 ships.
National Committee for Free
Germany. Citadel & Kursk.
—turns over.
Crowley & Office of Economic
Warfare. Bougainville Island.
Palermo.
O'Hair, Duckworth & Hurricane.
Hamburg razed.

—Stroke my chest. —Softer. —Lick my belly.
—Below there. Lower. —Longer now. Slower.
—Somehow now, here, we're one, while allready
somewhere nearer we go on apart.
Untouched. Our between. Our across.
Dying weirdly. Which feels tight but loosens.
Feels loose but opens wide up.
—US? —US.
—Fleeing US? —Only US.
—Does anyone ever allow US?
—Only our yearning out racing.
—These Worlds of ours.
—United if unforgiven.
—Because we're allways unpermitted. We're
various. We're extremely dangerous.
—Don't be afraid.
—I threaten more and more.
—I want you more and more.

May 23 1984
Kristine Holderied.
Second Hand Smoke.
Colleen Renee Brockman goes.
Saudi Arabia's 400
Stinger missiles.
—monstrous carbuncle on.
Hawaii land. Punjab, 22 go.
Golden Amritsar, 308 go.
Jarnail Singh
Bhindranwale goes.
—These are the.
Bogdan Lis. Maui morning.
Celtics over Lakers.
—fully under control.
Uniondale disabled.
Paris, schools & 850,000.
Jesse Jackson's 22.
John N Turner.
Gomez vs US Jaycees.
Albany seat belts.
Lange over Muldoon.
Kari A Swenson. Penn Square
Bank of Oklahoma.
—and the despised.
San Ysidro, McDonald's
& James Oliver Huberty, 20 go.
Geraldine Ferraro.

—Everyone dreams the Dream
but you are it.
—I won't help being.
—Your tears can't ever stop me.
—Allready drying.
—So sad.
—Is that surviving?
We take nips of a saltier equity. Mixed.
Our HONEY. With just 6½ Jars left.
Sticking on our lips, our fingers.
Our Leftwrist Twists of Gold too.
Sticking US together.
Sticking US to the World. When soon
our CHANGING HOPE visits such snuggles.
Union rocking up from a snooze:
—Everlasting Whims & Everlasting Loss.
Against Horrors passing with Love's passing.
Between Them you must choose.

March 28 1943
—severe defeat on enemy.
Eighth Army. Desert Rats.
Mussolini, Hitler & Salzburg.
Katyn thousands.
Martinique & Guadeloupe.
Cape Bon, 59 Luftwaffe
transports & 10 fighters.
Jurgen Stroop &
Warsaw Ghetto uprising.
Pittsburgh strikes.
War Powers.
Major Martin, Pam &
Operation Mincemeat.
Count Fleet's Derby.
United Mine Workers.
Bizerte & Tunis.
Attu's 7th Division.
—Tunisian campaign is over.
I-777 sinks Centaur.
Comintern. 56,065 go.
Guy Gibson's Mohne &
Eder Dams.
UN Food Conference.
SC-130. Me262.
Dortmund.
Mengele. DC & V.
3¢
Amy N Stannard.
Office of War Mobilization.

—Choice then is allways Them?
—Love & Horror's impermanence forever against
Loss & the Caprice of endurance.
Too soon gone, a snoozing Labor from such
struggles, our CHANGING HOPE rocks away.
Leaving US to the World.
Leaving US together with
our Leftwrist Twists of Gold.
Our sticky fingers, our lips.
With just 5½ Jars of HONEY left.
Our liquiditty. Sweetest mix of all we sip.
—Here's to deciding.
—So glad.
—Allready welling up.
—Laughter won't ever stop me.
—I can't help bleeding.
—Everyone dreams the Dream
but we are it.

July 21 1984

James F Fixx goes.
Suzette Charles.
Svetlana Savitskaya's stroll.
Continental Illinois, FDIC &
$4.5 billion loan.
Tehran's Air France.

Joan Benoit's marathon.
Carl Lewis.
Mary Decker & Zola Budd.
—We begin bombing.
US Navy & homosexuality.
Lee Trevino.
Manila's 900,000.
Mont Louis, Olau Brittania
& Uranium hexafluoride.
Gulbuddin Hekmatyar &
Burhanuddin Rabbani.
New Jersey schools
& asbestos.
Typhoon Ike, 1,363 go.
Montreal, 10:22 AM &
Brigham's rail, 3 go.
Pieter W Botha.
Hirohito & Chun Doo Hwan.
Nicaraguan contras &
$10 million.
Dennis Banks surrenders.
Miami's 10,000.

—Choice then is allways Them?
—Love & Horror's impermanence forever against
Loss & the Caprice of endurance.

Too soon gone, a snoozing Labor from such
struggles, our CHANGING HOPE rocks away.
Leaving US to the World.
Leaving US together with
our Leftwrist Twists of Gold.
Our sticky fingers, our lips.
With just 5½ Jars of HONEY left.
Our liquiditty. Sweetest mix of all we sip.

—Here's to deciding.
—So glad.
—Allready welling up.
—Laughter won't ever stop me.
—I can't help bleeding.
—Everyone dreams the Dream
but we are it.

Jan 28 1943

16–65 & 17–45.
Mosquitos over Berlin.
Paulus, Univermag
& Stalingrad.
—to the last man and
last round.
Marseilles. La Motta rounds
Sugar Ray Robinson.
3 shoes.
—Take her down.
Chindits & Burma.
Naples. Kursk. Tenaro.
—Total and complete defeat.
Globalloney.
Bess Houdini goes.
Faid-Sened.
—War with the life of.
Patton, Rommel
& Kasserine Pass. Mareth.
Sbiba & Ousseltia.
Kolomyia, 2,000 go.
Soviet's Rzhev. Operation
Cannibal. Gloster Meteor.
500 lb skip. Bismarck sea.
Essen & Krupp Arms.
—no other road.
Genoa, Turin & Milan.
—to the east.
HX-229.

—Everyone dreams the Dream
but you are it.
—I won't help being.
—Your tears can't ever stop me.
—Allready drying.
—So sad.
—Is that surviving?

We take nips of a saltier equity. Mixed.
Our HONEY. With just 6½ Jars left.
Sticking on our lips, our fingers.
Our Leftwrist Twists of Gold too.
Sticking US together.
Sticking US to the World. When soon
our CHANGING HOPE visits such snuggles.
Union rocking up from a snooze:

—Everlasting Whims & Everlasting Loss.
Against Horrors passing with Love's passing.
Between Them you must choose.

Sept 20 1984

Lebanon, 11:44 AM
& US Embassy, 8 go.
Reagan & Gromyko.

Italy's anti-Mafia roundup.
Peter V Ueberroth.
Kathryn Sullivan's stroll.
Brighton blast, 2 go.

—democracy by terrorism.
Mary Sue Bello goes.
Detroit over San Diego.
Duarte, Guillermo Ungo
& Rubén Zamora.
El Salvador & CIA, 4 go.

—Mr. Mondale but I am.
Baby Fae. Ethiopian
starvation. Solidarity
& Grzegorz Piotrowski,
Jerzy Popieluszko goes.
Gandhi goes. Rajiv Gandhi.
Margie Velma Barfield goes.
Svetlana Alliluyeva returns.
Johannesburg strikes,
10 go. 49/50

—the beginning of
everything.
Suchitoto.
Chile's mass arrests.

—Stroke my chest. —Softer. —Lick my belly.
—Below there. Lower. —Longer now. Slower.
—Somehow now, here, we're one, while allready
somewhere nearer we go on apart.
Untouched. Our between. Our across.
Dying weirdly. Which feels tight but loosens.
Feels loose but opens wide up.
—US? —US.
—Fleeing US? —Only US.
—Does anyone ever allow US?
—Only our yearning out racing.
—These Worlds of ours.
—United if unforgiven.
—Because we're allways unpermitted. We're
various. We're extremely dangerous.
—Don't be afraid.
—I threaten more and more.
—I want you more and more.

Nov 29 1942

Coffee & 4 gallons of gas.

3:45 PM, Stagg Field &
Fermi's Atomic Pile.
Petroleum
Administration for War.

—honorable discharge.
US planes over Italy.
USS New Jersey.
Hasler, Sparks & Laver.
Operation Winter Storm.
Washington over Chicago.
Splendid's Aviere. Sandur,
8 go. Bonnier de la Chapelle's
umbrella, Darlan goes.
Barents Sea, JW-51B &
Admiral Hipper. 110,000
Japanese Americans.
32nd division's Buna.
Leclerc's Free French.
FDR, Admiral Q & Mr P.
Siege of Sixth Army.
Schluesselburg.
Cooperative Health Groups.
Dorothy & Tripoli.

—unconditional surrender.
Messe. Wilhelmshaven
& Emden.

—I want you more and more.
—I feer more and more.
—I'm afraid too.
—I'm so strange now. Unmissed.
We're impossible to dismiss.
—To be apart of this?
—Whirls of ours.
—Still racing to. —Stinging. —earn.
—But who all chases US?
—Only US. —And outlaws US?
—US. —How?
—By something wide which feels close.
Open but feels closed. Lying weirdly
across US. Between US. Where we're
closest, where we touch, where we're one.
Somehow continuing on separately.
—Hold me tighter. —On top of me.
—Behind me. —Harder. —Use your teeth.

Nov 19 1984

Mexico City & petroleum gas, 334 go.
Korea's DMZ & Vasily Yakovlevich Matuzok, 4 go.
New Caledonia & Eloi Machoro.
Bhopal, Union Carbide & MIC, over 1,600 go.
Reagan & Tutu.
US & UNESCO.
Warren M Anderson.
Cuba's 2,746.
Erick Dickerson & 2,007 yards.
Muhammad Zia ul-Haq's Islamization.
Bernhard Goetz.
Vietnamese overrun Rithisen. New Orleans & rotating power failures.
Pedro René Yanes goes.
West Germany & Pershing II, 3 go.
Edward Kennedy, apartheid & economic sanctions.
San Antonio blizzard.
Addis Ababa & train, 392 go.
Hun Sen.

—My violence?
—I feer you feering me.
—Now? —Yes. —Again? —Yes.
—Everytime and everyway.
—Let'S just do it all at once.
—Because except for US
everyone goes away without US.
—Over with so fast. —So sad.
—Except it's allready going out.
—Yes? —O. —Again?
—O. —Yes. —Now.
—Whenever we roam be beside me.
When you're allone. When you go.
When no one comes along. And for all we
Wander, Encounter and Open
allways curl up with me.
Give me Pain, Past and Fury.
Betray my way. I won't abandon you.

Oct 1 1942

Stanley's XP-59.
Herriot arrested.
—War of the races.
Cardinals over Yankees.
—My fighting days are over.
Bengal cyclone, 40,000 go.
SC-104 & Wotan. Victory tax.
Clark reaches Algiers.
Hornet & Enterprise.
Monty.
—miserable strip of land.
Bihac. Madagascar.
—get the paddles.
Vichy & US.
Algiers capitulates.
—But it is perhaps the.
Morocco's Cap El Hawk.
—among you to repulse.
Djebel Abiod & Medjez el Bab.
Over the Volga. Vatutin, Rokossovsky & Eremenko.
Alcan Alaskan Highway.
Stalingrad offensive.
Darlan's Dakar. Kalach.
Toulon scuttle.
Cocoanut Grove, 492 go.
Blade Force.

—I want to let you go. Betray US.
Give US Torment, Deaths and Futures.
Then curl up with you through
Reunions, Abuses and Departures.
Too when you arrive. When you're allone.
When I go. When I'm allone. But
allways beside you wherever we roam.
—Now? —Yes. —O.
—Again? —O. —Yes.
—Except it's allready going.
—So sad. —Over with so fast.
—Why does everything go
that way except US?
—Because we're allways at once?
—Everything and everyone's?
—Yes? —Now. —Yes? —Again?
—O. —O. —I hear you hearing me.
—I'm not content.

—That's too difficult.

—What's easier?

—My rudeness. Besides I curve when I'm cruel.
Bring sorrow. And terror. When I'm defenseless.
When I'm crazy, anguished and brutal to behold.
Ravaging the best. The rest. Taking away their
breath. Their lives. For US. For me. Until all's
away and our Love is clutched by no one.

—And the World works?

—We're that poor.

—Let US go gently.

—Yes.

—Taking our time?

—Dancing on.

—How iz forever?

—Taking everyone.

Except US. Fan rattling. Linen rolled up.
If pacific still. Before the passing World.

Jan 20 1985

Super Bowl XIX,
49ers over Dolphins.
Sub-Zero DC.
—free to follow their.
Florida grapefruits.
David Lange & US Warships.
Lima power outage.
HPA-23. Phum Thmei.
Karpov & Kasparov.
Ramu goes. Cape Town
& Khayelitsha, 8 go. Evert van
Benthem's Elfstedentocht.
Nathan Pritikin goes.
Gambino, Genovese,
Lucchese, Colombo
& Bonnano.
Dennis Goldberg free.
Lee Iacocca's Liberty.
Julio María Sanguinetti.
Nuclear winter.
British coal strike over.
Ahwaz Steel.
Beirut's suburb & Hizballah,
80 go.
Mikhail S Gorbachev.
Raymond J Donovan.
71 Savings and Loan & 3 days.
Terry Anderson.

New allways. And pacific too. On a
tossandturn of bedding. Rattling fan.

—How's life?

—Taking forever.

—Let'S dance?

—And take forever with US?

—Yes.

—Let'S go.

—We're so poor.

—We'll work it out.

—I want you just this way. To never have to go away.
From you. From US. Allways kissing, adored.
The rest. And smiling. To hold you when we're
happy, we're lazy. Sad. When you're stubborn.
When you're brave. When you're mad. When you're
scorned. But allways beside me and my moods.

—That's too easy.

—Then be difficult.

July 30 1942

WAVES. Maly Trostinets,
30,000 go. Düsseldorf.
Florida Island.
6 German saboteurs go.
Mitchel Field.
Solomon Islands.
—We will stand and
fight here.
NJ General Cable Plant.
Operation Pedestal.
Eaker's 12 Forts & Rouen.
Harriman, Churchill &
Stalin. Tommy.
Dieppe, thousands go.
Brazil vs Germany.
Don River. Fletcher's carriers.
Kent goes. Willkie's globe.
Alam el Halfa.
—Give me your.
Rommel retreats. Me210.
U-156's Laconia &
Italian POWs, 1,500 go.
Treblinka. Jacqueline Cochran.
Kiska. PQ-18's 27. OPA.
Voyager & Sparrow Force.
Georg Stumme.
Yamschchikova. Hopkins &
Stier. Richard Sorge.

March 20 1985

Anchorage, 1,135 miles & Libby.
Uitenhage South Africa, 19 go. Khaibar Brigade & Marcel Fontaine.
320,000 & Denmark's strike.
Christos Sartzetakis.
Tulane basketball.
John McEnroe's challenge.
Medium-range nuclear missiles & Soviet freeze.
Gaafar el-Nimeiry.
—an amount sufficient to deter.
Galápagos, Isabela & fire.
Enver Hodja goes. Nigeria & 700,000 illegal aliens.
Discovery.
US Steel, LTV Steel, Bethlehem Steel & Steel Armco.
Spend A Buck's Derby.
Bergen-Belsen & Bitburg.
British Soccer & Bradford West Yorkshire blaze, 53 go.
Cathleen Webb & Gary Dotson.
Philadelphia's MOVE & firebomb, 11 go.

I'm off soon.
Out. About.
With Sam of course but often uneasy,
exploring a World just for two.
US, The Mishishishi, The City. However
curious and so many ways pretty, ever
only from. Because we're allways near?
Dangerously dear? **Amaranths** now wilting?
On roundabouts. Thruways. Sam pedals,
shifts. I just sit on the handle bars.
And allready our schedules diverge, thanks
to what our employers demand.
Still without flacking & slacking
we bumble back.
Grmmmble, grooooan. Our
time apart waxing.
And both of US taxed by
how this is so.

June 1 1942

Mexico & Axis.
Reinhard Heydrich goes.
442 Combat Team.
Kaga, Akagi, Soryu & Hiryu:
Midway. Kisak and Attu.
Lidice, 1,300 go.
—better World.
Elmer Davis.
Office of Strategic Services.
Tuttle. Pastorius 4.
Hyde Park.
Tobruk falls.
—for a German victory.
Commander of
American Forces.
Libya, Egypt & Desert Fox.
Amagansett & Ponte Vedra 8.
Don River. Tires & boots.
Bataan march.
Congress of Racial Equality.
Sevastopol.
El Alamein.
Castillo's neutrality.
PQ-17. Von Weichs.
Zagreb, 700 go.
—This is it, chaps.
Vélodrome's 13,000.
FBI & sedition.
Czerniaków goes.

—You're hoarding wild comb?!
Both of US crowd.
—Nope. Just slaughtering the swarm.
Sphhhhhht, sphhhhhht.
More gas. Stumbling US back,
spitting with backcaps & hacks.
But thank you, curfew, at least our
shifts relink. Over together. At last.
Hailey handlebars it. Shifting gears.
I pump and steer.
By whispurring **Larks**.
By solemn parks. Kilroy's here.
We're allways here. And overcome by
no distances, surrounding, fastening US to
The City, Our Mishishishi and US. Just two
for the World. Relying allone on a course
of unity. Faltering, altering
alliances we lead.

May 20 1985

1,150 for 3.
John Anthony Walker.
US Navy's General Dynamics.
Bradford's Mohammed
Ajeeb. Michael Lance Walker.
Bangladesh cyclone,
10,000 go. Sullivan's 500.
Brazil's prison lottery, 13 go.

—second American
Revolution for.
Alabama's one-minute.
Lakers over Celtics.
Israel out of Lebanon.
Thomas Sutherland.

Karen Ann Quinlan goes.
Frankfurt Airport,
1 leaves, 3 go. 747 over
Atlantic Ocean, 329 go.
Beirut banquet.
Damascus 39. Atlit.
Navratilova over Lloyd.

—of misfits, Looney Tunes
and squalid criminals.
Auckland's Rainbow Warrior,
1 goes.
—it's long overdue.

Polyp. F-14s, Iran & 5 arrests.

Now'z alive with
Buzzing Buccaneers of Trade. CEOs
confident with leveraged buyouts and
junk bonds. The Securities Exchange
Gang out long. I drop off Sam
and take over the Bike: —*Sideways.*
From his strong arms & long hold. And
those Green Eyes with flecks of Gold.
I return to my ride
along starved roads. Palatine plazas
doubling me back away from
my laboring & unwavering Sam,
hustling to keep US put,
slow US down for US.
But The River keeps ripping.
Splish and Shlapshlish.
Our unquitting flow still
overdoing everything.

April 3 1942

Flying Fortresses & Burma.
Ceylon, Hermes & Vampire.
—Over the hump.
Bataan Peninsula, King &
76,000 surrender.
New Delhi Congress.
Nelson over Hogan.
Coughlin & Espionage Act.
Koenigstein Fortress
& Giraud. GI Joe.
B-25's, Tokyo &
Shangri-la. Exeter.

—will ruthlessly eliminate
everybody.

Pryor storm, 100 go.

—hard work, sorrow and
blood.
Baederkerblitz & York.
Shut Out's Derby.
Burma road. Wainwright,
Masaharu & Corregidor.
—one flattop.
Shoho, Lady Lex & Coral Sea.
Malta & 60 Spitfires.
Lively, Kipling, Jackal
& 31 Ju87. WAAC. Kerch.
Harris's Cologne.
Kharkov. Izyum.

I don't confront anything.
Not even the flow. AWOL.
Slish, Shlap and Splish.
How The River goes. Bridges of Os.
Which for Hailey might allmost slow.
Nearly stays put, enjoying the trouble.
Hailey happified, satisfied,
even when pulling a double.
Until by Grant Road,
I again return to my post. Anxious for
those Gold Eyes with flecks of Green.
And her long legs with sugary knees.
—*Snazzy,* I wave, allmost desperately.
—*Just finishing up,* mashing me
dimples, while Pest Control, jerking
around, sprays Zyklon mist.
—*Whaz buzzin?*
—*A beehive, Miss.*

July 16 1985

Private Sector & NJ Hack Shack. Fiemme Valley & Dolomite Dam, 208 go. South Africa & Police Emergency Powers. *—sitting on silver bars!*

Steve Cram & 3:46:31. Alan García Pérez over Fernando Belaúnde Terry. Delta's Dallas, 133 go. Baseball strike. Flotilla For Peace. Charleston, Union Carbide & Aldicarb oxime. 747SR & Mount Ogura, 520 go. Hanoi's 26 handover. Kharg Island's Exocets. Harchand Singh Longowal goes.

Mount Vernon's 21. Hans Joachim Tiedge defects. West Germany's spies. Stalker. Samantha Smith goes.

—road to abdication and.

Suroit, Knorr & Titanic.

Oversupplying. Ever irremeable.
How all the banks go bust.
Roll over. Buy US. We're every ordeal.
High. Low. Adjusted. Fixed. Dutch Auctioned.
Killing **Honeylocusts & Jewelweed**. By
Blisted, slanging criles of crills for hourly
puffs. Mayflower thrills with padded cuffs.
Along Nazionale towards Raccordo Anulare.
Addicts. Underage. All wavering.
Linden & Chicory dying.
Along Leonor K Sullivan to Washington.
Tucker Boulevard allone.
Unsparing. Hands on. Hardly.
Now here, just coasting. Excited
most by the remotest streets.
North Florissant Avenue. Hebert to
Garrison. Natural Bridge. Union.
Over these blurring curbs. Aboutandout.

Jan 31 1942

Franz Stahlecker, 229,052 go. Gilbert & Marshall Islands. Empress of Asia down. Minister of Munitions. Kurochkin surrounds 90,000. Japan's Singapore. Savings Time. Sir Stafford Cripps. Operation Sea Lion. Percival surrenders. Executive Order 9066. Port Darwin. Edward O'Hare's 5. Struma down, 768 go. Kizo Nishino's Santa Barbara. De Ruyter, Java, Electra, Jupiter & Kortenaer. Crimea counterattack. RAF bombs Paris. Diego Suarez. *—Assembly.* New Guinea. Belgian deportation. Rangoon. Brazil & Axis property. *—I shall return.* 40 MPH. Supreme Commander. Belzec. 3rd Draft. Strike ban. HMS Cambeltown. Francs-Tireurs and Partisan.

Aboutandout. Cycling crunchy around
Horseshoe Lake. Down Edwardsville Road.
Rhodes. 6th. Madison. To Broadway.
Where avenues afford no distraction.
No boredom. So I coast. Here for now.
Forever. No hands. No fair.
Down La Fayette.
Italiens. Capucines.
Pandas & Penguins warning me. Afraid.
I wave. All badgy. Rearranged.
Around Place de la Concorde to the Seine.
Past tailors, capos and butter hoarding
tabacs. Soap, molars & ash. Blotto.
Meerkats & Sloths shivering.
Hazardous wobbles for this advancing
grunt. Allways a ghetto. SNAFU to JANFU.
The FUBARed front.
What allways confronts.

That's how I turn.
My returning conduct
allways heading me back
to my want's obligation.
The hurt of roaming solo.
When it clears. When it rains.
Docs. Hair shorn. All thumbs, but
tough. No dough, but brave. Grimly so.
I've only manners.
Pleases. Bells and Brakes. After Yous.
And all that manners fail to do.
I strive to give way. Oblige. Honor.
Defer ambiviolence towards Ho GIRLS'
advance on Sam. Business isn't
business ever when
soft sighs challenge commitments to
lives vanquished, regions anguished.
So I pedal back: —*Hayo, Hops.*

Sept 9 1985

South Africa
& US reversal.
Ines Guadalupe Duarte Duran.

Pete Rose's 4,192.
F-15's anti-satellite missile.
Ariane III. Oleg Gordiyevsky.

$31.8 billion. Benjamin Weir.
Mexico City shake, 4,200 go.
Richard Ramirez charged.
—we are of, from,
for the people.
Hudson goes.

Raisa Gorbachev's Paris.

Mediterranean, Achilles Lauro
& Mohammed Abul Abbas,
Leon Klinghoffer goes.

USS Saratoga's jets.
—You can run but.
Welles goes.
Fermi National Accelerator.
Benjamin Moloise goes.
Orlando Pizzolato.
Kansas over St Louis.
Charlotte's Shree Rajneesh.
Vitaly Yurchenko returns.

Humphrey. Hurricane Carter.
Bogotá Justice, 100 go.

173
188

—*Au Reservoir,* I yipe, pedalling on.
Conqueror of seasons, conqueror of drives.
Softly exiled by only sighs.
Hers. Wondering, if business
busies business, could I ever just hand
Hailey over to some stronger CRINITE OAF?
Bombs are falling. Elbows off the table.
I'm manners beyond commerce.
Ladies first. Brakes and Bells. Alerts.
I've only manners now.
Hardly tough. Unshaved, no beard. Rough
hands, weak. Whiffle resistance. Beret.
It clears. It rains.
Roamings roam. Impressed by
obligations. Embargoed by trade.
I'm allways moved by
conducts on going away.
So I stay.

Dec 1 1941

Malaya.
—climb Mount Niitaka.
Russia's Kalnin. Britain vs
Finland, Romania & Hungary.
ABCD encirclement. 7:58 AM.
—Air raid. Pearl Harbor.
This is no.
Arizona down. 2,403 go.
Kota Baharu. Singora. Guam.
Hong Kong. Philippines.

—which will live.
—over the forces of savagery
and barbarism.
Arcadia Conference.
Wake Island. Kowloon.

Bogdanovka camp,
54,000 go.
26. Bataan Battle. Manila.
$52 billion.
Kuala Lumpur.
War Production Board.
PQ-8, Matabele & U-454.
TWA crash, 22 go.
—It is Them.
Kimmel & Short.
Office of Civilian Defense.
Benghazi. Emergency Price
Control Act.

Nov 13 1985

Nevado del Ruiz, 25,000 go.
Dublin & Ulster.
Mamelodi, 13 go.
—we are not.
Xavier Suarez.
Malta hijacking, 60 go.
Ronald Pelton.
Israel's Jonathan Jay Pollard.
Robert McFarlane quits.
Texaco & Pennzoil.
Gramm-Rudman
Balanced-Budget Act.
Gander crash, 256 go.
Big Paul Castellano goes.
Aaron arrives.
—not going well
down on the farm.
Pakistan martial law.
Vienna, Rome & El Al, 18 go.
UCLA over Iowa.
Pretoria fight, 10 go.
Gore, Kerr-McGee &
nuclear exposure, 1 goes.
Super Bowl XX,
Bears over Patriots.
Libya's assets.
Ampie Mayisa goes.

At The St. Louis Club
where Sam can't stay, leaving me
tragic & jonesing.
If still managing the traffic,
politely, I guess.
But this life boosts my stress.
More longing for him, slouching my
shoulders, ever bleaker with the skinny
tossed around, about my Sam, by
VIAZOZONACCI of course. My scoffs
hardly chearing my gloomiest feers.
Some NEW HOTTIE, stacked
& round, busting moves on
my mack, turn me over
outmoded to some Lost & Found,
and then seize Sam. Doesn't help
that to BILL BAZALI
I'm the Flaky FuckUp.

172

189

Oct 2 1941

Elias goes.
Yankees over Dodgers.
CIO, AFL & Michigan tanks.
Operation Typhoon.
Moscow's T34s.
2,000 West Coast Japanese.
5,000 miles of Moscow
trenches. Fumimaro Konoye.
SC-48 & German Wolf Pack.
USS Kearney, 11 go.
Karl Holz goes. Nantes 50.
Odessa gasoline, 19,000 go.
Kharkov falls.
USS Reuben James, 115 go.
Joseph Grew.
Maxim Litvinov.
Aurora, Penelope & Lively.
Murray & Kennedy quit.
Sevastopol.
—the saddest thing.
Nomura. 130 miles
& Sidi Rezegh. Sydney sinks.
Edenborn strike. Bauxite.
—dash for the.
Gambut. HMS Barham
& U-331. Kurile.
Ravenstein. Sidra.

But if I'm CheezlePeezle,
when BAZALI BILL drops by
it's Hailey who keeps pleasing
these crowds, all buzzing to
chow down and hang out for the hops on
what's going around. She's killerdiller,
natch. Zazz girl cooking with gas.
Chearing the Gloomiest Mug with the
gentlest laugh. So certainly VIAZOZONACCI
wheels up, bumping gums
for gravel if ever bleaker, shoulders
slouched, yearning long for her.
Even when with THE WIFE.
Hailey, allways polite,
leaves him heeling snipes.
Hung up. Tragic.
Even I dig his desire
at The St. Louis Tavern.

Jan 18 1986

Mayan crash, 90 go.
Aden.
Ismail over al-Hassani.
3 Sikhs go.
Voyager 2's Uranus.
Super Bowl XX,
Bears over Patriots.
11:38 AM.
Smith, Resnik, McNair,
Onizuka, Jarvis & Scobee go.
Christa McAuliffe goes.
—belongs to the brave.
Haiti's Jean-Claude Duvalier.
—monkey's tail.
Dartmouth shanties.
Mary Beth Tinning.
Palermo's 474.
Tontons Macoutes.
Anatoly Shcharansky free.
Quirino heads. Larry Chin goes.
Clark Air Force Base
& Corazon Aquino.
—finally free.
Olaf Palme goes.
ANC 7, 7 go.
Vega 1's Halley's comet.
Flight attendants strike.
Donald Manes goes.
3,000 shoes.

Allways feeling deprived.
Down and down.
Without even a smile's relief.
Carelessly flinging patties & rings.
Coffees with cream.
Which I'm spurned for.
Bagged on, woofed and deplored.
Never tipped. While Sam
with his Leftwrist Silvergold Twist
keeps earning more. Hours stall.

Callery Pears fall.

And I serve more pie slabs for Bollas
and thick shakes for Janes.
Seatings on seatings, I'm weeded
with orders, until finally, only, can I kick
it to the back where Sam
on the bounce greets me loose with
Wassup? Hi Yeahs. Kisses & Boos.

Kisses, Soons, Swing Yous,
allready coasting loose but only
around to the front where by a bench
I kickstand the spokes, vanny to follow my
fly chick working her sidewalk tables.
Go Givers swilling soda floats,
Joltin Joes bashing slabs of pie.

Wood Ducks waddle by. Dem bums.

Their hours go. And though
I've my Leftwrist Twist of Silvergold,
Hailey's more. Allways greeted,
bonused, thanked and assured.
And of course returned for.
Slinging mud.
Artillery & beagles.
Assurances of a smiling gentle relief.
Up and up.
No one leaves deprived.

July 31 1941

—final solution.
US supplies Soviets.
Smolensk falls.
Surrounding Odessa.
Argus. Atlantic Charter.
—abandonment
of the use of force.
Iran's German tourists.
Drancy. Dnieper Dam blows.
—ground to rubble.
—I will smash.
Supply Priorities.
Kamenets-Podolski,
23,600 go. USS Greer.
Leningrad surrounded.
Gare de l'Est, Hoffman goes.
Riggs over Kovacs.
Pierre Roche goes.
Ho Chi Minh & Vietnam's
Liberty. Volga's 600,000.
Spitsbergen coal. Josef
Terboven. Hawker Typhoons.
Montana. Kiev encircled.
Ponary's 3,434 go.
Reza Shah Pahlevi.
Neptunia & Oceania,
384 go. Crimean Peninsula.
Halbert. Babi Yar, 33,771 go.
Changla.

March 20 1986

$100 million Contra aid.
Chirac over Mitterrand.
Honduran Army aid.

Tracy Ann Winston goes.
Rome acquittal.

Mexicana Airlines, 166 go.
—dreadful.
—American arrogance.

West Berlin's La Belle club,
2 go. Eastwood's
Carmel-By-The-Sea.
Dodge Morgan's round.
—at anytime by anyone.
18 F-111s & Tripoli.
A-6s, A-7s & Benghazi.
Vandenberg's Titan 34-D
blows. Peter Kilburn goes.
Nezar Hindawi &
Murphy's suitcase.

Dhaleswari River & Ferry,
300 go. Sri Lanka reservoir,
100 go.
Rob de Castella's marathon.

—shall do it again.

Garrison Diversion Project.
Chernobyl's No 4 reactor.
Ferdinand's Derby.

Ready to part,
tilting the Bike over to me,
amused even by the
winging metal edges
SALAD PREPS hurl but
allways fail to land.
—On it, Kid. Bus that floor.
Time of his life. Airplaning this Naples
for a World separated by five tables,
where hovering over more,
with a sissonne doublée, plié,
Sam fast clears the trash and then by
dishrag cleans & dries every spill.
Brim fills his dish bins. Replenishing
condiments and sides. Peppermills too.
Hosing down mats. Dollying flats. Then
overturns chairs. Replaces all wares.
Immaculates floors.

May 27 1941

—can be done. It must
be done. It will be done.
Bismarck down, 2,200 go.
Noc-out Hose Clamp Special.
Rashid Ali al-Gaylani.
Hughes retires.
Moshe Dayan's Vichy wound.
North American Aviation.
Damascus & Dentz.
Azuma Maru & 252,000 gallons.
Turkey & Reich.
Fair Employment Practices
Commission.
Germany, Russia
& Operation Barbarossa.
Bialystok, 2,000 go.
SS Einsatzgruppen.
—blood thirsty guttersnipe.
von Leeb, von Block,
von Rundstedt.
—must not leave.
Scorched earth.
Syrian freedom. Luga River.
Joe DiMaggio's 56.
—full-scale revolution.
Japanese assets.
Cattistock, Mendip, Quorn.
Panevézys, 288 go.

Until ascrubbing I go. Diving
for pearls with steel wool, soap and
buckets of boil. Whisks, colanders,
skillets and foil. Spatulas, tongs,
beaters and bowls. Dish bins too.
Dried then with dishrags on racks.
Bag the trash. With a half managed
digshuffle flap.
All over again.
Brushes, lye and steamy spray.
Circling the drain. All O the time.
—Quit the splash, Sloop. You're off
Racing then
the winging gauntlet of THE SOUS CHEFS'
serrated sharps dicing air.
Glad at least to find Hailey
waiting, holding the Bike,
reready to start.

May 16 1986

Jackie Presser's raketeering.
Costa Rica's Eden Pastora.
Botswana, Zambia
& Zimbabwe.
Hands Across America.
Crossroads & 30,000.
Rahal's 500.
Zbigniew Bujak arrested.
$2 trillion.
Celtics over Rockets.
Austria's Kurt Waldheim.
Tamil separatists & buses,
40 go.
Tutu & Botha.
Kimberly L Nelson goes.
South African millions strike.
Warren Burger retires.
Len Bias goes.
—judges that will.
—O boy, what a round.
Asian immigration.
Afghani rebels
& Soviet plane, 100 go.
Affirmative Action's 6-3.
Staten Island Ferry
& Cuban sword, 2 go.
Reagan & CIA's Contras.
Bolivia's cocaine.

And what's more dodges,
without winces & lurchings, blizzards of
knives hurled by PORTERS & SERVERS.
—*You're hurtless and dap. But man, I'm
rounding a Cool Mountain,* cancerous
CHEFFINGER sighs, *too early.*
Blades whirling
playfully after my guy who by
Shirk, Outie, and kiss, spares me
all of time's curve.
A cleaver misses, swerves. Very ill
CHEFBERG dotes only on Sam.
His loaned Bike handed off again.
Leaving when I arrive.
Arriving when I leave.
Departing Them with shifts
only we survive. Our cycle allways
putting everyone out to work.

April 1 1941

Rachid Ali's Iraq.
El Agheila breakdown.
Stafford Cripps.
Pál Teleki goes.
Germany attacks Balkans,
30,000 go. Thessalonika.
United Auto Workers.
Alain le Ray.
Office of Price Administration
and Civilian Supply.
Belgrade & Tito.
Zamjam down, 220 go.
Emmanuel Tsouderos.
Halfaya Pass to Bug Bug.
Athens. Corinth Canal.
Arthur W Mitchell.
400,000 Harland miners.
Defense Saving Bonds.
Whirlaway's Derby.
Selassie returns.
Liverpool's 7th.
Iceland, Somali &
München. Scotland &
Rudolf Hess. Westminster.
Vichy's 5,000 Jews.
Aosta & Amba Alagi.
Thanksgiving.
U-69 & Robin Moore.
Hood down, 1,300 go.

All work. The JustGettingBy
cycle of surviving. Where shifts
must shift, drifting US apart.
Hailey arriving when I'm leaving.
Hailey leaving when I'm arriving.
Handing off again the Bike still on loan
from CHEFBERG who dotes on her
and throws cleavers at me.
Leaving US only a curve of time
for Kisses, Laters and Byes.
Before braving another assault
of whirling blades.
—*Late, Drizzle Bag,* CHEFFINGER
complains. *You got
mountains. Pots, pans, plates.*
While FRYGUY & GRILLMAN hurl knives
which I, protected by Stock Pot lids,
just manage to escape.

July 18 1986

Chile's 25.
Harry Claiborne's impeachment.
Andrew & Sarah Ferguson.
Weyerhaeuser strikes.
LeMond's Tour.
LTV Steel bankruptcy.
Thatcher, EEC &
South African sanctions.
William J Schroeder goes.
Edward Lee Howard defects.
Karachi & Benazir
Bhutto's arrest.
Malakal, airline &
Sudan People's
Liberation Army, 60 go.
Tehran car bomb, 20 go.
Oklahoma's Patrick Sherrill,
15 go.
Cameroon, Lake Nios &
carbon dioxide, 1,700 go.
Soweto protests & police,
11 go. Lockheed's C-5B.
Jerry A Whitworth &
365 years. Moscow's
Nicholas Daniloff.
Istanbul, machine guns &
hand grenades, 21 go.

Letting go though sometimes
works a wider road.
Because it's free.
Because it's close.
European Hornbeams go.
Slowly. So Sam & I bury the Bike.
Chef dies. Everybody grieves. Ashes fly
across bankrupting skies playfully. Until
Sam grabbing my hand turns US out:
—*Catch US on the flip side.*
Because wherever toast drops we're both.
Jam Down. Jam Up.
Sam allways around. The sweet abrupt
between something ever restless:
The Losses of all Left
and me outcast by all
personal bends to love him beyond
him. Though nothing's beyond him.

Feb 3 1941

Vichy's Laval.
United Service Organization.
Benghazi thousands.
—and we will finish the job.
Howard Florey & Ernst Chain.
Hanover raid.
Tripoli, Afrika Korps
& Rommel. Sofia.
Kismayu. River Juba.
Singapore's ring
of British mines.
Formidable & Massawa.
Unsteady & Armando
Diaz. 250 Koufra cases.
Dardanelles. Martial law
& Holland. Laos, Cambodia
& Thailand. Halifax bomber.
Glasgow & Clydeside.
St Lawrence Seaway Plan.
Jarabub falls.
Grand Coulee.
CIO & Bethlehem Steel.
Yugoslavia joins Axis.
—plow under every
fourth American.
Cape Matapan:
Pola, Zara & Fiume.
Private Coe escapes.

it's allways their loss. The long across
rushing towards a personal
cost. Not me. I'm free.
I'm Unrest under
the Rest of their contests.
For something warm. Something sweet.
Jam Up. Jam Down.
When toast falls it's jam all around.
—*Catch US on the fip side,*
we exodust. Hailey seated behind, under
sleekspending skies where clouds of US
fly and everyone sighs. Because The Chef
lends US his Bike. On we ride. Slowly.
Lowland Gorillas panic.
Because I'm slowing here.
Because I feer
the irreparable loss of holding
someone dear.

Sept 12 1986

Hormel strike over.
Gennadi Zakharov.
Paris blast, 5 go.
Aquino's $200 million.
Tokyo's 1 million commuters.
Ulster Prison & 38.

South African sanctions,
Reagan's veto & override.
Beatrix & Oosterscheldedam.
Eugene Hasenfus.

Bermuda's Plutonium-239,
3 go. Malargo I
& 4,620 lbs of cocaine.
—Star Wars.
PLO's Yemen.
Samora Machel goes.
—must end.
New York over Boston.
—Big bang.
Sheik Ahmed Zaki Yamani.
Sandoz, Rhine & 1,000 tons.
Afghanistan, 2,000 go.
David Jacobsen free.
Muhajir & Pathan riots, 51 go.
—regain control
of our borders.
Iran Arms Deal.

And besides we're allways sixteen.
—O bet my sweet life!
—Tackhead Towelheads!
—Hadji this!
—Kiss my Waki Paki.

Chuckles for hucks given US with every
lap around a NASCAR oval. Rumping bets
placed by our Hussy Fusty Conventicle.
While with safe dials stopped,
employee earnings skyrocketing,
returns at The St. Louis Bar jump quick
because Bill Baazali keeps shorting it.
Even if our manager's Wife's dissatisfied,
cramming for Sam, anyone close, me,
to spare some concotion, emotion,
give her the clouds
which some New Roller finally does.
Under Viazizonacci's nose.

Dec 8 1940

Chicago over Washington.
Tom Harmon.
Western Desert Force &
1,000 Italians.
Operation Felix.
Marita plan. British Raids
over Italian Somalia. Office
of Production Management.
—No man can tame a tiger.
—arsenal of Democracy.
131.6 million.
—Did you do this?
—No you did.
Léon Degrelle & Rexists.
Bardia's 45,000.
—four essential human
freedoms.
—from feer everywhere.
Lend-Lease Plan.
Garden hose & fire.
Illustrious & X Fliegerkorps.
Swansea. Greyhound,
Neghelli & Phalconera.
Gnat, Ladybird &
Terror. Tobruk.
—any consideration left for.
Romanian riots. Chum.
Alexander Korizis.
Phelps Dodge Copper.

Yet Viazizonacci seethes for revenge.
The New Bim turned from him.
Hailey turned from him.
But if he'd quick with shin
come after me, anyone near, Hailey,
The Wife lurking around chills him.
Baazali Bill too, strolling
The St. Louis Cantina, checking the bank,
employees all thanked, spinning dials
on his safe.

While The Fussy Mussy Conventicle
hucks for Craps. Betting yards, rolling
cubes. Giving US wrinkles for luck.
—Ask me how Jigaboo!
—Agree then now Chillicracker!
—Live it big Hound!
—Rolling! And all fogged.

Because we're allways sixteen and

Nov 17 1986

Renault & Direct Action Group,
Georges Besse goes.
Ivan Boesky.
—by top officials.
Justice Department &
Oliver North. Fawn.
Tyson 2 rounds Berbick.
Stanley Friedman scandal.
Tennessee's MX, 4 go.
B-52s, Cruise missiles &
SALT II. McFarlane,
Poindexter & Meese.
Larry Davis.
Karachi riots, 54 go.
William J Casey's tumor.
Howard Beach,
Michael Griffith goes.
50,000 Chinese students
& People's Square.
Richard Rutan, Jeanna Yeager
& Voyager's 25,012 miles.
Dupont Plaza blaze,
over 50 go.
Beijing protest. Chad's Fada.
Maryland Amtrak, 15 go.
Nebraska's Kay A Orr.

Until this NEW MULLET scams
on me, all busy and wild,
getting down and dirty to drag me out
for a dancefloor ride.
VIAZAZONACCI digging these
haps chumps quick on Sam:
—*She puts out for any player, eh PJ? Time*
to find someone on your own team.
NEW BALLER still working his stuff:
—*Vicious biz. You're*
everybit and then some.
And me: —*I'm his. But*
thanks again.
HIM I won't suffer. I've got my limits.
This scrub's even jerking me
jewels which I decline
leaving HIM to
retreat, bruised somewhat,

Oct 5 1940

27,591.
Cincinnati over Detroit.
Eagle Squadron. Bucharest.
Brazil & Chile bases.
16 million & US draft.
Dönitz escalation.
Persian Gulf, Italy
& oil fields.
—We are waiting for the.
40 hour work week. Gabon.
Mussolini attacks Greece.
Henry L Stimson & 158.
—resistance to Reich occupation.
Dordogne, 4 boys & a dog.
Tangier.
—Roosevelt you have.
Jervis Bay. Yanina drive.
Uruguayan bases.
Taranto attack.
449, KG100 & Coventry,
568 go.
Korçë, 2,000 captured.
8 ft up.
Iron Guard's 64.
Liverpool bombs.
Greeks & Pogradec.
Navy over Army.

somewhat confusedly, I retreat
from her lowheel squeals. Gently first
but firm. Even when leaking,
a tumble of updo and fuss,
I offer HER a doily only:
Me: —*Please forgive*
me. I'm hers.
And HER: —*No, forgive*
me. You're spoony.
Kopasetic. Until NEW CHICK allso jives:
—*If you free up, I'm here Mr. Nine.*
Your fass prang just about anytime.
Fizzing hot for a fix!
Which VIAZAZONACCI just slipping loose
of a dancefloor jitterbug
gets a strong whiff of.
While I, relieved and
free of this NEW BREE, go find Hailey.

Jan 16 1987

Zhao Ziyang over
Hu Yaobang.
Dwyer goes.
Cumming Georgia
& Forsyth County.
Super Bowl XXI,
Giants over Broncos.
Glasnost. Perestroika.
Fidel V Ramos.
Robert M Gates over
William Casey.
Stars & Stripes cups
Kookaburra III.
RAWA & KHAD, Meena goes.
—tempest through the ashes.
Carlos Enrique Rivas.
Jerusalem's Demjanjuk.
Ford's $3.3 billion.
Brazilian debt. NSC. Supenova.
Howard Baker over
Donald Regan. Handicapped,
AIDS & Federal Protection.
—full responsibility.
Zeebrugge, Dover & Herald
Of Free Enterprise, 193 go.
Thomas Rizzo, Thomas
Olton, Cheryl Burress
& Lisa Burress go.

before cruising back at me:
—You're a Skank Scunt. A decked tease.
And I should reck you.
But HE doesn't. Only
Slubslobbering,
moves unsteadily towards Sam. Who,
surprise!, drags HIM aside. Throws a smile.
Whereupon this NEW SAD SLUG all
low and sulking
actually goes ahead and hugs him,
briefly becoming Sam,
though Sam's
satisfactions reach beyond all hold,
longed for, over,
by all who sip, nosh, roll, fuss,
throw punches, dare to not, give up,
win, fit. NEW BANGER splits for later.
Wants a group of his own. Whatever.

July 30 1940

Pan-American Union.
No 17. 150 Stukas &
Messerschmitt. RAF's Poles.
Spitfires & Hurricanes.
Berlin-Baghdad rail.
35 Luftwaffe. 1,485.
50 destroyers.
FDR & Mackenzie King.
—so much owed by so many
to so few.
Coyoacán & an ax,
Trotsky goes.
Berlin bombed. Tonkin to
Japan. East Asia's revolution.
—stop the rush
towards War!
Cocos Island.
London burns, 370 go.
Bucharest. Buckingham hit.
Switzerland's neutrality.
Selective Service Bill.
Italy, Greece and Yugoslavia.
HX-72, 12 down.
De Gaulle fails at Dakar.
Steel & iron exports.
Japan joins Axis.
Annamese troops.

Whatever. Everyone circles a want.
THE NEW WHIRLY even starts ganging
for Hailey, rubbin boobies,
coyly licking her teeth.
Spiffing for rounds, Hailey passes along.
A pass, Hailey passes off.
Crushing to be her, Hailey passes on.
SHE is her if only momentarily.
So kissing Hailey only withers HER.
Until hung up and sad,
THE NEW ZEAL GIRL grabs me.
Forcing a smile. Drags me aside.
With a screwed out squeeze.
Rubadubdub and allready
down on her knees:
—Saludos Amigo, want me to
gobblepipe your beeze?
And O my, while

March 18 1987
65 MPH.
Jim Bakker & PTL. AZT.
Jerry Falwell. 6-3.
Moscow's US Embassy,
Clayton J Lonetree &
Arnold Bracy.
US duties & Japan.
Steve Newman's 22,000 miles.
Jack F Matlock.
Al Campanis quits.
Texaco's bankruptcy.
—What are you afraid of?
Gregory Robertson's
freefall & save.
Toshihiko Seko's marathon.
Raul Alfonsin & military revolt.
Palm Bay &
William Bryan Cruse, 6 go.
Meech Lake.
—society.
Alysheba's Derby.
Philippe Jeantot, Crédit
Agricole III & 27,000 miles.
Gary Hart, Donna Rice &
Monkey Business.
—stand on their own feet.
Energia.

That's Sam too.
Bending the outskirts of popularized
hedges, oversized corporate feers.
Because enough's never quite here.
—*Mergers and Acquisitions.*
— *Our Global Agios.*
Stirring up all the static
these Long Traders & Yuppified Brokers
need to keep wired.
Sliding him riches
for a tip of his head when we're
packed, a scoop when we're cool,
Jacksons & Grants, jacketed smooth.
And while I'm just overalls, a gofer,
he's silk tie, suspenders & loafers,
up the ladder promoted, deserving it too.
While copper for tin I'm spiralling down.
Without a dish.

May 21 1940
Dunkirk.
Peruvian quake, 249 go.
Hitler halts Panzers.
Operation Dynamo.
Norfolk 90. Leopold
capitulates. Shaw's 500.
Somme.
200 planes & 1,100 bombs
over Paris, 254 go.
Paddle Steamer
Gracie Fields.
338,226.
—whatever the cost may be
we shall fight.
—We shall never surrender.
—We will conquer.
—the back of its neighbor.
Malta. Tobruk.
—auf allen Fronten.
—Finest hour.
—resistance must not go
out and will not go out.
Stimson & Knox. Pétain.
Alien Registration Act.
Wendell. Vichy.
Mers-el-Kebir. Lithuania,
Estonia, Latvia. Burma road.
Priscilla.
6 RAF's 80.

Without place.
And if Hailey, all overalls, keeps turning
Gaspers for Cuters, I'm togged to
the bricks, dicer, pulleys and pegs,
to valet the Valets.
Around I go, picking up Deeces & Deuces
for a park when we're slammed,
for a wash when we're through.
Which only goes to juice the crew.
I've no need for Them's lucre.
High Steppers & Moochers
blow rich for all I travel.
—*What's up, Doc?*
—*You Bobby Socks.*
I'm The Never Enough ever
letched for. And hit.
I'm their underage permit.
I'm that kid.

May 18 1987

Islip, Mobro
& 3,200 tons of garbage.
Unser's 500.
Raymond Donovan's acquittal.
Matthias Rust, Moscow
& Cessna. Sergei L Sokolov.
Oilers over Flyers.
Rashid Karami goes.
Alan Greenspan.
Seoul's Roh Tae Woo.
Danny Harris over Edwin Moses.

—Gorbachev!
—above the law.
—tear down.
Sachio Kinugasa's 2,130.
Lakers over Celtics.
ARGK & Pinarcik, 31 go.

—go for him again.
—radical reorganization.
Cindy Anne Smith goes.
Texas boxcar, 18 go.
Billionaire Boys' Club
& Joe Hunt's life.

—have never carried out.
Molly Yard.
Homoine massacre, 386 go.
Hulda Crooks.

Without recourse.
Allways their stunt.
Fondled havoc streeted to the gutters for
loads of troubles never outdone.
That's the run I run.

Certainly not Sam.

He could easily rise on these
bumps. Amidst such Tweekers & Drunks.
He's heavy on ice, shots sloshed to the top.
More still clamoring up with
desires to wump, their times
allready compelling Them to
seek out his wellbeing to restore Them
on the dancefloor. Toes tickling toes.
Jump for a swing & fling,
wheelaround with parTiers.
Large, juiced & ready to
bust it out.

April 1 1940

America First Committee.
British Defense Council.
Jimmy Demaret.
Mines & Norwegian waters.
Germany's Denmark.
Attack Oslo. Gurkha down.
Skagerrak.
Maple Leafs over Rangers.
Narvik landing.
Gerard Cote's marathon.
50,000 Allied forces,
Norway, Lillehammer &
Trondheim. Losey goes.
Steinkjer.
Dombås & Støren.
4,000 Allies from Andalsnes.
Gallahadion's Derby.
German hair & felt.
—and let US have
done with you.
Prime Minister Winston
Churchill.
42 gliders & Eben Emael.
Belgium & Holland. Krupp.
—nothing to offer but
blood, toil, tears and sweat.
Sedan. Winkelman's
surrender. Rotterdam.
Niagara Bridge. Weygand.

And HE's on, pushing
to buzz and tumble. The Big Dance.
Nifty Gals swingarooing for
tight flings and stomps.
Fingers circling fingers, all over the floor,
allways imploring me come, wanting
more to join Them every time their
romps grow and human desires
exceed what's escorted. For still more.
Coastered highballs repoured. Spicy topped.
Bebop. Smuggled muggles and birdwood.
The hubblebubble of contact I easily refuse.
Hailey too.

We do what we do.

Dishing herds and soda, sweeping
up the havoc had to let go.
I'm their vanquisher.
Without return.

July 23 1987
George Shultz.
William Sessions' FBI.
Air Afrique, 1 goes.
Namibia firefight, 193 go.
California freeways, 2 go.
Iranian riot &
Saudi Police, 402 go.
Tyson 12 rounds Tucker.
Mary R Stout.
Tamil's Velupillai Prabhakaran.
Joe Niekro's scuffs.
Costa Rica, Nicaragua,
Honduras, Guatemala &
El Salvador. South Africa's
282,000 miners strike.
Emily.
Hess goes. Donald Harvey.
Michael Ryan, 16 go.
Bayard Rustin goes.
Ben Johnson's 9.83.
Concord Naval
Weapons Station &
Brian Wilson's legs.
Ozone's 24.
AIDS & James R Thompson.
Mario Biaggi &
Meade Esposito.
NFL strike.

—*This The Shit!*
our manager pips, turning up the party.
—*Going wide,*
New Tender trips,
tight now with Viatotonacci, because she's
flush at last with stacks of long years,
played & spread around to overcome
uptown, tardy, very cheap
Lombards throwing out cold
shoulders at all newcomers raging to
overturn the present order. Of agreement.
All at The St. Louis Grill where she
now courts and marries the New Guy.
Whereupon our manager, despite
The Wife, starts flirting again.
Offering me his human
ruin. Just me and
Viatitonacci of course.

Jan 19 1940
Grenville down, 81 go.
Finland, 54th Division
& Kuhmo, 5,000 go.
000-00-00, Ida Fuller.
$22.54.
Bell Airacobra.
Mannerheim falters.
Hasty over Morea.
Cossack free 299.
—*The Navy's here.*
Auschwitz. Air Defense
Command. U-33 & Enigma.
Berwick over Wolfsburg.
Dunedin over Heidelberg.
Britain & 6 Italian coal ships.
Staten Island, Elizabeth
& Pier 90. Blenheim, U-31
& Borkum.
Michael O'Dwyer goes.
Karelian Isthmus surrender.
Nahum Goldmann's 90,000.
Brenner Pass.
Fortune, U-44 & Narvik.
RAF bombs Sylt.
Reynaud over Daladier.
IRA & Dartmoor prison.
US grants
Britain & France
Warplanes.

Of course Viatitonacci's rehired,
bumped up, handsomely
paid too.
And while still girking The Wife,
pesters Hailey less. Because now there's
The New Cake to walk. Here at
The St. Louis Lounge riffs starting to
ride, slide the comers!, then
kicking it ticktock, Hep Gees, Swing Kids,
dicty, all city, burnt to the crisp,
come over to bop, upscale the lowdown
for mucho tabs. Geetchie. Mezz.
CMC the MCM and leave jit.
Viatotonacci digs this turn,
especially his New Dilly:
—*Ooolie Droolie!*
Our manager freebizing her needles.
—*You're too grooby.*

Oct 1 1987

7:42 AM, Whittier Fault
& 6.1, 6 go.
Chicago Teachers Union.

DC's AIDS quilt.
Georgia sodomy.
Football strike over.
Midland's McClure.
US Navy & Iranian oil rig.
Donald Woomer
& Linda Despot.
508.32 down.
Bork over. Twins over
Cardinals. Herbert Ernesto
Anaya Sanabria goes.
Titan 34D. Arthur Kane goes.
A long crawl.
Gorbachev's Khrushchev.
—common prosperity.
Caspar Weinberger quits.
Ginsburg's marijuana.
Enniskillen blast, 11 go.
Boris Yeltsin fired.
—Iran-Contra affair must rest with the President.
$30 billion reduction.
Oakdale detention.
Harold Washington goes.
Typhoon Nina, 651 go.

Enough of this Public and
everything I have to put up with
here. And for what? Sam & me.
Stuck to these dismal routines slogged
out about jabbering crowds pausing
amidst our rush. Relentlessly

going on

even if I'm
all freaking with
tremors. Sam rubbing
my back to calm me. Terrrrrifying when:
—I'll ice Sam if he ever laughs at US again.
Cause now, for the timebeing, he's unsafe.
But Sam's solid.
Relaxed enough to even grin.
BILL BAIZALI's sure surprised. Sends this:
—Haaaaaaaaaaaaaah!
Laughing despite how brave Sam is.

Nov 23 1939

Scharnhorst & Gneisenau
sink Rawalpindi, 300 go.
—I am irreplaceable.
Fritz Kuhn's larceny.
Russian Army &
Finland, Helsinki burns.
Capone's syphilitic parole.
General Winter.
Arms to Finland.
Vidkun Quisling.
ERA.

Exeter, Ajax & Achilles vs
Graf Spee, Langsdorff goes.
Finnish troops &
Bielaja Smert.
Turkey shudders, 11,000 go.
DDT.
Clara Adams around.
—free at any moment.
Southern California
over Tennessee.
$1.8 billion for defense.
Dáil to de Valera.
Soviet 18th Division &
Lake Ladoga. Seahorse &
Undine scuttled.

Sugar, meat & butter.
Bartley mine, 92 go.
Weather.

Yard dog quits mad. I laugh:
—Haaaaaaaaaaaaaah!
Which is not so dapper. BAIZALI BILL,
allready salty, ready to spit, wheeling
back to grit:
—For now, here, go find your thrills. But
laugh at him again, ever, I'll kill you.
Terrifying. Hailey presses her palm
on my back. I'm Unsteady Eddie.
No breath.
But we get by.

Ongoing.

Punching our duties among
the rest of Passing Clickers prodding
for adds, subs and negotiations.
Me & Hailey allways around. Ever now.
But with all we go through here
is this Community enough?

Nov 29 1987
Haiti elections, 26 go.
Alderman Eugene Sawyer.
Atlanta's Federal Penitentiary,
89 hostages go free.
US, USSR & Cruise Missiles.
—that will enable US to.
Argentina's General
Confederation of Workers.
—send our people plowshares.

Lee Hart. Sicily's 338.
Japanese Public Works.
Tablas Strait, Doña Paz &
Victor, 1,600 go.
West Bank, Gaza &
1,000 Palestinians.
Yuri V Romanenko's 326 days.
Russellville &
Ronald Gene Simmons.
One second. Amerasians.
Ashland Oil &
Monongahela River.
David Bloom. Joyce Brown.
Lakers over Pistons.
John Connally.
Super Bowl XXII,
Washington over Denver.

Eventually a chill. Patrons dwindle.
Seatings for lunches, dinners, slim.
—*What did you do?* snorts
VIARORONACCI. *Yeah you.*
—*Leave her allone, Cabrón,*
exiting BILL BEEZALI rasps.

I shy back but that's a bust.
Slicking his hair over, VIARIRONACCI
advances through The St. Louis Café,
wending around scattered idlers. Impossible
to duck. All strut & front, slaying
no one with his props, but still
cocky enough to tug on his crotch with
that VIARARONACCI grin: —*Want some?*
—*Tough luck.*
Whereupon among these trife peeps,
he slaps me hard across the cheek,

Sep 16 1939
Russia attacks Poland.

U-29 & Courageous, 500 go.
Bzura's 170,000.
Brest-Litovsk. Calinescu goes.
Schrecklichkeit. Warsaw
surrenders. Hel falls.
1 Corps of BEF.

New York over Cincinnati.
U-47 & Scapa Flow:
Royal Oak down, 800 go.
La Guardia airport.
Warren Billings.
Land Army Girls.

Western Front.

—threw down the gauntlet.

Committee on Uranium.
Hans Frank.
City of Flint.

Schlieper, Carroll & 30 days.
Arms Embargo over.
Cash & Carry.
Paul Thummel.
Georg Elser's beer, 8 go.
Lagunillas blaze, 500 go.
Simon Bolivar down, 140 go.
Wilhelmshaven.
Piccadilly blast.

leave, HE
cuffs me. Hard across the cheek.
A cheap chuck here amidst
these dining Bims & Pips:
—*So tough.*
—*What's that?* VIARARONACCI respins,
flinging tables over, plates of sauce
suddenly tossed, flying globs of pesto
spraying everywhere. Which I dodge
completely, though the ensuing shatter
causes The St. Louis Grill to evacuate.
VIARIRONACCI with barstool overhead
allegroes after me. Grim. I stand firm.
Unfortunately BEEZALI BILL saves him:
— *Fessacchione, get outta here.*
—*Me?* VIARORONACCI stumbles
short. *What did I do?*
—*You? Throwing punches, pans,
start a stampede? You're fired.*

turning me around.
Viapoponacci even more riled
up by my shock and my tears:
—*You've pretty much zip to hold onto here.*
All nappy & thin lipped. Purge bag on
stilts. Act now Miss. Cause I'm the shit.
Shack you, stack you, slosh your slit.
Puhlease.
And because I allone must allways leave
everyone, I frown:
—*I'll never quit Sam.*
Viapiponacci the unflumstered slob just nods:
—*Come here now and gobble my nob.*
This hustle probably only amusing
the Teaspooners near. Where's Sam?
Gladiolas & **Zinnias** topple.
Chrysanthemums perish too.

Feb 2 1988
Tuscaloosa, James Harvey & 84 hostages.
US Justice Department & Manuel Noriega. Ethiopia & Government Troops, 20 go.
—*unrestrained epidemic of violence.*
New Hampshire, George Bush & Michael Dukakis.
Supreme Court Justice Anthony Kennedy. Jimmy Swaggart & Debra Murphee. Azerbaijan Armenians. Prithvi's 150 miles. Calgary. 540 Hondas to Japan.
Willie Darden goes. Halabja, Kurds & chemical weapons, over 5,000 go.
FDIC's $1 billion.
Eritrean People's Liberation Front. Operation Golden Pheasant & US troops.
Moishe Katz goes.
Sapoá, Daniel Ortega & Adolfo Calero.
Robert Chambers & Jennifer Levin.

—*Some puffstuff, her. Bloomers to corset.*
Chipmunks huck nuts.
Mockingbirds & **Buntings** wheel off.
Hailey hangs back, smiling clientele,
impressed perhaps by this tussle over her.
—*She'll gargle my cream,*
Viapiponacci flings.
—*She won't leave me,* I sling.
he's frowning. The googie. Because
to me allone everyone must cleave.
Allways.
—*Greaseball, you're such a wet smack.*
She's a niftic minx. Ready to act.
Curves, urges, eager hips. Juicy. Too
much for you to hold onto for long.
But I keep steady, barely
riled by Viapoponacci's
threats.
Except, when turning to

July 18 1939
Danzig's 2,000.
US trade treaty & Japan.
London & 2 IRA bombs.
Reich through Trieste to Libya. The bomb.
Standard Oil Company of California & Saudi Arabia.
$85 million for aircrafts & engines. AFL parade.
14 U-boats to North Atlantic.
Polish troops to border.
Normandie to Manhattan.
Stalin, Molotov & von Ribbentrop: Moscow non-aggression treaty.
—*Now Europe is mine.*
Soviet troops west.
16,000 out of Paris.
Blitzkrieg.
Britain & France & War.
Bydgoszcz massacre.
Unity Mitford.
—*will keep out of this.*
US embargo.
Warsaw battered.
Sikorsky's VS300.

April 4 1988

Fort Smith & 13 supremacists.
Lyn Nofzinger.
Seto Ohashi Bridge Complex.
Leona Helmsley's
tax evasion.
Aegean Sea, Kanellos
Kanellopoulos & Daedalus 88.
Mayor Sonny Bono.
Maui & Boeing 737, 1 goes.
Orioles 21st.
—most closely guarded.
Winning's Derby.
Mormon bombing.
Lenin Shipyard strike over.
Cabildo fire. Kim Philby goes.
Soviet Union, Afghanistan &
115,000 troops.
Károly Grósz over János Kádár.
Bess Myerson's arrest.
Mears's 500.
Debra Lorraine Estes goes.
Sydney, Fiji &
12 tons of weapons.
Moscow State University.
Presidential commission
on AIDS. Vietnamese leave
Cambodia. Osprey.

Scary
VIAPAPONACCI,
slick with spittle, lips atwitching,
grips me by the back of
my head to winch me down.
I don't resist.
I don't even try to kick
his shins, merely twirling my
Leftwrist Rosegold Twist
if with a tired stammer adding:
—Go on, shtake your shot. Give me everything
you got. A Whambangbangmeslam. But then
it's my turn. Civil & Criminal. Harassment.
Assault. You'll lose lots. And you'll do time.
Which hardly worries him. Even if
VIAMAMONACCI does release his stranglehold
on my throat and curiously shoves me off.

May 19 1939

Rochester food program.
Italy, Germany
& Pact of Steel.
Squalus sub down, 26 go.
688 executions.
St Louis reaches Havana,
907 refused. Ruth Karliner &
Walter Karliner. George
& Elizabeth, bagpipes
& midgets.
Byron Nelson.
Moscow's Mendel.
Phoenix down, 63 go.
Martin T Manton
& judicial favors.
Brazil accepts 3,000.
23 hours 52 minutes, Lisbon
Portugal & The Dixie Clipper.
WPA's $1.5 billion.
Lou Gehrig retires.
—but I have an awful lot
to live for.
Kentucky floods, 100 go.
Marble over Stammers.
Yankee Clipper.
Harlan County strike.

And I'm still horrendifying when
VIAMOMONACCI yanks me up at the scruff.
Uses me to mop slop by forcing me to sit.
Worries me a bit.
—Hey Half Portion, time to get busy and
lift it. Enough with the slam. Your hers
but she's mine. So scram. I'm the sock's
gonna roll that sexjob. Dig?
Hailey gripping hard her
Leftwrist Rosegold Twist.
Waiting for me to kick
both his shins.
But I don't resist.
Even flinching when HE reaches
back to wallop me.
His lips twitchy,
spittle thick.
VIAPAPONACCI's
scary:

I plop on

handsandknees while he grunts:

—I'm over you, Cunt.

Stomping off.

The gentle VIAMIMONACCI.

And shifts follow shifts,
me passing by table & chair,
clumsily, hardly able to keep up with
Sam, solid & down for the fuss over
NBA bets, netting long shots. Their charmer.
Up to speed, every lead and spread, a wheeler
dealer getting the big win allways wanted.
Too cool to suffer fools, ever, so all
around keep patting his back. Bow.

—He sticks it!

THE GUSSY HUSHY CONVENTICLE
living gratefully off his tips.

June 13 1988
Liggett Group.
FBI, Pentagon & bribes.
Lisburn blast, 6 go.
Henry Namphy's Haiti.
Carl C Icahn. Trabzon & Çatak mudslide, 300 go.
Tyson 1 rounds Spinks.
10:54 AM, USS Vincennes & Flight 655, 292 go.
Stefan Edberg over Boris Becker.
—Experts agree! Meese is a.
Wedtech's Iraq.
Northeast beaches & medical waste.
North Sea & Piper Alpha oil platform, 165 go.
$59.1 billion.
Carlos Salinas de Gortari.
Sandinista sugar.
—Now is the time.
—Where the big boats are.
Iran-Iraq War over.
Ne Win ousted.
Jordan's West Bank.

And my flips do exonerate these brittle
from doubts about living. So little.
THE THRUSTY LUSTY CONVENTICLE thankful:
—Quite heroic!
I bow. Back pats all around. For a
walloping time my warmth's
allways desired. I'm their table's gyre.
A great ball of desire, plenty rugged,
lending their Poker knocks pluck.
Follow Hailey then, fusses first, away
from their nods. Riffing ably, I trip barely
on a chair, steadied by a table. Square.

Shifts follow shifts.

VIAMIMONACCI plies Hailey
with gifts:

—I'm balling for you.

While I

handsandknees

blot up soup.

March 3 1939
Autocratic rule & Gandhi's fast.
Laurence Steinhardt.
Gestapo's Prague.
Moravia & Bohemia.
Hungary's Carpatho-Ukraine. Palestine failure.
William O Douglas.
Port of Memel.
20,000 anti-Nazi march.
Franco & Madrid.
Gable & Lombard.
FDR & George Washington Carver.
100,000 Spanish arrests.
Spratly Islands.
Britain, Poland & Mutual Aid Treaty.
US lifts Spanish embargo.
American Civil Liberties Union. 10–18.
Mussolini, Albania & Zog.
British Fleet for Greece & Turkey. US Fleet to Pacific.
571 planes.
The Trylon & Perisphere.
—open to all.
Nicaragua, President Anastasio Somoza & US.
Johnstown's Derby.

Aug 8 1988

Wrigley Field.
Angola-Namibia cease-fire.
90–4 & $282.6 billion.
Sein Lwin quits.
Mohammad Zia ul-Haq goes.
—America moving forward.
Lucchese 20. Ramstein Air
Base, 46 go. Dene, Metis &
Northwest territories.
Bangladesh flood, 490 go.
Stars & Stripes cups
New Zealand.
Steffi Graf's Grand Slam.
Hurricane Gilbert, 260 go.
Haiti & Prosper Avril.
Greg Louganis.
Nargona-Karabakh
state of emergency.
Flo Jo's 100 meters.
—hasn't been easy.
Gorbachev's 5.
—You're no Jack Kennedy.
Millikan wayside cry.
Pinochet's plebiscite.
Algerian riots.
Columbia over Princeton.
William Proxmire's 10,500.
Dodgers over A's.

—Without you our World
couldn't turn,

OSCARPOROSIS jibs Sam,
with NASDAQ returns allready
overflowing their IRAs. While over the way,
buzzed on the oblivion of his philandering,
VIAMEMONACCI keeps knocking back booze.

—Just merciless.
—And an absolute waste.
—Nothing but a charity case.

Which BILL BIZALI resents:
—And what then? Promote Sam? Man am I
glad I'm the one who runs this trashcan.

But Sam's the action here. The win over feer
when, yes, hard work finally pays off and the
dividend's a Mercedes 560, all thanks to him.

—Kataplikitiko!

Jan 5 1939

$1.3 billion for defense.
Thomas J Mooney,
Culbert Olson & pardon.
—chaos of bloodshed
and revolution.
Social Security extension.
CIO, 2 Teachers Unions
& 5 Communists.
Frank M Andrews
& 400 planes.
Hjalmar Schacht.
Chile shake, thousands go.
Franco's Barcelona.
Enrico Fermi, Otto Hahn
& 200 million volts.
Naismith & Zone Defense.
TVA's Constitutionality.
130,000 refugees
to Spain. Hainan.
Louis Brandeis retires.
University of Wisconsin
& donation. Madison Square,
Fritz Kuhn & 22,000 Nazis.
—kick.
DAR, Roosevelt
& Marian Anderson.
National Labor Board
vs Fansteel Metallurgical
Corporation.

—Straordinario.

Easily I twirl my rake even if I'd rather
take their American Bantam for a spin,
which this sodality hard at its Parcheesi
feers too often to use. I'm only action.

—Beetle, we're glad
you brought your man here.
Would he accept a promotion?

BIZALI BILL complimends.
Hailey: *—No, he prefers leisure.*

—Perhaps my manager's culo?
—Probably not.

VIAMEMONACCI, the Big It, louses around
over drink, oblivious to his tenuous hold
on employment, bantered while
Dominoes continue their click.
ARTHURITIS to Hailey:

—Without your Ace
our World wouldn't turn.

Still Bill Biazali blows his lid, promptly
throwing out The Gutsy Gusty Conventicle.
Though I plead for Them:

—Wait up, these're your friends.

And: *—Not junk.*

And: *—Just don't.*

Which accomplishes zilch. My begging
hardly stopping our owner from ordering
these regulars to gather their belongings and
get lost. To gutter & sidewalk. Dirty
streets for the *—dirty lot.*
Hermanoids pats Sam's elbow. Edema's funny:

—You're our oligopsony, our money.

And: *—Take care kids.*

Only Sam keeps me strangely confident.
Somehow retaining a certainty that we will,
without effort, absolutely

Oct 22 1988

Anti-drug Bill.
Philippines & Typhoon Ruby,
500 go.

3 California whales.
Yitzak Shamir.
Morris Worm.
Maldives, Maumoon Abdul
Gayoom & 1,600 paratroopers.
Burmese quake, 938 go.
George Herbert Walker Bush.
Curtis Strange.
—the state of Palestine.
South Dakota & B-1 crash.
Belgrade's Serbs.
Romania & 7,000 peasant
communities. Kohlberg, Kravis
Roberts and Company, RJR
Nabisco & $25.07 billion.
Charles bester.

—The World economy is.

Armenia, Leninakan
& 6.9, 45,000 go.
Robert Pelletreau & Yasir
Abed Rabbo. Drexel Burnham
Lambert's $650 million.

Lockerbie & Flight 103, 270 go.

absolute without softness, vagueness.
But now here with Hailey somehow
strangely unsure. My confidence
faltering. Missed.

So long Charley.

Toodleloo with a kiss.

Stanosis pats Hailey's elbow. Rickets too.
I turn back to broom the street.
Sidewalk & gutters requiring a sweep.
It's a dirty job for silly pay but at least
Bankers, Bakers and Wrens passing by
beg me to play. I'm not. When

—Okie!

some Trash Heap ambushes me.

—Arkie!

I pulverize him.
The Rusty Crusty Conventicle
throws out applause and cheer.
Biazali Bill joining friends with nods:

Oct 21 1938

Canton razed.
Guangzhou.
—the World is coming to an end and I have a lot to do.
—please have someone send me a pair of.
Seabiscuit over
War Admiral.
Paris, Reich embassy &
Herschel Grynspan,
Ernst vom Rath goes.
Berlin & Kristallnacht, 90 go.
Kate Smith.
England's Jericho.
CIO & AFL.
—race.
—nationality.
US Policy, East Asia &
The New Order.

Corneliu Codreanu & 13 go.
Czechoslovakia & Emil Hacha.

Sydenstricker.

$50 million to China.
F Donald Coster, Mckesson &
Robbins, Philip Musica goes.
Somaliland force doubles.

Dec 30 1988

Presidential subpoenas.
45 Nuclear Defense facilities.
2 US F-14s & 2 Libyan Mig-23s.
Chinese & African students.
Chrysanthemums.
Kegworth's Flight 92, 47 go.

Cuba & Angola.
Colombia & M-19.
Stockton California &
Patrick Edward Purdy, 5 go.
Clement Lloyd &
Overtown riots.
—a new breeze is.
Super Bowl XXIII,
49ers over Bengals.

Tadzhikistan quake, 200 go.
Ted Bundy goes. Bahia Paraiso.
Joel Steinberg.
Frederik W de Klerk.
Andrés Rodríguez over
Alfredo Stroessner.
$126.2 billion. Salman Rushdie.
—left behind me.
Chlorofluorocarbons.
Vaclav Havel's arrest.
Bush & Deng Xiaoping.

change the outcome for all.
Away from their roundtable, these hobbling
continue their bold procession of pains,
fever & aches. That's me. And I'm Sam's.
Getting on without any praise.
—*Missy, growing old*
ain't for sissies,

PARKERSON, DEANENTIA & PAULYP grumble,
pleased at least to find Sam & me now,
somehow, just holding hands.
—*Don't lose your youth,* ALLENZHEIMER
plucks, advice jovially given
amidst this sad clusterfuck.
Cold coffee left to their cups
which Sam then refuses to bus. He's the
diaspora of these scoffed, flatulently adding:
—*Never return again!*

Aug 18 1938

Japan's One Million.
US-Chinese airliner
& Japanese machine gun.

Arab blast, 21 go.

Eyston's 345 MPH.
Italy & Jews.
Pittsburgh's 55,000
& a Republican feast.
Don Budge's Forest & Slam.

—My patience is
now at an end.

—it is Peace for our time.

France, Italy,
Germany & Britain:
Four Power Conference
& Czechoslovakia.
German Army's
Sudetenland.

—of a long Peace.
—regime strange and
hostile to US but one that is.

Yankees over Cubs.
Jerusalem's Martial Law.
Hitler & Lindbergh.
Ochsner, DeBakey,
Cigarettes & cancer.
Robert Johnson goes.

—*Forever!* Each raucously adds,
suddenly flatulent. Over me.
I'm the euphoria of these Masses.
So of course Hailey brings Them
more glasses of Iced Tea,
while allways agreeing happily
to their solemn advice.
—*Don't lose him,* PAULIO smiles.
Because I'm her winning hand.
Theirs too. Further ratified
by the clinging raves of
JIMJIVITIS, DONABETES & JERRYATRIC:
—*So grave, so young.*
—*So brave.*
Though I require no honk.
She's allready mine. And I'm hers.
Hailey's No Ifs Steady who these Prunes
still huddle on my behalf to punchup.
Allone I'm unchanged,

March 8 1989
Lhasa Martial Law.
Sudan's Sadiq al Mahdi.
Semiautomatic assault
weapons. Joe Runyan.
FDA, Chile & cyanide.
—*confusion and violence.*
Afredo Cristiani.
Martin Fleischman
& Stanley Pons.
Hazelwood's Exxon Valdez.
Boris Yeltsin over
Yuri Soloviev.
Cold War over. Polish solidarity.
Barents sea & K-278, 42 go.
—*life!*
Abbott Hoffman goes.
Sheffield, Liverpool
& Nottingham Forest, 95 go.
USS Iowa, 47 go.
Moscow purge.
Takeshita's Recruit.
Austria-Hungary barbed wire.
Atlantis & Magellan.
North guilty on 3 counts.
—*no slowing down.*
Silence's Derby.
US Naval blaze, 6 go.
Guillermo Endara.

—*For now,* Sam tries.
—*You're only ever yours.* Is their reply.
Too: —*Byebye Miss.*

Around the way then,
rolling on at last for the shortest turn.
Them allways go.
Their agonies at least relieved some
when Sam kindly takes care of their aids.
Handing back wheelchairs. Walkers,
crutches and canes.

And certainly Sam's extraordinary poise
distinguishes these lads wearing sleaves
long with gritty baseball caps, holding
out for Social Security.

This Busty Busty Conventicle banished
from their roundtable, from Sam, me,
The St. Louis Bakery and all anyone ever needs.

June 8 1938
—*barbarous bombings of civilians.*
—*most elementary principles of human conduct.*
Chinese river dikes fail,
150,000 go.
Montana train, 30 go.
18 Reich spies.
Emergency Relief
Appropriations Act.
10 million unemployed.
Civil Aeronautics Authority.
44 hours, 40¢ & Fair Labor
Standards Act.
—*followed by a much needed.*
Hankow battle, 10,000 go.
Morris Goldis, William Goldis
& William Snyder.
Moody's Wimbledon.
Depressed South.
Abd Nour Khativ Imam goes.
Westwood & CIO workers.
Curtiss Robin J-6 &
Corrigan's Dublin.
Sudeten concession.
Japan & USSR truce.
Dustbowl grass.
One million reserves.

Everyone adores The St. Louis Café
and it me. Roundtable lads for sure.
That Musty Dusty Conventicle allways
bunched about playing some Checkers.
Regulars with palm panamas
& short sleaves approving of the extra
distinguishment I lend the ordinary.
Hailey certainly.
Taking care of their staves, crutches
and canes. Wheelchairs too. And by
kindness allone soothing their pains
which my presence redeems entirely.
Them's here to stay.
Braying over every turn.
Every throw.
Every round of fizz.
—*Over here Missy,* these steadies motion.
—*I'm only yours,* Hailey grins.
—*For now.*

May 13 1989

OPEC & Egypt. Apples & Alar. Argentina's Carlos Saúl Menem. West Beirut & Sheik Hassan Khaled, 21 go. FAA & 2,200 jets. Lithuanian Liberty.

—*We are the people's soldiers.* Paul Touvier. Deng Xiaoping & Li Peng. Jim C Wright retires. Ufa train, 190 go. Ayatollah Ruhollah Khomeini goes. —*counterrevolutionary rebellion.* —*chaos.*

Tanks & Tiananmen Square, 2,000 go. Sri Lanka floods, 310 go. —*thugs.* Pistons over Lakers. Minimum wage veto. Chinese arrests. —*Social volunteerism.* Arnaldo Ochoa Sanchez & Medellín cartel. Daniel Arap Moi & 12 tons of tusks.

Yes, maybe it's time to move on.
Spare some our hurt before
the World retakes what we allways
elude when we run.
4½. HONEY. Ours only.
Sycamores & Columbine collapse by
the Liffey, Tigris, Spree, the Nile.
River by City where
we part freely until
our next shift starts. Except now
Sam suddenly throws: —*Let'S quit.*
I only gnaw my thumb. Worried sick.
VIALOLONACCI: —*Muscle the mop, Traduttore.*
BILL BIOZALI snipping: —*He's the boss.*
Though not until THE WIFE delinks does
VIALILONACCI spin around to
have it out with Sam

April 4 1938

Lincoln-Washington Battalion goes. US & Austria. Otto von Hapsburg & German aggression. Daladier's anti-Communist Cabinet. Nationalist Neo-Destour & Tunis riots. Hawks over Maple Leafs. Albany, medical tests & marriage. 157,000 French auto workers & 213 factories. Taierchwang, China & Japan, 40,000 go. Dizzy Dean. Italy from Spain over Ethiopia. 100 Iron Guard. Spanish Civil War over. Lawrin's Derby. Ickes, US helium & bans. Belgium's Paul-Henri Spaak. 400,000 Czechs on German borders.

Revenue Act & Corporate Taxes. United Rubber Workers.

Louis 1 rounds Max Schmeling. Freud for London.

an uncommon footfall amidst our grind,
if I'm quick to bidness by the time
VIALILONACCI whips around, further
squelched by Ballandchain. His leery WIFE.
—*You too, Traditore!* BIOZALI BILL hefts.
—*But he's,* VIALOLONACCI contests.
—*Fine,* scowls, biting his thumb.
—*Let'S go,* I throw Hailey.
Another shift down
to wander around
City by River.
Tagus, Amstel. Danube.
Hummingbirds & Caribou weeping:
—*Not again.*
Only for US. HONEY. 7½.
Because we're every happy trail,
enjoining a World free of US
to have fun. Enjoy. We're all anyone
must absatively fail to destroy.

July 19 1989

John Bardo.

Sioux City, Flight 232
& a cartwheel, 148 go.
Mauritanian moors.
Oppressed of the Earth,
William R Higgins goes.
Bolivia & Jaime Paz Zamora.
Mickey Leland goes.
West Point & Kristin Baker.
Moriyama & Takahara.
Hering's Leap.
Assamese & Bodo.

Logan Airport
& Edward O'Brien.
Huey Percy Newton goes.
Bensonhurst gang,
Yusef Hawkins goes.
Giamatti & Pete Rose.
Kenya poachers,
George Adamson goes.
War on drugs. Steffi Graf over
Martina Navratilova.
Hungary &
60,000 East Germans.
Niger's French DC-10, 171 go.
Hurricane Hugo, 86 go.

even with BILL BOZALI still near:
—Unclog the toilet, Juliet.
Which Sam does until VIALALONACCI clogs it
again. Refuses then to attend the overflow
of all behinds left to pollute a floor.
—Okay let'S break north,
I cry.
—You can fuck off too, the lunkhead roars.
Which achieves zero.
VIAFOFONACCI determined now to damage
something. The St. Louis Trattoria stills.
And it's even packed.
—Careful friend, just go about your way,
Sam bravely stands.
—Get a loada that!
Peel your fuckin cap!
Sam just throws back his head and laughs.

Jan 22 1938

16 Oil Companies,
30 Executives &
gasoline prices.

US military spending.
Endymion down, 11 go.
Germany's Military
Chief. Alcira down.
Transcontinental highway.
Second Agricultural
Adjustment Act.
Emory Land & Maritime
Commission. Roberto Ortiz.

California floods, 144 go.
Premier Milan Hodza.
Arthur Seyss-Inquart
over Schuschnigg.
Germany, Vienna &
Anschluss.
*—never be broken by
anyone again and shall
never be torn apart.
—for the overthrow of
the Socialist regime.*
Bukharin & 17 more go.
Saudi Arabia & Aramco.
Barcelona Air Raid,
1,000 go.
—Mexicanization of.
Jimmy Caras billiards World.

—Gleam it again snooze while
I clean up your Sweet Patootie's cooze.
Tidy bags, messy ass.
Square up. Shrug.
Me: *—Ready to die screeching?*
But VIAFOFONACCI scarpers off through
rattling turns of
The St. Louis Dinette, readyset to molest
Hailey with his hose.
I grin.
His ludicrous splish: *—I'll take it whenever you*
wanna give it to me.
Hailey's don't careish:
—You're tired, Biff.
Wry only for antics behind him.
My spins and cheeky flips giving
VIALALONACCI my share of waggling hind.
When: *—Can the twatter!*
BOZALI BILL surprisingly sharps,

Sept 27 1989

Johannesburg, buses & swimming pools.
22 tons of cocaine.
Dubai's Fox. Copenhagen civil ceremonies. Shell's Raiders.
Andrea M Childers goes.
Israel, MIG-23 & Syrian defection.
—not possible to despair.
Krenz over Honecker.
5:04 PM, Oakland Bay Bridge & 880, 270 go.
Atlantis, Gallileo & Jupiter.
Maximum Bob Potter.
A's over Giants. David Dinkins.
Douglas Wilder.
—no longer divides Berliners.
SWAPO. Walesa's US.
El Salvador's Jesuits, 6 go.
Buck Helm goes.
West Beirut Motorcade, René Moawad & 23 go.
Abu Nidal arrested.
Azerbaijan SSR.
Gregorio Honasan's 4 T-28s.

Disaster follows. Sam though, by
jeté passé from the rampaging
VIAFIFONACCI, nimbly flies across
the floor, up over tables, above
flutes of champagne and dainty cakes.
Not even disturbing a single plate. His
Leftwrist Platinumy Twist spinning fortunes.
Diners stand. Applaud. Sam just floats on.
Still no wonder
The St. Louis Brasserie evacuates
with stools allso tearing up the place,
hurled by VIAFAFONACCI, now
plowing after Sam, spreading a ridiculous
wake of clatter & shatter.
Wacky mad. Rockets whatever he grabs:
shot glasses, platters, cutlery, allways
missing dear Sam completely.

Nov 18 1937

Gandhi & 1,100 prisoners.
Washington over Chicago.
Walther Funk.
Army over Navy.
$16 billion.
Rome, Fascist High Council & League of Nations.
The Rape of Nanking, 250,000 go.
Spanish Republican forces & Aragon.
Japanese, Yangtze & Panay, 5 go.
NLRB, Ford & Labor Laws.
$2 million.
—Growing concern for World events.
Octavian Goga.
Irish Free State & British Commonwealth.
—I am the law.
Krebs cycle.
TVA Dams.
California over Alabama.
7.8 million wandering.
HH K'ung. John Woodhead.
Teruel falls. Qingdao.
Ludlow Amendment.
Camille Chautemps.
GM's diesel engines.

Lying down for
a lazy shuffle. A clit is just a clit
until it's a moan. Bare touches
slipping gentle dips until her sides
drip over US from US
for blurring lives we won't abide by.
VIAFAFONACCI can't abide our affection,
turns aside, hunkers, throws over a chair,
even if The St. Louis Hashery
cherishes our wonder.
On I go, scrubbing dishes.
Up to elbows. Even with
my Leftwrist Platinumy Twist.
On all fours too.
Circular challenges of foam.
Under tables. Scouring floors,
which VIAFIFONACCI,
with muddy boots,
gobs up.

Dec 7 1989

William Lozano.
Nadia Comaneci & US.
Gregor Gysi.
—tense economic.
Bulgaria & Yugoslavia.
Robert Paz goes. Laszlo Toekes.
Robert E Robinson goes.
Panama City, 24,000 US troops
& Noreiga's Dignity Battalions.
Maryland's John P Corderman.
Baton Rouge, Exxon & 5 tanks.
Nicolae & Elena Ceauşescu go.
Prague's Vaclav Havel.
—of well-rounded people.
—bye pineapple.

Sukkur rails, 210 go.
Beijing martial law.
Zaragoza disco, 43 go.

Azeris, Armenians & Baku.
Marion Barry arrested.
Avianca, 73 go.
England storms, 94 go.
ANC ban.

Super Bowl XXIV,
49ers over Broncos.

And I, our
time together challenged,
quickly follow. Hopstep, doubleflip,
Sam slips out of reach, gliding past
Waiters & Platers, by leaping easily onto
a nearby dessert cart and speedwaying on,
slipducking nonchalantly
the astounding mess left wrecked behind.

And stacks of dishes still go heaving by.
Exploding around Sam. Pitchers too.
Sam just rolls on through the Kitchen
dodging flying blades of razor steel.

VIADIDONACCI doesn't. Stopped. Struck.
Dropped, near the sauté
station, by sharp knives flung by
still surprised & shocked RELIEF COOKS,
wincing over his scream: —*Aaaaaaaaaaaargh.*

Sept 3 1937

Hong Kong Typhoon, 300 go.
600,000 Nuremberg Nazis.
9 Powers & Mediterranean.
Jacqueline Cochran's
292 MPH.
Nanking Air Raid. Galilee,
Lewis Andrews goes.
Clarksdale, Route 61 &
Richard Morgan,
Bessie Smith goes.
Submarines & fishing boats.
Chiang & Mao unite.
44¢
KKK &
Supreme Court's Hugo L.
—Quarantine the
Aggressors.
—all will be lost.
US condemns Japan.
Oswald Mosley,
Liverpool 10,000 & stones.
Yankees over Giants.
Maine & G-Men, Brady goes.
Sudeten Party.
Franco's Gijón.
Prinz.
Mexico, Lázaro Cárdenas &
350,000 acres of oil.

Moscow one million.

Too tuckered out for more. Just
Eskimo kisses she adores. Oddly tolerable.
Even if THE KITCHEN BRIGADE chucks knives at
me every time I pass by their stoves. Lives.
Dodged.
Ignored. Even if VIADIDONACCI
foams to have her gored.
I roll relaxed from anything that
peevish bore serves up,
heaving to wring still
my whirling blur, strangle me dead.
Nonchalantly I MeltO such threats,
each shift spinning free from
his Surly Sneers & Objections.
Sliding smoothly away,
by glide, outside turn,
to a stride
resuming my together time
with Hailey.

Busboys gawking the wound:

—*Wack!* —*Cold!* —*So Very Dope!*

Though I'm zip around the block, where's
Sam?, past sales for ACs, Futons, Sinks.
September's Recycling Rinks.
To the front of The St. Louis Dive where
nearby **Bald Cypress** lie cut.

I whip through the skid & blast of traffic,
finding Sam nowhere. Somehow gone.
Me allone
lingering amidst turmoils of arriving
Paramedics, sirens whining.
While Laggers, Slackers &
wiggin Knotheads do the sidewalk slag.
Until behind me, turning to find me,
I find Sam, allready kissing &
holding me snugly.

Feb 11 1990

—to freedom is irreversible.
—Amandla!
Victor Verster &
Nelson Mandela.
Douglas 10 rounds Tyson.
Perrier, benzine &
160 million bottles.
Bangalore airbus, 92 go.
UK, Argentina & Spain.

—I will never obey
the orders of.

Peru, peasants &
20 Maoist guerrillas, 9 go.
Petit Goav,
Roseline Vaval goes.
Patricio Aylwin.
Farzad Bazoft goes.
Lithuania's Kazimiera
Prunskiene National Salvation
Front, Tirgu Mures & 500 troops.
Sam Nujoma. Estonia.
Bronx & Happyland, 87 go.
Trafalgar Square. North Sea
& Scandinavian Star, 166 go.
Poindexter conviction.
Nick Faldo.
Constantine Mitsotakis.

I clean up the messes without rush.
Sit down strike with a dustpan and
brush. Missing Hailey though she's close
by, flying high on Slick Usuals slying
propositions and still armed
with Skirty Flirts.
Oblivious that I allone
can roll with her.

Now. Here.

When work's over, strolling free.
Only then do I stretch, traffic's toot to
bell veering wide, **Okapis** trotting aside.
St. Louis Beanery refreshed. Despite
creosote, Carousels and August. Until
at last we crash. One meagre mattress,
basin and Limit Fan.

—*Dead!* —*Fatigued!*
—*Beat!*

Massaging our feet.

June 30 1937

Oklahoma shopping carts.
Hitler & IBM.
—gas is low.
—We are flying on.
Dorothy Round over
Jadwiga Jedrzejowska.
Peel Commission
& Palestine.
—typical hoodlums.
Tehran Pact. Train accident,
95 go. New Guinea,
Howland Island
& the search is over.
Florida lynching, 2 go.
Lapébie's Tour.
S1392 & 70–20.
4 Alabama free. 4 20–99.
1 to go.
George, Belfast
& IRA bombs.
Peaceful Chamberlain
& Mussolini.
37th, Polo Bridge
& Pei River.
Ranger cups Endeavour II.
Shanghai's 32.
Palestine negotiations.
—unity and capacity.
Sachsenhausen, Lichtenberg
& Buchenwald.
USHA.

148
213

April 22 1990

Earth Day. Robert Polhill free.
—prevention of a return.
Frank Reed free.
Unbridled's Derby.
Carpentras vandals.
Bogotá & Cali bombings, 27 go.
Zagreb soccer riot.
US Military bases
& Manila protests. Bergen,
Global warming & 34 nations.
Starfire-1. Ion Iliescu.
Republic of Yemen
& Ali Abdullah Saleh.
Colombia's César Gaviria
& drug cartels.
Russian Republic's Boris Yeltsin.
PLO speedboats
& Nizzanim beach, 4 go.
Off Monrovia.
Gorbachev & Bush.
State of Emergency over.
Mega Borg.
Northern Iran shakes,
40,000 go.
Checkpoint Charlie over.
—tax revenue.
Kiko Kawashima.

—There!
The Crowd abruptly parts. And I'm
stunned by the bandaged & stitched
grimace still crawling after Sam.
Plaster bound with sling & splint, yet
allso maniacally swinging a broom,
eager to slap, jab, beat even
me from anyone's hour, when
by some threat Sam okays,
VIADADONACCI's bravado is suddenly dumped:
—Don't leave US, please.
Betrayed by the way his life wanes.
Slows. Worsens. Lets US go.
Continuously. Sam devastating
VIABIBONACCI with his freedom's allowance.
Even if BILL BOOZALI steps forth, violent:
—You laughed at US. You're dead to US.

April 16 1937

Flying Fortress.
New Revolutions &
Overthrowing Stalin.
Britain's Aircraft Carrier.
Guernica.
Third Neutrality Act.
Cash & Carry.
Barcelona's anarchists.
7:23. Naval Air Station.
—O the humanity. And all the passengers.
War Admiral's Derby.
Social Security.
3 million for 2 hours.
Harry Bennett, Frankensteen
& Reuther.
—to the bridge.
Neville Chamberlain's
Premiership & Europe.
Reich battleship blaze.
Little Steel, SWOC &
South Chicago
—A plague on both your.
Duke & Duchess.
—Progress is not a mad mob march.
Harlow goes. Chicago glass.
Louis 8 rounds Braddock.
Youngstown 18,556.

and Hailey with grins and staggering
spins. Rolls of tin assuring US he's
better off without much. Because
BOOZALI BILL grants him too much
leeway, VIABIBONACCI loathes my
ubiquity. Desperate to get me dismissed.
Stomps butts, drops
cups, any loaded plate.
—Mop that muck, Boy.
Shucks. I'd banish VIADADONACCI
if not for Hailey. KO the bully with
a brutal hurry of knuckle kisses. Bucket
hat his nog, acquaint his flap too
with a broom rod.
But Hailey cherishes these
times so I just, ooftah,
let the recession
fly by.
There.

July 2 1990

110° & Ka'aba stampede,
1,426 go.
8,000 Albanians.
Silverado Banking's Neil Bush.
Cabanatuan quake, 900 go.
William Brennan retires.
LeMond's Tour.
Iraqi tanks, 30,000 troops &
Kuwait.
WHO, AIDS & women.
Krahn soldiers,
Gio & Mano civilians, 600 go.
Bulgaria's Zhelyu Zhelev.
Saddam Hussein, Sheik Jabir
al-Ahmed al-Sabah &
Iraqi attack.
UN Security Council &
Trade Embargo. Annexation.
—the sand.
US Reserves. Operation Desert
Shield. Armenia's liberty.
Brian Keenan free.
Yugoslavia coal mine, 178 go.
Mohawks' Mercier Bridge.
China's Typhoons, 1,802 go.
Sampras over Agassi.
Samuel Doe goes.

And with that,
teeters off.
Calms these streeted
with offers of tables. Free pastry puffs.
Even helps out troublingly
bewildered VIABOBONACCI:
—Just a couple of stupid kids.
And this gig's up. Chunked.
Sam superwilling to dip. And despite
my awkwardness even readies me to go.
Sending out:
—We go to free the World.
But BILL BUZALI tries for the last jab:
—You go to lose the World. You allways do.
—No, we go to free you.
And we do. Stumbling free of
The St. Louis Take Out stuckery.

Feb 4 1937

San Francisco Dock strike
over. FDR's court challenge.
*—cui prodest? Who
benefits? The hand of Stalin.*
GM, 44 days
& wage hike.
Nylon.
—road to.
National Revolutionary
Guard.
Ethiopian rebels, 3,000 go.
—I have work to do.
*—three-horse team
provided by the Constitution.*
Bernard Fantus &
Cook County.
Chicago taxi drivers.
New London Texas burning,
294 go. Chrysler strike over.
William Hastie.
AFL & illegal property
seizure.
West Coast Hotel vs Parrish.
United States Steel
& the Union.
Helena Arkansas
& 5,600 acres.
Collective bargaining.
Detroit tears.

before returning to her duds,
returning me to my suds. The Dig Hop.
All at The St. Louis Bagel Shop.
Chomp, Slurp and Relax.
Run out back by owner BUZALI BILL
handling the oops hat &
kalamazoo jack. Sure, a business man.
Rarely around but, thanks
to him, our current employer.
Won over by Hailey's awkwardness &
willingness, if begrudging
how overqualified I am.
—Couple a dumb teenagers, he swells.
Though VIABOBONACCI's a problem.
Our freeman lobotomy
managing shifts. Swaggering
tables & clientele.
A hick fisted prick
harrying every Hairpin

Sept 14 1990

Saudi Arabia
& 8,000 British troops.
Michael Dugan fired.

Israeli bulldozing.
Serbian National Council.
General Aoun's siege, 25 go.
Waslala & 200 rebels, 10 go.
East, West & the Federal
Republic of Germany.

Bush vetoes stopgap.
Jerusalem, 19 go.
David H Souter.
Cincinnati over Oakland.
Holyfield 3 rounds Douglas.
New Zealand, Conservative
National Party & Jim Bolger.
—going to do about it?
South Africa's imprisoned.

Jewish Defense League
& El Sayyid Nosair,
Meir Kahane goes.
Democrats. 56-44. 268-167.
Pakistan's Nawaz Sharif.
200,000 more.
Oder-Neisse.
Mary Robinson's Ireland.

I kiss his cheek:
—*What now?*
—*Who cares.*
—*But how? Where?*

Passing pedestrian blurs,
sold, broke, bankrupt,
rushing around US, until someway
we're approached by an anxious Exec who
on behalf of the Round Table Regulars,
long dead & buried, hands over to US
at their bequest all we own.
Amortized. Fueled. Ready to pour it on.
Our new 911 Cabriolet, nelly, natch to lay
a batch from St. Louis. Budapest, Santiago,
Warsaw. Amsterdam, Shanghai, New Delhi.
Lisbon. Every city. Roam. Air sharper.
Promises harder. Driving US from the ages.

Nov 22 1936

Japanese & Mongolians,
1,200 go.

Burning Crystal.
Trotsky's Mexico.

Simpson & Windsor.
—without the help and
support of the woman I love.

Chang Hsüeh-liang &
13 days.
Nehru & British Imperialism.
Flint, Fisher Body 2 &
Sit down. Gene Sarazen's
drive. Steel Workers &
Organizing Committee.
—do-nothing government.
—about the despised,
the defeated, the last ditch.
Halfway revolution.
Harold Ickes.
—driven by the wind.
Juliana & Bernhard zur
Lippe-Biesterfeld.
Mufti's Palestine.
—comfort, opportunism
and timidity. We will carry on.
Frozen citrus.
Allegheny floods, 1,000 go.
Piatakov goes.

Lingering around's The Drip
Lag. But that's The Big
City. Lisbon, New Delhi,
Shanghai. Amsterdam, Warsaw.
Santiago, Budapest.
Here's to St. Louis!

Way to it. Way from it. All. Without
defense. Studebaker Dictator dumped
for the price of staying put. Rent.
Just a scrubandmop grub for wawa plinks
from Lolleos and Dolls while Hailey's all
smileandgreet, thiswayplease,
calm, working Minnies and Heels passing
through for a pause, passing on tips,
passing up favors. All just passing.
—*Do me a flavor?* Hailey sneaks me.
—*Check Lemonette.*
—*Hang near.*
Sweet kisses my cheek

Nov 17 1990

Michael Tubbs, Jeffrey Jennett, John Tubbs & Stephen Fussell. Farabundo Martí National Liberation Front offensive. $600,000,000, 10 years & Michael Milken. Sikh separatists & Chandigarh buses, 25 go. World Solar Challenge. Felix Houphouet-Boigny. John Major.

—it's a funny. Singapore's Goh Chok Tong. Graham Fagg, Philippe Cozette & Chunnel. Chad's Idriss Deby over Hissen Habré. 3,400 hostages.

Lech Walesa over Wojciech Jaruzelski. Slobodan Milosevic. USSR Food Aid Package & US.

—disorder and violence. Shkoder & Durres riots. *—second revolution.* Haiti's Jean-Bertrand Aristide. Emory Highway 80 pileup, 7 go.

A way we go.
Speeding for all we pass and
refuse to slow down for.
On our own. Top popped,
bashing on topfuel and grit.
We're big engines without brakes.
Outracing faster still roaring to astound.
Catch our blur. We sure whirr.
By Chokia's grave labor. Dried hard.
Wrecking balls, back hoes. Rusted cranes.
Pin **Oak** falling.

Everyone wants the Dream but we give it.
Four lanes. Eight lanes.
Only one way about it.
Sam & me with nothing at all,
overtaking every onramp & merge.
Punch it & roll. Y'all!

Oct 4 1936

US imports over exports. Yankees over Giants. Louis 3 rounds Brescia.

Albany's Social Darwinism. Bombay riots. Britain's 300 Boeing planes. Germany's Condor for Spain's Nationalists. Stalin's goings. Spanish Loyalists & rebels.

—for which we must sacrifice some part of the freedom of.

—roll the roll of honor of those who stood with US.

—men at starvation wages.

—sweatshops.

—at looms.

Mussolini & pact with Reich.

523–8. Landslide.

—We cannot avoid this period. We are.

—come with a unity not imposed from the top, not imposed by force.

I nod then. And she nods. Slowly.
—*We can't go on.*
I sigh. She sighs. Slowly
taking a turn for a narrowing curve,
rattling wobblings, swerving US
by Concrete Walks, Sad Shops and Shut
Schools. Through Neighborless Parks.
Everyone sells the Dream but I live it.
A lone **Moose** bows stoically.
Hailey headturns our where's:
—*But how can we stop?*
—*Flip the car.*
—*O.*
—*And get a job.*
—*For how long? Until when?*
Wishes threaten departure
except Hailey holds all three
just by reaching over and
cradling my hand carefully.

Jan 12 1991

Bush, US Congress
& military force.
Bruce Gelb.
Operation Desert Storm.
Tomahawk cruise missiles,
F-117s & Wild Weasels.
Michael Speicher goes.
Eastern Airlines over.
Salt Lake City crush.
Louisville. 10 scuds. Patriots.
Wafra burns.
Siad Barre flees.
Super Bowl XXV,
Giants over Bills.
Khafji falls.
11 US Marines go.
USAir jet & commuter plane,
34 go. Hindu Kush shake,
200 go. GM's 15,000.
10 Downing Street's IRA mortar.
2,900 sorties.
Winnie Mandela.
150 oil wells.
—control of everything.
Warsaw Pact over.
American VII Corps.
—Kuwait is liberated.

Eazy Victor.
Aloft. And Sam laughs,
Green Eyes with flecks of Gold.
Brazen cheeks, strong nose. Bold. He
shockwaves the brave. Earblasts the bewildered.
All allone, an economy of passage outstripped
by haste. And still he drops more.

Flying over dip, pots and chucks,
by Elsah, Mozier and Hannibal,
until Lover's Leap slows US for a roadside
Fair Of Sorts where Sam wins a pie throwing
contest. Cash prize. Nuzzles me:

—*Guess.*

—*Yes.*

Our Toyota MR2 never better. Purring
from turbo to clutch. Cool and quick.
Lubricated. We never clutch.

Aug 16 1936

100 meters, 200 meters,
running broad jump,
400 meter relay &
Jesse Owens. Hitler exits.
1,200 Badajoz Rebels go.
14 Trotskyites go.
Grigori Zinoviev &
Lev Kamenev go too.
Egypt's liberty & Suez.
Mary's 30.7 knots
& Riband.
Beryl Markham's Atlantic.
50,000 spades march.
Iceland & Pourquoi Pas?,
Jean Charcot & 32 go.
—Around his neck is.
Maqueda.
France, Switzerland,
Holland & Gold Standard.
—down here
with their millions.
Detroit's Legion's 11 guilty.
General Varela,
General Moscardo &
Toledo's Alcázar.
Terre Haute &
Earl Browder.
Franco's regime.

collapsing valves turning to powder,
bearings jerking US left,
brakes weakening with each press.
The spavined Ford Half duressing.

—*Guess.*

—*No.*

Over the hill for any turnoff where we
might shirk, sluff and leisurely, perhaps,
partake.
There's the most worthwhile pay.
To experience this want by waiting.
Even if Hailey's allways for gaining
the next with a zip, she too needs
to do the drag.

Hailey. All drippy shnoz, wan cheeks
now, weary and teen. Yet somehow still
her Gold Eyes with flecks of Green
keep smiling tenderly
for me.

March 3 1991

Rodney King, 56 baton blows &
6 kicks. Stacey C Koon,
Laurence M Powell, Theodore
Briseno & Timothy Wind.

Failaka Island &
1,450 Iraqi soldiers.
Sebastião Ribeiro da Silva goes.
Charles E Roemer.
Alexandra, ANC &
Inkatha, 34 go.
Jerusalem, James Baker & PLO.
Conor Clapton goes.
Kurdish rebels & Kirkuk.
Safwan's 7,000.
Poll Tax Riots.
$4.25.
Diego Maradona.
Georgia & Zviad Gamsakhurdia.
Livorno ferry, 140 go.
Denver snow.
Genoa, Haven supertanker &
30,000 tons of crude.
—safe zone.
Yanomami gold.
500,000 Kurdish refugees.
NLRB & Hospitals.

Bolting smoothly on. Outrageous.
Our Mazda RX7 macks
crudely throughout every impedance.
Passing tows, oversize loads,
rolling out behind US excarcerated roads.
Sam: —*Faster baby. Let'S never stop.*
By Quincy. Ursa. Marcelline. Tioga.
My Leftwrist Silver Twist cooling.
Dairy Farms and shallow ponds spilling soon
with stars, where Calloused Workers slow
against hay wheels, chewing windlestraw,
wave US on
to foggy Nauvoo.
River slipping ever down. We go with the
current. Our own current. Ahead. Fascinating
stones plinking our trunk and bumper. While
Rivertrucks heavy with iron just let go.

July 3 1936

League of Nations
& German Acts,
Stefan Lux goes.
Perry over von Cramm.
Jacobs over Sperling.
Triboro Bridge's 200,000.

LA Police, tear gas
& 2,500 citrus farmers.
José Calvo Sotelo goes.
US heatwave, 3,000 go.
Cantonese Chen Chi-tang
escapes.
—Fascism will not pass,
the hangmen of October will
not pass.
Madrid revolution over,
25,000 go.
Mola & Burgos.
—our triumphant
movement. Spain is saved.
Berlin's 100,000 &
Summer Olympics.
Greek Military & Council
President Ioannis Metaxas.
AFL, CIO & 10 unions.
4/4 swing.
US & Strict neutrality.

Further erumpenting: —*Splendid!*
But here's a surprise: midchuck for
another murkgeyser thublunk I actually
commence celebrating her panache.
My hands repeatedly clapping.
Fascinating.
We continue on our travels, blowing
gaskets and steam, backfires gatling
US along on unrevelling wheels.
Pip, pap, whoooosh. Three more flats.
Even with her Leftwrist Silver Twist.
Past Blytheville and Cape Girardeau.
—*You slay me,* Hailey suddenly
mimbles. *Absolutely.*
And she's so delicate now. And soft. And
pretty. That I allso burn, barely able to
even pat her knee, while
the Packard Twelve
grinds gruesomely onward,

We let go and barge on.
Berm over herm, bridge across ridge,
up this Great River Road swerving US
for still colder climes.
We overtake motorcycles, sedans, flatbeds
loaded with spools of cable, pallets of
propane, lashed down sailboat keels.
Granite chips skimming off our fender.
We pass bonfires. Serial Anarchists. Car chases.
Junkies, Molesters and Assassins.
Even when traffic sticks for Worried Kids,
washing windshields and rims,
wanted by the Most Wanted,
we swing by.
Because we are traffic.
Heedless of all we far.
And yeah, never pocked, never

April 26 1991

70 tornadoes, 23 go.
Seoul protests.
Kutubdia, Maheshkali
& Bay of Bengal cyclone,
138,866 go.
Bush jogging.
Strike The Gold's Derby.
William Kennedy Smith.
SS-20. Mandela's 6 years.
Edith Cresson.
Rajiv Gandhi goes.
Israeli Hercules C-130,
El Al Boeing 747
& 14,087 Falashas.
Lauda Air's Thai jungles,
223 go.
Olivero Chávez Araujo
& Tamaulipas State Prison.
José Eduardos dos Santos
& Jonas Savimbi.
Glenanne's UDR base, 3 go.
South Africa's Lands Act
& Group Areas Act over.
Mount Unzen, 37 go.
Broadway parade.
Bangladesh cyclone,
125,720 go.

to Chattanooga, south to Baton Rouge
even skipping horizons north, for
permanently icelashed ports.
Ooodles of hops, rippling bitsies,
leaping by fifties with spinning arches,
on and on, down, up and across
this ever aching flux.
I am the flux.
And all gambols too.
Hailey of course allso tosses her
weight around, chucking boles of
stone wobbling out and down, only
once, with such a dismal plop.
No hops.
Typical.
But on and on she prances over such
Durham splashes, frisking proudly:
—*Asheville! New Orleans! Nome!*
She's a confounding one.

May 9 1936

—*Italy at last has her Empire.*
127.5 million. Cortes.
New Orleans & FBI: Thomas
Robinson & Alvin Karpis.
Stanley Baldwin's league.
Kurt Schuschnigg's
Austrian party.
Samuel Reshevsky.
50,000 Mexican
railworkers strike.
Havana's Miguel Gómez.
Tony Lazzeri &
2 grand slams. Norman
Thomas for President.
Louis Meyer's 24th 500.
Nicaragua & National Guard.
Superchief's 39.75
transcontinental hours.
Canton's War on Japan.
Léon Blum's
labor agreement.
Hoover, New Deal &
fascism. Puerto Rico's
Eleanor Roosevelt.
Himmler's police.
Compulsory prostitution.
Schmeling 12 rounds Louis.
Lemke's Union.
Ethiopian embargo.
Virgin legislature.

June 12 1991
Boris Yeltsin.
Mount Pinatubo erupts.
South African Assembly &
Population Registration Act.
Colombian police, Medellín
cartel & Pablo Escobar.

PV Narasimha Rao.
UN Weapons Experts &
Abu Gharib.
Algiers, Police &
FIS, 8 go. Krajina, Croats &
Serbs, 5 go.

—against the security of.
Hussein & Jordan's freedoms.
South Africa &
US trade sanctions.
Hitoshi Igarashi goes.
G7. G8.
UNITA & FLEC.
Australia, Greek tanker &
69,000 barrels.
Milwaukee, chocolate factory &
Jeffrey Dahmer. START.

Baku train, 15 go.
Palm Springs &
60 Girl Scouts, 7 go.

grimed by tar.
Rocks abruptly bounce deadon. Miss.
Haulings overtake lanes overtaking stalls.
And when the generous cut out
of our way, we giggle. And when
the bitter cut US off, we snicker.
Because we're rampant, impossible to
flex. Impossible to equal. Even challenge.
Sam allways the ongoing outcome. With
great hands. Freak legs.

—Why didn't the skeleton cross the road?
—Why?
—He didn't have the guts for it.

Sam cackles, a dozen stations fiending our
here temptation. Speed. Terrifying
everything beyond the perimeter of our way.
We are without

March 19 1936
US floods, 134 go.
200,000 wandering.
Harold Campbell's pacifism.
State Attorney General
Vincent & 17,000
Kentucky Colonels.
99% plebiscite. Harar burns.
38 British Warships.
New Hampshire floods.
Austria's military draft.
Trenton's 8:44 PM juice,
Bruno goes.
Southern tornadoes, 421 go.
President Zamora out.
Natives Act.
Turkey, Dardanelles
& Lausanne Convention.
Racketeer Lucky Luciano.
Tel Aviv–Jaffa of Palestine.
Public Enemy #2:
John Torrio arrested.
Akron strike over.
John Aiken.
Farouk's Egypt.
Mustard gas
& Addis Ababa.
—and this annihilation
cannot fail and is not
distant.
Bold Venture's Derby.

And so, glum, thirsty,
low on gas, I slump over
to The River Marsh.
Hailey, on blistering feet, limps up
smooching my mouth and wandering
with me. Wondering too
of a way to continue our blitz from
the impedance of the World.
Her scrubby legs. Dimpled knees.
Still exquisitely free.
Wanting all she may allways have of me.

—Let'S skip stones,
she glees.

And we do.
Gathering slim, fleet earth rings,
which by elbow and wrist,
shoulder and hip, ditching our grip,
I flick skimming chips
across the water east

perimeters, perpetually unwinding, unifying.
All around receding before
our freedom. Even the Vengeful & Needy.
Because we're mighty. We are the feer
every Itinerant longs to scoot clear of.
Catch US & miss US,
reach US & fail.
Any cockiness allready frails before US.
Sam quiet now, his palm on the air,
every tilt endangering lives,
hillsides shivering, each bend wailing
his horrible presence.
Fun outstanding! What joy!
Our wheels turned by the road,
radials unstressed, compression refreshed,
socketing ahead. And Sam such a gas
with our Nissan 300ZX bent,

Aug 2 1991
AIDS & US.
Crimea, Foros & Gorbachev.
Madagascar's 400,000.
Phoenix & Wat Promkunaram,
9 go. Edward Tracy free.
Strathfield shopping, 7go.
Turkish immigrants, North
Africans & Bayreuth's 1,000.
Moscow coup.
—unwell.
Hurricane Bob, 16 go.
Gavin Cato goes.
Crown Heights riots.
Yankel Rosenbaum goes.
Boris Yeltsin, KGB
& popular support.
Boris K Pugo goes.
Gorbachev returns.
South Korean typhoon, 75 go.
Carl Lewis's 9.86.
Powell's jump.
Hamlet blaze, 25 go.
Union of Sovereign States.
Slavonia & Zagreb.
Latvia, Lithuania & Estonia.
Thokoza ambush, 18 go.
Priština's 15,000.

But getting on, a tire pops,
the VW V2 hardly stocked, no longer
rocketing, soon after stops,
spilling air defeatedly.
Hailey kicks fenders, wheel, her
own shins. Sprawls out on the dirt.
Oi, her mood's long!
Deporting joys!
And worse, standing still, getting
at last the peril pursuing US,
counter to our tour, a reverting
at hand gathering to control, hold
and destroy US.
Here then my choke of feer:
I'm no longer strong enough
to defy such want.
Vengeance against caprice.
To deny, squander US
and finally find me.

Jan 24 1936
8,000 Ethiopians go.
Veterans, Veto override &
immediate redemption.
Ozie Powell goes.
Alfred E Smith &
Liberty League.
George V goes. Edward VIII.
Richard Loeb goes.
Mabel Eaton & more.
Davos, David Frankfurter &
5 shots,
Wilhelm Gustloff goes.
Rafael Franco. Attorney
General Cummings.
Jawaharlal Nehru.
Action Française.
Machine Gun Jack
McGurn goes.
Manuel Azaña.
Walter Johnson over
Rappahannock River.
Russian skies &
25 miles high. Ferdinand
Porsche. Mount Alaji.
Korekiyo Takahashi goes.
Second Neutrality Act.
Tennessee Dam & Norris Dam.
*—iron ring around
the Reich.*
Cologne.

Sept 13 1991

Baker & Bakatin.
Naqoura & UNIFIL, 1 goes.
Ingvar Carlsson quits.
Jackie Mann free.
2,400 US Nuclear Weapons & unilateral reduction.
Kevin McGovern goes.
Haiti, Aristide & Raoul Cédras, 100 go.
Apple & IBM.
Yugoslavia, Federal Air Force & Croatian Zagreb.
Anita Hill & Clarence Thomas.
Killeen Texas, pickup truck & George Hennard, 23 go.
Paris-Nice collision, 16 go.
Himalayan shake, 360 go.
Jesse Turner free.
Berkeley fires, 19 go.
4,000 Turkish soldiers & PKK.
Yugoslavian Army, Serbs & Dubrovnik.
Twins over Braves.
Philippine mudslides.
David Duke.

terrifying
craven
OWNER MAN, clipped allready by our approach.
Unprotected for all HE hoards and betrays.
Wizening, slumping. Slain.
Because everyone we blow by, we blow away.
Never paid, we never delay
for traffic barrels & cones,
Migrants, Jumpers and Joes.
Our Acura NSX
detouring East by fleets of Median Mowers,
Fast Mix Boys, Cement Slewers. One Dude
perched up a cherrypicker lifts his arm. Wants
to join. Holds onto US long after we're gone.
Our Mercury XR7.
High outputting the curves of our worst
by lanescapes strewn with unescapables

Dec 1 1935

Iraq, Afghanistan, Turkey, Iran & Non-aggression Pact.
President Chiang Kai-shek.
DC-2, 14 passengers & Air hostesses.
Tomas Masaryk.
Detroit Lions.
British Foreign Secretary.
Douglas DC-3's Wright Cyclone engines.
Nuremberg Laws & Private Hospitals.
Lindbergh for England.
Cold front, 212 go.
North Dakota's Gerald Nye.
—If we win the debt won't.
—and if we lose, the debt won't.
Stanford over SMU.
South African hailstones, 19 go. Ethiopia, Daggha Bur & Italian bombs.
Supreme Court & Agricultural Adjustment Act.
—We can get along with butter but never without cannon.

Kickin for speed. Past Pettifoggers
and Boondoggling Dindys.
Rugby Games and Judo Belts.
Only now the American Austin can't
keep up. Shift glitching, spring hitch,
pipe hissing. My Hailey ever
glummer. Me too. And to top
it off we're low on fuel.
Fuel?
The Chevrolet EC richters on
past WPA Crews slickering tar and CCC
backs hacking splinters for Beer Cans.
Gasoline dwindling.
At least there's a pump but
STATION GLOM only wants Hailey.
She offers the spare. OWNER LUG nods
fair. Fills the tank a ways.
Lip licks.
Unafraid.

Nov 7 1991

Chicago furnace, 10 go.
Earvin Johnson & AIDS.
Norodom Sihanouk returns.
Abdel Basset Ali al-Megrahi
& Lamen Khalifa Fhimah.
Edwin Edwards.
Terry Waite
& Tom Sutherland free.

—remove without bloodshed
the people who govern US.

Boutros Boutros Ghali. Choshi
Japan, Ilwaco Washington
& Gerard d'Aboville's row.
Vukovar falls.

Coalinga's dusty pileup,
17 go.
John Sununu quits.
Pan Am over.

Joseph Cicippio, Alann Steen
& Terry Anderson free.
Kimberley Bergalis goes.
North & South Korea's
Non-aggression pact.

Salem & Safaga Port, 533 go.
Alma Ata's Commonwealth.
Taiwan's Kuomintang.

only we easily escape. Because we are
untouchable. By all we blur by,
Sam stays jiggy & cool.
My Shimmy & Par.
Yup, he still turns me on.
—*You too,* he smiles.
—*Anytime soon.*
And we go for miles.
Air wet with our sweat.
Carnations dread. Wilt. Dead.
Not US. We gnaw on woe and quench
on sadness. It zazzles him. It shazzles me.
Pumped, stomped, by US churning.
Our Dodge Stealth kicks up
arcs of icy clouds splitting to exile.
Except there is no exile anymore.
There's only US.

Oct 16 1935

Britain's embargo &
American Oil.
AFL.
Geraldine Kollmann goes.
Mao, 6,000 miles &
Yenan, 100,000 go.

New Jersey Chop & shots,
Dutch Schultz goes.

—boy has never wept
dashed a thousand kim.

Mussolini takes over
Ethiopia.
Atlantic City's CIO.

Milwaukee Dynamite &
the Mad Bomber,
Idzi Rutkowski goes.
Albert Stevens,
Orvil Anderson & 74,000 ft.

Ripley West Virginia &
a rope, JS Gunnoe goes.

Columbus Texas & 700,
Benny Mitchell &
Ernest Collins go.

Italian Air Raid,
2,000 go.
Jacob Ciemiengo.
Zaimis out.
Peking & Tientsin.
18–45.

It's a Memphis rendezvous.
Whiling all the rotaries,
the Graham Supercharged burping
exhaust on Union and Riverside.
I'm exhausted too.
We stall by Escape Alley.
Stretch and stride.
I find fancy loaves of Missouri's finest,
served on trashcan china, while Hailey
wrestles some ribs from spitting **Jaguars**
tossing these along with
moldy cheese rinds upon used pie plates.
—*Thanks,* she chomps.
And I am violent too.
—*What a splendid medley for two.*
—*Whatever there, Scooter.*
Hailey searingly chopfallen, suddenly,
which gets me itching to shake a leg.
Road roar ahead.

Dec 22 1991

Texas floods, 15 go.
—fell apart even before.
Gorbachev out. Free elections
& Islamic Salvation Front.
Moscow's milk, bread & meat.
Mogadishu, Ali Mahdi
Muhammad & Farah Aidid,
20,000 go.
Pascal Carpenter, Johnny
Hincapie, Emiliano Fernandez
& Ricardo Nova.
Yugoslavian Army &
UN helicopter, 5 go.
Bush & Kiichi Miyazawa.
Croatia, Slovenia &
European Commision.
John Santora.
Super Bowl XXVI,
Washington over Buffalo.
83 military bases. German
Navy, T-72 Tanks & Godewind.
—friendship and partnership.

Venezuela's Carlos Perez.
Maastricht's 12. Alberto Tombo.
UN's 14,400.
Nicholas Bochatay goes.

Neat. Some heaty hubadub grub along an
uneven course. Under bipolar skies.
Behind Wrecking Yards, Fast Food Chains,
Truck Stops. Clubs.
Sam, all New World Order,
globalizes with a relentlessness only
he can coo through so
tenderly.

I hardly hold on, though I'm barely off.
Where there's a Wheel, there's a play.
And we're allways playing.
Yozing the peeps, honking up sticky
tendencies for all we avert.
Sam disarms everytime
the sweep of lives we zip by.

And all Advocate Ladies rock solid
for even a breath of him again.

Aug 31 1935

Neutrality Act
& Shipments Abroad.

Tropical storm & Florida,
400 go.

Bonneville Salt Flats
& 301.337 MPH.
Louis Brodsky.
Carl Weiss & 61 bullets.
—I'm shot.

Geneva, Edvard Benes
& League Council.

—I have so much to do.
—to use ballots not bullets.

Nuremberg NSDAP.
Huey P Long goes.
Allison's Forest.

Cordell Hull & apology.

Howard Hughes
& a flying 351 MPH.
Manuel Luis Quezon.

Joe Louis 4 rounds Max Baer.
$90 Million pay raise.

Italy & Ethiopia,
1,700 go.
George Condylis.
Tigers over Cubs.

Mussolini's Adowa.

This time, I stroll the banks while
Hailey retries wading against the rush.
Hesitant. River only hip high.
Dismayed by her biff:
—*You're so plush.*

Me just lounging, ambling
outside her slow dip.

Where there's a chance,
there's a bend. Hailey marvelling
how I ignore the current.
I am the current. And currently frisky.
The currency of every risk.
But I marvel over Hailey too,
enjoying her then,
however meek, fawning when
I leap towards the adoring
ripples to take her hand
and her beneath broiling skies,
on cool earth.

Feb 23 1992

Albertville Olympics.
Ford's $4.5 billion.
GM's $2.3 billion.
London Bridge station bomb.
Montenegro & Serbia.
Michelangelo Virus.
Bill Clinton's primaries.
Erzincan quake, 3,000 go.
Buenos Aires, Israel Embassy
& car bomb, 10 go.
FW de Klerk & apartheid.

—for the cause of Peace and Justice.
—Yes!

Kalenjin warriors, Luo & Kikuyu.
Flushing Bay & Fokker F-28,
27 go.
Desiree Washington
& Tyson's 25.
Gulab Sharma's warrant.
Sarajevo's snipers, 1 goes.
March for Women's Lives.
Arthur Ashe & AIDS.

—There are no safe havens.

Maraga attack, 100 go.

Away to Dullstown.
Pull short for a stretch.
Chill a park bench. Howyazall.
Quarrelling Couples glitch to flick US
coin. Enough change to return dancing
down the street. Two Liberty Spikers dropping
cash lose their shyness and rollerblade off
together. Even Vagabonds leave savings before
scatting spooked. We save no one.
—*Give it here,* a MADAM bashes,
jabbing at my Leftwrist Crystal Twist.
—*Beg your pardon?* Sam backats.
—*O, clowns.*
Then stupidly, THE PIMP attacks.
Sam curbs HER with a turn.
HE shakes. Wastes. Until
all of HER spins out.

July 5 1935

—national run around.
Senator Robert Wagner &
National Labor Act.
—unfair labor practices.

Fred Perry over
Gottfried von Cramm.
2 battleships & 28 U-boats.
Champs-Elysées military
parade. Communists,
The Radical Socialists &
France's Popular Front.
PWA & 100,000 jobs.
Boulder lake.
—mishmash.
—without a sincere bone.

151 free.
Communists, Hudson &
Bremen Raid.
China & River flood,
200,000 go.
Romain Maes' Tour.
Special Prosecutor
Thomas Dewey.
Germany's Jews.
Turin Dam fails, 1,000 go.
FDR's Social Security Act.
Alaska & a plane,
Rogers & Post go.

Vitamin E.

I stroke easily over, swiftly
halting her drift, so panicked
she rips hold of my hair.
Clenches and bawls. Fine. With
mighty kicks and crawl, I deliver
her trembling back to the shore.
—*Thank you,* Hailey blurpples,
unsteady, callow, fidgeting there with
her Leftwrist Crystal Twist.
So terribly destitute. Poor.
But Lovely too.
Hiking back we pass TWO LOVERS
struggling upon our paths.
Howls, clutches and ouches.
Both of US snicker.
We damp on around their
silly snabble, and with little
else approaching, just scramble
back to The River Landing.

April 15 1992

US air embargo &
Libya. Afghanistan &
Mohammad Najibullah.
Robert F Kelly Jr.
Guadalajara sewer explosion,
190 go. Germany's Public
Service Workers.
—*Not guilty.*
—*Not even a bone.*
Los Angeles riots.
Reginald Denny. 58 go.
Thousands of National Guard.
Lil E Tee's Derby.
27th Amendment.
America[3] cups
Il Moro di Venezia.
Josef Schwammberger.
Bhumibol, Suchinda &
Chamlong Srimuang.
Lop Nur's 1 megaton.
Cosa Nostra, Capaci &
Palermo Airport,
Giovanni Falcone &
Francesca Morvillo & 3 go.
Bush, US Coast Guard &
Haitian refugees. Oscar
Scálfaro. 12,000 Sudanese.

And Sam never even balls
a fist which would destroy
passingly any question over what's so
fine about him: remorseless glee
ending life's only conviction.
—*Let'S Scatter Batter,* I flip,
but Sam's allready with it. Moving out.
Squealing hard & far, past
Ginkgo, **Sweetgum** and **Lyre Sage**
strangely cut down and hastening.
Our Alfa Romeo screaming on from some
transcontinental terrortory
seeping after what we only drop,
hunching wisps of cold for battered rocks
of fading clamor, shrilling helplessly.
Even **Kudzu** dies unnaturally
amidst ribs tangled apart by the wind.

May 18 1935

Maxim Gorky down, 49 go.
TE Lawrence goes.
Patman Bill Veto upheld.
Kenesaw Landis,
Cincinnati & 7 games.
Unconstitutional NRA.
Works Progress
Administration.
Poultry Corporation vs US,
NIRA illegal.
Quetta quake, 26,000 go.
Ruth's Boston Braves.
Dubuque to Appalachia:
Dust Bowl & Dust Storm.
Reforestation.
Anti–soil erosion.
National Parks.
Nebraska tornado
& flood, 250 go.
Lumber, 6 miles & a blanket.
Atlantic, Normandie
& 29.7 knots.
Omaha's Triple Crown.
Bill W, Bob S & AA.
Japan & Northern China.
Omaha strikes, riots
& martial law.
Chuck's heart.

to free geysers
clear to mudballing **Cows**.
I am astounding.
What I evoke. Both of US
so joed now
if allso pretty much dinged.
The Willys 77 soon slugging US on
by bramble and field ploughs where
Minks, **Toebiters** and **Snowy Egrets**
whimmer solemnly:
—*It's not all about sex.*
Sure. If glom.
—*Let'S pop for a swim,* I sock.
And hop, we stop, head for
a waterlogged dock.
Hailey drops a toe. I dive
for foreign flux, Hailey following at
once, too slim though to take
on such opposing peril.

June 5 1992

Omniflox. Waldemar Pawlak. William Pinkney. Hiroshi Yamauchi's Mariners. Rio Earth Summit. Supreme 6-3.

Boipatong & 200 Zulus, over 40 go.

Yitzhak Rabin. Tailhook Association Convention, H Lawrence Garrett quits. Mojave quake, 1 goes. Islamic Salvation Front & Annaba, Mohammed Boudiaf goes. Willie Williams over Daryl Gates.

Mongolia & MRRP's 70. Glasgow's Minkes. Daytona Beach & 18 ft wave. Olivia Riner's acquittal. Austria's Thomas Klestil.

Columbia's 221 orbits & 5.76 million miles. Poland's Hanna Suchocka. Ross Perot. Slovakia. Paolo Borsellino & 5 go. Newfoundland, Plymouth & Dwight Collins.

We are killers naturally.
The goings of all around. Driving by
drivebys whose EXECUTIONERS
catch Sam's blown kisses, abruptly feeling
every executed lip their own. Over
and over again.

Radishes & Turnips bloat, seep & run.

—*Roust The About,* I plead.
—*Allready Clocking out,* Sam agrees, chill
torquing US over riprap & grade. Morgue &
slate. At speeds allways beyond where

Frost Daffodils die helplessly.
Sunflowers go too.

On we tear.

Litigation's death. If it were that great
all the time, it would allways be fair.
We are never fair.

133 228

April 1 1935

Supreme Court & Scottsboro Jury. Italy's Somaliland. Danzig rejects Nazis. Emergency Relief Appropriations Act's $5 billion. Stressa Conference. Sandstorm. Kansas, Colorado, Wyoming, Oklahoma, Texas & New Mexico. *—nation's bread basket.* Pan American Sea Clipper.

Geneva League Council & German Ways. Johnny Kelley's Boston run. Boris Bulgarian revolution. Formosa quake, 2,000 go. Polish parliament over. Soviet Moscow transport. Front seat New York three. Nazi divorce. Rexford Tugwell's RA. Boulder Dam. Omaha's Derby. *—help men keep their chins up and their hands.* Rural Electrification Administration. Orleans & Howard Johnson.

up and down, squarely of course,
fairly banging her bank for flat blanket
macking, over scoops,
under, plunging the fat, by benches,
tables and campfire stones.

On we go.

Wild Boars grow up around our trestle.
Sandhill Cranes chwerrr to our wrestle.

And I hurry close, unhurriedly
taking a turn on Mount Pleasant.
A fourknee romp behind Hailey.
Rubadub pump. Tomming
my wingding for a bump.

Gopher Tortoises & Plovers here

moolying muds. Snickers.
And though Hailey still can't come
I'm allmost done, smiling,
mellow and sweet,
removing my treat

July 27 1992

Giovanni Lizzio goes.
Russian & Ukrainian accord.
Milan Panic &
Detention Camps.
Barcelona Olympics.
—we'd get back.
Roman Gventsadze free.
US, Canada, Mexico &
North American Free
Trade Agreement.
3,000 Georgian soldiers
& Abkhazia. Bosnia
& Serbian prison camps.
Nagorno-Karabakh, 44 go.
Hurricane Andrew &
3,300 National Guard, 91 go.
US Air Force & No Fly Zone.
Kevin Harris & Randy Weaver
surrender. Todor Zhivkov.
Ciskei & ANC marchers,
28 go. Lima, Peru &
Abimael Guzmán Reynoso's
arrest. Mae Jemison.
Jhelum River &
Mangla Dam, 2,000 go.

I slide over to Sam, for his wide
shoulders, protective arms, against the cool
he drapes over the yards of every Shower,
Pool Dunk and Kegger we fleet by.
—Take it away!
O even the bravest Bailiffs twinge.
Probate Judges ripple gloom.
—So so get!
And every peck Sam shares
nixes somewhere someone's
desire to stay fresh. Our slide
& slam languishes the boniest Scammer.
McBabe and Shredder scram sorry.
—*We allso do,* Sam admits,
despite all that's frantic and young.
Because we're allways young flowings.
And we're never frantic

Feb 5 1935

15 rounds.
Argentinian troops
& La Plata. Macon
& Pacific winds, 2 go.
Hauptmann guilty.
Oklahoma prison's 31,
1 guard goes.
Nazi beheading.
Tennessee's anti-evolution
law. Paraguay
& League of Nations.
Ethiopia. Italians mobilize.
—my saarlanders.
Prajadhipok of Siam quits.
Malcolm Campbell's
276.8 MPH. Venizelos &
Greek Military revolution.
German Air Force.
Paris, National Assembly
& Warships.
Organized Crime's 2,000.
Treaty of Versailles.
German Military Draft.
500,000 & Germany's
Military Parade.
Harlem riots.
British troops & 20,000,
23 go. Persia & Iran.
Chinese Eastern Railway
to Japan.

Not too soon bared, stretched out, long
kissy moans, leisurely sips,
sucks and Dixie slaps.
The River, Our Mishishishi,
Rolling Along The Long Gone
Sadly Sliding On,
too slow to ever catch up with US.
Dilly & dally, spanking her fanny,
fressing her busby,
pressing her boobies
to mollock steamy with.
—O, o, give!
Dripping for bone. Until slippled with
bumbucking buttonring gasps:
—Can't take anymore!
I gasp too. She melts. Both of US
locked, she clawing my back, me
pawing her ass, grinding faster
this brunch, puddles of fun,

because frantic's what we give
even a COP we
only briefly stop for, hurling up from
around a bend with impudent sirens, trotting
to arrest what can't be arrested. Even lived.

Watermelons, Kumquats & Satsumas rot.

—*Got a license to land this thing?*

—*Sure,* I pip. But
Sam's peril provokes what my
kneeknocking fails to risk: how even
this HIGHWAY PATROL frails to resist US.

—*Hand over your identity,* CHARLIE tenses.
Underage ain't okay around here. Stealing's
gainst the Law. County's where we'll
defer y'all.

Our Maserati 222 idling.

—*Sure,*

Sept 20 1992

European Community's
Treaty On European Union.
Trans-Atlantic balloon race.
NHL's Manon Rheaume.
Vietnam's Le Duc Anh.
Gregory Kingsley.
Joel Rene Valdez.
Helge Hummelvoll
& UNICEF's Myint Maung go.
Subic Bay. Boulder's trains.
São Paulo & prison riot, 200 go.
Turkish destroyer &
USS Saratoga, 5 go.
Iraqi assets.
Schipol Airport, 70 go.
OPIC. Gradačac
& Serb planes, 19 go.
Germany & 4.4 lbs of Uranium.
France's National Blood
Transfusion Hub & HIV.
Toronto over Atlanta.
Charles Taylor, National
Patriotic Front of Liberia &
Liberian Army, 5 go.

Dec 29 1934

—*Fiery and feerless*
revolutionary.
Stalin's purge, 100 go.
Japan & Washington
Naval Treaty.
—*We do our part.*
Harold Ickes, John Collier &
Reorganization Act.
Alabama over Stanford.
Cyrenaica, Tripoli &
Fezzan now Libya.
Reich Steel.
Welfare's 3.5 million jobs.
Pickford & Fairbanks.
FBI & Karpis Gang,
Fred & Kate Barker go.
Saar Basin.
Mao's Army & Zunyi.
New Jersey, Mohawk liner
& freighter, 46 go.
Louisiana,
500 National Guardsmen &
Square Deal Association.
—*the wealth.*
Court of Justice.
Soviet Army's 940,000.
Flemington, Lindbergh trial
& lapel ladders.

By turnoffs, holdups and deadends,
the Terraplane KS turns for more grit.
Yowsah!
How'd I get so oodles for this nitwit,
zazzling strong, dingy and giddy
by my shazzling side?
And all we pass by.
Every PASSENGER's byebye.
What the jell YOKELS never try.
How LOCALS dwindle on what I half.
Pull over to Bean and Spindle. Laugh.

—*Why for?*

— *For just a quickie?*

Mourning Doves, Darners &
Armadillos stir. All experience,
Hailey hauls US beyond a shore tide,
where grabbing my poler,
free from LOLLERS,
procures some antic rides.

Nov 4 1992

New Democrat.
Bobby Fischer over
Boris Spassky.
US, European Community
Imports & 200% tariffs.
Peru's Alberto Fujimori.
ECOWACS. Trade War & Farm
subsidies. Australian military
& homosexuality.
Mölln & Turks, 3 go.
Arges Sequeira goes.
—annus horribilis.
De Klerk's non-racial
government.
Venezuela's Carlos Pérez.
Azanian People's Liberation
Army. Spain & Aegean Sea.
Ayodhya, Hindus &
Muslims, over 700 go.
Somali & 1,800 US Marines.
Flores quake, 2,500 go.
Teaching Business & Labor.
Straits of Florida &
Cuban defection. Tritium &
Savannah River.
Caspar Weinberger &
Duane Clarridge.

Sam eazes, taking back our age
which I give up with
squeamiest obeisance. Except
THE LIEUTENANT's stumbling then, beholding
Defense Highways heaped high accidently.
—*How the?!*
—*We're without agency,* Sam sweetly seethes.
Agings of all. Seek your Calm.
But his Calm ends, and with it
jurisprudence, allready disarrayed when we
pull away, leaving HIM heaving
amid grinding collisions, trucks burning,
scattering glass, sedans warped by miles
of brakes, totalities tossed across dividers
& rails, which only retire HIM,
allready excarnated by illness, and US,
recombining HIM for tourbillions of dust.

Oct 24 1934

Gloria Vanderbilt's
$2.8 million.
East Liverpool Ohio,
Charles Arthur Pretty Boy
Floyd goes.
Union Pacific
streamlined diesel.
Mao's Army & South China.
Huey's Louisiana secession.
Rome's Fascist Schools.
Joachim von Ribbentrop
& Rearming The Reich.
—unfit for custody.
5–5–3.
Istanbul, Premier Kemal
& Ataturk. Karl Barth.
Daniel Salamanaca Urey
overthrown.
German Air Threat
& Winston Churchill.
A ditch & 17 bullets,
George Nelson goes.
Egypt's Constitution
& Parliament.
Sergei Kirov goes.
Navy over Army.
60 MPH tank. Ualual
& Somali-Ethiopian border.
Ambassador Davis,
Pacific Security & Japan.

My busty baby.
—*Ain't this Liberation, on our own.*
—*Whatever wherever we please.*
We're both pleased.
—*Just US allone.*
—*Free from responsibility. Obligation.*
From anything and everyone.
Frowning: —*What about me?*
Lessenings driving her anger.
Starting to hurt.
But I take her hand, rounding one fist
from two, wrist on wrist, palm on palm,
calmly turned.
—*Except from you.*
Both of US suddenly hit by a chill
gust rising up just around the bend,
any bend, goosepimpling our arms
until we separate and shudder. Searing
Summer returning with a heehaw.

Jan 1 1993

Czech Republic & Slovakia.
START II. Z goes.
Israeli Army's 22.
Italy's driving kissies.
Domingo Arroyo goes.
Campidoglio longings.
Somalia stonings, 5 go.
Tamilgate.
Erich Honecker's Chile.
Palermo & Salvatore Toto Riina.
Persian Gulf & 50 cruise missiles.
42nd, William Jefferson Clinton.
Warren Chistopher, Lloyd
Bentsen & Les Aspin.
Zoe Baird.
Vienna's 250,000.
200,000 for Ugur Mumcu.
Super Bowl XXVII,
Cowboys over Bills.
Mayon volcano, 67 go.
Cincinnati's Marge Schott.
Bob Packwood.
12 weeks unpaid leave.
Arthur Ashe goes.
GM's $23.5 billion.
Janet Reno.
James Bulger goes.

Allways away with Sam.
Even if I've scraggly hair. Gross
overalls. Have to pick my nose.
He's why September never goes.
Our Subaru SVX releases curves.
I'm a thousand Septembers. And he's
all deserts east when the payloads explode.
Allready we're gone, Falun Gong, among
Dismembered & Harried until even Tarried &
Disenfranchised are carried off by our roadways.

Sassafras dies.

From Bloomington.
To Brimfield, Galesburg and Gladstone.
—I'm glad we're on our own, even if we're solo,
Sam softly slips, me kissing him yes. Our
Mitsubishi 3000GT
raging. Blown.

Sept 5 1934

Reich's 1,000.
Long Louisiana rule.
Asbury Beach Park &
Morro Castle, 130 go.
Westchester KKK.
Aristid Van Grosse's
Proactinium 91.
421,000 textile workers
& 20 days.
Bolivians at Algodonal,
1,400 Paraguayans go.
Rainbow cups Endeavour.
Bruno Hauptmann.
—Where O rain?
—Unless something is done
for the American farmer, we
will have a revolution.
Barcelona & Catalonian
secession. Marseilles
& Croatian Kalemen,
Yugoslavia's Alexander &
France's Barthou go.
Cardinals over Tigers.
Waterfront strike over.
Long Island's 1,155 slot
machines sinking.
1,200 Hungarian
miners refuse.
Mao's Kiangsi &
northern march.

Arounding circles with hooks,
shimmying duckily, if
the Bentley Mulliner blasts clouds
now of hotoil seizure. Rusty shrapnel
plinking Picnickers, Fishers, Weary
Laborers failing at leisure.
Towards worse.
By Bobo to Hushpuckena.
By dinkering **Eskimo Chickens**.
Lake and drought. Husks and bracts.
Scabbed knees, clotted coughs, rough
hands. Only some will stand. Slowly.
And I'm all soils west when the earth
lets go. I'm a thousand Julys.
The Pontiac Sport teaching
the idle why July never dies,
while Hailey picks her nose.
Riveted overalls. Flouncy ringlets.
Fidgeting fingers tangling braids.

Feb 24 1993

Kinshasa.
Virginia General
Assembly's ration.

12:15 PM & WTC blast, 5 go.

Waco Texas, Branch Davidians
& .50 caliber volleys, 6 go.
Voinovich & Quilter.
Ben Johnson's testosterone.
11 Bombay bombs, 50 go.
31 military bases.
East Coast blizzard, 184 go.
Jonathan Ball goes.
51 Sandymount & Ann.
Ozone low.
South Africa's 6 weapons.

Dakar peanuts, 60 go.
—stop.
France's Édouard Balladur.
Sarajevo War crimes.
39,000 Azeris.
Vancouver, Yeltsin & Clinton.

Philippe Morillon surrounded.
ANC & Januzu Wallus,
Chris Hani goes. Guerrillas &
Manila troops, 42 go.

Dual headers and chopped,
past Oquawka and Keithsburg,
our Cadillac Allante hauls top down.
And for Sam I ball top down.
Big Trouble for Educational Enforcement
employed to ticket what's allready given up.
We give Them a brake, a necksnapping
doubletake. Setting off school alarms.
Dismissing every class. Leaving schoolbound
frowns turning over for the chance
to set out from academic regulations for
something much more reckless.
Town after town, a rampage
through Joy, Millersburg and Preemption.
Ringing every bell. Class excused.
Principals not amused by
all principles we abuse.

July 13 1934

Heinrich Himmler
& concentration camps.
SS over SA.

—accordance with laws of
iron that are eternally the.
—of the German people.

Tibet's Everest,
Maurice Wilson goes.

San Francisco's
General Strike over.
Minneapolis 50.

Midwest heatwave, 206 go.

Chicago, J Edgar Hoover's
G-Men & Public Enemy #1,
John Dillinger goes.

—shot him down.

Chancellor Dollfuss goes.
Louisiana Governor Allen
& Ledbetter's swamplands.
Hindenburg goes,
65 mile march.
Silver's 50.01.
Niagara Falls
& 15,000 falling tons.
Haiti's Last US Marine.
William Beebe, Otis Barton
& Bathysphere.
President Adolf Hitler.

struck out,
walked, tagged out,
thrown out, though all
with grinny pluck.
My turn up and I'm relentless.
Load the bases, clear the fences.
More gathering round, shabby Wools,
shredding Pants, lifting thin smiles
for wheels, speed and miles
of road. Them all want to go.
—*You can,* Hailey glows.
—*How we start?*
—*Just depart.*
But Teens wait on worms and
afraid circle off to counter change and
burn one all the way with straws.
The Plymouth PG shaking
each one, taking US on,
until lingerers flee our haste.

April 19 1993

FBI, CS gas
& Waco burn, 85 go.
David Koresh goes.
Bernard Eric Miller.
WHO, tuberculosis
& global emergency.
China, Taiwan & Singapore.
Pentagon & women pilots.
Monica Seles's stabbing.
Sea Hero's Derby.
Pierre Bérégovoy goes.
Ranasinghe Premadasa goes.
*—people cannot allways live
under the pressure of.*
Juan Carlos Wasmosy.
Bangkok toys & blaze, 200 go.
Eric Bache.
Sabino Gutierrez
& Maria Martinez.
Cairo blast, 7 go.
Rodney Pearis.
Lhasa & 4,000 protestors.
Elizabeth & Mary Robinson.
Turkish women &
German arson, 5 go.
Bosnia's UN Peacekeepers.

We are unprincipled.
Impossibly prevented. The dissent
every freeway requires
US to consent to.
We do,
allways swerving lanes for
OFFENDED TEENS, jumped, pumped &
organized for turf battles over handplay,
street sway and dreaded bandanas.
All Them needs iz to get away from
the Pitcher's trap and Jake's joint,
but soso sniffing our HP and speed
itch to chump Sam's Leftwrist Ruby Twist,
dump me on the ho stro,
each of this CREW, fresh dipped with caps,
gaffled by badges and flags, procedure and
conduct, only feanin to go

May 23 1934

50 Texas bullets.
Sawed-off shotgun,
revolver & saxophone.
Clyde Barrow &
Bonnie Parker go.
*—if it hadn't been her it
would have been US.*
60,000 Bolivian goings.
US, Cuba &
Guantánamo Naval Base.
*—progress of
the Cuban people.*
Marriage rush.
$525 million
drought relief.
The Securities and
Exchange Commission.
Farm Mortgage
Foreclosure Act.
Hitler & Germany's
foreign debt.
—all but Finland.
Federal Communications
Commission. Italian fleet,
Durazzo & Albanian
resistance. FHA.
*—Blood Purge.
—of Long Knives.*
Ernst Roehm & Karl Ernst go.
Japanese Premier,
Keisuke Okada. Bubonic.

Here though, City Juice, Split One &
Spla. Slinging Misery & Swill. EPIC
Monopoly. Legions of Decency.
Caps, Bow ties, vests.
But I can't give these Bettys and Johns
my best, my Leftwrist Ruby Twist's not
liquid enough, Cleveland enough,
for these Jungles we leg along through
with their Skulking Wolves and Burning
Fruiters lurking around abandoned
factories, closed shops, dustblown lots,
where aboundoned TEENERS circle
round with exuberance for parks.
We do too.
Batting balls for fouls,
strikes for hits, flys and grounders,
even if Hailey
misses by
swipes,

June 5 1993

Colonial Affair's Belmont.
René Bousquet goes.
Naruhito & Masako Owada.
2-0
Harley-Davidson &
Milwaukee's 60,000.

Kim Campbell. Tanzu Çiller.
ETA, Salamanca &
2 car bombs, 7 go.
Templehof Air Base.
Nigeria & Ibrahim Babangida.
Lorena Bobbitt.
Siddig Ibrahim Siddig Ali &
FBI's 8. Iraq HQ &
US missiles, 6 go.
Gian Luigi Ferri's Petit &
Martin, 9 go.
Sheila Widnall & Air Force.
Shevardnadze, Sukhumi &
Abkhazian rebels.
—all citizens of.
Davey Allison goes.
Ada Deer. Missouri levee.
Mishishishi's 15 million acres.
—Don't pursue.
Louis J Freeh.

kick back. Dunk hoops.
Clowning on US for doing that too. Run.
—*Where you from?*
—*Now you're our fun.*
And I'm so conciliatory, dishing gratitudes,
sorrys. Wobbly knees. Worried. Sam though'z
his own legal tour, not withdrawing one
toe before their menacings.
And ALL GANGBANGERS charge ahead too,
too L12 to guess what each is up against.
Even with irons, pipes and hockey sticks.
Sam'z sacked up. Blunt. Doesn't pick fights.
Answers Them. Ready set for their front.
—*Wogs!* Them stunt.
—*Muzzies!* —*Feathers!* —*Provos!* —*Dots!*
Surrounding our Honda Accord.
—*Jigabrew!*

March 24 1934

US, Philippines & Freedom.

Vinson Naval Parity Act.
Kansas City violence.
Samuel's Greek Steamer.
Latvia, Estonia & Lithuania.
Queens Stadium's 9,000
& Heil Hitler Rally.
William Wirth
& head trusters.
Nye Commission
& Munitions profiteering.
—Dust, dust, dust.

10,000 ft high & 100 MPH.
Rhodes bombing.
M Sodoroff's Fontainebleau.
Fort Worth's Washeteria.
Paris riots.
Cotton Control Act.
William Bullitt.
Panchen Lama.
Austria's Dollfuss.
Berlin & ennobling labor.
Saudi Arabia, Ibn Saud
& Yemen.
Cavalcade's Derby.
Congressional sugar control.
350 million tons of
topsoil & wind.
New York dust storm.

oggles then my great cojones.
Yanks for more.
The Morgan Super Sport spanking
turns, cranking the burn. I am the
spurned, unburned, unspent, jazzed
juicy for the next Rest Stop.
Soda For Sale.
Jawbreakers. Candied Sandwiches.
Slow hirsle yearnings.
Dusty Miller To Mortgage. First Lady
For Purchase. Big Trouble For Free.
Some ambling over our way curiously.
—*What you need?* THE JERK slings.
—*What you need?* I flings.
—*No works here.*
—*We never work.*
—*Then knock the slam, Jelly Bean.*
—*Lucky US!* Hailey spleems.
We work enough. Ways too much.

July 23 1993

Rio de Janeiro, 8 go.
Tajikstan offensive.
Kenilworth, 10 go.
John Demjanjuk free. Yohei Kono.
Mount Bjelasnica &
Mount Igman. Serbs &
Maslenica pontoon bridge.
Shenzhen blast, 15 go.
Chad Security forces &
anti-government protests,
100 go. Crossbows &
Moscow's anti-terrorist troops.
Morhiro Hosokawa.
Woodruff goes.
Ruth Bader Ginsburg.
Joint Chiefs of Staff
& John M Shalikashvili.
Josephine. Johannesburg,
Namibia & Walvis Bay.
Antonio Sanchez
& Eileen Sarmenta.
—great blow to the planetary.
Guguletu,
Amy Elizabeth Biehl goes.
Joceylyn Elders. London 9
& Quaddus Ali.
Uew-Wilhelm Rakebrand.

Every race,
except we're the only race, so fast there's
never a race. Judgements razed. Still our
BALLERS encircle, hateful & aching, and
even if some GUYS & GALS pull back then,
Them're allready too late, over & out,
soaking with doubt. Sam never doubts.
He turns their impudence to fever.
Their arrogance to rout.
—*NnnnnnNnn,* ONE ROUGHNECK flinches.
—*NnnnnnNnn,* ONE THICKNECK winces.
—*nNNNNNnNN,* EVERYONE hitches.
Their roll stopped cold.
Now Here'z all Corrupt.
Rushes & Reed buckle.
Sam's the Justice each gave away.
Even our Grand Am brooms up.

Jan 31 1934

Federal Farm Mortgage
Corporation.
—Get fed.
—get shoes.
35¢ & 60¢.
Revolving Pension Plan.
Police, mobs &
Place de la Concorde,17 go.
Broadway Taxi riots.
Gaston Doumergue.
Civil Works Emergency
Relief Act.
Federal Emergency Relief
Administration.
CWA's $950 million.
Roads, schools, airfields,
parks & playgrounds.
Albert of Belgium goes.
Managua airfield &
National Guardsmen,
Augusto Sandino goes.
Habib Bourguiba's
Neo-Destour Party.
Mishishishi's Citizen Trap,
3 go.
Moeur & Parker Dam.
Salvador train, 250 go.
Latvia's Ulmanis.
5,000 negroes & NYC police.
Hitler's highways.
Hakodate fire, 1,487 go.

The LaSalle Coupe diverging from
Vicksburg brodies bends for secluded
banks where for water slaps
Rabbits & Robins splash, impossibly
urging US back. Chomp & drag. Guzzle
& hustle. Scrag. Hoover up. Lapping fluff.
Can have my JellyRoll and eat it too.
—*MmmmmmMmm,* she moans.
—*MmmmmmMmm,* I groan.
—*mMMMMMmMM,* we blow,
front seat bunked until federating
on the front hood, jaunty jounce and
snizzle, horizontal sloshes galoshing,
we're hummering clappers & jack,
bending US up,
I pop lobgobs of orifice missing
globblobs, swiggling thrushrushed
to populate deltas.
Hailey flushed, blushed,

Sept 13 1993

—no kissing.
11:47 AM, South Lawn,
Yasir Arafat, Yitzhak Rabin &
a handshake.
China's Wei Jingsheng free.
Angola famine, 1,000 going.
Killari quake, 30,000 go.
US helicopters &
Mohammed Farah Aidid, 12 go.
Russian uprising.
Yeltsin, 15,000 &
Tverskaya Street, 187 go.
Aleksandr Rutskoi,
Ruslan Khasbulatov &
Lefortovo prison.
NATO's Joulwan.
Shirley Sears Chater.
West Sea Ferrry, hundreds go.
Greece, PASOK &
Andreas Papandreou.
Cowbridge Driving.
Benazir Bhutto over
Toronto over Philadelphia.
River goes. Maastricht treaty.
Malibu fires, 3 go.
Cliff Young goes.
Darío Londoño Cardona goes.

—*Super!*
Sam swells,
so ragupsick the earth quivers
and the sky sharpens with streaks
until around US roars our iceharped
air, wrapping around their knees, until
Sam, pleased, and pleasing to me,
levies the effects of our rush:
each shuddering without recourse
before Sam's ending remorse.
—*Outta my way Jakes,* he slams. *I'm the beat*
you cry to. I'm the beat you die by.
And each ATTACKER sobsnots gore.
Crushed. Amputated. Swallowed by crime.
Me: —*Come on Mobile, let'S ditch these slimes.*
You're all that's happening.
—*Racer, we never happen.*

Dec 15 1933

Out of Tennessee court,
rolphed by mob.
Opposing armed reaction.
Romania & Iron Guard,
Ion Duca goes.
Heavier brains.
6,000 pigs go.
—Together we cannot fail.
—Can't carry out of this
bank all the corn that half-
dollar will buy.
Commission on
Social Trends.
—throughout the World,
leaving orthodox and
revolution to fight it out.
Chamonix France
& Bayonne bank,
Alexandre Stavisky goes.
Supreme Court, mortgage
foreclosures & temporary
Minnesota bans. Catalonian
President Lluís Companys.
Carlos Mendieta.
Victors Congress.
Paris & bank riots.
Chautemps Cabinet quits.
Solar systems.

Anyway we're jelly. My Butter &
Egg Fly filling her skirt with air and
care and me, dancing my fingers over
her sweet quim, easily dewed with
each turn, tickle and dip.
Pike for Silver Sardines. Strike out teens.
Her fingers nimbling my nubbin
past the slumbering
river wash
past the lumbering beat of
Tie bound Trains pistoning wheels
rolling and railed. I'm pleasing and
pleased. I'm tropics of heat, her tropical
breeze. With loads and loads.
—*Mitt me kid!*
—*Okey dokey, what for?*
—*Because you're slick.*
—*You're swell.*
—*Repus!*

Nov 9 1993

19.7 million refugees.
Mostar, Neretva
& Stari Most.
UK, China, Belgium, France
& oceanic nuclear waste.
—will turn this around.

Andrés Espinosa's marathon.
Puerto Rican commonwealth.
Kiev & START I. Tek Nath Rizal.

Colombian Police & Cali cartel,
Pablo Escobar goes.
Rafael Caldera Rodríguez.
—enjoyment of all.

Russia, Liberal Democratic
Party & Vladimir Zhirinovsky.
Geneva, GATT &
Uruguay Round. John Major,
Albert Reynolds & Peace Pact.
Somalia & US troop pull out.
US & Alina Castro's defection.
237-45.

*—We took South Africa
over the.*

Chiapas & EZLN.

And he agrees.
Our Oldsmobile Cutlass zips roaring over
bituminous pavements, past Halted & Raffled,
Municipally Dismissed on Local Charges.
Uncontended. Even Warrants out now for our
arrest turn out to be exurbanite diseaze.
And dubs twin tight. Dropped crates of
blasting caps tumbling toward US turn to fat.
Milkweed long gone. Hacked.
We drive faster & afster. Unmolested by
rearendings, flats, objections and motions.
Our Geo Metro
easily, allways, beating the World.
And when we pull over to amble,
feeling lumpy, I treat my boy.
3½ left. Sweet
HONEY.

Oct 18 1933

Maryland 2,000 & lynching.
Primo Carnera 15 rounds
Paolino Uzcudun.

RFC's Gold.
Haifa, Nablus &
9,000, 20 go.

—Share the wealth.

*—One of the two most
dangerous men.*

*—Long from the left
MacArthur from the.*

Mayor Fiorello LaGuardia
& Tammany.
Harry Hopkins &
Civil Works Administration.
Austria & Martial Law.

Chicago Fair's 22 million.
US & USSR. 8,000 Trotskyites,
Stalinists & Manhattan.
—War will.
Welles from Havana.
Gold Standard refusal.
Army over Navy.
Storm Troopers.

Alabama death request.
36th State.
Utah & 21st Amendment.
5:32:5.
Prohibition Ends.

HONEY.
8½ left.
One jar for two. Halfandhalf.
Ladling lumpy spoons. Liponlip,
tonguetotongue doubling an amber
moustache. Caressy, refreshing and messy.
Sticking US again to the World.
The Chrysler Wimbledon kicking
the roads, around pokey Trucks hauling
loads of Yogurt & Ghee by
Caravans of Poor beating an
Alpaca hawwing for butter.
Lost saddles turn to dynamite. While
the radiator dings a cap, alternator
and axle zzhinging out taps. Even if
hoses split, blow, and Thirstquenchers
& Starving force US to slow,
the Hupmobile 322 bops on anyway
without stops.

Jan 6 1994

Zviad Gamsakhurdia goes.
—Why me?
Nancy Kerrigan & crowbar.
Mexico City bombs & Zapatista
National Liberation Army.

4:31 AM, 6.7 &
Northridge quake, 34 go.

Kandahar course, 60 MPH
& soft snow, Ulrike Maier goes.
Super Bowl XXVIII,
Cowboys over Bills.

—ferocious and strong.

Yeltsin & Shevardnadze's
Friendship and Military
Cooperation Treaty.
Jaafar bin Abdul Rahman.

US & Vietnam
trade embargo over.
Byron De La Beckwith's life.
Costa Rica's José María Figueres.
$4.75 billion.
Finland's Martii Ahtisaari.

Bill Richardson &
Aung San Suu Kyi.
Greece & Macedonia.

Passing spoons around.
While nearby, over a pot of ashes,
a slew of PostTransients stir truces.
I do too.
Sam might jettison me here
but would I balk? O.
Beets & **Knapweed** poxed. Dead.
Such are the statutes against any attachments.
Snatched. We're the only match.
I let go of Sam's hand and there on
his knees, by national crossroads, proposing
with only a plea,
he officially asks me to him
and I agree.
Our Hyundai Excel flies on.
—Here's to letting Autumn fall where it wants.
Sam sixteen grins.

Aug 22 1933

Irish Fascists.
Poona Civil Hospital's
90 pounds. Salvador's
American Peace Treaty.
21 Nation Wheat Agreement.
Italy & USSR Non-
Aggression Treaty.

Air France.
Dachau.
NYC Grand Jury's flogging.
New York Flier, 14 go.
Céspedes out.

Texas Hurricane, 33 go.
Manuel Azaña over.
Chesebrough goes.
Grau San Martin.
Louisiana Prison break.

Civil Disobedience
Moratorium. Clothes, food
& $75 million. Port of

Tampico storm,
hundreds go.

—Feed the needy.

George & Dorthy Rea.
AFL's 1.3 million workers.
Giants over Senators.
Kingsford speed. Alcatraz.
Hitler, League of Nations
& Disarmament Conference.

My Hailey sixteen grins, toes wiggling
the wind. Racy. A hummer.
Lifting a chill smile:
—Here's to keeping it Summer.
Pinkieing back *—agreed*, while
the Auburn Cabriolet groans harder.
Laters smearing ground. Cheese it
with Zeal & Gleeful ruckus, for Stirs, a
slick torsion blur by Volleyball Courts,
Running Rounds and Strange Graves
spinning above ground. Fields of Rust.
Salt & Rock.
Snails and **Pelicans** bawk
but we're allready by Long Jumps,
High Jumpings and Discus. And
while PreTransients
stir a kettle of stew
with spoons.
I happily pass around

Feb 19 1994

Phoolan Devi free.

Hebron & Baruch Goldstein,
40 go. Lillehammer &
Diana Roffe-Steinrotter's gold.

4 planes, Novi Travnik
& NATO F-16s.
San Cristóbal peace.
Burundi, Hutus
& Tutsis, 200 go.
Chile & Eduardo Frei.
Henry Louis Wallace.
Nuclear testing moratorium.
Tonya Harding.
Tijuana, PRI & Mario Aburto
Martínez, Luis Donaldo
Colosio goes.
Alabama tornadoes, 41 go.
Italy's Silvio Berlusconi.
10,000 Zulus & ANC, 53 go.
Hungary & NATO.
Cobain goes.
Kigali & Bagosora, Ntaryamira
& Habyarimana goes.
Mokdad Sifi.
2 US Warplanes
& 2 US helicopters, 26 go.

Chill
allways. And unfastening.
Our Buick Riviera whirring North.
He is my North. My Northern Lands.
What Half a Ferris Wheel loaded on
a long Barge continues to tugptuppering up
The Mishishishi after. But even with hand
around, one darting the Wheel, I feel jittery.
Why? Our Chrysler Concorde races on.
Allmost carelessly. By military jets, comets.
And **Persimmons** putrefy.
Sam squeezes and nuzzles me.
Cotton & **Rosemary** die.
Along with **Peppermint** too. But we
spin on by Moline, Princeton, Clinton. To
Sabula. Our Range Rover now
only wedding bound.

July 1 1933

Circus 400.
Turner's 11 hours
30 minutes.

USSR's Cotton loan.
Man O War.
Kentucky election, 8 go.
Copper Gulch gold.
Schmeling & Ondra.
Matten safe.
Moody over Round.
Finland fires.
Chaco, 3,000 go.
Shorter hours,
higher wages &
one million laborers.
1,000 SPM.

Nuremberg 300.
Hyde Park protest.
DC-1. Speicher's Tour.
Madrid 500.
26,789 political prisoners.
Wiley Post's 7 days 18
hours 49 minutes globe.
Afghanistan bombings.
—to be bankrupt.
NIRA dance. Havana Riots.
Machado's Nassau.
China floods, thousands go.
Perkins employment.
Iraq & Syria, 600 go.

Heading the roll. Rattle &
bounce. Barrel & steel. Away
we go on tattling wheels.
The Nash Eight roasting the land.
For Our Great River Macadams.

Porcupines follow our route.
Raccoons scamper loose.
Alligators snoot pollutedly while on
the side a **Timber Wolf** woofs gently:
—Go careful you two.

The Hudson L bucks on through,
around vermicular shores lapped with
waste, Our Mishishishi, hoisting a
low Paddleboat loaded with
Half a Ferris Wheel puppuppering for
Southern Fields. I am the South.
The DeSoto Six humbering on,
extracurricular, vehicular.
Allways canicular.

April 19 1994

$3,816,535.45.
Paul Touvier.
Kigali's Amahoro, 20 go.
Belgian UN soldiers, 11 go.
Moorer 12 rounds Holyfield.
El Salvador, ARENA &
Armando Calderón.
Nagoya's Taiwanese airliner,
264 go. Top Quark.
KGB, CIA & Aldrich Hazen Ames.
South Africa's All-Race elections.
San Marino Grand Prix,
Roland Ratzenberg goes.
Ayrton Senna goes.
Michael Fay's cane.
Go For Gin's Derby.
Ernesto Balladares.
—let freedom reign.
John Wayne Gacy goes.
Chen Ziming free.
Armenia, Azerbaijan &
Nagorno-Karabakh.
MFN. Lawton Chiles.
Rwanda, Tutsis & Hutus,
500,000 go.
Beinn na Lice crash, 29 go.

Sam's filthy fine.
I'm not.
World's too petulant.

But we drive for it.
And where five roads startle,
Sam poops a cairn of marble.
The air smiles deciduously. He smiles too.

We keep driving. Searching now for someone
to legitimize our union. Worries so plenty get
me turning my Leftwrist Tin Twist.

But no one can challenge our run enough
to stop me. Iowa Rads just jawdropping our
blurby. So astounded Them don't even try.

What comes around goes around.

Horned Bladderworts desist pitifully,
while our Ford Bronco streaks for

May 10 1933

Paraguay, Bolivia & War.
Berlin University & bonfire.
Moscow jazz.

Federal Emergency
Relief Act. Agricultural
Adjustment Act.
Emergency Farm
Mortgage Act.
Havana troops
& Cuban revolt.
Federal Securities Act &
Federal Trade Commission.
Century of Progress.
Nazis & Communist Party.
Louis Meyer's 500, 3 go.
Chinese & Japanese truce.
Chaplin & Goddard.

The Rome Pact.
Protectionist tariff rates over.
100 days.
NIRA.

National Recovery
Administration.
France's Trotsky.
Hitler outlaws Social
Democratic Party.

—to be governed decently.

Great Lakes, Gulf of Mexico
& Illinois waterway.
Jobs, Jobs, Jobs.

We manumit it. THE CREEP's irritated.
By turns riled, elated. Until we boil.
The Lincoln LeBaron smoking US by
WhipPoorWills whippowing:
—What goes around comes around!

while we rubble river roads & leans,
nerving the curves, even if Hailey still
feers LOUISIANA POLICE too thuggish &
sluggish to halt our ride for chips.
This time. Anyway by Hailey's
Leftwrist Tin Twist we're slimps.
And suddenly
I'm gutthumping agony.
My turn to startle.
Ass out,
poop Marble:
—If it's not this World,
then it's of this World.
And I'm not.
Zazz.

June 4 1994

Kuwait's 14, 6 go.
Bay of Bengal's missile.
Nicole Brown Simpson
& Ronald Goldman go.
Vannatter, Phillips, Lange,
Fuhrman. Glove & a Bronco.
Ernesto Samper.

—this alliance and
my country for more.

Russia's NATO Peace Accord.
Tomiichi Murayama.
Algeria's Peaceful 15,000
& 2 blasts. US prisons & 1 million.

Arafat's Gaza Strip.
Texas highways' 43.
Leroy Burrell's 9.85 seconds.
Kim Jong Il over
Kim Il Sung. Paris mugging.
Shoemaker-Levy 9.
Buenos Aires explosion, 96 go.
Ervin M Graves.
Mullah Rocketi's 9.
Dawda Jawara.
Clinton, Rabin & Hussein.

the Protensive Hitch
we so wistfully slip for,
loose, off & ripping it.

And though a creepy chill starts
racing my heart, Sam & I mosh on.

Stopping soon amidst throngs of
Dirt Bags and Zekes, I'm even these, lost,
trapped, a flannel circle of needle grabs and pipe
glass, circling ever back, to their garageband
blast of pluck, drum & guitars, offering
The Ongoing Hangover no apologies. Sam just
scouting the skinny for getting tied. He persists.
Pervasive, even if everyone rebukes:

—Not permitted.

—Not together.

—You're too young.

March 6 1933

—for action and
action now.
LA quake, 123 go.

FDR's fireside.
Nazi Concentration Camp.
Raiford Florida's
charged chair.
Beer & Wine Revenue Act.
Hitler's governing powers.
Estado Novo.
Reforestation Relief Act &
Civilian Conservation Corps.
Hertzog & Smuts.
Banning German Merchants.
Clydesdale & MacIntyre
over Mount Everest.
Germany's exiting
Foreigners.
Hague, Norway & Denmark.
1 million barrels of beer.
Broadway riot. FDR, US &
Gold Standard.
Ramsay MacDonald.
Macon.
Prussian Police &
Gestapo.
Farm Relief Bill.
Sáncho Cerro goes.
Tennessee Valley.
Brokers Tip's Derby.
New York Life.

Away from The Goups allready lost:

—You're too young

Thanks.

—to belong. Stop.

—This.

—is not permitted!

But it's our persuasion. I'm every
evasion. And even if Hailey's skitzing,
no one's chasing. No one cares.
We buzz by The Party Ongoing,
scud baps & hot cats groaning
tram, gobble pipe, git, stick, skins &
woodpile, swing out!, give it a ride!,
frisking the whiskers—

Smoooooooooth!

Me & Hailey waltz through to
frenetic Creep still trapped by
The Chain. Too rigid for
the wistfulness of our gift.
—*Hey Villain,* I lift.

Aug 11 1994

AIDS, Africa & 10 million.
Baseball strike. Nick Price.
Woodstock's 350,000.
Carlos the Jackal &
Illich Pamirez Sanchez.
2,700 Cubans. 234-195,
$30.2 billion anti-Crime Bill.
Moscow, Bonn & plutonium.
Typhoon Fred, 710 go.
Nigeria's Sani Abacha.
Lockheed & Martin Marietta.
Dagestan cholera, 19 go.
—complete cessation
of military operations.
Moscow, Yeltsin & Jiang Zemin.
Viking Serenade's shigellosis.
Berlin.
Aliquippa's USAir 427, 132 go.
South Lawn landing,
Frank Eugene Corder goes.
US troops & Raoul Cédras.
Jimmy Carter, Colin Powell &
Sam Nunn.
Surat's pneumonic plague.
National Healthcare.

Manitoba Maples succumb,
Tulip Poplars too.

We hurtle along by roadside
disputes and property feuds. Counselors.
Bounty Hunters. Traffic Busters.
But no one bothers US. We are unpursued.
We cannot be stopped heading for the Courts.
All closed. Temporarily. Curious.

We wait around the block. At a park.
Sam takes my hand, reassuringly.
Security, racking their rounds, leaves US allone.
Departs. Then along comes a GROUNDSLASS
dragging a rake. Lounges on our bench.
Smokes a cigarette. A pack. Smokes a week.

—Do you have the time?

—We are the time.

118 243

Jan 23 1933

20th Amendment.
Peru, Colombia & Leticia.
German Chancellor
& Hitler.
15 million US jobless.
Bucharest mob
& Standard Oil Office.
Leningrad thousands
& Passports.
Oimekon's –90º F.
Death Valley.
Bay Front Park, FDR
& Giuseppe Zangara,
Mayor Anton Cermak goes.
The Ranger.
Golden Gate Bridge.
Reichstag fire.
Clem Sohn's bat wings
& parachute.
Yokohama quake & wave,
3,000 go.
Jehol's Ch'eng-te falls.
—the only thing we have
to feer is feer.
—We must act and act
quickly.
—Our greatest primary
task is to put people to
work.

—Let'S drift this brawl, I loft over.
Before the Damp Smacks return.
And I'm allready rolling,
slapping on my cap, waiting
impatiently for Hailey to
get moving.
When the reckless squabble
of DISCIPLINARIANS reapproaches.
Hailey grabs my hand. Weakly.
Around the corner we go.
Hospital alert. Pursuit.
Blood Cross and Collectors game too
for the chase. O the depravity!
Along with the mess of the Penniless
trying to scrounge US up.
But I'm ever won.
Put down, consumed. Debunked.
Sprinting towards roadsides where
frisky **Ocelots** and
Longtailed Weasels must tumble.

Sept 27 1994

Chad Hundeby's Channel.
Turku Finland, Baltic
& Estonia, 912 go.
WHO & polio.
Palau liberty.
Goma Zaire
& 470 Japanese soldiers.
Brazil's Fernando
Henrique Cardoso.
—This party is a living.
Switzerland &
Order of the Solar, 48 go.
700 tanks, 60,000 Iraqi soldiers
& Kuwait.
Eric Morris goes.
Christopher Myles Croston,
Paul Ridout & Kashmiri militants.
Tel Aviv bus, Qassem Brigades
& Saleh Abdel Rahim al-Souwi,
21 go.
Songsu Bridge collapses,
32 go. Clinton, Assad & Syria.
Dwingeloo 1.
Durunka flood, 500 go.
Foreman 10 rounds Moorer.

—Too cool for school, you two, SHE hi's.
Kind of you to stick around though.
Even if you do bring up how
much I miss my gal. Sharing
with someone's so dope.
And SHE's kind, pausing each time on her
rounds to kick back with US.
—We're getting married, I try.
—Drop Dead Twice!
Sam & I both shrug.
HER: *—It's a rigamarole that depends on*
Social Permission. Mutual approval's not enough.
Then SHE cries for a while.
—Perhaps you can still find her,
Sam gentles.
—O no, that's over.

Nov 13 1932

Paraguay,
500 Bolivians go.
Third Round Table
Conference.
US National Labor
Committee.
Anglo-Persian Oil
Company. Committee on
Cost of Medical Care.
USSR, France &
Friendship Pact.
German Chancellor
Kurt von Shleicher.
Army over Navy.
Lithuanian National Union.
South Africa &
Gold Standard.
185 tons of food.
China quake, 70,000 go.
Hirohito & air attacks.
2 million vagrants.
Committee on Technocracy.
—well for my country.
—not worth a pitcher of
warm piss.
Shuangyashan, 500 go.
Irving Langmuir.
Spain's revolt:
Seville, Granada &
Jerez de la Frontera.
Waite Hoyt.

and wheels over to
Hailey:
—How are you feeling?
She's fine, okay maybe frail,
but certainly still a hoot:
—Sweet with teeth.
—Yes, DOCTOR FRITZ kindly nods.
What you swallowed, dispensed by the
Quack, Bee Pollen. Harmless
to most but you're allergic.
Tremendously so. It could kill you.
—What should I do?
—Don't mess around with bees.
—Honey?
—Honey you need, smiling
strangely, allready wheeling off then
for his own rounds, if hesitating
for our last moment:
—Stick around. Repair the eggs, break the
yoke. Slowing down's your only course.

Nov 7 1994

Republicans, 53-47 & 230-204.

—I got it.

Newt Gingrich.
Chandrika Kumaratunga over United National Party.
Caribbean storm, 830 go.
Joaquim Chissano.
Smoking & Texas State Prisons.
Mario Ruiz Massieu quits.
Ami Olami goes.
Bihac. Dahmer goes.
Julio Sanguinetti.
Achille Lauro burns.
Afula axe. Sinn Fein & British.
Dzhokar Dudayev, Chechnya & Russian tanks.
Kungang & OH-58 helicopter, David Hilemon goes.
Pale, Carter & Radovan Karadzic.
Air France A300, Algiers & Islamic Terrorists, 3 go.
French Commandos, Marseilles & hijackers, 4 go.
Geneva's World Trade Organization. 104th Congress.

—What went down?
—Just how it sometimes goes.
No round hat. No square hat.
Just the mush of wants & needs
that never add up. But life's big.
If you can't fix it, give it a spin.
Which stings me something awful
until Sam's tender touch soothes me.
—*Here,* The GroundsGal coughs.
Somehow strange. Someway weird.
I suddenly want to run.
—If the Courts deny you, catch up
with my friend. Halfway illegitimate but.
Giving Sam then the way there
before returning to her mower.
—I'll leave me allone now.

245 116

Oct 4 1932

Nationalist Ministry & Hungary.
USSR's Dnieper River.
Illinois & striking miners, 1,200 arrested.
15,000 unemployed & London's overturned cars.
5 day work week.
Eleftherios Venizelos.
Federal Aid.
George G Blaisdell's Zippo.
Berlin Transit strike.
Nazis' 35 seats.
Labor Defense, Supreme Court & Scottsboro retrial.
—bold, persistent experimentation.
—restore this country to prosperity.
—but above all try something.
472–59.
—Destruction, Delay, Deceit and Despair.
Nadya Aliluieva goes.
—allone are responsible for the terrors that have fallen upon the.
Cuban hurricane, 1,000 go.
Secretary of War Patrick Jay Hurley.

—Leave US allone.
And Wet Socks immediately depart
obeying Doctor Friendly, on his
rounds, gently wheeling over to
determine our progress:
—I'm just around to check on your
wellbeings. For the timebeing. I
want you both back up and running.
How are you feeling?
I feel weird. Somehow strange, small
and fond near him:
—A bit knocked out.
—*Yes,* he tenderly motions. *Your*
heart's suffering some worry. Arrhythmias.
Tachycardia. Suddenly disorganized.
Just beats too fast.
—What can I do?
—The Valsalva Maneuver. Relax.
—What causes it?
But he just sighs

And turning to stroll,
the blood of Bounty Hunters, PIs
and hovering Huddas runs cold while Sam
passes by. Longings without answer. Ever.
Who can suffer that strength?
All scatter. Profoundly afraid.
Sam laughs at their shaking rears
streaking away and does
a headstand.
Stands on the wind. Holds the World up.
When I tickle his ribs Adulterers split feering
the World will fall. Though for Sam it ellipses.
And pretty quickly too. Even
if I am paltry against our binding course.
—*We're off for more fun,*
Sam bounds on

Jan 12 1995
British troops, Belfast & Ulster.
Bilbao & 2 ETA, 1 goes.
Bahrain riots, 2 go.
Kobe quake, over 5,000 go.
Netanya bus station, 21 go.
Kashmir snowstorms, 240 go.
Grozny tanks.
Yurt's Russian Planes.
Super Bowl XXIX,
49ers over Chargers.
Algiers bomb, 42 go.
Netherland evacuation.
Discovery, MIR & Eileen Collins.
Guy Delage's 2,400 miles.
Yeltsin's CIS Summit.
Charasyab, Hezb-e-Islami forces
& Gulbuddin Hekmatyar.
Taliban surrounds Kabul.
—a bag full of money.
Steve Fossett's balloon.
Antarctica iceberg.
Barings Bank, £650 million
& Nick Leeson.
Vladislav Listyev goes.

We will
until HOOVERCRATS barge over,
spilling their doldrums
and taking away our fun:
—*Knock that off!*
Parting US with
our Debt due at once.
Pretty steep too.
For taking care of US.
Hmph. THESE RELIEF OFFICERS
are only taking care of business.
Hailey does a headstand.
Spins. Her slipping dressy giving
FAST COMPANY some rear end.
Aghast, Them bunch, all mercury bent.
I'll suffer THESE FOLLY FEDS no more.
Though before I can knock off
their heads and splash
the Ward with their mash,
a tender cough changes everyone:

Aug 14 1932
95,000 at closing.
11 million jobless.
RFC's $49 million loan.
Controller of the Currency
& Foreclosure Moratorium.
Hermann Goering,
President of Reichstag.
Doolittle, Cleveland &
300 MPH. Peru's Military &
Leticia, Colombia.
—Gentlemen, Jimmy has
many kind friends.
Catalonia's liberty.
Excursion liner &
East River, 37 go.
Reichstag over.
—had become great
uncontrolled and
irresponsible
units of power.
Hindus, Untouchables &
Poona Pact.
Gandhi's fast over.
Lindo Lugar.
16,000 Bolivians.
Gyula Gömbös.
Lytton Commission &
Japanese aggression.
Chicago &
Yankees over Cubs.
Iraq & League of Nations.

March 3 1995

US Marines, UN Peacekeepers & Mogadishu, 6 go.
Lucien Sakubu goes.
Picabo Street & World Cup Downhill. Gerry Adams.
Tokyo, Sarin gas & Shoko Asahara, 8 go.
Valeri Polyakov returns.
Achkhoi-Martan.
Burundi's Karosi village, 100 go.
Mireille Durocher Bertin goes.
Major League strike over.
Gaza City & Izzedine al-Qassam Brigades, Kamal Kheil goes.
Major, Clinton & Ireland.
Russian soldiers & Samashki village, hundreds go.
Tahiti's Cheyenne Brando goes.
Yokohama's gas.
Oklahoma City, Alfred P Murrah & explosives, 167 go.
Timothy McVeigh. 95 057.
Terry Nichols. James Nichols.

outwardly, even
mischievously.
—*The Court's Open,* I flutter, which somehow
creeps me out. Sam though whips around and
—*Whoot, there it is!* commences to bounce,
ballerific, swinging me
around, popping revoltades, ballonné,
with both toes pointed and
arms flung overhead, while I bumble
pirouette on pointe, hop, until he scoops
me up, lifting me high, tossing me higher,
for a turn, drop, catch, effortlessly controlled,
until at last I'm laid out beneath
his Green Eyes with flecks of Gold
relaxing me with gentle kisses.
—*We'll be married soon for sure.*

June 29 1932

—*Peaceful revolution.*
Bangkok Monarchy over.
—*Hundreds of niggers.*
Ellsworth Vines over Bunny Austin.
—*New Deal for the American people.*
Portugal & António de Oliveira Salazar.
League of Nations, Austrian loan & Anschluss.
20% salary reduction.
Chiang's campaign, 10,000 go. Turkey, 56th.
von Papen over Prussia.
Relief Act.
Federal Loan Act.
209 female fishers.
87 female trappers, hunters & guides.
General Douglas MacArthur, Major Dwight Eisenhower & Routed Bonus Army.
Bunny, bayonet & eviction.
—*revolution.*
—*a pitiful.*
—*pfutt-pfutts across the.*
Los Angeles Olympics.
Paraguay, Bolivia & Chaco War.

—*You two must be separated soon,*
Nurse Ninny scolds.
It's not decent. When Doctor Friend
drops by, he'll do the splitting.
Bong the booshwash, I'll split her.
But Hailey easies US with those
Gold Eyes with flecks of Green.
Long legs and scrubby knees.
Until we're at it again,
a pillowmashing
duo dance. Bedtop, hitting
the socks with a Lindy Hop &
Piperoo. SusieQ. Swing.
Jack Fevered & Consumptives
joining US.
Until breathless, amidst
feathers, I wonder:
—*Is The Nóose still wound up?*
—*Yup,* Hailey mischiefs.
Let'S let The Creep go.

April 22 1995

Rwandan Tutsi Troops,
Bizimungu & Camp Kibeho,
hundreds go. Iran's
US Trade Ban. Ho Chi Minh City.
Serbs & Zagreb.
Alabama chain gangs.

Gulch's Derby.
France's Chirac.
Lawrence P Rockwood.
Alison Hargreaves.
New Zealand cups Young America.
Menem. Pennsylvania Avenue.
Bush quits NRA.
Sakhalin Island quake,
2,100 go. Zaire's ebola virus,
53 go. Bosnia-Herzegovina
& 320 UN hostages.
Brazil's Oil Workers strike over.
US Navy & Adriatic.
Kamenge's 20,000 flee.
Budennovsk, Shamil Basayev
& 200 rebels, 20 go.
—Too tight.
Esmor Immigration Detention
riots. 63-35. 55 MPH.

How tenderly now
he holds me. His careful breath
warmly caressing my ear.
And I'm confident again:
—We mustn't waste a minute.
Zippitydoo,
fast passes and kicks, and we scurry, I trip,
over gardens, by ponds,
down a sodpath towards all I want.
I even giggle. Both of US so excited
we pause for kisses and hugs, allmost a tumble,
down on the ground, allready fumbling
for a fast fool around, except we don't.
—Let'S hurry.
—Hurry it is, I hustle. Sam's
Open auricle, so wonderful to me, leads on.

April 28 1932

Wilbur Sawyer, Wray Lloyd
& Stuart Kitchen's vaccine.
Sandino Camp raid, 10 go.
Mount Washington,
Florence Clasr & a dog sled.
*—have got more energy
out of something.*
Burgoo King's Derby.
Paul Brède & Paul Gorguloff,
Paul Doumer goes.
Sourland Mountains,
the Fat Lamb goes.
*—that there are two sets
of law.*
Across the Atlantic.
—I wanted to do it allone.
Washington DC, Anacostia
River flats & the 11,000
Bonus Expeditionary Force.
Sharpe goes.
For Bonus Bill,
Edward Eslick goes.
Marmaduke Grove,
Eugenio Matte &
Easter Island.

Dear Hailey dishes swell nods
even if her cheeks are pillow
snaked. Big ear too poking out
over the blankets.
—Hurro.
—Hurro.
Yiggle & stretch, then a hop
over to her bed for cuddles,
muzzles and a caress.
And tickles too.
Hailey giggles.
Plush. And I'm ready get set
to rush on for more kicks.
Fast passes and tricks.
Route 66.
—Get back to bed this minute,
Nanny Nurse pounces. Seizing
my lobe and turning me again
to my mattress. I turn all frilly quilly
and prick her to death.

June 21 1995

US vs Aguilar.
Sarajevo snipers, 9 go.
Addis Ababa & Hosni Mubarak.
Mandaithivu Island & Tamil rebels, 132 go.
Capitol Square vs Pinette.
Seoul collapse, over 63 go.
Pavlos & Miller. Srinagar, Kashmiri rebels & 4 hikers.

Ajuchitlan del Progresso & a ditch, 11 go.
10,000 Sri Lanka troops.
Sampras over Becker.
Portadown riot.
Srebrenica, 7,000 go.
Vietnam's diplomacy.

Park Sung Hyon.
Bill Richardson, David Daliberti & William Barloon.
Wadi Kelt, 2 go.

Karadzic & Mladic.
Steven & Lorelei Turner.
Beit El & Kidumin. Knin.

Peace Park.

At his desk, The Clerk ignores US.
Unimpressed. More wait our turn.
Summoned, subpoenaed. There to confess,
object, pay a fine. At the Court's behest.
We are not the rest.
We are unrequested, neglected.

But Sam kisses me back. Patient.
Turning slowly then to renegotiate the stall.
—*Improving*, he nods,
letting go of my hand to return to the counter.
—*Can we speed this up?*
But even Sam's dismissed with a sneer.
He scratches his head. Taps his foot.
I stay back.
This hold up, oddly, starts racing
my heart.

March 2 1932

Norris-La Guardia Act & worker protection.
Ford Motor Company & Dearborn Michigan, 4 go.
Pu Yi's Manchukuo.
The Dáil's Éamon de Valera.

Ivar Kreuger goes.
Babe Ruth & $75,000.

Finland, prohibition's end & 875,000 bottles of booze.
Robin Lee's National Skate.
Southeastern tornado, 365 go.
Hoover's balanced budget & recovery.

Pittsburgh's Vitamin C.

—*man at the bottom.*
Run-off election & 6 million votes:
Hindenburg over Hitler.

—*it carries a heavy obligation to continue.*

Diaghilev goes.
$2 billion deficit.

Deportation of jobless aliens.

National Congress, British & 450.

Calm. Allready the flutters subsiding.
—*Shock?* —*Cardiac?*
But Hailey's kissing me. Smiling.
Wiggling my toes. Petting my head.
—*It's slowing!* —*It's evening!*
And The Wheel rolls on.
—*How'd that happen?*
Relaxing now. Head cushed on the
pillow. My hand mushing Hailey's.
—*Improvement.*
Ahhhh. General relief. Rush.
Gurney slowing. Turning.
And Hailey kisses me back to her
soft pleasure and no one stops her.
And we're whisked away to recover.
Together.
With allready The Convalescent
craning for the hot stuff on my rapidly
recuperating condition. Impressed to
death by my presence.

Aug 13 1995

Hans Ostro goes.
AZT.
James & Susan McDougal.
Shannon Faulkner.
Tyson 1 rounds McNeeley.
Firozabad collision, 360 go.
Shevardnadze & Tbilisi blast.
Bosnia Serb Military
& 60 NATO Warplanes.
Paul Bernardo & Karla Homolka.
Tahiti, French commandos
& 2 ships. 12:30 PM, Mururoa
Atoll & French A-Bomb.
Anothony George goes.
Ryder & 5,000 Teamsters.
Turano Hill, 10 go.
Hurricane Ismael.
—progressively narrowing the
sphere of human freedom.
Tanzu Çiller quits.
Uruba bananas, 24 go.
West Bank Palestinians.
IRA hand over.
Second Tahitian blast.
OJ Simpson.
—not guilty.

—Get back to your place.
It's a oneatatime procedure here,
The Pimply Clerk snaps.
So Sam shuffles back:
—Nothing else to do.
Me: *—Will we have to pay?*
Me: *—Is there a fee?*
Me: *—What's the cost?*

Because free's too much. Though that's US.
And my chest thumps faster. Harder to breathe.
Sam, suddenly concerned, rubs his hand over
the back of my neck. Touches my forehead.
Then pats my cheeks. Even strokes my hair.
—Slow down there.

Though allready somewhere **Aloe Vera**
& **Pansies** warp, bind up and die.

Jan 12 1932

Oliver Wendell
Holmes retires.
Benjamin Cardozo.
Hattie Caraway &
US Senate.
8.2 million jobless.
RFC.
USSR, Poland &
non-Aggression Pact.
Salvador revolt, 600 go.
M-2 down, 50 go.
—that Movement
cannot be destroyed.
Massie, Fortescue &
Jones on probation.
Santiago shake, 1,500 go.
60 nations & Geneva
Disarmament Conference.
Lake Placid Olympics.
Army Comrades Association.
20,000 Japanese &
Shanghai.
Benjamin N Cardozo &
Supreme Court.
Glass-Steagall Banking Act.
Federal Reserve, credit
& money circulation.
Chadwick neutron.
Helsinki, Finnish Army &
Kurt Wallenius.
Charles A Lindbergh Jr
kidnapped.

Nearby **Swainson's Thrush** and
Snapping Turtles reeeshnup with the
Hroo Ray of approaching wheels:
—Hurry up!

And Hailey wallops The Hospital
Administrator twice? More curses and
claps during which there's time for a
Staff Physician to press hard my neck:
—He's dying.
His heart's going too fast.
—He's dying?

Hailey: *—O you'll owe.*
Hailey: *—You'll owe.*
Hailey: *—And then O you'll pay.*
Me: *—Everything. At away my*
strumpy fine Lass!

Now flustered & unsure,
The Clinic must relent:
—Well do what you can. And
get her back to bed fast.

Oct 4 1995

Hurricane Opal, 19 go.
Aurora 8, 11 go.
Balkans, Richard Holbrooke &
60-day cease-fire.
Manzanillo quake, 60 go.
Esther's emancipation.
Banja Luka & Prijedor. DC Mall,
Louis Farrakhan & 400,000.
Moses Sithole. Michael
Schumacher's Pacific Grand Prix.
Sliema, Fathi al-Shiqaqi goes.
Atlanta over Cleveland.
—Peace yes.
—Violence no.
9:50 PM, Tel Aviv &
Yigal Amir, Yitzhak Rabin goes.
—acted allone.
Lake Kivu's Rwandan soldiers,
300 go. Nigerian rope,
Ken Saro-Wiwa & 8 go.
Shimon Peres. Slobodan
Milosevic, Franjo Tudjman &
Alija Izetbegovic.
Harry Kaufman goes.
Javier Solana.

Sam grabs my hand:
—*Chill out sweetness.*
And he softens and attends to me
even while my heart thadabumps
exasperatingly. Cupping my head, sliding
his thumb over my cheek:
—*Do you want me to get US out of here?*
Not on my life.
I'm dying for him to be my husband.
Dying to be his wife.
—*I'm okay. Just not used to this pace.*
Endings for a comfort
Sam holds out to me.
His place, this race, his company.
And if someone objects, no one objects.
We are left allone.

Nov 19 1931

Princeton athletics
& subsidies. Japanese
& Manchurian offensive.
Tammany millions.
Nazis & Nordic dominance.
Spain's Niceto
Alcalá Zamora.

Legs Diamond goes.

Gandhi, Britain & Freedom.
Communist exploitation,
Clarence Darrow
& The Scottsboro case.
Air-conditioners.
Kingfish & breadlines.
Star goes.
George Reyer.
John Reed clubs.
Anti-Fascists
& bombings of 5 US cities.
Marines leave Nicaragua.
Occupying forces &
Manchukuo government.
—Discard cloth. Discard
narcotics. Discard violence.
Defy all orders calculated to
crush national.
Casey Stengel's Dodgers.
Harry Young
& Jennings Young, 6 go.
Henry Stimson's
China & Japan.

And I'm allone.
Palpitations reassuring the ground.
Muffled footfalls. Someone's elbow.
I'm prodded, poked
and pressured.
—*Riffraff,* The Hospital Heel kicks.
Get this boy out of this place.
He's probably just jiggered.
A ruckus. Shrill with comfort.
—*Hey now? You pig fucker.*
He's dying!
Hailey heats. All bleak, decked out
with Hospital sheets.
—*Take her out of here. We don't*
handle his sort. Those're the breaks.
Hailey presumedly wallops him hard.
—*His heart's galloping,* an RN paws.
The Hospital Head curses and stomps.
—*His heart's failing.*
Hailey grabs my hand.

Until we're taken over
to The Prickly Clerk who appraises
US both. All shakes & nos.
—*We want a marriage license,*
Sam confronts.
A guffaw. Grunt.
—*Two Kings?* he stunts. *Ahhh nope.*
—*Two Queens?* he snitters. *Ahh nope.*
—*Too young?* he bitters. *Uh nope.*
I fall. O falling. I just sit down.
But Sam swings around, paces, heaves a big
breath, surly enough his footsteps
allone might leave everyone here bereft.
How can this administrant deny US the pleasure
of our together? I'm confustigrated. And dizzy.
The World suddenly revolting

Dec 5 1995

Jaffna falls.
Bryan Freeman. Galileo.
UNICEF's 6 million & 10.
Nablus hand over.
James Irons, Vincent Ellerbe
& Thomas Malik. Euro.
Buga's Flight 965, 159 go.
Latvia's Andris Skele.
Mandi Dabwali, 500 go.
Philadelphia zoo, 23 go.
Gloria Canales. First Cavalry
Brigade & First Armored
Division: Zupanja to Orasje.
Yahya Ayyash goes.
East Coast snowstorm.
Arkansas, Travelgate
& Hillary Clinton.
Amber Hagerman goes.
Juan García Abrego.
Pervomayskoye & Sovetskoye,
151 go. Sumatra ferry, 154 go.
John Shattuck's Bosnia.
—horrible crimes against.
—era of big.
Council of Europe.

I shuffle back. Round the World.
Hardly concerned:
—*I'm quite dizzy now and confustipated.*
Springing drags ahead, away
from These Players of what?
What sport? What dead?
Until heave up, once, I can't
leave another time. I can't breathe.
Stop. Racing. Flutterumfed. No
one around. O I'm falling. I've fallen.
And I fall down, swinging easily
towards stillness.
Some hubbub's cranking up here.
Clutter and clicking around
towards me. Where's Hailey?
How hazy. And strange.
Gasping. Caught.
All of me
allmost stopped. I'm losing
so much. But why? Over what?

Sept 20 1931

Nautilus dive. Harlan
County coal field strikes &
exploding soup kitchen.
Westhampton Airport,
Jackie Chapman & biplane.
Clyde Pangborn,
Hugh Herndon & Pacific:
4,400 miles & 41 hours.
Run on US banks, 800 fail.
Cardinals over Athletics.
Sharkey 15 rounds Carnera.
Spain, Left Republicans &
Manuel Azaña.
Tax Evasion, Capone
& 11 years.
Edison goes.
George Washington Bridge.
Hoover, Laval &
Gold Standard.
Geneva, 21 nations &
truce. DuPont rubber.
Buckingham with loin
cloth, shawl & sandals.
—gives encouragement
not.
Landslide & Panama canal.
Frederick Allison's
Halogen.

Jan 28 1996

Newton Square's John du Pont,
Dave Schultz goes.

Super Bowl XXX,
Cowboys over Steelers.
Alberton, 8 go.
Colombo's 400 lbs, 86 go.
Nuggets over Bulls.
Hazel R O'Leary's 99.5 tons.
Puerto Plata &
Alas Nacionales 737, 189 go.
Gerry Adams &
London Docklands, 2 go.
Gary Dockery.
Amtrak, Maryland Rail Commuter
& Silver Spring, 11 go.
Port at Cádiz, 50 go.

French draft.
West Jerusalem &
Ashkelon, 27 go.
OPSEU's 50,000.
Drazen Erdemovic.
LRA & Karuma Falls, 130 go.

Megan & Morag. Dunblane's
Thomas Hamilton, 18 go.

me.
And fluttering abates.
Cooling steadily. Evenly. Still.
Everyone chases the Dream but we leave it.
THE FINICKY CLERK pales and there, facing
Sam's fleet return to his desk, goes
woozy with feer. Head rolling. Tiny tics.
Until finally, to Sam, HE admits:
—*Who are you?*
Here too among the Arrested, Charged and
Guilty. Accused, Acquitted, Appealing. Armed.
Defendants, Plaintiffs, Experts. Citizens on Grand
Juries. District Judges & Prosecutors with
disputes over felonies & misdemeanors.
—*And who allso is she?* THE FALTERING CLERK
finishes, leaving US nowhere to go but

July 26 1931

Carlos Ibáñez del Campo
to Argentina.
Wickersham Commission
& Prisons.
Beer War, 1 goes.
John Cockcroft, Ernest
Walton & Lithium atom.
Yangtze River floods,
200,000 go. Bix goes.
Ohio's USS Akron.
Basle Commission.
Walter Gifford.
Brooklyn gangland
execution, 3 go.
Ford employees
& vegetables.

France's non-aggression
& USSR. Dornier Do-X,
12,558 horsepower
& 100 passengers.
Round Table Conference.
Doolittle, California
& Newark: 11 hours
16 minutes 10 seconds.

Chilean Communist revolt
over. Parliament's
wages & taxes.
London riots.

Naval crews & mutiny.

Japanese aggression,
Manchuria & Mukden.

Back at last to the Visitors' Desk:
—*My Hailey. Where is she?*
It's imperative I reach her.
Here among Murdered,
Gored, Drowned, Burned and Boiled.
The Neck Broken, Back Broken, Bled,
Leaded, Stabbed, Choked, Stroked,
Tumored and Disemboweled, stretched
out and canvased, seeping their ends
to the loss of their wind.
—*Who?* THE NURSE asks.
A Curious Vertigo gives
me the spins. Woozy with feer,
I take hold of THE CHARLIE GOONS
surrounding me by force.
Everyone shares the Dream
but I need it.
Something pounding.
A fluttering trouble.
Me.

March 19 1996

Quezon's Ozone Disco, 150 go.
Hague's Zdravko Mucic,
Hazim Delic, Esad Landzo &
Zejnil Delalic. Comet Hyakutake.

San Francisco's 175 couples.
Freemen arrests. Cigar.
Lincoln Montana
& Theodore J Kaczynski.
Dan Rostenkowski.

Operation Grapes of Wrath.
Riley Cycle, Dupuis goes.
York divorce.
Clinton, Ryutaro Hashimoto
& Alliance of the 21st Century.

Pyramids, Greek tourists
& Islamic terrorists, 18 go.
399-25. Robert Kupransky.
Port Arthur, Broad Arrow Café
& Martin Bryant, 35 go.
Grindstone's Derby.
ValuJet's Everglades, 108 go.
Tangail cyclone, 600 go.

Bulk Challenge
& 2,000 Liberians.

around the bend
to ponder zazzing off to
Vermont it, Vegas it.
We still got our wheels to
take US on out of here. Blow off
the ceremony. Dis authentication.
Bag whistles & shouts.

Even if **Sweet Pecans** pass.
And **Chapman Oaks** can't last.

We stand amidst the traffic streams. Gnarled
and regulated. Flowing and Open. Flatbeds,
sedans, Maui Cruisers and buses. Sued
winners. Petty losers. Teenagers & friends.
Accidental Hurt & Law Abiding Bruisers.
Traffic's rush now slowing down around US,
nary a dash, everyone stopping. Allways a wait.

June 3 1931

Mussolini's purge.
Madrid lynching,
mayor goes.
Venezuela &
Juan Bautista Pérez.
Loire sinking, 350 go.

USSR, Poland &
Friendship Treaty.
Bank of England &
Credit Anstalt.
China, British &
Nguyen Ai Quoc's arrest.

—That's me.

Bank of United States:
Marcus, Singer & Singer.
Lissant Beardmore's
channel glide.
One-year moratorium
on War reparations.
Austria's Karl Buresch.
—wise creditor.
Capone & Flegenheimer.
Benguela-Katanga &
trans-African railway.
Wiley Post, Harold Gatty
& The WinnieMae:
8 days 15 hours 51 minutes.

Danatbank bankruptcy.
All German banks close.
Pittsburgh fire, 30 go.

hardly abating, delaying.
Nary a stop.
To Algiers.
The Garden District, Metairie.
Across graveyards and Bayou.
To Pontchartrain. Bywater.
Haddlebollering by Stutter Buses,
Merry Cans and Lizzies honkings to
screechings to crash. Hot Blasts and
Sacks wringing their hands over
me allready way past.

Elisa Skimmers: —*The last laugh.*
Thistle Butterflies: —*Flip that hash.*

Ahead of whistles & shouts.
All The Devoted are about.
What Them want but don't have.
Have but can't hock.
I can go Over Land. Island Hop. But
without Hailey I'm once just
around the block.

May 16 1996

Landmine ban.

Palermo, 400 police officer & Giovanni Brusca. Kremlin, Yeltsin & Zelimkhan Yandarbiyev. Little Rock & Jim Guy Tucker.

Ariane 5. Zhang Xianliang free. Susie Maroney's Florida Straits. New Zealand's Mount Ruapehu.

—of abuses.

Michael Johnson's 200 meters. Dhahran, Abdul Aziz Air Base & truck bomb, 19 go.

—protect and defend our own.

US vs Virginia & 7-1. Awami League's Sheik Hasina Wazed. Mongolia's Democratic Union over MPRP. Boris Yeltsin over Gennadi Zyuganov. Colombia returns. $5.15. Sheff vs O'Neill.

Hurricane Bertha, 6 go.

—wanton and freakish.

Because we're what everyone waits for
even when the waiting's over.

Sad Crocuses go.

Around US clutter Nons, Burnouts, Zekes
& Herbs along with Players, Stoners, Outcasts
& Limps, far from any Fly Buds
& Babes, allready on their way to quick nosh
and grip, whack, hit and rack. Work it. Turbo it.
Curb it. That's that though what's next? US.

Musk Mallows cinch and molder.

Our stand stilling every transit, disjoining
every link, until Sam swings around:
—*Let'S go back.*
And with major tugs we're
around again.
—*This way.*

April 9 1931

Andy, Roy, Haywood, Clarence, Charley, Ozzie, Eugene, Willy & Olen.

Ruth Nichols & 210.5 MPH. Spain's republic, Alfonso flees.

Egypt & Iraq. Reactionary Hoover. Empire State. 2 minutes & a Reno divorce. Kentucky United Mine Workers of America strike, 14 go. Norway & Farmers' Party.

Martial Law & Seven Spanish Cities. Twenty Grand's Derby. Doctor of Applesauce. Moorehead & 1 tornado. Stratospheric gondola ride & Piccard's 52,462 ft.

—Valley Forge of depression.

Lou Schneider's Bowes Seal Fast Special Racer & The 500.

$800 million of Treasury bonds.

—*Hold up Buster,* a Bogey objects.
Sure there's offense but what we
got here's a minor. Now kid—
What's the bug?
O I'm allready scramming:
—*Abyssinia!*
So outta there, Blam!, lickitysplit,
streeted to zip, streaking past concrete
and brick, over corner and curb, by
rail line and strike lines,

Glossy Ibis: —*Poppin it hot!*

through clusters of Clinchers
diving for Dinchers, Whangdoodle
Hoofers slumming for lessons, Parlor
Bolsheviks working their Trotzkies,
Drugstore Cowboys skirting &
shirking their Shebas,

Whirligig Beetles: —*Skeeya!*

Flatfoots hot on my heelas,
trading off new shifts,

Out of our way.
Through the Courts to the bureau of
The Frail District Clerk who terribly perpilexed
why we still haven't left tries to close up.
Sam stops that.

—We're here to get hitched.
Don't let me kick twice.
—Yes but you. I.

Sam's mash rocksolids his rashness: —*Why not?*

—First there's an application. Second there are tests. There's certification. And above all, there's the Law. You're both unfit. You even have ID?

Sam: —*No.*

—What about you?

Me: —*No.*

—Then no. That's the way it goes. It's protocol.

July 17 1996

8:45 PM, Long Island &
TWA Flight 800, 228 go.
Deadliest forest.
Karadzic quits.
Bujumbura & Buyoya
over Ntibantunganya.
Centennial Park blast, 2 go.
Hurricane Cesar, 62 go.
Aidid goes.
Typhoon Herb, 400 go.
Jim Kolbe. Thugwane's gold.
Russian Federation President.
Hard Livings gang & PAGAD.
UN Zone & Turkish Cypriot
police, 2 go.
Canberra protests.
—pain and suffering.

Amaranth snowstorm, 239 go.
Alexander Lebed & Aslan
Maskhadov.
Charles, Diana & £20.
Dick Morris & Sherry Rowlands
FARC & ELN, 96 go.

Arbil, KDP & Massoud Barzani.

Nervous Nellie, I leap after Hailey
but The Admitting Agent
prohibits it. Official protocols required
before each and every visit.

—Are you her Custodian?

—No I'm.

—Are you her Guardian?

—No I'm.

—Of course not. Are you married?
Of course not, you're too young.
Your presence then is forbidden.

—Yes but we're dating.

—She's under our care
now. She's fine.

Whereupon The Skullbusters
rearrive, their Nab barnstorming
free on a tour. Even if Mr. Transport
with a mauling widescowl is still all
too eagers to press charges:

—Seize the scamp.

Feb 16 1931

Viceroy Irwin & Gandhi.
Admiral Aznar.
Peruvian troops, riots &
Callao, 61 go.
Bernard Marcus & 5.
Dry Law.
Scripps-Howard.
Senate overrides Bonus Bill.
Federal Loans & veterans.
Peru's Ricardo Arias.
Delhi Pact.
Nationally Spangled.
Hoover vetoes
Muscle Shoals Bill.
Oswald Mosley ousted.
Wincenty Witos &
Polskie Stronnictwo Luodwe.
$2,977.
Iraq & Transjordan.
Alabama's Ruby Bates,
Victoria Price &
the Scottsboro 9.
Managua shakes,
1,100 go.
Knute Rockne goes.
Chattanooga's
Jackie Mitchell. New York's
$1 million of opium.
Berlin Custom Union.
Madeira, Azores &
State of Emergency.

Sept 3 1996

27 US cruise missiles & Iraq.
Hurricane Fran, 12 go.
Bondi Beach, Brian Hagland goes.
Alain Van der Biest.
Defense of Marriage Act & 85-14.
Brazilian logging.
Tupac Shakur goes.
Umberto Bossi & Padania.
Irving Texas 10,000.
Guatemala & UNRG.
Maricopa County &
female chain gang.
Bob Dent goes.
Diarmuid O'Neil goes.
China, France, Russia,
Great Britain, US &
Comprehensive Test Ban Treaty.
Kabul & Taliban, Najibullah goes.
39,000 shoes.
Panjshir Gorge.
KJ's meet. Kimberly Smartt.
—can no longer tolerate.
Yankees over Braves.
Eugene de Kock's imprisonment.

Mopped up, tossed out, refused. But I'm
allways refused, even refusing every
bend we contend with along the way.
To the GroundGuy's friend. No contest.
We waste no time. Together.
Motoring, Sam's hand on mine,
by Correctional Facilities, Juvenile Detention
Camps, Low Grade Security Pens. Where
the detained feel US pass and
needing
our liberty scream until, for a closeness
none will survive, all lose US.
And Sam grins
again because there is only me besides
him. He holds my head. Strokes my lips.
Electric currents flowing off his fingertips

Jan 1 1931

Alabama over Washington.
Guatemala's Jorge Ubico.
Panamanian revolt.
Burmese Golden Crow goes.
—We want food.
Vyacheslav Molotov,
Communist Party &
Collectivized agriculture.
George Washington Bridge.
Hamilton Fish
& Deportation.
Wickersham Commission
& repeal.
European unemployment.
—the coming winter.
Gandhi out.
Soviet penal camps
& 662,200.
Pierre Laval.
Mine explosion, 31 go.
Civil Government
& Virgin Islands.
Napier earthquake.
Malcolm Campbell,
Daytona Beach & 245 MPH.
*—No, comrades, it is not
possible! The tempo must
not be reduced.*
Amelia Earhart
& George Putnam.
Smedley D Butler &
Mussolini's hit-and-run.

Panic. Doctors furious for time.
—It's pulmonary! *—It's shock!*
Patting her face, slaps for attention.
Hypodermics, alcohol and gauze.
—It's allergic! *—Anaphylactic!*
A sudden scramble for vulneraries.
—Adrenaline!
Losing her. Closer. Now.
But all I can do is hold on.
—Needle!
Ow. Outandout retreat. Pause.
Yet if there's success, before the effects
can play out on her tepid mouth,
All Practitioners unclasp my hand
and whisk her away to recovery.
Allone.
Then The Paddywagon Driver,
hair stinking of vomit, and
Butterboys guarding The Sorry Sure
motion me to join Them.

electrocuting, executing
a Penitentiary Parole Officer who out
allone wonders a task while hanging a kite. Even
the Imprisoned, snide, blocked & callow, wail.
And somewhere even Vanillas fail.
—*Circumstantially,* Sam yields.
We're irresponsible.
Me: —*Irresponsible.*
US: —*Irresponsible.*
And impossibly sure, on the gonzo charge by
riverring shores, through Beetown,
Patch Grove and Bridgeport. Latronic Lynxville.
And where Prisons adhere to the lurch of laws, we
roar by. Confined to no loss. Beyond stops we all
boss. Because we're urgent. Allways divergent.
Pulling over only when we reach La Crosse.

Oct 31 1996

Tutsi forces, Zairian army & 500,000 Hutu refugees.
—*humble government.*
—*comeback kid.*
Andhra Pradesh cyclone, 1,500 go.
Aberdeen Proving Ground.
Holyfield 12 rounds Tyson.
Saudi Airlines & Ilyushin 76, over 349 go.
Emil Constantinescu over Ion Iliescu.
Bangalore's World & riots.
767 & Comoros Islands, 123 go.
Toutatis. Paris Metro, 2 go.
Daniel Carr, Gerald Laarz & a tire dump.
Nelson Mandela, Democratic Constitution & Sharpeville.
—*I'm not a diplomat..*
Zajedno & Belgarde's 250,000.
UN & Kofi Annan.
Grozny nurses, 5 go.
Lima, Japanese Embassy & MRTA.

The Police swing around,
now hotly clutching The Pill Giving
Dope who keeps on protesting:
—*By the rules, friends. I*
assure you it's O Naturel!
—*Can it Pal!*
Alerting then The Hospice Nurse:
—*Since her current disposition is due to*
substances dispensed, procured, and
—*swallowed, digested*
—*on your premises,*
The Staff: —*you are responsible.*
Mr. Sane: —*you are responsible.*
Me: —*you are responsible.*
All: —*Financially.*
Even a **Silverfish** sweems: —*Haaaailey.*
Now all ire & feer, The National
Commissioner about faces:
—*What's the delay? If you don't save her*
you're fired.

Oct 23 1930

Shanghai & rebels, 8,000 go.
—*prevent hunger and cold.*
State Governors & Private Business.
Brazil's Getúlio Vargas.
Greece, Turkey & Treaty of Ankara.
Haile Selassie's Ethiopia.
160 Ohio miners.
Austria's Social Democrats.
London elephants.
Hamagushi.
Oklahoma tornado, 19 go.
African sandstorm, Paris mud.
500 Communists & tear gas.
Bank of United States, 400,000 depositors & 66 closing branches.
Spanish revolution.
Surplus apples.
Soviet food supplies.
$45 million for drought.
4.8 million unemployed.
—*satisfied with the circus.*
Grain, cotton & copper.
Joseph Louis Barrow.
Ellen Church.
Maginot line.

Dec 23 1996

—ready for battle.
Assam bombing, 26 go.
Naom Friedman's M16.
Tony Bullimore & a chocolate bar.
Comair 3272, 29 go.
Huambo minefields.
—that is going on all around the World.
—to solve our problems.
Martina Hingis.
Super Bowl XXXI,
Packers over Patriots.
Andrew M Cuomo.
Vucitrn & Serbian police,
2 UCK & Zahir Pajaziti go.
Bakhran Sadirov, Rezvon Sadirov
& Tajik renegades.
Bucaram Ortíz.
—El Loco.
CDC, US & 73%.
Raurimu ski resort, 6 go.
Heidi Fleiss. Rafael Martinez
Emperador goes.
—and prudent.
Seoul's Lee Il-nam goes.

Where we're allready met, except
emerging for our appeal, eccentric & genteel,
our WIDOWER expects little out of all
we've come here to fetch. HE's going.
Slender Silphiums go too.
—*You can't take umbrage over*
Love and still find it waiting there
for you.
—*O that's pretty,* I stastammer.
—*No, that's devastating.*
Wild Orchids shatter. Pulp. Go.
Fragile wisps of hair, withered left arm. Soft
tumbling lips. Stirs a cup. Offers US some.
Sam nods no.
—*Quit coffee. Had a life supply. Only tea.*
HE enjoys Sam's vitality. Maybe me.

Sept 2 1930

Costes & Bellonte,
Paris to New York.
Yen Hsi-chan's Peking
government. Hoboken
& Montclair electric train.

Dominican Republic &
160 MPH winds, 2,000 go.

Frank Kellogg's
World Court.
Uriburu over Argentina.

State Department
& foreign labor.

US out polos Britain.
John Doeg's Forest Hills.
Nazi Party 2nd.

Enterprise cups Shamrock V.
New Jersey Gang raid,
dry agents & brewery.

Soviet executions, 48 go.

East Texas Field
& Joiner's Well.
US Navy, 49 ships
& 4,800 men.
Athletics over Cardinals.

TWA.
Legs Diamond's 5.

Committee for
Unemployment Relief.

Poor Hailey won't let go,
fingers moonslivering my wrist.
Clatter of wheels. A gurney arrives.
Hailey's lifted, shifted
and levelled.
—*Stop,* a RUDE COMMISSIONER bells.
No one will treat this girl here.
No one will touch her.
Dispense with her.
Human Lice skitchy: —*Huh?*
—*She needs medical assistance*
at once, I confronsate.
—*Out of the question,*
THE HEEL COMMISSIONER harps.
We don't administer to her kind.
Shad Roaches: —*Huh?*
—*She's fading,* a PHYSICIAN croaks.
Even THE TROLLEY DRIVER, BUCKET on
head, pipes up: —*But iz an emergency.*
Hailey's grip softens.

Savoring by US
all HE no longer finds around.
His wife's fragrance. Her willowy hair. Protests
under a cough. Her walk. Paired. Fedup. Spared.
Carried forth. When the cradle of her soft touch
once gave HIM their only pulse.
Returning later HE
brings US the dead.
—Him, a Private, Them gored. Untried.
By some Liquor Store. Ball Player sprawled
across a hopscotch. Over by a parking lot.
Where he flowed. And left just this.
Handing over then all Sam
needs to legally marry me.
LICENSE. O yes.
With every heaviness.

Feb 18 1997

Cocha & Pumaranra
mudslides, over 250 go.
New York & Ali Abu Kamal, 2 go.
Hizb-i-Wahdat fighters
& Shibar Pass.
20,000 Bonn Miners.
Albania's Sali Berisha.
Bauby goes.
Anton Smith, La Capitana
& £5 billion.
Daqamseh's Island of Peace,
7 go.
Louise Woodward.
Ben Gurion Boulevard,
Apropo Coffee & 2 bags, 3 go.
Algerian forces
& Jihad Armed Islamic Front,
Abdelkader Seddouki goes.
Rancho Santa Fe, Marshall
Apple & Hale-Bopp, 39 go.
Villeneuve's Grand Prix.
Kamina & Kasenga.
Tshisekedi & Kabila.
Theisen's detox.
23 anti-tank mines. Woods.

July 23 1930

Chinese Communists
& Hankow.
Chicago heat wave.
Turks & Kurdistan uprising.
People's Commissar of
Foreign Affairs.
Maxim Litvinov.
Naples & Ariano quake,
1,500 go.
Leducq's Tour.
Gallant Fox's Triple.
Odessa, Soviet troops &
strikers, 200 go.
122.7 million.
—Hicks and rubes and
drivers of second-hand
Fords.
Marion lynching, Tom Shipp
and Abe Smith go.
RB Bennet.
Drought, corn &
690 million bushels.
British bombers &
Afridi rebels.
647 hours.
Peru's Augusto Leguía
ousted. Jimmy Walker's
petty graft.
Labor & legal beer.
Harry Socoloff &
King Kullen Grocery.

Hailey wobbles but stands.
I steady her shoulders.
—I shfeel szho shfot not.
Then starts plodding ahead, weaving
the Minnies & Scrubs, something's
going around, rubbing her gut until
she coughs once, stumbles confused,
now wheezing to breathe.
Stops. Breathing. Brows pinch.
Ears wiggle?
O! Hailey sags to my hands,
crumpling fast.
Calmly I fustigate NURSE BOZARK
to react. She doesn't, filing her toes.
Fortunately EXTERNIES race over.
Checking for pulse.
Hailey heaves her tiny chest
but finds no relief. Not even
an allowance of release.
—Pulse wavering, ATTENDANTS scream.

April 15 1997

City of Mina, 343 go.
Sussex County Pizza.
Peruvian troops & MRTA, 17 go.
Armavir explosion, 2 go.
Chemical Weapons
74-26.
Italy's Victor Emmanuel.
Abraham J Hirschfeld. 419-165,
Labour Party & Tony Blair.
Silver Charm's Derby.
War Crimes Tribunal &
Dusan Tadic.
Northeastern Iranian shake,
2,400 go.
Donna Ratliff.
—not a United Ireland.
Laurent Kabila & Kinshasa,
Mobutu Sese Seko goes.
Kelly Flinn.
Banjarmasin shopping mall,
130 go. 16 Nations &
Russia-NATO.
Republic of Congo.
Delmar Simpson's 18 counts.
USS Kearsarge. 5,000 Cobras &
Brazzaville. Drexler's Dance.

Our WIDOWER then turns to me,
allready pleased to the buckets by how
much relief these improprieties bring HIM.

Even if
HE won't last much longer. We're who outlasts.
We're allways last. HE'll finish this last task and
go. For US HE waited too long.

Carolina Jessamine. Gone.

—She, she shot. No recourse. All business.
Blew her brains out with a laugh. Swish.
Just flowed all over the bath.
Around some Fins. Left just this.

Handing over then all I
need to legally marry Sam.
LICENSE. O yes.
Without levity.

May 17 1930

Derby's Gallant Fox.
Young Plan reparations.
Syrian constitution.
Amy Johnson solos
London to Australia.
—a mad risk but it is a justifiable risk.
New Zealand's
George Forbes.
Billy Arnold, Miller Hartz
Special racer & 100.4 MPH.
United Airlines
& Female Flight Stewards.
Chicago Gang War
& Fox Lake, 3 go.
Clarence Birdseye.
Carol's Romania.
Dry Laws Condemned.
Hoover, Hawley-Smoot
Tariff Bill & Protectionism.
The Jonsong 6.
Isma'il Sidki Pasha.
1,000 attack
British consulate.
Rhineland,
Gustav Stresemann
& French departure.
Northland Transportation
Company.
Greyhound Company.
Veterans Administration Act.

But before I then demand
that someone locate Doctors
something peculiar happens.
There among Famished,
Scrofulous, Polio Mangled,
Smallpox Vanquished, Factory
Dislocated, Amputated and Banished,
spoiled with Fractured Tibias,
Fibulas, Festering Boils and Mashered
Noses, some LUNATIC, all friendly
bendly, offers Hailey a CURATIVE.
Which she takes! Wait!

While **Mosquitoes** flit elatedly:
—Superlative company!

I excuse. Flip. Slip quick to my girl.
THE REGIONAL DELEGATES promptly
tackle THE IDIOT. While THE LIMOUSINE
DRIVER, desirous to further crescent
my esteem of him, throws the CUP OF
UPCHUCK on MADMAN and HATTERS.

June 11 1997

—*So you can have,*
HE cordially extends,
his gratitude bruised by
confusion. HE needs US. HE feers US.
—*The question of my youth*
concerns only the bitter
comfort and chear of whatever
possibilities you now allready exceed. Behave.
Because we're every extreme.
Sam outside of all HE can never
leave allone. We leave everybody allone.
So what? Everyone misses US but we're never
missed. Despite Sam's Leftwrist Sapphire Twist.
The gracious offer of his hand.
The firm shake. Mighty Sam. Our WIDOWER
wobbles. Goes. And where a slack River joins

$4 billion
& Swiss Banks Associations.
Britian's handgun ban.
Afrikaner Resistance Movement's
Eugene Terreblanche.
William Hague over Ken Clarke.
US Tobacco, Medicare
& $368.5 billion.
Harry Shapiro's 10.
MIR collision. Montserrat
& Soufriere Hills eruption, 19 go.
Tyson 3 ears Holyfield.
Tung Chee-hwa, 4,000 troops
& Hong Kong.
Mumbai & Dalits, 12 go.
Spain's Popular Party
& ETA, Miguel Blanco goes.
Ocean Drive & Andrew Cunanan,
Gianni Versace goes.
New York's 60 Mexican
immigrants. Mo Mowlem.
Jarrell tornadoes, 27 go.
Gordon McMaster goes.
Thredbo & Stuart Diver.

March 12 1930

NOW THE TAXI DRIVER
approaches. A question
of the fare. And vomit.
All over his cab.
Big fellow.
Hands a fury of hair.
At once I offer, graciously,
my Leftwrist Twist of Sapphire.
But deemed beyond the worth
of his puling breath DERAIL accepts
gratefully the BOWL AND RAG.
Bows aside then for COUNTY
ENVOYS anxious to Edison me:
—*Dear Sir, how may we assist?*
—*Provide comfort and chear?*
—*We're most concerned.*
—*It's a question of youth.*
My sophistication overwhelming
their demeanors, I step back cordially.
So Them can live.

Gandhi, Gulf of Khambhat
& Salt March.
Primo de Rivera goes.
Hermann Müller. Ras Tafari.
Congress, $300 million &
public roads.
British Law & Monopoly.
Los Angeles plane crash,
16 go. Clarence DeMar's
Boston Marathon.
Ohio State prison burns,
320 go.
—Peaceful methods of
diplomacy can eventually
take the place of War.
London Naval Treaty.
Peshawar Riots, 20 go.
Chiang & Yen Hsi-chan's
Northern forces.
Gandhi arrested.
Nashua's fire.
1,028 for
Hawley-Smoot Tariff Bill.
Turkey's Ali Fethi Bey.
Burma trembles,
Pegu falls, 6,000 go.
John Parker over.

The Mishishishi, up on Grand Bluff,
we soberly behold some city outstretched
below and feel our peril.
The West outgrows the West
but we never outgrow US.
And it exhausts me. I'm beat & buffeted
by the teflon threat of our slipperiness.
We're without pause.
But allso never less.
And over Lock & Dam 7 few care that
Sam scatters tiny storms
and I feel queasier, uneasier about how
diminished and rough I'm becoming.
Which is when I find, all teen & shot up,
loping alongside me,
my LAST HOPE.

Aug 4 1997

—overload.

Cathy Freeman's 400 meters.
Guam & Korean Air 747-300,
228 go. Andes snowstorm, 6 go.

Mombasa machetes, 15 go.

Typhoon Winnie, 140 go.
Egon Krenz's 6 years. Rais &
Liamine Zéroual, over 300 go.

1 AM & Pont de l'Alma,
Dodi Fayed goes. Diana goes.
Hamas & Ben Yehuda Street,
7 go. Lebanese ambush, 14 go.

*—Life without you is
very, very difficult.*

Oslo's 89 countries &
antipersonnel land mines.

Borneo burning.

Medan's Garuda Airlines, 234 go.

Assisi shake, 10 go.

Thrust SSC & 763 MPH.

SWEET HOPE, allways a pain.
I shew HIM away. Kick his lynched ass.
Limps off amusedly.
Trailing his branch.
And we keep waiting
on the Administrative Staff.
Hailey filling up HATS I walk
over and slosh down a bowl.
Retch, fetch and drain.
Storm over to Triage again.
*—We're aware. She
must still wait her turn,*
NURSE GIMLET deplores.
Flapdoodlewaggle!
Hailey is the turn. I'm the turn.
And I'll burn all their beds.
Gently but firm:
—It's a question of some peril.
—She's stewed to the hat,
NURSE WURP flats.

Jan 20 1930

James Doolittle quits.
Carnera first rounds
Big Boy Peterson.

Alcoholism, Crime & Revolt.
Britain, US, France, Japan,
Italy & Naval armaments.

New Zealand shakes,
800 go.
Sonja Henie champion.
Hans Stuck firsts on ice.
Federal Grand Jury,
31 Corporations
& Bootlegging Ring.
Chief Justice Charles
Evans Hughes.
Flagstaff, Clyde William
Tombaugh & Pluto.

Manhattan & traffic.

Jack Sharkey 3
rounds Phil Scott.
Collective work,
Russians flee to Poland.
Unemployed, Communists
& NYC police.

Southwest French Floods,
200 go.
*—Prosperity is just around
the corner.*

Howard Taft goes.

Sept 30 1997

—the Giving Age.
Scott Krueger goes.
Trevor Rees-Jones.
Romantica's 700.
Foale returns. Prodi quits.
Hurricane Pauline, 400 go.
Quebec bus, 43 go.
Gilford, Gilford & Parry.
A hitchhiking umbrella.
Gyorgy von Habsburg
& Eilika von Oldenburg.
Sassou-Nguesso over Lissouba.
Florida over Cleveland.
—I didn't do anything.
Typhoon Linda, 130 go.
Three Gorges Dam. 279 days.
Brazil's Ronnie Biggs.
Gama'a al-Islamiya
& 6 headbands, 65 go.
Yamuna River plunge, 29 go.
Nathan Thill, Oumar Dia goes.
Dushanbe,
Karine Mane & 5 go.
West Paducah's
Micahel Carneal, 3 go.

—What gives?
—Grow up. He's haste. You ain't. Time to
slow down. Give him a shove. You don't Love
him. Besides, Love's not enough.
Enough?
I speed up but
HE keeps up easily.
—If you stick with him, you're over.
He's over. So debond quick, Hot Stuff.
It'z all you can do.
Enough?
—Life kid. Lost unless you
cut some loose. You're too young to keep it.
Too young to leave it. Life's the death a Love
still gets when Love is finally over with.
So departs my LAST HOPE.

Nov 24 1929

Chinese revolution
& Russians.
Clemenceau goes.
Byrd & Balchen over
South Pole.
Allies out of Rhineland's
2nd Occupation Zone.
Manchuria &
Secretary of State
Henry Stimson.
Marines to Haiti.
Root Formula.
Sino-Soviet truce.
—basic strength of
business.
Detroit's 5.3 million.
16 billion gallons of gas.
695,000 paved roads.
Ford's $6 to $7.
—My rackets are run on
strictly American.
Muncie feer.
Southern California
over Pittsburgh.
4,000,000 unemployed.
Stalin, Rye Farm
Cooperatives & Russian
Soil Belt.
Wickersham Commission
& Crime Rate.
—and far reaching.
Lockheed Vega's 171 MPH.

A SWEET HOPE lopes up. This one
a sporty fellow. Neat with
coalfine feet. High sox.
—Awwwww shucks, enough's enough.
Cain't keep an All World.
Pats my back. Sits me on his bench.
—Shiiiiiiiiiiiit, get all loose,
juiced, hot and lucky. Boy,
there're better ways to live.
Live?
—What every stompingest kid,
runaway, throwaway, outtaplay,
gots to heed if—
Live?
Grins my feers and streets away.
—Life's big, Champ. Hit the
saws and the jazz. And laugh.
It's not so sad to taste but never have. So—
Live? Allways?
—Give.

Dec 3 1997

Siberian coal & methane gas,
68 go. Northern Iraq,
10,000 Turkish soldiers & PKK.
AN-124 Cargo plane & Irkutsk,
85 go. Mandela retires.
South Korea & Kim Dae-jung.
Kenneth Kaunda arrested.

The Republican Irish National
Liberation Army & Lisburn,
Billy Wright goes.
Polhó's 3,000 Tzotzils.
Ouled Kherarba, 21 go.
Aspen skiing,
Michael Kennedy goes.
No smoking. Rafiq Ra.
Stockholm's 314.
Relizane's Had Chekala,
over hundreds go.
Northeast ice storm.

Terry Enright goes. Slupsk riot.

—deep remorse.

Les Orres avalance, 11 go.

Super Bowl XXXII,
Broncos over Packers.

Away. Tuned & bottlefed. Tricked out
& Slammed. Sam's all I have.
All I won't abandon.
I can't keep my hands off him.
Sticking to him. Missing him. Even while
we drive, even while, with a tumble of guts,
I let go a belch. Putrid sluices of muck.
Blurring on through Utica. Rochester.
—Never too soon,
Sam bumps US, pumps US wide.
By Mantorville and Owatonna.
Through Waseca, Madelia, Windom, Baltic.
To Hartford.
Highway Badges too plodding to even try.
The Bankrupt too broke.
Lolling Hemp twisting to smoke.

Oct 3 1929

Yugoslavia's Serbians,
Croatians & Slovenians.
Colorado prison riot.

US, Britain & War.
Athletics over Cubs.
Little America.

Transcontinental.

—had become a living.
Thursday.
—a speed and ferocity
that left men dazed.
—is on a sound and
prosperous basis.
Hitler, Hugenberg
& Young Plan.

Tuesday.

—the boys I can't pay
Them what I owe Them.
John Schwitzgebel goes.
Griggs's Lithiated
Lemon-Lime.
Fall's $100,000 & one year.

Hankow's Chinese Rebels
& Nationalists. Jimmy
Walker over LaGuardia.

One ball,
James J Riordan goes.
Baghdad's
Abdul Muhsin goes.
Stalin expels Bukharin.

Whereupon **Polar Bears** suddenly
rush among US, slashing, spending,
crashing boondoggle rackets and
chargé d'affaires. Too many heiresses,
not enough air. Sell, sale, sail. Angry
Bulls stampede for the swamp. Gone.
Janes, Jaybirds & Groundgrippers
slump stupefied
on the lawn.
Then little Hailey sniffs and
desnoots:
—Ahhh choooooooooooooo!
Grab the last taxi. Depart for the car.
Except Hailey's throwing up,
spilling sluices of muck
and the ever unstuck.
Caught with my hands.
All I won't abandon.
All that I have. She's all I have.
She's all that I'll ever have.

Jan 26 1998

Clinton & Monica Lewinsky.
Karla Faye Tucker goes.
Dolomite Ski life
& US Air Force, 20 go.
Rostaq quake, 4,500 go.
—never.
Roderick Ferrell.
Maine's homosexuals.
Sierra Leone, Freetown & ECOMOG.
Diane Zamora.
Tara Lipinski's 7 triple-jumps.
El Niño & Florida tornadoes,
42 go. Osama bin Laden,
World Islamic Front & Al Qaeda.
—kill the Americans.
Foday's pay.
Ezer Weizman. Sonia Gandhi.
Mazar-i-Sharif. Wales devolution.
Atal Behari Vajpayee's Bharatiya
Janata. Sergei Kiriyenko over
Viktor Chernomydrin.
Jonesboro's Golden
& Johnson, 5 go.
Norodom Ranariddh.
Muhi al-Din al-Sherif goes.

O No. But Sam laughs off
the slaughter we allways wheel past.
—*South Dakota,* he shares.
—*Our pair,* I dare, rumbling by
a KOA. Concertina wire & damp grills
dead by scrambled charcoal, while
the thrill of murder still tickles the air.
Sam celebrates. Full Contretemps.
We're onwards to Mitchell.
Ohlman by 8th Avenue
to Rowley Street where
I loop his arm, play with his hair.
Unable to stay away. Trembling
to scoop even closer. While pedestrians
wave at Sam, throwing US flips of weal.
Donating to what's allready forsaken.

July 22 1929

Russia & China border.
Rosselli, Lussu,
Fausto escape Lipari.
Auburn Prison &
1,700 rioting convicts.
Maurice de Waele's Tour.
Leavenworth riot,
1 goes.
National & Local farmers.
Weizmann's agency.
Sultan's 500th swat.
Manchurian crisis.
Soviet gunboats
& Sungari River.
Jerusalem battles, 47 go.
Graf Zeppelin rounds World:
21 days 7 hours 26 minutes.
San Juan down, 70 go.
Revolt & Damascus Syria.
One million.
British troops,
Syrian border &
1,000 captured at Hibbon.
Aristide Briand &
United States of Europe.
Manila typhoon, 200 go.
Lithuania's Voldemaras
overthrown.

Though bets are still cast,
Buccaneers on a roll, while
Caterers circle and Top Hats,
Stickpins all blingbling, continue
their stroll. At least I'm
with her, carrying these
trembling wings from the ball.
She knots up my hair, slurps
on my shoulder, so sobsloppily
tortured with shame and
remorse, though I'm the only
one here to blame of course.
Riff shuffles with crossover couplets
dodge fleeriest Folk, grungier Damps
here splattering yolks.
—*Will these ever!*
—*Seetie bohunks!*
—*Nigger and his slunge!*
—*It just slaughters me.*
O yes. Yes, it does.

April 10 1998

Stormont, Blair & Ahern.
England floods.
Paula Jones. Pol Pot goes.
US Peace Envoy's Dennis Ross.
Amy Grossberg. Andrew Wurst.
Juan Gerardi Conedera goes.

Zagoria's Connecticut leaving.
Quiet's Derby.
Sarno mud, 81 go.
Pokharan blasts. G8 summit.
Ravenswood hospital,
Christopher Sercye goes.
Kinkel's Thurston High, 4 go.
Serbian troops,
Kosovo's Albanian rebels.
Chagai Hills & 5 nuclear blasts.
—die for our.
Eschede train, 93 go.
Ethiopia, Eritrea & Badme, 40 go.
João Bernardo Vieira.
Jasper's John King,
Lawrence Brewer & Shawn Berry,
James Byrd goes.
Bowling's Bonfire.

By US. By Them.
Together without
everything we won't offer.
Outside Jackpot & Lucky Casinos,
Stalkers heap Sam's hat with fortunes
we allready assume. We refuse every price.
We're without price. He has no hat.
But Benders keep tossing tips:
—You two bring US so much luck.
Sam: *—All of my apologies.*
Me: *—All my apologies too.*
Which leaves The Absolved tear streaked.
Shysters, Muggers and Hooks on the take
circling their temporary bonanzas.
Them are all temporary. Only we recirculate.
Not moved by. Not moved towards. We move on

May 2 1929

Southern tornadoes,
25 go. Alain Gerbault's
World sail around.
Cleveland hospital
fumes & fire, 124 go.
Capone's gat.
Clyde Van Dusen's Derby.
Englewood, Charles A
& Anne Spencer.
Unconstitutional
Pocket Veto.
Ford autos
& Soviet Union.
Tacna to Peru,
Arica to Chile.
Owen D Young,
War Reparations
& $7.8 billion.
Ramsay MacDonald's
Margaret Bondfield.
Federal Farm Board.
Aviators Assolant,
Lotti & Lefevre:
Maine to Paris.
Charles G Dawes'
silk knee breeches.
Coco. Hot weather
& a Hoover handshake.
Fly by day,
train by night:
Transcontinental Air
Transport.

I cyclone this orgy, darting appalled
from their groaning engorging. And
then one tear falls. Two. Tears still
streaking her cheeks when I sweep
her up with my weeping arms.
Me: *—I'm so sorry.*
I'm sorry sorry.
And she: *—I'm sorry sorry.*
I'm so sorry.
And a Louisiana Dancer
bubbles: *—Oooooo where are you*
two going?
Swaying wantonly back and forth.
But we are allways going.
Allready gone.
The compass of all
that's never discovered,
leaving the rest to come
on their own and wither.
The Ongoing Party, so Over.

June 22 1998
Andrés Pastrana. Derry's kill.
Clinton vs New York.
Adana quake, 144 go.
Linda Tripp. Sampras's 5th.
Florida fires.
Moshood Abiola goes.
Ballymoney arson, 3 Quinns go.
Ryan Harris goes.
Papua New Guinea, 1,300 go.
Obuchi Keizo.
Pantani's Tour.
Patricia Robe goes.
Tanzania & Dar es Salaam
US Embassy, 10 go.
Kenya & Nairobi US Embassy,
247 go. Omagh IRA blast, 28 go.
—nobody's business but ours.
Grand Jury & Clinton turnaround.
Kendall Francois.
—Pan, pan.
—let peace slip away.
Million Youth. McGwire's 62nd.
Clovis growl.
Flo-Jo goes.

allone from these dirty sidewalks. O Ooo my Sam
still smiling gently for me. Gives me a
hug. And I'm nothing but failing,
just welling up over his attention.
I even hiccup. Hiccup twice.
I'm The Luckiest Fool Ever.
While all around US keeps dying.
Sam smiles. I smile,
buzzing with desire
to drive quicker. Happy to
nosh, cuddle, nog him & knob.
By Kimbal, Pierre and Midland.
Shredding past Mechanics, Motorheads,
Methracers, LiverBashers & more.
Scores more. Hundreds more. Revving it,
punching it, ripping it here, allatonce, to try

Jan 30 1929
Trotsky banished.
Éamon de Valera's arrest
& Ulster.
Lindbergh's Morrow.
Hoover's 15
10,000 ton cruisers.
Windy City &
Valentine massacre, 7 go.
*—This is a War to
the finish.*
Antarctic &
Marie Byrd Land.
Rebels, Nanking & Hunan.
Sleeping Car Porters & AFL.
8 State revolt.
Mexican rebels,
Vera Cruz & Nogales.
Seagrave's Golden Arrow.
Oslo's Olaf & Martha.
Coast Guard & I'm Allone.
18 US planes to Naco.
Williams, Grand Prix &
Bugatti Special.
*—I wouldn't change mine
for yours.*
Shipwreck Kelly's
flagpole sitting.
Greyhound
double-deckers.

Except before I commence,
one all at once, these wiggling hips,
jiggling tits, Amateurs, Tarts,
Secretaries, upturned derrieres,
pairs, sevens, baker's dozens,
fivescore and doubletime,
Hailey plops down aways
from my rodeo. Just sits there solo.
Rigid back, legs locked. Shoulders
drooping. Sad.
Though saddest of all, forcing
a smile, her beestung mouth
bending up for nowhere.
And I'm dying.
The Luckiest Fool Ever.
Hailey hiccups a cry. Hiccups
twice. Face splotched and welling
but lips never failing.
Still smiling so gently for me.
O my. What am I doing?

Sept 24 1998

Lesotho's Maseru.
Benoît Lecomte's Atlantic.
Germany's Social Democrats.
Hurricane Georges, 374 go.
Ferderal Reserve & LTCM.
Matthew Shepard goes.
258-176.
IMF & World Bank.
Augusto Pinochet's arrest.
New York over San Diego.
Amherst & James Kopp,
Barnett Slepian goes.
Hurricane Mitch, 7,000 go.
John Glenn orbits.
—progress over partisanship.
Newt Gingrich quits. USS
Enterprise, 4 go. Global warming.
—backed down.
9374.27.
Galina Starovoitova goes.
Israel & PNA's Gaza airport.
Japan & Jiang Zemin. 81.
Silas Cool goes. Islamic Iran
Participation Front. Ruth Dreifuss.
Operation Desert Fox. Impeach.

their hand at overcoming our joyride.
No one comes near. No one survives.
We're the pleasure accidents supply.
What no one seeks out. Who none ever find.
We're the duty to Societies not even
the stiffest Upper West Side kid can obey.
Untoward. Sam & I pleasuring only our boredom.

—Oooo.

—Ahhhh.

A pleasurable grind on private grounds. Without
much burst. Mmmmmmmmmming
then Ooooooing. All over the place.
Just two of US screwing human embrace.
Allone. And even if I still can't come,
Sam's ardor and pace leave me
quivering.

Oct 22 1928

—Rugged.
—and free commerce die.
Mansfield Robinson's Mars.
Harry Tucker's Coast.
Oakley Harris,
Sara Kellaway & acquittal.
Grieg's seaplane
& 319.57 MPH.
—every pot and a car.
Governor FDR.
Emperor Hirohito.
Etna, Catania & lava.
Vestris down, 111 go.
Grand Canyon Rapids
& Hyde's scow.
Heavy Trading.
Boulder Dam Bill.
NAACP's 9.
New York police
454 roundup. Broccoli.
Ascheim-Zondek.
Opals, Cotton & Saturday
Evening Quill Club.
Kiwanis. Dance Derby.
Alexander's Yugoslavia.
Sheffield Farms
over bottles.
Fokker Trimotor
& 150 hours 40 minutes.
Cascade Mountain way.
Afghanistan's Amanollah
abdicates.

and quivering thighs.
It's feathers & a first, fast over the
flirt, ready and dirty to blurt,
spreading out on silky sheets,
cotton towels, umpteen bodies oiling
up, rubbing down, Oooooing
the clutch, Mmmmmmmmmming
a taketurning touch, so gently started
on areolas, labias and tongues.
Public fingerings of pubic parts.
And arse.

—Ahhhh.

—O.

I'm every pleasure. I am pleasure.
Every Lower West Side patchjacketed
kid running to discover the worth of
his life. And everyone seeks to
please me because when I pleasure
enjoyments surge.
Which I allways deserve.

Dec 21 1998

Sihanoukvilles' 1,000.
Knesset's 81-30. Khieu Samphan.
Nuon Chea.
Euro. NBA & Players Association.
Foca & NATO troops,
Dragan Gagovic goes.
KLA & Racak, 45 go. UN, Angola &
UNITA. Colombia quake, 878 go.
200,000 Bangladeshi women.
Super Bowl XXXIII,
Broncos over Falcons.
Amadou Diallo goes.
55-45. 56-43.
Clinton's Senate acquittal.
—*profoundly sorry.*

Leaving. Nunavut. Skip Away.
Anthrax.

Truong Van Tran's Ho Chi Minh.
Galtür avalanche, 30 go.
Olusegun Obasanjo. NATO's Czech
Republic, Hungary & Poland.
Lewis ties Holyfield. Argaña goes.
Melissa. Wang Ying-zheng.
Jack Kevorkian. Narberth spit.

On we carouse, through Cactus Flat,
Caputa to Mount Rushmore granite,
cold cloaked & soaked,
where freezing there
beneath such naked lips
and mist kissed cheeks
some ALTERNACHICS gravitate toward our Laws.
Nice, tart, experimental & hard.
National, Territorial, Unifying & Progressive,
along a Presidential Trail following only US.
—*Wait up yes,* ONE lows.
—*We're going with,* ANOTHER blows.
—*Stay together,* still ANOTHER ONE sharps.
—*Please, we need you,* THE LAST ONE moans.
—*Flake off,* Sam growls, storming ahead. He's the
way even rock goes. Off for a Crazy outstretched

July 4 1928

Lussier's Niagara barrel.
Angomoa & Arauco Gulf,
290 go.
7,000 from Shantung.
Obregón goes.

Amsterdam Olympics.
Tunney's Sorbonne.
Idzikowski, Kubala &
Samos. Elizabethville.
Percy Williams golds 2.
Haitian storm, 200 go.
Hurricane Lake
Okeechobee, 1,836 go.
Hilda Sharp swims over.

Kellogg-Briand Treaty.
—*triumph over poverty.*
Albania's Ahmed
Bey Zogu.
Fleming's Penicillium.
Rockford tornado, 100 go.

Juan de la Cierva, Autogiro
& English Channel.
5 Year Plan.

Argentina over US.

Ondine down, 43 go.
Chiang's chairman.
Poisonous liquor, 21 go.

Yankees over Cardinals.

Graf Zeppelin & 111 hours.

On tiptoes, knees, high stools and
rollerskates. Nuzzle and dance.
One Two TwentyOne osculate!
Three Four FortyThree mash!
—*Gather round,* I bugle. *A bath!*
Their fugleman's charge.
Hailey with DOLLY, a threesome for
moresome. What's to subtract?
Here's POLLY & MOLLY. Cloche hats
removed! GOLLY GALORE. Garters
abused! CHATSOUS HOLLY,
gores and stockings despooled!
Scores to defile. Sweet, naughty,
beguiling and rude.
Cases of Dom filling a pool.
We all lap together, everyone nude.
Barneymugging their curls, while
Them mollycoddle to swallow
my national endowment's prize,
dowsing for tonsils, hymens

April 14 1999

Lahore missiles.
—out of control.
Columbine High,
Harris, Klebold &13 go.
Charismatic's Derby.
Oklahoma tornado, 47 go.
Belgrade's Chinese Embassy.
Stepashin over Primakov.
Chih-yaun Ho.
Baruk. Snowtown's 9.
Little Rock's MD-80, 9 go.
Agassi's Grand Slam. THAAD.
Korean crab fishing, 37 go.
Kathleen Ann Soliah.
ANC's Thabo Mbeki.
Tyrell Dueck goes.
Hicham El Guerrouj's 3:43:13.
Atlanta & Cyrano, 7 go.
Rafael Resendez-Ramirez.
280 mass graves.
JFK Jr, Carolyn & Bessette go.
Robin, Damien, Steve & Louise.
Kashmiri. Armstrong's Tour.
DARE. Phoenix Liberty.
US heatwave, 200 go. Dagestan.

arm beyond the grasp
of anyone. Not even grasping US.
—*You're too Lovely,* THE SPINNERS chase.
We just idle away:
—*Time to give up.*
Whisking off
for bends more remote.
If only I wasn't so
frail & frisked, with just
my Leftwrist Bronze Twist.
And THOSE GALS still humping a boo bus,
desperate to catch up until Them don't.
KATE, MENOLD, NICOLE, MCCLANAHAN & SUSAN at
last fazing sorrowfied before what bloody sweeps
we proceed and precede to release. At speeds beyond
guts. Because we're. Now. Here. Not even close.

March 10 1928

German Nationals
& US compensation.
Britain's Malta.
Santa Clara River Valley
& St Francis Dam, 450 go.
4,790,270 shares.
Chiang over River.
Hunefeld, Fitzmaurice &
Koehl, Ireland to Manhattan.
Milan, 16 go.
Costes, Le Brix
& 45,000 miles.
Lockhart goes.
200,000 Romanians
& Alba Julia.
Chinese & Japanese
hostilities over.
Jones-Reid Bill.
Haywood goes.
Reigh Count's Derby
Shipping subsidies.
Italian Embassy, 22 go.
Coolidge vetoes
Farm-Relief bill. Chrysler
& Dodge merge. Smith,
Southern Cross & Fiji.
Chang Tso-lin goes.
Peking falls.
Earhart's Atlantic.
Amundsen goes.
Calcutta violence.

I'll arrange for something extra.
Something strange.
Something rich.
Not just this smudger, however
outgoing for the odd pinch,
but a choice bit of Calico Stitch.
Sling to the Big Band swing, I'm
Ready Set Hot to highfive dingdang
with my thingthang for the coochity
coochcooch de l'Orage. And despite
Hailey's Leftwrist Bronze Twist,
a PIFFLED PATOOTIE, beady
with fringe, comes over,
tongue tickling her
smolder holder.
—*Hey there comer,* slipping
her hands down my pockets.
—*You're swell too.* Hailey blushes but
keeps close for this
stroke & gasp grope.

Aug 9 1999

Stepashin. Buford Furrow.
Kosovo Liberation Army
& Bernard Kouchner.
Izmit quake, 13,009 go.
START III.
—leaving behind.
East Timor. Rachel Goldwyn's
Yangon post. Fort Worth's
Larry Ashbrook, 8 go.
LAPD's Rafael Perez.
Hurricane Floyd, 42 go,
Mars Climate orbiter.
Mexico mudslides, over 500 go.

—turned its back on.
Orville Lynn Majors.
Yankees over Braves.
Super cyclone, 9,000 go.
27:28.
Gamil al-Batouti's Egypt Air,
217 go. Aude, Tarn
& Pyrénées Orientales, 31 go.
Lewis 12 rounds Holyfield.
Alex Witmer & Jason Powell.
Elián González. WTO protests.
Tori Murden.

—*Kifaya.*
—*You're all I need,* Sam coughs.
And we tear outandout for Custer Swerves
on wild spirals, smoothly and briskly,
rounding menacing drops,
paved and unpaved, by Grace Coolidge,
to Sylvan Lake, Anna Tallent.
So fast, I just clutch Sam.
Until we come among what's only left over,
strewn across our way, unconsumed,
untouched, here lying doomed upon
the frosty dash of our road, the powerful
blurring we breeze past wherever we go.
Sadness. The wastes of all survival.
US, a havoc upon the land.
Iron Weed turned to scabs.

Nov 5 1927

Gray's Tennessee treetops.
New England freeze,
150 go. GM's dividend.
Hudson's Holland.
Petroleum Law
Unconstitutional.
Moulay Hamada.
Machine guns &
Colorado Strikers.
Garvey to Jamaica.
Folsom Prison revolt.
Mei-ling Soong.
395, Coolidge &
World Court. Iraq Liberty.
Canton uprising.
—revolution is not
a dinner party.
2,000 Marines.
Nicaraguan rebels, 5 go.
Thames overflows, 15 go.
Trotsky to Kazakhstan's
Alma-Ata.
Hoover against repeal.
Detroit prison escape,
19 to Canada.
1,000 more to Nicaragua.
Beth & Betty Dodge.
Anastasia Chaikovsky.
Ontario shafts.
Sinclair, Burns & Day.
Lockhart's 225 MPH.

Mooch those doldrums. Meet the
Colossus of Clout out for a swing.
American Bisons approve.
Stuff the baloney, Mustard Plaster.
Gerry Flappers, Biscuits and Weeds.
Laughter's the taste of my surviving.
So sure I'm hursty. Thungry.
Gin mill for swills.
Moon Pies & Meat.
I never chew.
Bite everything off. Esculent!
Then Cy foot for hip shining,
fox trot and feather mining.
Hailey so piehighed and mine
she just follows.
I'm allways the lead. Every lead.
Speedy and rough.
But with all she puts me through
Hailey now's
not enough.

Dec 4 1999

Albuquerque van, 13 go.
Goran Jelisic. Panama.
Barak & al-Sharaa.
Vargas mud, 40,000 go.
Li Chang, Wang Zhiwen, Ji Liewu &
Yao Jie. Putin. Larsen's sled. Y2K.
Ricardo Lagos Escobar.
Gustavo Noboa Bejarano.
Super Bowl XXXIV,
Rams over Titans.
—not be tolerated.
Alaskan Airlines, 88 go.
George Ryan's moratorium.
$184 billion surplus. Stipe Mesic.
Ulster's power-sharing. Majlis.
Congo's 5,000. Rampart Division.
New Zealand cups Luna Rossa.
Joseph Kibwetere, over 900 go.
Pistachios & Caviar.
Alexis Herman. Merkel.

—extreme wealth and
extreme poverty.
Mafiaboy.
US Immigration & Elián.

Nodlow sour Thankless,
I let go of our Despised.
We are the despised.
And we just pass on by
unsure.
Sam's chin dips. He even slims and
next to me waggles for me. We're unaccompanied
even if something allready moves alongside US.
Still. Stalking.

—Do you feel that there's?
—Yes, but it's okay. I.

Except it's not. Feer around US. Allovers
I can't shudder off even with shivers. Though
Sam's not concerned. Unscathed & Steady.
Relaxed & Smooth. We'll never pull over
anymore until at a roundabout we do.

June 23 1927

Gehrig hits 3.
Marines & Bulldog.
Palestine quake, 1,000 go.

Vienna Justice burns.
Drinker, Shaw
& Iron Air. Coolidge
& South Dakota.
—to run for President.
Peace Bridge.
Rushmore.
Goebel & Davis.
—anarchy.
—forgive some people.
Japan's wave, 700 go.

Nice scarf.
Jonathan Thompson Walton
Zachary & Ruth's 60th.
Tornado & West St Louis,
69 go.

General Francisco Serrano
& 13 go.

Yankees over Pirates.
Ruth Elder rescued.
Iraq, Kirkuk & oil.

Trotsky
& Zinoviev expelled.
Principessa Mafalda
down off Brazil.
Pan Am's Key West
& Havana.

But we do.
Though I'm still unsteady. Shaking
and scathed. Unscathed. Hailey too.
At least The Party's Ongoing.
And I'm the bee's ankles, and
bimbo attired, holding Hailey
up from wibbling spills.
Soon among Slackers & Punch
Rustlers, Neckers & Petters offering
egg harbors for laughs and some ass.
Harmonicas grubbing to suckle me.
How hungry this crowd.
Loud, direct. Mad. Barons,
Oil Cans, Priscillas & Cuddlers. I wave.
Grin. My hard chin
assuring.
But Hailey lob, fogbound
to this mob's danger, rankles
my anger. High hatty
without even thanks.

There's The Creep:

—You can never quit me.

The Nóose at hand.
And though I'm HairyVonSkitters, when
The Creep charges, Sam immediately
thrashes back, bashing for time.
While I, all dangly arms, twittering fingers,
go for a dirt kick.
Sam then expertly circles behind. Tries to trip
The Creep who jumps, ducks, slips aside easily,
and with feersome sneers nabs both of US
viciously by yanking both of our ears.

Pitcher Plants die.

Mud Plantains die too.

And then The Creep commences hucking
The Chain, each time heaving with certainty

April 26 2000

Vermont's Civil Union License.

Gobi Desert dust.
ILOVEYOU.
Israelis, SLA & Hezbollah, 5 go.
Vieques' 200 protestors.
Fusaichi Pegasus's Derby.
Sierra Leone & Foday Sankoh, 19 go.
Edwin Edwards.
15-6 & 3 West Bank villages.

Thomas Blanton & Bobby Frank Cherry.
Montoya's 500.
Kim Jong Il & Kim Dae-jung.
Lakers over Pacers.
Gary Graham goes. Vincent Fox.
Tiger Woods' Grand Slam.
Concorde crash, 113 go.
George Speight.
Epsilon Eridani. To Tangier.
Kursk blows, 118 go.

LA Democratic convention riot.
Clinton & Castro.
Wen Ho Lee. Bobby Knight.

Maybe.
The Creep shrieks this reverso, drops
the pilot to knot me, though I swan
easily from every throw.

—Slip, **Recluse Spiders** divaricate.

—Step off, **Dwarf Sirens** prevaricate.

The Game Official bows out.
But I yank The Creep's Wedding
Ring free. Mr. Lariat of spin. Here
a minatory Nóose. MerryGoRound.
Lie Down. Retiring. Ready
The Wind Up until spurred
over huddling hunch,
shudder & scrunch,
The Creep falls over Hailey.
Fortunately not before I loop
that Hardboiled thrash with
The Chain at last.

—You can't quit me,

The Creep quakes.

Feb 9 1927

Carmona stops revolution.
Sarajevo landslide, 600 go.
California storm, 24 go.
Tamatave hurricane, 600 go.
Japanese shake, 1,700 go.

Chiang Kai-shek & Shanghai.
Bow's It.

—am never guilty, never.
—because I am a radical.

West's guilty. Davis & Wooster go. Mishishishi's 30 million acres.
Charles Nungesser goes.
Whiskery's Derby.

Louisiana, 15,000 Acadians & 30 ft high.

Bath blows, 42 go.

Lucky Lindy. 10:24 PM.
Le Bourget airfield.

—Cette fois, ça va!
—Well I.

15th Million Tin Lizzie.
Borden goes.

Chamberlain & Levine,
Manhattan to Berlin.
Ticker Tape.

Sept 19 2000

83-15. Robert Ray.
Aleksei Nemov.
Strategic Petroleum Reserve.
Johnson, Pettigrew, Alvin & Calvin.
RU-486. Ariel Sharon's stones.
Vojislav Kostunica over
Slobodan Milosevic.
USS Cole, 17 go.
—everything to me.
Yankees over Mets. Hillary Clinton.
Butterfly ballot & dangling chads.
US, Tran Duc Luong &
Phan Van Khai. Endeavor.
Supreme Court 5-4.
Michael McDermott, 7 go.
271-266. Kabila goes.
Rolling power failures.
176 pardons. George W Bush.
—everyone belongs.
Bhuj quake, 20,000 go.
Chest scratchings.
Super Bowl XXXV,
Ravens over Giants.
Hawaii & Ehime Maru, 9 go.
Harlem.

that we're set. Huh?
—Twerps. I'm your salvation.
Your hard times. Your tough spots.
Without me, you're both zot.
You'll slip away and never find a role.
Time's up. Time to tie you down. Now.
The Creep slings then The Cord
around US both, something free about US
allready perishing with this bunched tugging
and tightening about our throats, our hips,
fastening US everlessly. Until:
—*Uh, hey,* I shrug. *This can't do.*
The Nóose is never big enough for two.
The Cord allready undone
around our looseness.
—*We're allways sixteen,*

Aug 29 1926

Nepalese slavery abolished.
Germany's League of
Nations.
Florida Hurricane,
1,000 go.
Capone escapes.
Tunney 10 rounds
Dempsey.
Nation of steak eaters.
Cardinals over Yankees.
Havana winds. Debs goes.
Myers vs US. Peritonitis.
Mussolini, Rome & a boy.
—Credere, obbedire,
combattere.
Marie of Romania quits.
Seven-car Chief. Hoover's
standard of living.
Canadian prohibition
overturned. Hall-Mills
acquittal. Georgia crash,
20 go. German
& Italian arbitration.
Remus Parties.
—Americanize the
Americans.
Peaches & Browning.
It girl. Joyce Hawley's bath.
Massachusetts Auto
Securities. NYC Stock
Exchange & women.
9 million automobiles.

—So?
—We're only sixteen.
To which The Creep just spits.
Geee, that frisbee toss sure scores shit.
Because we're allone,
we're unmissed, savage
and loose.
—If only The Cord were large
enough for all,
The Creep yanking it tight,
Hailey squealing with tears,
prompting something terrifyingly
dear, waggish & flip, to surrender. And
then The Creep with Cudgel readies
for button butchery: *—Time to pay up.*
Whereupon The Game Umpire
arrives: *—Your Trophy, Sir.*
Unexpected win off a wild play
now exceeding The Creep's
rack. Though how so? Stocks up?

Feb 18 2001

Earnhardt goes.
Charles Andrew Williams,
2 go. Workplace Regulations
overturned. Uganda's Museveni.
Arsenic. Macedonian offensive.
Soft Money. US & Kyoto Protocol.
—harms our economy.
Hainan's 24. 65-35 Tax Cut.
Cincinnati's Stephen Roach,
Timothy Thomas goes.
Khan Yunis Camp, 2 go.
—very sorry.

Stone's clot. Junichiro Koizumi.
Chandra Levy goes.
Kinney hail. Monarchos' Derby.
Nablus & Ramallah, 9 go.
James Jeffords. Castroneves's 500.
Kathmandu's Dipendra, 10 go.
Mamoru Takuma, 8 go.
McVeigh goes. Allison.
Lakers over 76ers.
Andrea Yates, 5 go. KDoe goes.
Climate Agreement's 178.
Super Bolide.

I sputter. *So Jainky, so rare.*
THE CREEP falters, jiggying back
such roilings, trying to regather.
Which is when, bravely, fast,
Sam just takes away the trap:
—*We're free.*
And: —*Sqwimp Dunks, that's me.*
And: —*No more Dude.*
And That's That, wrapping up such twinings,
leaving THE CREEP bare handed & dumb.
Except for THE STAFF. Raising THE STAVE:
—*Return it here at once!*
But we don't. Both of US putting up our fists,
lowering our shoulders, popping our necks.
Physically fit beyond fitness. We're fit
beyond physical. Beyond gain.

March 26 1926

190,000 tons of kerosene.
V Gibson &
Mussolini's nose.
Passaic's 5,000 riot.
*—navel up and down
and from.*

French War Debt.
11 Farmbelt Senators.
Bennett & Byrd's
North Pole.
Bubbling Over's Derby.
—sackcloth and ashes.
Democracy deceased.
Air Commerce Act.
Abd el Krim's
Targuist surrender.
Polish troops &
Workers Strike.
Pilsudski's rule.
20,000 Natives &
Little Big Horn.
Judiciary Committee,
Crime & Prohibition.
Weimar Nazis.
Dover Munitions Plant,
19 go. Filipino plebiscite
& veto.
*— had to be done
and I did it.*
Britain's South African
diamonds.
Krishnamurti.

I stretch, crack my neck,
my shoulders rolling
their worth. Astounding physique.
Forcing CREEP to compete, executing
several thousand
pushups, situps, pullups. Even
sprints past municipal limits.
—*Congratulations,* I concede.
—*Where's my Guerdon?*
—*Yours allready,* I slide. *At
your skirmish. I gave it back.*
—*No. You flubbed it. So the plunk's
mine but you still owe. Her.*
—*Hold on, you glued US that Junk.*
—*Nothing's free.*
And then I retreat, all jittery
and, well, cowardly.
—*Now fops, ease me a Season.
You're way out of bounds.
There're Feds all around.*

Aug 2 2001

226-203.
Jerusalem bomber, 16 go.
Cam proposal. Condit.
Mustafa Zubari goes. Durban's 160.
—bleeding.
8:48 AM, North Tower &
American Airlines 11.
9:03 AM, South Tower &
United Airlines 175. 9:37 AM,
Pentagon's American Airlines 77.
—Let's roll.
3,030 go. $15 billion Airline bailout.
—civilization over.
528,000. Robert Stevens goes.
Beckham's kick. Kandahar's B-2s.
Barry Bonds's 73. 98-1.
Diamondbacks over Yankees.
American Airlines 587, 265 go.
Northern Alliance's Kabul.
John Walker Lindh.
Reid's shoe. Sydney fires.
Nathan Chapman goes.
Charles Bishop goes. Enron.
Mount Nyiragongo, 45 go.

Chill beyond pain. So of course, patsy & dork,
THE CREEP's CANE begins to fall short.
—*Fool,* Sam stings a circumwithering
terror THE CREEP can't avoid.
—*I feer you risk too much.*
Sam: —*Whaever.*
And then THE CREEP allmost weeps,
all hum dillyla, which pauses Sam,
at liberty to banish so much
with a snap.
—*O no.*
—*Sure. We won't tie you up again.*
—*Grateful.*
When, sudden slyly, THE CREEP swings with CUDGEL,
scandalous batterings at all I'm powerless to slow,
arrest, prevent. Except all aim turns to FLAX and

Oct 16 1925

Locarno Treaty
& Austen Chamberlain.
—nothing will.
Billy Mitchell removed.
NSDAP Protection Squads.
Noblesville, Stephenson
& Madge Oberholtzer.
7,000 British & Cologne.
William Dwyer
& Rum Ring.
600,000 Florida tents.
Kamenev, Zinoviev
& Stalin. 20 million autos.
Carrie Finnel. American
Basketball League.
—the whirlwind.
Petting parties.
Izzy & Moe.
Berlin & Mackay.
Reichswehr's 6.
Wilburton explosion, 65
go. Manhattan winds,
12 go. Obolensky goes.
No resin pitches.
Utah avalanche, 28 go.
$388 million tax cut.
China & League Council.
Goddard's liquid fuel.
*—I've been here long
enough.*

Choking. On all fours. I'm afraid but,
quick on my feet, fly smiles
for THE CREEP, unclenching those
fists for a shake. My lalapazaza truce:
—*Scandalous Brooksy boy. Thanks
for taking Miss Storm & Strife
off my hands.*
—*Our pleasure.*
—*Toss and hike.*
—*Jive fer sure.*
I chuckle hard, wheezing too over
poor Hailey's state, backslapping
desperate for some way around
THE CREEP's horror.
—*You're pretty fit.*
—*Fittest.*
—*Sure, among dog jocks back there,
all barreled, oiled. But hey sport
you're not that robust. Patsy &
dort. Still, so what.*

Jan 25 2002

Clifford Baxter goes.
Lagos depot, 1,000 go.
—against terror.
Super Bowl XXXVI,
Patriots over Rams. $2.13 trillion.
Abdul Rahman goes. Derek Parra.
Daniel Pearl goes.
—leads US anywhere.
Operation Anaconda.
Burka quake, 800 go.
Rachel Levy & Ayat al-Akhras go.
Hebron. Law & Shanley.
Rop's Marathon.
Arctic National Wildlife Refuge.
Robert Steinhaeuser, 16 go.
Espinoza's War Derby.
Pim Fortuyn goes.
Abdul Goni Lone goes.
Elizabeth Smart. Surf orbitals.
Lakers over Nets. Karzai.
Terry Lynn Barton. Virginia's
Atkins. Hesham Mohamed
Hadayet, 3 go. Alejandro Avila,
Samantha Runnion goes.

bungles off around US because we're unwinding
The Nóose.
Sam, with my help,
loosens, undoes, finally throws what's no
longer left of The Creep's hold on US.
On the World.
—Foshizzle zup.
Might The Creep pass on?
—You'z all US. Everyone.
Unbound, The Creep falls down with the anguish
of all who go on without US. Wookaslump &
Dumped. Messed up. And because I'm here now by
this agony, how The Creep, discommobulated &
finally unspared, keeps rotating by our fingertips
until even there seized with pleas,
turns me free

April 18 1925

Osceola mob.
German presidency.
Sande's Flying Derby.
Canadian beer.
John T Scopes.
Sinclair, Doheny & Fall.
Chrysler Motor Company
& 6 cylinders.
Taxis & collars.
—brunettes more careful.
Santa Barbara shake.
Feisal, Baghdad &
Iraq Parliament.
American Automobile
Association &
Women Drivers.
Dayton $100.
Mr. Darrow, William
Jennings Bryan goes.
Smallpox vaccinations.
DC parade & 40,000 KKK.
Philadelphia &
150,000 miners on strike.
Coral Gables, Florida &
land frenzy.
—wet and worthless.
Big Bill Tilden's 6th.
Navy dirigible
Shenandoah down, 14 go.
Lackawanna 7.
Pirates over Senators.

never survived.
The Creep's close, gripping those
lips. Phooey, for sure. And sure
I'm blooey for losing my sip.
Hailey cramped tight with that
pushingest Joe, lallygagging for mugs,
until her pal flips her around hard
for the mazuma.
And that's it, I'm througha.
Slump. Plop. Awshucksing the dump.
Hailey, my gal, rolling steady for
seed with The Creep.
She even swoons.
The Creep croons. Except whoa.
Uh O.
There. What Creep's doing now so
casually. Hailey overcome by how
easily Creep will torment
her evermore.
Greek Nóose. Around her.

Sept 28 1924

3 Army Planes around.
Gandhi & hunger.
Senators over Giants.
ZR-3, Friedrichshafen
to Lakehurst. Chicago
speeders & cripples.
Stone ousts 10.
—What time is it?
Federal Troops & Niles.
Miriam Ferguson.
—Keep cool with.
Coolidge, 30th.
O'Banion goes.
Thanksgiving Parade.
Duke & Charlotte.
—grow better day by.
Hitler free. Klaverns.
Notre Dame over Stanford.
—revolution.
—of America is business.
Forbes & Hospitals.
Kasson, Balto & Nome.
Floyd Collins goes.
Presidential Proclomation
& Glacier Bay.
Tennessee evolution.
Sun Yat-sen goes.
Chiang Kai-shek.
Breakers blaze.
Midwest tornadoes,
950 go.

That's for sure.
Hailey! Where'd she squirrel?
O I'm aches allready. Golddiggers &
Boob Ticklers begging me stop.
Drag a sock. Gayly. Except
I'm away, over puddles of dull mash
to a place beyond the band, estate,
the staff. Outside The Party.
Over potter's fields
where something nastier waits.
Jeepers. Even for me. And I
am the heebiejeebies.

—*Don't stay,* warn the **Leeches**.
—*Get lost,* **Coral Snakes** scorn.

But I'm allways lost.
Impatiently calming
opening graves, wringing my hands,
chewing my lips.
Feel thirsty. Hungry. Deprived.
I am every deprivation

July 19 2002

Harold Shipman's 215.
Salah Shahade & 14 go.
Peri Van Brunt.
Cassandra Williamson goes.
9 Pennsylvania miners.
Tokhtakhounov's arrest.
Ratliff goes. Safed, 10 go.
Alvaro Uribe Vélez.
Elbe overflows. West Nile virus.
Mi-26's minefield, 117 go.
—Regime change.
Sustainable Development.
Gerhard Schröder.
Iraq, al-Qaeda & Rumsfeld.
—breathe Jess.
296-133. 77-23.
Bali, 180 go.
Muhammad & Malvo.
Anaheim over San Francisco.
Mossy Grove tornadoes, 36 go.
Hussein rejection. Trent Lott.
Minor shindy.
Typhoon Pongsana, 40 go.
Yongbyon facility. Roh Moo-hyun.
Mwai Kibaki. Ryan's 167.
62,000 troops. Tom Ridge.

of such deprivations because I am.
Because Sam can. We are deprisal's hands.
And Sam with his thumb caresses my lips,
touches my scrubby elbows, his
patience finally calming me.
Because we are unclaimed.
Sphagnum Moss up petrifies. Dies.
Woolly Groundsel tumbles down. Decays.
And then Sam, who allso needs me,
I console too. Touching his face
over and over, my hands subtly
pattering over him, around his dare, tenderly
easing him, slowly smiling him with cares. Even
missing him. Affectionately. The next attraction.
I could never lose Sam.
Never.

Jan 26 2003

Super Bowl XXXVII,
Buccaneers over Raiders.
—Columbia is lost.
101st Airborne. Picadilly.
Epitome pepper, 21 go.
West Warwick fire, 100 go.
Djindjic goes. SARS.
Operation Iraqi Freedom.
Basra. Jessica Lynch.
Umm Qasr. Karbala.
Holland reunion. al-Arabid goes.
Baghdad. Kirkuk. Tikrit.
Amber Alert.
—have ended.
Funny Cide's Derby.
US tornadoes, 48 go.
Algiers quake, 2,260 go.
Ferran's 500. Spurs over Nets.
6-3. Loeb goes.
George Russell Weller,
10 go. David Kelly goes. Uday
& Qusay go. Reed's 135 miles.
ECOWAS. Mozdok, 50 go.
Jakarta, 12 go. Foil victory.

—*Ever,* he smees.
—*I'm yours,* I splee. *Forever.*
—*And never again,* we agree. Ready to power on.
US: —*We're over you.*
Long goneing from THE CREEP for
more turns of a road. Wild & amped.
We're chears across fields & gully, pasture &
parklands without exception. Except US.
We're every exception. Exceptionally stoked
how we ricochet away by Iraqi forces, UN forces
and rainbow ravers floating civilly below.
Where's the spaceship?
Everybody flips.
Even if nobody gets a whiff.
The slinkiest gist of who
it is we allways shplit for.

March 8 1924

Utah mine explosion,
173 go.
*—No politics and
no outside.*
Republic of Greece.
Daugherty. Harry Sinclair.
5 years for Putsch.
Dupont profiteering.
Lasker's Chess Mastery.
Ruhr & Reichsbank.
Warren McCray's 10.
Veterans' Bonus veto.
Gold's Derby.
Army Bonus Bill.
Owen Valley Farmers
& LA diversion.
Leopold & Loeb,
Bobby Franks goes.
Japanese barred from US.
Johnson-Reed Act.
Native American
Citizenship. Lorain
tornado. Cardini's salad.
Calvin Jr, Tennis &
Septicemia. Battle Creek.
Paavo Normi golds 4.
—Common sense.
Dawes plan.
Ford, KKK & Patriots.
Marino's cocaine & heroin.

Absolutely all wet, letting me
allone here with only my steps.
Where'd she get to? Goose loose
without even a check?
But the band's boiling.
Airedales, Fire Bells and Birds
snapping my taps. Dumkuff Prances
can't even try to catch my moves.
Whizzbang. Muckymuck. Raceman.
That smoooooth. Up to Them,
I'd Oliver forever. For nuts.
So abrupt, I bow, quick to skip
out this blow from their
following chear. After my girl!
I hurtz something fierce.
By softshoe on flatshoe
slipping clear.
—*O stay!*
—*Marvelous more!*
—*You have US all!*

Aug 11 2003

Charles Taylor flees.
French heat, 14,802 go.
Northeastern outage.
Baghdad's UN HQ, 22 go.
Joseph Druce, Geoghan goes.
Mumbai taxis, 46 go.
Najaf, 74 go. Jeffrey Lee Parson.
$87 billion. Anna Lindh goes.
Hurricane Isabel, 40 go.
—*ELFs are mad.*
Amina Lawa. Akila al-Hashemi goes.
Montecore's Horn. Treadwell & Huguenard go. Taikonaut.
Smith's Staten Island Ferry, 10 go.
Marlins over Yankees.
Gary Leon Ridgway.
Schwarzenegger. Portland 7.
—*I am Saddam.*
Bam shake, 25,000 go.
Reem Riyashi goes.
Super Bowl XXXVIII, Patriots over Panthers.
AQ Khan. Guy Philippe.

Dayrunners for Throesville, we batter it.
All we scatter.
Deucedeuces whipping our cruise.
So early we find nothing we lose.
Our allaround escapes. Not US.
Scouler Willows collapse lifeless to the side.
We lose nothing. By Hill City,
Seth Bullock, Hisega. Dakota Peaks.
Yeah, crossing Rapid City too. Of course.
And everything goes down for US.
Yeeze. Because we go off. Off route. We're pleased.
The only ones unleashed over Meade.
Tempt US. Fuck it. Fuck it all.
—*Seksellent,* Sam clucks. It rains. I'm stunned.
We're free of so much.

Aug 13 1923

US Steel's 8 hours.
Kalamazoo ordinance.
Tokyo & Yokohama quake, 300,000 go.
San José del Cabo's wave.
Walton's National Guard.
Germany emergency.
—*Join Ruth.*
Yankees over Giants.
40 billion to $1.
50,000 quit South.
Height restriction.
Schick razors.
Hershey's gift.
—*The National Revolution has begun.*
Hitler, Ludendorff & Putzi.
4 trillion to $1.
Kessler. Cal's tax.
Dawes & Young.
Zworykin. Cellophane.
—*won't be Long now.*
Lenin goes. NYC pearls.
Chamonix slopes.
—*I am a broken piece of machinery.*
Gandhi free.
Gas Chamber.
Shandaken Aqueduct.
IBM.
Ataturk's Customs.

And only by Hailey shunned.
—*Huh?* I grunt, zankzink zigzag
tight on everyone's
Charleston clap.
The Creep with Cane and Hailey.
Hooking my sweet bait's hair,
turning her quick from my yoyo flips
with terrifying resolve.
Hailey wiggling. Giggling? Gone.
But I'm the only one
she
will get down on
she
will want to with.
Crowd nodding my tripleriffling rings.
Bolivian Llamas
spitting: —*Hurry escape the hurry.*
But all's too late, finding by her
departure terrible reach. How
I answer. How I gather.
How I teach this World to travel.

Dec 4 1922

1.6 million shoes. USSR.
3 o'clock raisins.
—Big whorls have little whorls.
Clara Bow & Charles Atlas.
Lenin & Stalin.
Senate & Peyote.
Citroën's Sahara.
US from Germany. Senate Immigration Committee.
—until she gets complete satisfaction.
New Mexico mine, 122 go.
World Court rejection.
Agricultural Credits Act.
Lenin's stroke & troika.
KKK judges & police.
Carnarvon goes. Harvard.
Dance marathons.
Kelly, Macready & T-2's nonstop.
Zev's Derby.
Bryan's ban.
Persian quake.
German collapse.
Nenana's last spike.
Villa goes.
ERA.
—Goon.
Ptomaine.
Dresden Bread Riots.
$1's 3.3 million.

I scuffle tiptap from table edge to
chair back, disturbing not cup,
serviette, saucer. Not even a hair
on astonished Owls and Big Timers.
Cakewalking fastsnazzy over
cultured Pearls and Earls who

  —*Nerts!*

keep applauding.
Happily Hailey's flat tired to
the rear, leaving my dancing sizzle
foot razzmatazz unhampered.
Double Perrididdle on wings,
setting flo with low slaps. Thanks for
the Buggy Ride. Paddling fiddle claps
with flaps & roll. Hummingbird
fast to a flicflop stroll.
The World stunned by such
swan flings for fun.
I'm everything restrained
  Boooooooomblastandruin
undone.

March 8 2004

Baghdad Constitution.
Abul Abbas goes. Madrid, 190 go.
Ashdod, 11 go. Ahmed Yassin goes.
X-43A's 5,000 MPH. Tillman goes.
Smarty Jones's Derby.
David Reimer goes.
Akhmad Kadyrov goes.
Nick Berg goes. Dessi España goes.
—brought US dishonor.
Mapou floods, 860 go.
Pistons over Lakers. Saleh al-Oufi.
Stonehenge circles.
—shameful for.
Friends. Williams 4 rounds Tyson.
Letourneau & Fualaau.
Hurricane Charley, 19 go.
Carly Patterson. Jeremy Wariner.
Hockaday's gal.
Cael Sanderson's undefeat.
Beslan school, over 340 go.
Hurricane Ivan, 70 go.
Vancouver flower.
Samarra offensive, 96 go.
SpaceShipOne.

Here to abort any
lostlastandloooooooomin.
Through Sturgis, Deadwood, Lead.
Driving towards protections unable to
protect US from any defense. Sam protects me.
So with him, I'm but US,
beyond the eager touch of Cultures dying
to achieve Our Open Anticipation of Life's Rush.
Except our refusal leaves Them to the mashup
of their compromises, now tragically
unified & organized. Just doing time.
But away we roll. Out of order.
Because we're items of time's bend. Smited.
Divided. Beyond all United. To the end.
Wreck & writhe. Skid & slide. Lie

Oct 11 2004

Baquba ambush, 50 go.
Boston over St Louis.
—unify this country.
Arafat goes. Scott Peterson.
Falluja, 1,100 go. Wisconsin's
Chai Wang, 6 go. Yushchenko
dioxin. Base Marez, 22 go.
Sumatra tsunamis, 166,840 go.
Graniteville chlorine.
La Conchita mudslide, 10 go.
Huygens. Abu Umar al-Kurdi.
Mahmoud Abbas.
—our hands.
—I'm not scared.
Super Bowl XXXIX,
Patriots over Eagles.
Jordan snow. BTK. Ebbers.
Paris tornado. Schiavo goes.
John Paul II goes. Ferrand's
crossing. Osaka train, 57 go.
Syria withdraws. Giacomo's
Derby. Tobias & Hobbs go.
Bobur. Villaraigosa.
Milagro Cunningham.

still. We drive by
lostlastandstrewn funeraling the deceased,
lugged by Pallbearers and Jodys. Heaves
our swiftness allways blurs beyond grief.
Behind the Wheel. Behind our Vs.
Behind every mist. We're every chilly gift,
shredding closer to every Drifter
we spinor off to oblivion. Depressed & comely.
Aladdin, Alva, Hulett.
Passing lane. Fast lane. One way.
Revolving rims overturning our countering World
over and over. On we bounce, tricked on fumes.
Krumped out for horizons of willowy plumes
from every snort our exhaust pipes broom.
Kinnikinnik Dogwoods dead on the road.

May 22 1922

Federal Narcotics Board.
Brennan's helicopter.
Rathenau goes.
Henry Wilson goes.
400,000 shopmen.
Coolidge.
Schenectady blocks.
Hip Flask War.
Dancing Garden.
Michael Collins goes.
San Francisco Tong War.
Mustafa Kemal, Smyrna
& 27 Allied Warships,
30,000 Armenians go.
Britain's Palestine.
Shopmen return.
—Bread first then
reparations.
Frank Cobb. Rebecca
Felton. Prohibition
& ships 3 miles off.
Giants over Yankees.
Harris Caterpillar Club.
Suburbans
& Station Wagons.
—So am I! It is.
—Mussolini is the
government of Italy.
Ottoman Sultan.
Clemenceau's admonition.
Carnarvon & Carter.
Savage skies.
Hitler's 50,000.

where clarinet, keys, banjo,
breeze and snare tickle
the swell air.
And **Five Barbary Lions**
bland dewyly:
—Check out the band.
Cause I'm posalutely wild for such
Cats zesty with slide, ribbing out a
stride shufflestomping shimsham
shimmy to time. All mine!
Toetickling digs, I'm so looose for
these hands, brillo, di mi, splifficated
on reed, brass & pluck. Dance.
So sure I'm blocked,
Corn Shredders, Hoppers & Heelers
who can't get hot.
I take off,
allready atop an air of dare
with a shave and a
Booooooooomblastandruin
haircut where

May 29 2005
France's Europe. Wheldon's 500.
O'Connor. London blasts, 53 go.
—covered with blood.
Dennis. Way's leap. Lopez goes.
Emily. Hackney. Granulomatosis.
Armstrong's 7th. Mumbai rains,
hundreds go. Notting Hill arrests.
Jennifer & George Hyatte.
Gaza. West Bank.
—change is taking.
—open your.
Hurricane Katrina, 1,383 go.
Tigris River trample, 695 go.
Gadahn. Rita. DeLay. Stan.
Pakistan shake, 40,000 go.
Thornhill Broome Beach.
Wilma. Chicago over Houston.
Paris burning. GM 9. Sam.
Peanut kiss. Alpizar goes.
Pryor goes. C29300 goes.
Cheatham. Young.
—I love you.

Hajj stampede, 363 go.

And if occasions collide around US,
we punch it, snubbing allwheel ABS discs,
leaving this tip: when the goings grind down
you're over.
We clip on no slower.
O and wherever. We whirl
a wind of withering & death.
Extortion. Mopery. Homicides. Chief Justices
rehnquished. Turntablists & Trendbeggers
sanctioned. Even State Park Officials flee for
any haven from the tempest our worries allways
confess. There's no defense. Because we are explicit.
Our encounters illicit. Our engagements
exquisite. We're the fickle implicit
the weary feer to implisigh when by halting we

Sept 30 1921
Pig Stand.
Giants over Yankees.
Triple-barrel gun,
2,000 SPM.
Sanger & Dennett.
5 Power Naval Treaty.
NYC Milk Dump. Duce.
DC Rotunda.
Harding's warning.
Henri Désiré Landru.
Southern Ireland.
Pacific Peace.
Debs' pardon.
China's Communist party.
—where is the omelette?
Polio. German slide.
World War Foreign
Debts Commission.
Paris Dancing.
US, Britain &
Japanese fleets.
Annie Oakley's 98.
—to run this maddest risk
which a sane man can.
Rapallo Pact.
Teapot Dome's
Albert B Fall.
Wu Pei-fu vs
Chang Tso-lin.
Virginia meteor.
Morvich's Derby.
Russian loans due.

Tough luck, sweetie.
I'm quite the berries.
So speedy.
Hailey rocks. Whimpers.
Socks down more hooch.
But I'm on a roll now. I am the roll.
And ball. And field. And point. Each
run confirming my yield.
Golly dolly I'm boss!
The Baron's loss!
A high mumuring with
loads of apple sauce.
—How exceptional! *—How Ritz!*
—So monstrously rich!
Charging goal for a
kitandkaboodle win. Except, rhatz,
I miss
even if I'm allready gone. Though
losing first Creep's Cup. No four
flusher but floorbrusher racing dogs
for the beat around

Jan 18 2006

wonder what's the trauma with THESE LOPING
DINGBATS & RAGTAGS. Armed. Poaching.

—It's just sport, SOME peevishly shnort.

—Until you can't return, Sam sterns.

—Hey, that's life.

—So you'll get over it.

Over which THESE HUNTERS try and forfeit,
Sam guaranteeing their bribes & transgressions
with a desiccation clawing skull & spine until
even their wills huddle outlawed beside
their abandoned caps and fatigues.

Sam's pleased. He's taught all.
O Gee! Round's around. Le paths Odela.
Me though, only a calendar begging for whirlds.
Tiring. Without purchase on even tricks.

Jan 28 1921

swinging for Knock Outs. Hat tricks.
Aces. Kicks and assists.
Free Throws to Baskets.
Touch Down passes.
Fans parading for me, Hailey timidly
hanging back. I'm all Them support.
Nature of Sport. Favored, Unfavored.
Sure Thing. Long shot. Staking
The Creep's PRIZE on me.
THE SCORE KEEPER wincing my losing
streak though everyone still toasts
my bravery. Ahhs for each Quarter &
Half, Chukker & Match.
PIPPINS sidle closer
halooping each play
with air kisses and sighs.

—Flipper!

—My Slicker!

—A find!

Naturally Hailey's uneasy,
so unpleasing to THESE WHOOPEES.

Triomphe's soldier.
American Relief
Administration.

—and take our pay.

Immigration & Typhus.
9 million autos,
20,000 going.
Ice storm.
Harding, 29th.
Sunbury skirts.
$56 billion.
Hamilton's fall.
Walter & Waldo's Castle.
Plymouth Rock.
Paddock's 10.4.
MacCarron goes.
Smiley's Triple.
$33 billion. Chanel No 5.

Behave Yourself's Derby.
199 loops.
Emergency Quota Act.
Tulsa riots, 79 go.
Arkansas River overflows,
200 go. Bromwell goes.
AFL. Chief Justice Taft.

Dempsey 4 rounds
Carpentier.
Shoeworker & fish peddler.
Mitchell & Ostfriesland.
Grain Futures Trading Act.
Logan County. Margaret
Gorman. Depression.

Sept 21 2006

So sad.
Around somewhere
a whirl of solitary risk.
And me by Sam with his
Leftwrist Diamondy Twist. To twistor off richly he
sure could but he doesn't. Keeps my side, sliding
tall, wily: —*I'm gonna do something ballzy.*
Along 90, through Rozet, Wyodak and
Campbell County we verge, rounds of US
gripping the earth, spreading out across orchards,
playgrounds, pastures, streams lumped with ice,
foothills slumped beneath frost. Enough to
drive me off. But Sam tenderly keeps me near:
—*We're all around.*
Shattering these copses with our coming freeze.

May 19 1920

Dash through
oatmeal mush for glasses on ice,
crushed, flutes of champagne, gin
fizzles and splashes.
—*One round of sharp sauce*, glibs she,
The Bartender nodding approvingly,
Hailey gleeful with cherry
smashes only to gluggub
at once both servings with a
burruuuurp for more syllabub.
Round after round
our Charlie pours.
Brandy, Glögg. Sherry, Bourbon.
And Port. Hailey gugluggling
the works with gurgling chugs.
Not a sip for me. Though thirsty.
Twirling my Leftwrist Diamondy Twist.
I'm ready to bolt for a crowd
roaring amateur Rounders
somewhere around,
terribly loud,

Matewan, 12 go.
Carranza goes.
Merchant Marine Act.
Shell's Long Beach.
404 Bosses. Big Bill Tilden.
Bedford 150.
Resolute cups Shamrock IV.
Villa surrenders.
—*bleeding World.*
Russia's Warsaw.
Garvey's back. Loyd's 19.
Antwerp Olympics.
19th Amendment.
Brooklyn's longshoremen.
Rappe. Shidehara's
Sacramento.
Shoeless.
—*ain't so, Joe.*
Pilsudski's prisoners.
Cleveland over Brooklyn.
1 million coal miners.
Reed goes.
McSwiney goes.
Hadjin, 10,000 go.
—*Return to normalcy.*
Ankle curtain. 41.
Hymie Weiss.
Chevrolet goes.
—*Civilization and profits.*
Man O War. 105,710,620.
Pogosticks.
Negro Baseball League.
Trade unions.
Loss of teachers.

June 3 2007

Only the most damaged & twacked
Teenage Wastrels taste the lip & tongue
nipping rip of our farflung distress.
On standards, fencepoles & chains.
Of pricklings now frore to take hold of all we let
diminish and establish. We establish nothing.
—*The crowd's thin,* Sam bends, steering by these
Ravaged, crawling for a breath.
—*Then let'S feed it?* I wonder,
our awful bolt freeing up for
such Dislocated, Starving & Failing a way to
slip away. Trail US. With modesty.
Only none ever trails.
We are all strays.
Allways astray.

Aug 31 1919

Garden spread, silver and silks. With
Custard Pies, Chiffon Pies, Mince
Pies, Ice Cream Pies.
Pies! Pie! Pies!
Bunches of Crumb, Meringue and
Cheddar Biscuit Crusts.
Cheese Tarts too. Crepe Hangers and
Sugary Tartlets topped with
Sour Cream. Whipped Cream.
And Rum.
Towards which my mockadite
scrams with a snort, cramming down
stacks of Shoofly, Chess, Chocolate
Mousse, Caramel Bottom, Egg.
Buttermilk, Frangipane, Vanilla.
The rest.
Yomps Beignets, Galettes, Turnovers
and Streusels too. Confection
powdering Hailey's nose and mouth.
And ears. Though I avoid all deglutition,
disgusted by Hailey's hogging.

Workers of the World.
—*anybody, anywhere, anytime.*
Southeast hurricane, 876 go.
Steel strike.
—*guess I'm all.*
Cincinnati over Chicago.
Volstead Act.
—*rid of this pestilence.*
Gary Steel. Arizona reservations. Palmer raids.
Everest goes.
—*entangling alliances.*
Tucson airport.
—*policy did.*
68,000 runaway girls.
—*revolution is repression.*
USS Buford.
Italy's Fasci di Combattimento.
Palmer's 6,000.
Herman to Yankees.
Couztlan quake, 1,000 go.
Ukrainian pogroms. Dry.
London's League. El Butini.
Esch-Cummins Act.
von Kapp.
Senate rejects treaty.
8 IWW. Ruhr occupation.
Butte 14.
Leaving Siberia.
Paul Jones' Derby.
Debs' presidency.

Nov 24 1918

—*fit country.*
Denmark Union Act.
Spartacist Revolt.
—*Yankee Doodle Dandy.*
—*Please put out that.*
Boston Molasses. 18th.
Liebknecht &
Luxemburg go.
Prophet, Tiger & Wizard.
League of Nations.
—*Vive!*

American Legion.

Zapata goes.

Amritsar, 379 go.
Hoover, Smuts & Keynes.
Jim Europe goes.
Java volcano, 16,000 go.
16 bombs. Thelma Jean.
Scapa Flow scuttle.
Versailles Treaty.
Sir Barton's Triple.

—*seek the aid of America.*

US from Russia.
Nguyen Tat Thanh's Paris.
Manassa Mauler.
Wing Fool explodes,
11 go.
Lynching Summer.
Godefroy.

—*break the heart*
of the World.

Snugglepup's bowwow crash!
New Orleans! My town!
Cake baskets, wheels and
toetoheels allready hep for
a fête and set to get cream.
Here's the party. I am the party.
The long scream.

I part Grubbers and Johnny Walkers
with my ducky barlow on arm.
Just overalls. Unpopular. Unstacked.
Obediently trying to keep up with
my attack past these admirers,
ooooooing,
clamoring for Popularity's Conquest.
A hem.
Grab a flop. I'm too fast.
—*Joe please,* I relay.
—*Sure thing,* nods THE VALET.
And flipping him change,
we pass by unchanged.
Welcome.

Feb 22 2008

Unwelcome.
Continuously unchallenged, unchanged by all we
legally & illegally dissuade.
—*Are we betrayed?* Sam sighs.
—*No. Just played out,* I try.

By Ucross, Ulm, Wyarno and Ranchester,
past a roadside jog of Recruits, marching along
with crew cuts and raingear,
shouldering packs, rolled flags and extra
pairs of Government supplied boots. We're
where these troops each want to fly. And die.
Our cuddle & caress, stretch & renitence whirring
now a storm fleeing east the feeling of you.

While Promises hang above the immortal puddles
we allways splash through.

April 16 1918

Federal Food prosecutions.
von Richthofen goes.
Princip goes. Overman
Bill. Château-Thierry.
15,000 shells.
Exterminator's Derby.
Sedition Act.
Dublin arrests. Mobile fire.
Amiens. Cossacks fight.
Labor Law overturned.
Cantigny falls.
—Retreat? We just got.
Belleau Wood.
—no halfway Peace.
Quentin goes.
Ekaterinburg.
—three days.
Annette Adams.
Fowler's Folly's barrels.
—Tenacity,
Audacity, Victory.
Fanny Dora Kaplan.
Boston over Chicago.
—I am of it.
Mihiel Salient.
Spanish flu.
3 million drafted.
Lost Battalion.
Sergeant York.
Rickenbacker's 26th.
Princess Sophia, 343 go.
Turks surrender.
—Down with.
Piave River. 11:11:11
War's over.

Off to her ring. After which
she irksomely stings:
—I can't ever come.

Again. Fokker her circular cocard.
Biplane Baron her cannister.
Sideslips and spins for ardent
hardened kisses, my largest trench
tool and cartridge, finally upending
Big Bertha and letting Wilhelm's
Warriors loose. Storm front's away.

Hailey so burning I must ask.
—How's that? You Jass?
—Can't.
—O. —Nope.
—How many times
you done it?
Hailey's squeam to divulge.
Then deluges *—forever.*

Dog and a lifeboat. I allmost snooze.
But determined to exceed her thrills
hold her hand endlessly.

Nov 22 2008

Hastily we go. MT Garryowen, Little
Bighorn and Hardin. Leaving even
Billings behind. Me and
my stormy guy. Unperturbed,
unturned and untouchable.

Him sliding THE DISTRICT COURT CLERK two LICENSES
who overturning both returns one MARRIAGE LICENSE
with appointment: *—Go here and bring your test.*

Weeping allready because we're allways so snap.
Bringing no happiness. Only torment.

THE CLINIC STAFF needling US then, crying, hypodermics
exploding. Streaks splattering across their gasps.
Covering every cap, dress and sash with our
freezing blood. Which of course TECHS check easily
because we're bloodless.

Sept 23 1917

Wilson's shipyard strike.
Guynemer. Zelle goes.
Chicago over New York.
Looneyville.
—dustbin of.
American front.
Bathelemont.
Passchendaele Ridge.
Bolsheviks' Winter Palace.
324 tanks & Cambrai.
MacArthur's
Rainbow division.
Halifax blast, 1,637 go.
Allenby's Jerusalem.
Lawrence. Brest-Litovsk.
Patch shrapnel.
Iron Fist & Sword.
War Production Board.
—Yanks are coming.
—for human liberty.
14 points.
Mondays closed.
American planes.
Germans attack Russia.
Mecca. Jedda. Aqaba.
Gompers supports.
Russian Peace.
—We need an army.
Browning Automatic.
Foch's Joint Allied Armies.
Kaiser offensive.
—staking everything.
Savings Time.
National War Labor Board.

Thrills then at the Wheel,
whirring for Cinch City, allways
grinding the turns.
Ahead, a bash with oodles
of fun. By a blurrrun past
Porters, Munitionhaulers
and Trams.

I'm the most of the moment.
Every moment. Seed for the quick,
the slickest of Ricks.
While Hailey's a waddydoo pail,
free maybe but frail.
A limpid fluke.
Pimply simply.
Tangled and teen tail. Bumbling for
bucks with allways an excuse.
Blithe. Weedy. Except O those
Gold Eyes with flecks of Green.

—And her smile,

Carolina Parakeets preen.

I slow. Pull over.

July 2 2009

Pulling away.

Smooth Azaleas dead. Windthrown
& cold. Sam beyond cold.

Green Eyes with flecks of Gold.

With me just along for the ride. Without excuse.
Weak. Tangle of teen by pimply cheeks,
which I'm too afraid to tweak let allone clean.
While Sam's soothing to pristine. The ravishment
of every peculiar moment, tearing along 212, 90,
by Laurel, Park City. At terrible speeds.

Because we are the littlest part of we
and I'm the littlest part of me.
And allways we will leave US
behind US.
Because we're free.

Feb 10 2010

Terminating gamillions on our journey. Sam's
Toyota Scion-S overrunning all static rebellions
launched by the chemically determined. So many
so set. Unflinchingly defleshed. Met only by Sam.

—*Thank you,* I mummer.

His rushon You're Welcoming me to Columbus.
Allen Street over to Pike, where we find
by the Yellowstone River,
THE GENERAL. Someway familiar?

—*At your command,* THE GENERAL attentions.
Leading US around the overgrazed graves allready
decked out with chairs, benches, tables & linens,
circling a stump covered allready with iodine silk
edged with hardfrost.

Sam so fantastically boss.

Jan 22 1917

—Peace without victory.
League for Peace.
Housatonic, Lyman Law,
Laconia.
Immigration Act.
California Steamer.
Smith-Hughes Act.
Jones Act.
Baghdad. Algonquin.
—Bread and freedom.
—safe for democracy.
90–6.
Hindenburg.
373–50. 1:18 PM.
—Over there!
Lenin's Petrograd.
Nivelle's Soissons
& Rheims. Liberty Loan
Drive. Free Ireland.
Omar Khayyam's Derby.
Selective Draft Act.
Liberty Measles.
Draft Registration.
Speculator Mine, 164 go.
10th Isonzo.
Espionage Act.
Soviet congress.
Pershing's Doughboys.
St Louis riot, 48 go.
—Lafayette, we are here.
Baker's 258. Hoover's
Food Administration.
Tsarkoye Selo.
Houston riot.
Bainsizza & Chiapovano.

Hailey's obtuse.
THE CREEP palpating his CANE.
Afraid, obviously, but dignifies me.
I'm allways dignified.
And every dignity.

—*You're expected,* THE CREEP presents.
To The Party of Bets. Please attend.
I don't request.
Only beg.
Handsels with maimed hands.
PREMATURE HONORS. TALENTS.

—*On our behalf I accept.*
And with that CREEP hobbles off,
and overthere amidst LOST vasicants
departs.

—*Thanky thank now,* I yazz Hailey.
Due to me we're all set.
But oddly, she's all looped. Weirdly
spooked. So I carry her back to
my Commonwealth Tourister firing
off Diphenylchlorasine.

June 8 1916

Butte 162.
—*Readiness.*
Somme. Mexico ambush.
Ralison's offensive.
Kolomea's 200,000.
Boeing. British 60,000.
Farm Loan Act. Armed
Preparedness Parade.
—*This is nothing.*
Casement dangling.
Chewing gum.
8 hour day.
Keating-Owen Act.
Adamson Act.
—*We want it now.*
—*One big union for all.*
Tanks.
Boston over Brooklyn.
Brooklyn's clinic.
Ford's equal pay.
Wobblies, 5 go.
—*US out of War.*
Jeannette Rankin.
Wilson over Hughes.
Western Front's 1,265,000.
Verdun's French,
700,000 going.
Rasputin goes. IQ.
—*He's crazy, isn't he?*
Fighting Bob. Petrograd
strikes. Zimmerman &
von Eckhardt.
Virgin Islands.

Am I that terrific? Of course. I bow
allowing adoration a chance to
breathe. Hailey burning, ashamed.
Slacker. THE CREEP, so surprised,
falls back, shellshocked,
except not.
THE CREEP's miles of
Machine Gun Nests and Trenches.
Social imperatives. Allways bidden.
Exquisite. And if
Booooooooomblastandruin
goes with this terrortory, so what?
I'm every territory. Besides THE CREEP's
fond of me. Ragtime cackles,
ignoring Hailey, saluting my
impartiality. Quick batch then of
Chloropicrin with a dash of
Dichloroethylsulphide
to emphasize my unapplied ways.
Of course congratulates me.
Even a CREEP's sometimes okay.

Sept 24 2010

Slowly I go over our nuptials while Sam on a swing
spins full circles, up, over and around, stirring the
clouds, before doubleflipping
for a toetip landing. I smile.

THE GENERAL salutes, frightened by Sam but fond
too. After all Sam comes with the terrortory.
He's every territory. And drive.
Lostlastandstrewn.

Many soon arrive.
Cripples, Retarded, Beggars and Paranoids,
tearfully & desperate, taking up stations
on crates, pews and logs,
avoiding feerfully The River's edge.

—*Shall we begin?* THE GENERAL bumps, setting
our PROOF & LICENSE carefully on that stump.

May 10 2011

—We gather now to forever bind these two,
The General continues, ribbons withering
with the growing gazzle, a harrowing
cold creeping out of viny woods.
He nods to Sam. To me. To these rest,
fidgeting uneasily. Commanders,
ADCs, Warrant Officers and ODs.

Something old. Something new.
Someway restricted. Someway loose.
Somehow allways familiar. Too.

Sam grins, killer elited with
highneck collar, cuffed polymer & grids.
Me, overalls. He squeezes my hand. His hair soft
& long. Lips tender. Virginia Creepers gone.
Ice and smoke thirsting and hungering for his share

who despite me lingers. Ending my
thirst along with any hunger.
Creep even touches my property.
Killing every appetite.
My mouth dry, bitter. Tight.
—You can find a Creep anywhere,
Eastern Creepers bite.
Of course I will challenge.
It's too annoying.
Too me.
By shuffle on snaps,
I slide for satisfaction:
—Go carefully now.
Past broken vats of Xylyl Bromide,
palleted crates of Benzyl Chloride,
and with stomp, and flap,
overthetop, kick loose barrels of
Chloromethyl Chloroformate.
Clouds erupting then.
Hailey cowed by my tocsin.
The Creep? Creep actually claps.

Oct 23 1915

Suffrage Parade.
Peabody char.
French 100,000.
German 65,000.
4th Isonzo defeat.
Washington goes.
Masaryk.
—Organize!
Simmons' KKK.
Joffre's Command.
von Papen. Standing
Army. Millionth Ford.
Haig's Britain. Galt.
Persia sinks, 335 go.
—fight against.
Dardanelles. Youngstown
Strikers. 18 Americans.
Zuiderzee bursts.
Philippine freedom.
—sooner we are
wiped out of.
101,208,315.
Verdun offensive.
Philippe Pétain.
Villa's New Mexico.
Mideast division.
Lake Naroch attack.
Pershing routes Panco.
Dublin Nationalists.
—We have not lost.
Border militia. George
Smith's Derby. Gallieni
goes. North Sea clash,
9,452 go. Waterfront
strike. Army doubles.

Sputtering amidst havoc, even
my Mitchell Roadster revs to outrace
the wrack. I'm nothing if rash.
But allso fascinated.

This vapor of human waste, bitter
twin to honey's gift, sets upon my
teeth a satisfying taste. And I want
more. Vanquished years.

Brutality's alarm.

To relish these fumes wrenched
from Charred Vacationers and
Vandals dangling Bandoliers.
—*Wonderfully sweet dear.*
But not wanting Miss Pipsqueak near
to lessen my reach, I slink off allone
amidst this putrescent seep.
I'm No Man's Land.
Turpinite.
Chloroacetone.
While Hailey's detained by some
trenchcoat CREEP

McManus goes.
Zeppelin's Paris rail.
Pottawatomie Giant
26 rounds Johnson.
Gallipoli.
Naval Oil Reserves.
Lusitania, 1,200 go.
Artois.
—*nibbling at Them.*
Japan & China.
—*not need to fight.*
8:15 PM.
Bryan quits.
Turks slaughter Armenians.
League to Enforce Peace.
Slaton surrounded.
Argonne.
200,000 to Isonzo.
Eastland steamer, 800 go.
Zapata over Carranza.
Vimy Ridge.
Erich Muenter. Caperton
to Port-au-Prince.
Germany's Warsaw.
Leo Frank.
British gold for arms.
Nicholas II's Russian Army.
Resta's 108.
French offensive.
Townshend's
Nur-ud-Din Pasha.
Salonika landing.
Boston over Philadelphia.
$500 million. Serbia drive.

of what longing must allways depart for.
Suddenly cemeteries heave with churning soil.
Currents bloat The River and gouge
the bony shores.

—*Will any here object to their,*

THE GENERAL quakes. But who would stay?
US? Too afraid, ALL dash for their lives, lunging
off for anywhere anyway else but US.

—*By The Powers beyond,*
by The Power Powers abhor, take you
young woman this young man to be
your lawfully wedded husband?

Except THE GENERAL flees too,
the storm's campaign lowering upon
Sam's Saturn Spin, our wedding and escape.

Aug 13 2012

Tall Corydalis flung up. Killed.

Coldsnap slicing across schoolyards and roads.
Even breaths ice. And slide.

Wild Grapes curl, burst and die.

Sam though, calm & reassuring, patiently
waits for my response. What can I do?
He's all that is over all I'll never touch.
Me just bunched up & clinging,
wondering now about the somuchmore
Sam with his Cadillac Casimir
could soar far for without me.
Even though he's my honey. My everything. My me.
All that need desires to have to expire.
His Subaru SUSY even overdrives
Hahei!

July 29 1914

1,200,000 troops.
Austria & Belgrade.
—*consult her own.*
Attack Germany,
attack France.
—*Neutrality.*
—*Impartiality.*
—*Fairness.*
—*I attack.*
von Kluck, von Bülow
& The Marne.
—*We have lost the War.*
—*clear out of my way.*
U-9s.
Braves over Athletics.
—*woman's body belongs.*
Sydney's Emden.
Butte Mine Fight.
Hindenburg's Austro-
German forces.
Raggedy Ann.
Aerial battles over
Southend-on-the-Sea.
French to German
trenches. Fortino Samano.
Triple Entente.
River of Doubt.
—*going out all*
over Europe.
Italy quakes, 29,500 go.
Blücher down.
Coast Guard.
800,000 to Prussia.
Champagne attack.
Total Sub Warfare.

And goosies & veers
recklessly through crossroads
without pause.
My Speedwell MC snorting steam.
Air smoldering. Roiled. It's me.
Gasoline. And oil. Fuel for this
drive. Spooning up HONEY.
Fuel for the fuel. Keeps her alive.
My OWeGo Cyclecar
suffering Rebel Girl's
cranks past taxi and train.
Until she reaches a
Strange Accident of
times, burning charnel
to the end. Variable dead
by Monkey Bars, Sand Box &
Slides. Melting.
—*O beware,* **Passenger Pigeons** climb.
Yet for this carnage, Hailey stops.
Bilious smoke. Dripping fat.
On which **Turkey Vultures** gorge.

Dec 13 1913

Perugia.
Federal Reserve Act.
213 Banks.
—sex o'clock.
—I'm glad to be going.
Pancho Villa &
Emiliano Zapata.
Five Liberty Nickels.
Zippers.
The New Freedom.
Trehawke Davis's
loop the loop.
$5 and a share
of the profits.
Tokyo eruption, 300 go.
Jim Europe.
Caillaux &
Gaston Calmette.
—There is only the
revolver.
Ludlow Mine massacre,
18 go.
USS Dolphin seized.
Vera Cruz's 1,000 marines.
Old Rosebud's Derby.
Sarajevo & Gavrilo Princip.
Franz Ferdinand &
Hohenberg go.
—Horrible. No sorrow
is spared.
—assassination comes.
The Butcher's
counterrevolutionaries.

Dragging dirty low, Hailey slogs
along cratered roads. My
Overland 71 pounding pots from
Swannanoa to Knoxville.
Still she's flirty.
Wants at every bend to take a bend
over. Pants, whines and begs. But I'm
all wait, hello!, Whoa!, refusing even
her precocious toes.
No thanks.
Though thanks to me allone,
she survives.
—Why the drub, Sassy Man?
Just a quick belly rub?
But I'm suddenly serious.
And by dangerous Wind:
—I Promise to marry you.
Flash follows, searing lime to wide.
Hailey's reply? Hiccups over her
shoulder, uneasy,
suspicious.

April 4 2013

Only then does Sam release me. Cheek streaks.
Chin raining. And I'm allone again. With him. By
our Worldhurling blur.
ThuuUuuuuUuUuuuunder.
—I do.
Chimes! Chime! Chimes!
The stump lost. License & Proof too.
Still Sam rubs my round belly:
—Heya wifey!
Kissing me, I kiss him more. Can't hardly wait.
Having a ball and wanting still more. Somehow
allso unsure. Unconvinced. Even alarmed. Greedy
for his caress, attention and populace thinning
charm, until arm and arm, we return to his
Lotus Event rumbling ready for the rest of our life.

Nov 25 2013

Ambidextrous travels over asphalt and orient pavements. We're married amber, frosting exits, closing down canyon roads. No load spared by all we leave. Spurn. Bridge.

There's not a bridge around we can't burn. We build no bridges. Just overturn. Bystanders eager for Sam. There on the outside! I'm dismal.
He's the elegantic one, graciously waving byebye.

Where there's a way, there's a Wheel.
And he allways Wheels US gone.

If allofthetime confused & ashamed
I'm allso game for anything:
—No more games Rover.

Flazing by Big Timber. Springdale.
Extrastate runaround.

April 8 1913

Hailey growingly grumpy,
failing all Rocks, soaring Taws
galore over felled Chumps lost.
Until finally
I grant:
—For you from me.

Parting such
Riled & Violent,
with the largesse of Empires.
Where there's smile, there's a wave.
Hailey, blushingly thankful, confused,
hands over the Moonies she can't use.

Immies returned then & replaced,
multitudes resurrounding, until by
my rule, their constricting gawks
finally snap
with a Fin histing for Dubs.
Every angle, from bottom to top,
ups, downs & drops.

It's that easy. I clear the ring
with one shot.

17th Amendment.
Deirdre & Patrick go.
Linderfelt's Ludlow.
Donerail's Derby.
—emotional accompaniment of elation.

New Mexico's grasshoppers.

Railway Clerks vs New York, New Haven & Hartford Rail.
Hudson Stuck's McKinley.

—We won't scab.
Heat wave, 100 go.
Frank & Phagan.
Keokuk Dam.
Pegoud's loop the loop.
Triple Alliance.
Heligoland's Zeppelin LZ.
Underwood Tariff Bill.
Highland Park assembly.

Panama Canal & Wilson's 8 tons of dynamite.

Athletics over Giants.

—never again seek one additional foot of territory by conquest.

—There it is, take it!

—rests upon consent.

July 21 2014

Passing Livingston. Along with shaved, lathed
Cruisers of breeze. Sam bounding on by.
Every Tug & Junk locking our way blocked
from our transit. Every route.
Just Married whirling above. Kites
tight to the draft. Shaverings streaming cream.

And when THE MPs' ATVs chase we halt for fun.
—*Kids, there are speed limits here.*
—*Not my limit,* Sam defies.
—*Aaaaaaaaaaaaaay,* THE ENFORCER tries,
collapses and wastes. Dies.

We're impossible to confine. Past all extremes.
When pinched by my Leftwrist Twist of
Myrtle & Tamarisk Sam advocates quick
a Wedding Gift.

Aug 6 1912

—bull moose.
Parcel Post.
Nicaragua's Marines.
Progressive Party.
Stockholm Olympics.
Serbia, Montenegro,
Greece & Russia mobilize.
Teddy shot.
Boston over Giants.
Balkan route.
—New Freedom.
Arizona, Wisconsin &
Kansas women.
Jim Thorpe.
—trying to clutch a.
Wobblies clubbed.
Grand Terminal.
Gallipoli, 5,000 go.
Scott's freeze.
16th Amendment.
Pujo Committee
concentration: Morgan,
First National, National
City, Lee, Higginson,
Kidder, Peabody,
Kuhn, Loeb. DC Parade.
—your troubles to
Woodrow.
—Men's hearts wait
upon US.
Harriet Tubman goes.
Electrical storm, 100 go.
—we'll starve under
the flag.
Ohio River flood.

an Aggie and knuckles down.
Though but for my shake,
THESE MONETARISTS would drub her
at once from their club.

Hailey commences. If grumbling
BRAHMINS still wait for a bet.
Hailey offers her Leftwrist
Twist of Myrtle & Tamarisk.
Affrontery. Extreme.

THESE ZABERNISTS seethe:
—*Away ragged tramp.*
Continentaldrift from our ranks.

Hailey bowls anyway. Flailing
with Commies, Crockies and Mibs.
Snoogers all. Though some bounce
and loft, knocking IMPERIALISTS
off of their standing. Efforts to
apprehend Hailey send more
Hoodles flying, donking more
UNIONISTS to the ground,
bewildered and achey.

March 18 2015

But I protest, even while Sam attacks
the steep towards Bozeman Pass.
Curious. Allready up to something,
resourceful & rich, whizzing coolly by
traffic, until suddenly driving the center,
he slambrakes and slides.
Smooth rearspin for gotoo thrills.
Screeching to a standstill. Barring behind US all
transport modes. Junkers, Grimmers & Tam Bents
turned here to an impound lot. Dead
Mulberries & Morels ignored by every horn.
And no wheel can pass these wheels.
Sam's Jeep Gluon flung across every start.
From Bangor to Los Angeles by
Barrow to Wailuku.

Dec 12 1911

Stinky & hot. Still I find her spot.
Hailey astounded.
I'm so smooth,
she's soon grabbing my hair
and scratching for joy.
Afterwards needs a long break.
And bipbippitybap my
Republic Four blasts on, smoking
the swerves, passing with verve.
If **Goldfinch** & **Bobcat** chilper
sadly too. Something forlorn
by way of this route.
Unrescued, unprecedented.
Undeserved.
—*Marbles!* Hailey suddenly wakes.
And I'm fastbraking so she can go
straightracing for a field
surrounded by MAD ROBBER BARONS.
Avoiding her sugary smiles
and impertinent walk. Who before
any can balk grabs

Roald Amundsen,
Robert Scott & South.
Cork tips.
Jennie Hodgers.
Kissimmee chloroform.
Sun Yat-sen. 423.
New Mexico, 47th.
Lawrence Massachusetts
& textile strike.
Flagler's Folly.
—*I am confident of success.*
Arizona, 48th.
—*My hat is.*
Elizabeth Gurley Flynn's
crusade & police.
Italy, Beirut & bombs.
Albert Berry
& Kinlock Field.
Juliette Gordon Low.
—*cloth with bayonets.*
President Yuan Shikai.
Treaty of Fez.
Titanic. CQD. SOS.
—*Every man for.*
WorTD's Derby.
Gahring's Waterford Farm.
Mount Novarupta erupts.
Kodiak ash.
4,000 strikers, Perth
Amboy & fleeing police.
TR loses.

April 17 1911

Ellis's 12,000.
Cordova coal & 350 tons.
Iceland's vote.
Meridian's Derby.
Standard Oil's restraint.
500. Alaskan Creek
nuggets. Nation goes.

London march.
CW Post & TNT kites.
American Tobacco
Company's 14 way split.
Kettering starter.
Casimir Funk's vitamin.
Panther to Agadir.
Pelagic Seal.
Unionville,
Monroe County.
France & Germany.
Frank Gotch over
Georg Hackenschmidt.
30,000 go.
Zach Walker.

Italians, Turks & Tripoli.
20,000 routing rebels.
Athletics over Giants.

Revolution &
China's Dynasty.
Mary Garden kisses.
Durant & Chevrolet.
Northern Congo.
Maine dry.

Huerta, Madero &
Café Colón.

And I'm off road. Wandering.
But I am the road following.
Everyway's a road by me going.
Evers, Tinkers to Chance.
Joyriding the middle line by Camps,
Chautauquas and Cavorting Dreggs.
160 Pale Oxen snorting:
—*On you we all depend.*
Sure thing. Whatever.
With a twostep. There's a nice plop.
Park quick to Tango.
Fly it with Hailey.
Fish Walk. Fox Trot.
An **Opossum** chikering our tease.
Dancing a breeze.
Until down
on my knees
I'm licking her pot,
tonguing her sling,
my pinkie snug up
her slink little swing.

Nov 15 2015

A globally hubbed hork.
Sam so glee driving to a halt the endless surge of
travel. Delicate pleasures allso surging through me.
Even if hacked Chestnut Sprouts lie strewn upon
the slopes and we're allready out of the way.
Reparked. Beyond this road block, nerve block,
jaws aclopping and popping over
such a pause without cause.
No accident, leak, something hard.
Just the peril of an unanticipated stop,
where Poison Ivy dies
poisoned upon our medians.
What Transapocalyptics will never suspect
unless Sam suspends even their breath:
here's our mess.

July 15 2016

Unified, together, across. By all byeways,
freeways, lowways & highways. Each corniche,
curve, roundabout & merge. US.
—*O some task! A traffic jam!* I gasp.
—*Will you accept?* Sam asks.
—*It's soooooooooooo just,* I giggle,
wild for this clog we admire
from our hilltop pog.
—*Jam down,* Sam toggles for liples & gropes,
generosity allready surpassing my meagre efforts to
afford him.
Plains Larkspur stop stirring but I try:
—*So blur & shaggy.*
And Shagbark Hickory fails while lurching turns
keep braking for all we're no longer there to deter.

Aug 15 1910

Japanese typhoon,
800 go.
—*New Nationalism.*
—*steward of*
public welfare.
Blanche Stuart.
Fishing Newfoundland.
Claude's 33.
Orchard & Hester.
Ely departs cruiser.
America off Hatteras.
Athletics over Cubs.
Naples wave, 1,000 go.
Johnson & 9,714 ft.
Berger & Seidel.
Schrapp's laugh.
Llewellyn blast.
—*When we shake hands*
we shake the World.
Camp Fire Girls.
No clipping.
—*The final aim is*
revolution.
Chinese Famine.
La Follette's National
Progressive Republican
League. McLean.
—*the canal does allso.*
—*C'mon, let's run.*
Triangle fire, 146 go.
—*Steal a shirtwaist?*
Blanck & Harris.

Hailey's turn at the Wheel, sure.
Blobbling the curve,
beefing a ramp.
Shuddering gas & stamps beside
a skydrenched Shenandoah ridge.
Rat Snakes histing:
—*Aspire!*
A **Woodchuck** crying:
—*Go wider for a higher course!*
So I take over. Take off. Fly.
Wings, wind & prop. And hot air.
Drifting lazily. Landing for a query:
—*What's your burden, Giggles?*
—*Dirty Shoes. A Chump.*
Chewed over I'm cutting
em loose. You?
—*Jam up! Cutting em loose too.*
Hailey laughs,
and greedily tonsils my staff,
clumsily nipping, mirthy rewards
finally overslippling her lips.

Corn gold.
Equitable Life.
Labor vs Steel.
Zelaya quits. Dry.
—Shoyn Fegessen.
Pinchot crank.
Latham & monoplane.
Uruguay revolt.
La Libertad.
Seine overflows.
—I am a Scout.
Eleanor Alexander.
Pourquoi Pas?
Canton plunder.
Ghali goes. Dalai Lama.
Miller & nail.
Pavlova's turn.
De Laroche's license.
Chinese slavery.
—day of rest.
Cannon muted.
Immigration Act.
Bwana Tumbo.
Harries' rubber. Briand
campaign. 91,972,266.
Boer equality. NAACP.
Birmingham miners,
145 go. 9 Kings.
Donau's Derby.
Halley's return.
Mann-Elkins Act.
Liabeuf goes. Arctic Tamm.
Johnson rounds Jeffries.
Curtiss fruit.
Crippen's arrest.

because here's so much fun.
And allready I'm smitehot to
bobhop for a twirl, pulling
my Moon Landaulet over
where **American Sables** blunder:
—Summer's here!
Yes, I'm Summer Sizzle.
The mighty pizzle. Wrizzling to go.
Hailey too.
Flip forward, head first, onto the
hood, ecstatically under, bottoms
asunder, over, upside down,
shizzling cute, lippling twirler,
dippling her chute, round after
round until I'm shooting my loot—
skyward fleets of billowy seasons.
Cumulonimbus. Cyclones. Flow.
31 turns. Hailey's all hooked.
Squirms. Another load.
Horizontal storms across horizonal
plains to alpine roars.

Timeout to stretch, couple and melt.
Nibble and gobble. Melt again.
Skies swirling battlebleak, sought,
while on the road tires still grind for hard jolts,
over and over, every driver agonizing
over a weird halt for only a halt.
Semis to Humvees, Abrams, Pattons, Bradley APCs,
slamming armor, grinding tread, crunches
crumpling knocks for this Pass's persistent block.
—How long will it continue? I stammer.
—While journeys abound, it can't ever cease.
But we are beyond ceasing too.
Autumn's here. Displeasing US.
And Morning Glory goes.
Sam's Audi WZ goes too.

Nov 21 2017

And the journeys are long over. Traffic undone.
Leaving US allone on desolate roadways sliding by
closed Rest Stops & Common Junk.
Where I'm afraid. Chatters too while
Sam arrests all he evades.
Nothing ever overtakes his liberating speed.
I just hold on meekly.
Nodding Trilliums bend. And die.
And with the sharp stretch of creekice comes
the faint dread of all we must now somehow
regret veering for.
Whims outracing purpose, whirling
ahead, amidst all the collision of confounding
convectives, dangerous flurries. Waiting there.
Even if Sam's everyway aware

March 4 1909

And allways flowing.
Hailey: —*Where you going, Foxy Fiend?*
—*Everywhere away.*
She glides knee on knee:
—*Peachy keen! Everything clean?*
—*I'm on the lam.*
—*I detected.*
But not what she suspected. She'd
splash my seat if I suggested
all I'll kill.
Ringnecked Pheasants quailing:
—*You're allready too late.*
Because I'm anarchy. Axes
and raids. Find me at morgues and
bloodspattered parades.
Still Hailey tickles my back.
My leg.
—*I'm allso evading the rest.*
Her too? Well maybe then she does
get how what I must do's
become a won't do

—pushed around anymore.
Warships & Nicaragua.
Shackleton's South.
Roosevelt's Africa.
Popova arrested.
Peary & Henson's North.
Payne-Aldrich Act.
77,000. Ada hanging.
30,000 Armenians.
—Let me live.
Wintergreen's Derby.
Veto equal pay.
700,000 acres.
Emma arrested.
Zeppelin II.
Alaska–Yukon.
Hawaii sugar.
144 Warships.
Queensboro Bridge.
Boothby by Morton.
Weston stroll. Azad Mulk.
Reno splits.
—Bully!
Blériot's Dover.
—straining around US and above US to crush US.
Swedish strike. Sommer aloft. Oldfield's Benz.
Monterey flood, 1,200 go.
Peck. Morocco Moors.
Peking–Kalgan. Ferrer.
Pirates over Tigers.
Racconigi Pact. Ito.
Cherry.

of how briskly we race and where
from. Abashed by his stamina & urges.
Get out of our way. There is
allways this way. Not even a swerve.
—You're my October sighs. And I'm yours,
to which he smiles, unrounding
balances of desire.

Sam's Lincoln Phase fast past overpasses
and Junctions of Trade. The worthiness of exchange
somehow spinning away. Past Avon, Ovando and Apgar.
Sam, Sam, Sam.

His Pontiac Planck bending the bends.
Value finally betrayed. Ending.
Because we're taking it all. Taking our time.
We're leaving everything behind.

West Point hazing.
Young Turks. Koepper.
Persian parliament.
Thomas Car encirclings.
Ewry hops.
Country Life Commission.
Edward & Ischl.
Springfield lynching.
Abd-al-Aziz deposed.
Thumb bandit.
Winston's Clementine.
General Motors.
Left propeller, 1 goes.
Russian cholera.
1.75 million kids.
Bosnia Herzegovina.
Wilbur's hour.
Suffragette storm.
Cubs over Tigers.
Taft's progress.
Hamm explosion.
Tz'u-hsi goes. Takahira
Agreement. Pu Yi.
*—and we can beat
the World.*
—Hit here Tahmy.
Spangler gowns.
Messina shake,
200,000 go.
Bethune beheading.
Virginia hundred.
Gomez. Crowley run.
—are very few of US.
Great Fleet returns.

Niggles the stew barrel, that's me
and my Baker Imperial:
free, free, free.
Chief of every cost,
all around, lost and never lost.
By The Potomac.
Around Dupont Circle.
Down Connecticut. B Street.
Arlington.
If snarls of rush merkle up
Trade and Transport crust. For the
tyranny of cush. And I'm every snarl
and jitney begged for and tossed.
My Model T klunketing on. Capitol
thrill. I'm Capitol Hill. Trembling
Capital's dill.
Hailey glawps. Dowdy drub
abashed how I can
move without appeasement.
Higgledy Piggledy.
So beyond Occident & Orient.

April 6 2019

Idiotic repeat offender. It's all my slack. Misled by
romance. We're reckless, far to dak desolations
beyond. We're unprized. We haven't a chance.
Though Sam's Ford Merge still
marches on across thick brigades of ice.
O my floppy ears, dirty cheeks, wobbly arms,
how'd we wind up on this drive?
Deprived now of all we might have played with,
remained with and enjoyed. But any mightifness
allready skids loose from the potentials of
Sam's accelerating turns.
There's only one turn. Naked
with the centripetal
loan of all
I never owned.

Nov 4 1907

Then with a bow which should end
the World but doesn't,
I slide onto Hailey's feet
Stupendous Slippers
of Cordovan Sooth:
—From me to you.
23Skidoo,
an unsurpassable fit
surpassing by every bit
Hailey's lamentable condition.
Suited more for piebovine clogs
she's flabbergasted by my charitable
charms, at once terribly tearful
with lobbly arms.
So I kiss her dirty cheek and
how her floppy ears perkle.
Back at the Wheel, I race
my Oldsmobile Roadster
reacquainting Hailey to speeds so
beyond the horizon of her quaint
emotional expertise she faints.

—All is well.
Tennessee, Coal, Iron
& Rail. Cornu's heli.
Oklahoma, 46th.
Mauritania.
Congo Transfer Treaty.
Army over Navy.
Monongah mines.
Nasir ul-Mulk. US Fleet.
Jacob's Creek. Vyborg .
—I want you.
Somaliland.
Farman's circling.
—No man shall.
Vanderbilt & Szechenyi.
Deputy dogs.
Don Manuel.
Danbury Hatters.
Anarchists.
Collingwood blaze.
Inglis heart. Asquith.
Chelsea fire.
Morrissey marathon.
Hepburn Law activated.
Stone Street's Derby.
D'Arcy concession.
Aldrich-Vreeland Act.
—resources but so
use Them.
Pinchot. Bay of Reval.
Houston lynching.
Shah Muhammad Ali.
Nizai Bey.
Gould & de Sagan.

Feb 19 1907

Zelaya. Honduras,
Nicaragua & El Salvador.
RCAG.
—*ignorant labor.*
Army's canal.
Hamburg dockworkers.
Petkov goes.
Japanese & Korean
laborers. Waterways
Commission. Glasgow's
Cruiser. Paris drivers drag.
Oudja & Muchamp.
Voisin. Guatemala
resistance. Manchurian
evacuation. Lady Cooper.
Minder's Star Derby.
Bengal riot.
Trolley collision.
Arab revolt.
Peking to Paris.
Schmitz graft.
Norway's 95–26.
South African Free State.
Nazarro's Dieppe.
Brookes over Gore.
Haywood & Orchard.
Boy Scouts. Harlem riot.
2 tons of balata.
Kuomintang.
2,000 Chinese. Lucy
Gaston. Iman's sables.
Keir Hardie.
Cubs over Tigers.
Heinze copper.
Pommern.

to Plumey Hats, racks of Taffeta
& Fleece, stacks of Silver Espadrilles,
Slingbacks and Satinbowed Heels.
I negotiate.
Offer THE MAYOR all.
But my Leftwrist Wealthy Twist
stuns him.
Much too much.
NAMBYPAMBY CONGRESSMAN shaking
head feebly:
—*Forgive me, your eminence.*
I can't accept such riches.
Relentless then to hand over,
complimentary of course, his finest
pair of Buff Chaussures, there
daring to outdazzle all.
These'll do. And
I'm through, though THE SENATOR
still clings. Hailey squeaking and
trembling. Until with a pinkie, I
shoo him back to his ESTABLISHMENT.

Dec 15 2019

And then Sam's tires lift off,
disastrously above all we move upon,
zinging US around and around,
fullcircles on this roadtop freeze, beyond control
of steering & brake, traction & speed,
do nots swinging for impacts which just won't do,
impossibly tolled, never tolled,
the way we'll total a somesome who
none will ever happen on again.
Cadavers of anguishing collateral. Gone away.
At least Sam's Leftwrist Wealthy Twist
spins splendidly despite this accident.
And my toes wiggle loose too,
strangely without tongue & sole,
my shoes somehow flung away.

June 12 1906

Maybe. Maybe not.
—*Halt,* I demand and
my Buick G jerks to a
stop before a
Sideroad Fair of Frippery & Wares—
Society's Share.
Everyone reveres the Dream
but I take it.
Out I go, top hat & vest, for
CIVILIZED MAN waxed from
moustachio to spats, allready
rushing to greet me, his tears
splattering my slacks.
—*Enough Sir,*
stifling his awe.
And yet for my handshake, HE
offers his business. For my back pat,
unbacks his future. I decline, shaken
by my decency.
Probity, Propriety and Property.
Turning then

Bialystok. Gneisenau.
Sysonby goes.
Nesbit, Thaw & Stanford.
Hepburn Act.
Pure Food and Drug Act.
Norge, 800 go.
Mujiks rampage.
—*my honor.*
Salva.
Valparaíso quake,
5,000 go. Stolypin.
Hamburg revolutionaries.
24. Hongkong Typhoon,
10,000 go.
Atlanta riots. Magoon.
—*mere plutocracy.*
Oriental segregation.
Sox over Cubs.
Elliott Key, 2,500 go.
New Hebrides.
—*curs & dogs.*
Liberia renegotiating.
—*the ditch.*
Aoki. U-1 submarine.
Caffeine for cocaine.
Schmoller's acquisitions.
Licorice. Kingston quake.
Muzaffar ad-Din goes.
—*The savage
and woman.*
Argentina revolt.
Larchmont at Block,
150 go. 600,000 tons
to Russia.

Aug 27 2020

I get out. Ice stabs my feet. Harmlessly.
Cold is cold is warm. I shrug. Sam
slides happily around our stalled vehicle.
I slide too:
—*Is it time for your Wedding Gift?*
—*O Please!*
I oblige. My fingertip stilling his prancing lips,
until stillness pours off the sky.
—*Shhhhhhhhhhhhhhhhhhhhhhhhhhhhhhhhhhhhhhhhhhhhhhhhhhh.*
Anywhere Them congregate Them catch the fall of
a pause. Everyone feers the Dream but he frees it.
War & Fray sure fumble but Sam, steadfast
beside his Chevrolet Outbound, undoes all trait,
gang, environment & culture
for continuing on dumbly.

New York stoning.
Giants over Athletics.
Hemery's Darracq.
New Orleans Fever.
Cocknaye rounds Reine.
Hilda down. Sevastopol.
Sinn Fein.
Campbell-Bannerman.
—*No danger.*
Amundsen returns.
Steunenberg goes.
Dubasov. Willie Hoppe.
Wobblies & IWW.
—*condemned to repeat.*
$E=MC^2$
Langtry carpet.
The Forward Pass.
Valencia, 119 go.
Sheppard's mile.
Tahiti cyclone,
10,200 go.
Dreadnought.
—*cannot possibly.*
—*warn the government.*
Hale vs Henkel.
Ustica. Burns.
—*never sets.*
Wilkes-Barre collieries.
Vesuvius. San Francisco
quake, blaze & goings.
Paris May Day.
Sir Huon's Derby. Simplon.
Weston's walk. Nixon's
ears. Alfonso spared.
Ricketts' ticks.

ravaging the flats, skirting
a pond and with but a Pippipity Yip,
wheeling on, unalarmed, kicking
over pebbles & mud.

By Fairplay and Marsh Creek,
through Emmitsburg and Motters,
by Appolds.

—*Hello Sharretts,* she glees.
—*Hello Fountain Rock,* I agree.
—*Hello Linganore,* we sclee,

greeting Frederick and even
Reels Mill.

Hailey happily carrying
out our overflow.

And this is allso the way to go.

And so everything else around
US allso goes.

Except there's allso my Hailey's
poor feet. Something
I must do now. Get her quick
some comfysnappy shoes.

Yet maybe still appreciates me? How
even with these barefeet I apprehend for him
the outer rush with the feeblest brush. How around
bases, by tents, barracks, bunkers and dugouts,
suddenly everyone just shuts up. Them must.
A suspension for US without explanation.
Because we're off.
We defy. O Bye.
Sam blighs. O Bye.
I sigh. O Bye.
Without breach, strike, onslaught, when actions
just curiously cease. Momentarily. The hazards of
an unanticipated COF, we're allways the farthest
away from, a Preemption that Tactics can never
expect: we're what's left.

Jan 2 1905

Wipe my hands and with what's left,
a Leftwrist Bracelet—
Priceless.
And there's Hailey. How sad.
Around her Leftwrist a Twist of Scat.
Me all doggy too with
scarves & long boots
while she's just rags & feculent
overalls.
O well. Goggles.
Nobly I let her drive.
She can allso crankstart. Her
first try. Bump & jerk. Sidewind to
wayside. Unbearably slow.
Still this is allso a way to go.
And so everything else around
US allso goes.
But what poor coordination.
Her clumsiness slave to
cabbageheadedness, scattering
River Otters,

Stoessel surrenders.
Mr. Gran.
Petersburg Massacre.
Cullinan gem.
Gorky. Hoch's 9.
—*not at rest.*
—*no Czar.*
Soisalon-Soininen goes.
Nifka & blood.
Aleksandrovich's lap.
Jacobson vaccination.
Mukden. Rotary Club.

—*duties to.*
Costermans goes.
Venizélos.
Customs.
Khamarsia station.
No max hour.
Pellagra's B.
Pickney & Brown.
Belmont. Agile's Derby.
Moros & Wood.
Nadashidze. Strait of
Tsushima. Lodz chaos.
Potemkin & Odessa.
—*One great union for all.*
Bureau of Forestry.
Hart 12 rounds Root.
—*refuse to kiss.*
Stevens & Panama.
Duma. T'ung Meng Hui.
Portsmouth Treaty.
Baku oil.
Italy's trembling.

Jan 27 2022

Live Forevers leave then.
Never to return. For so by every greeting & wanting,
taking & selling steers his warning.
For him. This stall. Sam's all.
Hssssssssssssssssssssssssssssssssssssssssssssssss. I appall.
So Very Vonscary, he swoons, happy for such scutch.
Wherever there's a hush that's US.
My pleasure. If allready again now
Hiatus turns away.
The lag revoluting against delay.
Forays returning. Raids resounding.
A way back to the motion of attack.
And though I'm by my Leftwrist Twist of Scat
all stinking with rags, Sam's
Leftwrist Twist of Forever reassures me,

April 13 1904

Petropavlovsk down.
Carnegie Hero.
Yalu & Zasulich.
—I am for Socialism.
Elwood's Derby.
Canal Zone. Cy Young.
Cripple Creek.
Tangier Marines. Tanya.
Raizuli & Perdicaris.
Nanshan, 7,500 go.
Schron. Bullfight mob.
Slocum, 1,030 go.
Bobrikov. Obolensky.
Meatpacker strike over.
Chelyabinsk to
Vladivostok.
Kuropatkin surrounded.
Trotha's Waterberg.
Statesborough lynching.
Liaoyang. Sheridan's
hurl. Congo atrocities.
Hottentots Germany.
Cha-Ho River, 60,000 go.
—No circumstances.
Square Deal. Yale over
Harvard. Port Arthur
assault, 12,000 go.
—elasticity.
Monroe extensions.
Conditioned responses.
Schwab's Bethlehem.
Samar rebels.
2 million bales. Ice tea.
Ziegler's brothel.

Out the yaperdoo. Rear too to dance
the kickapoo. Stinky sap but crap's
that. I veer another way.

My own belly tumbling. Amusing.
What for? The ride? Her?
Got me.

Over a trap, I perch & lift.
O Lucky World.
My gift.

Leading from my anus, stampeding
Muskoxen, **Camels**, **Roosevelt Elk**,
even **Siberian Tigers**.

Next, **Giraffes**, **Gibbons** and **African
Elephants**. Finally relieved Topaz
and Tourmaline, Onyx and Jade.
Coast to coast. Granite and Volcanic.

Psssssssing allso rivers wild with
Coho Salmon and
Brassy Minnows.

Brrrrp Cirrus and Altocumulus.
Rainbows too.

Oct 15 2022

bending rainbows, Lotuses rent, Starworts
swept up, Arrowheads gone filemot on sere bogs.
The howling notnot of detonations rendering
squalor, race, and the toxicity of crowds beyond all
asylum. Encounters mystified by such dying
for only a rattle. Grief & hurt cut down.

Trailing Arbutus, Rugosa Roses, Yew torn up,
until not even Downy Hawthorn, Junipers
and Giant Sequoias persist.
Our gift.
Lucky World.
How long will it last? Sam can't ask.
While we stop, it can never stop.
But we never stop. We only depart
from such amnesty. Weary.

July 23 1903

Passing through Gettysburg,
Chambersburg Pike to Taneytown
Road. By Round Top.
By farms, stacks and plows,
blurring fences and furrows of
handtilled land. Each way we go.
Until Hailey begins moaning,
knees TeddyBear clutched.
Braaaaaaaaaps rolling up.
Briiiiiiiiiiiiiiips rolling down.
—*O Stop! Stop!*
I oblige, gliding my Cadillac One to
the gentlest halt. Hailey, allready
fast from her seat, tumbles a ditch,
Splash!, circumstepping a **Northern**
Racer. Fascinating. And though fat
Bullfrogs jugorum: —*Nay.*
I take a gander anyway. To ascertain
my Pumpkin's sitch.
Out of both ends.
Squatting. Sick.

Model A.
Jackson's crossing. Babis.
Kiev, Odessa & Tiflis.
Dan Patch.
Fetch & Karrup.
Hay-Herrán Treaty.
Reliance cups Shamrock III.
Deakin. Langley's plunge.
Boston over Pittsburgh.
Russian fleet at
Masampho.

—across the isthmus.
—want the canal.
Lebaudy. Petropolis.

—sat upon.

Wrights & Kitty Hawk.
Iroquois, 578 go.
Mary Mallon.
Gonzales vs Williams.
1,000 dervishes go.
Herero.
39 seconds.
Palma's thanks.
Maryland disenfranchising.
Coal Creek. Retvizan,
Czarevitch & Pallada.
Missouri Kid.
Shemsi Pasha.
Springfield mob. Togo's 7.
Coal & Iron. Northern
Securities dissolved.
Arkansas lynching.
541 Achinese go.

July 6 2023

Encounters long gone. Actions dismissed.
Leaving US to twisty routes,
ever uncertain and disturbed and allone.
Bracken Ferns dead without mourning. And I'm
horrified. What stillness founds US? And why won't
we turn around, especially with Bee Balm
lifelessly defiled? Because we are irreparable?
Beyond the closures of living? So seldom of life?
Sam's Ferrari 720 pulling away.
O Go! Go! I O.
Howoooools troubling down.
Howoooools rolling down upon our thrust.
The sadness of the World after US
but we are allready before US
and sadly surpassing even US.

Oct 28 1902

Uribe-Uribe. TR's UMW.
Molineux acquitted.
Williamsburg burning.
Colombia's rejection.

—No bar to office.
Aswan Dam. La Guayvra.
Education Act.
Thérèse Humbert.
Ammonia to Nitric.
Jell-O.
Minnie Cox. Guatire.
1,000 Tuamotus go.
Department of
Commerce and Labor.
Porcelain teeth.
Elkins Act.
Gilmore's spit.
Undesirables.
Karmania cholera.
Coal Strike Commission.
Dry Niagara. Okhrida.
Kishinev pogrom.
Turtle blows, 95 go.
Barrows & Renault, 6 go.
Judge Himes's Derby.
Petty's Persian Gulf.
Niuchwang.
Turkey quake, 2,000 go.
Gainesville tornado,
100 go. Polonium.
Draga goes.
Corwell's George.
Jungfrau. Garin's Tour.
Macedonian uprising.

Away and free. I'm not weak.
The weak are not weak.
I outdo all weak.
Even the strong.
GrowGrowling, sure hot.
Spin PitiPasPasPutter PoP!
I'm leaving The Mountain.
East. I am The East.
Master of the Wheel. All mine.
From Piston to Rod.
Rotoring the decline.
No stopping this prime
plundering speed.
My StevensDuryea Runabout
freeing up dust. Freeing all ruts.
I am the ruts. And rush.
There goes I. There goes. Not I.
Allways.
Smooth blow these curves, killing it
dead, allways ahead, Hailey hardly
breathing. Clutching me. Terrified.

March 28 2024

So I grab onto Sam
who keeps blasting up, climbing by what's allways
waiting, mustering curves, exits and dead ends.
Here goes me. Here goes. Me too.
Roads crumbling, expanding, coming undone,
blunting US with rut and crust entrapped stone.
Until Sam's Bexxer 60 slows,
fast stops, enginings going tock.
The Wheel his no more.
We're stuck and he's my West.
But we've reached The Mountain.
And though we're not strong, the strong are not
strong. So we outdo all strong.
And weak.
And then by foot we continue on.

Feb 1 1902

soaring the sky, while
I gently sigh:
—I'll allways only come outside.
She thanks me, kissing my fingers.
Bites her lip. Because under
me she's so entirely unsure.
She'll cry.
So I cuddle her for a while.
Then lift her gently.
My Hailey.
So what if somewhere behind
US
Them shreds & bashes?
Beside her I'm terribly free.
Sure Them're still after me.
Boooooooomblastandruin.
But I smile because I'm faster.
For now here, weirdly, where
my butchered **Horse** died
and Hailey's betrayed timber lies
waits a Ford 999 Racer. Idling.

Imperial dissolution. 30,000 Russian students. Hookworm. Trieste riots. Baku, 2,000 go. Tillman's nose.
—That can't be done.
Colorado Avalanche. Tochangri. Polish schools. Sipyengin. Bocas del Toro. City of Pittsburgh. Dominican revolution.
—Undigestible mass.
Bengal tornado, 416 go. Alan-a-Dale's Derby. Pelée's Martinique, 25,400 go. Crawford.
—don't suffer.
Palma. Vereeniging Treaty. Oregon's referendum. Newlands Reclamation Act. Spooner's Bill. Twentieth Century Limited. Falling bell. Wollongong. Supreme Holmes.
—Take it away.
Gobin's orders. Ladenburg skirt. Agram. Roosevelt's lip. Transcaucasia landslide. Panther. Katalla oil. Fram. Yacolt Burn. Return Reliability Run. Mitchell's UMW.

Dec 20 2024

Leaving Sam's Sumover Linx to cold surroundings
we attack sweeps of needles crusting over
Green Ash, toppled. Dead.
Bafflements of ice to trudge across. Allmost sufficing,
Lostlastandstrewn,
except snow on the ground won't do.
We must find ours falling our wides
freely. So on we climb, puffing, fatigued,
until Sam pulls me aside and among boughs
evergold & sweet lays me down with
sloping kisses. All of him taking me.
I could cry. Uncertain, unsure, giving Sam's
nudeness my sighs. Gliding his lip. Sliding.
Until O suddenly O
I'm becoming—

May 9 1901

Stock collapse.
Morristown speed.
Salisbury's opposition.
Columbia cups
Shamrock II. D'Arcy's oil.
Nationals Not Citizens.
Vlakfontein. Becquerel.
Cuba & Platt.
Staten Ferry sinks.
Fournier's Berlin. Hecker.
Gore over Doherty.
Malvas. Socialist Party.
Venezuela's Castro.
Anderson slaves.
Carrollton lynching.
Battlefield's Armstrong.
Machias.
Oklahoma lottery.
Cresceus trotting.
Walthour's 15 miles.
Czolgosz fires. Borodino.
President TR.
Jennings Field. Columbia.
Steamer Hating.
—crime equal to treason.
Santos-Dumont dirigible.
Taylor's barrel.
—depreciated and.
Brakenlaagte. Hay-
Pauncefote. Alabama
disenfranchisement.
De Wet & Smut.
Norway vote. Hurry Up
Yost. Carvallo. Konia to
Baghdad. Panama route.

O. My. Hailey!
Not corking the chance to fork on
my Bindle, I ravenously bounce,
sweeping her off my feet.
Muskrats scattering.
Cast away blouse & togs. Overalls.
Shrugging suspenders, dropping
my wools. Leave socks.
Gigantic.
Kisses first, soft and hot.
Breasts bitty. Boggling. Until
hips grinding gobble me up.
Until
I'm sliding smooth. Riding her nude.
Sweating. Scratching of backs,
rump and sides. Jiggling too. Long
powerful drives. Perhaps too long.
Until. Out.
I release with a jerk torrents
of me, turning freely to playfully
racing **Southern Bog Lemmings**

Sept 16 2025

Flushed on top with tingles
now overtaking me, shaking loose
his roaring admission: —*I won't pull out.*
Not aside but this time
remaining gigantic up my thighs.
I can't breathe, pricklings overflowing me,
until I scratch, paw and sob against
my sorry palms with my first
heave releasing everything I'm allready
allways coming to him for:
my appetite, my time. Our unbuttoned bellies
wiggling each cool, kisses smooth, sidling smiles,
while I still carry on crying even when
we continue our ascent, overalls on,
by fuscous slicks of Sticky Geraniums.

Though this ragamuffin?
Hordes to those loins!? Hers?!
And still I'm steady.
Some steps merely to shed my
surprise. But that rattypuffin?
Summer assaults?
Placidly ambling I greet nine
Western WoodPewees up a tree.
—*Who cares? Leave her be.*
Some wandering **Kit Foxes**
snort:
—*She's out of your league.*
While a **Striped Skunk**
peevishly exhorts:
—*If you're not with her,*
Them's gonna get you. And her.
And she has the HONEY too.
Is it ever too late
to destroy the World?
Then surprisingly Hailey sadsighs
and hands me the pack.

Aug 10 1900

Davis. Peking.
Powers & Goebel.
Carroll's mosquito.
Greyling grippe.
Dublin Nationalists.
Amur's 5,000.
Bobs' Transvaal.
Galveston hurricane,
8,000 go.
Bostwick's rush.
Minnesota primary.
Loubet pardons Dreyfus.
Arthur Griffith.
Reed's Fever. Boer
Republic. Salisbury &
Hatzfeld. Khaki election.
Chartenus. David Fag.
Catalonia Carlos.
—*Isn't that fine.*
Kitchener's concentration.
Jenner goes. Porter's stake.
Tennessee tornado, 50 go.
Mercier's attack. Planck.
Cudahy.
Nation & Nethersole.
Spindletop gusher.
—*burden over to you.*
Yaqui. Chi-Hsin
& Hsu Cheng-yu go.
Bogolepov goes.
Pobyedonstzev.
Aquinaldo seized.
Mercedes Jellinek.
His Eminence's Derby.
Tinio surrenders.
Jacksonville fire.

June 13 2026

I carry the pack
of all we have. Just a taste.
Because I Love him
and it's never too late to keep a World.
So we're tender with our honeymoon
and all we guard, laid to ruin upon this
plated snow, fixing water & flame. Lands bound.
Airs tamed. Undertaking paths
by petrified Primrose,
our only course no longer untried.
Sam, my Federation, ever peacefully by me,
hiking over Soft Elm charred, dead,
up these cold grades, towards our sumiblity,
barely touching such sifting grains
allways drifting down these slopes.

Dec 12 1899

Samoa.
Botha's Colenso.
Boston Back Bay.
Delhi thirst. Kansas corn.
Peavey's Folly.
—shores hitherto bloody.
Blossom.
Hatfields & McCoys.
Gibson Girl. Tenements.
Prosperity Panic.
Germany strikes.
Redmond revolt.
—Carry a big stick.
American League.
Buller's Ladysmith.
Czar's Finland.
Bloemfontein.
Gold Standard. East River
passage. Golden stool.
Colorado River. Foraker.
Ottawa & Hull.
Honolulu plague.
Casey Jones goes.
Lieutenant Gibson's
Derby. Boxer Rebellion.
Lake blaze. Deutschland III.
Tirpitz fleet.
Harmonious Fists.
Cape Coast.
Hoboken pier, 200 go.
LZ-3D1. Doherty over
Smith. Sandras.
Angelo Bresci,
Humbert goes.
Salsou misses.

if gawpingly flushed, presses me to
share. Uncertain. Maybe.
But I fancy her
so I spare nothing.
Naturally.
—*And you my dear?* I politely redare.
Hailey hitches & mmmbles,
but doesn't refrain.
— *Laid allot by every Boss, Boodle,*
Immigrant, Native & Galoot. By
Breakerboys, Oil Rich, Railhands,
Convicts. One for the great bunch.
By turn and at once. Even gals.
Wooed, forced, scorned, adored. Pals,
perverts. The bored. Nothing to lose.
None of me at any time untouched.
Repeatedly.
Unexpected.
Of course I'm unruffled.
By me who's everybody else
anyway?

March 12 2027

And all the while laughing,
happy, dancing. Terrifyingly expert,
the mobilization of his way.
His chuckles hurling typhoons. Smiles releasing plagues.
Quakes just by rocking a hand. Brows mauling arctic
currents, headturns storming cosmic years.
Continental sieges and deep galactic colds.
Sparing only me, giddily,
because his attraction is too fleeting to lose.
We follow our fleeting arrivals together,
joined beyond value, unlinked links
forever relinked by all ways we've lost now,
all I'm new to, new by, streaking
over all we'll never again have
the time to return for.

Feb 6 1899

And Hailey drools & pools on,
tongue spooning for
more. With ankles & knees,
wrapping me quick.
Rolling me up & down, with a
backaround and no please.
Until panting I lull.
—*Whoa, Cherry Gal*
take five. I won't
run out.
She nods, chompmunching
the air. Any whiff breathed
by me.
—*You done this before?*
she quizicks.
Me?! Do I get around? I'm the
desired surrender of every Doll
and Long Ear. Curls the circle over,
wanton, far, feeble, near, weep to
encounter me. Even once.
But Hailey, still curious,

One vote ratification.
Mariana, Caroline
& Pelew.
Federal elections.
Ice floats & Mishishishi.
Third Isthmian
Canal Commission.
Dover to Boulogne.
MacArthur & Malolos.

—*we do not admire the*
man of timid peace.

Otis rejects.

Manuel's Derby.
Hague Conference.
Geneva Convention.
Wilcox Station
& Wild Bunch.
Charles Murphy's ride.
Turin Fiat.
Sonoda & Nishijima.
Alger's dereliction of
duty. Ford's Detroit.

—*Criminal aggression.*

John Hay's Free Trade.
Ragtime King.
British Guiana–Venezuela.
McKinley's wheels.
Boers & Glencoe, Natal.
Columbia cups Shamrock.
Joubert's
Nicholson's Nek.
Luzon, 8,000 civilized.
Governor Brady's State.

Dec 11 2027

And after those subtle steps, all will follow
relentlessly, if never occurving to
him, unapproached, unruffled.
Whichever way he travels US.
Among these frosty whispurrs.
—*Will anything outlast all?* he wonders.
—*No,* I gruntgasp, scrambling to catch up,
the slow wade holding me up, while
he keeps flitting our outandup with
buoyant skips and turns.
I grumble: —*Hey won't you wait up, please?*
—*Why my sweety,* he about faces, so I can
eventually, coughing & steamiling, clutch
his knees, cling his waist, embrace the spin
of our ever contesting pace.

Sept 11 2028

Beneath limbs bent by the briefest wait
of all we fail to prolong.
Here surrounded by crystal falls & flakes.
How is it though,
with him close, I still feel so partial?
How with kisses, long ones,
do I kiss longing for still more of Sam?
So profound his taste, I barely turn.
So profound his taste, I unbravely return.
Until snowsurrounded he kisses my fingers
and retrieves for US our last jar
of HONEY. All we've left.
Not half enough to crave.
Not half enough to save.
Just half.

Swoon and drool O butter girl.
from ear lobe to neck nape.
down with a swizzle round
I'm darb for this babe, steaming
kiss her extra.
exchanges, I generously
acquainted with these tender
And since Hailey's so fresh
Lips, lip and cheek.
Half kisses.
A dozen kisses competing.
She rises. So profound my taste.
She faints. So profound my taste.
I kiss her back then.
Sunnysurrounded
untroubling meat, she'd starve.
Without which, such dear
Bringing appetite too.
ecstasy I bring her.
swallows every squirty
Half a Jar goes. She greedily

May 12 1898

Navy & San Juan.
Battleship Oregon.
Santiago &
Merrimac blockade.
100 Days.
Guantánamo landing.
Guitterez, Glass & Guam.
Las Guasimas.
TR, 10th Cavalry &
San Juan Heights.
—*Follow me!*
Rough Riders &
Kettle Hill.
—*Bully time.*
Puerto Rico & Yanquis.
War over.
Manila Falls & 20.
Kitchener at Omdurman.
Blumenschein & Taos.
Cixi.
Anvil to Nome.
Virden scabs.
George of Crete.
Portland sinks, 163 goes.
Treaty of Paris.
—*A splendid little.*
Brad's drink.
Gatling's 3,000.
Heroin. Frères.
Cuban Liberty.
—*A strenuous life.*
Schurman's post.
Filipinos & freedom.

June 15 2029

Honey's departing power,

with Mistletoe gone,

joining our snowastounded lips with an awful
ache only I follow. Sam beyond such
savage separation. Our Jar over.
Uncapped, unwaxed, timetrapped
stickiness of some no more.
—*Let'S move on,* he grins uneasily.
And uneasily I move after him
towards cries of compacting ice, a higher razing of
our weather's colder grind. Coulds now turning
upon the vagueness of our climb. Vagaries without
a place for Directives until he halts sharply.
Surprised. Shepherd's Purse dead for feer.
Because yes! not all is death here.

July 17 1897

deprived of all dignity, flyblown
and bloating, unburdening no
burden, septic meat upon which
Blow Fly Maggots feast:
—*We're the cleanup crew.*
Hailey blithers forth tears. Snot.
Not me, no niminypiminy, I'm
manly, serene, fantastically
handsome. Soon finding amidst
this slaughter a Strange Pack which
under brass buckle & flap offers:
Jars! One dozen Jars!
Twinewrapped with
plugs of smooth wax.
I decap one. Certainly vile. I give
it to Hailey. Savagely she noses
a scoop. Then fingers her mouth.
Sunnyastounded kisses my mouth.
Storks bliss:
—*Consume only this.*
Honey!

Yukon Gold Rush.
Argonaut I. Tremont.
Hazelton & Latimer.
—*Yes Virginia.*
Wilhelm der Grosse.
Evangelina. The Butcher
& reconcentration.
Marshall Field
Company's tock.
Jiaozhou occupation.
Constantinople Peace.
Niagara Bridge.
GrapeNuts.
—*I'll furnish the War.*
Electrons & Stanley
Steamers.
5 Boroughs.
—*J'accuse.*
Havana Harbor & Morro.
Butter & Egg Board.
9:40 PM & Maine, 269 go.
Supreme Court & Utah.
—*the Maine!*
Weihaiwei & Kowloon.
Citizen Wong Kim Ark.
Volunteer Army Act.
Nashville
& Buena Ventura.
—*whip the dagos.*
Dewey destroys fleet.
—*fire when ready,*
Gridley.
Plaudit's Derby.

—without feer.

Treaty of Addis Ababa.
McKinley.
Emancipation Run,
33 vehicles & Flag Act.
Nicholas & Brooklyn
Skating Clubs.
1/3 owns 7/8th.
Diamond Match.
Montana's Lamonte.
Wanamaker's emporium.
Carver's peanuts &
sweet potatoes.
MH Cannon.
Alderman Sidney's
ladies. Crete & Greece.
Cleveland &
immigration restriction.
—We want no Wars
of conquest.
US vs Trans-Missouri
Freight Association.
Hammud bin
Mohammed's slavery.
Typhoon II's Derby.
American relief & Cuba.

—The supreme
triumph of War.
Alaskan criminal codes.
Debs & Berger.
Macleay Park.
75,000 coal miners strike.
Dingley Tariff Bill.

Yammer & yabber, this girl is all
jabber. Deluge of thanks. More
oblivious yanks. Expected. But
sheesh what a scrub.
—*Without you I'd perish,* she grubs.
Your presence allone salvates
my mug.
I nod. That's a given
I'm her stoic. Tectonic heroic,
accepting such gratitude mildly.
—*Your whatevers amuse,*
I crumb her.
When abruptly there,
what we pass around,
slumped to the ground,
a crop of tortured bones, agony
of all I skitter by so easily.
My **Horse**! At last.
Unlasting. Sad corpse.
Beside timber & rot,
allso unnaturally cut,

There upon
burning crest, palms aflame, bark convalesced,
my Silver Birch!,
scowling upon my distress over this crumbling stuff,
whickering with disgust, limbs free from such
fluff, offering me her strength, stretch
and stand off.
Which I refuse by holding onto Sam,
so leaving behind all of me.
Higher on, to alpine groves, glades of powder.
Avalanche chutes we cross over.
Oblivious to all to all Wishing oblivion.
Sam's my oblivion. For once. And allways.
Beyond even time's front. Because now
we are out of time. We are at once.

Dec 25 2030

Ever around. Over the World. Down, yup and up.
We reach the top where cottony air threatens
blizzards. Sam allready rejoicing, rounding, carefree,
lying back on this summit plateau,
while I cartwheel off, finding too quick
the vertical precipice, here, near, a jagged drop
slick with sharp ice.

—Ooooooooeeeeee!

Dangerously edgy. A slippery ledge. Which I scramble
to avoid, Sam's end, upon my heels,
offering no way to freeze my whirls, sliding stupidly
towards what I can't prevent, fail to arrest,
until abruptly with a plunge of feer

I fall.

Jan 18 1896

If up ahead,
a warming labor, thousands
of **Honey Bees**.
Gentle wings and pollen sacs,
spread out before Hailey
whose turns oddly someway
soften Breezes and Wax.
Aerials and roundoffs.
But should she, her waif feet and
hands, curvings confused,
ever meet these sad bees—
O what hurt!
Hailey, too stupid though, back
handsprings ahead!, obligating me
to commence warning my friends,
bzzzzzing then joyously for me,
abandoning anther & bud,
to scatter the wind
where alltogether we reel with
her round wonder of palms
leading everyone somehow
feerlessly on.

Francis Scott, Coomassie, Ashanti & Prempeh. Grubbe's X. Crete's revolution. Boise Canal & Diggers.
Rio Grande, Fitzsimmon KOs Maher. Charles King's Detroit. Oklahoma & Texas. Nicaragua revolution. Panathenaic Olympics.
Plessy vs Ferguson. *—Separate but equal.* Ben Brush's Derby. Spain rejects Cleveland.
Missouri tornado, 306 go. Quadricycle.
Tsunami & Sanriku, 27,000 go.
—shall not press down upon the brow of labor this crown of.
—Kansas?
Carmack's Bonanza Creek. Oak Bluffs waterspout. Constantinople, Turks slaughter Armenians. Connolly triple jump. *—Get a horse!* Narragansett Park. Waco trains. Gladstone pleas. RFD.

April 17 1895

Formosa, Liaodong
& seven ports.
Shimonoseki Treaty.
Halma's Derby.
Port Arthur returns.

Unconstitutional Tax.
Paris-Bordeaux,
a roundtrip.
Nikolov Stambolov goes.
Guiana boundary.
Selman & Acme Saloon,
Hardin goes.

Fourneyron turbines.
Brailler's toss.
Defender cups Valkyrie II.

*—Put down your bucket
where you.*

Constantinople massacre,
Turks & Armenians go.
Rawlins over Dunn.

Fox Hunt & Min.
Sunkist.
Lake Michigan race.
Selden's clutch.
Laramie dance.
Chicago to Evanston.
Amba Alagi.
Iola Kansas gas.
Jameson Raid.
Ida B Wells.
Russell & Diamond Jim.
Silent steeds.
Michelin. Doornkop.
Utah, 45th.

Then, eager to honor me, she goes
grubbing for stalks. To soften her
roughness?
How about a rasp?
She just grabs weeds brittle
and wilting to stuff up her hair.
Though what of her
disgusting feet?
Sores, blisters & corns.
Squeeeeeeealing
suddenly then,
she dives on her head,
only to avoid breaking her neck,
just, with spastic hand pivots
rereturning heels to ground.
My frown a smile a frown a smile.
Allways a frown.
Around and around.
Across warming meadows and
fields, she impressively whirls, her
cartwheels somehow overturning
everything.

Oct 2 2031

But O what a slip! How? Me? Over with? Now?
Tumbling down unable to cry, reach
out, leap beyond my own unstoppable loss.
A prison. All here's imprisonment & tumult.
Snow, air and sheer rock. Around and around.
Spastic grabs for pivots nowhere found.
My head. My fragile neck. Allways down.
Away from Sam, nowhere close to catch me.
—O no,
plummeting faster and farther, icier and harder,
towards what? That roughest landing,
mortality's hand, lifting my cold hands,
my cold mouth, my cold feet
and hurling me to Peace.

July 11 2032

Hit?

But softly. A feather's fall. Wheelings continuing.
Gossy air still threatening snow.
Below this cliff. Unharmed.
—*Sam!* I round but Sam does not return.
This stony plunge from crowning peak
bleak beneath a circling storm.
I shudder. Dumb. Tense.
At least I can reascend by gradual slope. Stunned
Uncertain. Amiss. Feet blistering for my delay, despite
ringing jolts, to rejoin him on the top.
—*Sam!* I fleet but Sam does not return.
No longer around now. Above, yes, but why still?
No. Time's askew here and all too near

June 26 1894

But a touch of my splendor
could colliquate her.
So, on her behalf,
most magnanimously,
I allso turn my head.
Yet little matty urchin keeps
sticking around. Still unaware
of unpleasant jolts far
ringing my expanse.
—*Can I offer some assistance?*
she biffles
—*Listen pesky wench, isn't it plain*
I'm just trying to relax?
To which she laughs.
A halfwit. Tragic.
Earnest though
and for an idiot cute.
Graciously I offer my hand
which with slideo blushes
she rushes to grab.
I weigh cliffs.
But I'm glad for her touch.

ARU boycotts Pullman.
Labor Day.
Pennsylvania strike over.
—*The dignity of an.*
—*Thugs, thieves &*
exconvicts.
Dole's Presidency.
Panhandle Yards
& 700 cars. Kassala.
Korea. Panhard to
Rouen. China's War.
Carey Act.
Wilson-Gorman Tariff.
Hinckley blaze, 480 go.

12,000 tailors strike.
—*Labor will organize.*

Bubonic plague.
Dreyfus arrested.
Sheriff Royal goes.
Port Arthur. Madagascar.
—*Stop Niagara with*
a feather.
Jaw cancer. Bull Run
River. Kenyon-Cornell.
Liliuokalani's treason.
Weihaiwei.
Frederick Douglass goes.
NAM. Cuban rebellion.
16–1.
Georgia to Liberia.
Wyoming Canyon blast,
60 go. Abyssinia.
—*Blundering foreign*
policy.

there's a stillness I cannot stand. Fluster & panic.
Sam. My spiral of cycles. When evers go.
And play. Beyond what even Quality
could never qualify. Cannot go missing.
Missing him would find all missing.
Yet here I hike & struggle allone,
switchback on switchback, spiked
with raw firn, under churning skies for falling twice.
Stuck, blundering me, scrambling only higher and
with just a tattered shawl to repel a World somehow
still ongoing without the wonder of Sam's spin.
Until at last, limping past another turn.
ThuuUuuuuUuuuunder
Flakes finally

all the falling snows of Winter.
And then a Flash sears lime to wide.
And Hailey gimps over,
shrugs:
—*Neato*
She's not so neatly changed,
smattered, battered and by
claw, club and dirt,
mauled, scuffed and worked.
Ragtail scampering about,
frowzy with fetoring goo
while I hurt. Yes.
Though I'm allso
calm & ferg. She's oblivious.
—*How's you, Mr. OneandaHalf?*
missy nincompoop
gutturally gullucks.
So wretched sprung & wrung out,
my Quality shocks her
blotchy cheek. Too much and
she might pass on. So,
desperate to live, she turns away.

Cherokees' Oklahoma.
Everett's Northern
Railway. Springfield
motor. Cheniere &
storm, 1,500 go.
Vigilant cups Valkyrie II.
Russian fleet greets
Toulon. Rolling back
Sherman Silver.
Leander Jameson, Matabele
revolt & Bulawayo.
Vailland & bomb.
Italians over Mahdists.
Stanley cup.
Chicago Cafeteria.
World Columbian ash.
Federal Bond &
Reserves. Repealing
Enforcement Act.
Isabella Beecher Hooker.
Jockey Club. Doolin Gang.
Vetoing Silver Dick.

—*the World over.*
British Uganda.
Ohio's 140,000.
Coxey's Army crushed.
—*manage his own
property.*
Trenton's employers.
Chant's Derby.
New Haven squeeze.
—*need more money.*
Marie-François-Sadi
Carnot goes.

Because everywherethereandhere's
Hailey
wambling by, hardly able to stand
let allone walk, now somehow
managing to halt without toppling
over, a feat I euphorically celebrate
with a leap, flipping high up and
over, backwards, around,
then over and down. Too over.
Uh O.
Feet freefall for clouds.
Still spinning.
Until I backhammer the ground.
Ow.
Face up. Still now.
Only my heart flutters fast. Faster.
Still faster. O no. The me I
terribly feer. Sickening, sinking
with falling vulnerability.
Until by shuddering Wind
I slowly whipper:
—*I Promise for her*

Krakow's Pan-Slavic.
Painter's cap. José Martí.
Texas Boll Weevil.
Muir & Sierra.
1,400 lynchings.
Marquis's Fife & Variety.
Polygamist amnesty.
Boston overthrows
Liliuokalani.
Philadelphia Railroad.
Diplomatic
Appropriations Act.
Gerald.
24th. French Guinea
& Ivory Coast. Anti-trust
Amalgamated.
Boston Bells Chicago.
8,000 businesses fail,
1 million jobless.
Bowen Burke's long tie.
Blount's dismissal.
Alexander I. 600 Banks.
74 Railroads. 999's
112.5 MPH. Kunze's
Derby. Geary Exclusion.
American Railway Union.
Debs. Altgeld's pardon.
Crash.
—*Frontier's over.*
France's Spain?
Minneapolis blaze.
Charleston & Savannah
wave, 1,000 go.
Goldman arrested.
—*arouse.*

of falling snow.
Chimes! Chime! Chimes!
Quiet endings. So sad. Fluttering doubts without
Sam's shouts to catch these varied nows, floating
whims, landing briefly on my tongue.
Melting just once. Gone. O.
I continue up. Higher on for that whirling peak
I lower with each stubbing toe and twisting ankle
against this impounding thick. Confounded
if surrounded allways by an uneasiness
I cannot reach. I even run, spilling often.
Grappling rocks, wedging, shinnying up, gaining
ground, fighting the graupel, soon hobbling across
mellowing rises hung with the passing of forevers.

March 26 1892

—Each of US limitless.

$25,000 for Italy.
California temblor.
Extended Chinese
Exclusion Act.
Azra's Derby.
Honolulu Monarchy
& Liberal Leaders.
Japan's Hirobumi Ito.
Frick's thousands strike.

*—Colossal fortunes
for a few.*

Populist Party's
Silver & Gold.

—Tramps & Millionaires.

Pinkertons &
a river on fire.
Frisco Mill. State Militia.
Idaho Bull Pens.
People's Party.
Sault Canal.
Moravia's cholera.
Gentleman Jim 21
rounds Sullivan.

—pledge allegiance to.

Springfield's Charles
& James Duryea.
Coffeyville's Daltons go.
Montana Crows evicted.
George Ferris wheels.
Hoocheecoochee.
Cleveland.
Union broke.
Belgian & Arab
slaveholders.

nearness I feel veering for me,
her every racing step removing me
farther from

Them
and that terrible Out Ranked
role I carelessly forestall with
each of my own steering footfalls
racing for Hailey along **Lynx**trod
wends, by purr, hisss & peeep,
sweeping from meads, gleeping:
—Ooooouuuiiiii!
Pine Squirrels too and
Pocket Gophers puppling
forth. Rampantly.
I'm sooooo from these highlands,
sharp tor and scarp.
From hogback and horn. From
the firn cached and low splashed
gushslushings through spilling vales
under such wheels of a soaring
American Kestrel killying:
—Hello.

Nov 15 2034

One bye?
Removing all Will. Summary
of living lost on a hill. Above softening vales,
below horn and hogback, scarp, firn and tor,
past highlands and solitary bluffs.
Ahead. Panting. Mad.
Desperate to regain all I had.
And yell at him. Bawl at Sam. Clutch.
Because if there's a wind, I'm not the wind. Sam's
the wind. There are no winds. Only the collapse of this
tumbling storm I keep stumbling up through.
Abandoning the borders of
even the Remotest Orders, no longer locatable
with even my own nearness to

Aug 30 2035

him?
His radiant place? His quickening race?
That frightening pace reending a World.
Vengeance. Greed.
And Vanity.
No! There though, still on top, across this frigid top,
just ahead of me. O no. Lying among that arc of heavy
boulders. His arms struck back, ankles kinked,
a frozen splay following my weird topple.
Sam! I slog on. Up to my waist. Through these
still rising drifts, across their wide reach.
And sharp short of breath. Now soaking with
sweat. Bogging me down. Tripping me up
with grief I can't outrun.

May 13 1891

Kingman's Derby. Cincinnati's Populist farmers. Jackson & Corbett 61 round tie. Koenig's meteorites. Cary's Paris dash. Franco-Russian entente.
—where one wife sits.
Cotton strikes. Harrison's 900,000 acres. Boulanger goes. Cripple Creek & Crede. Leland Stanford. Baltimore's Chilean fight. Madison Square's 6 days of circles. Mino-Owari quake, 7,300 go. Melbourne's rain. Naismith peach baskets.
—Kansas we busted.
Rainbows & zippers. Burroughs's additional turns. Strowger's dial. Panhard & Levassor's wheels. Wahehe War. Annie Moore & Ellis Island. Coeur d'Alene's mines. Abbas over Tewfik. Henry Clay Frick's cut. Verkhoyansk freeze.

something else trailing even
Them, beyond outrage & relief,
a Kindness
never outdone, never survived.
A horror I should easily outrun
but can't leave behind, traversing
all winds except for this one,
which dares me, dogs me,
bewares me to burn
the World quick.
Even if **Silver Grizzlies**,
Whimbrels and **Snipes** grunder:
—Humility.
And **Sandhills Hornets**, **Pine**
Weevils and **Wolf Spiders** munder:
—Charity.
And **Least Flycatchers**
blegger: *—Mercy.*
Because all around me
the World rebegins. For my saunter
and smile of course. And these but
quickening and radiating for her

July 14 1890

Silver Purchase.
Rhodes's Cape Colony.

Lawrence cyclone, 8 go.
Kemmler's Auburn
charge. Narva.
People's Party.
Forfeiture to rail.
McKinley Tariff.
Weather Bureau.
Polygamy. Clément
Ader. Hennessey goes.
No vote.
Navy foots Army.
Parnell & O'Shea.
Sitting Bull,
Kokipa-Koshla &
a Circus horse.
Lugard's Uganda.
Wounded Knee.
—hoop is broken.
—Nation I am.
Macadamia. 63 million.
Half by 1%.
Lambert's ride.
—Surrounded by
thieves.
Mahan's navy.
Colt revolver. Kalakaua
goes. Boepple's mussels.
—Hawaii for the.
Candalaria. Circuit Court.
Forest Reserve Act.
11 Louisiana Italians go.
Pan-Germany.
Lucy Long.

Every **American Robin** and **Sage**
Thrasher chears admurringly
my tremendous blur:
—*Whirrrrrrrrrrrrrrrrrrr!*
Newly fidgeting **Bats**, **Wrens**
and **Newts** by ponds and rill,
Hooknosed Snakes tumbling
over banks and logs, **Wolverines** &
Moles grrrrring by brittle rocks, all
breeeing for my impossible stir:
—*Whirrrrrrrrrrrrrrrrrrr!*
And I'm allready gogone, their
only On and On, shooooshing
beyond these thickets and marsh.
By **Chorus Frogs** and
Western Turtles with a
Gyrfalcon circling above:
—*Whirrrrrrrrrrrrrrrrrrr!*
From palisade and powdery saddle,
fumarole, flume and falls,
I hurtle free, even if Them allso
hanker to follow me,

June 16 2036

Until he's at my feet,
cradled by my arms. O Sam. So still & stiff,
and gone from falls, flume, fumarole and saddle.
Palisades of change.
I shake him. Sob. Beat his rigid chest. Parting
those lips, driving down my breath upon
his strange freeze. And allways prompting How?
Here? To me so near
without even a cause.
Impossibly gone. Just still. Dead.
To where I'm allready gonegoing.
Yet over him still slobbering, kissing him,
plugging his nose, pounding his heart. My breath
pounding. Allone. Too left. Now. Here. Only.

April 3 2037

Yes run. Bundle him up. Sprint back.
Little gained though. My feet failing the stinging
cold. Falling through its wasting crust,
fleet bursts of powder everfleeing this mead.
I heave on. But to where? What assistance? Who?
How to return Sam from his unturning presence?
And me allways too frail, allready overcome
by all I hardly haul.
Beyond even the drive of rancor.
The hurrying of concern. Hardly able
to hold on let allone move on.
His uncrossed arms against my breasts,
chin rocking up,
each time kissing my cheek.

Oct 2 1889

Not here with this impertinent
wreckage & rout, anger surpassing
anger's fastening doubt, misusing
me, abusing me over
and over for such
Violent Wrenchings of Want.
But it's no concern. I'm unharmed.
Unaffluenced. Unmarred. Though
Them's continuance gives me the
rancor I need to abolish cause
for even a pause.
And Them.
Only Hailey's absence stays
me. Offers Pain.
A fascinating gain I'm not
so keen to encounter again.
So turning for
a Wish
still Wishing one Wish's loan,
I obey my charge,
wriggle free of these Bashers
and run.

Jingo Jim.
—Friendship not force.
—of a mighty presence.
Milwaukee's Bijou
Judgement.
North & South Dakota.
Montana. Washington.
Elizabeth Cochrane.
Wooden shoes
& Lynn fire.
551 buffalos.
Tenements,
sweatshops,
opium dens.
Harrison's touch.
Jones & Laughlin.
Mayo clinic.
General Federation of
Women's Clubs.
Locusts over
Erythraean Sea.
Topeka & Santa Fe rush.
—Unity! Unity!
Nellie Bly. James Duke &
American Tobacco.
Roll Call by head.
National American
Woman Suffrage.
Bank of America fails.
Riley's Derby. George
Francis Train. Pemba &
Heligoland for Zanzibar.
Sherman Antitrust Act.
Wyoming.

Dec 12 1888

Ethiopia's Menelik II.
Jack the Ripper.
Whooping cough
& measles.
Wovoka's trance
& Paiute Dance.
France's Ivory Coast.
Roseburg 's Cowbells.
Provident Hospital's
nurses. Mayerling's
Rudolf goes.
Norman Coleman.
Bering Sea's control.
Rural rebellion.
Samoa Hurricane,
Warships & Calliope.
Pabst's.
Boulanger flees.
Oklahoma Land Rush.
Freewheeling Boomers,
Sooners & The Strip.
—One flag encircles.

Spokane's Derby.

Johnstown flood,
over 2,200 go.
Russian Flu,
over 500,000 go.
Brussels abolishes
slave trade.
Gluepot & Seattle fire.

Sullivan 75 rounds Kilrain.
Wilcox & Honolulu, 7 go.
Union Party.

South Halstead Street.

By this flurrious fury
what here just won't fade,
a pang—
Hailey.
Somewhere too amidst this
relentless rush of living refuse
untouched—
Hailey. On her own. Lost.
So even with Them, their consular
disgust reclustering to envy my
consummate Fame, I wonder of
her Gold Eyes with flecks of Green.
—She's around,
assure **Heather Voles**.
But then Them returns.
Where's her ringlet spleshes?
I meander until seething Mobs
reaggress, battering my ass,
pummeling my twanger, ringing
my spine. I slide and lose compassion.
I'm their only World.
Where's her smile?

Jan 21 2038

Though missing a smile.
My only World. What's left of compassion.
Beyond any feer. Removed from the seething of drift
I allways move with. I'm a waste of time but here
with his soft hair mashed against my chest
lies the wastes of time. No longer around.
Green Eyes with flecks of Gold.
A cold Glory
found without satisfaction,
unbound without release, leaving me
lost, too allone, still somehow
rushed by the relentlessness of a pang beyond
even my reach. Sam fading with this flurry
I keep trying to clutch.

Feb 19 1888

But at least I'm whipped up too
to gather all under my heel
and crush it.
I'm corpses of ruin. Now
here, suffer my affections.
How I belong. How I long.
Because that's how I'm here for.
Even dirt smolders with feer.
—Spare something far?
hoooowee **Western Tanagers**.
But my consolation demands
their annihilation.
Offered with carnage & gore.
And, yup, plenty more.
—Spare something near?
slimpump **Longtoed Salamanders**.
But I'm unavoidable. No beneath
underneath. No over
above. Just one side.
Only I'm nervous.
Hands shake.
Breaths bruised and slack.

Mount Vernon's
Cyclone, 35 go.

Yonkers Fairways
& John Reid.

Louisville Kentucky
& Kangaroo voting.

The Great Blizzard,
800 go.
Anglo-American
Oil Company.

AFI & 8 hour workday.
Mount Rainier meet.

Britain's North
Borneo & Brunei.
Dom Pedro II
abolishes serfdom.
Macbeth II's Derby.

Belva Ann Lockwood
for President.

David B Hill turns
from hanging to
electrocution.
Union Pacific's
Oregon steel bridge.
Thomas F Bayard &
Latin American Nations.
Coastal Arabs,
Germans & East Africa.
Spa contestants.
Arbitration Commission
for railroad workers
& management.
Harrison over Cleveland.

Nov 12 2038

And now my breathing bruises.
Legs cramp. Everything about me unsteady.
Unable to shoulder him more. No way on.
Walking the edge of a sob.
Weaving. Tripping to a stop. US.
Collapsing to my knees, tendering his brow.
No kiss, retching over his missing.
The ultimate annihilation I can't console.
Too feeble to ever lift him again.
So I shove him. But not much.
He's too much. I can go no farther. Shivering then,
slick with feer, here where I won't belong,
among bodies of want,
upon The Mountain's heel.

April 20 1887

George Bouton's steam.
Huang He floods Honan.
American Cattle Trust.
Montrose's Derby.
René Goblet.
Flags unreturned.
Zululand annexed.
Lottie Dod.
Kalakaua's opium ring.
Chatsworth Bridge,
100 go.
Lillie Bridge
Stadium burns.
Volunteer cups Thistle.
Sears over Slocum.
—Our silence will
be more powerful.
—voices you
strangle today.
Trafalgar Square's
Bloody Sunday.
Thibodaux & Cox men go.
Sugarcane strike over.
Arkansas Bauxite.
—Stay the flowing of
the streams.
Cassius Merritt's trip.
Alphonse Bertillon.
—Hasten forward
quickly there.
Foxburg golf.
Marvin Chester
Stone's first straw.
National Geographic.
Sprague's trolley.

About me, around me,
spinning me, galling me,
doublenelsoning me until
before it's begun and after it's done
I'm overwhelmed by Them.
Raped. Defied. Tried.
Lynched. Staked. Despised.
Everybody gets a turn.
—*You,* Them bash.
—*Me,* Them smash. Earned
without yearning, and for such
Woe & Shame, flinging their
frustragings upon me. Freeforall.
From balls to bones,
by sticks & stones,
jabs, swings and brawling slugs.
I don't move.
Them don't stop.
All Them. One by one. Allatonce.
Until abruptly Them's gone.
Leaving me menacing
and, well, okay, slightly startled.

Sept 4 2039

And only the chill menaces me.
Because there's No One to turn to. And None will
ever turn for US. I can't continue with him.
Only hold him, cling to him. A shield
from jabbing ice, covering ears and face,
protecting him from this freeze,
allmost okay & Ohio enough to need,
if condemning too such afflictions with frantic
fingers circulating the end.
—*Sam,* I wail.
—*Don't leave me,* I flail.
Drooping over him, battering him, spinning him,
for depriving me of his calm
where longings cannot long for me.

So I stick to.
Minutely concerned. Doubts?
A chance. Certainly some perpilexing
bashing rolling this way. Slightly
vexes tendencies to recline.
Unwind. Not that I can't with both
hands behind my back
devastate all.
Except I'm somenowsomehow
changed. Snagged perhaps. At least
deferrent. Even when, by these
encompassing centuries,
clatchgrabbing my wonder,
pullulating over ridge, peak, and crest,
and across, Mangy Angry Naked
Urges rampage towards me.
—*Them!*—
Every last one of Them.
Steller's Jays racing away
from this suffering convergence.
Still most peculiarly, I do not
beat the riot.

June 29 1886

Trade Unions & Congress.
Canadian Sealfishing
ships. Bogus Brodie.

*—Sedition, tumult
and riot.*
Sofia coup.
George over Cumming.
Miles over Geronimo.
Mayflower cups Galatea.
Railroad Company
vs Illinois.

*—your huddled masses
yearning.*

Satin Lorilland &
the Tuxedo Club.

*—Big prairies, big
wheatfields.*
AFL.
*—Our labor movement
has no system to crush.*

Witwatersrand
Reef Gold. Styth
Pemberton's kola coca.
Sears. Mead Johnson.
Thomas Crapper.

Dakota blizzard,
millions of cattle go.
Bismarck army.
Kermadec Islands.
Honolulu reciprocity.
State Commerce Act.
Dawes Severalty Act.
Hatch Act. Repealing
Tenure Office Act.

June 28 2040

I must go. Race for help. Though for
that chance I'll have to leave him here.
Must if I'm to find from
this suffering coalescence some alexiteric
against his stillness. Over crest, peak and ridge,
down beyond field, stream and trail, towards
another encircling of life to lend a life
and revive my Sam.
But what if, if by such time,
if he's even then not revived, I find I'm changed?
Somehowsomenow prevailing?
By astral conversion willing to remain
on without his devastating blaze?
How repulsive. Would I betray him?

Sept 15 1885

Puritan cups Genesta.
Rock Springs Massacre,
28 go. Tacoma wagons.
—No official shall
discriminate.
Louis Riel hangs.
British Mandalay Burma.
Wade Morrison's
Alderton Pepper Girl.
Curtis heavy.
Furnaces & garbage.
—Unsafe.
—turn bristles,
blood and.
Odlum goes.
Thank Daws.
Talented Tenth.
Banff. Upper Burma.
Tournament of Roses.
Succession Act.
200 Chinese to ship.
California citrus.
Hall's aluminum.
Alternating Current.
Iceland Rule.
—Eight hour
day with no.
Revenge Circular.
—your might. To arms!
Haymarket Square.
—Hang Them first and
try Them afterward.
Corporated.
Ben Ali's Derby.
Frances Folsom.

Weals dragging wheels. Lost to
misty glens drifting down by
stoped hills wet with slipping nets
of loosened dew. Until soon by
every wandering trail,
Whistling Hares itch nervously.
Mountain Marmots gitching too.
Over the way the strangest looming.
Boooooooooomblastandruin.
Gathering sooooooon.
—Them!
bolt a hundred **Barn Swallows**.
Aphids & Gnats panic. **Mayflies**
too. Not me. Nothing frantics me.
I'm the all. The all available.
Ever now. Ever here.
Allways unavailable. But
Mountain Goats still stampede:
—Run away, you dumb yuk.
If somewaysomewhere on batten
winds, a sadder neigh.
Hmmmmm.

April 23 2041

And nah, with only a maybe
halting me, yeah.
I'll stay.
Beside him, with him, for him. His Peace, his wrack.
What even now his stillness commands.
All I can never get from me. Not me.
What frantics me. Those returns
No One ever permits.
So way out. The strangest yearnings. By every
meandering allready slipping from here. From
him. By frost and ice, the frozen ground of hill
and grove, down to where common bounds bake
their way with warming fingers and warmer grins.
Where I will not go.

Feb 18 2042

What's this?
A Bee?
Still clinging to Sam's swollen wrist? My poison!
His poison? With nix of even paucities left over.
Still I scratch its sad sting over my skin.
Across my gums. My demise denied by Sam's demise
denying me here what's my affliction.
Because I can't start what I don't own.
Though there must be someway I can go too?
I lose it. Skeeking, shaking.
On my back. Streaks unstopping slogs of goop.
—*O here. Release me. O please.*
Still harnessed to this toothy World.
I'm so terrified.

Oct 29 1884

Until ballchangearound for a
frightened whinny. **Horse**! Tooth
long. Queerly harnessed to haul
by knobbly hands:
—*O, over here. Release me. Please.*
Yipyawketyay!
Strong Back. High Withers.
Mighty Flanks, Oily Wild with
mane of Every Dust. Hooves, now
shoed & cracked, under roughshod
lash, to cart attached
by that Spiteful Spinster:
—*You'll never own*
what you don't start.
Lacerating and cackling. I sprint,
slaughtering divides to still her
whipafflictions upon my **Horse**.
Strong Head. Warm Heart.
Neighing laments to just stay
awhile except overridden
by violent flays
allready taken away.

—Rum, Romanism
& Rebellion.
Greenwich.
Maxim's 600 shots.
Parsons' steam.
Mayenberg's evaporation.
—Ha, ha, ha!
New Orleans Expo.
Burlington Rail.
Walker, Wilburforce
& Toledo Stockings.
Charles Sweeney drops
19. Appendectomy.
Ahantchuyuks.
Benz 3. Khartoum's
Dervish massacre.
Leopold's Congo.
Massawa, Eritrea.
—Finger pointing
to the sky.
Barbless Public West.
Foran Act.
Vail's state to state.
Fortifications
& Coast Defenses.
Grover Cleveland.
Sparks' 2.75 million acres.
Convention of Tientsin.
British Korea.
Joe Cotton's Derby.
French Liberty.
Meister & a rabid dog.
Grant goes.
Dumont & Métis
flee to Montana.

Jan 1 1884

No more Russian Poll Tax.

City of Columbus, 103 go.

Atlanta tornado, 700 go.
Alice for Alice.
Ohio's 71.
Khartoum &
Charles George Gordon.
Greenbacks back.
Susan B &
100 DC suffragists.

Pocahontas coal, 112 go.

For a hammer.
—Let's hang Berner.

Treaty of Valparaíso.
Cyclone Assemblyman
& no re-election.
Murphy &
Long shot Buchanan.
Baraboo.

Treaty of Hué.

Mugwumps.
Cape Sabine rescue.
Knights of Labor.

Kansas Spanish Bullfight.
Knight &
Bentley third rail.

Bureau of Labor.
Krebs & Renard's
circular La France.

Dervish followers
over Omdurman.

Lost then. Her. Me. But my
laughter's still sinister,
a sweltering Spring blister.
Anyway, I'm footloose now and
kicking out. Doing what I won't.
I never don't.
—Do what you do, **Great Spangled**
Fritillaries summon.
—What do you do?
Camel Crickets ricket.
All. Allways. Pervious.
Marching cendiary by icy Mountain
wides and wooded barrows. Mine.
Ladybugs fliburring
confirmations: *—Impartially.*
Sweet hails all around:
—Come sta! Comment ça va!
—You've nothing to lose.
Meet all ears with a wave.
Kangaroo Rats to **Rubber Boas**
and **Squash Bugs** figgling:
—Morning! —Howdy! —Heigh!

Dec 17 2042

Out! So long! Over!
Just beat it. Skip it. Turn it loose.
I'm nothing left to lose.
Addio! Toute a l'heure!
Clutching a certainty overdue,
and, excepting the how, ready for too.
But electing that now, still stuck on manner.
The Mountain he lies upon, The Mountain
by a Bee he dies upon. With
agony, terror and welt. Brutally successful.
And awful dread still upon this face, these cindered
cheeks. Tenderest hands. Fingers wrapping
thumbs. If mouth's so sinisterly armed.
He for me, O. Me for him, O. Allone here.

March 20 1883

—All of it's yours, New Hope *wickets.*
But not a lick of it if you
stick with that gonus.
Even licks his lips.
Misfit but spinning.
Very.
Though allso paltry.
—Me? he winces. My turn to
lick. Relishing his flinching.
Though weirdly I'm wobbling
with mighty frail knees.
Where's Hailey?
The New Hope goes ballistic if
ritualistic, thrashing on dung.
Dying Hope returns
following the tantrum:
—Carry out every task.
You allone can. But grasp:
none may ever accompany you.
Couldn't care less.
Though curling up
find only the rest.

Eleven's Convention for
Protection of Property.
Astor, Vanderbilt,
Duc de Guise &
The Power of Electricity.
Kruger's South
African Republic.
Cody's Wild West.

Leonatus's Derby.

—What multitudes
democratically
organized can do.

Gregory's ore.
Kimball blaze.
Thank's Flynn.
French Annam & Tonkin.

Krakatoa skies.

—No golden spike but
an iron one.
J Montgomery's glide.
Horlick Milk.
Edison Effect.
Paris to Varna
& Orient Express.
Harlan's dissent.
Peace of Ancón.
Ahmed of Dongola
over Hicks.
4 Zones.
2 Free &
Congressional balance.
—a Navy able to cope.
Sumner's socializing.

Oct 16 2043

Away with the rest.
Except for Sam I couldn't care less.
Left above such stealing drops
beside all the ways I dash so easily. Bent, unmet, if
pathetically imposed upon, begged, by Sam's
Dead Hope. Sauntering over now. Shaggy. Mauled:

—We're the unwelcome, the lost,
poor journeys beyond cost. We're the frail,
orphaned, unweathered and uncrossed.
We're the unwashed and rude. We're the once missed,
dismissed and allways misused. Because we're unfinished
and feered and we're never pursued.

—We? I cavil at this Caped Wreck foolishly
blandishing his broken sword.

May 2 1882

Kilmainham Treaty.
Chinese Exclusion Act.
—Chinese must go.

Greely's Pole. Hurd's
Derby. Triple Alliance.

Bombay storms,
100,000 go.
Hague's 3 mile
territorial waters.

Lindemann's slice.
Hailstone's 2 frogs.
Amalgamated
Association of Iron &
Steel strikes.
T'ang-shan to
Feng-nan.
Rivers and Harbors Act.

*—Such persons shall
not be permitted.*
Maamtrasna's Joyce.

—Labor shall.
Appleton power.
Myra Belle Shirley.

*—That which
no living man except
me has touched.*

Italy's Assab Bay.
Pendleton Civil
Service Act. New
Jersey's Trade Unions.
Wilmington's
Shaft #2, 70 go.
Rolling cigars.
Ohio River rampage.

But I'm freest, skimming the far
slides. Down by **Stiletto Flies** and
Comstock's Netwinged Midges
buzzing rapturously above flats
of sandstone:
—Wait. Enjoy. Relax.

But I'm irate. Distraction's
bait. Endlessly misplaced.
And coming across a clearing,
with **Leopard Frogs** hopping,
a Dying Hope greets me.
Creamy. Opium addict. Rankest.
But not too difficult to avoid.
No mannerly shake required.
Though too quickly disturbed
by a gnawing up through
hardpan and loam.
A New Hope slashes
with clacking jaw.
Flesh of leprous rot.
Hands? No Hands. Peddler.
New Hope. Dangerous meddler.

Aug 16 2044

Dead Hope. Very dangerous. Though not to me
even with millions of hands. I shrug menacingly:
*—You're through. You're Disease Control when
the disease is beyond cure. I'm the fever ongoing.*

Dead Hope screeches. Whumph! to that:
—Live longer you brat! Get back!

—*No*, I plumph, banishing this addict's
petty banes to splintering rasps.

And so misplaced slump
again to my storm's curling and bludgeoning
blasts, abating at last, with only me and Winter,
rolling here, impersonally present,
heedless of the frozen pyre
we prepare together with shocks of ice.

June 16 2045

Gelidity binds Sam. Currents of sofslimmering
rime harden over his face.
Hands a claw of icicles curving
down to The Mountain of World.
Even his hair joins the surrounding freeze.
Struck, claimed, needlessly seized.

Where's The Hive of venom warming? More stabs
warning one. A ball heedlessly near this.
A clustering bzzzzz offering a way to steer free
of my eternity. Near, a Queen killing sting,
allready tugging me too, assurances of
the quickest slip, which amidst a
swarm's breeze will shock me from

Sam's perverted halt? With one drop?

July 2 1881

Onto a steep slope, where
I by nosetwitch mix a breeze
until
THAT SCORCHED LURCH OF A DUDE
lunges suddenly by some ornery
Hens. Hate his only clemency.
His only aim. Perfectly claimed.
Even if,
by simple sideskip,
I easily slip out, ushering
his bawling pounce forth,
over, round, around, down,
splitbattering the ground.
THAT SCORNED BAR OF A MAN
railrolling **Lubber Grasshoppers**
and **Thrips.**
Over and over. So solo.
Clemency his only age.
His only fist.
Completely missed.
Until a Creek accepts his splash
and Currents free HIM gently.

—I am a Stalwart.
Tuskegee.
Bonney & Garrett.
Kate Shelby.
—Now it is over.
A hard time I.
Durango-Chama's
Rockies.
Gompers' Federation.
Carpenters & Joiners.
Greely's Greenland.
Arabi Pasha.
—O Swaim,
there is pain.
Chester.
Mischief cups Atalanta.
Long Drive over.
Haiphong typhoon,
300,000 go.
—and now you have it.
De Long's gone.
Beer Ball.
Atlanta's spike.
Tenino to Olympia.
Ring fire, 850 go.
Disston's Everglades.
Coney Island.
Jim Crow. The Nine.
Sullivan rounds Ryan.
Edmunds Act.
Bob Ford backs James.
Federals to Arizona.
John Fox Slater.

Oct 13 1880

Transvaal Boers & Freedom. Tenafly. James Garfield, 20th President. Chinese Exclusion Treaty.

One mile of Broadway. 93,000 miles of rail.

Joe Juneau, Frank Harris & Alaskan gold. English muffins & plimsolls.

Boyd Dunlop's tire. —*Go dry.* Safety razor & Kampfes. USC. Gossima & Ping-Pong. Springer vs US Supreme Court, constitutional tax. Nationalist Egyptian Army. Majuba Hill & Boer victory. California quarantine. Alexander II goes. Alexander III. Bizerte from Algeria. Sheep vaccinations & anthrax. French Protectorate's Tunisia. Hindoo's Derby. Clara Barton.

Three Emperor alliance: Germany, Austria-Hungary & Russia.

Prompting THE FAST ONE
to beat THE SLOW ONE until
both bleed their mud.
I'm ever so unbegun.
Shaggy **Sheep**: —*Roam on!*
Provident **Pigs**: —*Orgulously!*
But where is she? Awkward rush.
Is that who I amble for?
Ridiculous.
I roam free. Effortless if Haileyless.
She can't be far.
Probably lost.
Trails cross by heaps of stone
left on behalf of painful regrets.
Feer begets every regret.
So scoffs a TAXED STEELMILL WORKER
to a LAX STORE CLERK I pass:
—*Love! The second most*
misprised of
human goals.
—*What's first?*
—*Liberty.*

April 14 2046

Love?

Stirring wings to refuse a possibility
of anything more. Liberty following then from
this wake of violence. Because allready I hover
murderously over an amber slumber and waxy bed.

Begetting no regret. Pursuing no dead.

Because I'm allready discovered and never
discovered. I am discovery and all discovery loses.
Because allways found about, I'm allready lost
without all ambles his absence excuses.
So I crouch, ready, over this just discovered Hive
for the poison still necessary to lose him.

Roam no more. Proudly.
Allways done. If now undone, tied

Nov 1 1879

The Gargantuan Hurl of a Dude
allso lunges but
tripping lands face down
where he
screaks.
And crisps. And chars. Finally
bolting loose for damp retreats.
Continuing to screak.
I calm the crowd.
Their President, their tyrant,
their crown. If not long for such
folk. Only my exits let any exist.
So despite encores I limbo off
by ravines where convene
a Wizened Clerk
and an Irregular Farmer:
—Love's all.
—Liberty, The Broke One objects.
—Love and Liberty are one.
—And Marriage? Where
Love accepting Liberty's end
secures Love's undoing.

Chile's War.
French Clamor to Paris.

Tay River Bridge falls,
300 go.

Denver
& Rio Grande Railroads.
Wabash Street.
Samuel R Lowery
& Belva Ann Lockwood.

Winter Palace bomb,
10 go.
Saccharin.
Strauder vs West
Virginia Supreme Court.
Ferdinand de Lesseps,
the Canal Company,
& France.
British Salvation
Army & US.

—Unite the farmers
of America for their
protection against.

Fonso's Derby.
Battle of Tacna.
Paddy Ryan 87 rounds
Joe Goss.

Senator Blanche K Bruce.
Tuscumbia's Keller.

France's Annexation
& Tahiti.

US delegates & Moroccan
liberation movement.

Feb 14 2047

to Love no more. To Liberty no more.
Their marriage untied here with life.
Life's all. Death's only toll.

And where Irregular Winds outflank
Wizened Clouds, such rollless ranks
defeat little but each's own bounds.

Only my existence lets any leave. Aborted grasps
I move on past. Because I don't exist.
A diadem of only weather, when abruptly

The Hive stirs a churn of feer.
Small wings of sorrow. Crowds of heat.
I'll quit tomorrow. I won't repeat.
So without Sam, and facing down,

I plunge my arm for stings.

Jan 1 1879

Coin. Zulus, British & Isandhlwana massacre. Arrears of Pension Act.

Chile, Peru & Bolivia. Buffalo Springs Texas, last of Southern Bison go. Hayes, Army Appropriations & veto. Boston's Safety. Wyoming. California's Chinese labor. Murphy's Derby. Gandamak's Khyber Pass.

1,500 Negroes stranded. Radicals & Anarchists. Progress & Poverty. *—Boob from the country.* Chelmsford over Cetewayo at Ulundi. Jeannette Expedition. Afghans, British & Kabul massacre. George Selden's horseless carriage. Carlisle School. Amir Yakub surrenders.

Carbonized cotton & Edison's burning bulb.

Pacific Northwest Tribal Wars over.

Jetties & Callie French.

—*Get gone!* bellowing strong.
But I don't respond.
And I certainly don't run.
—*Adios Muchacho!* bellowing out.
—*On what charge?* I courteously ask.
But THE ENORMOUS HURL OF A DUDE,
rage racked, just charges.
All around stunned, pulling back.
Though my furnaced nay
immediately ends all such frivolity.
Cremates HIS bravado
and suicidal abandon.
I chase HIM around the fire.
My pursuit so fast, HE chases me.
Now. Here. HE's most afraid.
Time for one more
grave redirection.
I wade through coal & ember.
Unrestricted.
Unafflicted.
Spilling sparks.
Killing starts.

Dec 16 2047

Killing starts. Spilling barbs.
Except there are no starts. There are no barbs.

And a googolplex of bees succumbs to the freeze.
Now a dust of practice shunned by my hands.
No point surviving. Venoms lost to the outside.
A mystery of season massacring their poor lives.
Which I clutch and fling, littering
nival wastes with everything
Them might've given up for me.

My greedy sadness even envying their bed.
Now a crowning roundringing for Sam's unwhirl,
my unflinching Emperor
who despite me, to spite me,

still refuses to go.

Oct 16 2048

I attack the air. Can't even stir it with a swing.
Sam so unprovoked. And unjoined.
By me unrevoked. Busted. Nothing remotely
threatening near. All puffy and soft.
Departure's prohibition.

Is there even a poison? Is there ever a sting?
Sam's hurt now haggering me with its
Open exodus. Vulnerability beyond stealing.
How he somehow succeeded.
His weakness beyond feelings.

I splat down on my chest.

Could I just obliviate from this mess. But I can't.
Because I'm allways stung by him
and ever after and allready before only warned.

March 3 1878

THESE EIGHT BUCKAROOS then repose
upon encircling stones, Duck
Duck Goose blowing their noses.
Cowed by my rank.
All plead but I do not sit.
A **Great Horned Owl**
upon my shoulder:
—*Obliviate the lot.*
THESE TEN WADDIES
swooning over their Dodgeball.
THESE TWENTYFOUR EXODUSTERS
dropping their Medicine Ball.
—*Omniviate the fools,*
my **Snowy Owl** lofts to the moon.
Then THESE FORTYFIVE
SOD BUSTERS cluster & filibuster,
spooning up mustard chears.
Honey Do You Love Me?
I exude.
Whereupon, disgruntled
kakistocracy stands, some
HURL OF A DUDE, and attacks me.

Treaty of San Stefano &
Russo-Ottoman War.
150 Sheepeaters.
Day Star's Derby.
Karl Nobling & Emperor
Wilhelm I of Germany.

—Let all our
dealing with.

Kansas
& the Exodusters.
Chester A Arthur: Port
Collector. Treaty of
Berlin. American Bar
Association.
George Leslie's
Manhattan Savings.
Democrats
regain control.
Southern Democrats
& political murders.

Bronze John, over
14,000 go by wagon.
Greenbacks & gold.

Albert Michelson's
speed. Deadwood &
Martha Jane Cannary.
Pope bicycles.
Alexander Winchell
ousted. Cuban cigars
flee to Florida.
Chinese thousands
migrate.
Corn Killer.
Auburn Milking.

May 1 1877

Four rails.

End of Dominion.

Crazy Horse turns.
Baden-Baden's Derby.
General Howard,
Wallowa & Nez Percé.
Flag Day.
Flipper.
Joseph & Bird Canyon.
10 Mollys go.
Martinsburg
B & O strike.
Maryland militias, 9 go.
Flaming Pennsylvania,
20,000 go.
Chicago strikers, 19 go.
Young goes.
—no sass but
sasparilla.
Satsuma Rebellion.
Sam Bass's Union
Pacific. GTT.

—I will fight no
more forever.
Wolfe Mount.
Enrico Forlanini's heli.
Joyce twirlers. Antibiotic.
Redeemers & Bourbons.
Battle of Senova.
Shipka Pass.
Hall vs De Cuir.
Samoa Treaty.
Adrianople. Thessaly.
Bland-Allison.

I mosey on. Diverging all ambling
with every step. Trailblazing.
Nothing but freedom
ringing with protest.
Bringing unrest.
—*Give over the tenderest,* rawrrrawrk
snarling **Coydogs** ready to fang
whoever dares by. I dare by.
Casually.
Each canines each. Savagely.
I'm every dare's hullo.
THREE STOVEUP COWPUNCHERS
cock their resolvers. Aim at me.
My chuckle buckles their knees.
Panic fells their killing.
All run off afraid.
I walk over their shame.
I'm sick of fighting.
But with their anger turning
fast to sighs,
All follow my lead.
And find a fire.

Aug 16 2049

Icy comfort. But allso too my own warning.
I return to Sam with fastening sighs and
allready each stomp of snowy chunk
heaves mountain ranges up.

I crave fighting, the pleasures of killings.
Crippling peace. Alltogether resistant.

I'm every dare's byebye,
unleashing with each grunt
Spoilations of civility. And now the fist I finish
brings down a ringing sting of Katabatic Winds.

Storms too. Why? Because I feel rotten.
Worse. Rotten's got something left to give.
I'm not even worth taking. But I have what it takes.

Rage. Rage. Rage.

June 18 2050

Now's my way. Never gone.
What none can evade. For I am
every pass. And I'll savage every chance.
The sickle. The blaze. Expressways.
I am that fury at last
no hope will prevent. Not even this ravaging cold,

tossed along by blizzardy groans, Open,
will help. Wipe it all out. Because
I've no hand to kiss, fondle, hold.
How uncomplete I am. Neglected. Missing and
unmissed. Even the cold's sympathetic touches now
go unrejected. Because he's not jealous

anymore. Beyond powder and ball. Cannons.
Where there is no hope.

July 2 1876

How too HE flirty smarms,
tawdry crack & crick of
his rotting arms.
Cannon wound still discharging.
Hailey's enthralled.
But no NEW HOPE can evade my
harm. Even this seedy gum.
To cinders by my fulgent blast.
When suddenly gaunt,
with shivers sympathetic,
HE holds her hand!
Strokes it! Tenderly!
I wipe out something.
Somewhere.
Allot of something.
Allot of somewhere.
O NEW HOPE, by
Drum, Fife & Horn, prepare!
For I'm a turnhurling madness,
driving fire upon ice fields of air.
Except Hailey's allready gone,
taking HOPE with her.

Montenegro's War.

Colorado 38th.

2 Aces, 2 Eights & Bill.
Madeline cups Dufferin.
Murad's madness.
Northfield Minnesota
shootout.
Battle of Slim Buttes.
Warren Powder
Company Mills.
Beecher's hung jury.
Juliet Corson.
Conway's fire, 300 go.

—I admit.
Blair's prohibition.
Ottoman constitution.
Ashtabula Express,
90 go. Delhi drought.
Famine & Northern
China. Melvil Dewey.
Bakarganj cyclone,
200,000 go.
Henry Heinz.
John Harvey Kellogg.
Nikolaus Otto.
Hoosac Rail.
Vanderbilt goes.
—I am not.
Serbia Peace.
Munn vs Illinois.
Desert Land Act.
Rutherford B Hayes,
19th. Earmuffs.
Russia & Romania.

Aug 24 1875

Matthew Webb's Channel Crossing.
Molly Maguires, Buckshots & Sleepers. Isaac Parker's rope examination.
Fort Laramie's broken treaty. Sioux Cloud stays. Egyptians fall at Gundet. Helena Petrovna Blavatsky. Ludlow Jail, Tweed & Cuba. Bessemer. 40,000 miles of crisscross. Snooker at Ooty.
Marcus's auto. Snapping & stretching chicle. National League. Ottomans & Bulgarians.
—Watson, come here, I. Cruikshank. Harvey Girls. George Hearst. Eli Lilly. 13 bells, 100 cannons. Vagrant's Derby. Japan's Tsunami, over 28,000 go. Chief Sitting Bull & falling grasshoppers. Little Big Horn. *—Ho hechetu!* Commanche trots free.

Still with surprising pluck
she ambles off. **Angus** & **Herefords**
mooing her losses, disturbed how
she chitters honeymad at every
plant she crosses.
My **Magpies** & **Chickadees** smirk.
But I follow. I'm every following's
work. Allways at ease.
And readyset to
offer her station: Maid.
Only before I can,
wheeling backwards with yikes.
Flummuxed. Frantic.
There amidst some grove,
Hailey cavorts with
the upstart antics of
a preposterous dope:
a NEW HOPE, flabbling
precociously. All squirty, with
putrescent boils and oozing skin.
Digitless too.
NEW HOPE. Silliest of the bunch.

Silly. A billion filickering digits without
one turn of sympathy. Not even empathy.
All here now and but once. Where rancor's
touch stayed by frozen slush refrains from
releasing all I miss so much: his mayhem,
his closeness, his warmth. Unguarded. Struck.
Wheeling away.
With no hope long gone. What is
there ever the reach of? Only
Winter waiting now upon Sam's left palm.
Along with a generous comb of HONEY.
A waxing amber that doesn't ebb.
Enough to nip. Worth a bit.
Jibbs! what weird fire devours my limits.

April 19 2051

Nov 3 1874

Through muck & harm
she crawls, contemned by
clods & barbs,
until stalled, dung among their
shins & clogs, she curls up a ball
and whimpers.

Whereupon the surrounding
Mob, waving Steel Quoits,
spits on her, arcs of
offal & clay. Sooooo
behooves her too, if my own
heehawing turns to ache.
Where's dear Horse?

Eventually some pluck her up,
brickandbind the mess, & chearing
—*Kick The Can!* pinwheel the
nuisance loose. Near undress too.
On to lovely ruins.

Until with topsyturvy thump
she's stump stopped.

American Wigeons laughing
fippantly.

Democrats rebound.
Cantor's endlessness.
Joseph Schlitz.
A Nasty Elephant.
Washings & Wringers.
Mary Ewing
Outerbridge's tennis.
Philadelphia Zoological
Gardens. Henry
Stanley's Lake Victoria.
Annie W Henmyer.
Joseph Glidden's
Barbed wire.
Greenback Party.
Elizabeth Township,
12 workers go.

Vicksburg ejection,
75 go.
Peavey horse
walking the Wheel.
Specie Resumption Act
passes. Western Farm
Relief. Clay County
Pinkerton raid.
Juries & Transportation.
Hawaii Reciprocity Treaty.
Pattee Swing Lottery.

Whiskey Ring.
Colombia & Venezuela
shake, 16,000 go.
Aristides' Derby.
—What did you do?
Don't change anything.

Herzegovina
& Bosnia risings.

Feb 18 2052

Limitless on the fipside.

And just that simply, on my behalf,
I come around. Because I'm blazing.
Because I am too soon.
Because without him I am
only revolutions of ruin.

The harvest of War reaps only the seeds of War.
And I'm now just for sowing.
Here's how my agony frees.
Annihilate everyone of course. Because I'm disdained
& unsafe. And I'll take jeers away with castrations & rape,
murders & feers not even the dead will escape.
Surrounding the Scoundrels, Relevants, Culpables and
Tamed. Resolved. Annihilating their tolerances.

Jan 13 1874

Yet despite their retreat,
she officiously skips closer:
—Over here fellas!
And Eighteen Trappers all leap
appalled with Whirligigs and
Bilbo Catchers:
—Get lost.
Twenty Ranchers turn their
backs on this mewling reprobate.
Whipping Tops for PickUp Sticks:
—Get lost now.
These ThirtySix Prospectors
Capturing The Flag by
holusbolus Tag & Roundabout:
—Get lost. Now.
These Ninety Hard Rock Farmers
even threatening to brutally
repulse her clutch. Rover Rover
Come On Over. Fireworks & fuse.
And Hailey still lunges for a boot.
Astounding all around
with a mouthful of dirt.

Crime of 73.
Vanderbilt,
Czar of New York Rail.
Adolph Coors.
Tompkins Park riot.
Congress repeals
salary raise.
Morrison R Waite.
Blanche K Bruce.
Lokomaikai goes.

Garnet Wolseley's
Kumasi, Ashanti's
Kofi Kari-Kari &
human sacrifices.

Emma, David Kalakaua
& Honolulu riot.

Freight Rates &
Granger Laws.

Grant vetoes Legal
Tender Act.
Ten Hour Act.

Ashfield Dam &
Mill River, over 100 go.

Gold & Dakota Territory.
Bolivia-Chile border.
Beecher, Tilton &
Elizabeth.

*—Meet brute force with
brute force.*

Grasshoppers
& Great Plains.
Turkey Wheat.
Britain annexes Fiji.

Dec 20 2052

Temperaments. Their Gall. Because I'm without worth.
I'm the march of every genocide. Turning none aside.
Riving organ, tendon & joint. Excepting no hurt.
From this Mountain I'll move, unprorogued, stalking
the Poor by their fields, Hungry with their buckets.
And every town will burn.
I'll hunt the Strong. And the Lucky. Skulls splashed.
Rolled. Limbs hacked. Tossed to creek beds.
Along every road.
Cities swept loose by fire.
And for those who beg and plead,
Organizations and Outstanding Citizens, I'll gnaw
through their teeth.
And every nation will burn.

who yelp and reverse with her
approach. Such is their abhorrence.
Their immediate disdain.
But Hailey's all over
THESE FIVE TENDERFOOTS,
whinging for a little
Mublety Peg:
—*Get lost.*
Their mugs charged with disgust
over her rank impudicity
& whealpocked filth.
Yet from
THESE NINE EXPLORERS
she still seeks some exchange.
All scatter, fleeing her fingernails
clawing after their distaste.
She's just too strange,
circling wide their Hoop & Stick,
trampled by snide hoots & quips,
heedless of their need to
have her quit. Their attentions
evaporating. Every lust too.

March 3 1873

Congress & Salary.
Dutch
& the Sultan of Achin.

Slaughter Case.
Colfax Massacre.
John Kirk,
Sultan of Zanzibar
& the abolishment of
slave sales.

Richard Greener.

—*Resistance to*
tyranny is obedience to.

Bengal's Famine.
Sphairistiké.
Truss bridge by Ends
spans Mishishishi.
Jesse James & a train.
Nob Hill's cable car.
Great Fire of Portland.
Russia's suzerainty over
Khanates of Khiva
& Bukhara.

NYC Stock Exchange
& closing panic.

Kansas City stockyards.
General ERS Canby goes.
Virginius apprehended,
12 crew go.

Buda & Pest unite.

Fred Hatch silo.

Oct 22 2053

All I won't forgive. Forfend. Fortake.
I forsake it all with massacres.
Seethe supercooled, jacketed, enriched for
troubling velocities. Artillery lobs, hydrogen bombs.
By me all berms will undefend. All strategies end.
I will walk heavy.
And I will walk strange.
Wealpocked plagues from cities to plain. No graves.
A compass of journeys never
exceeding the reach of my rage. Even the poles
will char. Change our polarity. Until Jupiter,
Neptune, fedup, will shudder loose and go.
Tomorrow's Five Horizons goes too with a tap.
Superclusters, singularities, every megaverse recollapsed.

June 10 1872

Freedmen's Bureau
& lapse.
Australia &
Britain together.
Grant & bribery.
Oakes Ames to
Henry McComb.
Berlin's Wilhelm,
Alexander & Josef.
Alabama,
Shenandoah & Florida,
Britian's restitution.
John H Conyers.
—Turn the rascals out.
Second Term.
Tebbets, Baldwin &
Davis, Boston burning.
Horace Greeley goes.
Leagues &
Policed Elections.
Amédé Bollé's steam.
Mary Celeste.
Fort Dodge &
Dodge City.
Columbia River stops.
Attorney Charlotte
E Ray.
Luther Burbank's
Idaho potato.
William Lunalilo.
Tule Lake Lava Beds,
Modocs & Captain Jack,
9 US soldiers go.
Silver Coinage Act.

Until such dashing takes her away.
From me. Much obliged.
When O what hurt strikes!
My Promise threatening to break.
How longings long me then
from here.
—Never leave her,
mitter **Deer Mice**.
—Allone,
moan **Fireflies & Antelopes**.
I go on, allone, by curving paths
and sloping passes.
By lolling **Shorthorned Lizards**.
Follow after her
below the cackle of **Brant Geese**
following baleful lakes.
All I pass begging my stay.
Lifting up heads for me.
But I just keep rolling through.
And come upon
Two Boys,
Paddleballing on a hillside,

Aug 24 2054

And more still. All following to death my death,
ever allways beyond extinction. One and on.
For I spare endlessly only
the pursuit of all I extend.

I'm the prophecy prophecies pass.
Why desire dies at last.

How mountains fly. And deserts swim.
And sandstorms glass before the wind.
I defy the mighty. I turn the meek.
Only an **Ass** feasts along desolate streets.

And I allone am left to laugh
at all my slaughter Promises to keep.
Where by my staying no else remains.
All now I'd never take.

July 8 1871

Leisurely I lope, stride, my way
beyond wide, victor of all sides.
The obliteration of place.
Hailey sputters and spits. But my
pace exceeds her stumblebounds.
I'm a shudder overground. A
stampede of flame. Absolute
devastation. Quite dashing too.
Preble's Shrew stretching the new.
—*Pick up*,
brrronk aerial **Ravens**.
But I pick up nothing.
Not even speed.
Just rolling after her, that ragtail,
all wobbling, slobbering about
on the trails I command.
Ordering nothing.
And everything.
—*Pick up*,
gatutter **Fleas & Ticks**.
And I pick it all up.
Especially me.

Tweed
& the Tammany Ring.
Scotch-Irish parade,
33 go.
Staten Island Ferry &
Westfield's boiler, 72 go.
US Arctic Whaling Fleet.
Cochise surrenders
to Crook. Young &
lascivious cohabitation.
Peshtigo blaze,
1,100 go.
O'Leary's lantern, Danny
Sullivan & De Koven
Street Cow. Girl aflame.
Columbia cups Livonia.
Tongs & Arcadia, 19 go.
NRA.
—*Dr. Livingstone,*
I presume.
Jim Williams.
Traveller.
Grand Train Depot.
Earl of Mayo goes too.
Pago Pago.
Roller skating.
Mugwumps.
Lone Pine shakes, 27 go.
Stager & Gray.
Jesse & Frank James.
Martin goes.

June 26 2055

Because I'm the laws I allways change
and by their change allready regain.
Because I'm the commands every outlawed
command will still demand, and by my Sam,
what I'll ban with appetite.
For a greater nation shall follow US
and it will be outdone.
And a greater devotion shall follow US
and it too will be outdone.
And a greater emotion shall follow Love
and it too we will blow to dust.
For I'm longings without trust. The pendulum rush
emancipations from Sam allways punishes.
Dust cares only for dust.

Sept 1 1870

Prussians at Sedan.
Napoleon III.
Louisa Swain.

Siege of Paris.
—Strike the tent.
Metz.
All States for 41st.
Joseph H Rainey.
Sarsaparilla,
Hops & Hires.
McIntosh.
Democratic HeeHaw.
Wilhelm & Versailles.
Civil Service Commission.

Sioux Treaties disallowed.
Appropriations Bill
& wards.

Southern Power.
Charles Sumner.
James Kerns & Baseball.

London Conference &
Clauses.
Requisitioning cannons.
Commune.
Sarah A Allen driven
from Cotton Gin Port.
Railroad Act.
Phineas T Barnum.
Pillsbury boy. Force Act.

Camp Grant Apache
Massacre, over 100 go.
Legal Tender.
Victoria Woodhull.
Peace of Frankfurt.

Anyhow, I've plenty to torch.
No lingering for me. Even if
this picayune giglet spurts ahead.
Ashamed she's not fast.
Ashamed she's so slow.
Everyone's afraid because
no one goes the way I go.
And everyone will go.
But still her bellwether
sluggishness mildly amuses me.
—*I'm late*, she coughs.
Pathetically.
Concerning her poverty,
I resort to generosity. But
my offer's too great. She panics.
Accidentally kicks my nose.
A burst of sting.
Odd.
What a bug.
I'm too much to accept.
There's a fork ahead.
She runs over it.

April 27 2056

And time only for US.
No more spooning anyeveroneway. Not here.
What I must accept. Except
I'm too presently too late.
Sam somehow allways separating me
from painlessness I'd now so gladly take.
But his offer's too great, a
palled generosity I can never afford.
So here's my hideous toll. What solitude
enforces. Wrath assures. Juggernauts of one.
Everyone will go because no one lives the way I go.
I'm the only. Beyond speed.
That eager to feast on sacrificial smoke.
Starting up now with his leftover comb of HONEY.

Nov 13 1869

—*You okay?* She quires.
My fumey snorts blistering mesas.
Waving her hand: —*Slow?*
My severity burning out her
possible plans.
—*Simpleton?* she concludes.
No biggy. I need shoes. Too
I'm off to find some falling snow.
Shrugging, I
gift her my laugh.
Its lift so staggering.
Overcomes her. She
hyperventilates. Bends agonized.
What hurt I deliver with just a
hatless shuffleandflap. When
suddenly by a wild of only Wind,
I strangely blurt:
—*I Promise I'll never leave you.*
Flash follows, searing lime to wide.
Fascinating.
She curtsies.
—*I'm Hailey. Hi.*

Princeton over Rutgers.
Lesseps' Suez.
Stone's suffrage.
Knights of Labor.
—*to one is*
the concern of all.
Wyoming women vote.
Frederick Douglass
& CNLU.
Hail the Cutty Sark.
Arabella Mansfield's bar.
Jane Addams.
Catharine E Beecher &
Harriet Beecher Stowe.
Rockefeller's Standard Oil.
Baker's Piegan camp,
173 go.
15th Amendment.
Hiram Revels. Compton
& Wilson swing on
hangman's tree.
Constantinople fire,
900 go.
Department of Justice.
28–28 rejection of
Dominican Republic.
Robert E Lee over
Natchez riverboat.
Ems.
Transcontinental to NYC.
Worth & Spicheren.
Comstock cups Cambria.

Feb 28 2057

Dumb me with a curtsy. It's the HONEY.
All along. By it I thrive.
Without it I recede. Start to die.
ThuuUUUuUuUUUuunder.
My hand drops. I'll eat no HONEY.
Chimes! Chime! Chimes!
Because by earth's urgings over World's want
all's gathered up from the partial labor of
value and need. From field, flower,
bower and stream, slow amber of every bee,
gold's master hour & ore, source of games, pleasure,
commerce and War. Though no more.
And without? Without me. The only way
my agony can now find sweetness. Maybe.

Jan 1 1869

Ice skating.
Chief Tochoway,
Fort Cobb and
a Comanche going.
Justin Morrill's tariff act.
18th.
Public Credit Act.
Wright shortstop.

Judiciary Act, 7–9.

Secession, illegal &
Unconstitutional.
Haiti's Consul General
Ebenezer Bassett.
—Atlantic and Pacific
joined together never to
be parted.
A Golden Spike.
Grenville Dodge.
—Gentlemen.
—Done.
Powell's Grand Canyon.
Cheyenne at
Fossil Creek.
McGaffey's vacuum.
Missouri River span.
Avondale Mine Disaster,
108 go.

San Francisco riots &
Chinese immigrant labor.

Grant by foot, by horse,
to Mount Washington.
Gould & Fisk gold.
Canadian River
Rebellion.

Only before my lips
can afflict—
Giggles. Bustles behind
skawffing **Crows**.
Gold Eyes with flecks of Green.
Bumbles out bootless upon her
King. She even stumbles over me.
Terror & Awe.
Paralyzed.
After all I am her sigh's
redemptions.
—This way to New Delhi,
Mallards & **Hawks** preen.
—Lost my balance, she skeens.
Loosening a fumble of wild hair.
My nostrils flare, my shoulders
catch continents, my Open palms
detach horizons.
I stand and scorch her falling sky.
I'm her World.
Of course dear tyro trembles.
What a capavating smile.

Jan 1 2058

I kneel down beside him. Though his smile's
so sad I can't help but tremble. Blur.
My coldest sky. My fallen land. No more tears.
Enough of tears, turned for a deadlier wake.
His careless hair soft upon my hands,
his continents, my quakes, ringlets by which
he still redeems, reconciles and warns.
Cold so paralyzing.
O here my Curving & Pining King.
Green Eyes with flecks of Gold.
Free and never sold.
Reproaching me, his bumbling girl, for
this kiss now I couldn't hold.
Left gently upon his brow.

March 5 1868

That's the end.
What wroth & withering woe
just stole my friend?
Yet here I am.
Again. Allone.
No more soft nose.
Time to just
set this fucker off.
No big deal.
—*But what about Peace?*
Bighorn Sheep & **Worms** romp.
My destruction is
the ultimate Peace.
Over with a hit. A flick.
—*There's so much more to greet,*
tocks a **Woodpecker**'s beak.
Couldn't care less. I elect to kiss
the World away.
Won't take much.
That's it. Pitiless. Kneel. Kiss Hag,
Horse, Mountain & All.
A byebye. By this.

—*Gibbet of everlasting obloquy.*
Constitution's Simple Majority. Moshoeshoe I.
Crispin Knights.
Kit Carson & Boggsville.
Six Southern States.
—*Not guilty.*
Senate acquits Johnson 19–35. Muir & Yosemite.
—*Let US have Peace.*
Velocipedes & Paris.
McIlhenny's spice.
Bareknuckle boxing.
Wheelcutters & coal seams.
—*viz. Extermination.*
Oscar J Dunn & lieutenant governor of Louisiana.
Florida.
Reed's requests ignored.
Titokowaru's War.
Organic Act.
14th Amendment.
Peru quake, 25,600 go.
Georgia legislature & 28 Members.
Kansas Warpath.
San Francisco quake.
Grant elected President.
Bozeman treaty.
Battle of Washita.
Asunción.
Hewitt steel.

Nov 4 2058

For him
the World spins and to blow it away
would forfeit all the World allready Loves of him.
What resolving he allways bends.
What ending he allways evolves.
How here without, he still someway,
over with, consoles what I'd now devastate.
And he's just curlin on the snow.
He relies on more. More relies on him.
And I cannot destroy more.
For I cannot destroy him. Ever.
So let ice cavalcades gallop his hair.
And though withering & wroth,
all he cares enough for to let go I'll spare.

April 9 1867

Seward's Folly.
—*useless.*
—*perpetual snow.*

Caged Eagle free.
Franklin, Camelia
& Carpetbag Rule.
Querétaro &
Benito Juarez,
Maximilian goes.
Ruthless & Belmont
Stakes. Settlers &
Cheyenne, Wyoming.
Military Governors.
Scalawags & satraps.
Midway Islands.
Abilene, Texas &
Chisholm Trail.
Chinese Mary goes.
Giuseppe Garibaldi.
Matsuhito.
—*High crimes and*
misdemeanors.
Oliver Kelley &
National Grange.
Shuttlecock, Battledore
& Badminton Clerkenwell.
Vanderbilt's Railroad.
—*Now is the time for all.*
Tenements & Slums.

Chinese strike on
Pacific Rail fails.
Edward P Weston's walk.
Diamonds & Vaal River.
Tokugawa Shogunate
abolished.

Somehow wider, someway stiller.
Out there, somewhere,
another killer.
Exciting.
But spinning round to share
suspicions I find some CRONE with
fleam lassoing my terrified **Pony**.
—*Git gone Scalawag*, SHE'll spit
even if fourteen teeth split
and crumble.
—*Free him now*, I brash.
Ready to burn HER, turn HER,
blow HER to ash.
But allso amused.
I calmly approach.
SHE tightens the ropes
until **Horse** groans.
Then abruptly
both are gone.
A long tear quits me, tumbles by
my strife and on the dry paths
lashes my earth with life.

Sept 7 2059

Except me. I'm allready over too,
retreating from this life.
So he goes I allso go. Twist about,
cross legs and ankles. Guard over him.
Winter's shock lending Winter's fall
quickly on my shoulders.
There is no more way for US.
Here's where we no longer occur.
We're the mixed up, the ever unfixed.
Freezoids for the hadits. Sad bits. And nixed.
No longer pairs. Gone.
Dancing around. Goofing on. Not even valid.
And cold allone O cannot numb how I miss.
Me with him. Beyond return. Beyond all starts.

June 7 1866

By and by I round the bends
thrillingly.
My **Mule** on my back
comforts curiosity.
—*Tranquility & Civil Authority,*
Wasps & Cottontails flurry.
I'm no hurry.
But what now worries me?
Terribly unique. Heartendingly
sharp. Out there, my only harm.
Of course I approach the edge.
Roams below drippling the extent
of my thawing ramble. Surely.
I'm The Mountain which
The World climbs down from and
I laugh because it tickles.
Martins wheel.
And though with a wave I could
raze it,
I'm fascinated.
My **Donkey** trots off:
—*Never fall.*

Bismarck troops
nudge Holstein.
Admiral Wilhelm von
Tegetthoff, Lissa
& Italian fleet.
New Orleans riot, 200 go.

National Labor Union.
—*Peace, order.*
Lemochi goes.
Ottoman Authority,
Revolution & Crete.
—*swing around
the circle.*

Treaty of Vienna.
Oglala Sioux
& Fort Phil Kearney.
Chain gangs.
Cattle Trails.
Winchester rifles.
—*Kill the buffalo and
you kill the.*

100 million go.
Forts & Desert Ribbons.
Bergh's ASPCA.
Cholera.
Colorado with a
paddle wheel.
Bozeman closed.

Ireland's Fenians
& County Kerry.
The Great American
Desert. Nebraska 37th.

British North
American Act.

July 10 2060

Sure no picnic
stinging for him all over again,
allone.
Too alive with all he still provides
and risks, touches and assists, his green
amidst these blushing golds, tickling
hill and meadow, brook and hedge
for swerves of Peace. Heartrendingly Open.
All that these roams allready keep of him. Explosions of
Roughlegged Hawks, **Mallards** and **Crows**. **Bighorn
Sheep** charging by **Cottontails**, **Wasps**, **Milk Snakes**
and **Toads**. **Brook Trout**, **Badgers**, **Ants** and clowders
of **Cats**. My wide. **Deer** bounding by **Crickets**, **Coyotes**,
Beavers, while **Golden Bears** range and **Bald Eagles** rise.

Aug 12 1865

Lister's phenol.
Taranaki War.

Otto von Bismarck,
Napoleon III & Biarritz.

Henry Wirz goes.
Johnson &
habeas corpus.
Thaddeus Stevens.
27 States &
13th Amendment.
Pulaski & Ku Klux Klan.
Kekule's Benzene Ring.
Chicago Union
Stockyards, Burlington
Railroad & 761 pigs.

Pasteurization.

Mendel's proceedings.
—lastingly condense a
Nationality.
Peru, Spain & War.
Idaho, Governor Lyon &
$41,062.

Forty Acres & a Mule.
Western Union.

Andrew Johnson,
Confederate States &
Texas.
US Citizens.
—of every race and.
Memphis riot & George
Stoneman, 46 go.

—Our time is now.

Top of such heights, my salutations
ring down and from frozen fields
cataracts surge loose racing
whorls of egalitarian wisps.
By Forrests of pale harm.
And from slate scattered screes
where blabblating **Brook Trout**
glee, I start the ball rolling
by ambling off.
My fiery Mountain Top hollers:
—He!
A thousand **Starlings**
soar through dissipating
mists.
I will sacrifice nothing.
For there are no countries.
Except me. And there is only
one boundary. Me.
Of course **Boreal Toads & Milk**
Snakes applaud: *—Run on Master.*
Neighing, my carried **Yearling**
agrees.

awaken among these cataracts of belligerent ice
around this animal streak of orbit & wind,
that would by harming Sam's play, ever wayward
a warning upon the back of every life
spread my polar chill, reaching even the warmest climes,
By him now. My only role. And for that freedom,
from The Mountain top.
He, I sigh
for all his seasons miss of soaring.
I will sacrifice everything
Only ever contemporary of this way.
But I'm no tomorrow. I'm no yesterday.
me to stay.
Him. Him. Him. Future winds imploring

May 14 2061

Turning around a **Foal** wobbles
over with soft nose:
—*You're impressive.*
I pick him up. **Coyotes** add:
—*You impress everyone.*
Approval unanimous. I'm
a Yankee Doodledandy. Vanguard.
Surrendering nothing. But April
does. This land is my land. Treats me
reverentially. My force earning
thiricckity **Field Cricket** legs.
Mule Deers snort.
—*You're our end*, **Cougars** perrfel.
By my hand **Fire Ants** &
Badgers feud. Glaciers move.
That's a beginning.
Kingbirds hatch and peeekaboo.
Monarchs wake too.
I'm a new horror upon the earth
releasing floods, sluicing rapids.
No big deal.
Me.

Bloody Bill, 24 go.
Calcutta cyclone, 70,300 go.
Nevada 36th.
Atlanta char.
New York Arson.
Sand Creek Massacre.
Franklin 6.
Nashville fog.
Gift of Savannah.
Salk Swamps.
—*With Malice Toward None.*
—*Treat Them liberally all around.*
—*Don't kneel to me.*
—*I have done the best for you.*
—*It's all over now.*
General Order 9.
—*great rapidity.*
—*Sic semper tyrannis.*
—*I'm mad. I'm mad.*
Fort Sumter's Anderson.
—*Now he belongs.*
—*O Mr. Welles.*
—*Useless.*
Sultana.
—*Then all is lost.*
John J Williams.
—*have nothing on earth.*
Four graves.

me.
And my Justice.
At once.
The Vengeance of my awful loss set
free upon this crowded land. An old terror
violent for the delirium of
ends.
But to those who would protect him, frightened
by such Beauty & Savage Presence to do more,
my cool cries will kiss their tender foreheads
and my tears will kiss their gentle cheeks,
and then if the Kindness of their Love, which only
Loving ever binds, spills my ear, for a while I might
slip down and play among his foals so green.

Nov 22 1863

The Cause.
—Abolition of slavery, confiscation of property, and territorial vassalage.
Battle Above The Clouds.
—Chickamauga!
John Hunt Morgan flees.
Capitol Dome.
Hemolytic Streptococcus.
Amnesty.
Meridian.
CSS HL Hunley.
Ulysses S Grant.
Copperheads.
Fort Pillow massacre.
—mostest.
Prisoner exchange ends.
Joe goes.
Battle of the Wilderness.
—hunt to the death.
—Go back General Lee.
—No turning back.
Mule Shoe.
—all summer.
Bloody Angle of Spotsylvania.
Jeb's Tavern.
Cold Harbor.
—This is murder.
Jubal Early.
Fugitive Slave Laws.
—down, you fool.
Crater.
—Full Speed Ahead.
Atlanta Fairly Won.

Haloes! Haleskarth!
Contraband!
I can walk away
from anything.
Everyone loves
the Dream but I kill it.
Bald Eagles soar over
me: —*Reveille Rebel!*
I jump free this weel.
On fire. Blaze a breeze.
I'll devastate the World.
No big deal. New mutiny all
around. With a twist.
With a smile. A frown.
Allmighty sixteen and so freeeeee.
Rebounding without even a cap.
Golden Bears bow at my knee:
—*Go ahead Lieutenant General.*
Take it all.
American Beavers allso chitter
scared. Bowing. Fawning too.
Why don't I have a hat?

My barrenness. Sam's solitude.
And all his patience now presumes.
Luster of Spring's Sacred Brood.
By you, ever sixteen, this World's reserved.
By you, this World has everything left to lose.
And I, your sentry of ice, shall allways protect
what your Joy so terrifyingly elects.
I'll destroy no World
so long it keeps turning with scurry & blush,
fledgling & charms beading with dews,
and allways our rush returning renewed.
Everyone betrays the Dream
but who cares for it? O Sam no,
I could never walk away from you.

Jan 19 2063

S

You were there.

Only Revolutions

The Democracy Of Two
Set Out & Chronologically Arranged

THIS IS A WORK OF FICTION. THOUGH SOME CHARACTERS, ACTIONS, AND EXCHANGES ALIGN WITH HISTORICAL EVENTS, THE TOTALITY OF THE NOVEL—FROM MECHANISM TO MOTION TO MOOD—IS A PRODUCT OF THE AUTHOR'S IMAGINATION.

 Published in the United States by Pantheon Books, a division of Random House, Inc., New York, and in Canada by Random House of Canada Limited, Toronto.

Originally published in hardcover in the United States by Pantheon Books, a division of Random House, Inc., in 2006.

Pantheon Books and colophon are registered trademarks of Random House, Inc.

Library of Congress Cataloging-in-Publication Data
Danielewski, Mark Z.
Only revolutions / Mark Z. Danielewski.
p. cm.
ISBN 978-0-375-71390-3
I. Title.
PS3554.A5596055 2006 813'.54—dc22 2006040996

Printed in China
First Paperback Edition
2 4 6 8 9 7 5 3

abOut

O-Color
Polythiophene Ink
&
Bipowered
Decks

TriColor
Pantones
356 U, 146 U
&
2602 U

B/W
Double Volumes
without
Concordance

Fonts by order of arrival:
Life (Endpapers), Dante MT (Title), Lucida (∞), Perpetua (Dedication), Tempo (Dates), Myriad Pro (Chronomosaics), Spectrum MT (Sam) & Univers 57 (Folio).

www.onlyrevolutions.com
www.markzdanielewski.com
www.jessicagrindstaff.com

Special thanks to VEM™
for Imaging & Cultural Resonance Tracking

Expiration Date: Now

Only Revolutions

by

Sam

Volume 0 : 360 : ∞

V.O.

Pantheon Books New York

Mark Z. Danielewski's

Only Revolutions

II

"[A] towering achievement . . . A bittersweet love story saturated in American mythos . . . Provocative, mischievous, and thoroughly dazzling."
—*San Francisco Chronicle*

"Sweeping ambition and fierce intelligence . . . A quintessential novel of our time."
—*Los Angeles Times*

"Rewarding . . . A palindrome of a book . . . Appears destined to become a classic."
—*The Oregonian*

"Heartbreaking . . . [A] celebration . . . and chronicle of America . . . Adrenaline pulses through the book."
—*The Denver Post*

"Exceptional . . . Heavy with wordplay and heady with love . . . A crib sheet to the universality of teen angst."
—Minneapolis *Star Tribune*

"A startling and versatile pair of voices, and a manner of storytelling which is at once hallucinatory [and] slyly punning, and also possessed finally of an authentically tragic register . . . Once you are attuned to its extraordinary music, there is no way out except through the end."
—*The Guardian*

"It's difficult to decide whether Danielewski is merely reinventing the novel as a medium, or has constructed his own, entirely original platform from which to destroy literary convention."
—*New York Press*

"Engaging . . . A marriage between pop-culture fanaticism and postmodern nihilism."
—*Time Out New York*

"Poetic . . . Elegant . . . The more the novel's structure is decoded, the more lyrical and poignant it becomes . . . Ambitious, undeniably astonishing, and contemporary."
—*Bookforum*

"In his new novel, the author of *House of Leaves* is up to his old tricks—multicolored and upside-down text—and some flabbergasting new ones."
—*The New Yorker*

"Turning readers upside-down [*Only Revolutions*] is the road novel as if imagined by John Cage . . . A true revolution—it wants to overthrow not just how we read, but what we read."
—*Newsday*